As the Wolf Howls at My Door

ALSO BY CHANDLER BROSSARD

As the Wolf

CHANDLER BROSSARD

Howls at My Door

Dalkey Archive

Library of Congress Cataloging in Publication Data
Brossard, Chandler, 1922-
   As the wolf howls at my door / Chandler Brossard
   I. Title.
PS3552.R67A9   1992
813'.54—dc20   91-28630
ISBN: 0-916583-97-X

First Edition

Partially funded by grants from The National Endowment for the Arts and
The Illinois Arts Council.

Dalkey Archive Press
1817 North 79th Avenue
Elmwood Park, IL 60635 USA

*Printed on permanent/durable acid-free paper and bound in the United
States of America.*

for Steven Moore

Mum's the Word, South Carolina

Man cannot live by equivocations alone. Nor can he be expected to sell his soul as often as he sells his ass. (It is said that the dollar is holding its own against the surging Swiss franc and the German mark, but only weekend dervishes will be buoyed by this news.) There are walls and there are walls—some protecting gardens, others surrounding restless nuns—but the one we've been keeping in mind is the one against which man has his back. This is where he'll be for the rest of his pimply life. He cannot be pushed any farther, even if he would offer to be. That wall does not move (and bribers will be wasting their time, no matter what the color of their money).

Every split second of the above is known by heart by everybody here with two eyes and a nose. That is why they are all into last-ditch dignity. And that is why they are not blabbermouths when it comes to meat 'n' potatoes existential matters—like survival.

One cold-eyed nipper put it cleanly in a school essay contest: "Holding one's tongue and clamming up are no more the same thing than corn muffins and ragamuffins. The person who would confuse them would shower in a toilet bowl."

The contest was sponsored by a stone quarry. The theme was Cleaning Up Your Act. The aforementioned scribbler won it, sitting on his hands. We will surely be hearing from him again before this day is done.

Young mothers and fathers—who are doing their best to keep their own two feet on the ground—are not bugged blind by hearing their issue whimper such statements as "I wanna be a fireman when I grow up" or "I'm gonna be a nurse when I get big." Youngsters hereabouts don't tell their parents anything. Many years later they stride through the front door and announce, "I am a policeman. I arrest people." "I am a baker. Doughnuts are my game." "I am an actress. I make believe." Of course, Denmark is not the only place where something might be rotten, hence there are invariably those who fling open the parental front door and shout, "You'll never guess what I've become!"

Such a one could be Carol Lynn Mobley, who at this particular moment is swallowing a Frenchman's joint in the Place de l'Odeon, in gay Paree. Be assured, Carol Lynn will come out of this alive, and with fifty bucks in her pocket. Carol Lynn is a part-time hooker and she works in a surreptitiously elegant, well-behaved (in the most complex sense possible) whorehouse at 15 bis on the Place. Which does not mean, of course, that there is not plenty of good fun to be had. Her customers are not smelly brutes just off an assembly line with a monkey wrench up their ass. Oh no. They know that a vulva is not a Swedish car, just as they absolutely know that a chocolate mousse is not something you set traps for. Her customers have class. Just listen to some of their conversations:

Monsieur Le Blanc: —Mitterand must be defeated at the polls this summer. Otherwise his little commie rat followers will eat us up like dirty cheeses.

Or Monsieur Mohrt: —The French film will inevitably return to realism. That is where its roots are. Our art should always show life as it is really being lived. In spite of what people say, we Frenchmen are very down-to-earth at heart.

And what does Carol Lynn have to say? Not much. Because she must attend to her work. There is not a great deal you can say with a stiff prick in your mouth. Naturally, it is a bit different when she is being fucked in a somewhat more normal fashion. This gives her some breathing space, so to speak, and she can more reasonably keep up her end of the conversation.

—I would certainly agree with you, Monsieur, she will say, looking up toward heaven as her customer pumps away at her vividly obliging cunt. —If it is steeped in anything, France is steeped in naturalism. Why, just look at Zola. Or glance even at Balzac.

Or just look at the divine hunchback. What was he steeped in? The blood, shit, and piss of Our Lady, that's what. And you cannot get more down-to-earth than that. But that's another story, and you can be sure that we'll get back to it.

Staring at the ceiling (or at heaven) where Carol earns her bread is not the unrewarding, catatonic bit it is in normal rooms. Her atelier—we are surely entitled to call it that, are we not?—She is an artisan, and she is not to be cold-shouldered or patronized by the likes of some crapulous painter or a self-deceiving plumber with spooky hemorrhoids—has mirrors on the ceilings. So looking up, she will be talking to herself. She can watch her bourgeois gentleman's sweating, roiling ass and back if she likes, but this need not distract her from her train of conversation. In point of fact, she can work the two operations in and out of each other, in very much the same way that a gifted, crazed, red-haired Languedoc weaver with a vacuous childhood spent in the limestone caves can work bizarre patterns and freak scenes in and out of her calm browns and whites.

There is a very good chance that Carol will say, —Political extremists of ... oh! Monsieur! Your raging plunger! ... all kinds must ... mercy! Such divine skill! ... be avoided. Oohh! Monsieur ... I come ... like ... a ... river! She collapses and sighs, —Oh Monsieur Balaban! What exquisite lust you summon from my very soul.

Monsieur Balaban will roll over on his back and grin at his face on the ceiling. —A decent Frenchman will always try his best, Mademoiselle. We know our duty when we see it.

Carol will tie the Legion of Honor band on his limp dork and sing what little she can remember of the French national anthem.

—Oh, how thoughtful of you, my dear. Très, très gentil, the smug dorker will say, and gratefully he will kiss her drowned snatch. —My own mother could not do better.

Carol's interest in her client's mother is very limited indeed, so she does not ask him to explain the ambiguities of his last statement. Was he referring to his mother's singing abilities? To his carefree days as his mother's lover? Or to the varieties of genteel gestures his mother could pull off? We will probably never know. Certainly his mother is not going to reveal all, not with her strict Catholic upbringing. Don't breathe a word of it, that's the code of those Neuilly types when it comes to something juicy and personal. Tight lips, tight asses.

Carol knows a thing or two about mothers herself. Her own, for instance. —She'd rather go to an anticommunist rally than fuck my father any day, Carol told her friend Burke, the frail, shifty-eyed poet, one afternoon over a cappuccino in North Beach. —She thinks Ron Reagan is the Pope.

We must hear from the mother. What does she have to say? —If you don't like this country of cold, mountain springs and spanky fox-trots, why don't you leave it? Maybe you should try living in one of those cold, grey, politburo places where the government buildings don't have any windows. See how you like that.

Mrs. Mobley looked in mirrors in a frugal way. She did not really look *at* herself but over her shoulder. She wanted to get a good look at whatever it was that might be creeping up on her.

Her "rootless" daughter Carol—"You just don't have any roots, Carol, in your head or out. You're rootless"—was into mirrors in quite a different way. Particularly the large no-questions-asked mirror on the ceiling above. This mirror was not to be used to pluck your eyebrows in. This mirror was a larger-than-life sort. It gave you highs. It turned you into a movie so that, in this case, you could watch somebody called you being eaten by a slightly bald Monsieur Balaban (whom you may or may not have caught in other ad hoc flicks and whose industrious, shameless tongue was certainly not working for scale, though it was indisputably slavering to scale). And it took you places, this mirror. I mean like, here's this cool, neo-Winesburg, Ohio, ex-cheerleader cunt Carol stretched out on her naked back, legs spread to accommodate bobbing head and darting tongue, staring up at Famous Performer Herself and being carried beyond the simple Herself, by the magic surface, beyond The Watched Self, beyond the tongue and deliciously aroused cunt, to other tableaux where she was both doing and watching, both herself and others, both participant and spectator. The mirror teased and plucked fragments of her always-fluxing reality and the several Carols (while the insatiable tongue licked away). Several Carols and Herselves could not keep from smiling at one another as they glided in and out of their shared roles and bodies. (Spanking sounds and sharp squeals of exquisite pain-pleasure penetrate the walls from another Sacred Stage next door, where that divinely lewd Brazilian performer Alita "lives." Though these sounds, or "innocent" manifestations, are not intrusions; they become absorbed, unannounced guests at an overflowing banquet whose mystery host had long since vanished.)

Carol was now watching herself at the Café Beaux Arts near the cold, green, somnambulistic waters of the Seine, at the bottom of the Rue Bonaparte. She was with Stephan. Stephan kept lighting and puffing on his short, surly, black pipe which refused to stay lit. He was the natural prey of small despairs. Waiters sensed this and served him at something of a distance. Small dogs also picked this up and inevitably tried pissing on his shoes.

—I think a bat has shit in this pipe, Stephan said, and jabbed into its malevolent bowl with a matchstick. —Last week I was certain a squirrel was hiding in it. Stephan banged the bowl on his heel. —The fucking thing must have been a park in its former life.

This relatively lithe young man emitted other mysterious vibrations which obviously dislocated some people's minds and forced them to ask him unorthodox questions.

—Why is it you always seem to be out of breath?

—How can a man answer such a question but in kind? I have been running from the authorities all my life, he would reply.

—You are hiding a dirty comic book somewhere in your clothing.

His rejoinder: —My very existence is a dirty comic book.

And in the Louvre a wart-wattled guard whispered to him, —It will be very difficult for you to dispose of the Egyptian scarabs you have come here to steal.

What could Stephan say but, —When was the last time you had a good enema?

Stephan had for quite a long time suspected—or, rather, had stopped resisting the phenomenon—that there were many people in the world who, without understanding why, without giving the matter a second thought, felt that he was a floating extension of themselves. Or, in other cases, that he was a predestined mediator (predestined by whom is a question we must leave up to Those Who Know) between warring aspects of themselves; or simply between themselves and themselves.

—I just don't understand how all this got started, Stephan confessed one afternoon to his dentist while getting a cavity filled, —and something tells me that I would be ill-advised to find out why, or how.

(His dentist nodded in total agreement, and told him that he had creeping gingivitis which must be attended to —at once, mon chéri, before the swallows head for the south.)

Here is a perfect example of this, well, endearing or eerie problem: One light, grinning morning, when not a soul in Paris was thinking, we're sure, of the crimes of the Third Republic or of Marie Antoinette's chronic menstrual problems, Stephan was sitting in the Café Mouton on the Place Contrescarp. He was having *un café*, smoking his sneaky little black pipe, and letting his mind collapse in the *International Herald Tribune*. He was beginning to sink into a simpering article about the vile, plump Dutch royal family, a cluster of assholes who are suppurating in their own mediocrity and self-love. Their grinning faces oozed up at him from page 12 of the newspaper. His glance shifted momentarily down to his left: a woman's unshaved, bare leg, ending in a purple espadrille (from Spain?) and a half-hidden red toenail (her big toe). An enticing leg, especially enticing because of the soft blonde hair that still covered it as God and His close associates had intended. Stephan wanted to lick the leg. He had been licking women's legs for many years, to everyone's pleasure, and his plans were to go on licking for an indefinite period ahead. Though he had never before seen this particular leg, he was already savoring its taste and its special texture. His tongue was twirling down toward the delicious hidden toes.

—Why did you leave Rome so suddenly? the owner of the legs asked huskily.

—I have never been in Rome, he replied, keeping his gaze down on the ankle. —And certainly, one could never leave a place as tricky as Rome suddenly. Oh no.

—You left without a word to anyone, the voice continued. —That wasn't very nice.

He simply had to look up. There was no way out of it. Her face was accusing yet amused. Sardonic, you might say, with a genteel lewdness. In other words, it was a face that Emma Bovary could certainly have used. This woman was smoking a thin cigar with a style that spoke for itself: it was not born yesterday. And of course, this woman was not to be resisted.

—OK, said Stephan, looking into her face. —Have it your way. I split. But what did you expect me to do under the circumstances?

Artfully and boldly, as a Japanese calligrapher ending an intense moment of concentration suddenly strokes the paper before him and in that stroke brings the bird into being, this beautiful stranger who insisted, as so many did, that Stephan was an inhabitant of both their lives and their imaginations, blew her cigar smoke at Stephan. —To let us all know what you were doing so that your departure would not leave us feeling so vulnerable.

Stephan let himself go, breathed in her fragrant, suggestive smoke and in so doing breathed her into himself and became a willing, passive ingredient of her moment, her vision and need, a vision so intense, so demanding, that it was of course quite erotic, for the very soul of eros is in the metamorphosing of the other. Her half-bare foot brushed against his calf as she moved her chair closer . . . and he was immediately in the howling streets of Rome with her, running over the gleaming cobblestones of the Via della Croce with the absurdly crazed carabinieri chasing them and the other demonstrators, shouting panic-stricken obscenities at the young demonstrators and firing tear-gas canisters into their scattering groups.

—You are worms in the belly of the Virgin Mary! they screamed, waving their long black truncheons over their helmeted heads.

—You want to shit on all that is sacred!

—We are going to cut off all your communist pricks and shove them down your dirty throats!

Stephan and Juliette held wet handkerchiefs over their faces to protect them against the burning tear gas. The vile, searing gas was consuming this ancient Roman street, evilly transforming it into an unspeakable, sulfurous cavern shrilly presided over by the raging carabinieri who, got up as they were in tight black nylon costumes, white crash helmets with plastic masks, holding walkie-talkies with long antennas, and whirling truncheons, seemed really to be giant insects on an extermination rampage. Shouts and screams and sudden wild laughter careened through the evil vapors. All of the small shops along the street were sealed tightly behind steel shutters. But above the terrified little shops (which cringed so wretchedly behind the protective steel curtains), the ancient wooden shutters had been flung open and the thrill-starved inhabitants of those tiny, sunless apartments were hanging out of their windows and participating in the hellish spectacle below as best they could. They waved their arms and banged their shutters and yelled their bloody heads off, mostly to encourage the police insects. —Don't let the little rats get away! Stomp them! Stomp them!

A demented, half-naked old bag with a red wig shouted that piece of advice—no doubt she had shouted the same thing as the Nazis rounded up the Italian Jews—and to show her sincerity she hurled a flowerpot onto the running masses below.

Perversely, an occasional window spectator yelled something in favor of the persecuted fleeing demonstrators. —Keep your peckers up, comrades! These carabinieri cocksuckers are playing a losing game!

As you would imagine, and as is always the case with such impromptu mass spectacles—in collapsed modern times, that is—there was the inevitable spectator who seized upon the embattled street scene as his own private theater, and like an itinerant, hallucinated actor, hurled proclamations that had no bearing at all upon the action at hand or the scene before him. —My sexual preferences are my own business! howled a bald, red-faced nut. —You work your side of the street and I'll work mine.

Stephan and Juliette are still fighting and groping their uncertain path through the heavy chaos in the street. They don't know how to escape. They can barely see as they hug the buildings. The insect cops are beating at them and their comrades. Whack! Thunk! Smack! Some comrades are falling down drenched with blood. Others also drenched with blood are fighting back (and why not? what have they got to lose?) and our ears are delighted by the squeals of a cop as he is kicked and beaten. What precious sounds they are! We shall treasure them as long as we live. They shall be collected in our slim album of victory sounds.

Without any warning whatsoever—minus a premonition on everyone's part—the sky opens up and a deluge of rotten fruit and vegetables pours from the rooftops. Swarms of shrieking street children (who, one can be sure, do not get too many vacations from their sordid boredom and poverty) are up there dumping crates of this garbage into the street far below. A freak storm of Mother Nature's shit. Cabbages, squash, grapes, tomatoes, lettuce.

—Up Garibaldi's ass! the avenging children screamed. —Mazzini's mother fucks donkeys!

How can one explain such off-the-beam references? Because Garibaldi and Mazzini, however noble they were, are not the issues here. The explanation is very simple. These poor urchins, existing as they do only in history's sneezes, have been denied modern education. Classrooms are not for them. All they know about historical moments is what they read under the statues in the parks.

Stephan and Juliette are suddenly inundated with rotten melon rinds and pumpkins.

—Merde! howls Stephan. —Der zigguashion iss disindergrading!

—Quite clearly, says Juliette, flicking a chunk of lemon off her shoulder.

—Sshniddzel! Vee must schplitt! He raised his arm and blocked a bunch of grape bombs.

—Undt on der dubble, Juliette said. —Hopefully.

They lock arms and push through a gas-shrouded cluster of giant insect cops and crazed demonstrators who were beating one another with sticks and wrestling to the cobblestones, yelling and groaning. Fascist mother-fuckers! Oh mamma mia! Help! Pigshit eaters. Thump! Whack! A fallen cop grabbed Stephan's ankle. Stephan kicked him off. Shoulders hunched, heads bent down, he and Juliette plunge into a skinny, secretive alleyway that abruptly decides to make itself known to them. It is a blind alley. At the far end an old lady with a black shawl over her soft grey head sits on a stool and watches two snow-white toy poodles serenely fucking.

—I believe she's whispering to them, says Juliette.

—That's a lewd and ambiguous statement, says Stephan.

—Perhaps, but it's better than talking that fake kraut talk of yours.

—Dot remens to be zeen, he says.

—You must talk straight for a while.

—OK, he said. —"That remains to be seen" is what I said.

They are now on the cool first and least demanding floor of an old, old house that, quite obviously, has been broken up into apartments. Perhaps this was done at a time of economic stress or family disorders and vilifications. It is, of course, too late to tell, and ... and naturally everybody's got his side of the story, and nobody within earshot ...

—Mmm, murmurs Stephan, nosing the air. —Smells of Plutarch and upper-class madness in here.

—And early marriages and badly kept secrets and velvet suits and malpractice suits and ...

—Calm down, says Stephan, putting his suspect finger to his devious nose. —You're getting carried away.

—I've come out of the closet, thanks to you, she says, and gooses him. —We can't stand here forever. The cops may crash in here at any moment swinging their penis substitutes. She points upstairs. —Andiamo.

The softly worn marble stairs gave them no trouble. Live and let live, they seemed to be saying. —The air pressure in here is different, says Stephan. —Odd, very odd indeed.

—Not at all. This air is back in the Renaissance. Less tension in those days.

—Oh.

—Men obviously don't think of everything. You'd better get used to that, Comrade Stephan, before you get lost in the shuffle.

—Well, yes, he replies, peering about, —but I have many other priorities.

One of the two doors in the next landing is slightly open. Stephan points to it and Juliette nods. They sort of creep up on it. Stephan raises his fist to knock on the door, and as he does this he realizes that he feels like one of those furtive, underfed characters in a contemporary Polish movie.

—They always wear their coat collars turned up, like it's going to rain at any moment, he says.

† 14 †

—This is no time for an identity crisis, Juliette says. She does it for him. She grabs his wrist and thumps his troubled fist on the door. —Permesso! she shouts.

—Avanti! a rose-twined voice calls out from inside. —Avanti! And may your sweet ass depend upon it!

Stephan quickly whispers into Juliette's ear. —In Italian, that would not translate into "the ass of your sweetness."

She shoves him inside.

They are in a large studio with an ominously big skylight. (And why not? Where should they be? In the locker rooms of the Colosseum?) Obscure, challenging, imminent cleverness permeates the air here. A woman in a blue smock is painting a small, elegantly gaunt man seated on a model's stand in front of her. Another woman is stretched out on a red velvet chaise. She is eating Ritz crackers and peanut butter, and she is naked, as naked as the bold first page of *Les Misérables* as Hugo sat fidgeting before it, only her breasts are much larger than anything Hugo could have had in mind. Cracker crumbs and peanut butter are dropping onto these breasts, but she does not seem to be bothered by that. Of course, it may well be that she is unaware of it, which is an entirely different department of speculation.

—If you are running away from anything, you've come to the right place, says Naked Woman, licking peanut butter from the corner of her mouth.

The woman painting turns around to face Stephan and Juliette. —Don't listen too closely to my sister. She is only an amateur soothsayer.

Stephan and Juliette (holding hands now, inexplicably, like Hansel and Gretel) nod and smile. —That may be, says Juliette, trying to be amenable while keeping her options open, —but we must always remember that Cassandra was not exactly working on salary.

Stephan, too, would like to keep all options open, but he doesn't know how. He can't help himself, if the truth be known. He wants to work both sides of the street. So, while presenting The Painter with a shit-eating grin, he quickly darts over to Naked Lady and, dropping to his knees with a disconcerting savoir faire, furiously but skillfully licks up the crumbs and peanut butter from her succulent breasts.

—There now, he says, —that's a little better.

—For whom? shouts the gaunt man sitting for his portrait without moving his head or changing his rigid position. (He could have been in a dream, but he wasn't.)

—You sure have a quick tongue, Juliette says to Stephan as he returns to her side.

—We always knew that. Quick tongue, silvery tongue, sharp tongue. Tongue! Tongue!

The man modeling gets up. —All this talk about tongue is making me hungry.

—Presto, says the blue-smocked painting lady. She rings a little bell (how imperious its gay tinkle!). You can see guillotines hung with such tinkling bells. Don't fuck around with a tinkle like that. —Porti cena! she calls out. —Subito!

—Ah, food, says the small, gaunt man, doing a ballet arabesque in slow motion. —How wonderful that it has escaped the philosophers.

This little man's presence had the airtight exactness of a question mark. We cannot deny it.

Without any of the traditional effort, the naked woman withdraws her disinterested succulence from the chaise of velvet and glides over to Stephan and Juliette. —You'll see, she says. —He's very loyal to the dishes of nostalgia. He is always eating in the past.

Stephan grins expertly at Juliette and the nude woman. —Really makes you wonder, doesn't it?

Juliette shakes her head in friendly despair. —Your statements are becoming less and less dialectical. We'll have to sit down one of these days soon and have a good straightening-out rap. That's for sure.

The nude woman, whose succulence is quite irremediable, puts her arm around Stephan. —Whatever you do, caro mio, don't sell yourself short in the interests of collective wisdom. She squeezes him, then pats his tushie, just for good measure (one would hope).

Stephan looks at Juliette. —You realize, of course, that this woman, whose identity may never be revealed to us, represents the world's history of ad hoc nudity.

Juliette has not lived her life in a bottle. —Are you trying to tell me that you have something up your sleeve?

—Do fish swim? Do birds fly?

It was true, the gaunt man was not into modern foods. Archeological handbooks, that's where his plats du jour hailed from. Cow udder, hog jowls, duck feet, sheep tongue, reindeer bladder—it was all piled up before him, much as the Middle East must have been piled up before Alexander the Great's depraved imagination. Steaming and oozing in self-aware defeat. Drowning in its own reluctant juices.

—That should keep you quiet for a while, Mirko, says the painter.

Mirko seizes a dripping tongue. —To each his own. He bites the little tongue in half. —Someday we must look into *your* vices, cara sorella.

The rest of that sacrilegious crew eat as human beings should under the circumstances. Prosciutto sliced very thin, estimable cheeses—parmigiana, fontina—and fruit. And wine, of course. It should likewise go without saying that Stephan and Juliette—who, as I have candidly suggested before, are disturbingly similar to fugitives from the Brothers Grimm—nudge each other with unashamed yet sly pleasure. But we are not bothered by this.

We are not present as tight-lipped moralists, nor are we here as shabby, penniless informers seeking employment.

The servant who brings in these tasty treats is a short, muscular young country woman who has the exalted flashing brown eyes of the virtually extinct peregrine falcon. Her powerfulness is quite erotic but it is both self-contained and, in a sense, self-referent. It does not reach out to seduce you; it has no plans for you.

—I know. You don't have to tell me, whispers Juliette, folding a slice of prosciutto. —You are dying to kiss her hairy, muscular legs.

The noble servant woman slams a big loaf of brown bread down on the long, rustic table. —It is touch and go in the streets today. Our side is taking some beatings and dishing out some beatings. But sooner or later, we shall win. She looks triumphantly around at everyone with those dazzling falcon eyes, which gleam with such precise, elegant hunger. —And when we do, it's the firing squad for the bourgeois oppressors who have been sucking our blood ever since the wheel was invented.

As the servant woman is striding from the room, the woman painter— what a divinely forgiving smile she has! It is forgiving before you have even done anything—says, —It's quite all right, my friends. You may shout bravo or right on, if you like. We won't be in the least offended.

What can Stephan and Juliette say?

Stephan turns to me (I permit him to do this under certain circumstances) for help. Soundlessly—for he has of course learned to read my lips—I say, Why don't you say, Ah well, let them eat cake?

He shakes his head.

My lips move again: How about, Everybody's days are numbered?

He makes a face and turns away, giving up on me. So it goes.

Juliette speaks up: —The class war is going on all over the world. Capitalism has had it. She gulps down some red wine. —So you might say that all of us in this room will soon be extinct.

The painter lady shouts across the vast ancient studio to the naked woman, who is archly turning this way and that in front of an enormous mirror. —Did you hear that, Giovanna? I think we should all hurry to the zoo and turn ourselves in. We can be put on exhibit with all the other rare, vanishing animals.

—An exquisite idea, Giovanna calls back, continuing to admire her voluptuous body. —I've always wanted to have an affair with a giant panda. She caresses her gorgeous breasts. —Can't you just see it, Anna Marie. We would make love in its cage, in front of all the Sunday visitors. The children could throw popcorn and candy at us, and the fat papas could take our pictures. Bravo! Che bellisima! She laughs with unbridled delight at this lewd but, in essence, angelic prospect.

Everyone in the studio joins in her laughter. It is the exquisitely liberating and purifying laughter of complete absurdity. Their spirits float and play and bathe in it. They are joyful, weightless creatures in a primeval, oceanic scene.

—Ooolala! howls Stephan, hugging Juliette.

—Hot dog and holy shit! shouts Juliette, rubbing her face on his as she would rub it on the stars.

—And I'll be doing it with the reindeer! shrieks Mirko, tossing tongues and pig bladders high into the air.

—Guess where I'll be? whoops Anna. —Doing unspeakable things with the seals!

Naturally, it will not stop there. (Dame Nature may be crazy but she's not stupid. She knows a good thing when she sees it.) Do you for one second really believe that the Sunday mobs at the zoo, double-jointed and bug-eyed as they are, are going to stand by and be satisfied with just watching? No indeedy. Not in a million years. They're going to want in. And then, my good sir, you're going to reap the fruits, if one can say that, reap the fruits of your depraved imagination. These slavering, popcorn-crazed, family-structured hordes will leap into the cages too. The poor animals (who were peacefully minding their own business in the first place, way back when) won't have a chance. The hordes will sexually assault every square inch of them. Please, sir, I beg you on my mother's knees to try to picture it. Young mothers gang-banging the orangutans. Biting their necks, gouging their backs. Young fathers frothing at the mouth as they bugger the rosy-assed baboons. Shrieking, toothless grannies tearing off their corsets and grappling with the giant anteaters. (Who have no Rape Hot Line. Who don't know what is taking place, really. Holy fuck, what is it with these goofs? They used to be happy with merely throwing stuff at us. What gives here?) Rolling all over the ground and forcing those poor, stunned creatures (with their two-foot long tongues) between their flabby, aging thighs. And the children . . . Oh heavens above, sir, this is where you force even our dear Lord above to cover his eyes with shame. The little folks, cherished blue-eyed readers of *Little Miss Muffet* and *Snow White*, howling through the cages and the trees, the dens, and the sacred grazing grounds, humping the aardvarks, debasing the noble mountain goats, ravaging the two-toed sloths as those cuddly creatures try to snooze their sweet lives away; seizing the gentle penguins by their pricks and swinging them round and round over their tousled, sex-crazed heads . . .

Oh sir, even though it is too late, I stand head and shoulders above Saint Francis of Assisi and implore you, just look at the dripping, lascivious carnage you have mustered up! Now look deep into your heart, sir, and ask yourself have you not, in your sinkhole whimsy, fucked up The Grand Design itself?

S tephan looks at me and says, I've got to get back to Carol and that table at the Café Beaux Arts, for just a few minutes anyway. I say OK, sure. That's part of our deal. I mean, after all, it takes two to tango. He can make such requests from time to time. Just don't overdo it. Because after all I have my needs too. From time to time of course there are those who do abuse our relationship, who think *they* run the show—"Gimme this, gimme that. No, I'm sorry, I don't like the parts you give me. No, I won't be free this evening" and so on—and I have to get rid of them, terminate their contract. There have even been . . . it makes me blush just to remember it . . . certain brutes who have gone so far as to say, "Where would you be without us? Nowhere!" Can you believe it? Anyway . . .

—. . . so naturally I can't tell my parents what I'm really doing to make out here, Carol said, sipping on her milky somnambulant Pernod-and-water drink. —They'd flip out. And I mean *really* flip out.

Stephan just adored her whole crazy picture. He laughed like an old hyena in a charity soup kitchen. He clearly saw her respectable, nice-smiling, clean-smelling, small-town parents going bonkers and bouncing off the walls and ceilings of their two-story frame house like eerie, weightless figures in a spaceship.

—A translator! A translator of children's stories. Oh Jaysus! I do love it.

—I thought that would grab you.

—You're a fucking genius! he shrieked, grabbing Carol's hand and anointing it with quick wet kisses. —And it's not a lie, really. I mean, actually and truly, when the artichoke is all peeled, that's what you're basically doing —translating children's stories in the most wonderful way possible, by becoming . . . he whooped again . . . —by *becoming* the story!

—Well, she said, —it certainly beats teaching English, or spieling on one of those sightseeing buses.

—Oh perish, perish the sordid thought. God, Carol, how I would love to watch it, you playing Red Riding Hood and Rapunzel and the johns doing the wolf and Rumpelstiltskin!

—Maybe we can arrange it. Lemme think about it.

—I could hide under the bed, said Stephan.

—You wouldn't see much. No, the big closet would be much better. But the best place, she took a long drink of the milky Pernod, playing her tongue in the thin glass, —the very best place would be through the mirror.

—You mean like Alice through the looking glass?

Carol thought about that (while the café's dappled cat sniffed her glistening new red boots). —Yeah, like Alice in a way. You'd be going into another world all right, the sex fantasy world. Uh huh. She dipped her finger into her Pernod and held it down to let the cat lick it. —Anyway, there's one room in the place that has a large see-through mirror. Some people . . .

—A lot of people.

—. . . like to watch. They look through a sort of window in one room that's a mirror in the room where the fucking performance is going on. She gave the cat more Pernod finger. —Performing because the girl knows they're being watched.

—The john doesn't?

—No. Not unless he wants it to be that way. On the sidewalk outside, a fat, blind beggar man began playing "The Yellow Rose of Texas" on a harmonica. (He is dressed like an Arab sheik, with a black top hat. Who put him there? Don't worry. We'll get to the bottom of this.) —Some guys do.

—Do you perform?

—I've done it twice so far.

—Why only twice?

—I guess I'm shy about being watched, at least by strangers. She laughed and playfully kicked him under the table.

Knowing Stephan as we do—from the ground floor up—none of us should be surprised to hear what he then said. —When you come right down to it, the whole world's a play and we're all on stage.

Now, that is a pretty hard statement to follow, so they both looked at each other for a few moments without speaking. Carol blew throbbing Gaulois smoke rings across the table. (This is sometimes known as playing both sides of the table.)

Stephan continued sniffing his coffee cup. —Having said that, I realize that it's just one step more to saying . . .

—That you would like to be in one of my children's stories.

—Precisely.

Two members of the French secret police sat down at one of the café's sidewalk tables. They had a fairly good view of the crowd inside the café, not an unhindered view but a good one nonetheless. They were about fifteen feet from where Stephan and Carol were sitting. They were Inspector Jean Pierre Epernay and his assistant, Subinspector Georges Leger. Their faces were modeled from God's least interesting putty, off-pink in color and shoddy in texture. And their expressions . . . Oh! It was only too obvious that these flics had lived lives of vivid emptiness.

—That's him, said Inspector Epernay in a voice that was not loud.

—Yes, said Leger, nodding, —and that's her.

—They are a tricky pair.

—That goes without saying, Leger observed.

—What if your children were like that?

Leger shook his head sadly. —It would be simply dreadful. He sucked his cigar. —But I don't have any children.

—You had just better keep it that way, do you understand me?

Leger nodded. —Very well.

—Because, Inspector Epernay went on, —we would find ourselves in the uncomfortable position of having to surveil them and perhaps eventually to seize them . . . his voice became clotted and raspy, —as enemies of the people of France!

Leger shook his head. —Dreadful, simply dreadful.

—Aren't you drenched with parental humiliation, Leger?

—But I don't have these children.

—You'd better keep it in mind nevertheless. Do you get me? the Inspector snarled, his voice now dirty and threatening and tired, like an animal trainer's in a shaky provincial circus.

Leger nodded again. —Absolutely, sir.

Inspector Epernay glanced again in the direction of Carol and Stephan, puffed on his old cop's pipe, and opened his soft old black leather notebook (a present from his wife Claudine upon his first arrest, a Tunisian pickpocket with a sad smile). —Here's the complete dope on him.

—Aha. Very good, sir.

—Absolutely nothing's missing in this little rat's picture, said Epernay.

—Oh I'm sure of that. Interpol is very thorough in its coverage. Doesn't leave anything out, not a turd, not a fart.

Epernay peered at him with older generation distaste. —If you must. He looked over at Stephan and Carol. —One must look beyond Interpol and the bulging data banks of the international intelligence community to fill the dossier of such types as these, my dear Leger. One must search through the medical books, the museums of natural history, the bureaus of engineering and technology, the departments of marine life and café dwelling... His voice was threatening to break and his face was, well, swelling. —Because such people are diseases, they are crop blights, prehistoric mammals that should have remained in the silent seas, faulty bridge designs, malfunctioning air valves. They are hailstorms in darkest Africa. They are . . . He shuddered. —They are a stench in the nostrils of George Washington's cherry tree. He could not go on. Gradually, he subsided, deflated, so to speak, came down from his soaring loony bird flight. He was able, in a couple of moments, to light his pipe and read the pages of his notebook for a few more smoky seconds. Then he handed the previous old notebook to Leger to read. Leger's brow went up a bit and his wine-mottled nose twitched as he read about Stephan. Here's what the pages told him:

Now or Never, Kentucky

Waiting for the muse to strike has always been an iffy business. A good many folks—a lot more than you'd like to think—prefer to wait for lightning to strike. They feel that the odds are better and the results about the same.

—Fatalism ain't got nothin' to do with it, some of us around here have been heard to say when pressed. —Anymore'n you could say that Judas Iscariot was just another stool pigeon.

And we leave it at that, whether you get the picture or not.

It is deep in the lifeblood of the community that every man, woman, child, dog, and furry chipmunk realizes and accepts his true self and his destiny. This crucial phenomenon can, of course, take place, occur, and materialize just about any old time with each individual. (Who has ever seen a mirror stamped with such warnings as Keep Away from Children, or Not for Use after June 1984?) In other words, there is no time plan or preordained day. Vlonk! It can happen.

Get an eyeful of these neighborhoods facing up to such moments of inescapable self-realization:

—Get it while it's hot! shouted Emma, the mayor's wife, lifting her skirt to expose her snatch. —Line forms on the right an' it's two bucks a throw! She did this right in the middle of the Rotary Club's Thanksgiving banquet. Standing on the main table.

—It's myself I've been chasin'! howled Sheriff Hasley O. Botsford about 10:30 one shiny morning on the courthouse steps. —I'm the archcriminal here! And he grabbed himself by the seat of the pants and ran all the way to the town jail, where he locked himself up and threw away the key.

—It ain't no use pretendin'! exclaimed town drunkard Alleyway Evans, waking up in his favorite gutter. —I'm a cabbage at heart. He promptly dragged himself to the community vegetable patch where he dug a hole and planted himself.

Nor is the collective sense of propriety apt to be suckered by practices and customs holding sway elsewhere in the state. A delectable case in point was the softball game, two weeks ago, between our team and the Blue Grass Bashers down the valley. They lost, 5–11. Now, the way it goes elsewhere is for the losers to be consoled, hugged, and feted, like it's even better to lose than to win, ya see. Know what our boys did? Marched the losers to the nearest cliff and pushed them off, one by one.

—Losers is losers, said our team captain Biff "Choo-choo" Biddle, peering over the cliff at the bodies strewn on the rocks way down below. —To hell with that hypocrisy stuff.

Another case in point, every bit as tasty as the one above, though salivating perhaps to a different drummer, is the annual beauty contest, held out at the lake on the Fourth of July. The contestants are not your traditional (!) tits-and-ass glamour girls with toothpaste grins and one foot in the movie magazines. How predictable and dull-witted that would be. Let others suck as they will. We have seen our star and we will follow it. Flash this: the female winner of this year's contest was a three-hundred-pound blimp named Imogene Wanamaker. She had warts on her knees, hair on her face, and barked as good as a coon dog. And the male winner—'cause we're not sexist pigs—was Jo-Jo the Hair-lipped Boy, who was four foot two and smelled like glue.

—Hurrah! Hurrah! shouted the happy throngs. —Three cheers for bein' true to yourself! Hip hip! Hip hip!

The winners' prizes: for Imogene, a three-week, all-expense paid vacation to the Black Hole of Calcutta. For Jo-Jo: a hundred bucks' worth of defective hand grenades and a week in the Alps with Typhoid Mary.

The thoroughly wonderful, unbridled festivities of this event were topped off by a mass, all-ages-welcome marathon swim in the lake. Prizes of unspeakable value went to those who swam out the farthest and stayed out the longest. The turnout was breathtaking. The lake waters churned as they must have churned in prehistoric times with spectacular monster animals. Three thousand and seven shrieking, wild-eyed townspeople swam their hearts out. Two thousand six hundred and nine eventually make it back to shore long after dark. It was generally taken for granted that the other three hundred and ninety-eight contestants had drowned. As the festival chairman put it so neatly and proudly many times long after the fact, —Hell's bells. I think that on balance we came off real well. Now just think—how do some of these other towns deal with the population explosion? I'll tell you. They spray their people with DDT, or they poison their drinking water, or asphyxiate them with fumes, or put cancer in their mothers' milk. Now I ask you: Does that sound like fun to you? Our way, folks get exercise and prizes to boot.

And tell me this: Why should Chairman Sutter have gone into the fact that the drowned ones—if that's what they were, and we sure hope it is, 'cause the other way's just too hard on your head—were the winners? Why?

Imminent, or, if you like the taste of it better, long-foreseen, head-on clashes or deeply sensed, preordained showdowns are handled by little folks and old folks alike, with what could hardly be regarded as furtiveness. (However cluttered the auditor's frames of reference and value judgments may be.) A tyke, for instance, one no bigger'n a short-order cook's memory, will whip a crayon out of his pants pocket and draw a line right on the pavement. —Cross that line, he'll announce to his surprised playmates, —an' we go to the mat!

A girl in her late teens, guided by nothing more than the aforementioned divinations, will charge up to a middle-aged woman who she suspects will eventually become her mother-in-law, and shout, —Keep your nose outta my marriage! Your dear little boy belongs to me now!

This preeminently air-clearing episode can occur at the seasonal "fire" sale (nobody's fooled by that "fire" bit) at Cyrus Gwaltney's Friendly Department Store; or it can suddenly materialize at the South Main Street bus stop, where if they knew what's good for 'em, everybody will be standin' round like a buncha undated calendars.

—Allors, said Inspector Epernay through the sad moan of a passing Seine tugboat. —Are you getting a firm feel for this young viper's past?

Subinspector Leger looked up from the file in his lap. —Yes, your excellency, I am, he lied with true Breton candor. —My fingers are touching the very grass from which he originally slithered.

Epernay nodded, at the same moment casting a sharp look at Stephan and Carol. —Bon, très bon. He sipped his vermouth in an official way. —It is not really necessary that you address me as "excellency," Leger.

—I am sorry, sir, said Leger. —It is just that I have this deep sympathy with the glories of the ancient regime and . . .

Epernay held up his hand. —Yes, yes. But when we are on the job you must do everything you can to remain in the present. Oh ho! His face flared up. —He has just passed to her a subversive pamphlet!

—Little swine! hissed Leger. —What gall. Phew! Leger watched the other table with righteous loathing. —By the way, sir, he went on, turning to Epernay, —what exactly have they done?

Epernay did not bother to look at Leger. His putty face remained stuck on Stephan and Carol. —That is entirely up to the President of the French Republic to decide.

Humble puzzlement registered on the, uh, official putty of Leger's face (but then, even fish gasp). —But does that mean that the, er, uh, Internal Security Police don't really have . . . anything . . .

Epernay's drink, on its way to Epernay's mouth, stopped in midair. —Do we ask at what times Joan of Arc took her pee-pees?

—Well, un, uh . . .

—Leger, my most sincere official command to you is this: Continue to keep your hand down in the snake's grass.

A flock of conceited, gluttonous pigeons, belching and dribbling from feasting at the Café Palette down the street, whirred into our scene. The patrons at the sidewalk tables showered them with tidbits. A pair of grinning American mannequins floated by and snapped pictures of this gripping tableau: In Keeping with the High Humanistic Values for Which Their Culture Is Known, Relaxing Frenchmen Feed the Pigeons.

A drunken clochard, dressed in bizarre rags and holding a bottle of red wine, pissed noisily against the giant sycamore tree in front of the café. Like a carnival balloon, he seemed to deflate to half size as a great whistling fart escaped his backside.

The sleepwalking blue-black Senegalese street cleaner (his tribal skullcap purple and yellow) turns on the flooding system in the gutter and smiles dreamily as the gurgling water whirls debris against the feet of surprised pedestrians.

—That pamphlet is very beautiful, Stephan said to Carol, filling up his little pipe for the second time. —It tells you all about how the People's Liberation Army swung into action to destroy Thieu's army during those last days. I mean, those people are incredible. He sucked and puffed furiously to bring the surly little pipe to life.

—Yeah, said Carol, leafing through the picture pamphlet. —They really are. I still can't believe it. I mean, that they finally won, you know. She shook her beautiful head in pleased disbelief, and through the magic in this lovely motion we see swallows burst upon a patch of blue sky and consume it with their wondrous wings. —I thought the fucking war would go on forever and that fucking America would eventually kill every single person in Vietnam. She turned these pages of final joy and our swallows swooped and darted in consummate abandon. —"The enemy was taken entirely by surprise when we attacked Ban Me Thuot," she read from these triumphantly blood-soaked pages. —"Thieu did not realize we could go over to the offensive so early and his forces were not ready."

She looked up and smiled at Stephan. —"The enemy was taken entirely by surprise." Wow. What a great line.

—Oh yeah. For at my back I always hear the enemy being taken entirely by surprise, said Stephan. —It drags poetry right up to date, right by the hairs of its silly ass.

Carol tucked the glorious pamphlet into her soft, seemingly obscure, self-effacing but deeply chic handmade (actually, she liked to think of it as mouth-made because she had bought it with her earnings from three blow jobs back at her "house") shoulder bag. She promised "faithfully" to return it. Three months ago she had lost a treasured copy of Malaparte's *Kaputt* which Stephan had loaned her. Though terribly sorry and contrite, she had maintained that the book had not been lost at all but had really been metabolized, absorbed by the spirit of the bordello where she worked, in the same way that the seemingly alien, nonhuman material stitches used to sew up a wound are gradually absorbed into the body, becomes part of its very life. —The stuff in the book was so much like the life in the "house" that they merged, she had insisted. —Really. Dreams or fantasies flowing into the other. Now that may sound crazy or mystical . . .

—Oh no! he had exclaimed then. —I completely believe it. And I also believe that the kinkiness of your "house"—though I prefer to think of it as a living theater—will in turn live on reproducing the stuff in *Kaputt.* Make its theater its own. He was very pleased at this absurd prospect. —The marvelously crazy scenes in the book will be played back in various forms in your wonderful "house."

They both suspended themselves—as two haughty hawks in the sky just hang there in the blue—and listened as an American couple, freaks, at a nearby table happily discussed the relative qualities of Lebanese and Moroccan hash and whether it should be eaten or smoked.

The waiter's worn, bony hand suddenly dominated the delicate space between them. He scooped up the coins on the table. —I've got to go . . . back to my theater, said Carol with a light vibration of amusement coming from her.

—You're not the only one, Stephan said, and he leaned across the table and kissed her.

They agreed to meet on Saturday at the American Cultural Center on the Rue Dragon where a bunch of them were going to harass and hopefully break up a lecture appearance by Harvard Professor Samuel P. Huntington. Huntington had devised clean, nifty ways for the Pentagon to more effectively wipe out the Vietnamese resistance in the war.

Stephan turned to me and I nodded of course. He had to get back to Juliette in Rome. Outside on the swarming, table-covered sidewalk a jaunty young man with an accordion materialized. He began to play his happy instrument and to sing a jolly French song. A disgraceful old woman souse, half collapsed at the bar counter, was wakened by the music from her trance of sordid boredom. Her swollen drunkard's face, which was a basket of discarded vegetables, exploded into a smile, the warped turnips and carrots, the sagging tomatoes and the crushed cherries came to life, and she began to sing too. But while she sang within the framework of the young man's popular tune, her words were her own, and they could not have been more brutally different. His words told of carefree young love and tender caresses under fragrant trees in the Luxembourg Gardens. Hers recalled degrading experiences during the German occupation. And her words and the in- human obscenities they revealed were given a quite special horror by their being sung within a gay, lilting tune. And let us say this, that the listener's senses were psychotically cut in two and divided against themselves: the heart gaily danced and laughed with the innocent catchiness of the tune, while the heart and the head were aghast by the blood and pain and shit- covered words. Let us imagine the effect of a child, sweetly and coyly dressed, announcing, as though she were reciting her arithmetic lesson, the number and the types of casualties of the atomic destruction of Hiroshima; let us consider your reaction as the smartly costumed waiter at the Tour d'Argent wheels up to your table the delicacies of the house, stylishly lifts the gleaming silver cover of one, and there on the silver plate is a coiled dead snake.

They tied my hands and feet together
Over a wooden hobbyhorse
The black and white Great Dane
Leaped upon my bare buttocks
And they howled with glee and
Slapped their German thighs
As it growled and whimpered and
Clawed and humped away at
Me. Its giant cock finally pierced
My ass. Oh, how they laughed and
Slapped their young German thighs.

Regarding the matter of young German thighs, past and present: we cannot ignore thighs because they're old; such thighs, while they may not involve us with the aching, spittle-covered carnality of the present, have memories, and these memories often can tell us more about history, that is, what really went on, than a whole shelf of books written by vain scholars who were not only not there but who are very happy indeed that they weren't; and we can be sure that they frequently congratulate themselves on this divine stroke of luck, as they stuff their faces at academic dinners where half the room is boisterously honoring the other half and vice versa. Anyway, German thighs . . . there were two men drinking Burgundy at a table in the back of the Café Beaux Arts to whom the subject of said thighs was of more than passing interest. One of the men was in his late fifties. His name? Michel Latour. He was a collaborator during the German occupation of Paris. The younger man—oh, in his late twenties, let us say—who was he? David Thorpe, an American in the part-time employ of the Central Intelligence Agency. Latour had spent many, many gorgeously happy hours in those bestial days being intimately involved with strong male German thighs; his plunging, sucking head between them, his own thighs entwined with them, thighs that scissored his torso in youthful wrestling, rows of thighs he had crawled through on his hands and knees being pissed on in giggling, drunken water sports à la Attila the Hun. Oh yes, thighs Latour knew well. And David Thorpe, what was he to kraut thigh? Just this: David's current lover was the effervescent but mysterious, thin-lipped but in general juicy cultural attaché of the German Embassy in Paris, Gunther Jaspers.

—You're like a Stefan George poem, you know that, Gunther? David might say while resting in Gunther's muscular arms after a love blast. —Puzzling, yet so very satisfying.

Gunther would pensively caress David's thick, rising cock, which seemed to have the noble tranquillity of a strong, young Roman gladiator who has but momentarily spent himself in a complex cause for which he is simply the innocent instrument. (Do cocks dream dreams of their own? do legs run races that we do not know about?)

—Hmm, said Gunther, —how nice to be a poem. He blithely turned David's cock this way and that. —And especially one of another age. He thought. —You have the cock of a Swiss yodeler.

Just outside the door of David's Latin Quarter studio, the blubbery, cat-reeking concierge was straining her hairy ears to catch what they were saying, even though they were talking in English, which she did not understand. Nevertheless, she would report Gunther's visit in her regular, routine chats with the Paris police, and she would invent conversations that she thought would please them, shockingly obscene, filled with heavy espionage items and gossipy revelations about the higher-ups in French politics. And the wasted young policemen would retell these lies to their wives, and their wives would pass them on to the hairdresser, and . . . oh shit.

David's conversation with Latour, a man with an almost arrogant furtiveness, was not quite so poetically lascivious.

—Are you absolutely sure you can get the plastic dynamite by Tuesday? David asked.

—Absolutely, Latour replied.

—Will you be buying it yourself?

Latour laughed. —Of course I won't be buying it. Do you think I'm crazy? It will be stolen. He shook his head slowly in surprise at David's ingenuous question. Mon Dieu, Americans were so childlike when it came to . . . Latour looked over the rim of his wineglass at a conspicuously handsome, grey-haired woman drinking coffee at the far end of the noisy, thickly entangled room. How astonishing. She looked exactly like a woman he had fingered for the Gestapo. They had tortured her to death while trying to force her to reveal information about the Resistance movement in Paris. Mon Dieu! What a fearful resemblance! He felt a weird urge to go over and ask the woman if she were the other, one Janine Salomon. Aren't you the woman the Germans killed? Of course, you were much younger then, as we all were. . . . Ah, those were the days, weren't they? she was saying in his head. Never a dull moment. One had to be on one's toes or else, isn't that so, Monsieur? I didn't get your name. What was the woman talking about really? And who indeed is she? And exactly what is she all about? And her companion, who the devil is he, sitting there so calm in his English tweed jacket as if he knew the answer to just about everything?

Obligingly, she steps forward. I am just a face in the crowd. Of no particular importance. Like that woman in the Dubonnet picture on the wall, someone for the idler to fantasize about.

Her companion now steps forward. I can't sit passively by as she tries to arrange for her own oblivion. Her modesty is against the rules of the game,

I'm afraid. She is a wonderful woman, and is waiting for that paragraph which it just knows it will dominate into blissful slavery. The girls' hands fluttered excitedly over the stage of their tiny black table. (We do not have here the desolate hysteria of the underpaid clerk.)

—Can you imagine! the miniature-faced one with monster-sized eyeglasses was exclaiming. —All I have to do for my room is give their two children breakfast every morning and then take them to school. Nothing more.

—Nothing more? said the pigeon-plump other. —You don't have to put out for the husband? Or for the wife? Or serve drinks at their dumb parties?

—Oh, Gilda! You're such a cynic. You don't even trust the birds in the trees.

—You'll see. There'll be a catch in it somewhere.

Elly looked at me (as one looks into a mirror at infinity on the other side) and shrugged as the whole world knows only the Frogs can do. —And I can do anything I like with the room, she continued, her hands never stopping their serial ballet. —I'm going to paint it into an enchanted forest.

We know about girls like her. They end up fucking trolls. They talk to rabbits and tickle turtles. They put flowers in their hair and play with traumatized snakes. They live on nuts and berries and poetry. And as I said, they wind up fucking trolls. (And sometimes, without even knowing what they're doing, really, they smuggle dope across heavily guarded borders, or they hide their boyfriends' stained shivs during a sudden raid at the neighborhood dance or at an otherwise well-behaved place like the Deux Magots, or Le Drugstore where everyone is mindlessly suspended in the middle of a movie magazine they are reading free of charge.)

Before we split this throbbing scene at the Café Beaux Arts, we must quickly check out the latrines for any messages that might have been left for us scribbled on the walls, those lewd bulletin boards of the unconscious (which is forever playing games with our dignity and tricking us into thinking we know what we are doing). Aha! "Martin Buber is a closet schizophrene." "God is a nigger fucker." "Red Riding Hood Eats Wolf Peter." "Roberto—Meet me under the bridge at 8 P.M. tonight." Ah, not only do we have naughty poetry, self-referent statements that exist in erotic solitude (like one's morning erection), metaphysical howls that speak only to themselves and the howling, but we have simple messages as well. Here's another, scribbled right under the French umbrella dispensers (2 francs; 3 francs for colors. Ooolala! A purple prick! A bright yellow rammer! Here now, lads, we must desist.): "Raymond, beware of Fornos. He kills people."

There is more—and those livid anatomical drawings, surely in the majestic tradition of Pompeii—but we must be on our way. Stephan is tugging at me. He must get back to Rome, and I am his only means of transportation.

(Fornos . . . that name sticks in one's throat, in one's troubled mind . . .) Our nose is the last to leave this toilet, inhaling that rare, lurking aroma of imagined pleasure. Mmm.

S tephan and Juliette were back in the bubbling, steaming kitchen with the muscular peasant girl Renata. The nude woman and the miniature man and the blue-smocked lady painter (whose soaring Byzantine eyebrows had surely leapt to us right out of a Coptic mosaic) had vanished into their respective (well . . .) bedrooms for the afternoon siesta without which the Roman middle class would be a disorderly band of lunatics.

—There's a lot more going on here than you would like to think, Renata said, or really promised, as she stirred a pot of heady tomato sauce. —I'm a simple, uneducated woman but I want you to know that my life does not end with the pots and pans in here and taking care of those crazy ones in there.

—Oh, we don't doubt that for a minute, said Juliette. —And we want you to think of us as friends, as . . .

—Comrades in the struggle, said Stephan. —We have the same enemies, Renata: all fascists everywhere, the enemies of the people.

Renata nodded her agreement to that all-embracing declaration—one finds sudden sanctuary in such statements: they are the hidden, warm mountainside cave in which the disparate fugitives can rest while their pursuers actively plot their death—nodded and simultaneously—because she was not one to isolate moments of self from the continuity of doing; that's for the alienated middle class whose continuity exists in historical abstractions—tasted the simmering spaghetti sauce with a long, ancient wooden spoon. —And the enemies of the people are always smiling and patting you on the back and saying that life is getting better now that Hitler's dead or now that bubonic plague is licked, but of course that's all sheep shit. She put the lid on the big pot. —Listen. Do you know that the chief of the filthy Italian secret police gets down on his hands and knees every morning and kisses the feet of Christ and then rushes off to torture his prisoners? I know this because one of my sisters, Orianna, is the nursemaid to his children.

Stephan and Juliette smiled because they knew about that sort of devotion. —Oh sure, said Juliette. —That's the way they are. Kennedy played touch football with his children in the afternoon and bombed the Vietnamese peasants at night.

—Si, si, c'è vero, c'è brutto, said Renata. —And in Iran . . . Come to my room. I want you to meet my cousin Elena. She has been in Iran working for a rich American family. You must hear her stories about what it's like in that insane place.

As they were leaving the kitchen, Renata plucked two garlic bulbs from the long, twined rope of them hanging against the wall. —From the Italian earth to you, a present, she said, and stuffed them into their jacket pockets. —And they might come in handy against werewolves and pickpockets.

They followed her down a long, narrow, darkish corridor to her room. Gradually, almost foot by foot, this corridor seemed to become older and smaller. The smooth white plaster walls became rougher and gradually turned into brick, and then into rough stone blocks whose cold, rough-hewn surface they seemed to be feeling, feeling their way along with their hands. The corridor had become an ancient passageway. They had begun their trip by walking normally behind Renata. Subtly, almost in slow motion, they felt that they were creeping (though not yet tiptoeing, though they sensed that as an imminent possibility; that is, their bodies, their senses, were prepared for that, just as when we stand on the edge of the sea our skin anticipates the gentle tides lapping all over it).

—Old, old, said Stephan, his voice lower than normal. —And I mean old.

—Michelangelo stayed here, whispered Renata, —and that's a true fact. He lived here when he was painting those ceilings at the Vatican.

Juliette squeezed Stephan's hand and put her mouth close to his ear. —Why do I feel we should all be holding candles or tapers?

The sensation of the ceiling's having become quite low (and vaulted) forced upon them a reflexive need to bend their heads and faintly hunch themselves.

—We're almost there, they heard Renata's now small voice promise them from up ahead in the semidarkness.

—Did you notice those symbols and names scratched into the walls back there? Stephan softly asked Juliette.

—Yes, but I somehow wish I hadn't.

Finally, they came to a small, heavy, planked door. Renata carefully tapped three times on its formidable, obscure surface. As one person, the three of them tensely waited for sounds within, for a response. (Were they holding their breath?) Footsteps . . . locks being turned . . . and the thick door was opened. One by one, Renata and Juliette and Stephan, all imbued with secrecy, with conspiracy, stepped inside the chaste room.

The woman waiting there for them was young, but, in the manner of all servants, her youth seemed to be, in a manner of speaking, withheld. It was poised in abeyance behind its "older" self, a calm, expressionless, soundless self which has been brought into existence in response to a lifetime of waiting upon, and being commanded by, others. A neutral, ageless servant "presence." So really two people stood there for our visiting trio.

Renata introduced them, and when she told her cousin Elena that —These are comrades, it's all right to talk freely to them, Elena said, in a sweet, matter-of-fact way, —Of course. I understand that. (All of us, of course, like to believe that saints throughout the ages have spoken like that at very important moments.)

They had not come to "visit"; they had come to "hear." The self-effacing, unseductive character of her room reinforced this point, or "understanding." (Because it did feel preordained, as a nun's habit preordains the actions and thoughts of the woman who, having cleansed her memory of her other life, slips into it.) A bed, a table, two wooden kitchen chairs, a thin self-effacing little vase with no flower in it, a frail lamp ... We naturally associate this kind of room with pain of one sort or another, either the physical recovery from it or the spiritual courting of it.

Renata said to her cousin, —These comrades are very interested in hearing all you know about Iran, the terrible things that are going on there.

The cousin smiled the polite, ritualistic smile permitted by the austerity of her room (one could hear laughter here but only of the most demonic sort, or the trilling ice giggles that curl in and out of the lewd medieval marble friezes of religious processions found on cathedrals), sat with a relaxed primness on one of the wooden chairs, her hands folded in her lap, and began her tale of pain and horror. Stephan and Juliette sat on the edge of the strict little iron bed.

—I work for an American family in Tehran. Their name is Hodges. Mr. Hodges is an electronics expert and he is a special advisor to the Iranian government. I take care of their household and its needs. I have been with them for a long time, because, you see, I first met them here in Rome when Mr. Hodges was doing the same thing for the Italian government. They liked me and that is why they took me too when he had to go and do his special things for the Shah. Mr. Hodges is a nice man but his head is wrapped in secrets. When he looks at you he does not see you. A long time ago Mrs. Hodges was an actress. Now she looks at the television all of the time and thinks about those old days.

—And drinks, added Renata.

—And drinks whiskey, cousin Elena continued. —When you look at her, she's not there. But she is not an ugly person, you know. She gives me her clothes when they stop doing the job. That's what she says: "Here, Elena," she'll say, "you can have these things. They're no longer doing the job."

Renata nodded at Stephan and Juliette. —The parts about her boyfriend will come shortly. She likes to tell things thoroughly. That's always been part of her nature.

Elena shifted herself in the chair. —All right. So there I am in Tehran. I hope you can see me in that picture little by little. Now for my boyfriend, who is going to be my husband in December. His name is Aram and he is a truck mechanic. He is a very good and kind man, and he feels very strong about the needs of the poor people and how awful they live and why things must change in Iran because so many, many people are living not even as well as animals. It breaks your heart to see how these people . . . they're human beings after all . . . how wretched their lives are in that country which is so rich with that stinking oil. She paused. She looked down at her hands. Stephan and Juliette closely watched her face as she tightened it against the flow of tears. She looks up, her dark brown eyes glistening. She is holding her hands firmly clasped, holding back . . . —So, I'll tell you what they did to Aram because he thinks and acts like a decent human being who wants his human brothers to have a life that is worth living.

She closes her eyes, and her deep, intense concentration—an utterly selfless concentration in the religious sense—unites all four of the people in this pure, ascetic room (whose very purity permits and mediates this unification), obliterating and consuming their individual identities (as a vision takes unto itself the spectators), so that they all become one, and that one becomes a being within Aram, and what is happening to him is happening to this composite one. Each one is Aram, there is not speaker and listener. His voice is their voice, his agony becomes The Agony, and thus it was that The Voice of Aram resonated in everyone's throat, and they all speak: —I was a member of a small group of students who met once a week to discuss the political and social problems of Iran, Elena says.

—We met secretly in the back room of a restaurant owned by the father of one of the group, said Stephan.

—Not all of us were communists, says Renata. —A couple were socialists. The others had no specific political ideology. They were simply decent progressives.

—And of course it is a lie that we received our orders and were controlled by Moscow, says Juliette. —It is a lie invented by the Iranian government with the constant help of the American Embassy in Tehran. And all of the American newspapers obligingly print these and other lies. So they are just as guilty of the crimes against us and the oppressed Iranian masses as the Iranian secret police. You must keep this in mind. All murderers do not wear uniforms and speak a strange language.

—We saw that, whatever your social class or your personal goals, you cannot be a person of conscience and not be appalled and shamed by the dreadful conditions of life that degrade and ultimately destroy such a large part of the Iranian population.

—I was arrested by SAVAK agents who came to my room in the small pension where I live, Elena recited, her eyes staring straight ahead. —They kicked open the door because I did not open it fast enough. I was immediately taken to the SAVAK station of Khorramshahr. Three men stripped me naked with punches and kicks for the purpose of so-called physical inspection. From 8:00 P.M. to 1:00 A.M. the next day, the interrogation went on accompanied by more punches and kicks . . . The next day I was transferred to the police station of Abadan and imprisoned in one of the toilets there. I spent one whole week in this toilet with only an old army blanket, one meal a day and no clothes at all. On the eighth day I was handcuffed and transferred to Tehran in a SAVAK Land Rover, to the Evin prison. Interrogation began upon my arrival, combined with torture. Two men, Reza Atapour, known as Dr. Hosseinzadeh, and Biglari, known as Engineer Yoosefi, beat me for nearly an hour. Then they sat me behind a desk and told me to write down that I was a communist and engaged in espionage. When I refused, Reza Atapour ordered two sergeants to come in and force me to lie down.

—They began flogging me with assistance from Biglari, using a black cable whip. The flogging and the beating and the punching and the kicking went on for more than three hours. My torturers were taking turns and resting. I fainted twice in the course of all this. My whole body had turned blue, and blood streamed down my back.

—The interrogation on January 21 ended here, recited Renata, keeping her eyes straight ahead in the manner of Elena. —On the next day, the same things were repeated, with the only difference being that they put the weight cuffs on me several times. They forced me to stand on a stool with the cuffs on, with one of my feet held free in the air. They knocked the stool out from under me several times, causing me to fall onto the floor with my full weight. The following day, as a result of slaps I received from Atapour, my ears started bleeding. The eardrum of the left ear was torn. I can no longer hear with it . . .

It may go against some people's grain, or it may merely get under their skin (like a chigger which has been carried away by its own chutzpah), but the fact of the matter is that the projectionist in Juliette's head—a person whose genealogy is as thrilling as a precipice—this person had gone bananas. Why else would this person who's got it so good keep interrupting the main show in Juliette's consciousness to flash on such surly, low-budget stuff as . . .

She was in a car parked on the deserted picnic grounds. It was nighttime. Paul kept working his frantic hand under her skirt and into her panties, pushing her against the inside of the car door with his urgent body. —Come on, Julie, please, he pleaded, plunging two fingers deep into her wet cunt. —Please, I promise I'll pull out in time. Please.

—No, no, Juliette moaned, writhing and riding with his plunging hand. —I'm afraid. I'm afraid I'll get pregnant. Ooh Paul. Oh . . . we'd better . . .

—I promise! I promise! Please, Julie! Let me put it in!

Juliette's hand, acting on its own it seemed, pulled down the zipper of

Paul's jeans and grabbed his hard cock. Her entirely autonomous hand jerked it, and in a matter of seconds, come was spurting on her hand and wrist.

—Ooh Jul . . . ie! he sighed, thrusting his groin, convulsively thrusting, thrusting. —*Ohhhh.*

Juliette relaxed against the car seat. Her (in a sense) disengaged hand still clasping Paul's soft, spent cock, she smiled. Suddenly her whole body stiffened and went cold. A grinning black man was standing at the car window. He was pointing a pistol at them.

—Yeah, said the black man, grinning and slowly nodding his head. —That's right, baby. You got it. Don' you yell or nothin' 'cause I'll blow yo' fuckin' head right off. Now come on outta thuh cah . . .

Her father was walking furiously back and forth across the large brown carpeted living room. Her soft, fat, nice mother was standing in the kitchen doorway. She was crying almost soundlessly, and a dead, half-eaten doughnut dangled in her silly, pudgy, little hand. Juliette and her brother Mike sat tensely next to each other on the edge of the long, squooshy leather couch.

—I don't give a goddamn what you say! he shouted. —You're going into the army and you're going to carry your share.

Mike remained stiff and shook his head. —No, I'm not, he said. —I'm going to Canada and nobody's going to stop me, Dad.

Juliette put her hand on her brother's. —I'm for you, Mike. I wouldn't go either. Why should you get killed for a bunch of lousy fascists like Johnson and Laird and Westmoreland . . .

—You! her father screamed from across the room. —It's your fault he's acting this way! You goddamn little communist! You're a disgrace to this family.

Her mother began to sob. —Oh please, Harvey. Please.

Juliette turned to her brother. —I'll go with you, Mike. We'll go tomorrow if you want to, OK?

They were all sitting around, lying around Helen Gilbert's studio on Green Street in the Village: Juliette; Henry Watts, who taught English at Bard College; his girlfriend Laura, who taught at Old Westbury College; George Maxey, who was a civil liberties lawyer; and elegant, blonde Helen. Henry passed the hash pipe to Juliette, who was lying on the floor pillows. She inhaled deeply and held the smoke way down in her lungs without breathing.

—And so those dumb bastards closed the college down for some chickenshit thing called black power, said Laura, sprawled next to Juliette right under Helen's huge red-and-blue abstract painting. —What a stupid fraud, what a dreary joke.

Juliette passed the pipe to Helen and, floating gently within herself, sweetly hash high, smiled as she looked at Helen's soaring, partly exposed, naked breasts.

—Well, it sure taught the white liberals a lesson, said Henry. —Until their black students started attacking them, the idiots were drowning in sentimental brotherhood bullshit.

Juliette was floating deeply in silent caves within herself and yet, within the same sensations, she was sliding deftly along the throbbing surface of herself. —I guess they don't know what to do with all their anger, she listened to herself say, could even see the words as they glided from her mouth. —I mean, I think they think that black rage is an ideology or something.

Big black George Maxey began to laugh, a somnolent, rich laughter that seemed to be coming from a hidden, well-to-do valley somewhere. —This poor, crazy, fucking country. It's going down the drain, honkies and niggers together, no difference. Just look at New York City and Philadelphia and Detroit. You think those places are cities? Man, those places are white outposts under siege. You know what I mean . . . *under siege.*

Juliette was beginning exquisitely to float to Detroit and those other swarming, crazed places when the studio door was suddenly and brutally banged on with clubs.

—Open up! This is the police!

—Oh shit! said Helen. —Is this a dope bust?

She snatched the hash pipe from Laura and raced to the bathroom as the brutal banging resumed. —Open up or we'll knock the door in! the dreadful, lumpen, blood-choked police voice yelled.

Juliette felt physically assaulted. That black-hooded executioner voice forced its way inside Juliette and immediately killed the tingling life of sweetness there, and reeking death stalked her very soul.

V oices . . . you don't have to be the head elevator operator at the Ritz in London, or the only homosexual in a five-man high-wire act, to know that, once sounded, voices live on and on. That, in truth, they insist upon it, no matter what your sentimental and simpleminded feelings on the matter may be. Only misguided Trappist monks and hopeless deep-sea divers think otherwise. And why should we hang around bums like that? Lurking in the perverted atmosphere all over the world are voices that won't give up. They wait there for you, for me. They've been waiting/lurking since yesterday in some cases; for thousands of years in others. *But they're there, do you understand?*

Like the voice of Richard Suckhouse Nixon saying, "The most fundamental weakness in American education is that students are not allowed to face the challenge of failure." Those fart-smelling words can come at you, quite unexpectedly and without being summoned, and at any hour of the day, in your favorite massage parlor, in the basement of your psychoanalyst's house, or even in the quiet, craven back streets of London. Make no mistake about it. And this shit-covered statement, "I'm no crook," by the same little scum. This one can quite easily be waiting for you in the stale air of an airplane over, say, Mexico City.

And just yesterday, as I sat my weary ass down in an Amsterdam strudel house, hoping for a little peace of the mind and quiet of the stomach between acts, from under the table, where it has been poised for God knows how long, came this voice: "I am not willing to accept the idea that there are no communists left in this country. I think that if we lift enough rocks we'll find some." Senator Barry Goldwater. I knew from the depths of my own personal records (not bought or inherited like a hooker's john book or a dental practice in Great Neck, but compiled with blood, sweat, and shit) that that voice, or those words, had been in the air since 1953. Later on, while strolling down the Avenue Rembrandt on my way to the No Holds Barred Sauna, minding my own labyrinthian business for a change, looking for no trouble or any fast-buck deals and all that, my gently bred ears were violated by more free-floating human statements: "And I repeat . . . the United States has in no way been involved in the Bay of Pigs." That as I turned my head to savor an especially tasty piece of Dutch ass. A few yards farther on, while observing an old man feeding pigeons around a statue of a nationally adored slaughterer of the innocent: "Female cardholders in the American Communist Party are required to show their loyalty to the cause through indiscriminate intercourse wherever it will do the most good."

In the sauna . . . Mmm. Nothing quite like steam and heat and nakedness, and of course firmly grounded Dutch hands, to loosen up the brain cells, to induce the body to abandon its secular constraints and its identity problems. Those sneaky, so dearly purchased masks we all hide behind, they melt here. The haughty styles of the boulevard vaporize. Male and female costumes that manipulate you, the grinning, open-mouthed dumbbell, into sly sociological mythologies are not schlepping around doing their stuff here. Oh no. You could say that in this vast, undulant Amsterdam sauna we were naked, glistening humans sharing the steamy primordial swamp, and in that eerie divine ooze, conscious and unconscious flowed in and out of each other as the same thing, as the birds and reptiles and fish and even hairy ape-man himself were glorious and bizarre composites of one another.

Barely to be seen through the dense steam, the long, bony man lying near me on the floor mats caressed and rubbed his arms with infinite slowness and care. —Government's gotta clean up the red-light district here. Filth and abominations. People doin' things that even animals can't do and wouldn't if they were given a chance. Spilling out into that street where mothers are walkin' with their young issue. Worse'n disease, 'cause you can cure disease with a needle. An' all those degenerates throwin' their arms aroun' Karl Marx in the middle of everything else putrid an' soul destroyin'. Clean ... them ... out ... Must ... stamp ... out ... worldwide ... whoredom ... and ... the ... hordes ... of ... anti-Christ ... commie ... lovers ... that're ... shittin' ... on ... God's ... head.

I could see only breasts and stomach through the shifting sauna mists. —Told him that I didn't care what official government spokesmen said. My brother didn't commit suicide, he was murdered, by killers hired in Amsterdam by the CIA. Because my brother knew too much, that's why. He knew all about those mystery visitors to Rhodesia. He knew they were American advisors to Smith and his gang. He knew because he'd been in the Green Berets with them in Vietnam, that's how he knew. My brother wasn't crazy. He wouldn't one day just decide to jump into one of these canals to drown himself because he was tired of it all or something like that. Not him. He was killed and thrown into that canal. And you can bet on it that I'm not going to let them get away with this. If you don't stand up to them, it may be your turn next. And you better not kid yourself about that, my friends.

Euphoric, muted, ecstatic splashing sounds in the distance, sounds refined and mediated, yes, filtered, perhaps, by having traveled through a collective unconscious ... All kinds of bodies were leaping and hurling into the chilly pool. The ecstatic thrills of hot/cold shock, the mind and body abruptly brought to the breathless edge of traumatic self-obliteration. Squeals and shrieks and gasps reached me in my delicious, sweating nonbeing, wafted through grinning/leering eons . . . and wafted also through my own sweating/melting/drifting self. The gates and boundaries of myself, and the sturdy, faceless watchmen on my high walls had been dispelled ... become benign clouds of human steam ... which was the whole idea of this place. Two men strolled past me with towels over their heads and shoulders, making them look like fearful priests in an ancient and dreaded religion.

—It's just a question of packaging now. Everything else has been solved.
—Right. The laser beam itself is the most powerful we've designed so far.
—Oh absolutely. It dematerialized that drone flying three miles up. In a puff of smoke.
—Never saw anything like it.
—Gives you an idea of what we can do to enemy cities one of these days.
—Boy, I'll say!
They disappeared into clouds of steam and clusters of naked, steam-shrouded bodies resting or suspended, somehow, in various positions. And the steam and the bodies were metamorphosing in and out of one another,

flesh becoming steam and steam becoming flesh, naked/talking/babbling humans vaporously merging one into the other, faces emerging from bellies, arms and legs drifting into and vanishing into faces and asses, cunts and cocks and balls, muffs and mouths mistily vanishing into hands and feet and shoulders. And voices . . . voices coming from everywhere, some with wanton boldness, some with skilled emptiness, others with the elegant shyness of a giraffe hiding behind a perfumed mimosa tree at midday.

—When the crunch comes, he'll run, I just know he will, said a voice emerging from a pair of looping breasts. —He can't stand real pressure or responsibility of any kind. He's a child, afraid to grow up.

—Of course. That's precisely why you married him, came a voice from a black-muffed pussy. —It's important for you to assume the dominant, maternal role with a man. What I'm saying is you picked Carl for exactly those qualities that are now so disturbing to you.

I began to wander/drift effortlessly through the swirling, timeless mists, hoping to find a massage somewhere. I was cosmically absorbent and detached from myself. My mouth opened wide to catch more oxyg i, and someone's words issued from it: "Reports that we had advance knowledge of this coup are incorrect." I inhaled deeply and exhaled. More words flowed out of my gaping mouth: ". . . to advise the Chilean military and assist them in their training and in the use of supplies . . ."

A bearded, sweating, disembodied head passed mine. —We are all like brothers, it said.

I glided through a ruddy tangle of arms and legs that were performing an undulatory, slow-motion series of group gymnastics. —Admiral Merino asked me for three thousand rifles. He wanted them flown in at night.

—Charles Horman, if you're here in the stadium, you're perfectly safe now, issued from a mottled back. —If you're here, please come forward.

Farther on in this sweltering, primeval miasma, near the slurping, dousing pool, a soft, large ass brushed against the sensation, the presence of my face, was absorbed into this face/presence, and as it was being absorbed, and my face/presence itself vanishing into it, a voice like a supreme fart came from the asshole: "I came here not to praise Caesar but to bury him."

Soon strong, gentle arms were manipulating my body on a table, and hands of soft steel were massaging me, rubbing and caressing and probing my entire mellifluous being. Voices came from the hands, and the hands were rubbing these voices into me, into my back, my thighs, my groin: —The point that I'm trying to make in my thesis, Elaine, is that women have been so subjugated, so colonized really, by a male establishment that even when they write novels they are afraid to see things in their absolutely own way.

—Yeah, yeah. You're right, you're so right.

Those voices became part of the tension in my calf muscles.

—The only debatable point is whether the victims of bomb testing should be counted in the thousands, the hundreds of thousands, or millions . . . into my ankles and between my toes.

Somewhere between my tingling, alcohol-saturated chest and my stomach, a voice said, —Have you got the address right? OK. Now listen, Anna. Just show up there and don't worry about anything. Everybody there will be friendly. You don't have to know anybody. You'll be there in an act of solidarity with the Vietnamese and with the American Left. We don't celebrate Christmas anymore. We celebrate Tet. OK?

The powerful, all-knowing Dutch hands (I must assume they were Dutch. What would Indian or Chinese hands have been doing there? But this only shows how simplemindedly logical I can be at times. You can come across yellow hands anywhere in the world, even inside your wallet pocket at times) continued their subtle business of infiltration. The fundamental structure of my being was no longer an integral sum. My tissues and cells were being rearranged, reordered, reinvested. The irresistible, fecund, antediluvial ooze, where tadpoles and lizards and fish were changing into birds and baboons and men, was coming into me, swallowing and reclaiming me, making me a liquescent part of the tidal wave of mankind. Other beings and their voices oozed through me: *I was that transforming, ineluctable ooze of human essence.* Gill gaspings, lowly tonguings, shrieks, beaks, calls were evolving into human sounds, and these sounds were boundless urging. They were me and I was them.

The mysterious masseur—even if he were a specific human with a name and I knew him or her and his or her name, I would not divulge it, at least at this stage of the (I mean our) game—brought his face down through the sublimely swirling vapors, put his lips to my moist ear and whispered (with the consuming intimacy of a cosmic voice coming from the clouds, or a vast cavern, suddenly without urging, speaking to you and to you alone), —They will come to see you tonight. They'll have some truly great Lebanese hash for you, and they will also have some important messages.

I heard a voice take shape from some part of my amorphous, collective self. —That's fine. I'll be at home around seven-thirty. I have a class until seven.

And as the words lingered there, in ectoplasmic steaminess, expanding and contracting, collapsing and reshaping, rising and falling and floating, I experienced the eerie exhilaration—a sort of inverted vertigo, a rushing up out of the abyss rather than a falling into it—of a self taking place who was connected with the words, who in a fabulous, magical, molecular way was being created by the words themselves. (Can't you just see, on a morning of virtually insane, bucolic clarity, the first huntsman's horn sounds suddenly, summoning forth/creating the hounds, and the fox from nature's awesome slumbers?) This process was completed by the caressing, kneading, knowing masseur's saying, —You were so great yesterday, Michael, the way you handled that tourist asshole at the bar. What did he say he was? A reporter for the *New York Times*? The kind of shit he was trying to pull!

And I was quite simply Michael in the bar on the Canal Vermeer telling this smug, tweedy little cunt—whose face had the expression of a monk who thinks he is in possession of some damning bit of gossip about the Holy Ghost—who was in the company of a woman, who surely must have been a store window mannequin every morning, I was telling him, —You are completely full of shit. American newspapers are not unbiased and neutral in their reporting. Every fucking thing they print, especially if it's about anything antiestablishment or political, is misrepresented and slanted. Reading American newspapers is a sure way of becoming simpleminded and right wing.

He smirked with ineffable self-love, and you knew right then and there what happens when farts begin to inbreed. —Oh really? And I suppose you'd say that the publication of the Pentagon Papers was an insignificant or right-wing gesture?

I presented him with a look that combined scorn with loftiness, the sort of look that is normally reserved for illegal aliens caught at the remote border disguised as watermelons or pregnant sheep dogs. —Publishing the Pentagon Papers hardly offsets the mountains of poisoned shit that rag has been printing since time began. Furthermore, I added, —they left a lot out.

His little mannequin suddenly came to life, leaped out of whichever shoddy department store window she had been obscenely posing in— modeling, to be sure, a provocative costume meant to help the female masses compromise themselves still further—leaped out (or scurried) and bleated, —But . . .

—But nothing! I cried. —Right up to the very end, that filthy paper of yours was begging for more American aid to that murderer Thieu and his gang!

Farthead made one last shameless attempt to plant the flag of liberal fascism on these decent shores. —Yeah, and look what's happening in Vietnam now. A million and a half people in concentration camps.

Could his running-dog consort resist throwing in her grubby two cents' worth? Of course not. —That's right! she said. —Try to explain that away if you can.

My only response to these star-spangled-banner suckers was to speculate on how to dispose of their bodies after I'd murdered them. But the bartender, a sensitive man with wide shoulders and the mouth of a Renaissance penitent, who from time to time functioned as history's town crier, came from behind his shiny mahogany bar and altered the course of things.

—To cast some light and final truth on this subject, he announced quite gently, —I wish to relay the following statement from the Southeast Asia Resource Center: "While most of the over a million people who had registered for 'reeducation' (in the camps) in 1975 spent only a short time in centers set up for this purpose, numerous former officers and civilians were still being held in camps towards the end of 1976—as many as 200,000 according to some observers. However, Vietnamese officials stated in February 1977 that about 50,000 people were still being held, equivalent to 5 percent of the total of those who had registered. According to the statement, issued by Vietnam's observer at the United Nations, they would have to 'remold themselves' before being released and they were being reasonably treated, although they could not expect a 'better life than most of the ordinary working people in Vietnam.' According to a broadcast by Hanoi Radio, those who would have to undergo prolonged 'reeducation' included members of the Green Berets, the rangers, the paratroopers, marines, policemen, prison guards, district officials, village chiefs and secret agents who were trained by the United States. For the remaining 5 percent the average length of 'reeducation' would be three years, a period which can apparently be reduced depending on the 'progress made in the reeducation centers.' "

The bartender continued: —Now this from Friendshipment, a people-to-people aid campaign consisting of over forty national and local peace, civic and religious organizations: "We visited Reeducation Camp #2. One unarmed guard stands at the fence. The gate opens to a large flower garden. Each building is built with the usual thatched roof, mud walls, and earth floor like hamlet housing found throughout Vietnam. The large kitchen area had fires for cooking, areas for preparing meals. The dormitory buildings seemed to sleep about fifty men each. Typical wooden beds, straw mats, and mosquito netting were surrounded by the personal items of each man, including bags of fruit, radios, clothing and books. Many men were making fish traps, sewing fish nets, and finishing bamboo handicrafts to send home as we passed through their rooms.

"Families are allowed to visit one weekend and stay overnight. The men are permitted mail and packages."

M ichael was surrounded by his students. That is, they were seated all around him in the university cafeteria. But really, they were swarming all over him, like bees on a juicy flower, or monkeys on a ripe apple tree (or even, he thought, like question marks on the shoulders of an unsolvable problem). He could feel their hungry Dutch faces rubbing every inch of his naked body. Their mouths, their tongues, their sniffing noses. Sniffing, licking, munching. Faces that . . . well, one of them would have been better off—or at least more at home—in a pastry shop, with raisins stuck in it. Another—those eyes, surely they had been stolen from a drowned sailor— had unquestionably been nurtured on equivocations (and barely suppressed parental longings for shoddy pleasures).

—Professor Smoot, isn't it possible, do you think, that Americans must be undergoing a severe crisis of identity?

—Yes, Professor, wouldn't you certainly agree to the position that with their complete defeat in Vietnam, Americans had to face the falsity of their chauvinistic mythology?

—Do you believe that the class struggle has come to a middle-class dead end?

—The time has come when America has no more culture heroes, and therefore social homogeneity is breaking up.

—Tell me, Michael, would it be hard for me to get some kind of job in New York City? I want to be there for a year just for the energy. You know what I mean?

Michael sucked at his pipe and said, —That isn't real energy. Just as violence isn't strength. New York has anxiety and panic and hustle. (A crazed spade runs before him with a drawn knife.) And death and the terror and emptiness of death. (Three black kids jump him in the subway and one of them fires a pistol into his neck.) Americans are dripping with blood, inside and out. (Two policemen grab a gay protestor and one of them hits him repeatedly over the head and shoulders with his truncheon until he collapses. Michael goes to his aid and is clubbed too.) "Hey meester, you wanna buy a nice secon'han' torture machine real cheap, no shit?" Dutch student giggles and chuckles. Laughter that seemed to be translated. Sounds that smelled of cheeses and pipes and hot chocolate, sounds over which wooden shoes were clomping and ice skates were skimming. And then one pair of flashing skates suddenly made a sharp turn, stopping, throwing up a spray of grated ice, and said, —The American peoples will not allow these Cambodian dwarfs to turn them into helpless yellow giants!

—Yeah, right on, Dirk, you got it, Michael said.

—As der fugging world becomes smellier and more lower-class, our vell-beings require more commitment at an early stage of puberty if der crazy, demented challenges are not to grow overwhelmingly and make us clean people zleep less.

—Perfect! Michael shouted. —God, you could all go on tour.

The shimmering Meerloo girl, who was sleeping with the Chilean refugee poet Catalana (whose poems were like trees sobbing in the wind), said, —Maybe your State Department would be happy to sponsor us, yes?

On one of your cultural exchange arrangements. "The Little Dutchies Sing Your Favorite Political Songs."

American Studies . . . what exactly is that? Michael asked himself (more often in the middle of something else: taking a shit, reading, cruising the Atheneum Bookstore for cultural/political news, for free-floating Dutch pussy—young or middle-aged, either one will be OK—though I think I kind of lean toward the older stuff, 'cause it knows more). Can I really teach these kids anything worth knowing about that lunatic, fucking place? Or can I at best merely trace with our collective finger the labyrinth? And when they get to know the dank, malevolent labyrinth, will this help them live their lives decently? Or will this (in a sense) technological-cultural information be the equivalent of a brochure on what to do when the Bomb is dropped? Isn't it a black joke to be talking about *Moby-Dick* when it is Lieut. Calley we should be analyzing? *Moby-Dick* isn't going to dismember their raped sisters, but Calley/Westmoreland will. Can I possibly convey to them the American Experience, somehow put them in my own anxious shoes? Yes, that's really worth trying; flip out together, get brain transplants, everybody in a daisy chain, put a finger up one another's asshole, hold my hand, me with my finger up my own asshole, and turn on the electrical current. That would do it. Pure American Shit racing through everybody's blood and brain cells. They could all be me, living it up in the American Maze. Like this funky, weird story—who put me up to it?—before my very eyes:

L eaves can lie. Clean light may hide shadows of black imminent rain torrent. Green that promises sweet firmness, beneath it soggily, in its indifference, could be the skill of snakes and muck and death. And what can you safely say of the birds? Darting of self-swooping, sharp cries, exclamations of small, uncontained discovery—can they not be the voices of recognized panic before the great bird kills? Just behind them, wings outstretched, wet, mad mouth open? But why? But of course! Soft sheets in their benign shifting change nothing, whoever you might be; what then can you do about it? Close the curtains, open your mouth, close it, then open it again and say, —I wish you wouldn't keep doing that, Earl. Can't you wait until they get here?

—That's tomorrow. I'm for now. How's your old now? You can't really deny that, can you, Willa old pussycat? I mean the now of you?

Wind shakes trees at the depot, enmeshes and thrills bushes, and isolated, bringing up cold speculation, and a question, —Is there a cab available? I'd like to go to the Hansens'.

—He's right over there, the depot worker said. —He's just coming back from a call. I haven't seen you before, his expression said. What are you up to?

That's the nasty part of coming out to the country to visit someone, Penny reflected, the thick-witted male looks of authoritarian curiosity that men have and that without their ever knowing it, the poor trapped idiots, turn them really into hateful old ladies, while they are all the while feeling they are so manly. Pathetic and disgusting.

—Is it very far? she asked the driver after she had given the address of the Hansens' house and he had begun pulling away from the railroad station house, a forlorn, forbidding, burnt brick-turreted structure that now, with the fleeing of the alighted visitors in bright, insect-small modern cars, sighed back into the impregnable nineteenth-century vacuum of its origin.

—About three miles, the driver replied, not turning his head. —Don't worry, he added in a flat, matter-of-fact voice that sounded as though he had arranged it and recited it all many times, —in no time at all you'll be sitting in front of a hot abstract painting with a cold martini in your hand, well on your way to a real fun weekend in the country. You won't be bored for a minute.

—Oh, that's fine, she said, though really being slightly taken aback by his intimacy. Does he know that I'm supposed to meet a man here too? Two unmarried, unattached people being brought together as weekend guests of Earl and Willa Hansen. Makes you feel you're being pimped for. But when it's being done all the time . . . and obviously it must titillate me or I wouldn't be here.

The taxi swerved suddenly, throwing her heavily against the door.

—That rabbit was surely bent on suicide, the driver remarked, gifting her only with the back of his head, an act which made his statements more like a soliloquy than human conversation. —Can you imagine a lowly animal getting so desperate it would want to destroy itself?

—Lowly animals . . . she began, without really knowing what she was saying; she did not go on. She was chilled and her equilibrium assaulted by his voice; he sounded so fastidiously cultivated, yet here he was driving a cab. Something was dreadfully askew. Was he insane? Had he fallen on bad times from a loftier place? Or was he simply a cabdriver out here because it amused him, while living, elsewhere, quite an understandable, reasonable life? She became, momentarily, a child. I hope he's not kidnapping me. What have I done to him? Mommy, please don't let him do anything naughty to me. I'll be a good girl. I promise. I'll do anything you say, honestly I will. Only don't let him make me pull my dress up and take off my panties. Please. Spankings from back then began to sting her legs and quivering buttocks now, and her shrill, futile child screams made her twist her head in anguish. She clutched her purse hand to her stomach as she had her doll, after punishments, for dear life. An amputated monster tree, sheathed in outraged mottled skin, a huge crotch eye squinting from memories of ancient tortures, mocked her from an abrupt clearing in the woods on her right. The other trees had drawn back in appalled disgust from it: its pain and abandonment were a contaminating blight.

The taxi swerved sharply across the road and into a gravel driveway. —'Ere we are, your loidyship, the driver announced gaily. —The cahstle at lahst!

Moments later the dazzling modern house swallowed her up.

—His mother is at death's door, Earl Hansen was explaining later. —And he had to rush off to Cleveland. I'm really sorry, Penny, because you would have liked him. Very bright, charming fellow. He took a consoling drink from his martini and smiled.

—We'd planned to bring you two together for such a long time, too, Willa said. —But we'll try to see that you don't get lonely.

Penny's second martini was helping her feel quite at home. She even felt conciliatory toward the arrogant abstract mural on the living room wall. —Please don't worry about it. Being away from dirty old New York for a weekend is enough pleasure in itself. Really. This was not entirely the truth; she had felt apprehensive about leaving the city and coming out here to be a houseguest—she had met them in the city at a party given by her boss three weeks ago—but whatever her uneasiness, it was much, much more bearable than huddling alone in her small apartment. She longed for people as a small plant longs for sweet, giving water that will keep it from dying, despite her inability to be as effective socially as she wished. Like her body, her personality was curved and dark and soft, and its natural motion was away from, gently off course, rather than forward in straight lines or sideways in hungry angles, as was the case with tall, Nordic-seeming Willa, sprawled confidently over there on the couch like a huntress returned from a successful kill, with the sure knowledge of many more. Sometimes, when Penny, who was twenty-five, imagined herself, it was as a friendless child covered in a huge black shawl hunched up in a street-level doorway in a deserted Mediterranean village, one bare foot exposed to the unforgiving passing eye of life. Self-pity bathed her then, as would womb fluids. —Excuse me, she apologized to Earl, reverie broken. —What did you say?

—I asked if you liked birds.

—Yes, I love birds.

—That's good, he continued, admiring the delicate stem of his glass, —because we have a lot of them out here. He chuckled. —Sometimes I wake up thinking I'm a prisoner in a bird sanctuary. Just can't imagine how I got there—if you know what I mean. Birds talking to birds . . . telling each other secrets and all that.

Penny laughed unrestrainedly. She liked the man. He seemed vulnerable in an affectionate way. Like a brother perhaps. He was an advertising executive. Willa was a designer. Through the open veranda door, peremptorily claiming the moment its own, a piercing bird cry broke through.

—See what I mean! shouted Earl, slapping his knee. —They'll be coming out of the ice cubes next.

—That's a golden-throated warbler, Willa advised them, smiling beautifully at Penny. —She's lonely, and she's calling for her mate.

—How do you know it's a female? Earl asked, going to the sideboard and mixing another round of soothing, conspiratorial martinis.

—A woman's intuition. I know that cry so well. But what would he know or care of that? Willa asked herself. When did I first hear that soul-splitting cry? I think it was from myself . . . oh, five years or more ago. When I realized that Earl and I had lost each other like two children becoming parted in a strange night-city. And by whose omniscient order or desire? Mine or his? Or just destiny like rain or snow instead of sun? That was when I first heard such a cry. Where was my mate? Not Earl . . . he became quite lost, even though he still goes through the rituals of mate demands and mate proximity. Nights and nights I would listen, still do, to the sounds therein, hoping, dying for a response to that great cry/question. How the nights go mad with calls and calls. But no responding call for me. Why? Or had there been one but was caught and strangled by the omnivorous ivy out there before it reached my ears? This Penny is so brown and delicate. I wonder if Earl is going to make a pass at her somewhere along the line . . . But of course! That's the idea. How silly of me to forget. And I was going to take . . . what's his name . . . to my own pillow.

—. . . so any way you look at it, the public's to blame, not the sponsor or the agency. They were on the lawn now, and Earl, between bites of an egg roll appetizer and sips of gin, was holding the floor. —You know what happens when you present *Oedipus Rex* in three installments? The last two parts are watched by half a dozen people, three of them in the control room. But give them Perry Blotto or Losers Creepers, you mow 'em down by the millions. So how is it possible to avoid the conclusion, assuming anybody wants to avoid it in the first place, which I certainly don't, that the general public prefers garbage to caviar? However, I wonder whether it really matters or not. You know? Why does everybody get so hot about raising the cultural level of the masses? Leave them where they are. They aren't bothering anybody, are they? Are they bothering you, Penny my dear?

She giggled and flicked a tiny, confused ant off her knee, an ant that quite obviously had no goal in mind at all, that was defying every known rule of successful living. —No, not in the least.

—That's fine, just fine. I think they're entitled to their base instincts just like everybody else. Agree?

—Absolutely, Penny replied. —To base instincts, she added, somewhat to her own surprise, and drank off a toast, which Earl joined while Willa merely watched, more or less amused. It feels funny to be getting drunk, Penny told herself; guilty and good and, I don't know why, dangerous. I wish that other person had come, then I wouldn't feel so—exposed, I guess it is. But why? Exposed about what? I feel naughty, a bad girl. But I am enjoying myself. No turning back even if I wanted to I suppose. Just see what happens? What am I afraid of? Mmm, Willa's perfume smells divine. Arpège? Yes . . . yes, that's it. I should wear stronger perfume. Maybe I will.

Buzzing of insects somewhere, neither far nor near, interwoven with the gentle rustling of leaves. All vengeance and purpose had vanished from the sunlight, and now it was utterly sensual and passive, soft and willing; it murmured and vibrated the message: enjoy, enjoy, no harm will come of it. Enjoy, abandon yourself. The air was calmly innocent there.

—You must be starving, Willa said without frightening off the complicitous mood with the ordinariness of her words.

—Well, Penny began, —now that you mention it . . .

—We'll eat out here. It's so much less . . . confined.

A young Negro maid heaped a table on the lawn with chilled vichyssoise, chicken and ham, salad, cheeses; cold wine in tall bottles glowed happily in superior resignation. Earl went to the john. Willa got up to stretch after drinking down the last of her martini.

—Have you ever been married, Penny?

—No. Why?

—Don't know. It just occurred to me to ask, and she laughed with sudden pleasure and gave Penny a peck on the cheek. —That makes you a virgin, in a sense.

—I suppose it does. Penny finished off the last of her own martini (the cheek kiss was still a slightly indecisive sensation). —Should I feel bad?

—No, God no.

Into the momentary silence that settled gently between them, laying down a threshold of discovery and innocence, appeared now—not really flying but defying time and space by suddenly materializing, motionless-seeming—a hummingbird. —Oh! Penny gasped sweetly in startled delight. Its exquisite, green presence precipitously shrank the tall trees and wide veranda and waiting women to its own awesome dimensions; all sounds, rustlings, chirpings were stayed by its wing whirrs; its imperious needle beak penetrated keenly to the very nerve centers of the two women, paralyzing them. They could do nothing at all but stare at the bird, waiting breathlessly. Then it vanished into the mysterious country twilight.

—I feel it was almost trying to tell us something, Penny ventured shyly after a moment.

—Yes, Willa agreed. —But what?

—I don't know. But it was something important.

Willa put her hand in Penny's in mutual understanding. Soft and firm. Strong, suntanned hand that poured the sharp, exhilarating white wine during dinner—Earl's hands, Penny observed through increasingly wine-obligated eyes, were mottled and clearly burdened with heavy self-contempt that pudged them too—clumsied all fingers everywhere they went, to knocking over his glass of wine—"Oh Earl, really! You are irresponsible." "Good for the tablecloth, m' love. Gives it that lived-on look." (That laugh, sounds like he's strangling, thought Penny)—strong hand that rang for the silent, self-abolishing black maid, and that then cut her a wedge of Danish Port du Salut, just enough to experience lightly rather than to gorge on as Earl was doing between quite uninhibited swallows of Frascati. Where, where in the ungiving past had she seen and felt that hand? in dreams? in life? in movies?—somewhere.

—Course, the thing is that nobody really gives a good goddamn when you come down to it, Earl continued, for he had been talking all through dinner. —They'll say they thought Kennedy did wrong here and goofed there and so on. But that's just a lot of bullshit. Talking so they can hear themselves and feel involved or something. They know the whole thing is a big gas. Only thing they care about is getting laid or making money or being top or bottom dog, I mean it.

—You're a cynic, Penny said, smiling a bit drunkenly.

—No, I'm not, Penny baby. Just wising up a little as I get more grey hairs. And he reached out and chucked her under the chin.

—Do I hear a faint note of self-pity? Willa inquired, but not harshly.

—From this old Stradivarius of mine? Not on your life, Mother baby. He drew in deeply and patted his stomach. —Soon as this chow's settled, let's all take a swimmerrooni.

Penny turned and looked at the pool. The flickering light and the breeze were making it smirk enticingly. Come in, come in and find yourself, it was whispering.

Penny's assigned bedroom at the north end of the flagstone terrace was elegant, yet simple, and so exact as to never have been violated or even intruded upon by human hand. It could have come into existence completely by itself, by its own power and desire. And that was where it happened. As she was stripping down to her pants and bra, not as effortlessly as usual because she was tight, slightly clumsy and hands strange-feeling, not quite themselves, she heard the door creak. She kept her hands on her breasts and turned around. Earl stumbled drunkenly into the room dressed only in his pink-striped undershorts. He was grinning.

—I'll do the rest of that, he said, coming up to her. —Can't stand to see a woman work.

He touched the back of her bra and Penny said, —Take your hands off of me and get out. She said this quite matter-of-factly; she was not frightened now or angry.

—But I'm just trying to be a helpful little scout. He started unfastening the bra, and Penny turned and pushed him away. —Get away.

—Oh fiddle, he replied thickly. —You don't know a good thing when you see it, and he walked uncertainly toward the door. —See you in the pool, old pal. He paused at the door. —You're not playing the game right. Naughty girl. Lose points. And he left.

Like a football coach. Like the last time, in the sleek young man's apartment-lair after the chic dinner—why is the pathway to rape always strewn with delicacies and wines and the corpses of exotic, almost extinct birds and beasts?—where she had gone quite willingly as though she were on the side of the young man's conspiracy against herself, like a third person, against her not submitting to his, or their, pleasures and ultimate rapture. But as enthusiastic or willing as her co-conspiracy was, something went bad. The third person of her who was supposed to be lying there on the sacrificial bed of her and his fantasy, legs apart and mouth slightly open in endless expectation . . . No, she simply said no, just as the man was unhooking her bra, having helped her take everything else off and dropped them, the things, on the living room couch. No! Unnatural! the other cried. Fills my veins with poison! And then her retreat from that scene—"What's the matter, anyway?" he asked. "Are you sick or something?"—was a crawling on hands and knees through a foul swamp of contempt and confusion and fear, hoping, head down, that all present had the human kindness and decency not to stare as you sneaked away.

The water in the pool was black and exquisite, and Penny played in it with drunk lack of self-torture. Willa was in the pool, too. Earl had passed out in a lounge chair on the patio; could be dead for all anyone knew or cared now. Suddenly, hands were grabbing Penny's ankles underwater, then Willa surfaced inches from her body, then face.

—Oh, this is glorious, Willa said, wiping the water from her face with both hands. —I feel like a child.

—I feel like a dream, said Penny.

Now Willa stripped off her bathing suit. —I want my body to be free, she said, —and yours too. And she carefully, while Penny smiled acquiescence, pulled Penny's suit off. —Your body is divine, and she began to kiss and caress Penny passionately. Penny had never felt so released of care.

They don't know that I can see them screwing on the grass, Earl said to himself, moving his lips. Never seen two broads do it. It's strange and sexy and funny. And oh God! Don't want to watch it but I can't stop. Do they get the same thing they get when a man does it? Who would have thought . . .

me. Knew it all the time I guess. On top of a boy for the past five years. Pig of a blob that I am. Got my finger in my drink, might as well drink my finger. I did. Taste of finger not good. Stick my finger in my ear and whistle "Dixie" but it might disturb their sex rassling. Jesus Christ, look at Willa go. A regular tiger on that girl. Maybe I should go over and referee just to see that the proper rules of lesbianism are observed. Without rules there's no game and without no game there ain't no fun. Churchill say that? Wouldn't surprise me. If I knew it all the time, why did I put up with it? If she's a boy, does that make me a fairy? That sure would surprise the hell out of my old daddy. Earl, short for Pearl. Yes indeedy. And . . . God almighty I wish I had my Nikon handy . . . and my tape recorder. Never heard such moaning and whimper-ing. Should go into the Library of Congress ballad collection. Jesus! She never carried on like that with me. Completely different person. Guess she was just putting up with me until the real thing came along. No man can ever get close to a woman's secret, whatever the shit that secret might be. Might as well try to sell mushrooms to Eskimos. It was OK to switch partners, as we've done to our mutual four-way satisfaction before, but girl on girl . . . that's the kiss-off. Rotation of wives a basic law of animal husbandry, but this . . . Knew a guy in the army whose brother screwed him once, but that's different. They weren't married. Oh screw this . . .

Earl grabbed the bottle of vodka next to his chair. On cushions of night-stealth he walked across the sympathetic grass to the writhing, white female bodies. He began, to their spasm-stopping horror, to slosh the liquid all over them.

—I don't think you people are being fair, he said. —You have no feelings for the third person.

Now wasn't that just wonderful? Ain't you glad you came along for the ride and in so doing became the ride? And there's a lot more where that came from as we diligently trace Michael Smoot's roots. Lying not too far below the experiential stratum you've just returned from is still another stratum, lying there patiently underneath the language, heavy-lidded, quietly confident, long, long ago forced down there beneath the surface, by The Authorities of course who would have been drowned in their own gravy train had they not done so (or, Has It Ever Been Any Other Way?). Take a close look at that portrait of George Washington hanging over the bidet in your mother's bathroom. Or at those Currier & Ives engravings on display in the electric shock room of the nearest madhouse. OK. Look real, real close. Take those people and scenes completely by surprise. Don't let them hoodwink you. Bore through (as you have never done before) those guileful facades. Deeper . . . be ruthless . . . whip up that granny's skirt . . . and you will see . . .

Letting Bygones Be Bygones, Oregon

You'll find a lot of burgs that are up to their ears in debt to memory. Their tiny, hand-stitched streets lie in perpetual darkness because their sun is always rising on the past and its deeds. Halfway through his morning plate of basted eggs, side meat, country fries, white toast and peach jam, an' a potta java, their fire chief will push his chair away from the table, strike his brow, and grunt Ach! and tear out of the house to douse last year's fire at the old mill. Or . . . smack in the middle of a heart-to-heart talk with his favorite turnkey, their Justice of the Peace will suddenly shout, Oh! Heavens above! and charge out to the courtyard gallows where he will deliver a stern lecture to a long-gone prisoner On His Way Out.

We don't go in for any of that. As far as we are concerned, past participles have their little quirks and we have ours, and never the twain shall meet. Likewise, every man, woman, and child here will tell you that a grudge in hand is worth two in the bush. Look at it this way: late this very afternoon, The Old Lady Who Lived in a Shoe will be appointed Director of Urban Renewal.

And another thing: soon as we lick the problem of The Absentee Half-back, our entire football squad, to a man, is going to chop down every cherry tree within five miles of the town square. You can bank on it. (Isn't it pretty clear by now that there are more ways to keep in shape than you can shake a stick at?)

Every couple of months on the dot we have our church social, town rummage sale, and cooking display, all in one fell swoop. Over in High-tower's Meadow, where the last runaway mule driver was caught and buried alive. —You gotta nip that kinda thing in the bud, otherwise you'll never know which side your bread's gonna be buttered on one of these fine days, said Gotch, the man who trapped him, in what many people of the day thought was a masterful statement that cut right to the bone.

These combo, all-purpose get-togethers of ours are a sight for sore eyes and just what the doctor ordered, even if, by some unfortunate coincidence, your old pal Time seems to be running out on you. As one chipper old gran said in a furtively conducted poll: —I wouldn't miss one of 'em for all the whips in whippoorwill, and I don't give a hoot who knows it.

As you've probably begun to suspect, our festivities are not quite the same thing, on a fun level, as your average day-by-day taffy pull. Folks show up with their eyes flashing and their cheeks flushed, and in some cases their teeth are bared. A real crowd favorite is the Swap Center. (An' it ain't so hard to see why, once you get right down to it.) You can really let your hair down here and swap your pants off. Like, there's some that stand around and swap lies.

—Caught me a jackrabbit this mornin' that could recite the Lord's Prayer.

—That ain't nothin'. My wife Juniper can whistle in German in her sleep.

Others swap husbands and wives, sisters and brothers, mothers and fathers. Even themselves.

—Had my eyes on you fer quite a spell, exclaimed Mrs. Martha Babcock, lassoing chubby little ol' Mrs. Botsford offin the platform.

—Sure had a stummick fulla you, said freckle-faced Jimmy Swenson, pushing his pouting mom into good viewing position.

You just can't afford to miss the booth marked Ailments & Afflictions. It's decorated with such *loving* care, there's no other way to put it, and the over-all quality of the action (not really performances, but by the same token not neutral exhibitions either) has such, well, panache, such bounce. —Lookie lookie lookie! I got stomach cancer! I got stomach cancer!

—I hear you, I hear you! An' I've got fourth-degree syphilis! I've got fourth-degree syphilis!

—Oh boy! Oh boy! It's a deal! It's a deal!

And the affliction swapping . . . How can anybody with even the smallest amount of civic pride help but be caught up in it and even, when things really hit their stride, swept away? I ask you.

—Obsessive gambling? Obsessive gambling! That's what I'm talking about! That's what I'm saddled with.

—Oiyez! Oiyez! And I'm offering incest, and I'm offering incest!

Nobody's to blame, least of all yourself, if you decide to hang around that glowing aspect of the festivities till it's time to go home. It's up to you, isn't it? I mean, one thing about us is that we don't tell people which altar they've got to worship at.

The food stalls, they're right up there holdin' their own too. And unlike some towns we could mention, we don't say you have to be a female to try your hand at whipping up a dish or two. Man, woman, and child—just the way God made it—anybody who fits into those categories is eligible. Now, the idea in this arena of the tongue is not only to come up with a mouth-watering culinary feat, but at the same time, in the same ecstatic, writhing gesture, to give it a title that will more than just decorate the halls of memory. The title must hope to *consume* those halls. You gettin' the point?

So . . . at hand or at tongue's tip, right in front of you, just waiting for your delectation, is Creamed Chicken That Was Last Tasted by Ahmed el-Akbar As He Fell Defending the Faith at Roncesvalles, 1422. And . . . Pot Roast from within the Eye of the Hurricane from Which No One Has Ever Returned. And . . . Lemon Pie Kirkegaard Who Was Not Afraid to Call a Hunch a Hunch. And . . . Tossed Green Mystery Salad That Will Never, Never Turn Its Back on You Even Though You Are as Guilty as the Day Is Long. (Whose grinning puss do we see in the winner's circle? Michael's, of course. And he's proudly holding aloft his Coddled Cherries for Girls of All Seasons. Little rascal!)

Those other rinky-dink towns . . . What nerve they've got tryin' to hustle decent folks with a bingo game!

When all is said and done, what is it that a body asks of a town? Of course, 'twas mine, 'tis his, and has been slave to thousands. But once you've gotten that off your chest, just what is it that you demand of a place? That it come through for you, right? Right. That's exactly the way we see it here in Bygones, and no effort, no single naked human body is spared in our single-handed dedication to pleasing our townspeople. The sky's the limit does not apply only to birds.

Okeydoke. Fer openers: the implacable fact of human mortality and how are you going to slice that. Let's say you are one of us (unless you are, there's no conversation). And you find yourself needin' a new kidney, I mean really hurtin' for it, no joke. Now, if you lived some other place, you'd have to break your ass to get that other kidney; or you'd have to be a millionaire to afford it; or you'd just die, period. Or maybe you need a new eye, having lost one of your own somehow or other. Do you work yourself up into a big sweat wonderin' how the devil you're gonna lay your hands on it? No sir. You just leave it to us. Our specially trained Medical Scouts take care of the whole thing. When the moon is high and the wind just right, they climb into a van designed to a spanky T just for their purpose (The Divine Replenisher, as the van is called, is a real knockout and, like several other unique "institutions" in our town, it's on display at regular times for schoolchildren to visit and learn all about, so's they know what makes things tick around here), give their hoods a last minute check, and away they go. And they know precisely every inch of Route 1, silent and empty and gleaming in the moonlight. And they know precisely the right town to hit. Some towns have better "defenses" than others: the night lookouts in some towns have had their palms greased; other towns may be in the midst of a drunken, ritualistic orgy and thus distracted; and still other places, much farther away of course, are completely vulnerable because they've never been raided. And of course our Medical Scouts know exactly whom they will seize, the "donor," for in their hands are the vital statistics and health records of all the inhabitants in all the towns for miles around, obtained through means that're nobody's business but theirs. Nothing half-assed about our people. They know their stuff. They don't mess around.

Once the "donor" is in hand, "our boys"—our fond way of referring to them, though in fact there are two female members of the group who take care of any delicate matters that may either be implicit or explicit in any "replenishment" situation—"our boys" can do one of two things: they can relieve the "donor" of the required organ right then and there in the van—

"on-the-spot liberation" they call it—and get this, 'cause it's real beautiful, no foolin': they are so skillful in their surgery and so deft and quiet in their seizin' that the donors don't even know what's happenin'. They are "taken" in their sleep, kept asleep with the proper drugs during the "liberation" procedure, and returned to their beds, just like that! Ex post facto, of course, they do notice certain, uh, differences or changes in themselves. Much too late for them to shout something like, —Hey! Whaddya guys think you're doin' anyway?

When the operation is a very tricky one, however, beyond the technological reach of the van and its staff, then the "donor" is whisked or bundled or trundled back to Bygones and the Skippy Hopewell Memorial Rooms Removal Wing, named after the great benefactor who over the years was the recipient of three whole new bodies, in pieces naturally, and acquired as I am describing to you—where no removal job under the sun is too difficult. In such "return" cases, the out-of-town "donor" must be disposed of afterwards, because we can't have these people hanging around clutterin' up the air with their damn ol' gripes. —Where's my lung? —Where's my kidney? —Where's my heart? —What happened to my eyes? I mean, Hell's bells, who needs that kinda crap? Those half or three-quarters geeks bangin' 'roun' makin' trouble, wailin' and whimperin' an' if we wuz to let 'em which we ain't never, askin' the nurses fuh all kindsa special favors, whimperin', pissin' in their pants. See what kine bedlam we would have on our han's without its doin' nobody no good 'tall? So, as you would expect, all things being a bit more than equal, our Disposal Squad is tops. They really do their job. They *are* their job. (What kinda hare-brained town you think we are?)

While we're on the subject of out-of-towners, it may as well go without saying that you'd want to be filled in on how we deal with, or actually what happens to, strangers passing through who, for reasons that may well defy gravity, or just plain orneriness, or heavens above, because they are simply unschooled in the death-defying ins and outs of our local laws, wind up breakin' these laws. If you think we've got the same rules for strangers that we have for our own folks, you're crazy. For one thing, there's naturally a curfew for strangers. Do you fer one split second suppose, for example, that we want these outlanders prowling the streets when our young uns are on their dutiful way to school, and most likely, if that were to happen, fillin' their heavily waxed little ears with all kinds of garbage about the outside world? Not on your life. So, no "aliens," as we call 'em, are allowed to be out on our streets between 7:30 A.M. and 8:30 A.M., or again between 3:00 P.M. and 4:00 P.M., when our offspring are on their way home from school. Then again, curfew strikes at high noon and stays struck for one hour while every single townsperson over sixteen is taking the daily, obligatory, ritual community cleansing in the big outdoor pool in our town square. Just let your poor mind wander and try to picture the unspeakable and self-referent lewdness and ogling, baboon barking and sickening self-abuse, that would most certainly explode if said "aliens" were to look on as our naked, possessed citizens scrubbed and doused and birched one another. Oh no. Perish the thought.

You don't have to ask: there are more than a baker's dozen of the special laws constraining outsiders that have the same impeccable pizzazz as the above, all designed with a hawk's eye to maintaining the built-in purity of Bygones. OK. So what do we do to "aliens" who violate and offend? Fine 'em? Jail 'em? Beat 'em? Bail 'em? No, none of that. We assign them tasks. We press them into our very own and, if we can be allowed a glancing blow of pride, our *unique* labor force. (About which, by the way, the U.S. Department of Commerce has wisely refrained from giving us any of its lip.) Some of the offending "aliens," for instance, may be assigned, for an indefinite period, to the Rickshaw Fleet. They pull the rickshaws and they are at the beck and call of any of our bona fide citizens. Even children, who, in their traditionally inbred, high-spirited, low-minded playfulness, often pile in two or three such prisoner-pulled rickshaws and, cracking their own special little whips (made just for the occasion over at Greb's Sporting Goods Store on lower Main), race each other furiously from one end of the town to the other, not infrequently until the hard-put puller drops, and drops for good.

Or they will be assigned to any interested citizen who requests one to perform chores that said citizen deems essential to the pursuit of his or her health, welfare, happiness, peace of mind, or internal security in general. Two specific examples over easy? OK. Comin' raht up with uh side orduh uh real-life sound effects:

—Hello there, Warden Hemsley? This is Olive Treaster. Oh, things aren't too bad, I suppose, I ran a couple good séances this week. Summoned two sixth-century Spanish black magicians. They were really top drawer. Helped me work the kinks outta that long-distance spell-casting project I've been workin' on . . . Oh no. I understand every word they said. No problem. That's the way it goes in trances. Uh huh. Right. And they also gave me a terrific recipe for a potion that completely, and I mean completely, wipes out memory. What was that? No, no side effects at all. That's the beautiful part. The stuff I'd been usin' was real tricky. Right. Sometimes caused blindness, sometimes brought on paralysis of the arms or legs. You just never knew. Oh, nothin' like that. Though from time to time I do get items through trades with other guild members. No, this was a family recipe, handed down from my great-, great-, great-granddad. He was a full Cherokee shaman. Very famous. He mesmerized a whole colony of early

English settlers and had them all commit suicide. Oh sure. It's all on record, over at Town Hall. Well, anyway, plus the fact that this new stuff is absolutely 100 percent *tasteless*. Isn't that something. Oh easy. You can put it in orange juice or coffee, or mix it in with morning porridge. Sure, anytime you want. Just call me a day ahead of time so's I can mix it up. Oh, we'll talk about my fee then. We'll work something out. Sure. Don't worry 'bout it. Professional confidence. Sure, I understand. Yeah. Listen, Jim, here's what I called about. You got any "aliens" in the pokey there? You have? Good. That circus that passed through town last week, huh. Three among them? Oh great. Anyways, I need two . . . can be men or women, don't matter . . . to test my new Dream-Sucking Machine on. Uh huh. Been workin' on it for quite a while. It's supposed to suck dreams outta people's heads while they're sleepin', and it also puts those dreams into other people's heads. You know, people are comin' to me all the time complainin' about their dreams. Well, thank you, Jim. I appreciate your sayin' that. Do you think I could get these two "aliens" by sometime tomorrow? Oh that's wonderful. You'll bring them over yourself around three? That's just perfect. OK. Thanks real much, Jim. See you then, anytime 'round three. Bye now.

(Know who was eavesdropping with his soft, young ear pressed to the floor grating directly upstairs? Uh huh. Our little Michael. Olive Treaster was his aunt, and he often stayed over at her house when his parents went visiting out of town for some reason or other, which Michael could never figure out why. "What you gonna visit about?" he would ask them. "Business things," they would say. "Grown-up business things." "Like what?")

M ichael and Trudie, each with an arm around the other's waist, walked happily and somewhat unsteadily down the empty, sound-less, serenely moon-bathed Avenue Frisson. They were both kind of bombed.

—Isn't it lovely? said Trudie. —We can hear ourselves walking.

—Yes. Like it's two other people, said Michael, putting his foot down hard on the glistening cobblestones.

—That's a funny way to look at it, she said. —But I sort of like it.

Two young hookers, waiting effortlessly under the streetlamp at the corner of the Avenue Frisson and the Avenue Beaudoin, watched Michael and Trudie. Breasts half-exposed, miniskirts barely covering their cunts for sale. They were motionless. An airless tableau. Insanely elegant. Moonlike.

—Do you know them? Trudie asked.

—In a sense, said Michael, guiding her up the steps of number 17. —We live in the same house, here.

The downstairs hallway of the old house was gently, dreamily dominated by the perpetually accumulating smells of marijuana. This pungent, provocative odor (like perfume and jewelry on a transvestite's body: it was not exterior to it, superimposed) was its presence, its inescapable essence, that which immediately, without any cute distractions, engages one's own self and essence: when we enter the police station, are we taken in by the neat blue uniforms and their shiny brass buttons? the ornate pendulum wall clock? the polished, solid-mahogany railing? the large official photograph of the president? The tableau, in other words, of imparted law and order? Of course not. We are alerted immediately by the undisguisable, ineradicable presence of brutality, lies, corruption, and aching despair.

—Oh, said Trudie, and deeply inhaled the marijuana smell. —I wonder how they make out.

Michael unlocked his own door at the end of the wanly lit, bombed, old hallway. —They're shop girls during the daytime. They softly entered his place. —They're lesbians. And the odd thing, an American guy, a Negro, is staying with them. I get the feeling that they're keeping him.

He and Trudie embraced in the room's simple darkness. Sucked each other's tongues, caressed and groped each other's genitals, thrust and ground against each other.

—I've got to take a quick pee-pee, Trudie said, and broke away, sweetly squeezing the big hard-on imprisoned in his pants. Michael sometimes thought of his hard-on (and only his hard-on, not his soft cock) as Charlemagne. And naturally it would follow that the tasty, suppliant cunts it plunged into were thus colonies, or colonies to be. He saw tribute-paying villagers, fields of wheat, ripe vineyards. He amused himself in this simple, arcane way while, wobbly, undressing. Sort of crawling into bed—the mattress was flat on the floor and served also as a sitting/flopping place for visitors—oh fuck taking my sweater off now . . . later as we're sleeping . . . for now the vital, throbbing parts are exposed and waiting . . . my strong but slender thighs are ready, nakedly ready to clutch/squeeze and lovingly cradle her sucking, bobbing, clever, dark, and soon-to-be-there head—he noticed the essay he's been working on, dropping onto the floor just under where his parts were gliding over onto the mattress. (Mmm. I could fuck a sentence while waiting for Trudie.) "Mythologies of the Mass Media: A Class-Value Analysis of the Mystification Process in American Magazines and Newspapers." While most of his being, physical and mental, was concentrating on the juicy reappearance of Trudie, a carefully disciplined and obedient person in his head reflexively—the lion resting in the shade suddenly sniffs airborne game and instantly it is up and stalking—slipped into the essay it had created. "Now you can easily see how you are being coded, and mystified, by this newspaper headline 'Vietcong Terrorists Sneak into Saigon Suburb and Bomb Restaurant,' " it was saying . . .

—Your bathroom has very thin walls, Trudie said, coiling her soft nakedness around him. —I could hear the American Negro talking when I was peeing.

—Oh? What was he saying?

Trudie's hand sweetly stroked his stiff prick. —He was saying, "They'll pay me fifteen hundred bucks a month to fight in Rhodesia."

Two men are standing in the tight, hunched doorway of an old stone building on the Plaza del Sol in Madrid. They are trying to appear casual, but they are truly furtive. One of the men is wearing a tan cashmere V-neck sweater and grey flannel pants. The other is dressed in the quietly surly garments of the Spanish lower middle class. His face? Cold and anxious.

—It will go off in three minutes, this man says, looking at his expensive gold wristwatch, which glows with remote arrogance.

—Yes, says the other, glancing lightly at the other's watch. His manner goes with his clothes. Cultivated boredom, at once removed from where he is. —And you'll get the other half of the money tonight, as I promised.

The other looks at him anxiously. —And if anything goes wrong, you say your contact at the American Embassy will help?

—Yes, yes, Felipe. Of course. That is what she is there for, to help us out. As I have told you before.

—Who is she? What is her name?

The other makes a characteristic body gesture of genteel impatience. —Her name is Marianne Leeds, and she is an old friend from my school days in America. But these facts are not important for you to know. You will always work only with me.

Felipe stares into the other's face, in the same way he would stare at a photograph of a strange, faraway city. Then he looks again at his watch. —Thirty seconds more.

They both watch the big Café Loyola across the crowded, noisy plaza. The seconds tick by. Slowly these two men, so different in every significant respect, merge into a single, conspiratorial presence that is utterly motionless, almost breathless. A terrific explosion in the Café Loyola hurls glass and chairs and blood-drenched bodies and pieces of bodies out into the street. Felipe gasps and crosses himself.

At the moment of the explosion, Marianne Leeds, sitting in her office in the American Embassy on the Avenue Mola, looked at her wristwatch, but quickly, furtively, so that her looking would not be noticed, because she was having a conversation with an "innocent," so to speak, an old friend and classmate from Swarthmore, Sue Dabney. While bloody arms and legs and heads and hands flew through the shattered air in the café on the other side of Madrid, Marianne was saying —. . . so that seems to me to be the main difference between European literature and American literature—the European writes from an existential position of sociopolitical necessity, you see, while the American doesn't.

Sue Dabney said, —But wouldn't you say that the American minority writers, I mean like the blacks and homosexuals and those writers who have come out of the poor classes, don't you think they write out of that kind of necessity?

Marianne glanced at the black telephone on her desk and shook her head at the same time. —No. They write out of alienation, which is completely different from . . . in fact, the exact opposite of political/social engagement.

Sue looked at Marianne and just thought about it all for a minute. —Hmm, she finally said. —I'll have to turn that one over a few times.

—Take Sartre, Marianne began, glancing at the phone again, this time not furtively; no, this time with a detectable impatience or worry. —Now, uh, Sartre's starting position . . .

The phone rang. Marianne coolly controlled herself as she picked up the receiver. —Yes? Oh good. Fine. Uh, OK. Tonight at nine then. Good. She hung up. Her freckled, tomboy face, unsullied by makeup—this was the Post Toasties face of everyone's kid sister—was relaxed and pleased. Her grey-blue eyes twinkled with murder. —Let's see . . . where was I?

Yes indeed. Where was she? Where is she? Where has she been? On the playing fields of death, that's where. We must, with astute apprehension, examine every corner of these stark fields.

—Cork, you ought to be a geologist, her friend Samantha told her one day, back in those delicious high-school years at McArthur High School in Fairfield County.

—Oh? said Marianne, who had been nicknamed Cork by her father for reasons as obscure as minnows in their Connecticut pond. —Why do you say that?

—Oh, 'cause you just look like a geologist. Honestly. I see you scrambling around in a dried-up riverbed examining pieces of exotic rock.

And later, at Swarthmore—a few months before she moved on, stroking with the flawless determination of a deep-sea diver, to Harvard Law School —Jeff Roberts, out of just about nowhere (but not really, of course) as they were having a beer after playing some tennis, laid this on her: —You know, Cork, I always wanted to have a gal like you for a friend. You know, just pals. No sticky, neurotic involvements. Know what I mean?

Oh boy. Did she ever. That that's the way the cookie bounces or collapses. Some folks were destined for the pits of passion, others for Girl Scout leadership in forest glens. You cannot, as the good Marie Antoinette pointed out, win them all.

In her very youthful days, days of tree climbing and 'jama parties, and even on up to all-night dorm gab sessions, Marianne lovingly used expressions like "he makes my skin crawl," or "she gives me the willies," and "so's your old man," which she picked up from her father, who had gone to Yale and who just knew that America was "tops." But those were the poetics of the past. More up-to-date, businesslike, and relevant poetics gradually climbed into the saddle. We might even say her tongue lost its cherry. Put your ear to this door and listen to her. "The pragmatics of the situation don't permit me to agree with you." And: "Let's get on top of this baby and ride it through." And: "Don't get sentimental on me, Mack. 'Cause I'll have to disengage you. You reading me?"

Getting the picture? Let's give it some depth. Take off your own shoes— that is, unless you are in some sniffy public place and such an action would raise eyebrows to your detriment—and slip into hers. Hurry, before she gets back from the shower. From time to time, when she was down, Marianne (Cork to you, maybe) played funny games, gloomy games with her head. She made up elaborate stories in which she played the lead roles, both male and female. Here's a typical story, in which she plays an out-of-the-way chap named Carl. Take it away! (Are you in her shoes now? Good.)

S ilver crashed around him: here, a sudden explosion of quarters, there a jangling avalanche of mammoth dollars. Directly in front of him a swarm of dimes burst shockingly into view. A flabby, middle-aged woman with a dark wen on her cheek squealed in hysterical triumph and began clawing at the silver like a famished dog. Carl wanted to bark for her. He was in a forest primeval of slot machines, and moving feverishly from one to another were packs of garishly dressed human beings. They all seemed slightly defective physically, and they vibrated that way psychologically too, rejects of the race. The lobby of this Las Vegas hotel was indeed a jungle.

Out of boredom, and because the grinning machines did draw him a bit too, Carl tried his luck with a quarter. A lemon and two clusters of grapes, clicking fatalistically into position, informed him that he had lost. To Carl's left, a man with a long, twisted nose and wearing a Hawaiian sport shirt, howled his own loss, baboon-style.

Not feeling at all like himself, the madness of the place had distressed his balance, Carl now walked through the crowded lobby and into the dim bar and ordered a double scotch on the rocks from a girl half-naked in a black leotard. This confused him. The rise of sexual desire caused by her unbridled appearance contravened his thirst for alcoholic numbness. The conflict of senses changed the chemistry of the drink, somehow, made it taste different, subtly unseated its own self-confidence. He wondered if the girl were a prostitute besides being a waitress. She brought his change in silver dollars.

—Don't you have any dollar bills? he asked.

—I'm very sorry, sir, she replied in a remote, silvery voice, —but we don't. She smiled slyly and drifted away into the darkness.

—But why don't you? he called after her. But the girl did not bother to turn around.

Carl knew quite well that the whole thing was rigged by the management. You were supposed to put the silver dollars into the one-armed bandits. Even if you did not want to gamble, you put them in the machines because you were sick and tired of carrying them around, clanking heavily in your pockets like dungeon chains. If it weren't for that damn plane goofing, he wouldn't be here. It had developed mysterious engine trouble en route to Salt Lake City from Los Angeles and had limped in here for overhauling. The passengers were told they had to stay the night. Carl was a teacher at the University of Utah.

He was on his second double scotch, and feeling a little tight, when he noticed the girl playing the machines in the lobby outside the bar. Dark, straight hair fell in anachronistic elegance down to shoulders that slumped indifferently. Her face was quite handsome. She appeared just the least disheveled, and about her, like a supersonic aura, hummed a kind of frenzy. Carl watched her with fascination and a mounting feeling of strangeness. She glided from one machine to another, machines catering only to silver dollars, intensely expecting something from each, but each one mocked her. She disposed of her remaining silver dollars in a machine near the door of the bar. She stared at the machine unhappily for a moment, then, like a sleepwalker following a new turn in a twisted interior labyrinth, she walked slowly into the dim bar.

Halfway inside, she paused and looked about the room. All of the tables were empty except Carl's. Slowly now she came across the room and sat down at his table. After a few moments of silence, during which she carefully examined her long fingers, she looked up and said, —Will you buy me a drink, please?

—Be glad to, Carl heard himself say. The waitress in the leotard was now standing next to him, smiling, omnisciently. —What will you have? Carl asked the girl.

—Oh, anything.

—Anything?

—Yes. It doesn't really matter, does it?

—No, I suppose not, he said, and ordered her and himself scotch on the rocks.

The waitress left. Carl turned to the girl, expecting her to begin telling him the statistical facts of her life as strangers always seem to do within the first five minutes of meeting. But the girl did nothing. She truly seemed to be asleep, or in some way softly disengaged from reality, as she stared over Carl's shoulder.

It was Carl who finally spoke. —Have you been here long?

—It's hard to tell, she replied. —Time is such a funny thing. Sometimes it lets you be part of it, and sometimes it rejects you completely. When you're part of it, you know exactly what is happening all the time, and how much is happening. But when you are thrown outside it, for whatever reason, you're not really sure what is going on. She smiled oddly. —It's like looking for a street in a town that has no street signs.

For a while a thin strand had been connecting Carl with outside reality. It had been straining steadily, and now it was about to break. He made a valiant, but he knew doomed, attempt to sustain it by asking the girl another question about herself. —Where did you come from?

She laughed lightly. —I've stopped trying to remember. With this, Carl felt himself begin to slip into another world, her world. —But I don't think this matters much, do you? I mean, it's more important where you're going than where you came from. She smiled, placidly, mysteriously, like a child who knows it is absolute ruler in a country of dreams. Carl was not quite certain now whether he was asleep or awake. But it did not matter anymore. He grinned conspiratorially at the girl. They drifted along together.

They had a few more drinks, then he followed her out to the gambling room. Each was laden with silver dollars from the bar. They journeyed from one machine to another. Sometimes they won, sometimes they lost. When they won, the girl (it no longer mattered to him what her name might be) giggled hysterically, and swaying as though in a slow-motion ballet, grabbed at the gobs of coin and stuffed them in Carl's pockets. He laughed wildly too, as did a cluster of people they had attracted. People they weren't, exactly; they were more like hybrid offshoots. They glistened and vibrated with an obscene madness. Their looks and shapes and sizes were caricatures of grotesqueness, among them being a small-eyed hunchback and a pin-head giant.

—This little beast is greedy, the girl shrieked before a machine that kept taking their money and not returning any.

—Filthy, dirty thing! howled a fat woman with vast breasts. —It wants to break your heart! and she threw the contents of her drink at it. The other clowns crowed with glee, and Carl found himself doing the same thing. The girl moved to another machine, and the others with them huddled around it.

—I know this little dear, the girl cooed, caressing it with excited eyes. —And it knows me. We love each other.

The machine indeed behaved like a lover, a coquettish one, elusive, teasing, unwilling to part with its delights quite yet without first extracting some anxiety and pain from its partner. Each time the girl made her bid of desire with the huge silver dollar, the machine responded with only a part of the total required. Instead of three oranges in a row, two oranges and a horseman appeared. The little mob moaned and whimpered in frustration. Two clusters of grapes came up, but followed by a pear. The little mob whined and growled. And then it happened, the third try. One sailor appeared, another joined it, and at the final moment of consummation, a third. She had hit the jackpot. Hundreds of dollars crashed out of the machine and spilled onto the floor. The mob shrieked with lewd pleasure.

—We gonna be drown in it! howled the hunchback, and began to hop up and down with furious delight.

—Ah want to rub all ovah maself! yelled a young matron with tiger eyes, and threw herself on the floor.

—Christ almighty! bellowed a little old man with a cocked eye. —Let's grab it before they take it from us.

As for the girl, she was undulating rhythmically with laughter, like a delicate tree bending in the wind's insistent caressing. —Let's have a party! she shouted, and the others bellowed their pleasure.

In a matter of moments they were gamboling through the lobby toward the elevators, each carrying the coins in little canvas bags supplied by the awed attendants. They were like a band of fairy-tale robbers escaping with their loot to their hiding place, a dark and dank place of trolls and gnomes beneath a wooden bridge. Carl was carrying a bag of money in one hand and was being led by the other by the girl. She whispered something to him. It had to do with promises of ecstasy and most secret abandon.

A bald, pop-eyed man in the band kicked the elevator operator in the rear when he turned his back. —That'll learn you to be nice to important people! and he laughed like a hyena in the night.

Then they were all roistering wildly in a suite upstairs. It was indeed a bacchanal of surreal proportions, led in its frenzy and design by the name-less girl, with Carl at her side. Champagne corks popped and whistled through the rooms as the babbling, howling troupe, each freakish member brandishing a foaming bottle, tumbled raucously back and forth in absolutely unleashed pleasure. To satisfy the appetite (at least that *one*), there were foods of richest, riotous fantasy: mammoth smoked turkeys; vast, exotic fish in aspic; glossy, radiant whole baby pigs choking on apples; thrushes skewered through their tummies, tongues that seemed ready to slaver obediently.

Gradually the place became a sea of madness, out of time, out of space. The incredible silver dollars carpeted the floors like monster fish scales, blinding the mind with their glitter. The giant with the patch over his eye and the huge fat lady with the big breasts were playing catch with the hunchback while he gnawed a turkey leg. While the girl guided his arm, Carl painted and wrote things on the wall with a lipstick. Staggering drunk, the pop-eyed man and two women—a demonic, blonde, young tigress in a swimming suit and a mottled, flop-eared lady in shorts—were playing hide-and-seek under the furniture. This was but a part of the howling whole. Someone jammed a sausage into Carl's mouth and he shared it with the girl. In the bedroom the others were conducting another carnival.

—I never, never, never want to be me again, the girl murmured in the welter of noise, and guided his hand to write something else. Carl said the same to her.

—Don't ever be afraid, the girl said to him moments later, as they left the wall, she leading him by the hand, and floated through and around the seething, grappling madness there, to the other room. A wildly dancing couple bumped into Carl. He tripped over a gurgling mass of bodies on the floor, fell into them and pulled the girl with him. She squealed in high-pitched pleasure as she fell, and then the mass of revelers on the floor, whose own howlings were being complemented by a child hillbilly singer on the radio, swarmed over them. Scores of hands were tearing Carl's clothing off. Paralyzed, it seemed, he watched while the mob ripped off the girl's garments. She screamed and so did he. Above them, the giggling hunchback began to spray champagne over everybody.

—You'll never get rich diggin' a ditch, inky dinky parlay voo! he yelled.

That revelry exploded into a climax sometime later with Carl and the nameless girl racing down the corridors banging on doors and, laughing with idiot delight, rolling silver dollars crazily before them.

When Carl woke up the next morning, the first thing he did was to look for the girl. She was not there. Carl became confused and panicky. He was about to call out for her but he realized that he knew no name to call. He leapt out of bed and ran into the bathroom. But the girl was not there either. That room had the fearful emptiness of an operating room awaiting the first body. Carl could not believe the girl was not there. Even though he was completely sober now, even though he felt *real* again, the girl was an essential part of him. She had shown him a part of himself that he had never allowed himself to know.

The clock in the bedroom socked him with the reminder that his plane was leaving for Salt Lake in an hour. As he frantically dressed and packed, he clawed through his memory for some clue as to the girl's identity, or where he might be able to find her. But he could not dredge up anything. He cut himself while shaving and the blood trickled unnoticed down his neck.

The scene in the lobby downstairs was quite the same: the crazy sound of the one-armed bandits, the crashing of silver, the foolishly dressed vacationers—nothing had changed. Carl looked into it for the figure of the girl, but she was not there. Over the loudspeaker, a lady's voice softly warned him that the limousine was leaving in five minutes for the airport. He was frantic. He was about to rush to the desk, when he saw her.

She was walking down the marble lobby stairs toward the swinging doors, carrying herself with an almost forced erectness. She was dressed in a quietly but obviously expensive linen suit. Walking with her, protectively holding onto her arm, was a stout, grey-haired man with a cane who reminded Carl very much of his father. Carl was overcome with anxious delight, and he sprang after her, shouting, —Hey! Hey!

The girl and the man with her stopped and stared at Carl as he ran up to them. —Thank God I've found you! he panted, and grabbed the girl by the shoulders. —I couldn't understand where you had gone.

The girl's face was uncomprehending and terrified. —I . . . I don't know what you are talking about, she said, with a foreign accent that she had not had before. The grey-haired man, squinting fiercely, began, —Vat iss? Vat iss?

—It's me! Carl shouted frantically. —Me! You know, last night and everything! and in his confusion and fear he began to shake her.

The girl tried to pull away from him as the old man cried, —Somezing iss wrong here! You are talking to my vife!

—I don't know you! the girl insisted, twisting in Carl's grasp. —I've never seen you before. Let me go!

—You can't say that! Carl screamed. —You do know me! You know me better than anybody!

Suddenly and furiously, the old man began beating at Carl with his cane. —Poleez! he shouted as he swung his cane. —Help! Poleez!

All Carl knew was that it would only complicate things if he were to run, so he just stood there, dazed, holding onto the girl, who was now watching him the way his mother used to do when he had done something wrong, while the old man kept raining blows upon him.

I n the Prado the man and the woman stroll with hesitant lifelessness from painting to painting. It could be that the museum air is malevolently heavy and is offering strong resistance. The way one walks underwater, that is the way all the people are moving about in these equivocal, unobliging galleries. From time to time they pause in their draining, slow-motion voyage to cast equally slow-motion—all right, somnambulant—furtive glances around the room. Could they be mutely pleading for help? Or is it that they are attempting, however pathetically, and without any verve whatsoever, to keep on the alert for a surprise and uncalled-for attack upon their being? Would this "attack," this, as they might be seeming to suggest, imminent "assault" result in their nonbeing? Of course, there is nothing to stop *us* from speculating. It may well be that these . . . these mutely anguished "visitors"—my God! "visitors" to their own enervated dilemma!—had somehow, in ways that had best not be handed down, managed to make themselves feel that at any dreaded moment the lunatic figures in the countless paintings around them would step out of their own ill-gotten tableaux and, holy shit!, have at them!

—That blond guy back in that other room looks like a fella I was in Nam with, says the man. Tattooed on his large muscular arm is the atomic mushroom.

—Don't you just love the way Velazquez does these people's clothes? says his wife. She has a teased, cutely premeditated look about her. She could be carrying secrets from Disneyland.

—He was a red-hot headhunter, says her husband. —Goddamn! He used to cut the heads off dead Vietcong an' stick 'em on bamboo poles. Can you believe it?

—You know what? I think we ought to get your picture painted like this. Wouldn't that be a scream! You dressed up in duke's clothes. Put a wig on you. Oh my God!

—Wonder what he's doin' here. Listen. I'm goin' back to see if it's the same guy. Wouldn't that be great!

Oh yeah, she thought. Real great. We'll sit around in some dumb café while you and whosi bullshit about how many gooks you killed with your bare hands, and getting drunk and whosi's little wife and I can swap recipes or talk about our menstrual pains. Oh boy. Great. Wonder how these jokers hanging on the walls were in the hay. This guy with the long, crooked nose. Does he have a long, crooked cock? And did they eat each other? Spanish . . . when these people talk, it sounds like they're going down on each other. It really does. Slurping and hissing and lisping sounds. Wonder what . . . you hear all the time what hot lovers they think they are . . . maybe give it a try . . . with that chauffeur at the base who's always giving me the sly eye. Claudio. These guys look at you like they'd climb right into your pants, hat and coat and shoes and all.

Floating gently before an elegantly surly and ambiguous landscape by an unknown fifteenth-century Spanish master in this aura of slow-motion somnambulism are two young men. Their beards are intensely carefree. Their faces are not empty, garbage-strewn lots where one can lose one's soul. No part of their bodies is waiting to respond to a drum march. No gas chambers in their hearts. We can all of us in our questionably ad hoc entourage approach them without hesitation and caress them if we like.

—We will meet at Pepe's place before the demonstration, one is saying as he examines the painting up close. —Don't forget to bring the photographs of the two informers.

—I won't forget. Is it all right for me to bring the American? The writer?

—Do you completely trust him?

—Yes. He's OK.

—Because you know the fucking American Embassy intelligence stooges are all over Madrid. Bring him then, but he's your responsibility. You understand?

—Completely, Alberto. Listen. Do you think we will kill the informers?

—This man's brush strokes are absolutely fantastic. Kill them? Oh yes, but not before we have extracted all the information we can from them. In any way we have to. It's them or us. We must find out all about their organization. Jesus, I can't get over what this man does with his little brush strokes. I can almost taste them.

The two lifeless museum guards float lumpishly together near the entrance to this somnambulant gallery. We must sniff them before leaving. (Don't believe for one second that the mobs hanging around Christ's cross didn't sniff it and even lick it. Yes, *lick it*.) These two pathetically ill-shaped men are truly cadavers. They struggled and lost and were murdered out there in society's magnificently rigged battle, and they have been plucked from the de facto cemeteries of the cluttered streets and installed here to "function," dead as they may be, bent and broken and even grotesque, their breath, as it rushes over those rotted yellow and black teeth, stinking foully of their putrefaction, their death. As we tiptoe closer to them (I'm pleased to say that we have got our traveling act together), we perceive that they are both wearing masks. What a splendid conceit! What a sublime dispensation! How inspired of the authorities to permit (or to require, who knows) these resurrected dead men to cover their dreadful faces with a mask, a "face" of their own choosing.

One of the guards is wearing the "face" of a haughty, mustached, young swell, in whose vanity the boulevards of the city all run through his living room. The other is masked with the patronizing, elegant "face" of a "personage" clearly meant to be a grandee of the old feudal order.

—My Rolls-Royce is in the garage getting its monthly checkup, the young swell is saying, but in an old, clotted voice that has nothing to do with the face or the statement. —So I must drive my little Porsche.

—I don't know what to do with the tenants on my Toledo estates, the other is saying in a coarse, broken voice that is clearly from the working-class slums. —They are always asking for more food and more money. Oh, what a bother!

We must go now. One cannot risk staying in such institutional tableaux too long. Beyond a certain point you can never leave. We drift through the large doorway. Those absurd, degraded, masquerading guards, what are they doing? They are approaching us. What gall! What madness makes them presume such intimacy. They'll pay dearly for such folly, you'll see. Rules of the game are rules of the game, and never the twain shall meet, as each one of us in the privacy of his own fall from grace knows only too well. Oh dear! These gutted chaps are touching us. What are they shoving into our jacket pockets? Pieces of parchment smeared with Christ's blood? Furtive copies of the latest American neutron bomb secrets? Joan of Arc's last poem? What sacred, ineradicable stains are they laying on us? Hurry! Hurry!

At last we are in the clean outdoor air. Free of everything but life itself. Now let's see what those eternal impersonators stuffed into the relative decency and innocence of our pockets. Is it humanly possible to read such handwriting, such surreal scrawl? Oy! We'll do our best to read it aloud. In this way we'll avoid the crass insinuation of conspiracy or masturbatory, elitist groupism. What is it that you are suggesting? That you want to climb up on that statue of Generalissimo Franco and read this message from there? Friends, one of our group has just asked that she be permitted to do that which you have just heard me describe. She says she will identify herself when the time is ripe. So be it. Climb away, my dear. Excellent. Well done. You are obviously in tip-top physical condition. All right, amigos. All right, you staring strollers. Lend her your terrified ears.

"It is inside Chile that our parties and militants have shown that the possibilities for unity of the Left have a broad and rich potential, which, above all, can be materialized today. These years of struggle against the dictatorship have shown that, in spite of inhuman repression, the workers' and people's movements are the motor force and center of activity of the antidictatorial resistance. Thus we see how, in so little time, the *legal struggle* has become active and spread through the industrial unions, neighborhood clubs, mothers' centers, youth clubs, and student and professional organizations, while simultaneously semilegal organizations develop, offering support and defense against military and economic repression— such as the Unemployed Committees, the People's Kitchens, the Committees to Defend Political Prisoners and the Disappeared, etc. But the Popular Workers Movement has also been creating illegal and underground organizations to give political leadership, such as the Factory Commissions, the Resistance Committees and other similar ones, where the highest example of the political consciousness of the working masses is expressed."

Bravo! Bravo! we all shout, and clap our hands vigorously. A few of the assembled, curious strollers clap also, but most of them, largely young, middle-class couples forever contained within a shoddy, leering altar constructed of convertible sports cars, washing machines, and expensive dinner clubs, well, of course, these shadowy types merely gawked, holding on to each other for some sort of low-grade reality reassurance.

Another of our members, a surefooted chap whom you will be meeting soon enough, pulls a crumpled, handwritten manifesto from his pocket where it had been so presumptuously stuffed by the preposterous mannequins lurking mistily back there in the Prado. He has no sooner read the first sentence, "Confronted with our strong attacks, the enemy's strategic retreat from the Central Highlands developed into a panic-stricken retreat rarely known in military history," no sooner has this leading statement been read, than a cop, one of those lewdly evil Guardia guys who wear the infamous black patent-leather hats and carry machine guns slung under their arms, this fellow, whose face was dark as a death warrant, eyes like rat turds, breaks away from the side of his fellow Guardia and grabs the paper from our friend's hand. For moments it seems this grey-uniformed little shit is going to stuff the paper into his mouth. He is making choking, muffled sounds. He has gone ape. Suddenly he leaps wildly up onto the roof of a parked car, losing his fine black hat in the process. He begins to scream/ read the rest of the paper. —"After the Ban Me Thuot victory we noted that, faced with decisive defeat, the enemy's morale had again fallen considerably and this was a favorable occasion to press on with our general offensive and pull off a great victory."

His fellow Guardia shouts for him to stop it, to get down off the car immediately. But the crazed fellow is in orbit. We in our group exercise our prerogatives and hold our tongues as well as our breath. He resumes his screaming/reading. —"From March 13, we were involved in blocking the enemy retreat from the Central Highlands. On March 16, when the enemy started to withdraw from Pleiku and Kontim via Highway 7 . . ."

The other Guardia can stand this outrageous exhibition no longer. This raving lunatic atop the car is endangering the dignity of the entire police corps—and spreading enemy propaganda as well! So he fires his machine gun into the pungent, whispering lime trees. But the other keeps on shouting. —". . . we mobilized our tank forces to seize positions along Highways 14 and 7, to block the enemy . . ."

His fellow cop screams imprecations that are both violent and mysterious. —You will go unburied when the time comes! Your name has spilled shame into the heavens! More machine-gun blasts. —Your bunk will be torn from its roots!

Of course . . . My entourage, my deepest companions, are now quite understandably motioning to me that we must go. Things here are clearly getting out of hand. The heart of Old Madrid is one thing, but really . . .

The well-dressed couple in their golden years hanging with such thuggish superiority at the edge of the crowd, these smug abstractions mutter, —What a pity that our good king Don Juan is not here. —Yes, yes. None of these obscene exhibitions would take place if he were here.

Indeed! Indeed! Would they like to know what that degenerate, self-satisfied little fart is doing right now? Trying to decide whether to finish his creamed chipped beef and poached eggs or race after the juicy little serving boy who has just bowed out of his royal Lisbon hotel suite. That's the sort of redeemer these pigs draped in cashmere are kidding themselves with. Is it any wonder, then, that their class is on the brink of extinction?

Does it come as a surprise to anyone at all that such bourgeois dodos find it so very difficult to reproduce their kind, no matter what kind of involuted (and of course outdated) kinkiness they may bring to their passion? Who among you, spectators or participants, can present scientifically acceptable evidence that pogo sticks can produce children? Va bene. Andiamo.

D ecca Aldridge tooled along the aisle of the huge PX. She was trying in an offhanded, circumstantial way to lose her mind among the shelves and lockers of food, food, food. Her shopping cart was approaching the delirious point of no return: it could not hold much more food. Decca stopped at frozen prepared dinners. Mmm. Yummy. Let's see now. I can get chicken potpie, beef stew, beef stroganoff, beef tips and wine, beef patties with cream of mushroom sauce, beef slices with sheep dip. No. Home-gravy dip. That's home gravy that's gone dippy and been frozen. Organic therapy for insane food. Terrific. People go nuts in my house, why I just freeze them up. So let's see . . . meat loaf with Spanish sauce. Hey you saucy Spaniards! How 'bout loafin' around with my meat? Could you go for a little of that? Bring your own gravy train of course. No, wait. I mean gravy boat. No, thanks. Don't think I'll fly this time. Got me an outside first-class cabin on this here gravy boat. Stops at a lot of porters who have stormy private lives. Well, what I mean is . . . Lady, does your porter have a hole in him? Because there's a lot of talk going around about these portholes, and I was just wonderin' . . . Braised tenderloin of beef Soixante-neuf. Mmm. Madam, I have nothing but braise for your tender little loins. Colonel, this here pussy comes highly braised. Ah yes. Braise the Lord and pass the aggravations. Friends, Romans, cunt sniffers. I come here not to braise Caesar but . . . Okeydokey hoky smoky. Smoky the Bear arrested on charges of indecent exposure. Picnicking families complain that Smoky brazenly showed his privates to their children while instructing them in the proper use of forest fires. Gerald Ford voices outrage on prime ribs of TV time. It's bad enough, said the former president from his home in the Detroit Lions' dugout, that the cherished Halls of Montezuma have recently been sullied by sulky students "flashing" for all they're worth and that's a mutant point as we all know, but it is absolutely too much for national park bears, whose current high standard of living they owe to the generosity of the silent American majority, for these bears who are living high on the hog rather than, as could very easily be the case, low on the berry bush because let's face it, that's where we found them, for these bears to mislead our beloved little folks by showing them their hairy privates instead of what they're paid to do, which is how to stamp out two Boy Scouts who have been rubbed together and thus started a flash fire wherein flashers, who have but recently been fired because of being national security leaks, are firing upon one another regardless of what depilatory effect they may have upon our remaining stands of virgins' timber. So I hereby authorize Congress to call in a surgical strike, 'cause Smoky the Bear, you gonna fry tonight . . . The American people will not allow their selves to be made a helpless giant by this bear's hairy hard-on.

Veal scaloppine marsupial à la go fuck yourself. We gon scallop yo peenie, Mistuh Al'rich, iffin you don stop pissin in thuh win and git yo plittikal repohts in heah wif mo jews in em, cause yo repohts is too dry fuh Kernel W. C. Fahtsmellah ta read. You heah? Mo jewsy. Yeah. Right. More juicy Jews is what we could use in this dump. Three pounds of Juicy Jews, please, and a pound of these nice frozen dog collards. Might as well throw in some of those lionized potatoes which as I live and try not too successfully to breathe, cause the air in this base—American atomic asshole base—leaves a great deal to be desired, I see you are offering at a reduced price. While you're at it, Mr. PX, you and your silent partner Mr. Y.Z. might like to consider reducing a lot more than prices. You say that I'll have to speak to the Grand Reducer myself? You wouldn't happen to have his number, would you? What's that? Ain't *nobody* got his number? Oh, of course . . . I see what you mean. What kind of a world would it be if somebody had God's number, right? Well, I've got news for you, Mr. Chicken Gumbo. *I've* got God's number. And just as soon as I get this fucking half-witted shopping done, I'm going to demand equal time on the networks to expose the devious, two-timing cocksucker, and you'd better believe it. I'm going to nail that bastard for good. I've got a bill of particulars here that will . . . Oh shit! Where is that little creep! Every time I turn my back, he starts undermining the human race. Never a minute's peace. He's driving me up the wall. Got to stop in the middle of everything and go find him. Where the hell can he be now? Not over there in the candy department. Hmm. Not in the ice cream department. 'Scuse me. Didn't mean to bump into your nice new carriage. Fuckin' Barbie Doll with a baby. All these moron army wives are defective Barbie Dolls. *Oh where is he?* Why do I hate my own child? Even though . . . —Oh, hi, Marla. How's it going? He's not really mine. I have been his fake mother for six years. Why do I think he's a midget Eisenhower? He looks like him, he acts like him, and he always wears that awful drill-sergeant cap he found in the parking lot. How is it possible to have an army drill sergeant for a child? Oh God, please help me bear my loathsome burden. I'm nailed to a cross of army jocks. *There* he is. In the war toys department, natch. Where else?

—Damn it, Ike! Haven't I told you a million times not to . . .

—My name's not Ike, my name is Wally Aldrich, and I'm a mean Green Beret.

—OK. You're a mean Green Beret. What in God's name have you got there? A machine gun or something?

—It's an atomic spray gun. It sprays radioactive stuff all over the enemy. Then they linger into death throes.

Help me, God. I promise not to expose you if you do. I'll do anything you say. I'll crawl on my hands and knees through every novel Henry James ever wrote. I'll join the army wives' bowling team and bowl my fucking brains out with those burly dike storm troopers. I'll swallow Ron's semen when he comes even though I'll puke. I mean, I don't even want to fuck for him. Please, God, because I can't stand wishing this little all-American monster would disappear and I can't stand living this awful life on this awful army base with a man who doesn't cast a shadow and who washes his hands after taking a piss even though he hasn't pissed on his hands. Where, where did I find him anyway? In a Cracker Jack box? An army internal security officer. Of course, where else would they come from but a box? Oh Christ, what in the name of all that is light and bright and human, what the fuck am I doing here? Why didn't I just sign on as a galley slave with a Death Ship and let it go at that? Maybe I'm not really me. Maybe I'm somebody else and just don't know it. Maybe I'm someplace else wonderful. Oh boy. But how do I find me?

Oh, this goddamn simple-witted, babbling check-out line. Worse than being trapped in a drowning ladies' room. —Ike, for God's sake! How many of those stupid magazines are you going to get?

—They're not stupid. They're for my dad.

—They're stupid.

Sports Illustrated, Sports Afield, Manhunt, Pursued, Caught, Spy, Master Spy, Master Key, Master Charge, Moon Hunt, Spy Mechanics Illustrated. "I Eat Spy Pussy," "I Eat Satellite Spy Pussy" . . . No, no. Good girls don't talk like that. Now lie back and let this nice man . . . Oh shit! And oh shit again! There's the boss's wife, Mrs. Colonel Leroy Fuckhead. Jesus. Gives me the shivers. She must have been a guard at Auschwitz. With eyes like that you don't need a gun. Oy Dios! She's spotted me. —Morning, Mildred. Sure is, absolutely wonderful weather . . . What's that? No, that's right. You didn't see me at the general's birthday party last night. I had one of my migraine headaches. Absolutely couldn't move a muscle. Oh, I've been to doctors. There's not an awful lot they can do. Uh huh. One of those things. Sure will. Maybe next week. Say hello to Leroy for me.

Thank you, God. She's gone. Say hello to Leroy my ass. Shoot the little prick in the head for me. Gestapo Chief of Internal Insanity at Rota Air Base. How wonderfully clever and dramatic of him to wear that rubber Himmler mask. And he's so studious, practicing that German accent so's he's got it down pat with our good friend. And those two killer Dobermans that trot at his heels. They're so *cute*. Feeds them on gook babies, no doubt. Oh boy, would I love to whip up a few intelligence reports for that mother-fucker. Internal Security Report No. 69. Subject: Suspicious Behavior of One Private I. P. Freely, Fifth Platoon, Sixth Regiment Royal Hot Steam Camel Floggers: Private Freely has been observed talking to his food during normal, routine, regulation-issue mealtimes in our wonderful, recently completed mess hall constructed in reverse record-breaking time by spic slave labor. On one occasion, he was heard to address a plate of perfectly fine mashed potatoes covered with pan gravy, with the following statement: "Love, let us be true to one another, for the world, which seems to lie before us like a land of dreams . . ." Subsequent words drowned in form full of mashed with gravy. On another occasion, specifically at our recent Memorial Breakfast in Honor of Our Comrades Who Loved and Lost at the Battle of Buggers' Hill, Private Freely whispered to a plate of sausages and grits and two over easy: "It ain't watcha say, it's the way thatcha say it."

Private Freely carries on a vigorous and widespread correspondence with certain nonexistent persons. We know this because all of his letters are returned stamped Person Unknown. The subject regularly misuses (and misunderstands, we perhaps should hasten to add) his weekend passes to the ancient and nearby port city of Cádiz. This city is thousands of years old. It was built by the Phoenicians when time was not of the essence. Cádiz is a city filled with memories of bygone things and, as often as not, with bygone people. It is a city that should bring out the best in a simpleminded, lower and lower-middle-class white soldier boy. It has many attractions. Countless brothels filled with short Spanish girls from the debt-ridden, rat-infested, and sorrow-sodden working class of this country that continually maintains that it is proud. These short, diet-unconscious girls flop down, pull up, and put out, and shut up. The ancient, reeking city of Cádiz also offers countless bars where Our Boys, the very cream of America's Cast-off System, can drink up and fall down. And no informant of any status or decency can fail to mention the slot machines, shooting galleries, dance halls, and desecrated park benches on and in all of which the lads from Rota Base can really let their hair down and pursue their congenital emptiness as best suits their whim and wile. But obviously our subject Private I. P. Freely, for reasons that we must determine if America's glittering bastions are not to be creamed one barfed day by some one-eyed Jew faggot, does not want this done to him. Private Freely, on his weekend pass, ducks into a big latrine on the Plaza of Virgin Pigeons, and after a bit, ducks out a full-grown monk. Yes, monk—which rhymes with sunk, lunk, bunk, and spunk. Just what does Private I. P. Freely, a pimply faced high-school dropout from Fayetteville, Arkansas, do now that he is a monk in Cádiz, Spain?

That's a very good question indeed and one to which this report will address itself with vigor as well as . . . —Well, hello, hello. If it isn't General J. Edgar Hoover come to pick up his little family.

—That's not General Hoover. That's my dad.

—Hi, Decca. Hope you didn't forget those steaks for the barbecue tonight.

—Daddy, why does Mom call you General J. Edgar Hoover?

—Well, to start with, old buddy, I don't think it's because she particularly likes J. Edgar Hoover and the FBI . . .

—Man, just look at the fucking mountains of food these fucking Americans are pushing out of that store of theirs, said one of the two Spanish chauffeurs waiting in the parking lot next to their black American limousines. —You could feed my whole fucking village with that. Man, that's all these crazy fucking people do is eat.

—I am not saying you are wrong, Pablo, said the other chauffeur, —but some of them are not so dumb, and they make the money, lots of it. You see that tall lady over there, with the blue hair and those eyes of a German Nazi killer? That's the wife of the chief of intelligence at Rota. Well, you know something? That elegant Nazi lady, Pablo, that smart American cunt, whose pussy must be as sweet as a razor, makes a big fortune bringing in the hash from Morocco. How do you like that?

—The truth?

—No shit. The truth.

—How do you know this? asks Pablo.

—I tell you, I know the angles around here. And something else. My girlfriend Sophia is her maid.

—Man oh man. That is really something to stick in your fucking brain. I mean it.

—And here's more to stick in your mind, my friend, the other says to Pablo. —You see over there getting into the yellow Mustang that little bald-headed guy, fat like one of Sophia's big, soft tits? Well, that fat tittie, Pablo, has got so many rackets going you just wish you could count them without the big tears of envy rolling down your very own face.

—Ah yes?

—Ah yes. He is in charge of ordering all of the goods and foods for this big store. Now I don't have to spell out to a smart man like you what a juicy tree that is to shake.

—Oh no, no spelling at all on a tree like that.

—And because we were not born yesterday afternoon, Pablo, we don't have to be told when we walk into one of those very fine and very dear tourist grocery stores in Marbella or Torremolinos, you know the places, they fucking look like jewelry stores, we don't need to be told where those internationally exacting taste thrills—smoked salmons that have jumped right out of the clannish rivers of Scotland, truffles that have been rousted in their forest sleep by the noses of smart-assed French pigs, thick, shuddering strips of bacon straight from the very soul of small but haughty Denmark—where these heavenly and almost beyond-reach savories digressed from and who just happens to be half owner of these shops devoted shamelessly as they are to the downfall of your inner strength, and that to buy one of those downfall items would cost more than one's sister could make selling her little ass on the Paseo on a brisk day . . . We don't have to be told . . .

—Señor Fat Tittie.

—Himself. And it takes no very big effort of the mind or one's inner will to go on from there, Pablo. The list of his hustles would be far longer than the catechism you were forced to recite on your hungry little knees as a helpless child by Father Xavier y Whip Stick. Like the imported topless girls at the American base, like the speedy, low-slung road hogs that you cannot even spell the names of unless you work through the arch smiles and lewd winks of . . .

—Señor Fat Tittie.

—The list, as I pointed out, is long, and it grips you.

—Oh, I can imagine, man I can imagine. But of course there's no doubt that one can see a few Americans here who are not drowning in their own shit. I mean, they may be eating some of it, yes, you know, but they are not turning into their own hot dogs. I mean, I . . .

—Like that long-haired cha-cha American princess getting into the jeep with the man and the little boy. Mmm. Whenever I see this one, I feel wings beating inside me because she gives you the feeling she has just hurriedly flown down from the sky. Dios mío! What my tongue wants to do for her tasty secret parts.

—I know these two Americans who have been living in my village for more than a year now. Now I do not understand the craziness that brings Americans to live in a small Spanish village where the action is, like, man, chasing squirrels and playing tarot when they can stay home in their own famous American cities where there is everything. But anyway, these two, they're living without marriage, that is for certain, and they are pretty nice.

They are not always singing "The Star-Spangled Banner" and waving $100 bills in your face. They are simpatico. And they can speak enough of our own language so that you don't have to ask yourself what they are fucking thinking because they can tell you themselves. And for yourself, you can tell them something too if the mood hits you to do that. What I am saying is, you don't have to look at each other through emptiness. The woman Señora Denise is out in the campo most of the time making paintings. She lets you come up and look at them closely if you have that curiosity.

—"The painting has feelings," she said once to my wife Marta. It had rained the day before and Marta was out in the campo looking for mushrooms. The woman was painting a picture of the old church that was half destroyed in the war. "It is more than just a picture of this church." Marta told me about it.

—The husband Señor Welles looks like a big question mark. He is always bent over a little bit when I see him walking in the village. I mean, he gives me the feeling of looking like a question mark. You know, the way you think people look? Like Father Cabrera who looks like a rainstorm. The husband is peculiar somehow, you just know that, but he is funny and he always buys me a drink when we run into each other in the village bar.

—"Pablo, we are going to drink to the sailing of the *María Pinta,*" this Señor Welles will say. Or, "Pablo, my friend, let me buy a glass of anise to celebrate the death of Senator Joseph McCarthy."

—From the upstairs of my house I can see him working early in the mornings in the rear patio of the house they rent from my sister and her husband. He sits in a chair under the big chestnut tree there writing in a fat notebook. That is when he most looks like a question mark. Bent over his notebook and his legs tucked under the chair. He has seen me looking at him, and our eyes have met and held, and that is when I feel we go into each other's spirit. In those moments people are going deep inside each other, not just at each other. I know he feels the same way. You can tell, and you can tell when the other person does not want to be in you and does not want you to be in him. But the American Welles does, and when our eyes held early the other morning, I know I was in him, I could feel him saying to himself, There's that Pablo, the driver for the AID official down in Cádiz. Those guys, they're all fucking spooks working for the CIA one way or another. What's with Pablo? Is he just another lumpen proletariat Spanish servant, like a waiter or a maid, who jumps when people snap their fingers? Or is he really himself belonging to himself? Is there a secret, real Pablo who is up to something divine? who is his own glory garden which nobody can get to? Something I feel inside his eyes suggests there is. Way, way inside him very carefully hidden is a gentle, sweet place, a pure place that is known only to him, like those spots in the woods that kids will lay claim to and not let any other kids in or near. Maybe your very best buddy, but nobody else. This guy Pablo has such a spot in him but he doesn't allow anyone to be there with him, not his wife, not even his children. He is a little boy when he retreats to this spot. He has had this hideaway of self since childhood. He plays one-man soccer there. Sometimes when our eyes meet in the morning, across this patio, it is the eyes of his sanctuary that look at me, the eyes of the child taken by surprise, and he sees right through me. It's so painfully beautiful. Poor Pablo. You are continually betraying yourself because you are afraid of betraying yourself. You think that if you hold out your hand to another, a pair of handcuffs will be snapped onto you.

Well, don't be afraid of me, Pablo. I'm not going to expose you. That's not in the deal I have with this village. They would not permit me such an intimate role in regard to one of theirs. I'm an outsider, and will be one for quite sometime longer, until they decide that I'm ready to come in. Then it's up to me to come in or not. They will then think of Denise and me as the Americans inside us. Until then, they will continue to feel, benignly of course, that we are the odd foreigners sitting on their skin. Meanwhile . . .

Ah yes, meanwhile . . . a black-and-white rubber soccer ball sails over the wall into the patio. Rolls along the ground and finally stops next to a fallen chestnut. The dismayed yells of the boys playing on the other side of the wall hang in the air, suspended in their flight or dissolution by my arbitrary/ warped mind that converts everything, Mother Nature herself, into fodder for my cannons . . . No sir, you are not the fodder of my cannon, or of my children, as that crazy, wonderful, tragically imprisoned Decca would say; or grist for my mill, or soup for my stains or something. What is that black-and-white ball saying to me? It is, of course, both the signified and the signifier in the tightly complex sociological boys' game outside my walls; the symbol and also the actual thing; itself and a symbol of itself; a real ball floating through the soft Spanish country air and an idea around which eight dark, slightly undernourished peasant-class and working-class kids are structuring into a game they will be furiously involved in until they are ladled into their graves on that hill over there with those somber, snooty cypress trees. (Why have these noble trees struck me as transvestites?) Does this ball have any messages for me? Like that other ball that had been left out here at night by what divinely sly hand in which I found, the following morning, that whole chapter on Mickey Mouse as Imperialist Lackey Colonizer, a vigorously presented and most convincing analysis. Or that extraordinary story in the manuscript, neatly packaged of course, handed me by the white-haired old lady dressed in traditional mourning black who hopped off the bus last week, toddled up here with it, like she was sleep-walking, then toddled right back to the bus. Story about how the United States was working with the Nazi intelligence services even before the war ended. Even helping some of them escape to America and other countries in return for information they had on left-wing groups in Europe and also on members of their own Nazi groups. Truly fantastic document. Gave complete files on all the Nazi war criminals living in the United States. Like the Ukranian Nazi leader who is now a county official in Passaic, New Jersey. And the honcho priest in Milwaukee who had been a top Jew exterminator in Rumania, head of an Iron Guard unit that went from village to village hanging live Jews, kids too, from meat hooks.

All these murderers say the same thing: "My hands are clean." They must all use the same strong soap, something like Fels' Naptha. Special murderers' soap. I must write a section—it's really a genre unto itself—called that, "My Hands Are Clean." Of course, I must first clear it with Socks Peelmunder. Have to clear everything I write with Socks. The Benevolent Tyrant, The Man Who Grabbed the Ball and Kept on Running, The Gatekeeper without Whom There Is No Gate. How did he achieve his present eminence? How did he creep in under the silky sound of the sleigh runners on hard snow? A cap was hurled into the air and, even before it began its gentle descent, the head of Socks Peelmunder was taking shape under it. He whom I invent now runneth me and my secret show—though in all truth, Mr. Dante, this seemingly private conceit which I am titling "The Fall of Rome: Another Capitalist Lie?" and within which Socks Peelmunder is concocting his own lewd mythologies is one in progress being called "A Jewish Version of *War and Peace*" (clearly, nothing is sacred to this fellow)—in truth as I was saying, these overwhelming divertissements may well turn out to be more nearly on target than the Rosetta Stone or the unretouched version of the Old Testament. This race is not over yet by a long ways, so just hold on to your tickets. There is far more to the blood-covered Washington merry-go-round than the Congressional Record (and its mottled, snoozing Old Boy readers whose yawning, open flies are that town's insatiable collective dreamer) would have you believe.

How very peculiar indeed, fucking strange, man, fucking strange, that a character I should invent in my fiction should take off and arrogantly start inventing its own fictions, rather like God's copilot taking over the plane, and not stopping at that, but, consolidating its malignant foothold in my imagination, should then tell me what to think and write. You can't match that for gall, or hubris, or simple home-fried greediness. Just shows you what can happen when you open up the hatch, peer down into the darkness, and shout, Come one, come all! Anything goes. Just no way you can tell who and what is down there and what might be going on in their pretty little heads.

Between the opening of the bird's mouth and the emergence of its song, into that delicate, sacred silence, that awesome void between the gesture and the actual creation, Socks Peelmunder flung himself.

Frantic running, barking from the fields beyond these walls. The urgent animal sounds overwhelm the delicate country ambience. The village dogs chasing a rabbit! What a disturbing, frightening sound. What does it sound like when bloodhounds or trained mastiffs are running a man down? Oh my God. And such did happen here when the Franco fascists hunted the losers after the war, hunted them in the fields and the forests and in the wounded, cringing little stone-and-adobe villages.

Allors! What is the high-and-mighty Socks Peelmunder up to? What is he doing to further exacerbate the world's already shaky condition? Glad you asked. Mmm. This coffee slipped in here so astutely by the sly-footed woman with whom I share my threadbare destiny is hitting the old spoterooni. As is this most lowly but powerful Celtas cigarette. "Socks, in a mood of black-velvet contained euphoria, completed the last paragraph of his anonymous paper, 'The Infrastructure of Fascist Ideology in the American Boy Scout Movement': '. . . making it an ideal pseudo-ideology/ institution for structuring the young male in a fascist mode. The abstracting of a young person from the existential crises of his own development into the "selfless" robotlike performer of absolute good deeds, which good deeds are preselected by a never-identified higher authority, leads inevitably to the development of a "clean-cut," selfless, soulless exterminator type: the smiling, sweet-faced little boy, dressed in the neat, ubiquitous Scout uniform, reflexively performing "good deeds" like a sleepwalker, becomes, in a society such as ours, the spotless automator/punisher/ exterminator of those who, according to the manipulating authorities, do "bad things," commit "bad deeds"; in other words, those who get out of line politically. We now have the cherubic tenderfoot become the glistening, marble-faced Death Squad member. The uniform has changed only slightly, and the seemingly innocent Boy Scout insignia of the lily of the valley, sewn there originally by his "mom," has metamorphosed into the skull and crossbones, the Death Head. Also proudly sewn on by his "mom." ' "

Welles sighing with satisfaction was Socks smiling with satisfaction, and vice versa, of course. Life is not a one-way street, mon ami. And the same goes for balls. A ball tossed up in the air must come down. Socks Peelmunder and Welles Ewing were, had inevitably become, the same person. Or at least they were not separable. Part of the time, in Welles's mammoth, organic fiction, Socks was his man. And part of the time, out of the fiction, tit for tat you would say if you were somebody's granny, Welles was Socks's man. And he did his bidding. 'Deed so.

As they thus sighed together, out there in the timeless, elegant simplicity of the stone-walled Spanish patio (where the falling of a leaf was exquisite and could be felt), the sounds of Denise opening the big kitchen windows, these sounds entered the patio, and so did her voice as she spoke to herself:

—Mmm. How I love the smell of the campo in the morning. It makes me dizzy.

Welles saw this lovely statement floating gently out across the dew-soaked fields like a silken banner. He almost shuddered as he saw the village dogs leaping and snapping at it. If they caught it, they would tear it to shreds as they would the panting rabbit.

Welles has recently completed two of Socks's assignments: (1) a psycho-sexual analysis of the Christ/Judas relationship, wherein Christ and Judas are seen as fag lovers; and (2) an exchange of letters between Cervantes and a younger sister, Arabella, in which it is abundantly clear that *Don Quixote,* as well as other, less-known works, was actually written by the sister. The first assignment was presented as a section of the Dead Sea Scrolls which had been secretly borrowed and translated by an eminent contemporary biblical scholar who had peddled it on the black market because he was very much in need of cash for a new Jaguar sports car. This apocryphal scroll, "originally" penned by an apparently sardonic and disgruntled second-echelon member of the Essenes, that offbeat (to put it mildly) sect that Christ was immersed in during a very "experimental"— there is no other way to characterize it—period of his life. The inside story (Welles, or Socks, had surpassed himself in scholarly mimesis) revealed bitter doctrinal bickering, feuding, power politicking, and crazy inter-personal carryings-on. Jesus was portrayed, and most convincingly, it must be said, as an inspired prima donna who got his way or else, and who, because he was queen of the hill, did not feel bound to monogamy in the manner of the lesser folk. Judas felt he had been jilted, and he struck back at the first opportunity. There was much more to the document—specific episodes, specific, verbatim-shouted accusations: "Judas: 'Where were you last night, oh haughty one? Don't tell me another council meeting because I simply won't buy it'"; dates and places, essential stuff like that—but that was the overall gist of it.

The Cervantes/Arabella letters were little jewels. They revealed, and of course exposed, a sibling relationship that touched all imaginable bases. Sister Arabella was a gifted loony, a weekend doper (Moroccan hash), a visionary, part-recluse, part-tavern show-off, occasional member of a traveling actors' group, and, quite obviously, a philsophical storyteller of high box-office quality. She lived through, and some may now say invented, her brother, with whom she had the by-now classic love/hate, inferiority/admiration, fear/need (and so on) deals going. Hints of incest there too: "Our meeting in Toledo last week left me drained in more ways than one, brother dear." And, "Who could wish for a more generous sister, who shares her God-given bounties so willingly." We all know, of course, that in those hand-to-mouth, short-shrift days, folks were not very fussy about drawing lines when it came to the nitty-gritty of basic human needs. You hustled and made out as best you could, eating what was at or in your hand, so to speak. You could die if you got too cute about life's problems.

Arabella was delighted to see her brother make out so well on her literary efforts—she lived through him in so very many ways—but at the same time she was furiously pissed that she would never have been able to present those literary masterpieces on her own because, you see, that sixteenth-century, chastity-belt-ridden society absolutely would not permit women to do such ballsy things. No fucking way. She would have been kicked down any number of old Spanish stairs. "Out with you, vile jade!" those grandees would cry, Arabella wrote in one of her letters. "Beneath your rustling skirts lurks blackest madness!" Oy Dios!

Welles loosed these breathtaking fabrications of Socks Peelmunder's upon the world by way of a nonexistent scholarly news agency, Scholars News Service, SNS, no dateline. Every time he/Socks concocted a historical document, he would sit down at his shiny Olivetti portable and peck out a "release" which he would mail off to a randomly selected newspaper or journal—the *London Times*, the *Washington Post*, the *Modern Language Association Newsletter*: high-type, gullible publications like that. "Bulgarian authorities unearth 'lost' Shakespearean manuscript . . ." Or, "Historical Society of Naples exhibits rare document on first aircraft design." In these handouts, in his best press-release journalese, Welles would summarize his own historical inventions. He had developed a repertory of sentences to assuage the simple raised eyebrows of whatever underpaid lackey at the recipient publications scanned his releases. "Leading experts throughout Europe unanimously agreed . . ." "Several scholars reached by telephone stated that the authenticity of the document was unquestionable . . ."

Welles had come to accept his, to put it calmly, labyrinthine, cross-pollenated, polysaturated way of being with philosophical simplicity. "Only fools believe the mirror tells the whole story," he said to himself, and to anybody else who got ambushed into the subject. "Look at it this way: I'll never be bugged by one of those acne-scarred identity crises. Y'know what I mean?"

A pair of mourning doves swooped gently into the giant tree sheltering the patio garden. They sat in the dense leaves with a lovely passivity, not hopping, not screeching, like commas subtly waiting to be summoned into a sentence. Welles sucked on the raunchy Celtas—this cigarette and its lewd smell properly belong in waterfront bars and small, surreptitious streets—and, his whole self swirling softly in that ecstatic inhalation, let go of himself and slowly sank into weightless spaces where his other selves, his supposedly fictional characters, were conspiratorially waiting for him. Their hands reached out to him, his to them, and, faceless, selfless, effortlessly, he began writing.

The Pied Piper of Hamel: Who Sucks for Mammon Sucks Blood

Hamel was a cute little middle-European village with nothing to hide. Quite the contrary. It blew its own horn so much that the surrounding mountains developed ear trouble. The reason for Hamel's self-love, smugness, and absolutely unbearable fucking hubris was this: It was the possessor of the world's only aspirin deposits. That is correct. If you wanted an aspirin tablet, you had to get it from Hamel (through your local pusher, of course), or get it not at all. To put it another way: Hamel's joy was the world's headache.

And you can be sure that the good people of Hamel were not about to let anybody forget this fact, not even each other.

—I hear that Prague is swept with migraine this month, said one saucy housewife to a passing burgher, grinning widely.

—Roll out the aspirin, we'll make a barrel of dough! sang the good fellow.

Or this from Preacher Fartblast to his Sunday congregation: —And the Lord sayeth, let there be headaches.

Oceans of amens.

And you know what that creepy village had on its coat of arms? Three white aspirin on a field of pain, that's what.

Well, that zilchy little place was laughing up its sleeve morning, noon, and night until a particular evening in June (the 12th, to be exact). Without warning, without any advance notice whatsoever, like the discreet Coming Events and Disasters paragraph in the underground press, without even an omen in anybody's noodle soup, the village was flooded with thousands upon thousands of shiny black rats. And they weren't on their way to Miami Beach or any other such grooving spot. *They stayed.* They took the bloody place over.

And I mean they were everywhere. In every nook and granny and crevice and crotch. In attics and basements and drawers and wardrobes. The tip-top, lovable folks of Hamel couldn't make a move without bumping into or falling over a black rat, or swarms of them. Por ejemplo: Judge Klaus von Quicklicker would dip into his marzipan jar and yoicks! a rat would leap out. Frau Erna Chopcock would open her cedar chest for her new spiked-steel corset and whoosh! out leaped a dozen shiny, squealing rats. Town Counselor Rolfe Kuntlove would open his latest porn mag and zoomph! rats spilled out instead of hot nooky. Like, ach! it was really murder.

All their silly-assed rat extermination attempts fizzled. Rat poison merely made them fatter; rattraps were tripped by the rats as a joke, and when one mind-blown storekeeper blasted at a rat one day with his shotgun, the pellets just bounced off the rat, who then grabbed the gun and whaled the living shit out of the storekeeper.

Not only that . . . the rats were organized six times better than the Medici.

They took the best seats at the opera, the best tables in the restaurants, creamed 20 percent off the top of all gross receipts, and boorishly monopolized the sidewalks to such an extent that the townspeople found themselves walking in the gutters. Boy! Were the villagers of Hamel climbing the walls!

—This rat scene is just too fucky heavy, said Town Surveyor Snatchgrabber to his drinking companion, dodging a half-eaten onion roll hurled at him by a rowdy, drunken rat at the next table.

—Something's got to be done about it.

—What else is new? replied Horst Lewdtongue, not batting an eye as a sausage end, lobbed from the unmentionable table nearby, caromed off his bulbous nose.

Just when the village was about to go under—things were so bad the villagers stopped screwing, because every time some couple was about to knock off a piece, there these pushy rats would be, making dirty cracks, giggling, and even taking pictures—a very far-out-looking stranger suddenly appeared in the town square. On one hand, he resembled a Cracker Jack prize, and on the other, a midget mountain climber. He wore a beanie with a propeller on top. He was about three feet tall, give or take a couple of smirks. He was wearing a big button on which was written "God Eats Pussy."

—Understand you folks have a few unwanted houseguests, he shouted in a high child's voice, and then giggled wildly.

—You don't have to rub it in, you little prick, Town Crier Twattickle shouted back from a bench there. —What's on your mind?

—I'm Piccolo Pete, he replied. —I'm to rats what James Joyce was to the contemporary novel.

There was a long silence as the villagers in the square tried to slice *that* one.

Finally, Mistress Lowbottom, the village hooker, said, —Spell it out, you little buzzard's fart.

—OK, said Pete. —I'll get rid of all the rats for you at a deuce a head.

A great gasp went up from the assembled loiterers. —A deuce a head, they howled. —Mama mia! That'll wipe us out.

—Take it or leave it, said Pete. —It's no skin off my ass if the rats do you in.

—OK, OK, said Town Negotiator Klaus von Slysuck. —It's a deal. He gave his fellow citizens a real big wink. —And our word is as good as gold.

—Oh, wow! they exclaimed.

—Yeah. Right on.

—Go, man, go.

Their chuckles of complicity were almost too much to hide, and a couple of the natives pissed in their pants in the attempt.

—You're on, said Pete.

That evening, when all the village adults were in the town hall watching some hard-core flicks from Amsterdam (the best seats, of course, were all taken by the uppity, boisterous rats, who were milking the situation for all it was worth), Piccolo Pete worked his magic. He stood in the town square and began to play his little silver piccolo. The tune was an oldie but a goodie. It was the marching song from the Children's Crusade. Old it may have been, but its box-office appeal . . . jeepers! The rats began to pour out of everywhere—basements, attics, sewers, the theater, shoes, you name it—and their frenzied rush down the streets to the square was so noisy you'd have thought Cecil B. was reshooting *Ben-Hur*.

—No holdouts, I hope, said Pete, surveying the rolling rat masses.

—Oh no! they chorused by the thousands. —Not when it comes to stirring, suicidal music like this.

—Groovy, said Pete. —Andiamo.

And away they went, through the tricky, self-satisfied, cobblestoned streets of Hamel. Piccolo Pete was playing at his best, and the hordes of rats scurrying obediently behind him were humming their crazy hearts out. If you don't think that was a sight to end all sights, then you'd better get your eyeballs fixed.

They finally reached Funk River.

—OK, you all, said Pete, pointing to the swirling, hungry waters. —This is it.

—Last one in is a blue-balled revisionist! shouted the first rat, and leaped to his doom.

They all followed suit, while Pete continued to play that very catchy tune. The last rat left was a fat, silvery grey old codger who had clearly been around. —We had a real good thing back there, he said, smiling philosophically.

—Yeah. Well, you can't win 'em all, said Pete.

—I'll drink to that, said the rat, and leaped into the river.

The next morning Pete showed up in front of town hall to collect his fee. The place was jammed with happy, grinning villagers. They were giggling and nudging one another. What a simply super joke they were in on! What a boffo coup they were shortly going to observe.

—Well, began Pete, —I took care of those rats for you. They're all drowned. He held out his hand to the Town Negotiator. —You owe me $206,000.

—Our deal, said the Negotiator, grinning and winking at the crowd, —was a deuce a head. Where are the heads, my freaky little friend?

—You know fucking well that's simply an expression, said Pete. —It doesn't mean I'm supposed to show up here with 103,000 bloody rat heads. Those rats are drowned and you know it.

More wild laughter from the crowd.

—No heads, no dough, said the Negotiator.

The crowd of lumpen shits howled with lewd glee. —Attababy, Horst!

Pete stared daggers at them. —OK, you double-crossing motherfuckers. But let me tell you something. When I get through with you, you're going to be laughing out the other side of your faces, if you have any faces left.

Somebody flung a coin after him. —Here's a nickel for a pickle!

Late that evening, while the adult villagers were all in the ancient Fuckatorium celebrating their sleazy fraud with a drunken sex orgy, Piccolo Pete returned to the village square. He began to play a very strange number on his piccolo, a number that could only be heard by the ears of the sleeping children of the village. As he played, all of the children left their beds and scrambled (noiselessly, on feather feet) out to Pete in the square. They crowded around him. They were not awake, but they weren't asleep either. Their eyes were glistening and wide open; they were in an ecstatic trance. Pete stopped playing and began to speak to them in an odd language. As they listened, their faces were suffused with an expression of beatific sensuality. Pete finished his message and began to play again, and the children raced soundlessly back to their homes. In a matter of seconds they came back out of the houses.

They were armed with guns, knives, pikes, hatchets, and hammers, and these glistened eerily in the moonlight. Pete paused in his playing to say one more sentence in the odd language. The white nightgowned children sped through the dark, moonlit streets toward the Fuckatorium. The drunken, sated, stupefied adults could offer no resistance to these avenging angels, and in a matter of blood-drenched minutes they were all slaughtered.

Piccolo Pete strolled on his way, and though he was not exactly what you would call throaty, his laughter reached all the way to heaven.

P.S. Hamel thus became the Original All-Children's Village.

I n the vast, pained, noisy numbness of Trafalgar Square, a man and a woman, with long colorful scarves curled jauntily round their necks and flowing blissfully down their backs, strolled through the hordes of scrofulous, picky pigeons that covered the area round the nostalgically bravo statue of Lord Nelson. Many depraved, scruffy, grey pigeons were shitting all over Lord Nelson. England's finest hour was disappearing under ominous layers of mottled, dried pigeon shit.

—I've asked everybody I know to come, said one of the pair. —But some are afraid. They think there's going to be violence. And the fucking British secret police . . . they're afraid they'll be hassled by them and maybe deported or something.

—Yeah, well, there won't be any violence unless those storm-troopers from the Nationalist party come and provoke it, said the other. —The police love those bastards. They never bother them, no matter what they do.

—Legally, you know, no foreigners are supposed to engage in any kind of political action while they're guests of the country. It's against the law. So you're really taking your ass in your hands even to show up at a political demonstration like the one tomorrow.

—What that really means is you're not supposed to interfere in the internal politics of the country. Like trying to influence the way these fucking limeys vote or whatever. Or trying to get them to feed their kids milk instead of Watney's ale and chips.

—No way you could ever do that. That's like telling them to stop sucking up to their idiot queen. Is it all set that Mrs. Allende and Mrs. Letelier are going to speak tomorrow?

—Oh yeah. It's definite. And Vanessa Redgrave has promised to show.

—She's so great, said the woman. —No bullshit about her, the way it is with all those liberal assholes from Hollywood. She's really committed politically. She was fantastic in the antiwar activities over here. Helped raise a lot of money for Vietnam aid. It's weird her being an actor and also a political ideologue.

—Yes, it really is. Look! In front of the South Africa building over there... Those cops are rassling that black guy down. Come on! Let's see what's up.

And they darted through the robot-strolling crowds toward the suddenly materialized moment of anguish across the honking, primly ugly London square.

—Fucking Nazi country! the black man yelled. —Bunch of murderers!

S tephan gently picked his way down the juicy Rue St.-Antoine, much as Marcel Proust walked through the brain of the Baron Charlus, arm in arm with nothing, beholden to no man, yet in debt to all, his pores wide open, his fly tightly closed, and his eyes and ears lurking greedily in the imminence of reality's collapse. As far as anybody knew, he could have spent the early hours of this day posing as an unemployed movie usher. Or he could have been relentlessly teasing the imported sociological secrets out of a paragraph by Colette (under the direction of that clever little owl Roland Barthes, of course). Or he could have been... Oh God, who knows?

As usual, certain people in the street thought they knew him, and as was his passive custom, Stephan made no effort whatsoever to set them straight. Had Polonius been able to tell Hamlet anything? Did the wives of Bath learn a fucking thing from the Romans? OK then. A gross woman inundated with running Camembert cheeses grinned at him and made a cabalistic sign.

—The time will come, she said to him, winking. He winked back. An enigmatically self-satisfied wench lording it over a huge pile of shimmering blood sausages shouted to him: —We know you made a killing at the races yesterday. How about spreading some of it around?

—In time, he replied.

A saucy, red-eyed chap scaling freshly captured sea bass (little did they know, right?) came right out with some advice for him. —You'd better stay away from that little Benoist girl, Philippe. She'll only bring you bad news, believe me.

Stephan smiled, and in a manner he thought would suit Philippe, said, —Oh well. What is life but bad news? And he shrugged (a very usable response he'd picked up watching French movies).

In a few moments he was sitting at his favorite café in that quarter, the Café de la Musée, sipping *un café*, happily polluting his lungs with a Gitane, and thinking about Carol, in and out of her classy bordello. One part of his tableau had Carol talking very carefully about intellectual elitism and at the same time, in the same tableau, dressed in black leather undergarments, she was spanking a fat, naked client as provocative obscenities leaped from her red-lipped mouth. He was trying to separate these two seemingly but not really contradictory images of Carol in order to get the most concentrated mileage out of one or the other. He was getting things more or less sorted out when a simply, tastefully, conservatively dressed woman sat down at his table out there on the sidewalk. It seemed to Stephan that she smelled of fields of clover more than anything else when you came right down to it. Stephan felt immediate confidence in this woman. In her unadorned way, she is onto something big, he said to himself. For instance, it would not surprise me in the least to discover that she is an authority on the behavior of nonferrous metals under stress. Or she has done singularly original work on the comparative development of speech patterns in rural and industrial areas. She doesn't fuck around, not this lady. She doesn't do a lot of tap dancing in front of the altars of revelation. She just lays it right on the line and you can take it or leave it, it's all the same to her. Truth is her simple, unadorned, clean-smelling, firm-limbed, nonshit, smiling business. —This lady can go through the eye of a needle, goddamnit! he shouted, slapping his hand down on the small table.

—That is very sweet of you indeed, I said, because I am of course the woman. —Your confidence means a great deal to me. In fact, I don't exist without it.

—Oh, it's you, Stephan said, slightly startled. —But that's OK. I meant every word of it. That woman that you're got up as is above reproach. She is everything I thought she was and more! Do you hear me? He leaned toward me and looked at me fiercely. —In fact, my good man, or woman, she is superior to you in every way. So there.

I could not keep from putting my arm around his slight young shoulder.
—You are a wonderfully loyal chap, Stephan. It's because of such feelings as
yours that our group has survived so many challenges and still kept up its
high standards of performance. Solidarity and mutual respect . . . I was
beginning to feel quite teary.

—OK, OK, Stephan said. —Let's stop before the whole thing gets sloppy
and embarrassing.

—You're absolutely right. Sentimentality is man's worst enemy. But I
must say that it's wonderful that people like us can have these little talks
from time to time.

—I suppose so, he said.

I pulled myself together, sat back in my chair as before, conservative,
cool, remote but at the same time inescapably and provocatively there,
vibrating exactly the same classic immediacy as the statues of Venus de Milo
and Winged Victory. I slipped back into my role as the irreproachable
mystery woman. Stephan likewise resumed his former position and self, so
to speak. A really quite decent pause of silence settled between us.

Stephan inhaled and savored his Gitane. His cig and his café were very
tasty. And very tasty too were his feelings and speculations about the excellent lady sitting at this table, right there on the thoroughly engaged Rue St.-
Antoine, where all the people were pursuing their lives, going about their
business, in ways that could not be faulted by even the most orthodox
existentialist. The fine woman (faultless chin line, matched by equally faultless gold earrings) sipped her Vermouth, kept her head high but not aloof,
and did everything one would expect to very subtly support Stephan's
feeling that she had something to say to him, a message of some kind, some
important information, *a rare but long-awaited involvement.*

He had to say, finally—just after she had visibly responded with a smile,
not a private one, to the incontestably amusing sight of an old man wildly
rolling a hoop down the middle of the street—had to say, —This balmy
street never fails to treat.

Now she looked at him. —You rhyme and that's quite acceptable. But
there are some other streets that you have perhaps forgotten.

—Oh?

—Yes. Streets that must be recalled. She moved her chair in a bit closer to
Stephan's, and this brought their shoulders into touching contact. —Listen,
she said, putting her marvelous-smelling field-of-clover face close to his.
—Those other streets run in a town called Barking up the Wrong Tree, New
Mexico. And she told Stephan all about the town as if she were one of its
inhabitants (he just knew she had to be borrowing a special voice from the
town):

We don't fool around down here when it comes to accuracy and mistakes and penalties, stuff like that. One just follows the other, and there's no way around it. Like, somebody will walk into, say, Hot Hanna's Peaceful Diner and without even so much as sittin' down and orderin' a bowl of her roaring chili and a glass of ol'-fashioned cold buttermilk, will shout, —Hanna, this place of yours is lurking behind a mask!

Hanna will just stand there behind the counter, wipin' her hands on the blue-flowered apron that she won at the Lutheran Church bowlin' contest last spring, look him right in the eye the same way she's looked at many an apple pie that's givin' her a hard time, and say, —Doug, you got it wrong this time, you silly old son of a bitch.

What happens next is this: any two of the customers, good, sound towns-people who have dropped by Hanna's for an order of jello and coffee, or maybe a dish of raisin pudding, will rise calmly from their seats, grab Doug —who could very well be grinnin' pretty foolishly by now—and hustle him outside to the nearest eucalyptus tree. There they will twist his arms till he falls to his knees and, looking up, begins to bark. The two civic-minded enforcers will then return to Hanna's and their desserts (to be sure, one of 'em could have been in the middle of a hot meat loaf sandwich with a side order of mashed with gravy).

—Lemme top up your java, Hanna will say to them on their virtuous return to their stools, coffeepot in hand.

—That suits me just fine, Hanna, each will say.

Perhaps they will have made that very powerful and all-too-clear gesture of dusting their hands upon their return to the diner. This would depend upon how old they were and how impinged upon by modernity—and its lackluster abstractions—they might be. Some very fine gestures are dying out among later generations, and there's not a darn thing you can do about it, lessen you wanna make a federal case about it. This, in turn, would raise the question, a tough one lemme tell you, of whether or not each new generation has an inalienable right to its own emptiness. Anybody who feels he has a clear view of this is plumb crazy.

But let's get back to old Doug and this penitential barking up the tree. That's nothin'. When the misapprehension season is in full swing, round the middle of August, you can see as many as twenty ill-advised, wrongheaded people down on their knees barking up eucalyptus trees for all they're worth. I mean, it's quite a sight and easily worth your serious attention whether you're a visitin' cultural anthropologist (tryin' your damnedest to make ends meet on your per diem) or an ordinary bozo who's just tryin' to get by till your number is up. Think it over.

In fact, our whole violation/punishment system is something you might want to pause and reflect on (unless you've risen above that kinda thing in your scramble to the top). You comfortable? OK now. Put your eyeball real close to this: Violation Number One—Adultery. Let's say the man is the guilty party. There's more'n one way we have of dealing with him. For instance: we let his aggrieved wife select half a dozen of the town's men that she thinks are the most desirable; then we assemble the whole population in the square, including the naughty hubby, of course, and while everybody's gawkin', especially the hubby, his missus screws these fellas to beat the band. That's one punishment. Then there's this one: we paint his dashing dilly with a luminescent paint—let's say a real hot orange or yellow—then for three nights straight we make him stand . . . we tie him naked to a cross on a scaffold in said square. Quite a sight. There are a whole buncha horse chestnuts. You're wrong if you think a lot of folks walkin' home through the square at night don't pick up a few of those hard, shiny chestnuts to throw them at that glowing dong up there. And can you think of a better way for our young folks to keep their throwin' arm in shape?

We don't mess around with dishonest business people. When we find out some store owner has been gyppin' its customers, we move with the speed of forked lightnin', no two ways about it. The offender's store is declared "free" public property for an entire business day. Anybody who wants can come in and help themselves to whatever strikes their fancy. We don't need to declare a place "free" for more than one day for the simple reason that at the end of that one day—actually, several hours before, to tell the honest truth—there's not one single item left in the place. It's been stripped to the bone, and of course it goes without sayin' that the owner is required to stay there and be a witness to his own purging. I'll tell you something: there's not one storekeeper on record who ever returned to his old gyppin' ways after such a "free" day. No sir. Not one.

Like to know what we do with wife beaters? You'll like this: the first Sunday of every month—after our people have finished barin' their breast to the Lord almighty and made whatever deals they could, and sung their hearts out with such top favorites as "Jesus Wants Me for a Sunbeam" and "Put Your Shoulder to the Wheel, Push Along," we rope off Main Street, 'bout four blocks of it, from Jed's Homemade Ice Cream Parlor to J. C. Penney, then distribute stout sticks to the hordes of happily grinnin' women who are always more than on hand for this particular age-old event. —Oh boy, what a great day this is gonna be. And, —I wouldn't miss this little party for the world.

The wife beaters—who don't have a stitch of clothing on, of course—are drug to the "payoff" area with ropes tied round their necks. Drug 'cause none of 'em ever want to come of their own free will, willingly. They're lined up at one end of the roped-off street. The specifics of their offense are read out real loud by Our Lady the Reader (a role that has been held for the past five years by Lily Briggs, girls' gym teacher at Tom Jeff High, whose late, mean husband had closed one of her eyes for good). When Our Lady Lily has finished, a starting pistol is fired into the air, and the naked men are given a good push on their way. Which is down the row of howlin' women armed with those stout sticks.

Now, you don't have to be told all the gory details, do you? Like the whimpers and then the screams of the men as they are beaten with the sticks; the blood coverin' their naked bodies, the funny little sounds of bones bein' broken, the unmanly sobbin', the pleas for mercy—"Oh help! Help! I won't do it again! Oh please! Oh God! I'll be good!"—the wild howls of pleasure comin' from the women. No, best we leave the rest up to your imagination. (And it's probably best we also leave up to your own imagination what we do to thieves and burglars and such by way of educational punishment.)

When it comes to religious worship and the four freedoms to do it therein . . . sure, ever'body knows that ever' town worth its salt has got its churches an' more than enough. Baptis', First and Second, Meth'dis', Luther'n, 'Nitarian, 'Piscopal . . . like ever'body else, we got all those 'nominations (up to here almos'). Plus we got some ain't nobody got. Church of the Three Fallen Angels, Church of the Cloven Hoof, Church of the Child Who Shall Lead Them, Church of the Friends of Salome . . . to give you a rough idea. Last count, we had thirty-eight distinctly separate and independent and sufficient-unto-theirselves religious groups over'n above the Big Ten. You don't have to have a guaranteed congregation of 3017 in order to set up a church in our town. That's not our style. You can open shop with just one person if you want to. For instance, Witnesses to the First Human Sacrifice Executed Not Far from the Garden of Eden under the Supervision of Certain Prominent Mesopotamian Family Men Who Hoped to Remain Anonymous, well, this church has only four members, one of which is a huntin' dog named Richard. And the newest, which opened its doors, in a manner of speakin', just last week, calling itself Friends of the Sacred Monkey Who Saw and Heard a Lot More Than She Was Supposed to Which Has Ever Since Made an Awful Lot of Folks Very Nervous, this outfit has a mere seven members, and three of 'em are identical female triplets, the Wort-Whistle sisters, the eldest of whom is thirteen. You beginnin' to see the shape o' things?

Hell's bells. Why don't we take a look-see at one of 'em 'stead a just standing here with our thumb up our ass. So happens that we're no further away than a choked throat from a spanky little religious commitment called Revelations from That Part of the World So Long Denied and Suppressed by the Church in Spite of Undeniable Evidence. You can see for yourself. Never been any substitute for that. With your own two eyes. Sure is a nice day, for just about anything you might want to get it into your head to do. Hmm. Old Pete Wallaby's barber pole ain't workin' again. Bet the red band is stuck down at the bottom. Mornin', Miz Emma. See you been to market skimmin' off all the best persimmons again. While there's still time? Uh huh. Well, here we are. They've been in this little basement here goin' on two months since the snow up on the mountain melted and we discovered the bodies of those runaway bird-watchers. Musta been a real strange kinda bird to lure those two up that high. Right? Couldn't a been no robin red-breast. 'Cause such a bird as that just wouldn't have no bizness up that high.

Well, we're just in time for a ceremony, I see. Thank you very much, Fred, for showing our visitor the town and for bringing him or her here. All of us on the council agree that you leave nothing to be desired as a tour guide. Good. See you around, Fred. You what? You want to complete this tour? You won't be interfered with by any uppity council member who thinks he's better than you? Now look here, Fred, you just . . . OK, OK. You don't have to threaten me with a gun, Fred. We've known each other for a long . . . OK, OK, I'm going. Just watch it with that gun. Take the gun away from my head, OK? All right, I'm going. You'll hear from the council . . .

Damn smart ass. Just 'cause fellas like him have been to college they think they got the right to run all over us workin' people. Well, they've got another thought comin'. Maybe I shoulda put a hole in that swelled head of his after all. Let out some of the hot air. Boy, just you wait. One of these days there's gonna be a showdown with those council cuties. They act like they own this town. Buttin' their big noses into everything. We been bossed around long enough. One of these days real soon you're gonna see a lot of bodies lying in the streets, an' they won't be ours, y'can be sure uh that.

You see what I mean by really diffurnt religious groups? You ever see people dress up like this in the Baptis' meetings? . . . masks an' animal heads on their heads, their faces painted up in this crazy way? What kinda animals they supposed to be anyway? And what's that they got up there lying on that altar? Well, I'll be damned if it ain't somebody wrapped up in a wolf skin. Let's get a closer look, they won't mind. They're all busy doin' their ritual. Damn, if it ain't little David Thorpe! If that don't take the cake. Why, I saw him just this mornin' deliverin' his newspapers. You'd never guess a mild kid like him would be up to somethin' as outta-the-way as what we're lookin' at right now. Just goes to show you, don't it? Golly! Did you see that? That person in the jackal head just cut that chicken's head off and is holdin' it over little David. The blood . . . Let's get outta here. I don't know 'bout you, but I like my religion with a Bible.

S tephan paid six francs for a steaming wedge of sausage pastry at the jolly, bubbly, open-air charcuterie at the corner of the Rue St.-Antoine and the Rue Tournelle. He liked eating on the hoof, on the wing, or even on the fly. (But not *in* the fly, because that would mean he was one of *those,* easily half of whose furtive lives were lived kneeling before an open fly here, and open fly there. Oh the wild world of dangled meat!) As he crossed the Rue St.-Antoine heading up the Rue Tournelle for the Place des Vosges, he was jostled by a distressed and furiously babbling old lady. The crazy old quiff almost knocked the cherished sausage pastry out of his hand.

—The dirty swine have stolen everything from us but our names! the disheveled and disorderly old thing was shouting.

—Madam! My sausage! Stephan cried out, recovering his balance just barely.

—Just wait! she went on yelling. —They'll grind us up into dog food next.

—Oh dear, said Stephan. —What a bleak view.

—She's right, said a passing chap in a very nice grey coat. —Every bloody word of it.

Conversations in the middle of moving traffic are doomed, Stephan said to himself, deciding to keep his trap shut until he reached a clean bench in the park. Surrounded by starched nannies and soft, dreamy young mothers, and all those kids who were just aching to grow up into a world that would fuck them over proper. Nothing was going to keep Stephan from smiling to himself. The Rue Tournelle was one of Stephan's very favorite streets in the Marais. It was gentle without being listless and amusing without being . . . without being what? Well, competitive. It wasn't competitive, period. In a store window filled with intimate and saucy female undergarments—devil-may-care bras, shock-wave panties—a woman who, at first look, seemed to be a mannequin modeling a black-and-red garter belt and a tiny peekaboo bra turned out to be a real live woman. She grinned at Stephan and of course —because where would he be without this sort of thing?—he had to grin back and wave at her.

—Until later, he whispered at her.

—Perhaps, she mouthed back. —I'm not promising anything.

—You have a strange accent, he continued. —You must be from Languedoc.

One can never be sure what Stephan has in mind during such exchanges. Even I am often puzzled, and who knows him better? Exactly. His soul beat as one with ambiguity. For the time being we must use that fact as our leaning post.

The park in the Place des Vosges was just what the doctor ordered. It was calm but not lethargic, innocent but implicitly game, and crawling with people who quite obviously were not punching time clocks in a tennis racket factory. And many young children—clean and fastidiously dressed by elders with a vested interest in that—who inevitably would grow up and join the ranks of bourgeois piggery. And that's how we got the pyramids (for those of you who have wondered). It can be said, in general, that in the Place des Vosges you could not go wrong. Throughout the centuries this grasp of the situation was held by a select group of people with the proper money to do so.

Stephan flopped on a bench that was within grinning distance of a couple of not-so-prim, young French nannies (who, in truth, may well have been au pair girls, which is an entirely different kettle of you know what) and a demurely catatonic youngish couple (cashmeres, flannel, quality blue-striped shirting) who, it is not completely out of the question, were dreaming of some obscure well-bred victory in the class struggle: i.e., the clubbing to death of a starving sixteenth-century peasant who dared to break into the granary on the estate of the Duc du Monet; or the finals of a competitive exam at the Ecole Normal when a gifted, profoundly motivated upstart from the lower middle class lost out to a member of the upper middle class because, when push came to shove, he did not have the extensive protein reserves to draw upon that his infinitely better-fed opponent had at his disposal. (Just to give you a model for speculations on your own. Anyone can do it. Though I do have something of an edge, I do not have a monopoly on this sort of historical reconstructing.)

He munched happily on his warm sausage pastry (Touraine) and sipped from a half-bottle of Burgundy he'd managed, in his usual unstructured way, to buy without our knowing it. One cannot watch characters like Stephan too closely. Such as he, brimming over with the possibilities of their own autonomy, have made it necessary for narrators to take out heavy mal-practice insurance, or to go about armed, merely to protect their vestigial rights. (Parents have been in this leaky boat for quite some time.) A child pulling a very small leopard on wheels stopped in front of him. She stared at him as if he were in the original German text.

—What are you doing here? she demanded.

—None of your fucking business, he said, and swallowed some sausage.

—My leopard will eat you, she said.

He was about to pour some wine on this little cunt's curly head when her young, ambiguous nannie/au pair darted up. —She knows not what she says, claimed the woman.

—You read that somewhere, said Stephan.

—Maybe yes, maybe no, but it's still applicable, don't you think? said the young woman.

—Actually, no, said Stephan, plucking the child's hand from his pastry.

—I think this mini jade knows all too well what she's saying. She's destined to become a fascist exterminator, exactly as her foul class has planned.

The little girl grabbed his wine bottle. Stephan quickly retrieved it. Had to apply strength, 'cause the kid had strong wrists.

—I have two policeman friends, the kid said.

—Listen to that, Stephan said to the au pair. —I'm being threatened.

—I think it's her way of playing, said the au pair, looking suspiciously at her well-dressed charge. —But I'm not sure. This one has a lot up her sleeve.

The child yanked the leg of his pants. —Where do you live? she asked. —I'll bet you live under a bridge.

—OK, that's it, Stephan said. —Take this premature plague away immediately. He looked at the au pair (who obviously had a variety of possibilities, otherwise, why all this business?). —We've got a lot to tell each other. Come back after you've returned this one to her test tube.

The young woman naturally smiled. —It's a deal. Now don't change benches or anything on me while I'm away. (So far, it is hard to tell just where she comes from. She may or she may not be yet another American.)

Guess what: after the au pair and the child had walked a few yards off, the child turned abruptly around and made a standard lewd gesture with her finger at Stephan.

Hmm, went Stephan. Very surprising. How would a child with her upper-class background learn such a gesture? And, furthermore, what trans-schematic urge would permit her to use it in such a public, and constrained, situation? Neither Durkheim nor Florsheim can help me here. In socio-logical crises like this, one must stand on one's own two feet or fall on one's own two faces. This brings up—a crazed blue jay attacked fat pigeons to his left—the existential question (which, in effect, is question numero uno): are intellectually acquired insights ever as good as one's own intuitive grabbings? Or, to put it another way (he chewed and swallowed the last juicy morsel of sausage pastry and sluiced it down with some vino, while noting, at the very same time, that the obscure-looking gent—a former accountant from the colonies?—sitting near the gate had slyly opened his fly and . . .): what good is it to read a lot of fancy books about life when you are up to your ass in it? What can you tell your ass that it doesn't already know?

—Oh dear! Stephan exclaimed aloud. —Upon the answer hangs the tenure of a thousand professors.

The wine and the rich sausage pastry were permeating him with Frenchi-ness. Saturating me . . . Am sodden with . . . No, not that. For one thing, *sodden* is actually a sociological value-judgment word, plus a moralistic word, whereas *saturate* is neutral in those senses of meaning. Sodden with drink . . . We're not talking about a bombed member of Giscard's cabinet. No, we're referring to—oh my. The obscure gent is exposing himself to the two Japanese ladies with cameras sitting on the bench just down from him. He's put his bowler over his hard-on and he grins and lifts it up to show them . . .—referring, in a superior way, to a person on the lower rungs who is a loser in most of life's endeavors. Like, all those bleak characters in Zola are sodden. Nobody in Proust is sodden. Saturated, yes. And permeated. Baron Charlus was saturated with his need to be flogged. And after the flogging (administered, the old fart complained, by ordinary married men whose heart was not in their work) was saturated with satisfaction. Now we can't possibly link sodden with satisfaction. Wait. Maybe we can. Plumber's-helper Smith was sodden with satisfaction. That is to say, this working stiff, by the very nature of the rigged game, can only be degraded by his satisfaction. Back to Charlus. The Baron was permeated by class snobbism, while his ass was penetrated by rough trade cock which has been both saturated *in* Vaseline and saturated *with* upstart cruelties, and which would moments or minutes hence, depending upon the trade's discipline and whose skill, be *sodden* (though limp) with lower-class smugness, because it had buggered (we must look at this at all levels of implication) an aristocrat, and it had been paid to do so . . . OK. We have that nailed down. 'Course, we could lob *sodden* into a wholly different, and classier, realm. We could, in effect, strike off its shackles. I kind of like "He was sodden but not forgotten," or, "His prose style, while not dazzling or provocative in any way that could be called original, did, however, have a certain sodden, self-contained authenticity, an authenticity that had been earned and not bestowed." Also we could . . .

The park gardener was suddenly sweeping most provocatively around Stephan's feet. Said the sweep, sweep gardener, —I should like to call your attention, Monsieur, to the shameless transnational hanky-panky taking place three and four benches down to your right, not one hundred feet from the sacred domicile of the late, great Victor Hugo.

Good grief! And b'gosh! And I'll be a stuffed brown owl. Remember those two Jap lady tourists with the cameras? And the cock flasher who planned to shock the living shit out of them by doffing his bowler off his raging tool? Well, guess what. Those Jap ladies, who always look so suppressed and repressed, good-behavior-wise and all that, must have been secretly trained in turnabout (did the French customs people know this?), 'cause in response to the seated flasher's display, one of them, without changing that Jap look of frozen eternal serenity, was standing with her skirt held high and rotating her nonpanty-covered snatch at the benched flasher, while the other lady, skirt also high, was shaking her fat bare ass at him.

—It is just this sort of thing, Monsieur, that has driven the dear little squirrels from our park, said the gardener, picking a fallen leaf from Stephan's lap. —Still another example of the deterioration of the social and moral structure of La Belle France.

—Ha! exclaimed Stephan. —The poor bugger is running away; the slants called his bluff.

—Exposing oneself has a long and honored tradition in the alleyways of Western society, the gardener went on, sweep, sweep, —but turnabout must . . .

Stephan lightly kicked the man in his fanny as he bent over to scoop up some dead oak leaves. —You're not a real, down-to-earth, bona-fide gardener, he said. —You're some kind of a spy. Or you're doing field research for a long overdue doctoral thesis. Right?

The man, whose eyes, it must be said, flashed the complex guile of rampaging question marks, deftly swept a bunch of leaves over Stephan's new Earth shoes. —Wrong on both counts, Monsieur.

Stephan kicked off the heap of dried leaves. —You are the alienated son of wealth who has decided to work because of nagging moral principles.

With precisely the same effortless élan that Nijinsky would summon in permitting himself to be buggered by Diaghilev, the "gardener" (who can tell how old he was? who can tell how tall?) swiftly scooped up and deposited the exhausted, exploited leaves in his lovely round refuse can. Then he sat down next to Stephan and lit up a meerschaum pipe. —This is not your day for guessing right, mon ami, he said, puffing away, not exactly like a chimney but not like a Parisian subway vent either. —I am going to prevent you from making yourself seem more preposterous than you already are, he went on, and if his eyes twinkled like Santa's on fire-sale day, we would not necessarily know it. —The simple, overwhelming facts are these . . .

—Mmm, murmured Stephan, glancing at me, as he often does, in a gesture of inextricable solidarity (the sort of solidarity you come by in prison or as you drown with your best friend while others around you are obviously making merry and each . . .). —What are you smoking? Sugar-cured camel shit?

—In point of fact, Monsieur smart ass, I am. Purchased at considerable expense from the tobacconist Fernet on the Rue du Rivoli. He blew some of the very tasty smoke into Stephan's face. —Allors. Who I am. A female clochard in her declining years, dressed, as you would imagine, in the cast-off clothes of the Third Republic, strolled by wearing a sandwich sign on which was printed this message: "It is later than you think." Directly across from them, on Victor Hugo's side, to be precise, Madame de Sévigné ducked behind a bush to make the pee-pee. Louis Pasteur carefully, as was his style, did push-ups on the grass to impress his young secretary Imogene who stood there beaming like a small alarm clock about to go off. Three feet away, under a giant sycamore tree, Baudelaire's pet green monkey Coco was slowly strangling a pigeon.

More heady, and very original, pipe smoke. —I am an unemployed character from fiction, the "gardener" said.

Stephan slapped his thigh (a tradition-soaked gesture which he seldom made, by the way). —Well, of course!

The man nodded. —Oui, oui. I have spent my entire life, in a manner of speaking, bouncing, leaping, crawling, walking through the dog-eared pages of short stories and novels. A certain self-serving poignancy was noticeable in his tone.

—A life well worth having, Stephan said, sounding, in spite of himself, like a provincial professor of literature or something. —And you certainly seem none the worse for it.

The man shrugged (as you would imagine). —Oh, I'm not in any way suggesting that my life in fiction has been hard or that it hasn't had its rewards. All in all, I'm pretty sure I would not want to trade it for another. He puffed away and scratched his small chin. —A provincial doctor's, or a minor government official's, or—he turned and smiled craftily at Stephan—or yours, for that matter. You don't look too substantial to me.

—Careful now, my friend. Let's keep it objective and at an arm's length.

The man chuckled. —Just funnin' you, as one of your own fictional types would say. Anyway, I'm hardly in a position to judge the lives of those on the "outside." He looked closely at our Stephan's face. —However, the more I "feel" you . . . I wouldn't risk asking you for an identity card, my friend. Oh no. Sooner ask a fish for a flashlight. Well, no matter. As I was saying, I'm not really complaining. It's simply that there is less and less work for a chap like me as time goes on.

—Hmm. And just why is that, do you think? said Stephan. —I mean, it couldn't be because people are writing less fiction. Holy shit. Every time I pick up a newspaper, there are ads and blurbs for ten thousand more novels. Phew! I'm up to my granny's asshole in novels.

The man—he doesn't have a name so far—shook his small, no-nonsense head. —No, no. It isn't quantity that's the problem, my dear chap. It's content and tradition. I'll put it simply: my type has almost gone out of style in fiction. I'm a vanishing breed, as they say, like the unicorn and the nightingale. Your modern novel has no place for me. Oh, I find a little work here and there, when some poor bloke who's stuck in the old-fashioned ways of fiction is putting together a cozy, fireside book or short story.

An old Chinese man wearing nothing more obligatory and oppressive than bright red shorts (which were obviously not cut in the current fashion) ran cleanly through the green, theoretically staid park, and due to a benign combination of genetic structure, plus personally developed skills, he was managing to run in slow motion—he was so elegant and rare—a long silk scarf writhing exquisitely in a wind of its own choosing. Bravo, said Stephan to himself. Bravo indeed. They'll never surprise that old dog in his sleep.

—Well, uh, just what sort of work do you do, Monsieur? Stephan asked, dragging happily on a joint of Lib shit he'd deftly rolled. —I mean, what characters do you play?

We do not have to be told that his bench companion reacted warily, in various subtle ways, to the question. How do birds feel about flying? Fish about swimming? OK. We must be able to assume a minimum of intelligence and sensitivity in this group activity, else the whole bloody show will go up in tears or smoke or something.

—I very much appreciate that question, the man said. —I hardly need to tell you that I don't get many opportunities to have such chats, and especially with, how shall I put it, a man of your wide and sympathetic background. I'm trying to avoid the words *fellow performer*, which I know would offend you, because, as a closet metaphor, you do not want your cover blown. Mostly I keep my nose to the park rubbish and my ear to the cries of children and the babbling of maids and grannies. Of course, I have my small circle of friends, out-of-fashion and therefore out-of-work types like myself who, poor dear souls, are daily pressed to keep body and soul together. Just as an example . . . A very dear lady who has been—and of course in a sense remains—in many ways a literary classic, both here and abroad, this lady is working now as a clerk in a charcuterie, if you please!

Stephan reluctantly, slowly gasped out more of the sacred, exhilarating smoke from his tight lungs. —The roles, please.

Two criminal-type pigeons calculatedly flew over a glistening, pink, snoozing, bald-headed veteran of the Siege of Paris and released two à la carte servings of pigeon shit on his skull. Plop. Plop.

—Long-lost brother who has quietly done very well in the colonies, the man began, more or less straightening up without really doing anything specific. —He is generous in an oblique way. He never signs his gifts. His strength reinforces his isolation. The man looked at Stephan and smiled patiently. —And he has a very secret kind of vice.

—Very good, said Stephan. —Other roles, please.

—Stop acting like the director of the academy. I am not sucking for a job.

—Yes, you're quite right. I sometimes get carried away by a number of possible positions. He was cozily stoned. —Indeed, I not infrequently feel like a composite of these positions . . . I think. He peeked at me but I did nothing more chilling than shrug my shoulders.

—Who is that sly-looking man over there in the red beret?

—The formidable Socks Peelmunder.

—What's so formidable about him? He looks like an ex-bouncer in a bonbon factory to me.

—I urge a little respect, said his friend, his voice dropping. —Peelmunder is a wheeler and a dealer, as you fellows would say, and a good many things would simply not take place without him.

—You're not scaring me a bit, Pierre.

—Let me suggest that, given the choice, you stay on his good side. He has been known to make and break people. Comprendez?

—Hmm, said Stephan. —I'll have to check him out some other time. Let's get back to your career, the many wonderful minor characters you've given your all for.

—A country priest who knows more than he is supposed to, our man continued, looking straight ahead into the park which, as we who have been watching know, could at any moment erupt into a fragment of self-serving drama, bound to no form of logic that could unequivocally be sold over the counter. —He takes long walks in the woods to calm himself. He asks Mother Nature for advice, even though he knows this is pagan and forbidden. He is the best chess player in the village. The young women there find him very attractive; however, when they do occasionally succeed in catching his eye, it is the same as catching a falling star.

—Begorra! Stephan snorted. —Madonna mia! And of course. I've read about you, in at least half a dozen novels, in past years of course, when I was still reading for sentimental reasons. He looked over at me in his characteristically uncomfortable way. (I must say, it is certainly taking him an unusually long time to "settle into," as they say, our special relationship, notwithstanding the fact that it is still only a part-time deal. You would think . . .) —I almost feel I was in there too, somehow.

—How nice, the man said. —Solidarity and camaraderie. Where would we be without them?

—Up shit creek, said Stephan.

—And without a paddle, I might add.

Stephan, still drifting wantonly on his grass high, was about to say something clever yet poignant, a sadly rare combo, it should be disturbingly pointed out, when his attention swerved to a strolling couple who seemed to be arguing. Strolling couple . . . no, not quite so bland as that. An oldish man and a conspicuously young and dishy girl/woman. "Gentleman," you might say, because he had the look of someone who eats steak far more often than hot dogs. —Who are they? Stephan asked. —That old man seems familiar.

His French friend nudged Stephan with guileful pleasure. —Familiar . . . of course he's familiar. That's the great Stendhal.

—Who's the young pussy with him?

His companion sighed and gestured in that way that has become of course (who doesn't recognize this?) a closely guarded French monopoly (I mean, it is against the law to make certain gestures unless you are French). —Oh, there's the bloody rub, my dear. He shook his head. —That abrasive and provocative little vixen is the great man's bête noire. She's a minor character he invented for *The Charterhouse of Parma*. A maid in the employ of the Montecattini family. He looked at Stephan in a benignly patronizing manner, the way a croissant might look at a Mex slice of bread on a given morning. —I'm not assuming you know the work too well.

—Don't get cute with me, you little pischer.

—Well, her name is Odile Lenoir. Life and fiction being the devious things they are, Stendhal gradually, and as far as I am concerned, almost reluctantly, became involved with her. Enmeshed, really. He threw up his hands. —Ah! Age and passion!

—And a couple other things.

Stendhal and Odile passed in front of their bench. —You never want to spend much time with me, the girl was complaining. (Mmm. What eyes.)

—But I keep telling you that I must attend to these other people who are . . .

—Who are what? the girl said (cruelly delicious mouth). —More important than me? Well, do they take care of you the way I do? Just answer me that.

—Now, Odile, said Stendhal, putting his crafty arm around her. —You must not act this way. You know very well how much you mean to me, so why . . . They passed on of course (because fiction cannot stand still, right?).

—Mmm, Stephan murmured. —Did you get a whiff of that jade?

—*Whiff* did you say?

—A mixture of fresh basil and violence, said Stephan, lighting up another joint (which he'd rolled, naturally, under our very noses without our noticing a thing!). —I wonder if she rubs it on her snatch. He inhaled deeply. (Who among you has observed a blue whale doing the same thing before descending into the deep?) —Mmm, he mumbled as he gently exhaled. —Wonderful idea. I'll suggest it to Carol or Juliette or whoever. Love it. Nothing quite like a faceful of basil, wouldn't you agree?

—It's really quite fascinating, his companion said, watching Cyrano de Bergerac fastidiously lay out a picnic lunch for himself and Colette on the grass nearby, —how that girl Odile has gotten on over the years.

—You don't say, observed Stephan, who saw the picnic spread too (natch) and immediately wanted some of the pâté, the little pig.

—Oh yes, his companion continued. —Once created, a character doesn't stand still or pass away after the primary performance. That would be too preposterous, and furthermore (he looked seriously into Stephan's dreamy, gluttonous face) it would be against The Natural Order of Things, you see.

—Got it. 'Nuff said. Mmm. This shit is sure great.

—Yes indeed. Once launched, so to speak, a character, however small, goes on forever. Some do better than others, of course. Not through any basic superiority, mind you, but through historical chance.

Stephan exhaled the exhilarating, goofy smoke, so precious, haltingly. —Listen, I've just got to have a bite of that pâté, no kidding. Just hold everything and I'll be back in two shakes, OK? He handed the man his joint and nipped over to the picnic spread, sweetly and with no effort, hurdling a soft green bench on his way there. —I just can't help myself, he explained to Cyrano and Colette, grabbing a piece of the pâté lapin and some bread. —You can do the same to me sometime.

Colette grinned *that grin*. —Oh yes. We'll be meeting again, mon ami.

—If I'm anything, said Stephan, sniffing the pâté, —I'm open to new possibilities.

Back at the bench, —Oh yes, that one often found that her services were wanted, the man continued. —She appeared in *Remembrance of Things Past* as one of those very dubious women whom Albertine was always sneaking off to see. A certain sly creature named Marik, who was employed in a dressmaker's establishment.

Stephan, piggy, piggy, licked a bit of pâté from his itchy fingers. —Oh yes, I remember. She was a raunchy dyke who also made it with men, for dough of course.

—Well remembered, my friend. (A sleek black squirrel attacked a disgusting, tiny white poodle that was all set to take a shit under the squirrel's tree. The poodle screamed. Drops of bright blood oozed suddenly from its snowy, manicured haunch.) —She also worked, as you may recall, in *The Counterfeiters*, by Monsieur Gide.

Monsieur Face-Stuffer Stephan brushed bread crumbs from his drooping young mustache. —Let me guess. She was, uh . . . she was Eloise, right?

The man clapped him on the shoulder. —Bravo! You are in very good form today.

—I keep in shape. In my line of nonsense, you gotta be ready for anything, ya know. Well, now tell me, Gaston, Ferdinand, or . . .

—At the moment I don't have a name, because I'm unemployed. I only have a real name when I'm working as a character, you see. But for this silly quasi job, you might say that my name is Raymond.

—Raymond . . . Has this dubious creature done anything lately, something I might have read while waiting in the witch doctor's office?

—As a matter of fact she has, now that I think about it. And a very interesting situation it was too. She plays the provocative wife in a fairly recent story called "The Closing of This Door Must Be Oh, So Gentle." An American fiction, no less, he added, and playfully (we hope) pinched Stephan's cheek.

—Aha! American is it? All is not lost after all, eh, Raymond? Ol' Moby Dick continues to spout away.

Raymond smiled into the day. —A good story, too. Mmm. He turned to Stephan. —Would you like to have it run through for you?

—Can you do that?

—Oh yes. No trouble. It's all part of the arrangement in the world I exist in. Now then, just lean back and let your mind sort of drift or let go. That should be easy, since you have smoked so much of that lewd marijuana of yours. All right? You may, by the way, wish to participate in this fiction by playing one of the parts, identifying with one of the characters. That is permissible. But you absolutely must not attempt to steal that character from himself. Comprendez-vous?

—Uh huh, Stephan said. Gently, he urged a swooning in his being, a tingling, somewhat erotic emptiness or nonselfness. Smiling, slipping, vanishing . . . And the story began, first in Raymond's trained, uncanny voice, then it was telling, or living, itself.

Harrison's wife Edith looked like a dwarf. Her legs were about two inches long, her torso about the size of a peanut in the shell, and her head was recognizable only as an odd bump on her shoulders. He wondered how anybody that small could possibly exist. The sea on her left side at any moment would wash her away; the dunes on her right were towering mountains that seemed fearfully about to fall upon and bury her forever. Harrison almost felt like yelling out to her to beware for her life. But would she hear me? he thought, and smiled sadly. Are people reachable when their lives are in danger?

Now she reversed her doomful course and started walking back toward Harrison, lying under the big beach umbrella. A sand fly boldly attacked his fine serenity, a bite on the leg, and Harrison slaughtered it with a blow of his hand. He squinted his eyes almost to closing and resumed his observations of his wife. Everything abetted his distorted view: the heat waves vibrating crazily off the sand denied the scene its customary reality; the surf, its sovereignty awesome, refused to yield entrance to any other sound, and thus cut him off from the world outside this moment; and his squinting, through trembling, enlarged eyelash filaments, revealed things in their microscopic hugeness (as if he were somehow a bug looking on). Edith thus gradually became bigger and bigger as she got closer, and in another few moments (can such time be measured?) a giant hand was reaching down to him with a terrifying object in it. He jerked away in fright.

—What's the matter? Edith asked, annoyed and surprised. —It's only a baby hermit crab. It washed up on the beach.

—And you naturally picked it up, he said, recovered now.

She remained standing, hands now resting on hips, and by doing this, rather than dropping down in a beach pose beside him, she made it clear, quite clear, that she was not, at least for this jarred moment, in harmony with the rhythms here. —I thought it would interest you, she said. The surf noise battered her words in midair, bruising their tender surface, making them sound weak instead of merely soft, giving them an unjust quality of supplication.

—A baby monster, he said. —Sure. What could be a more fascinating present! He was coming up now from his microscopic vantage point and feeling, the grotesque aura was giving way to a more or less normal one; he swung into a squatting position on the blanket.

Edith sat down now on the sand, not on the blanket, and looked down the beach, instead of at her husband. —It seems that everything I give you turns into a monster, she said, and threw a pebble into the foaming surf near her feet.

Well, now, I guess maybe you're right, Harrison thought. I wonder why that is. Am I responsible for such midair mis-magic? These things must start out as gifts, of some kind or other, but when they arrive at my threshold, something awful has happened to their shape and chemistry. Why? —All right, he said, getting up. —I'm sorry.

—I think you want them to become monsters, Edith suggested, her back to the raging surf, arms jutting geometrically from her hips, hair curling delicately in the sea wind.

She is like a Botticelli now, rising up miraculously from the sea, Harrison thought, and for a second or two, as he stared at her, he felt they were both transfixed in timelessness, in design, in motionless thought, in stilled heart.

—We'd better be going, Edith announced deferentially, yet not so deferentially that her words did not rob Harrison of his jewellike moment of timeless isolation. He nearly winced as she ceased, simply by opening her soft mouth, to be his Botticelli.

—That's right, Harrison murmured. —We're going to that cocktail party at what's-his-name's place, aren't we?

—Mason Bowler's . . .

—The rich queer.

—. . . and remember, you promised you wouldn't drink too much and act peculiar.

They were slogging off the beach, arms wrapped around the essential scenic props—umbrella, towels, lunch basket, for they had picnicked—toward the car.

—You know, he began, —for a few minutes you looked like a dwarf. It was very remarkable.

Edith opened the car door. —So I suggest that you absolutely stay away from martinis. Drink scotch or something. Promise?

He sighed heavily, a stricken sigh, for a terrible loneliness had come over him again, like a soft shadow of death. —Whatever you say.

—Something awful happens to you when you drink too much, Edith
continued. She got into the driver's seat quite naturally, not in the manner
of a reigning queen, nor with the aplomb of the aggressor, but rather with
the motionless ease of having gotten there by default. —I think you should
lay off it completely for a while. For your own good.

He listened to the meshing of the gears as Edith drove off down the
narrow, black, tar-smelling road. He listened so raptly that the gears seemed
to be inside his head. —I've thought of laying off everything for a while.

—Just what does that mean?

—I wish I knew.

He leaned back and closed his eyes, giving himself over completely to
being chauffeured by Edith, like a helpless little baby, he thought, being
taken for an airing in a carriage. As he allowed himself to gradually roll down
the long hill inside himself, to quiet nothingness at the bottom, he
wondered if Edith would take the wrong turn at the crossroads ahead and
get them lost again. But right now this possibility did not have any
importance for him.

—Are you and your wife spending the summer here on the shore?

—Just two weeks, Harrison replied, looking at a shy black mole on the
man's right ear.

—Oh, the man gasped, as though Harrison's reply had been a punch in
the belly. —It's a wonderful place to relax, don't you think? he went on,
apparently revived.

Harrison sipped his scotch and soda and wondered what this man did to
keep a roof over his head. —What do you mean by relax? Harrison answered
(he had made up his mind to ask into the man's occupation).

A freckled, pinkish eyelid quivered, a soft, blanched hand suddenly was
rubbing a cheek in sheer amazement, and a moist baby mouth, as if forming
its first words of defense, was saying, —Uh, well . . . to be on the beach . . . you
know, uh, swimming in the ocean . . . The mouth closed for a second
(Harrison thought of the mouth of a squid).

—Ah, that I tried, but I just became more uncomfortable. He smiled
somewhat. —I guess something must be the matter with me. My wife
frequently suggests that.

An eyebrow, hairy and sandy, lifted. —Really?

—Yep. He paused. —You don't have a wife, do you?

Mouse fear tensed the man's face. —Uh, no, as a matter of fact, I don't.

Harrison took a long, satisfying drink of the cool scotch and smiled at the
man. —Well, if you did, you would know *exactly* what I mean. He is afraid
now that I am going to expose him as a homosexual. But I'm not. Just look at
the terror at the corners of his eyes! —You see, wives are often suggesting

that something is the matter with their husbands. It probably makes them feel less inferior—that's what I might say if I were a psychoanalyst or something.

A dry, choppy sound came from the man's mouth, a forced laugh to fill the awful void between them. But his eyes, Harrison saw, ah, there was nothing smiling about them.

We'll never see that one again, unless it's in the Sargasso Sea with the rest of the eels. He looked around the room for the presence of Edith. All kinds of faces were animated in various scenes, to Harrison distressingly like the subjects in an impressionist mural, their faces flushed and mottled with the feverish colors of unreality. Voices he heard, of course, and familiar word formations, but the largess of meaning that usually accompanies those two things was not now forthcoming to Harrison. What he heard, poised as he was on the brink of his own definition, all of it sounded quite insane. While he was searching for Edith, his hand chilling from the highball glass, she found him.

—Are you having a good time? she inquired, appearing abruptly at his left side (he always thought of it as his weak side) like a secret agent.

—I'm certainly trying to, sweetie. He held up his highball glass to show that his drink was on a comparatively rational level: no disintegrating gin fluids. He felt he could have been holding up a scrap of the Constitution.

No somersaults of joy, or appreciation, came from Edith at this; a gentle nod, that's what she responded with, plus a patient look in her eyes. —That's fine, she said. —I met a rather nice couple, named Andrews. He's a furniture designer.

Between them now sprang up a pure greensward, an absolute pause of tentative exploration, and upon it, like children suddenly in a foreign country, they stalked each other, maneuvered this way and that, each utterly permeated with the need to hear the other's song first, whatever its words: I won't hurt you, please don't misunderstand me. So they listened, listened and watched.

—Do you know of him? Edith finally continued, returned, both of them, from that other land.

—I think I've heard his name, Harrison replied. He finished the rest of his scotch. Now he was a little high, but this was not noticeable. —Why do you say they were nice? Did he say surprising and amusing things? Was she sexy without being vulgar? Or do you just mean that they smelled clean? Which?

All of the gentle signs of female resignation, those incalculable changes of interior costume, showed upon Edith after his words were out. She allowed her attention, as if to rest it, to wander to strangers' faces in the room before answering her husband. —Why do you hate the human race so much?

Harrison thought for a moment before answering this challenge. —I don't really know.

—Maybe you should try to find out.

—How? By going to a doctor?

—That's one way.

His face untensed and he smiled at Edith. —Is it really so bad to hate the human race?

It seemed to Harrison, in reflection, that the reply came from the air rather than from the mouth of his wife, for she responded as she was drifting away from his side, in flight almost, and the words thus became, as in the thin hours of the night, disembodied Ariels. —It must be, the words whispered, —because it makes you feel so terrible.

Then he himself was traveling, in the other direction, for a refilling of his scotch-and-soda highball. He felt more at bay than before: There was absolutely no defense, worthy of him, to Edith's gentle thrust.

At the bar in this fashionable house, what had sounded to him before like zithers of mutual hysteria had now become, from those drinkers and talkers clustered there, a music of rancor counterpointed, oh so impressively, with chords of vilification. In fact, Harrison, sloshing scotch and soda inadvertently over his fingers, felt, heard, and saw it as a Renaissance horror opera; shivs flashed, garrotes twisted—what screams, what dark denunciations, what bleats of outraged innocence! The thuds of bodies falling offstage, these chilling sounds could be heard most clearly by Harrison. So he put his lonely mouth to the scotch business at hand.

—Have you had any experience with the restaurants around here? he heard a large-eyed blonde woman asking of him. Harrison gazed into those eyes and very nearly drowned in their self-pity.

—You mean have I been a busboy in them or something?

She looked at him as if he were crazy, or as if he had not quite understood her seemingly harmless question. —Oh, no, no, she blurted, her face wanting to escape. —I meant had you tried eating in any of them. You know, found any, uh, good food.

The words just had to come out of him. —I'm not going to hurt you, so please don't look so scared. I am not crazy or violent or even real drunk yet. (Her mouth was partly open now in readiness for something, like an oxygen mask.) —But, honestly, I take the word *experience* seriously, and I feel it shouldn't be misused for purposes of chic. See what I mean?

The woman regained herself in a split pause—apparently he really did not mean to assassinate her—her mouth smiled somewhat patiently, and she said, —Well, I suppose so, but I don't see why you have to be so goddamn rude about it. After all . . .

He did not let her go on. The scotch was allowing him too much freedom inside. —Now as for good food, why, last night I ate some incredibly delicious sea squabs. I had four of them, all for myself. My wife had only two, but that's because two is enough of anything for her. Anyway, they had been rolled in a perfectly divine egg-and-flour batter, then fried in deep fat. Mmm! Yummy! Well, I was so impressed by these delicacies that I spoke to the waitress about it. I said that I was not familiar with sea pigeons and their young, and were they members, perhaps, of the albatross family. Well, you can imagine my surprise when this young lady, she couldn't have been over nineteen, informed me that they were plain, ordinary blowfish and you could catch them by the millions swimming around Fire Island.

The lady's large brown eyes blinked slowly at Harrison, who, by now, had drunk nearly all his scotch. —Sounds like *quite* an experience, she said, and with the cruel deliberateness of a guillotine in slow motion, turned her face away from him and toward the others like herself at the bar there.

I'm getting a bit drunk and aggressive, Harrison whispered to himself—though audibly if you were standing very close to him—and he charted a course toward a crowded sun porch where he saw Edith talking in a group of four or five men and women very smartly garmented in summer styles. He felt now that the scene around him was a thriving insane asylum, filled with strangers, among them somewhere himself, whom he should try to find and help to escape as soon as possible. How and through what special unguarded aperture in the scene the two of them were going to slip free, this he wasn't sure of at the moment, as he moved thoughtfully across the large living room that was jiggling with gabbling bodies, toward his wife and others intertwined there on the sun porch. But he knew, quite beyond any questions, that this escape must absolutely take place. Or else.

—Do you know that you won't be able to recognize New York in five years? he overheard a woman say. —They're tearing down so many buildings.

The place they lived in was a converted barn; about a hundred yards in front of the barn was the original old farmhouse. This, too, had been wrenched from its self-enclosed and indisputably deserved grave and forced to serve generations more, except that these were not connected in any way with the warmth and the cold, the inscrutable breathing, of the soil. But what part of nature's body *are* they connected with? Harrison asked not only himself but Edith and whomever else of the human race might be tuned into him at this moment as he sat in the unself-effacing early American living room of the barn, looking out at the shy, green, and gently swollen Connecticut landscape.

—They're scavengers, he said aloud. —They leave scars and holes and garbage piles wherever they go. He looked at a wastebasket that was cleverly decorated with *Vanity Fair* drawings. —And I'm one of them.

Edith came in from the bedroom, where she had been napping. —What on earth *are* you talking about? she asked, and then stifled a baby of a yawn with the soft back of her left hand.

—Me. Us.

—Oh, we're doing that again. Please count me out. I came up here to get a rest. She sat down, one leg nestling secretly under the other, and struck a match to a Pall Mall. Persian tapestry was her natural design; she seemed to contain no straight lines whatsoever. Even the faint sleepiness and dark femininity encasing her felt almond-shaped to Harrison. Then I must be a bomb fragment in shape, he decided.

—What would you like to talk about then? he asked, looking at the hoarded beauty of her bare legs. Edith made the long cigarette her companion, rather than her husband, in that moment, and did not reply. Instead of words, thick sets of smoke streamed from her mouth. —Let's talk about sex, he continued.

Edith sucked in and exhaled a ferocious quantity of smoke. —What's there to say about it?

Harrison smiled wolfishly. —Oh, lots and lots. Just oodles, in fact. Let's take you and sex. (Edith slowly mashed her cigarette to death in a saucer.) Just what is there with you and sex, Mrs. Harrison? Does it make your little tummy just a wee bit sick? Does it make you want to grab your teddy bear and cry yourself to sleep?

—You're being very cute, Edith said, and put her hand to her throat as if to comfort it.

—Oh? I'm sorry, because I'm really trying to be very scientific about all this—in the interests of enlightenment. He tried to bring off an ironic smile, but it failed, and an unhappy compromise of a sneer appeared. —For instance, this afternoon when I came in as you were lying down . . .

—I explained to you that I was very tired and not in the mood.

He felt thousands of pricklings inside his body and mind now, as though he were a huge bar of metal being tortured for stress resistance in a factory. —Now which was it: fatigue or not in the mood? I'd like to be exact about these things.

Edith lit another cigarette and, as was her custom during strenuous conversations, presented him—as one, turning away, gives a beggar in the marketplace a stained coin—with her profile as she looked away at the blank wall to maintain an idea of her dignity. —All right, then. I simply wasn't in the mood to make love. Does that make me a criminal or something?

—No, Harrison replied. —It makes me feel like one.

—Well, I'm sorry, but that's your problem. If you want to feel like a criminal, that's up to you.

Harrison shook his head at the floor. —You're never in the mood. Even when you do have sex, you do it reluctantly: I can't remember when you have ever made me feel you wanted me. He made a noise like a snort, of both anger and amazement. —You ought to be in the Metropolitan Museum. You just lie there with your eyes closed like an Egyptian princess mummy. Tell me, he went on, hoping she would turn her head toward him just for a moment, which she didn't, —do you feel that you are dying or that it is really happening to somebody else?

He wasn't really waiting for a reply; for some minutes, like a lost explorer, he had been wandering, stumbling about, in the vast caverns of her being. He had never experienced so irrevocably such desolation, such hopelessness; each time he put his hand against a wall for comfort, it repelled his hand with dankness or cut it cruelly with sharp edges; the paths that promised to take him somewhere ended abruptly at sheer drops; he shouted for help and then had to suffer the mockery of hearing his own voice, distorted by distance and fatigue, thrown back at him. He felt that he would eventually just disintegrate there.

—If you wanted a sexpot for a wife, why didn't you marry one? Edith said, gliding toward the kitchen to make coffee.

—That isn't the point, he replied, and reached out for his highball glass. —What interests me is why did you marry me if you didn't want to share yourself? I suspect, he continued, the soothing loveliness of the scotch sluicing intimately down his throat, —that fundamentally you must dislike the hell out of me. He paused for sounds from her. —Come on, 'fess up.

That was the thing about his work these past few months—like Edith, it had become deaf, mute, so unresponsive and deathlike as to make him utterly despair having to engage in it every day or grapple suffocatingly with it every second. Each new project was an insidious challenge to his sanity.

—Don't you feel well? Evans had inquired one day at the office.

—To tell you the truth, Ev baby, he had confessed, —I don't feel at all.

Ha! Ha! That was Evans's reaction, but oh, Harrison knew that Evans was not really collapsing with humor; what he really thought, and Harrison could tell this by the patronizing tenseness at the corners of his field-mouse lips, was that something was a bit flibberty with Harrison. It was not at all unusual for him to be approaching the heart of a matter, there in his cubicle, and suddenly, instead of driving full speed ahead as other rational humans would have done, find himself floating abstractly in midair, like a balloon that a child has abruptly grown weary of. When this happened, he pushed his chair far away from his desk and went out to a movie.

Somewhat later, as he sipped a fresh scotch and water, he was listening to the sounds of his wife getting dressed in the bedroom. They were intimate and exciting and forbidding sounds: He wondered, very hazily, because he was drunk now, if women themselves were aware, in their way, of the world of unique sounds they created. A rustling of stiff material and then a snap, snap of a brassiere created Edith's opulent but indifferent breasts; a stretching of sheer nylon against fingernails and there was an elegantly outstretched naked leg; a pulling of tight elastic, a stress of breathing, the running of hands down the mesh surface of her girdle, and into view came Edith's completed underclothed body. Harrison held her there, like a connoisseur holding a china figurine, turned her this way and that, then, overcome with futility, let her crash to small pieces. Harrison's hand for stricken seconds ached; then he put it back around the chill of his glass.

—I'll be ready in ten minutes, she called to him.

—Wonderful, he murmured to the sweet glass as though it were Edith.

—I promise I won't run away. He felt somewhat crazy now; the old watchman who usually guarded the impervious borderline between the self of today and that other older self of childhood, this ancient had abandoned his post, and the two Harrisons began racing back and forth across this unguarded, sacred terrain, mockingly almost. The two of them alternately howled and whispered recklessly to each other.

Edith came in from the bedroom. —Well, are you all set to go? She plucked a wanton thread from her dress. —We're supposed to meet John and his girlfriend in front of the theater at 8:15. She smoothed the dress over her hips. —Have you ever heard of the author of the play?

Both selves in him stopped in their fevered roaming in that special country, looked questioningly at each other, observed her words in wingless flight across their land, then together, holding hands and staring into each other's fugitive eyes, worked on an answer to lift back into space to her.

—We played lacrosse together in San Marino, Harrison said, smiling.

Edith seemed to recoil into a huge, blazing question mark. —You did *what?*

His two selves grinned at each other. —He was the toast of the Andes. And I was the English muffin.

Not disgust, really, but rather a blend of irritation and hopelessness tinged with slight fear showed itself in Edith's reaction as she stared at him, before saying, —Oh, I see. It's going to be like that, is it? She walked partly across the room and turned around. —Why don't you just stay here and I'll go alone? You'll only wreck the evening—and I'm in no mood for another social disaster. She snatched her pocketbook from a tabletop and headed for the door, where she paused after wrenching it open. —I hope one of these days you decide what you're going to do about and with yourself. Because I can't stand it anymore.

—Sir Isaac *New*ton! he said just as Edith was disappearing and the door was being slammed.

Harrison was very concerned, for the trembling moments that followed, with the possibility that she might have hurt the door, in the way that you would surely hurt a person if you were to slam him shut. Who can prove that a door doesn't have feelings? he asked the other Harrison. This other self, recovered from his boyhood, was sitting on a large rock now, resting from some furious activity. He gently nodded his head at Harrison's question and said, I very much agree with you. Harrison was very pleased to hear this, and he smiled sweetly to show his pleasure. He drank off the remainder of his highball; then he walked, quite uncertainly, over to examine the abused door. He touched it gingerly here and there, as if he were a doctor and the door his patient, and strained his being to receive its vibrations. He was quite sure he could hear it crying, oh so softly, in such bewilderment. —There was absolutely no need to do this, he said, almost to comfort the door, and his other self, who was pacing restlessly, replied, Most people are dirty brutes. Take my word for it.

It was clear to Harrison that the other was anxious for them to go somewhere. —All right, all right, he said, —I'm coming. He turned away from the door, which was down to its last tears of injury, and looked around the living room before leaving. The invisible nerve that before had held it all together as a recognizable unity, a design of purpose, had apparently snapped, for what lay before Harrison now, as he prepared to depart, was an abstract of fierce isolation; the pieces of furniture seemed angry and abandoned in space, and the enclosing room, bereft of its previous property, emptied, was hungry and menacing. Harrison shook his head in sadness; then, responding to the bidding of the other one, left.

He and his other self walked around to the back of the building; he was being led by the hand, and the impeccable inside terrain, where he had first caught sight of and then gamboled with the other, had now become fused with the outside terrain. Gentle conspiracy was in the air. The grass beneath his somewhat stumbling feet refused to allow any sound of his escape to be heard; the long stone field wall, like a member of the family, firmly stated that no stranger should intrude upon this utmost privacy. As they walked toward the large pond which lay patiently waiting across the field at the edge of the woods, the other began whispering fabulous things to him, things that Harrison had never heard from any other human being. Each thing had the dazzling wonder of a secret that had been kept from him all his life. And with each awesome revelation Harrison became more and more aware of another world opening for him, one that had oh absolutely nothing to do with any other.

At the edge of the pond Harrison bent over and plucked a handful of small white flowers growing there; then, still listening to the stream of revelations, he followed the other (whose young boy face was beaming beautifully) into the cool water.

L urking in that story, smirking there in and out of the equivocated shadows (though it is not certain that Stephan ran into him) was David Thorpe. We know about David. We have seen him before, under circumstances that varied substantially in quality, meaning, direction, and sound grass-roots investment possibilities (Dow Jones averages may not be the last word but they are a definite improvement over chicken entrails). Little Dave, whose face had the threatening pallor of a peanut, the relentless, *fixed* shallowness of a peanut. A cupid's mouth to go with it, a mouth which his darting, nervous tongue kept continually wet. Lick, lick. Soft, sneaky brown eyes, not of a peanut, but of a reindeer that has been compromised again and again by a totally depraved Santa Claus. A reindeer that knows what the score is, *through and through.* And over those small brown cesspools, those jolly, humid confessions of anything goes, what? Arching, swooping eyebrows, that's what. Heavy mosaic eyebrows such as you see in early Roman mosaics, in Ravenna or Viterbo or Tarquinia (where you have undoubtedly been if you've had the brains and the bread). Can you see him now? A good, strong pix of David Thorpe. A comprehensive Bosch-graduate portrait. An exotic, dangerous little cocksucker. Exactly the type of person you should want on your side if and when it turns out that there is no God after all. You sure as shit don't want to be hog-tied to some simpleminded moralist. Some starry-eyed oaf who feels that there are certain vile things you simply cannot do to people, no matter what.

—You guys on the Left are all bleeding hearts, he said some time ago at Antioch College after a political exchange between progressives and conservatives. —You're moral romantics, and believe me, you'll always lose to the pragmatists who don't have weak stomachs.

How's that for a love-thy-neighbor manifesto? Isn't that just the sort of statement you'd like to have a nice petit-point placard made of to hang over your bed, so that you could look at it and take heart every time you felt guilty after fucking your little cousin Emma?

We all have culture heroes. There is nothing more juicily human than idolizing people whose characteristics or accomplishments send little shivers up and down our backs and make our lower abdomens swoon out with powerful identification plans. Long-distance runners, mountain climbers, movie stars who go boing boing boing, billionaires who buy entire jewelry stores for their mistresses, incredibly gifted writers who write masterpieces in their sleep. Etc., etc. Man cannot live by creamed chipped beef alone. OK. Smooth, self-satisfied David (who does not at all mind taking it up the ass, by the way) has his heroes too. And a loathsome lot they are. Vipers all. Let's play a cute little guessing game here, pick up your snoozing brain cells. We are going to identify David's heroes by quoting statements that issued from their very own mouths. All set? Eager-beaver tongues hanging out? OK. Quote 1: "The United States has exercised a degree of restraint unprecedented in the annals of war." Quote 2: "Peace is at hand." Quote 3: "We seek nothing for ourselves."

Now then, who is . . . Right! Henry Mass-Murderer Kissinger! The Mad Bomber of Hanoi! The Little Kraut Who Sucked Just Right. Slippery little David thought Henry was the cat's meow and then some. —Kissinger won't take any shit from the commies, David announced proudly. —He calls the shots, and that's that.

David was simply ecstatic when Kissinger ordered the mining of Haiphong harbor. He threw a party to celebrate the event, which he, in his impenetrably warped way, felt was one of the brightest moments in Western civilization, like the day penicillin was discovered, or the flight of the first airplane.

We do not have to be told, do we, that David was there clapping when they burned The Maid at the stake, and he was certainly in the front row, or better, when the innocent Rosenbergs were electrocuted. It would not come as a surprise, really, if the Securities & Exchange Commission were to announce that David owned the major voting stock in Bubonic Plague, Inc.

What is this smirking virus doing as we are discussing him?

—It is very important that the extreme Left be blamed for this, David is saying to Marcel and Bobo, two surly, pimply, rough-trade types in leather jackets. —You understand that?

—Oui, oui. Completely.

—And you're sure about the two French policemen in front of the embassy?

Marcel and Bobo grin at each other. —Very sure. We're old buddies. We belong to the same club. They both giggle. David is pleased with this. He slaps Marcel on the back.

—OK, says David. —So . . . when the Shah's wife and her entourage show up at the Iranian Embassy tomorrow afternoon, you and the two other guys you told me about will go into action. They nodded. —You already have the incendiary device for burning in a car? They nodded happily again. —And you say you'll have no trouble getting a bucket of animal blood somewhere?

—Marcel's cousin works in an abattoir in St. Denis, says Bobo, nudging his friend. —They swim in blood out there.

—They also swim in shit out there, says Marcel. All three absolutely break up over this. Shit and blood, blood and shit, the natural ingredients of joy for those who seek intoxication in violence and death. And of course they have found not only intoxication but ecstasy. Heavens above! Just think of the juicy, high-quality fun they have fucking one another in the shit hole! And blood . . . Consider their wild joy as they smash the heads and faces, with clubs and truncheons and brass knuckles of course, of young left-wing students protesting social injustices. More . . . Can you imagine how close to God they must soar, on their wings of horror, when they manage to murder another human being! Truly, one cannot easily find a language that would adequately describe such a heavenly experience.

Our Lad of the Naturally Arched Eyebrows is a sly one. Guile comes as naturally to him as breathing underwater to a fish. He is a smiling, punctual, hi there, everybody! student at the University of Paris VII. Why is he there, you should ask even if you are only half awake and your semi-eaten croissant fallen negligently to the floor of your nifty little garret up there on the Rue Mouftard. OK. The answer is overwhelmingly simple. Paris VII is swarming with lefties. They hang from the rafters. They spin eternally in the revolving doors. They stuff themselves into every nook and cranny, and if there were a granny around, they would stuff themselves into that. Not only French students from France, but lefty students from darkest Sweden, glaring, crazed Africa, blood-covered South America. It even has happy-go-lucky gringos who are only too willing to dance on the head of a pin at any given moment, singly or in pairs. So, if you want to get to know the international student left wing, in order to compromise and betray them, you would be well advised to do precisely what creepy, menacing David did, i.e., you will enroll there as a student and heartily pretend that you, too, are for social and political change the world over. And if you are exceptionally industrious, you will do as David did (quite a while back, of course, when it became clear to him that his calling was to serve under the Prince of Darkness): you will tie in with the Central Intelligence Agency. And they will give you all kinds of money and ideas and scenarios and connections. And anything else your loathsome little heart desires. I mean, shit, you just can't score any better.

Would you care to hear what an old inhabitant of David's hometown has to say about Young Judas Returned?

—We didn't have no clams around here, but that little Thorpe boy sure was clammy.

That was Ol' Jack Toomey, who owned all that lovely, rich bottom land down next to Fool's Gold Creek, until the durn state ran a coupla those big cement highways through it so's crazy people with big cars could drive to wherever the hell they drive to.

Another witness to David's character: —I went to a couple of high-school dances with him. He didn't do any dancing. He just stood around with his arms folded looking like he wanted to turn the lights out and plunge the whole place into darkness.

That was "Pinky" Aswell, who wanted to be an airline pilot; but she married Doctor of Dental Surgery Biff Trager instead, and together, heaving and humping, roiling and moiling, they produced four picnic-loving kids.

And now let us hear from Baba Das Murtha, né Bob Dalton, mystic now residing on a consenting green hillside in Nepal. He was one of David's teachers at Holier Than Thou High School.

—David was born with cancer of the soul. He crawls to the beat of the deadliest of drummers. The ear is offended by the sounds emanating from deep inside David: whispers, sniggers, hissing, obscene screams of pleasure, and laughter so dry and empty as to make your skin hurt. Gratuitous, utterly innocent curiosity was totally alien to David's desolate sensibility. He inquired into the nature of things solely to acquire power. David *seized* when other children merely reached out. And while these other young humans seemed to experience themselves in a joyous exchange between one another, David discovered his natural habitat in isolation. To observe him on the school playground, during those longed-for reprieves from study, was to see the abyss in its dreadful infancy. If one had been a prophet, one would have divined that this abyss fed and matured upon the suffering of others. It was always a joy to watch the young develop their taste for life. It was pure desolation to watch David develop his taste for death.

OK. Come in tight on David again.

The Café du Midi, directly across from the University of Paris VII-Jessue. Many students talking, talking, eating, eating (the long hot dog, the *croque-monsieur*). Smoking, smoking, my God. David is sitting in a booth with three students. He is exuding, pouring out, laying on his left-wing act. Smiles and vibrations of solidarity against repression. Rubbing shoulders, etc. He is always eagerly offering his pack of Gaulois filtre around.

—Did you see that fucking Nixon on TV last night? he says. —Jesus. He is one incredible fucking psychopathic liar. Shit, he can't even tell the truth when he's got absolutely nothing to lose.

—But, you know, your American public simply adores him, says the gleaming but delicious Nicole (an army surplus jacket, blue jeans). —They elected him president with, how do you say it? plurality greater than any other American president.

The muscular, heavy-faced, working-class boy Georges: —Obviously Mr. Nixon *is* America. America loves to lie and to cheat and to brutalize other peoples, especially if they are poor and weak but have the arrogance to stand up and shout No! We will not be fucked up the ass by your Yankee cock!

Marco, the sallow Botticelli angel: —The United States, they're hopeless right wing up to here!

David: —No, no, not hopeless, Marco. And it's just such pessimism as yours that we on the Left must fight to overcome. It will be the death of us if we don't. A new awareness is slowly growing throughout America. The Left is regrouping, grass-roots oppositional groups are sprouting up. Why, in time . . .

—In time nothing, says Dora, licking mustard from her gamy little thumb.
—You're pulling your own leg, David.

Marco laughs a very eclectic Italian laugh (in which you see satisfying thumbnail sketches of the greats: Lucretia Borgia killing one of her brothers, naked Da Vinci bat-flying, Caruso slurping tons of spaghetti). —You have stars up your asshole, David.

Close, very close indeed, Marco. Though more likely dead planets. But you are certainly on the right track. You are one smart guinea kid to watch, caro mio.

OK. Another close-up on Iago Thorpe: at the big Mutualitie hall. A mass meeting for Chilean Solidarity. Hundreds of comrades fiercely yet fluidly jammed together in the vast, smoke-hazed hall. Banners and placards. "Boycott Chilean Products!" "U.S. Stop Aid to Fascist Chile!" "Unite Against Junta Murderers!" Singing. Speeches. Wonderful total applause. Yes, a sea of applause. Every single hand clapping for all it's worth. (Outside, throngs of cops with truncheons ready, just in case. Still others, riot cops, are sitting inside police vans, just waiting, waiting for the go sign.) Individual shouts from the vast gathering. —All political prisoners must be released immediately! —President Carter's human rights program is a fucking fraud! Applause. —We denounce selective fascism! We denounce the shit of American duplicity! More applause.

David jumps up from nowhere. He stands up on his chair. —Fuck the military murderers! he screams, waving his arms. —Kill Pinochet! Kill the American military advisors! Kill the CIA in Chile! We won't take their shit anymore! Kill them all!

Moments of vast silence. Throats in abeyance, in check. Then from a spot here, a spot there, an extremist shouts approval. —Sí! Sí! Yes! Kill them! Kill them!

But then other voices. —Don't be provoked. They *want* violence from us. That will give them the excuse to kill more of us.

David screams again. —Comrades, don't be cowards! Fight fire with fire!

Shouts of agreement. Shouts of disagreement. Suddenly in three different spots in the audience fistfights explode. Shouts. Screams. A heavy fist crunches a nose. Blood, blood. David claps his hands and continues to shout his head off. A soft, black ecstasy oozes up inside him.

Outside, the police hear all this. They look at one another and smile. They will be moving in momentarily.

O K, says David to his Agency contact Meyers, —here's the new list of students.
—Great. That's really great, Dave.

—Two of them are particularly interesting: Hernandez and Villas. They're Cubans. There's something different about them. I don't know exactly what it is. I've got a hunch they're really part of Cuban intelligence. Can you find out?

—I'll sure try.

—Good. Listen, Meyers, he went on, —I need more money. The people I deal with are upping their fees. He watches Meyers's reaction carefully. Here in the Luxembourg Gardens it is soft and green and quiet. They are observed only by the row of white marble statues at their back. In the distance, tiny children play at delicate, obscure games, games that, upon analysis, would probably have meaning only for them. But that's OK. I mean why . . . —For instance, I had to pay out almost a thousand dollars to get that riot going at the Friends of China rally. He waits. His wet-lipped half-smile is a lurking, lewd presence. —And it's going to cost two thousand dollars more than we estimated to have the South African von Blucher delegate killed next week.

Meyers nods his head and smiles. This smile, like all his smiles, including the one he always presents to his wife Nikki after he has completed his clean-cut, missionary-position, Saturday-night fucking of her, is right out of the L. L. Bean catalog. He found it there many, many years ago while leafing through the catalog in search of a particular kind of boy's hunting cap. That's for me, he said, even though he was only eleven. This page-38 smile worked in perfectly with his button-down shirt and his red-black rep tie. It has wrapped itself around many, many good volleys at the Army-Navy Country Club in Neuilly and around countless chilled Beefeater martinis. It has never wrapped itself around any hot nigger pussy or around any unsettling paragraphs by Hegel. —Got it, he says after a couple of moments. —Inflation spares none of us, however dedicated we are to the services of truth and beauty. He looks up at a statue of . . .

—Yeah, David says. —That's one way of putting it, I suppose.

—How would *you* put it?

David shrugs. He has never liked Meyers's Ivy League type. —Guys in the demimonde or underworld—and that's where we are—are hustlers, naturally. They just always want more, that's all. Sometimes they try to justify it, sometimes they don't. You know, like increased risk, stuff like that. But basically, they know there's plenty more where I come from, and they're right, and they want it. He shrugs again. —C'est la vie.

—You've got a nice accent, Dave. OK. Sure. More dough. I'll bring you five thousand when we meet here next week. OK?

—That's fine. That'll make things a lot easier for me.

Meyers mildly slapped or patted David on the shoulder with his strong, clean, freckled right hand, a hand, however, that was quite obviously—and

in a clutch he would have been the first to concede this—more at home
throwing up a tennis ball, or quickly grabbing a telephone, than it was
clapping or patting or caressing, or goosing or tickling another human
being. In fact, now that the subject has been raised, his wife com. . .

—You're doing real well, Dave. The Agency's proud of you.

David (we mustn't forget that eternally lurking, wet half-smile) nods his
head. —Thanks. And I'm proud of the Agency.

—Great. That's just the way it should be. Steady smile, mannequin smile,
from Meyers. —I hope you don't mind if I ask you this, Dave, but, uh, you
haven't told anybody about us, have you?

—Of course not.

Not true. No sir, not true at all.

We must come in close on the cold facts of the matter. First: take one big,
round, stiff kraut prick. Rub Vicks Vapo-Rub all over it. OK? Now take one
naked male ass. Bend it over (so to speak). Expose the asshole. Sprinkle
lightly with . . . No. We're joking. Gently but firmly shove lubricated kraut
prick deeply into oven-ready asshole. OK. Now, using only natural ingredients, no chemical substitutes, prepare a sudden gasp, a sweet, high cry on
the part of the owner of the asshole. What you have is your basic recipe of
Kurt the German cultural attaché fucking David up his round, soft, cute
little American boychick ass. (Said his Boy Scout leader once: —Dave,
honey, you got an ass just like custard pie.) After a bit of reaming and ramming, groaning and gasping—the Vapo-Rub has produced a rather delicious
burning tingle for both participants—and as David has said on more than
one such fuck occasion, "It's the best way to treat a cold I know of"—
culminating in high sighs of orgasmic joy, they collapse onto/into/around
each other, and we have this as "pillow talk" (their expression, not ours):

—. . . and so it is enough for you to live on? Kurt is saying (his hand rests on
David's basket).

—Yeah, I get by all right on it. And of course whatever I have to lay out as
job expenses, they naturally take care of.

—And your Agency contact, he's easy to work with?

—Yeah, he's OK. Ivy League, you know. Smooth dresser, clean-cut.

—What did you say his name was? Meyers something? Kurt's hand is
bringing David's cock gradually to another hard-on.

—Corliss Meyers.

—Hmm. Corliss Meyers . . . sounds rather familiar. Yes. You know, I think I've
met him. At Klosters this last February. He was with an embassy skiing party.

—Could be, David says (his flat tones have powder on them). —Mmm.
That feels *good*.

Kurt is lying of course. But nothing new in that. Have you ever met a
German who could tell the truth?

For the benefit of those of you who have straggled late into this ad hoc saturnalia (this magical minestrone, this hyperactive labyrinth, this . . .), I feel somewhat more than obligated to point out, again and again if necessary, that, no matter what crap is printed in a handful of obscure, hand-printed, secular broadsheets, Carol is not your garden-variety, part-time satellite stewardess. Nor, for that matter, is she your run-of-the-mill thinner of privately owned aardvark herds. No, not at all. To put the record straight and to sweep out whatever polyester cobwebs remain in your belfry, she is (on one level, at least) nothing more, nothing less, than Your Fundamentally Prepaid Cornucopia of Cunt, Your Vaginal Foam-Lined Nonstop Midnight Magical Fuck Show, and, finally, ultimately, Just About Everybody's Long-Overdue Answer to the Sermon on the Mount. There now. If that doesn't satisfy your basest vestigial needs for definition, I have but one suggestion: go jump in the lake.

(There are, as I have rather strongly suggested, here and there, other dimensions to Carol's life, but the question each of you must ask yourself, after peering deep into your own heart problems, is: Have I earned the right to know about them? Am I ready for them? Is knowledge of them a pre-requisite for graduating magna cum better-late-than-never from this loony bin? When you have come up with the answers, call my answering service and we'll set up a wall-to-wall rap session. You hear me?)

Stephan! Behave yourself! Jesus. Every time that dybbuk gets bored, he does the weirdest things. OK. I told you we'd do something interesting this evening and when I give my promise I don't take it back. I ain't no fuckin' Indian giver. Uh huh. We're gonna do a gig with Carol. You'd like that, wouldn't you? I mean, shit. Are there cows in Texas?

Ah . . . who's that knockin' on my door? Aha. One of my fine-feathered friends from over the seas. From Vietnam, from the looks of his gib. Buon giorno, comrade. A communication for me? Don't have to sign for it? I see. OK. Thank you very much indeed. Hmm. Nipped off before I could even get itchy about a tip. Now then . . . let's see what this is all about. Can't imagine what . . .

"Around 8:00 A.M., and not 7:00 A.M., as their accounts say, fighter bombers came over and started circling. After a while they seem to have concluded that their own dead and wounded lying around the battlefield were our own troops, hiding in the grass and undergrowth. They had no ground-air radio contact because they had nothing operational left on the ground. Our troops were marching off with all their communications equip-ment. They started bombing the battlefield, bombing their own dead and wounded. Then their artillery joined in. The battle that 'raged all day,' according to their communiqué, never took place, except that between their own planes and artillery and their own dead and wounded. It was not until late in the afternoon that two puppet battalions entered the area to collect what was left of the two battalions."

See what happens to you if you're brought up with a hot dog jammed in your mouth and a yo-yo up your ass? It's a wonder to me that the whole fuckin' country hasn't fallen into a manhole and disappeared forever. The kinda shit you dumb gringo assholes have had to swallow. Like . . . "Determine to like your work. Then it will become a pleasure, not drudgery. A machine is an assembly of parts according to the law of God. When you love a machine and get to know it, you will be aware that it has a rhythm." Norman Vincent Peale, *America's Guide to God.*

"There are today many communists in America. They are everywhere— in factories, offices, butcher shops, on street corners, in private business— and each carries in himself the germs of death for society." The United States Attorney General.

Bone-building stuff all right. Truly mind-expanding. Sharpens your night vision. With that kind of stuff racing through your bloodstream, there just ain't no way you're gonna get caught by the Vietcong with your pants down, or while you're sleepin' on the job, or while you're aimin' down the wrong end of the barrel. Nope. No fuckin' way.

Now then, where did we leave Carol? Ah yes . . . she was getting ready for the Red Riding Hood Show, which she was putting on for/with a particularly kinky customer, a Monsieur Delon, who was heavily into suppressed childhood eroticism. The costumes and sets were all at hand. The House of Unbridled Pleasure was equipped to the teeth. As all of us old show-biz folks know, you don't just close your eyes and leap into a role like that. No indeedy. Not if you value your reputation. What you do is you research the material. Upside down, in and out, round and round. You get to know where the characters and their story lines come from, and where the fuck they're going. And if you have any sense of history and tradition, any feeling whatsoever, let us say, for the psychodynamics of role playing, you acquaint yourself with the various versions of your vehicle. All of which our own dear friend and comrade Carol did, and with feeling, it should be pointed out. She read every version of Red Riding Hood she could lay her gifted, sensual (when Carol grabbed a prick it almost immediately became the Cathedral of Our Lady) little hands on. She poured over this version, then that version, then this one, then that one. . . . Finally, as her exasperation was soaring—"Jeepers! I can't sink my teeth into any of these!"—she came across one that hadn't been done anywhere before. It was called "The Little Girl Who Went All the Way," and here it is! (Stephan of course had a part, but we'll let you figure out which one. And do we have to be told that his anxiety was so great, his fear of nonbeing so acute that even though he was firmly costumed on the inside of the curtain, so to speak, he still could not stop himself from shouting —Wait for me! as the curtain slowly rose?)

T here they were, mother and daughter. Mother (a composite of undulance) relaxed at the big walnut table with a jar of the homemade ale, daughter (coiled blonde promise) flopped on the windowsill and cleaning her nails with a porcupine quill. The mother was half watching her daughter and half watching something in her own head. At one side of the small but not degraded cottage a fireplace waited for a stick or two.

—Jesus! exclaimed the mother rather out of nowhere. —All the swell clothes you've got and you have to wear that bloody red hooded cape all the time. It gives me the creeps. What's the matter with you anyway?

—Stop bugging me, snapped the girl. —You make it your way, and I'll make it mine. OK?

Her mother snorted, blowing off some ale foam. —Cheeky little bitch. If your father were alive . . .

—He'd be out trying to stick up some fat traveling priest. The girl tossed the quill at the Maltese cat but missed. —Lay off me. I've got enough problems. She stared, gloom-eyed, out the window. —I'm going stir-crazy. This village is as dead as yesterday's mackerel.

The mother guzzled down half the ale, belched, and wiped her foamy mouth with the back of her strong peasant hand. For an obscure reason, she reached inside her blue blouse and scratched one of her fine boobs. —I've got a grand idea, she said. —Touch base with Grandma. The walk'll do you good, because you don't get enough exercise, and it'll remind her that she hasn't sent me any money lately, her poor and only daughter.

Her own daughter, whom she often called Little Red for reasons only too clear by now, sighed with appallment. —Boy oh boy. Some people's idea of fun. You could not tell who she was saying this to, actually, because she looked into the low-beamed cottage ceiling while saying it. —Besides, I can't stand the old bag. She's a disgusting prude and she smells bad. Old pee-pee.

Mother stood up, sighing a bit. She patted her tummy philosophically, but actually she had no worries. She was a handsomely proportioned piece of only thirty-seven and there was a lot of fun in her yet. She knew it, too. —Take her some of this headcheese I bought yesterday. Tell her I made it special.

As she paused at the doorway, Little Red (around whose heavy, sensual mouth one could detect communications of despair and mysterious plans) shook her head and observed, —Lies, lies. This little world of ours is filled with con jobs and hustles.

Mother not too gently patted and propelled her out. —Run along now. And try not to get into anything kinky on the way. I mean, take care, you know?

A few minutes later, while she was bathing her splendid full body in the big wooden tub, she muttered, —Wish to hell that kid would run away with a circus or something. She vigorously sponged herself under the arms and between her succulent thighs. In fifteen minutes a regular customer was arriving to, uh, have his palms read thoroughly. Widows such as she had to do what they could to get by, and she absolutely couldn't see taking in laundry. Not with a body like hers (plus her general flexibility).

Little Red moseyed along in the forest that stood between the dreamy thatched cottage where she lived and the rather similar cottage her smelly old gran holed up in. (Gran's husband, now dead, had done quite well as a forest warden for the Duke of Schlogg by selling a lot of the ancient walnut trees on the sly to city folk.) She could have taken the shortcut, a well-ordered path cut by the village council and used by the utilitarian villagers who had no inclination to mess around, but she preferred the longer, more arduous way that took her through the unkempt, raunchy parts of the forest where one's imagination could get a little nourishment. Odd and slinky animals abounded there, as did trolls, centaurs, gremlins, thieves, gypsies, mushrooms, marijuana, and brazen birds with long wings and big mouths.

After a while—during which while she gathered some divinely chewable, wild blue schikel berries (—Now I can throw away that lousy meadow shit Helga sold me! she cried out happily as she stuffed the pockets of her red cape with the shiny berries), passed a couple of lynx, a drunken tree dwarf, said hello to two well-known poachers (—Mum's the word, they whispered to her)—she ran into this wolf. Just about the furriest, strongest, hottest-nosed, longest-tongued wolf she'd ever laid eyes on. Big shoulders, big haunches, and a look in his boss eyes that was just too much. Oh . . . and there was just a trace—well perhaps more, but so what?—of blood on his jaws from the snack under foot, a fat, or was, Belgian hare.

—Well, hello, hello, Little Red sang out. —Where have you been keeping your big bad self?

The wolf looked her up and down. —You don't sound quite right.

—What? Me?

—Uh huh. You don't talk like you're seeing what you're seeing—a big bad wolf.

Little Red swirled her cape as coquettishly as she could and laughed. —Can I help it if I dig dangerous animals?

The wolf looked her over again, this time more carefully and with some savor. —I see, he said, licking his bloody jaws with that simply fabulous red tongue of his. —So you're one of those, are you?

She giggled and lowered her head. —Whatever that may mean. Knowing full fucking well what he meant.

—Not bad, he continued, casting good looks at her body. —Not bad at all. Uh, would you like a little lunch? and he motioned at the remains of the hare.

—Thanks loads, but I've eaten. Sure looks good though.

—Nothing like wild Belgian hare, believe me.

Little Red was abruptly reminded of her original mission by a tense (transference) finger that had worked its anxious way through the headcheese in her pocket. —Oh darn! Listen. Let's keep this rolling. I've got to make a bread-and-butter call on my old grandmother. Come with me. We'll knock it off in no time, then we can have a little fun. She grinned lewdly. —You know. Fool around and get to know each other.

A soft husky sound came from the wolf's throat. He licked his jaws a couple of times and raised his beautiful, savage head high in the air, flexing his neck. —Yeah, he said finally. —But, uh, you know what the local laws on bestiality have to say about that, don't you?

—Phooey on them! Little Red exclaimed. —Besides, what they don't know won't hurt them.

—Just the same . . .

—OK, OK. Perhaps we'd better play it cool. Being seen together might get those lunks up kind of tight. We'll take separate routes and simply meet there. You can't miss Gran's house. It's three blocks past the old pagan sacrificial ground and just a half block east from that funny-looking stone statue with the broken head.

—What about your old gran?

—Don't worry, she's in bed. And there aren't any nosy neighbors. So just relax on the steps in front, OK?

So they parted, and away, away.

Oh. The jolly woodcutters. Well, a few sighs and funny thoughts later, Little Red passed these woodcutters. They worked as official all-year-round choppers of wood for the old Duke. They were strong (each one had a lunchbox of good eats prepared by his very own mommy), clean-cut rather than dirty-cut, young and just brimming over with traditional modes of communication.

—Watch out, honey pie, one said smiling gooeyly. —Don't fall into any woodchuck holes.

—Say, sweetie, began another, —haven't I seen you somewhere before?

—Fuck off, Little Red suggested, and pulled the hood of her lovely cape over her curly head. Those fags, she said to herself. Who do they think they're kidding?

At Granny's. The very attractive wolf was stretched out on the grass in front of the cottage picking his long, sharp teeth with a pine needle. His brown-grey fur glowed sensuously in the soft amber of the afternoon sun.

—I'll check out the scene inside, Little Red said as she arrived, unable to keep from running back. —I'll be just a sec.

—I still feel a little nervous about the whole thing, said the wolf, spitting out a shred of hare. —I mean, you're a real dish and all that, but those laws . . .

—For a big bad wolf you sure worry a lot, she said. She blew him a juicy kiss and nipped into the cottage, after raising the big bar on the door.

Before going into the tiny bedroom where her old Gran was lying in the bosom of her illness, Little Red paused to look around the living room, just for laughs. The place was agog with symbols of peasant success. Petit-point homilies decorated the walls: "Work Is Godly" . . . "Be True to Your Owner" . . . "Down with Bad Thoughts"; tacked on a board over the fireplace was a parchment attesting to the fifty splendid years of her husband's servitude to the Duke; to the right of the fireplace was a sort of plaque honoring Grandad for flushing and beating to death a woods witch; scattered about the room—which was really quite *intime*—were knickknacks made of boars' tusks, soapstone, and cleverly put-together turtle shells and bird beaks.

—Great place for a weenie roast, she muttered, winking, and went into the bedroom.

—Hi, Gran. It's me. Little Red Riding Hood. I've come to . . . But Gran was either in a coma or was just snoozing the snooze of the aged. Little Red tiptoed to the bed for a closer look. An old crone's mustache grew on the woman's ancient leather face, which was partly covered by a lace night bonnet which had slipped down. Her bony hands, clutching the blanket, were talons of steel. She was snoring.

—You just won't let go, will you, you miserable old cunt, Red said, shaking her head in a more or less amazed way. She placed the little packet of head-cheese on the pillow next to the snoring grey head. —Just in case you get a sudden yen. And Red giggled.

She hopped to the front door and beckoned to the lovely vibrant wolf. —Come on in. She's dead to the world.

—You may not believe this, said the wolf as it trotted into the cottage, —but I've never done this before. Never.

—There's always a first time for everything, she observed, and gave him a real affectionate hug.

In a very short time Little Red and the wolf were chewing the wild blue schikel berries. They were lying on several large eiderdown pillows on the floor.

—Mmm, murmured the wolf, chewing away. —Strange-tasting things, aren't they?

—They're the greatest, she said, grinning. —Wait'll they hit you. Best high you ever had. She began taking off her clothes. —I'm feeling it already. Gee, it's hot in here. In a shake she was completely nude. —There now. That's much better.

The wolf licked its big, fangy mouth, grinned wide, wide, and slowly scrutinized every part of her young nubile body, said, —Kid, you sure got it all. I'll say that. They didn't leave out a single thing.

—Well, I'm sure glad you like it, wolfie. Her usually high girlish voice was now oddly husky.

Little Red's entire being shimmered and radiated like a rare sunset. A faint flush suffused her face, which had by now lost its youthful innocence and was becoming lewd and fierce in its expression and texture. Her eyes glittered and her lips were full and wet. She seemed to be modeling for the wolf: she arched and flexed and turned slowly around in front of him. A whisper and then a long low growl came from him.

—These berries are knocking me out, he said, staring at her golden muff, and whimpered, —I'm moving eight different ways.

—Oh Jesus, Jesus, she murmured hoarsely, rubbing her hands over her glistening breasts and belly and stiff red nipples. —I'm a soaring demon!

The wolf was standing and pacing now. His great red tongue was hanging out and as he panted saliva ran down it. The fur stood up on his heavy neck, and his eyes were shot with blood. His savage head moved back and forth and up and down. He stood in front of her trembling loins, and a sharp urgent whining came from his strongly muscled throat. —What lovely white arms you have, he said.

—All the better to squeeze you with, she panted.

—What a fine juicy mouth you have.

—All the better to bite you with, she said, her voice becoming stronger and huskier and her writhings more tortured.

—What rich, pointy breasts you have! he howled.

—The better to rub against you! Sweat was beading all over her ravenous, crazed face.

—What tasty, supple thighs you have!

—The better to rassle and fuck you with! she screamed and they sprang at each other.

They were embroiled in a frenzy of slaverings, biting, moans, growls and shrieks when Granny suddenly appeared in the doorway separating the two rooms. She was an apparition of gnarled nightgowned crone.

—Obscenities! she shrieked. —Unspeakable filth! And she hurled her lace nightcap at them.

An animal scream of rage came from Little Red, who was under the great wolf. —Kill her! she yelled. —Kill her!

Growling madly, the red-eyed wolf leaped upon the old lady and knocked her to the floor. She did not have time for even one more bad accusation. In moments, the wolf's sharp fangs had ripped through her scrawny old neck and separated her head from her body. Blood poured all over the wolf and the floor.

—Yes! Yes! howled the sweating, naked girl crouching like an insane beast on the pillows.

The wolf, covered with dripping blood, stood over the old lady's headless, twitching body for a couple of seconds whining and growling, then trotted back to Red.

—Roll on me! she commanded him, lying on her back. —I want the blood all over me! and her voice was thick and berserk.

The wolf obeyed her, and Little Red panted and writhed with mounting ecstasy as the dark blood stained her loins and belly and breasts. She gripped the wolf with her legs and arms and began to lick and bite him, and the whimpering, arching wolf did the same to her, up and down her twisting body. His long dripping tongue was soon in the wet blonde crevice of her loins, and her shudders and howls were evidence of the demonic pleasure his engagement there was producing. Her spasms of orgasm seemed to engulf half his head.

On and on they went. Each crescendo begat another crescendo. Little Red was soon applying her lustful expertise to him. Ultimately they combined and synchronized their tormented efforts, and in their cataclysmic joining the animal world was once again united.

Afterward they sank into a torpor of satiation and while the birds twittered and the squirrels played outside, they snoozed thickly in each other's embrace. The old grandfather clock in the corner ticked mindlessly away.

Little Red eventually opened her eyes, yawned, and sat up. She looked at her blood-smeared body, smiled at the wolf, and said, —Boy oh boy. That was sure a great piece of action, wolfie. She scratched his head. —You're the greatest.

—You're pretty good yourself, he said, and gave her a friendly little rub with his nose. —And you can tell 'em I said so.

—Oh sure, she said, laughing and standing up. —You can just bet I'll do that. She stretched deliciously and rubbed her belly for good measure. —Mmm. Those schikel berries are so terrific. And no bad aftereffects either.

—Yeah, agreed the wolf, yawning and scratching himself. —Leave a good taste in your mouth too.

She ran her hand through her messed-up hair, massaged the back of her neck, moving her head around as she did. Then she saw Gran's headless body and all that blood splashed about. —Golly, she remarked, shaking her head. —What a mess.

—Yeah, well, that's the way it goes, said the wolf, having a good stretch himself.

She continued to survey the bloody scene, and a slightly different expression settled on her face, a thoughtful, private expression. —Hmm, she murmured to herself, and her eyes, which had been soft and warm, were now serious and even a bit hard.

—How about a little chow? she asked.

—Sure, the wolf replied, grinning. —I can always eat. And they both tittered at the double meaning.

Red went into the little kitchen off the main room and began looking around for some food. She came upon the remains of a pheasant stew in an iron pot on the windowsill. —Aha. Here we are. This ought to put the kick back in the old kicker. She scooped up a bowlful, looked carefully around the kitchen floor layout for just the right spot, and set the brimming bowl on the floor in the corner to her right.

The wolf padded by her to the bowl. —Yums, he said, sniffing at the stew. —Good show. He wagged his fine bushy tail in appreciation. Since his back was to Red now, his wagging tail brushed her legs, and she twitched with the sudden tickle.

—I'll have a cup of tea myself, she explained, her voice now rather careful and flat. —I've got to watch my weight. She watched the wolf intently. His head was bent down to the floor away from her, and his side vision was completely cut off by the sides of the corner. He lapped and munched noisily. Little Red's hand gently closed around the handle of the heavy meat cleaver on the sideboard. In slow-motion, and without taking her cold eyes off the wolf's bent neck, she raised the cleaver high. In one swift, powerful chop across his spine, she cut him almost in half. He died without a sound.

—Sorry 'bout that, she said to the dead wolf. —But I just had to. The cops would've connected me and you and Gran's murder, no question about it. But this way they won't. I'll just tell them I killed you in a fight right after you killed poor Gran, being the very dangerous wolf you were. She looked at her arms. —And these groovy scratches and teeth marks will prove you attacked me. Neat, huh?

She started out of the pantry. At the doorway, she turned around and, grinning slyly, added, —And besides, you might have gone around bragging how you had me. Just imagine what that would have done to my reputation.

She laughed a sweet, lyrical child's laugh, and scampered outside to the rain barrel for a good wash.

To describe a nose is not really the same as annotating a Roman dissertation on road building. But while one activity may turn you into a road snob, the other could possibly bring you one inch closer to The Whole Human Truth. Therefore . . . Monsieur Paul Corot's nose, it seemed to Carol, raising a fine forkful of muffled *lapin* in *sauce pyrénées* to her mouth, was closer to an invitation to the waltz than it was, say, a summons to court for a traffic violation. Corot's schnozz suggested both provincial guile and at the same time a decidedly urban laissez faire . . .

—The American character, Corot said, stroking his way through a plate of asparagus, —is forged in contradictions. It is insanely innocent, yet relentlessly corrupt. Sweet Norman butter ran down the corner of his strict mouth. —Wouldn't you agree?

Whether to "date" a client of The House was a decision which the management (the owners were two aging sisters who had inherited the business from their enterprising mother and who for the usual reasons chose to live in the Swiss mountain village of Montluc, where yodelers were pitted against yodelers on the clearest and coldest of days) left entirely up to the discretion of "our consenting angels," as they were so affectionately called. Corot was one of Carol's steady clients. Once a week she performed with him a fairy tale or a "children's" story. Why not have a spot of supper with him. After all . . .

—Uh . . . yes . . . I suppose I would agree in prin . . .

—I give you, for example, Calamity Jane Wilson, the only too well-known wife of your seventeenth president James Fenimore Wilson. As sword swallowers "drop" their swords, so did Corot "drop" another dripping stalk of asparagus into his upturned cormorant mouth/neck. —Madame Wilson craftily made millions selling fundamentally outmoded state secrets to the British, on the one hand as you Yankees are fond of saying, and yet she permitted her life to be manipulated and savaged by a crazed, one-eyed Cherokee Indian posing with the utmost in cynicism as a seer and prophet.

Carol carefully dabbed his mouth with the soft white napkin (juicy rabbit, you see), and just as carefully, as soon as she spotted them, plucked two wolf hairs from Corot's chic blue jacket. —I didn't know that President Wilson's wife . . .

—And of course, Corot continued, expertly finishing off the asparagus in a blaze of dripping butter, —the blaring contradictions between the democratic dreams as they are lived in your official books of lies and the real nightmares as they are lived in the streets that are paved with black men's unlucky babies. He grabbed a rabbit leg and bit into it with the skillful abandon of one who has been there before and will go there again. —Therefore, the American character is continually fermenting in an unbalanced state of . . .

Of ear-to-ear horror, Carol thought. Pat Nixon is the Beast of Belsen. The Mouseketeers are storm-troopers with enlarged ears. J. Edgar Hoover maintained close professional ties with Nazi police chiefs right up to the beginning of the war, says the *International Tribune*. My God. And the CIA hires Mafia hit men to knock off Castro. While Cardinal Spellman was telling the GIs they had to kill more gooks for God, Beach Girl was taking it up the ass from Huckleberry Finn. She was in the showers at Sonoma State University, blissfully disintegrating in a rain forest of steam, when that fat dumb little cunt Marjorie Sams suddenly turned on her idiot transistor radio as loud as possible. It screamed, "Naturally, we kill and torture many Vietcong! The only way to combat these people who act like animals is to kill them!"

Oh yeah. Right. But the dumb thing is, politically I didn't know my sweet little ass from a hole in the ground in those days. Somebody, I think it was big Jo White who hopped out of the shower and yelled at Sams, —Shit, Sammy! Can't you get anything good on that little Jap yap of yours?

—Leave it on, Carol said.

—What? asked Corot. —Leave what on?

—Sorry. I was just thinking out loud of something that happened years . . . It just leaped out.

—Oh yes. The past. We think we have swallowed it, like this juicy little rabbit. But we are wrong. It's always there, lurking in the throat, waiting to leap out.

Lurking in the throat, like all the cocks I've swallowed. She was suddenly overwhelmed by a vision of scores of cocks leaping out of her mouth. A wild cock storm filled the air. —Oh my God! she cried out, and began to shriek with laughter. She held a piece of bread with runny Camembert before her lewd open mouth. —Ah, the secret humors of the American woodsman as he boldly prepares to burn his first bridge.

One of the hard-ons flying around Carol's head had a thick, red beard and was called Michael. Let us grab onto this airborne cock and soar with it right back to its rightful origins and owner. Hold on now, folks! 'Ere we go!

OK. Here we are. That hot but oceanically beautiful day in Washington, D.C., fascist center of the USA. Carol was marching down Constitution Avenue with thousands and thousands of other antiwar demonstrators. They were heading for the United States Capitol. Marching next to Carol in the dense singing/shouting mass was a beautifully satanic-looking man named Michael something, with a dense, red beard. They had been talking in between the singing and the shouting of statements against the Vietnam war.

—You've got to remember, he said. —There's a lot more to being political than just marching. That's just the romantic part of it.

—Uh huh, she responded.

—You've got to train yourself to think and feel politically. That takes a lot of reading, a lot of discipline.

—All right. Who should I read?

—There are a lot of people. Start with Christopher Caudwell. He's terrific. He analyzes capitalist society right down to the corncob up its asshole.

At the end of the wide avenue, high above them on the Hill, squatted the white Capitol building, a giant albino blob. It seems to be trembling slightly.

From time to time over the past few years Michael has wondered about the girl he marched next to in Washington. Carol something or other. Nice kid. But so were all the others. This particular one, he discovered later that day, sucked a very mean cock. She was the only woman he'd ever met who came while blowing him. A rare, divine talent. Where had they all gone to? Have they vanished into a song? Have they all married and changed their identities and dentures?

—When the Vietnam war ended, so ended mass solidarity, Michael says aloud to me. For it is not too unusual that a character I have merged with, or become, is still separate enough from me, at moments, to talk to me. This can be called double-identity soliloquies until we have come up with a more durable or desirable term. —Too fucking bad, he goes on, drinking his beer. —For a while there it looked like we had the makings of something. He looked more or less blankly at his beer and sadly shook his head. —No way there'll ever be a Left in that fucking country.

A chap with an elegantly nondescript personal ambiance hovering about him—yes, you could say radiating a purposeful (and conceivably malevolent, but of course we shall see about that) goal-oriented ambiguity—nodded from the intimate and, by implication, vulnerable nearness of the next tiny table.

—You are so very right, my friend, he muttered, with an accent and a "smile" that were somewhere between Middle European and lower pastrami. He was not so much "seated" as he was present at the table.

Michael looked him over (carefully licking beer foam from his red mustache). —I'm not in the mood to talk to anybody right now, he said.

The man nodded with that absolutely reeking grin. —Of course. As you wish. Whenever you are ready. Peelmunder's the name. Professor Socks Peelmunder.

—Hmm, Michael murmured. —I suppose so.

Nobody had to tell him that there was something fishy about that name. How did anything as footloose, as brashly ad hoc, as Socks ever get within shouting distance of the timeless tweedy dignity of professor? And Peelmunder . . . A name? Oh no. That just had to be an obscure local beer that had never really caught on.

—Yeah. Later maybe, he said. He felt like saying something like, why don't I just send you my contributions and you can keep all the literature, OK? I mean . . .

Where was . . . Ah yes. The utter fucking impossibility of a really progressive opposition in America. I should discuss this in my class, in relation to the counterrevolutionary function of the mass media. OK, OK. Finish the letter to Germaine LeClerc at Charles V. Snare yourself that nice visiting lecturer job for the spring semester. Squeeze the living pâté out of Voltaire's sister. Bring The True Living Word to the musky Marais. So: ". . .and the lectures will be supplemented/complemented by a substantial reading list, including such books as *The Cold War and the Press, American Power and the New Mandarins, The Manufacture of the News,* and *Culture against Man.* Parallel to the study of these texts, we will be analyzing the political infrastructure of the news columns of the *New York Times* and *Le Monde,* two paradigmatic middle-class newspapers, in order to . . ."

In more ways than one, a dark shadow fell across Michael's page. The American Negro Cleon passed his table, brushed against his big, striped composition book which extended slightly over the edge of the midget table, jarring the delicate letter to Madame LeClerc. This man was a black whippet, racing grimly at mystery tracks at unexpected hours. And though very black indeed, he was at the same time transparent; and this seemingly contradictory phenomenon (that is, ordinarily thought of as mutually exclusive by that part of us which holds certain things to be dear and self-evident . . .) evoked in the *other,* the observer/spectator (though it could be argued, if not here, elsewhere, and if not now, later, at a more precisely felt and delegated moment, that the self and the other are always one and the same entity), emotions of metaphysical jeopardy within which state one shouted, above the din of other competitive emotions, "Hang on to your hat!" And not entirely out of the corner of his eye, Michael saw that the black man's appearance had been recorded also by the rather forward, suggestively self-referent stranger who, without any show of conscience or embarrassment, called himself Socks Peelmunder. This aggressive ambiguity, Michael saw, was watching the black man (who was lighting up a Gitane cig with the studied aplomb of an unknown actress who has just captured a big role the official announcement of which you, and all others of course, will very shortly be reading about in your favorite newspaper) with the quasi-scientific detachment of him who has a turd in one pocket and the Golconda diamond in the other. You know that look? You have seen it suddenly manifest itself in situations where, because the game is rigged, someone has *inside information?* Va bene. I believe we know where we're at. . . .

Michael knew about this man through the bathroom walls of his apartment on Van Spiegel Street. He was between jobs as a mercenary. He had last worked, Michael heard through his wall, in Angola where, as an agent of the right-wing forces of Holden Roberto, paid directly by the CIA, he had done a fair to middling amount of killing. Spilled a lot of black people's blood—by machine gun, handguns, and hand grenades—men, women, and children involved in the struggle for liberty in the forces of the MFA under Neto. What had penetrated the Dutch walls of the bathroom—Michael shitting, showering, or peering deep into his hazel eyes for signs of unexplored psychic wealth—was that Cleon would soon be pulling down very good money as a soldier killer for the white fascist Rhodesian government.

—Get back my fuckin' self-respect, he said to his girlfriend/keeper one night about 6:30, a little while before she hit the streets to hustle. —Not my style to be kept by anybody.

His hooker friend said, —But isn't this nicer than having to kill people?

He shouted, —Fuck! It's my business to kill people! That is my profession. You got yours, baby, an' I got mine. You dig?

She said, —But in my profession I give the people pleasure.

What exactly is it? Michael asked himself. What's in it for her? Is black cock so different, so great? Great Day at Black Cock, first show 2:00 P.M. Or could it be black professional killer cock? Furthermore, Dr. LeClerc, our seminar at Charles V will make a dialectical analysis of the perpetuation by the mass media of the mythology of black cock. We will address ourselves to the following questions: Does the problematic of black cock (hereinafter, as an aid in future cataloging, to be referred to as BC) arise from the dynamics of class struggle? Or must it be understood as a purely white/black phenomenon? Is the BC mythology, then, a physiologically orientated one, comparable, let us say, to height, weight, ideals/values? Or, is BC a subtly constructed metaphor of a deeply hidden Manichaean-type fear, within which metaphorical construct BC is plague/death/evil/ultimate darkness? Is BC at the heart of darkness? Or is it more likely to be found deep in the heart of Texas? Can BC be stopped? Can we get at it by way of Income Tax Evasion? Can't the Food and Drug officials prevent the marketing of a low-tar BC? And if that isn't possible, can't we put our scientists to work on developing an all-purpose many-splendored filter tip with recessed genes to go with BC with mandatory wording on each over-the-counter package, to the effect that the Surgeon General has found that BC contains unknown agents who may well eat you out of house and home? In conclusion, Dr. LeClerc, I would like to say . . .

—I want a shot of iced aquavit and a glass of Tuborg, if that's cool with you, Cleon informed the waitress.

The young, very Dutch, blonde waitress stared at him for a couple of seemingly but not really blank seconds. Though she was not a large young woman, you just knew that deep inside her were muscles that would come in very handy indeed at critical moments. This was a woman who could run up and down hills with the best of them when that became the name of the game out there.

—You ken haf anyzing you ken pay for, she said. Her pencil whirred over her order pad, and away she darted.

—That's boogie, Cleon said to her nonpresence, to the air, to himself, to The Cosmic Ear. (Cleon's name, Michael knew, was Bunk, and that's what he'll be called from now on.)

Michael unwillingly looked over at the irreparable Socks Peelmunder, who, when their eyes made contact, winked. I'm still not ready to talk, Michael indicated silently, but could it be possible that you are writing that black man's dialogue?

Peelmunder—how can one, can he, have a face that personifies all of the indeterminate guile of an intransitive verb?—simply grinned. Anything is possible, he replied silently. I might ask if you are completely convinced it is you yourself who write *your* dialogue.

This question caught Michael at the wrong moment, caught him a bit off guard. He drank some beer and considered the whole thing. Hmm. What does this apparently unavoidable and hubris-filled spook know that I don't? Why does his question precipitate queasy frogs inside me? I mean, aren't I all me? Am I not the sole owner and operator of my own vehicle, that is, in the broadest use of that word? And if not . . . He returned to Peelmunder. I'll have to get back to you on that, he said. I can see that you play real fastball.

Whenever you are ready, said Peelmunder.

I wish to fuck you wouldn't keep saying it that way, said Michael. You sound like you're an abyss that I'm doomed to fall into.

Peelmunder's response, as one would expect, fairly oozed with self-satisfaction. What can I say? he replied. And he did not immediately wipe away a beer-foam mustache from his uppity lip. Chutzpah, and brazenness, that's what we're dealing with here and make no mistake about it.

Michael licked foam off his own lip. Something tells me, he thought, that I will have to dip into my inner resources when I deal with this creepy guy.

Lip-smacking sounds from Bunk over there brought Michael back to that dark man. He's got black mirrors all over inside himself, and he keeps running and running from one to the other looking for himself, but it's a fruitless search, as they say. That sharp gleaming face, he borrowed it from Queen Nefertiti. Quite a face to go with a dealer of blood and death. Shit, he goes right back to the ancient Egyptians and their death birds and jackal heads and scarabs and crazy tombs. He was the court's official killer, not to be irresponsibly confused with executioner, which is a horse with a different coloring book. Nothing elegant about an executioner, for one thing, and their jobs were totally different. One is just a mechanical man, an automaton with no class. *He's not family.* That's what you've got to remember, kids. But the other, I mean, like he's a priest, y' know? All kinds of religious and magical and otherworldly stuff are involved in his killer gigs. Sort of, he's the dark side of the soul, the sole authorized agent from, and to, the eternal world of the dead. The awesome universe of the infinite unconscious where you can be sure they don't have alarm clocks or flight schedules 'cause ain't nobody leavin'. Giant black birds with eyes of rubies eternally soar there. And sounds are as much felt as heard. Those Egyptians did things with style. *They took care of their own.* Serenely confident, sharp-featured types with all that Upper Nile class. They provided their boys with official costumes that would knock you dead. Top-grade threads. Nothing shoddy off the racks for their "in people." Like our boy The Court Killer over there . . . why, they provided him with easily twenty-two, twenty-three different changes for his work and place in the exquisite hierarchy. Shit, with no trouble at all I can see Nefertiti-face here draped from head to foot in flowing fuchsia robes and his extremities dripping with wild jewelry that flashes maniacally in the dry, brilliant sunlight. And he's always serenely and haughtily caressing one or another of these special mystical pieces of jewelry, just as he's right now turning and feeling those rings on his long, smooth black fingers. I mean, he's doing it with such calm, absorbed, communionlike intensity, he's making my own fingers vibrate. My fingers and hand and wrist are picking up his Egyptian Court Priest finger-ring magic signals, and, uh, something's happening here that's changing things, changing, commanding, somehow making all energy and self concentrate mindlessly in these fingers and hands, I mean, he's rubbing his way into my fingers and hands. I don't have to look to know that they have turned black and the thoughts in his arms and fingers, the elegant, intense, self-centered vibrations in that head are now mine. And these hands, black, long, jeweled, are now me and I'm utterly with them in their smelly, primitive, deranged, thatched village in Africa and my fuckin' M16 automatic rifle is firing into that hut and I'm shouting, —Show you cocksuckers what's what. Show you who's runnin' this fuckin' show! You hear me?

And their screams inside. Children and women screaming. They're running and crawling out bleeding, covered with blood. The naked woman holding the baby is yelling something at him in that funny language and holding one arm out to me. . . .

And then, in a mindless, thoughtless, silken swiftness, he was out of Bunk. But he was still where Bunk, or he as Bunk, had been. Only he was now Michael. Like waking up and simply finding yourself there. In a bar of eerie smells and malevolent, whirring ceiling fans. Eerie . . . he was smelling the deranged thoughts and bizarre feelings in the place. And why do those fans seem like huge, outspread birds? The hairy, viciously muscled white American in the camouflage field clothes sitting at the scarred wooden table—all kinds of crazy shit had been carved and gouged into it—slopped down half his glass of gin and tonic and said, —I'm telling you, man, you look close enough and you'll find the Yids are behind this whole thing.

—The Jews? Michael said, amazed that he was here, not understanding how he had got here. —What have they . . .

—International communist conspiracy. With all their gold bullion in those big banks of theirs, they're pulling all the puppet strings.

Michael, feeling that he had somehow become an abstraction, stared simplemindedly at the skull-and-crossbones tattoo on the man's forearm as he slopped down more of his drink.

—You know what President Richard Nixon said? the man asked.

—No. What did he say?

—He said anything that's against Christianity is a blow against our children's unblemished future.

—That ain't nothin', said the guy sitting next to him. —Sidney Hook said the lowest form of intellectual is led by left-bank American expatriates who curry favor with Sartrian neutralists. His submachine gun was lying on his lap. His face perfectly matched the hand grenades dangling from his shoulder belt.

Another white soldier in camouflage field clothes leaning in his chair against the wall giggled shrilly. —Fuck, man I can cap that. Jacques Barzun said our society fulfills more and more purposes, recognizes the desires of more and more different kinds of human beings. It gives me music, others cyclotrons, and still others camping sites, or football games. A small brown monkey was squatting on this soldier's swollen beer belly and eating a potato chip.

I've got to get out of here, Michael said to himself. He knew that at any moment they would "discover" him, the true him, the one who shouldn't be here, who was somehow mistakenly . . . Panic was hemorrhaging in him. He started to get out of his chair in a stealthy manner. Maybe they won't notice me if . . .

—Hey, red beard! shouted a strangely mottled guy whose nose had been mashed. His face said toad. —It's your turn. You gotta come up with something.

—Uh . . .

—Don't give us that uh shit! shouted a bony little white killer.

Michael was frantic. His end was near, he knew that. He looked around the room as if for help, although God knows . . . Peelmunder . . . Could that be Peelmunder grinning under that green beret over there at the bar? That .45 Colt strapped to his belt? . . . Peelmunder mouthed a whole string of words at him.

—Yeah! shouted Michael. —You know it! OK. Guess what Daniel Bell said.

—You tell us! You tell us! all the stained, filthy, lewdly grotesque white mercenaries shouted together, banging their glasses and bottles on the tables. Feeding time at the zoo.

Michael felt himself levitating as he responded. —He said the tendency to convert issues into ideologies, to invest them with moral color and high emotional charge invites conflicts which can only damage society.

The reeking bar rocked with crazed applause, and shouts and whistles of pleasure and admiration. Michael felt himself dematerialize into an epiphany of liberation. He was getting out! The last thing he saw in that foul jockstrap den was the sly I'm-on-top-of-it grinning of Peelmunder.

'Course, it goes without saying—I hope—that nobody else there had Michael's luck. (Naturally, depending on how you want to look at it.) That is to say, they all had to remain there, stroking their way through blood and shit and disease and their very own leprous hangups. Now, to most of these moral throwbacks, I have just described paradise. They wouldn't want it any different, and they would get extremely huffy if anybody tried to introduce any ideas or offers of change. There was, however, one lice-ridden, sweat-drenched, ball-swollen bucko who, on balance (don't you just love that phrase?), was beginning to have certain misgivings about the whole fucking mess. He was non-run-of-the-mill-stream in another way too, in that he looked like Genghis Khan, or, at least, what he in the grip of his furious role-playing need imagined GK looked like. His head was shaved bald except for a horse-tail growth of hair soaring up from the very middle of his glowing head. A mustache hung way below his often quivering youthful chin, as in old-style, you-better-hide-your-women-or-else Mongol hordes. (Do I hear some of you muttering, We are getting the message?) Plus . . . now get this . . . plus, swinging gaily or brazenly (whichever you prefer) from his right ear was a large, radiant, gold earring. Wouldn't you think that anybody with that kind of an identity come-on would absolutely fucking have to be happy?

"Dear Sis," he wrote early one swampy, imminently psychotic morning while sitting in his armored troop carrier just outside a freshly roasted village, "I am sinking fast."

Before things get out of hand, you have every right to (1) consult a lawyer of your own choosing; (2) refuse to eat foods prepared by any one of many loosely woven infidels; (3) ask who is Sis? Well, it just so happens that Sis is an inspired, blue-eyed misfit named Decca Aldridge, better known to herself and her demons as Decca Records (whom the more dedicated among the audience will surely remember meeting across a crowded super-market). His identical twin sister. He is to be known as Fall, short for Fallen, or more legalistically precise, He Who Is Falling. Fall and Decca had always been as close as two humans could be without offending God. Which is not at all the same as saying their closeness would not have offended the average idiot in the street, because it would have. Offended and scared the living shit out of. "Stop that at once!" the idiot would have shouted had he but known or seen. "You can't do that!" or this: "What kinda people are you? Who the devil do you think you are?" Stuff like that (certain types swimming hopelessly round and round in history's tide pools would have exclaimed "Good grief!" or "Jeepers!") would have poured out of the stunned, jeopardized mouths of such street idiots had they but . . . Decca and Fall were so tight, in fact, that they were at times *interchangeable.* When one had a thought or a feeling, the other more than likely had it too. They were continually in touch psychically when they wanted it that way. What this amounted to, as often as not, was that they were *both* present when something was taking place, you see: One being inside the other, or vice versa, if you like. Oh yes, very eerie indeed. There are scientists who have put their reputations on the line by maintaining that such twins carry around in their heads *one and the same brain.* (Keep your seat belts fastened, *pullleeease.*)

"I am sinking fast. This entire fucking misadventure was conceived of, by, and for the people in and on quicksand, four score and seven years ago to the contrary. Why am I here? Why are you there? Why do odds-on favorites break their legs at the starting gate and end up as glue on some schoolgirl's desk? Why was Lot's wife turned into a package of Epsom Salts, instead of, for instance, a whirling chili dog? Then, at least, wandering biblical freaks could have had a good munch or two, which she probably would have liked, my own theory being that nobody was eating her and as a result . . . These and many other deeply human questions must wait for the Day of the Big Answer. Meanwhile, pit opens up under pit, and behind each dark cloud there is an even darker one. Humanity is approaching zero point where I am. Cheek by jowl I live with the scum of the earth. Lift a big rock anywhere and you'll see us, a glowing group portrait. I am here of course because God, who is a raving, fucking maniac, wishes me to know the bottom before knowing the top. The scabby old loon is preparing me for sainthood. And what is also clear . . . That's putting it too genteelly. My brain is surrounded and under seige by the realization that our group is your basic archetypal collection. We are the personifications, the reifications, of antivirtue. We are Lie, Cheat, Brute, Sneak, Vicious, Suck, Kill, Betray, Evil, Degenerate, Glutton, Venal, basic types from the Nuclear Scum Bag.

Sometimes I think I'm in the middle of a primitive morality play, written by Swift or one of those other driven types back there when. Here: let me trot them out for you. I know you've just been dying to meet them. OK. Here's Suck (Frank Walters):

"The very first thing you may want to know about me is the title of my theme song: 'Sucking Will Make It So.' You folks out there name it and I'll suck for it. First thing I ask myself about anything is, Can I suck for it? Or, How can I suck for it? I was a tenderfoot in our scout troop in Milwaukee.

Got my first merit badge by sucking around Mr. Abernathy our scout master on an overnight hike in the woods. I did everything wrong but boy oh boy did I suck! It was just a coincidence that he too sucked ... my cock. But my rock-bottom feeling is that even if Abernathy hadn't sucked me off a couple of times, my own sucking around was so good I would have gotten my badge just the same. By the time I got to Nam I had got my suck together so good there wasn't anything I couldn't finagle. Shit, I was getting weekend passes when there weren't any weekends. And when it came to body counts, I sucked so many of them the fuckin' brass thought I was another one-man army like Audie Murphy.

"Here in boogie asshole country suck is different. Suck is black. Over there suck was slant. Black is leaner and meaner 'cause of scarcity. For instance, it took me any hour of my best efforts last week to suck a couple of extra cartons of Marlboros from Supplies. I got good mileage out of those filter tips: one solid week of ace-of-spades pussy in Buwalla. My sucking up to Major Bart for three weeks has finally paid off. (A very challenging effort, by the way, because Bart thinks he's some kind of puritan Captain Ahab, only this whale is coal black.) As a result, I am now in command of a work gang of half a dozen coons. And I don't have to spell it out to you that the more you work loading and unloading jobs, going to town for supplies, fixing my broken-down trucks, the less you get your ass shot at. Like, two days ago, during the time it took me and my gang to bring in fresh water from a pool way up in the bush, three of our guys were killed in an ambush. You can say what ..."

Enough! Git! Phew! Give Suck five minutes and before you know it, he's eatin' up all the fuckin' words. He's been sucking so long, his lips can't close anymore. He's going to put in a piece of screen so's he doesn't choke to death from all the flies buzzin' right into his throat. Next I'd like you to meet Vicious (as played right from the heart by Jack Seaton of Short Hills, New Jersey; weighing in at 270 pounds, wearing purple jockey shorts). Vicious, step up here and say a few choice-cut words to these nice people who've come all the way from nowhere to feast their beady little eyes on your cute little ass, so to speak. OK, friends! Let's hear it for Vicious!

Vicious: "Hi there, ever'body. Sure is swell to see all you swell folks in a godforsaken place like this godawful village dump Grinkonga or Lasagna or whatever in Jehovah's Witnesses they wanna call it, 'cause you know it's no skin off my ass *what* they call their fuckin' ..."

Come on now, Vicious. Cut the shit. What are you trying to pull here? Making out like you're some kind of Neanderthal comic-strip boob with a cleft palate or something. You got the wrong script, Vicious. Now straighten it and be out front with these good people who've had the decency and patience to pay us this courtesy call. Be yourself, Vicious. Your ineffable, inimitable, cold-blooded, articulate, Adolf Eichmann, born-to-brutalize self. You reading me?

Vicious: "Ah, OK, Fall, if that's the way you want it. I just thought I'd try it out. A lot of people like that style better than the real thing. It makes them feel more comfortable if they think that brutes are something different from themselves. You and I both know, don't we, Fall, how the middle-class propagandists traditionally portray the peoples they are subjugating and destroying as low and brutish, not at all fully qualified members of the human race. In fact, I'd like to quote something from one of our very own leaders as an example of the point I'm making: 'We must save these dark-skinned little Filipino people from themselves. They do not know what it means to be decent, civilized people, because they are just one step up from the monkey. We must teach them Christian ways, clean habits, respect for law and order, knowing at the same time that they can never be regarded as equal to their white masters.' President Theodore Roosevelt, if you please.

"See what I mean? There's a lot more where that came from, ladies and gentlemen, and I'd be more than happy to pass it on to any of you if you want to come by my tent after the show.

"Well now, as for myself, my own viciousness . . . It really came into its own during the Vietnam war. Before that I must confess that I was your well-washed, well-dressed, garden-variety, middle/upper-middle-class WASP American vicious brute lurking behind a Brooks Brothers blue oxford cloth button-down shirt, which I was continually flaring the collar of to take care of the nervousness of my fingers. In those prewar days I was vicious only within the mores and guidelines of my class. That is to say, I treated others, other people, with the smiling coolness, distanced 'friendliness' that was expected of me by the social institutions that had formed me. I was 'on top of it' and of course 'on top' of them. The idea behind me was unquestionable superiority. I was above the rules that governed people who were not from my class. Let anybody cross us and they're dead.

"And in Vietnam they really were . . . dead. With that green beret on my head, oh my oh my, I could do anything to anybody—to the enemy, to those beneath me, to 'the others.' Of course, the very nature and purpose of that green wool symbol converts everyone else into the enemy or 'the other.' Up until that divine point my inherited and educated brutishness had been expressed in social and professional ways only, meaning I could only degrade people. Now my brutishness could be unqualified. I could murder people. I could utterly dispose of their humanness. And the sky was the limit. Let me tell you good people out there that it is only under such circumstances that you get to know your true self. Absolute power precipitates absolute self-confrontation: I saw how thoroughly I was vicious, how complete was my contempt for human life. My puritan forebears, who made their pile by shipping black slaves in chains, lived on in my heartbeats. They would have been proud of me. *Are* proud of me! Will continue to be proud of me! The track record of my bloodthirsty hands speaks for itself. There is not a clean spot on them, nor is there one inch of open space on this desk calendar, nor for that matter is there one single uncalled-for beggar's holiday! Irregardless of what those irresponsible irrigation ditches . . .

   ". . . I hope you'll excuse me for that unwarranted burst of emotion, everybody. I certainly didn't plan on getting carried away like that, and I can assure you that these unfortunate tears you see me wipe away are news to me too. And you can bet on it that when I get them alone after this performance they're going to have a lot of explaining to do. Let not these wanton tears force their way to the head of the table in your heart. That's an old family motto and I am determined to have it stay that way. For the simple reason that before you know it the best and the brightest will be bringing out the worst and the dullest in your favorite and mine, Teddy Roosevelt, who, while he may have had his faults, through no fault of his own . . ."

   Whoa there, Vicious boy. Hold on to your horses. You're getting off the track and heading into the direction of going off your rocker. You were supposed to tell our visitors all about your vicious deeds in Vietnam and more recently in Angola, that reeking, third-rate abattoir where we now . . .

   Vicious: "Slanty-eyed peasant blood! Fish sauce! Glyop gloop! Ruptured spleens! One if by sea, two if by stealth! Crush their infrastructure out of helicopter doors at three thousand feet up! Female Vietcong genital surcharges with 16 millimeter handheld electrodes! Bloated gook baby bodies 'cause there's no business like row row row your boat business . . ."

   Sorry 'bout that, friends. Vicious has been keeping a real tight work schedule and I'm afraid it has gone to his head. An' it's gone rat to mah haid. You remember that wanderful old song I'm sure. Had a lil drink 'bout an hour ago . . . Such things do happen from time to time and in the very best of fumblies. The producers and sponsors of this show furthermore wish to apologize for any inconvenience caused by our having to use force in full view of your loved ones in subduing Vicious and taking him off our make-shifty platform and away to a far, far better life in the hospital tent just up the elephant track to your right, but don't look now if you know what I mean.

   Sis, I know exactly what you'd say if you were here right now in my shoes. You'd say, Fall, honey, you're overwrought and underlaid, and you've been spending entirely too much time talking to and for all those creepy soulless guns for hire, those free-floating zombies whose only reason for living is to make sure other people don't. What in God's name are you doing there? Why in God's name do you stay? I've never understood . . . You what? It isn't you, it's somebody else? What kind of high-wire bullshit are you trying to sell me, Fall? I'm your sister, Fall. I'm the one person in the whole bloody world you can level with, I mean, we're virtually one and the same person. Remember how we used to dream the same dreams when we were kids? And how we used to switch beings for days on end, blowing The Parents' minds? And the time you got cut but I did the bleeding? We were in and out of each other like a hermaphroditic metaphor. So OK. What the fuck do you mean telling me . . . In another life you were a member of the Pretorian Guard? A sword for Caesar? And seven years ago this guy Plotinius re-entered you and has been running your life ever since? Which explains why you, a perfectly harmless, far out, self-obsessed freak, enrolled in the Green Berets? And why you are here doing this perfectly loathsome, unspeakably icky work? Oh wow. Are you sure you've got this right, Fall? Are you absolutely positive that you haven't fallen under the spell of one of those fuzzy-wuzzy witch doctors? You say you haven't. Well, what have you been doing, doping with other than the usual? Nothing? Well then, fuck it: you've flipped out, Fall. You're not yourself, and I'm not punning. I hope you realize this and put a lot of effort into recovering yourself. I mean really give it all you've got, Fall. Don't fuck around. None of those Look, Mom, No Hands deals. You hear me? And if I can help you in any way I will. You know that, don't you? We're kind of in this together. What's mine is yours and never the twain . . . You've got to split for an emergency strategy meeting over in the headquarters tent? Well, OK. So long, Fall. My last words of advice are, defect as fast as your strong little legs will carry you to the MLA and do a lot of mea culpas.

I sure wish I could defect to somebody. Too bad the MLA doesn't have a branch office down here in Rota. Maybe I can defect to the Bolshoi Ballet which is doing its tour stuff in Cádiz. That would sure be a neat switcheroo, wouldn't it. Maybe one of those ballerinas who lust for the wonders of the West would like to defect into me and mine—oh boy!—and I could do the same with her. Yeah. I could vanish forever into Swan Lake. The life eternal of a Russian ballet swan. Forever suspended as a character in an art form. Yeah. It has possibilities. You don't eat, you don't breathe, you don't shit. All you do is perform, perform. That's what I do now, for a select nonpaying audience of three. One husband, Colonel Ack-Ack, one son, General Dwight Eisenhower, one daughter, Julie Nixon. Some family. I'm going to have a good long talk with God about this, or whatever armless juggler is running things up there. What I want to know is, how did I get the Republican right wing instead of a real live family? Why am I being punished? I was a sex-crazed college kid who married a man for his cock. But it turned out that he had Bomb Hanoi tattooed on it in invisible ink. When we fuck I feel like a helpless city under attack.

"We are approaching target area at 22 hours. Ground speed 500 miles per hour. Our speed 2000 miles per hour. Prepare to release ordnance."

How do you like that for a guy about to come? And there's more, much more, it grieves me to report, where that came from.

"Well, Ike," I'll say to my little son. "And how did the cookie crumble at school today?"

"Our foreign policy will be based on the need for America to obtain profitable foreign markets and raw materials to sustain her economy," he'll say.

Or I'll have a go at a little human communication with my "daughter" of a morning. "Wasn't that a funny show last night on TV? I'm crazy about Sid Caesar."

"Our boys in Vietnam walk tall and proud," she'll say. "While those draft-dodging peaceniks disgrace the American flag."

Need I say more? Real heartwarming stuff. Just the sort of thing you need to make that great all-American apple pie with. Sure. I'll bet if I had another child—somebody else's or my own—it would be Typhoid Mary or Benito Mussolini. Oh God. I don't get it. Was I seeded from outer space by one of those "things," a spore with a computer up its ass? I should never have gone to all those fucking space fiction movies when I was a kid. No doubt that's when it happened. While I was stuffing my mouth with hot buttered popcorn, *they* were stuffing *me*, entering me and *planting their evil seed*. So like maybe what we've got here is not a family at all but a piece of a science fiction movie. Oh great. That would certainly explain it. And everybody knows how much I've always ached to be in pictures.

Sure is weird what's going on inside my head, or some such place. Here I am in our apartment in Cádiz, sitting on the little porch above the Calle Spinoza with all the exploding crazy Spaniards and their crazy cars and motorbikes below me but I don't hear that. I'm hearing sounds that have nothing to do with the street below. Sounds from some other place. People shouting in one of those hubba-hubba languages. Machine-gun and rifle fire. Big trucks bouncing around. And smells. Never smelled such smells before. Body smells that are a funny mixture of sweat and herbs and crushed fruit. And air smells that could be of jungles maybe. Angola. It's got to be Angola where Fall is and where part of my being is too because at times we are extensions of each other. Yeah. And I can feel him crying inside himself. And I'm seeing white and black bodies with blood on them. Just look at me. I'm wiping my own arms as if they've got blood on them. Oh shit. A fine kettle of pickled fish fuckers. I'm going inside the apartment and try to turn Angola off. My God . . . those buzzards circling over all those dead bodies . . . Mix a drink. Milky Pernod and water and ice. Cozily anesthetize the top floor of my hyperactive, thirty-six-story brain.

—Those Vietnamese sure have a lot of gall, says Ack-Ack, reading his

International Herald Tribune, stretched out on that loathsome chaise his putrid pumpkin mother gave us. —Claiming we owe them reparations for war damage. What a laugh.

—Yeah, it's a scream, I say. —What if they did have their country destroyed and their people blown to bits. Served 'em right for being commies in the first place, right?

—Decca, your mind is getting warped, and I'm serious. I sincerely believe you should see the post psychiatrist. He's a good . . .

Fuck, and a good suck too. Can't say how good he is as a shrink, but who cares. It's such a lot of bullshit anyway. Dr. Bluestone, I had this dream . . . *The Creaming of the Dream,* in two acts, by Dr. C. W. Blueprick, the only psychiatrist in town whose couch has box springs. His box springs and my box lunch. My oh my, Mrs. Aldridge, said the doctor, what a tasty lunch your box is. He certainly has a fast tongue. A practiced tongue. So good maybe he ought to open up a tongue practice on the side. Dr. Bluestone, my snatch has been feeling kind of strange lately. I see, Mrs. Hot Springs. Well, I think we may have just the tongue for you. The place where we ran into each other for the first time, what a peculiar place to meet another American in, and a psychiatrist, and from this cruddy base. A hangover-from-medieval-times herbal medicine shop in the ancient Jewish ghetto of Cádiz. I mean, holy shit. You might as well say we met in a dream.

What on earth is a man like you doing in a place like this? I asked him almost immediately.

Ha, ha, he went. The very same thing that brings a woman like you here.

And what could that be?

We're both looking for a powder that will cure us of being human.

My God! I shrieked. You've hit it right on the button.

And what a button, if I may say so, he said.

A vanishing powder. Something made up of ground ostrich toe and tiger balls. You take it with a little Perrier water and phtt! you've vanished.

But where to? he asked. Into thin air, do you think? Or . . .

Into somebody else, that's where you vanish into.

Very interesting idea. Listen, he said, almost whispered. Why don't we buy this powder and then go to a café and vanish into a drink?

Not a bad idea when you get right down to it.

Good. Uh, what's your name anyway?

Decca, Decca Records.

Ha, ha, he went again. Can I play you on my machine?

All depends on your machine, I said. And if one thing didn't lead to another, what did, may I ask?

—What's cooking in the hot-blooded kitchens of Army Intelligence these days? I ask my dear husband, whose reading had now advanced to *The Spy*

Who Came in the Cold. My God, what a weird smell, really a stench, is drifting across my face. Burning leaves or grass? No. Burning meat? Something unnatural, sickening . . .

—You're not interested in my work, and you know it, he says without looking up from his book. —You're just trying to bait me.

—No, I'm not. I'm dying to have some kind of conversation, just about any kind, with another human being, and your work is just about all we've got, if you really want to get right down to it, although I'm seriously considering enrolling in a special bull-fighting course. . . .

—We're into a communist cell or something that smells the same, he says, still looking at his fucking little paperback book about spies that are always coming.

—Very special course in that it's going to be all women. And, second, it's going to be against bullfighters and bullfights. We're going to be on the bull's side. Women Strike for Bulls, that'll be our umbrella course title if you will. Or Women Strike for Turnabout. Yeah. That's probably better as a title. Snappier and more to the point. Turnabout, turnabout, snap, snap. Yeah. Well, anyway, we'll study the makeup and psychology of the bullfighter, all the better to eat him with, in a manner of speaking only, that is. We women will put on our own bullfights wherein the bull will be played by a bullfighter, and we'll just see how much he likes the sport then, if you get my meaning, which it would be a downright impossibility not to. We'll buy us or steal us or kidnap us a bullfighter or two, and then we'll dress him up in bull's clothing, horns and all, and then we shall see what we shall see. As I believe it was your own Joe Louis who said "He can run but he can't hide." Read that in a book way back when. Anyway, then us women, The Girls from Turnabout—I like that; you know, The Boys from Syracuse, The Girls from Turnabout—all dressed up in the elegant, swish, bullfighter drag, we'll go at the bullfighter dressed up in bull drag. And we'll see how that grabs him. Go at him with pics and poles and swords, and at the end, of course, because we'll be sticklers about the whole sacred ritual, we'll have the stabbed bullfighter's body dragged out of the arena, same as the bull, by horses. And as we stand before the crowd receiving its thunderous applause, one of us will be holding up high his genitals, his cock and balls, which we've cut off instead of his ear. Mmm. Should be a really dynamite show, I mean, I can see ticket sales literally in the thousands, can't you? What do you think, Captain?

—They've been holding kind of secret meetings and discussing revolution and communism, he says. —We're pretty sure the leaders of the group are in touch with the Spanish Communist Party here.

—Kind of secret meetings . . . just how would you do that, I wonder. Half in and half out of a basement, perhaps, or maybe they whisper during half of the meetings, the secret stuff, and talk normally the other half. Hmm.

Interesting tactic.

—Your mind is no longer in touch with the real outside world, he says, getting up from the couch in slow motion. —What worries me is how a person in your condition can discharge her duties as a mother. He glides out of the room and disappears into the back of the apartment.

I have the weird sensation of seeing this in a movie. It really is like a movie, one of those Godard movies. Now that makes much more sense. This idiot situation isn't real after all. It's a fucking movie. Well, thank God we finally got *that* cleared up. Boy oh boy . . . for a while there . . . talk about close shaves . . . wow . . . I don't even know this jerk, except that he's an actor who auditioned for this role and got it. Same as me. That goes for the two little spooks playing our children. Hollywood brats. Of course. They've been little hoofers ever since they were born, acted in more movies than you can shake a shtick at. And now they're playing in this one. Wonder who their real parents are. My heart goes out to them. Which reminds me, where are those two fugitives from central casting anyway? Oh yeah. That swimming meet at the base. Bluestone's kid is in it too. "He's a lot nicer than I was at his age," he told me. "I was so competitive I was an incipient murderer."

Mmm. I can feel his tongue on my cunt now, from the last and second time we fucked in his office. Ahhh Jesus. What a fantastic tongue. I've been eaten a lot in my time. I've had more tongues in me than they had in the Tower of Babel. But none of it compares to his. A tongue for all seasons. He really put his heart into it, none of your dip and run tactics for him. How did he get so good at it? Must have practiced a lot, trying out all kinds of different techniques before arriving at his present four-star cordon bleu style. Gee, maybe I could do a public testimonial commercial on the subject. Decca Records, would you please stand up and tell the assembled multitudes precisely what features of Dr. Bluestone's diving tongue set it above and apart from other tongues of your experience? I'd be delighted to, Your Honor. Bluestone's tongue has a tiger in its tank. I beg your pardon. A tiger . . . Precisely, Your Honor. His tongue has growl power. Both growl and power. Secondly, it has the courage to be free. Oh, indeed. The kind of tongue this country needed to open up the West. You got it, pal. Thirdly, it is not burdened with the mistakes of the past. Aha. I presume you mean by that that it is not weighted down by historical guilt. Bingo for you again, Your Honor. Fourthly, it is not afraid of the unknown. Hmm. A fearless, inquiring spirit, would you say, to be placed in the company of Galileo and Newton? Right on the nose, sir. I couldn't have put it better. And finally this tongue knows that a cunt in hand is worth two in the bush. Ha! By that you mean that it does not spend itself in idle speculations but, instead, gets right down to the suck of the here and now. Bravo, Your Honor. A perfect score! Allow me to present you with this autographed, in-depth photo of The Tongue in action. Full fathom five in my own divine deep.

Ohhh . . . that smell, that Africa smell is coming back. Oil and sweat and dust and rich jungle smell. My hand is shaking. "I won't shoot this innocent man! I don't care what you say!"

My God. I shouted that. Or Fall shouted it in me. Oh Christ. Push it out of my head. Push hard, push hard. Think of something else. Somebody else. Make up a story, quick. My hand is shaking again. Glug, glug, down goes my Pernod. Mmm. My head is leaving me. Quick. OK, I've got one. Something is coming through. I see a peculiar kind of boy, surrounded by very old-style people, in some Middle European country. The beat in me is changing. It's like I'm calling forth one of those children's stories or something. Like book illustrations are coming alive. It's coming in now.

A t twelve, when most boys are still tasting their mother's milk, Yeozel was already middle-aged and a maestro. Leers, winks, chortles, and whinnies—these advanced garnishments of the soul were second nature to him. His bemused, undersized agate eyes did not look at you but around you, and his walk, which in others his chronological age was part hop and jump, was the very essence of stealth and weightlessness; by some special arrangement with nature, he seemed not quite to touch the ground. His clothes—ach! who could have conceived, who could have stitched, such garments but a maddened Rumpelstiltskin! Even the dogs in the village were elevated by them. But enough of this. The central thing about Yeozel was that, with the invisible aid of his older sister Galina, he was the town procurer.

—Whatever your needs and dreams, he would say, —I can fill them for you. Tall, red-haired women with swinging hips, fat-breasted ones with delusions of sanity, black ones with wild eyes and blood-curdling screams, insatiable blondes more than willing to break new ground—they are all at my fingertips. There is not one inch of commercial flesh in this town that I don't know about. Just call your friend Yeozel.

And at all hours of the night too; he was no kosher absolutist. He knew that passion, like genius, has its own exotic timetable, and no amount of howling is going to change it. Perversions among members of the identical sex were the province of his sister Galina. One side of nature's street is enough for any man.

No one knew anything of their origins. They had simply appeared one day in our village, when they were both little better than babies, having wandered here from heaven only knows where, and they had survived, in their own way, by the most imaginative and devoted scavenging.

The favorite gathering place of our local sports was the Perfunctory

Abattoir, a restaurant of Babylonian odors, a bar of varied and unchastened flow, and healthy-sized wooden tables where, without breaking his neighbor's ribs, a fellow could indulge in a hand of pinochle or write to a wealthy cousin for financial aid. There was also a certain amount of music to be had, if you felt you needed it, and the splendid thing was that whatever the tune or instruments, it never offended the customers who had not asked for it. The decor was in the way of dimming oak, and the high walls ungrudgingly supported portraits of many of our national heroes. Here and there in the air would suddenly appear the high, lyrical laughter of the waitresses, like wreaths of wildflowers borne on the wind. It was here that we would see Yeozel.

The men treated him with what can only be described as a style oddly compounded of awe and throaty laughter. As a child he was not to be taken seriously, as one who knew and satisfied their weaknesses he was hated, and as one who seemed to exist on an abstract level, having apparently no vice of his own except principle, he was viewed as inhuman and therefore incomprehensible. They played with him endlessly. —What do you do at night, Yeozel? one of the sports would roar at him as he rested on a little stool near the bar.

—Count your blessings, he would answer, grinning lewdly.

—Who do you sleep with? shouted another.

—The memory of my childhood, he replied, slapping his leg with his black cap.

—Where do you hide all your money? bellowed still another.

In a giant's earl and Yeozel, giggling wildly, rolled onto the floor and spent himself in a spasm of self-delight.

A chap in the back, an owl-eyed fellow with a big mustache that looked as though it had been stolen from a circus performer, began pelting Yeozel with the small, scented rolls the Perfunctory Abattoir was famous for. —You'll end up in a pigeon stew one of these days, the man yelled, and the whole place exploded with delight.

—At least I'll taste good, Yeozel yelled back. —That's more than I can say for you, you Gorgonzola.

Now someone at the table nearest him, in a setting totally committed to the gassy fumes of beer, grabbed Yeozel and in a whirl of arms tossed him through that flatulent air to another roisterer at the next table. In another few moments Yeozel had been converted into a game of catch, and you could not hear yourself think, so great was the noise and heartiness of the players. There seemed no possibility of Yeozel getting hurt or taking offense: as a poem can be interpreted any number of ways by any number of people and still retain its insoluble identity, so Yeozel's organism could collapse and elude, melt and give way, disappear into its own smile, when faced with hard wood or animal hostility. I swear, he did not even make a thud the one or two times he landed on one of the tables instead of in a man's outstretched, drunken arms.

—Why don't we ever see his sister here? Shoyl at my right asked, gulping down a water glass of our local red wine.

—Yeozel thinks this atmosphere would corrupt her, answered Aba, the piggy-faced butcher who came here directly from his shop every night and stayed until it closed. —Besides, she has not time to play. She's devoted to her work.

—She'd have to be, ventured Levi Zagursky, the wolf-toothed bachelor who sold tombstones. —Why, I'll bet you that at this very moment she's snaring a dimpled, blue-eyed girl for that stinking old hag Madame Mindl.

—Or bargaining with a truck driver's helper who has caught the eye of the one-eyed Baron. Oh Lordy! Remember what that prizefighter did to the Baron and his apartment last spring? An absolute shambles. You couldn't identify him or the place. And this man, middle-aged Egon, pockmarked and glistening with the special, dank moistness of the denied and the unrequited, squirted a stream of spit and tobacco toward a spittoon.

The game with Yeozel ended with one of our fellows bearishly hugging him and exclaiming for all to hear, —If it weren't for you, you little hyena, I'd be in prison for molesting my granny. A few moments after this touching testimonial, while Yeozel was resting again on his little stool, one of the glistening, fuming crowd decided that he had to have a half-Chinese girl with black hair down to her navel, otherwise he would surely perish before the night was over. Yeozel was off like a whistle to execute his task. In our most graced village the voice of carnality was more frequent and far sweeter than that of the mourning dove, and not a soul would have had it otherwise.

Early one spring evening, as long pent-up rains, withheld for hours like the tears of an injured innocent, began sweeping over us, delicious in their young wetness, exuberant in their abandon, a stranger appeared at the Perfunctory Abattoir. Now, strangers are nothing new to us; travelers have for centuries used our village as a place of rest and refreshment, and in the words of an old housewife, not an apple complained of the eating. But this stranger was different. You knew immediately that he was not stopping en route; he was simply stopping, and you wondered why. It took us just a few critical seconds to realize that this man was not a traveler, but a hunter: he was not going anywhere, he was looking for something.

He stood just inside the tavern and looked us and the place over, most intensely, before selecting an empty table in the back of the room to sit at. Outwardly, he was not too exceptional; his clothes were of the kind worn by men who live in the open, not behind sooty windows; he was not large but he was tensely built, or athletic as a city person would say; his lined and heavy face was tanned and even a little on the handsome side, but when you looked carefully it disturbed you because it was not a face at all: it was merely an expression of fathomless hunger.

But it was to his eyes that one's apprehensive gaze was irresistibly drawn. They emanated a quality of simultaneous rage and surprise, as if all of his life he had been reading the same novel wherein upon turning the page for the climax and resolution of the story, the spectator's reward, so to speak, he was presented, not with words, but with a white sheet drenched with blood.

The conversations in the big room resumed after a few moments, the lull that had been now gently closed itself like a wound; but only the deaf would have been oblivious to the false tone of the drinkers' words: against their will, they were listening, not to one another, but each to the timorous beat of his own heart.

—How have the rabbits been running? one of my fellow drinkers asked me, looking into his mug of beer.

—Wonderfully, I lied. —I snared two just this morning. Fat ones.

—Nothing beats a rabbit for good eating, he mumbled into the beer.

The stranger called the waitress, and this girl, who had been known and adored by us for her saucy, bold spirit, approached his table hesitantly and stopped a few feet from it.

—Brandy and beer, he ordered in a loud voice.

This was a combination unheard of; you drank one or the other: drinking them together was like going bathing with your clothes on.

—But sir . . . the girl began.

—None of your back talk! he roared. —You heard my order.

—Yes, sir, she muttered and retreated as if she had been whipped.

Within half an hour the man drank off half a dozen of those powerful brandy blasphemics. Then he looked around the big tavern, from table to table. —Where's the procurer? he demanded.

No one stirred or replied. Then, in a few moments, as the place was gripped in a vise of silence, Yeozel got up from a distant corner. —Here I am, sir, he said respectfully.

—Come over here! the man shouted.

Yeozel walked slowly across the room, everyone's eyes following his progress, and stopped at the edge of the man's table. —Yes, sir?

—Is it true that you can procure a man anything he wants?

Yeozel looked down at the floor before answering; at that moment he was undoubtedly asking God a favor for the first time. —Yes, sir, he replied, lifting his eyes.

—Good! and the man slammed his hand down on the table.

An unnatural and frantic smile appeared on Yeozel's prematurely aging face. —What can I get for you, sir? A blonde with black eyes and hips that would make you weep? An Arabian girl with breasts like mountains? A fat woman who adores to be beaten?

—No! None of that garbage.

Yeozel's eyes now glistened feverishly, and one could almost hear him pant as if he were running. —I know! Twins! Identical twins! I have these two French redheads . . .

—No! the man shouted, hitting the table and upsetting his beer chaser. —I want a sixteen-year-old virgin who has never been seen naked by another man. She must have short, curled hair the color of midnight, eyes that reflect the drowning sea, and small pointed teeth that seem to have been stolen from a fox's mouth.

Yeozel stiffened, and his face turned white. The rest of us, our drinks suspended between the table and our mouths, looked anxiously at one another.

—She must be able to sing in the language of the woods people, the man went on, downing a tumbler of brandy and following that with a draught of beer, —and she must have a beauty mark in the shape of a crescent in the inside of her left thigh.

Yeozel looked like a dead man whose eyes have not yet been closed. The man had described his Galina.

—Well? the man shouted after a few moments of stark silence. —Do you have such a girl?

A little life, or something like it, came back into Yeozel's face. —I . . . don't . . . he stammered, putting his head to his mouth as if to catch whatever other words might tumble out involuntarily.

—You don't what? the man roared. He pointed his finger ominously at Yeozel. —I have come all the way across the country to see you because of your reputation. He looked around the big room, and the controlled rage in him charged the atmosphere with crackling vibrations. —And if I do not get what I need (he slowly drew from his coat an enormous black revolver) not a man here will live to see the sun again.

Yeozel's position was horrifyingly clear: present the man with his sister, very likely the one person in the world he loved, or be the cause of the death of all the men there. It was not that the men were necessarily cowards; because they had families, operated the shops or ran the farms, they represented the life of the village, not only the throb within their own skin. Yeozel's dilemma immobilized him. He would have remained rooted to that spot had not two of the men shaken themselves free of their own paralysis, walked across the aghast room and brought him back to one of the tables.

The distressed men hunched around Yeozel and poured out their pleas and arguments and threats and terrors. Though there was absolutely no need for discretion or secrecy—does the moon think, for one second, that the sun does not know of its nightly trips?—the men nevertheless kept their voices down to a whisper; and this absurdity compounded the situation, giving it a smell one usually associates with babbling old ladies. Finally, Yeozel got up and went to the stranger's table.

—Very well, sir, he said, bowing slightly. —Just as you wish. Please accompany me.

The man let out a shout—more of an animal's cry of pleasure, really—and they left together. Strangely, the sounds of their departing footsteps seemed to be walking across my face.

There was very little sound in the tavern after the two had departed. What mumbling occurred was in the form of fragments of soliloquies; no human exchange seemed possible in that void. The men finished their drinks and left, one by one. Within half an hour, the tavern was empty, the first time in its long history that such a thing had happened. It would be most revealing to know which of them slept that night.

Only one person in our town ever saw Yeozel or his sister again, the rabbi. Yeozel appeared at his small house on Dalnetskoyer Street in the middle of the night, and he was covered with blood.

—Rabbi Pakovsky, he said, kneeling at the holy man's feet, —I killed that man.

—Who was he? the rabbi asked, putting his hand on Yeozel's bowed head.

—He was my father.

—May God have mercy on you.

Yeozel explained, before he left forever, that he had not known this before killing the man. He had discovered it when going through his pockets after watching the man ravish his sister. There was nothing to indicate that the man knew the girl was his daughter: some mystical power of the most indecent sort had shaped his desires and led him to this place.

This happened just a year ago, but already our town looks like a shrunken shell. Most of the people have left it, turned their backs on themselves, so to speak, and journeyed to settle elsewhere. Day by day symptoms of its fatal illness appear: a dying tree is blown over in a mere breeze, the well water turns green, the fruit is poison to the tongue. And the birds, formerly one of the delights of our countryside in their variety and exuberance, are now to be seen only rarely, and always flying alone. Not until I saw that, always a single unaccompanied speck in the sky, did I understand the old saying regarding flying birds: "One if for sorrow, two if for joy."

S eize this picture: high cheekbones, low character. Lofty looks, basement behavior. Well-bred smile, ill-bred thoughts. Who is this masterly Rembrandt-style portrait of, friends? The colonel's wife, natch. She has a classy, airtight, almost condescending way of walking. When we see her in walking action we just know she is heading for the queen's coronation; or for a meeting of the board of directors of the *National Geographic* magazine. Those superior, light-blue eyes unflinching, steadfast, undoubtedly are focused solely on matters of high quality. That look of hers . . . one immediately recalls Balboa gazing out over the infinitude of the newly stumbled upon Pacific Ocean.

Oh yeah? Here's that holier-than-thou, my-shit-is-chocolate-ice-cream broad in the existential grease pot of action.

—There are simply no two ways about it, she says to the bald man in the black turtleneck sweater. —Suarez must be disposed of.

The man's smooth, chubby face contorts. —What do you mean, "disposed of"?

We can't see those exquisite Queen-of-the-May blue eyes behind her black, black shades, but we know they are there (we will bet money on it). —Killed, she says.

The man makes one of those Spanish gestures. —Killed? That is very strong. He has a family and all of that sort of stuff. Why can't we just perhaps give him the warning, or perhaps punish him with a smart fine? Would that not . . .

The colonel's wife looks straight at the man as she sips her glass of dry sherry. —Killed, my friend. He broke one of our laws. He stole from us. A kilo of hash which he attempted to sell himself. We trusted him as one of our couriers. We took care of him with good money. She sips carefully. —He betrayed our trust. That is unacceptable, Danzig.

The man Danzig makes another very Spanish gesture. —But, señora, he is my nephew.

She "fixes" him, as the expression used to be, with those black, black shades. She is highly skilled at not moving a muscle. —That fact is of no relevance in this circumstance. She sips. —And when I say killed, Danzig, I mean that the body is not to be found. Absolutely. Now she permits a slight lowering of the strict surveillance of the muscles at the sides of her mouth. The slightest of smiles appears. —He must vanish forever into the sea of your ancestors. To our utter amazement, this smile is permitted to widen. —Yes, I quite like that. The sea of your ancestors . . . That's rather like saying that he will be swallowed up by the collective Spanish unconscious.

Our man Danzig of the turtleneck simply looks at this imperial woman. We know that the Jungian reference she has just made is both outside his ken of knowledge and outside the ken of his interests. He just doesn't give a shit about that sort of thing. We know that he is thinking now what he allows himself from time to time to think: how much he would himself like to knock *her* off and take over her reigning position in this very lucrative drug-smuggling operation. But Danzig is not dumb. He knows, and of course we know too because of our privileged position in this whole shebang, that he stands about as much chance of swinging this part-time dream as he does of becoming the archbishop of Seville, shall we say. These most eloquent odds, however, did not discourage Danzig from frequently projecting, in his most private of screening rooms, a short, lyrical flick of his lady boss. As one would surely expect, she is the star of this flick. He plays her male lead. The costuming for the production presents no real problems: she is dressed as a nun, he as a priest. And the sets do not tax the budget (as is so often the case in these home movies, because the shimmering, pulsating producers simply cannot control their appetites). There is but one set and one scene (another cost-cutting idea, conceived within the admonitions of none other than the Great Director Himself: "Bring your movies in low an' you're in business till the cows come home"). The scene, the set: the radiant, gold and silver and marble and red velvet altar of the Cathedral of the Virgin Twat. She is kneeling before him at the altar as he chants, in a truly gripping voice, from a sacred text. It is a rich, deep, throbbing moment. But . . . slowly she begins to raise her head, for the sacred texts suddenly have become outrageously obscene. Not only that. Her head is not the only thing that is rising at the glowing altar. She has almost straightened up—though still on her knees, mind you—when her gaze is captured—seized!—by what we might term the hypnotic motion beneath his chaste white priest's skirt: slowly, majestically, like a primeval animal awakening after a winter's sleep, a hard-on was rising there. It kept rising and rising. And rising! And as it rose, so rose the Bach organ music that until now had been lying low in the background. The hard-on was monstrously lifting the priest's skirt up and up, and the organ music accompanied and surrounded this awesome phenomenon with wild leaps and demonic spinnings. The giant hard-on is now emerging from under the stunned raised priest skirt. It is about three feet long. She, the colonel's wife/nun, in a full-bodied spasm of fear and religious umbrage—there are visions and there are visions, right?—throws back her hands and head and screams.

Which is just fine by the super cock. It grows through the scream-filled air right into her mouth. And then it begins to devour her. His mammoth prick has become a thick, writhing pink python and she is sucked/chewed into its enormous serpent mouth. Slowly she disappears into its swelling, lewd, muscular coils.

—You seem to have gone into a trance, Danzig, she says. —And why on earth are you licking your lips in that disgusting fashion? Are you all right?

Danzig blinks his eyes and quickly downs the glass of Fundador in front of him. —Everything is just fine, dear lady, really just fine. I was dreaming about what I was going to do with my share of all the fine money we have made on this last fine run.

We must not be unsympathetically critical of Danzig's use of the word *fine* four times in two sentences. He is hard-pressed to make sense at all, because not only is his cool, elegant boss sitting across from him, acting like a fucking general in the Falange, but she is also still in the stomach of his big hard-on down below. So you can see . . . Or, how many of us here could . . .

Another small, condescending smile from Boss Queen. —Well, don't spend it all in one place, as we used to say in the States.

A man whose face is gentle but whose hair, red, is raging and writhing down to his shoulders strolls into this hidden, or at least out-of-the-way, café. The sudden sight of all this crazed red hair abruptly reminds the colonel's wife—behind those implacable black sunglasses that would seem to reflect/rebuff any intrusions into her head—of a "red" letter her husband the colonel in charge of base intelligence had intercepted on its way to a certain soldier stationed there. She had come across the letter while making one of her regular secret prowls through his intelligence files just to keep on top of any developments in his office that might relate to her hobby, as she liked to describe, to herself, the Africa to Spain to France drug-smuggling operation she ran. She had found the letter, actually a photocopy, in a folder marked "Sickle," her childish husband's code for politically subversive material. She knew—he often chatted, more to himself than to her, about his base intelligence work, as he would have chatted about clever backfield maneuvers had he been a football coach, or different kinds of bricks had he been a mason—his "team" (his word) had sniffed out a bunch of "commie punks," "raving reds," on the base and were surveilling them morning, noon, and night. Intercepting and copying all mail addressed to the several members of this "subversive" group was, of course, a standard procedure. The colonel and his boys were collecting evidence preparatory to moving in one silky night for the kill. So "red" for letter, "red" hair, the latter springing the former to mind. So the letter . . . it had been written to a Sergeant Claude Somebody by a Juliette Somebody, from Paris. The name Juliette had truly caught her, because way, way back in youth's heady flower, she had played that role in a school production of Shakespeare's half masterpiece. She had, therefore, read the stolen, we could even say violated, letter with an almost personal interest. More than that. She found herself getting into the character of the woman Juliette. That is to say, seeing or feeling her as a role to be played. Reading the letter was to take on somewhat the ways of Juliette's persona. She had loved those carefree years of playacting on the stage. Mmm. The letter, she made it her own. It was in her bones. She could recite it line by line:

"So gradually, bit by bit, we are getting it together here. Organizing people has been tough, because in a sense Americans living abroad feel that they are living in a political vacuum. They feel they are just spectators to the political struggles of the country they are sojourning in. An understandable failure of vision and political intelligence. We—Stephan and Carol and Gilbert and myself and a couple of others—have had to convince people of the need for solidarity abroad and that they must see themselves as participants in the world struggle. What this means is we have had to push people into reexamining their identities, their notions of who they are and just what it is they are up to. In other words, we've jostled them into an existential crisis. You might say we've backed them into a corner of their own ego room.

"We meet once a week, in a room of the University of Paris VII, over in the Marais. A friend who teaches in the American Studies Program here managed this for us. We discuss and analyze political developments in America and Europe and try to figure out how we can most effectively relate ourselves, our energies, to specific problems and projects here in Europe. One of our main concerns at this time is the increasing viciousness of the right wing in France, Spain, and Italy. They are attacking the Left constantly, and of course they work hand in glove with the fascist political police in each country. You certainly must see this in Spain where you are. The obviously right-wing, police-directed bombing of the Café Mola in the Plaza del Sol in Madrid, for example. Here in Paris, and also in Rome where Stephan and Gilbert and I spent some time recently, they attack peaceful demonstrations, create disturbances and incidents which they hope will be blamed on the Left, and have even tried to murder members of the Left.

"It is clear to us that a good deal of their vile work is coordinated not only through the political police but also through the CIA, which, as you certainly must know, is crawling all over Europe like lice. We are also aware that these unspeakable and shitty fascist police groups are employing Americans to do their dirty work at times. Two such American flunkies are at work here in Paris. We haven't identified them yet, but we will and when we do, oh boy! what a time we'll have.

"Did you receive the magazines I sent you? How does your own group progress? Are you hassled by the army assholes? Have you been able to make contact with politically progressive Spaniards in Cádiz? I know of two excellent people there. Their names are Carmen Alfau and Juan Portrero. They live at . . ."

The colonel's wife was so deeply into Juliette through the letter that she was with her now wherever she may be in Paris. She was feeling the chill of the morning air as it came in off the Seine and into Juliette's studio on the Rue de la Huchette. She just knew that Juliette was pulling the down comforter up over her bare shoulders for protection. Juliette's hands were moved by hers; and Juliette's murmur, willed so powerfully, so sympathetically by the colonel's wife, gently wakened the simple, lovely studio room high up on the fifth floor of the ancient building. She could watch the Seine from her window. She really loved this room. It was a delicate poem from her own inspired, elegant and, oh indeed, very strong hand. Many short-necked, rat-eyed oafs mistakenly believe that the word *inspired* must absolutely, as acorns are inevitably followed by squirrels, as creeping poachers are inevitably followed by panting game wardens, be followed by the word *fragile*, or *delicate* or *unreliable*, but that just shows how full of camel shit they are, and that's why it was so easy, while he was still alive and breathing, for the Naz to fix their bucket. OK. This sweet, idyllic room has been wakened by Juliette's murmurs (all the way from Spain). It takes this murmur unto itself, unto its bosom, as it does also the almost painfully sensual, leisurely yawn that soon floats after the murmur. Now the sensitive room awaits the First Words of the Day. The room holds its poem's breath as it waits for the First Words. Come on, Juliette! The words!

—We must destroy this village in order to save it, she says finally.

What? You don't mean that. There must be some mistake, you cry. Bullshit! There is no mistake. That is exactly what the lady said. What's the matter with you liver-lipped, redneck, sexist bastards? You think that women can't say complicated and stunning things, and particularly for openers? Must they always be mouthing such pusillanimous shit as "Oh dear. I absolutely must see my dressmaker today. These seams are killing me." Or maybe you lunks prefer something like this: "My oh my, Mr. Frothingham. What a long, red tongue you have. All the better to eat me with, I presume."

Idiot garbage like that, eh? No wonder you guys are still sweeping the floors in Plutarch's Pizzeria. What was that? Up my mother's ... Step outside and say that. I dare you.

The room is still trying to pick itself up off its own floor, when Juliette says, —There is no significant evidence that fallout from U.S. atomic tests will be hazardous either to people now or to future generations.

Whoopiee! How do you like those apples, Granny? Think you can make some tasty cobblers from them? You've abandoned the kitchen for primitive painting? Oh. Yes, Rosa? The switchboard is flooded with calls, is it? Thousands of people canceling their subscriptions? The Friends of Aristotle Society is claiming that basic principles of reality are being jeopardized? Fuck 'em all, Rosa. Lousy buncha deadbeats. Where were they when Galileo called for help? Yeah. A lotta good that does him now.

As the ineffable and, on record, irreproachable room reels and tries to collect its wits, our Juliette, naked as the first three bars of *Don Giovanni*, slowly rises from her understandably cozy bed and steps slowly to the floor-length windows facing the Seine. The room trembles with unconcealed desire for her uncontaminated, unequivocated voluptuousness. It would be more than happy to devour her/absorb her in a tear-jerking, final curtain-dropping act. Tough titty. Life has other plans for Juliette. She throws open the balcony doors. The sanity of the Seine, a fundamentally conservative family-orientated river, has seldom had its sanity so challenged. The fucking thing almost stopped flowing. Woman Revealed shook it to its very roots. Not since the birth of Venus—remember the awesome moment when she sprang from Botticelli's forehead?—has anything like . . . Radiance floods from our Juliette's noble and succulent breasts, her candid yet inscrutable cunt, her roiling, turbulent but, in the final analysis, unapproachably serene belly. . . . The tiny light-brown hairs surrounding her sweet, sweet belly button . . . She opens her excellent mouth, a mouth that . . . and . . .

—Recognition of the Supreme Being is the first, the most basic expression of Americanism. Without God, there could be no American form of government, nor an American way of life.

Well, I suppose that takes care of your plans for the weekend, right? You wonder what? Whether such a woman could be trusted as a mother in the event . . . Oh wow. It sure as shit doesn't take any great genius to see where you're at, vis-à-vis any human events beyond the Dark Ages. People like you should have their ID cards withdrawn. That would certainly make you think twice about trying to force your lousy two cents' worth down decent people's throats. You don't fool me for a minute. You'd have our dear friend J. fling the windows open and flood the fuckin' city with "Columbia, Gem of the Ocean." Know how long it would take the North African slave laborers cringing or loitering here in Paris to scrub that shit off all the beautiful money-making public buildings? About two hundred years, that's all. What's that? Same to you, Jack, and many of 'em.

Christ! The time you waste trying to talk to meatheads. All that baloney about keeping the dialogue open. Yeah, sure. Keep it open and those swine will drive a ten-ton garbage truck down it.

—I'm beginning to feel that any social revolution will have to bypass the lower middle class, the petit bourgeoisie as you call them. They're utterly impenetrable. They're immune to any ideas of collective good, or change, or spiritual awakening.

They're not my words. They were spoken by Juliette, who, I'm sure you will grant, is above suspicion. She said them to our very handsome and substantial Germaine LeClerc. After Germaine's class at the University of Paris VII. Germaine nodded her auburn head. —I'm afraid I would have to agree with you.

Do you see how fluidly things can move when two people with brains and breeding have a go at it? Don't you just want to bite yourself on the ass with pleasure? OK. Back at the window . . .

The entire city of Paris, its panoramic self, gamboled erotically upon Juliette's finger-lickin', lip-smackin' nakedness. The Seine went ape, and poured into her pussy. The infamous Cathedral of You Know Who threw itself upon her soaring boobs, sobbing hysterically. The Palais-Royal had no place to hurl itself but upon and all over and then up her saucy, shimmering ass. And Looie the Fourteenth, the Sun King, stood on the Petit Pont and barked like a dog. Mollify him? With what? Give me liberty or give me death! he howled, looking at the wrong page. Oy vey! Have you ever?

Juliette ultimately decided to turn away from the window. Enough is enough awready. Any longer would necessitate urban renewal. Now for a shower, that's the ticket. Announcing those three despicable statements made her feel good all over. It's very important that the whole world hear them. I refuse to let them hide on the pages of books that nobody reads, or on official pieces of paper buried in vaults in Washington, D.C. Should plagues be kept secret? Should the death of seas be suppressed? Once a week the loudspeakers of the world should be ordered to play chapters from *Mein Kampf.* Once a week all of the television sets of the universe should show Auschwitz and Dachau and My Lai and Hiroshima and the bombed and napalmed villages of Vietnam and Korea and all of the American Indians massacred by the United States Army.

And once a week every single piss-faced American schoolchild should be required, as should their teachers, to stand up and recite a list of the American crimes against the human race. Starting with those loathsome, scabby, long-nosed, self-loving Pilgrim assholes who murdered the Iroquois as happily as if they were knocking off turkeys.

Quickly now! Imagine an unencumbered, unpremeditated, brilliantly *uncompromised* animal in the jungle abruptly pausing, in whatever it is doing, just to think things over. Holding there, suspended in self-silence. If I take a shower, she thought, I'll wash off Stephan. He's all over me. I can still smell his smell on my body. I can still feel his hard prick in my cunt, raging there. And his tongue, licking me and licking me up and down and around in my armpits and my ass twirling and in my cunt whirling and swooping, darting, luring and pulling me, drawing me, *tonguing* me into suck-flooded spasms of coming, coming with his mouth over my cunt twisting and heaving, coming into his covering, sucking mouth, disappearing out of myself and into him, I came into him, my being, my whole self became my orgasm in his hot mouth. God, it was marvelous. Last night.

She broke out of the self-enclosed moment laughing. My God! I'm floating around in Stephan's mouth wherever he may be at this moment. If I'm not careful he could bite me in half as he eats his croissant. Or I could drown as he swallows his *grand crème.* His own *grand crème...* there must be half a pint of it in my stomach. What a big comer he is. Jolting spurts of hot, sweet come.

She does not spare the hot water once she finally decides in favor of the shower that obliterates. Urgent, intense hot sprays pour over her delighted, juicy body. She watches the gallons of shower water swirl and gurgle down the drain at her feet in the shower box. Just so much water under the bridge, she says aloud. That sounds like . . . that is . . . a place? Pictures that have been hiding and breathing under other pictures of other places start appearing in her head. Old-fashioned road sign . . .

Just So Much Water under the Bridge, Alabama

Voices: —. . . scared a their own shadows. Then there are folks that don't have no shadows. So they're scared of other things. That kind, though, they pretty much stick to theirselves. I don't see too much of 'em. But I'll tell you, that don't bother me.

Another fella here says, —I don't believe in askin' questions where there ain't no answers. That's a cardinal principle of mine. 'Nother one is, I don't believe in stickin' my nose in places where it won't fit.

'Course, more than a few diehards do, though, and as a direct consequence, you might say, they're always in the shop gettin' their noses refitted.

Time ain't stopped up here in these willy-nilly hills. It's just takin' a breather. You hear that? Long as your watches keep on tickin', you ain't got nothin' to worry about.

Maybe you've seen 'em—there's a whole string of people round here who're up to their necks in time an' wouldn't have it any other way if you ask me. Every chance they get they're lickin' up to it. Time we got started! they'll shout outta the blue. By George, it's a long time since that's happened here . . . Time and time again the town council's been put on notice . . . There'll be a hot time in the ol' town tonite . . . Just in the nicka time . . . Holy Hannah! Makes your head swim. Know what I think? I think that if you was to scratch around a little, an' I don't mean just under your arms, go over to where they hide the town's vital information, y'know, or maybe read the fine print on summa those old gravestones, why, you'd discover that all these time nuts are really brothers under the skin. That's right. An' now that I seem to be headin' in that direction, I don't mind goin' one step further an' sayin' that there's a better'n even chance you'll discover that they're all the same brother. Uh huh. Maybe you'd like to sit on that fer a while an' see iffin it'll hatch. Meantime, I'll just . . . Ho there! Damned if it ain't Carrie W. Beadle. Carrie, you ol' female-wrapped scallion, whatcha been upta lately anyway?

—I been keeping my nose clean and close to the ground. I've been keeping my desk cleared and my ears cocked. I've been keeping a stiff upper lip and running a tight ship. I have not been resting on my oars or my laurels. Neither a lender nor a borrower have I been. Nor have I been permitting my left hand to know what my right hand is up to. To put it simply, you old poop, like everyone else in this historical stasis, I haven't been up to a damn thing.

Ho ho. You always was a funny one, Carrie. Even when you was knee high to a grasshopper, you stuck your tongue out an' kicked high. Yessireesir, ain't nobody can accuse you a hidin' in a corner.

—And certainly no one can accuse you of being full of anything but baloney. Why a Harvard graduate and retired corporation lawyer, with a vast personal library attesting to his cultural sophistication, should decide to metamorphose himself into a classic, archetypal hillbilly is completely beyond me.

Hee hee, ho ho. Fan my brow, Carrie, if you don't put on as good a show as anybody kin find up here. Damn me, Carrie, iffin you don't belong on the stage with those purty speeches of yours. Pullin' down big money. Yessireesir, as the Lord is my . . .

—I've got to shove off. I can't spend all day explicating your profoundly obscure solution to existential angst. If your late and eminent father Judge Birdwhistle could see you now he'd have a fit.

Lordy, lordy. Have you ever in all yore borned days heard such fancy prattle? Whooee. Carrie's a good woman, fine and upstandin', but she's crazy as a bedbug, an' that is the truth uv the matter. Now I gotta poke my head in here for just a second to see if Doc Fossie's got my blood tonic perscripshun ready.

Name-callin' and hog-callin' are cherished activities here'bouts. Some people call them sports, whether rightly or wrongly is a question that eventually must be clarified by a rigorously ad hoc committee whose one and only item of business will be The Morality of Taxonomy, or Taxonomic Morality, or Morals and Taxonomy. And it should go without saying that each and every committee member must be on the lookout for his own taxi. You can't count on the two above-mentioned activities taking place at any particular time or with any particular order (any more'n you c'n look up at the heavens and expect your favorite hailstorm to descend). In so many words, they can bust out at any old time any old place. For instance . . .

Last Tuesday, 'long 'bout the traditional sassafras hour, Fred Boggs (his dad was the best darn game warden we ever had. Damn shame he had to go and lose it in a shoot-out with the best damn poacher we ever had, *still have*) came to a dead halt smack in the middle of the Dooley and Main Street crossing there—he was out walking his wife Dodie who was born with her eyes closed and decided to keep 'em that way—and shouted —J. C. Hamstringer, you ain't worth the powder it'd take to blow you to hell! You are a lyin', cheatin', two-tongued polecat!

Who's J. C. Hamstringer? Ain't no such person.

You want to hear some good name-callin', the best place to be is within earshot, or arm's throw, whichever suits your talents the best, of Big Harold's Hunting and Fishing—Guns, Traps, Lures, Snares, Hooks, Nets—Shop, and the same distance, because they're across the street from each other, from Toomey's Groceries and Dry Goods. For reasons that are either beyond town memory (on the one hand) or that are better left alone (on the other), that stretch of the imagination that lies between those two grassy roots enterprises happens to be the town's favorite name-callin' ground. And oh my, how the furriers do fly there!

—You are mean, lean, and green, Martha Dillworth! You are pinching, inching, and lynching! howled Emma Ludlow loud as she could.

And who is Martha Dillworth? Merely the regional director of the U.S. Small Business Loans Bureau, that's all.

Neck muscles tense, shoulder muscles bunched, thigh muscles straining, and arms akimbo if you will, Dubrow Walley—whose family is very well thought of on his mother's side—opens his big mouth and shouts —You listen to me now, Buster Willingham! You'd better stop spreading lies, rumors, vilifications, and reductio ad absurdums about me or else. Or else I'll be forced to expose you to the entire free world for the double-dealing, underhanded, overbearing, two-faced, loose-living, loose-boweled, scum-sucking pig you are. I'll start right at the beginning and tell everybody what you used to do in the boys' locker room once you'd got your greasy little hands on half a dozen or so pictures of George Washington's mother in the nude. I'll work my way up from there, you double-jointed, knock-kneed pecker wood.

You would be mistaken if you were to think we have not been asked, You folks give prizes for your name-calling, like you surely must do for your hog-calling? We have answered and we'll go on answering, Name-calling is its own reward. Hog-calling gets you only hogs. If you have trouble following that it's because you haven't been paying attention. Or because you're not in condition. Or because...because you're just too damn dumb to bother with. Makes us wonder what the heck you're doing around here in the first place. Could it be because you missed the boat?

If you can bear to think twice about the name of our town, you'll see why we think about history the same way it thinks about us. Takes two to tango, y'know, and history made the first move, long, long before we knew enough to keep a close watch on that ol' bitch. Too late now.

—The Declaration of Independence? Hmm. Let's see now...I know I've heard of it...Uh...Oh yeah. That was when the South announced that it was sick and tired of taking orders from the North, where a lot of uppity nigras were acting like they were free men and purposely letting their dogs shit all over the streets too.

Haley works half days at the Doobie Doo Beauty Parlor. What she does with the other halves of those severed days is none of your damn business.

—The Great Depression did you say? Sure. That was way back before doctors had microscopes, and some kind of bug was going around and everybody all over was catching it and getting very depressed, and acting funny in other ways too. They never did lay their hands on that damn bug. It was probably one of those Asian bugs that climb aboard their little banana boats just as they're about to set sail for the shores of our American free-enterprise system. It's a good thing we finally got our immigration laws going before it was too late. What do we need that kind of Asiatic folderol for, I ask you.

Wally owns, operates, calculates, and spawns in a gas station and general notions store, Wally's Come and Get It While We Still Got It. He married his boyhood sweetheart June Lee Potter late one March night thirty-two years ago and she hasn't been heard from since. However, you could not say hide nor hair of, because that wouldn't be true. Because we don't permit that kind of thing 'round here. Abattoirs are for the use of heavy-footed animals only, so you might as well save your breath. If you think that's the same as holding your breath, you're wrong. Same goes for holding onto your breath (which is what some people appear to be doing from time to time, 'specially when the weather gets that shifty look. Oh oh).

It's only natural, and frequently it's just as well, that the first thing that comes into an outsider's head when they think of a small town is cottage industry. (In the case of those who, on the other hand, think of cottage cheese, well, we must let bygones be bygones and refer them to their own Scandinavian ancestry.) Now, our cottage industry . . . Oh all right. To be more folksy, we'll call them cottage crafts, even though, and there's no getting around it, they add up to the same old thing, whether you like it or not. Our cottage crafts, unlike some we could mention, are off the beaten track. We don't turn out hook rugs, hook shirts, hook curtains, hook candy, hookworm, or hookers. Nor do we crochet, touché, or sashay. And we sure as hell don't bake, snake, slake, or crake.

OK. OK. Hold your horses. Want to take a gander at the craftiness in our cottages? OK. Come on down here and peek into this baby, the Plodgett family cottage. No busy little hands whipping up candy-cane models of the Bastille, or tiny square-jawed figures of our by-now disgraced national leaders in hand-painted chewing gum. Oh no. See the dark liquid in that small bowl there at Effie's right that she just dipped the little dagger in? Well, that's a real strong homemade poison that has been in the Plodgett family for generations. Over there sitting on that stool under the window is young Luther Plodgett, whose job it is to cut out and sew up the smooth, high-quality, leather sheaths to keep the daggers in. The Plodgetts' main market is south of the border where folks settle accounts with a flick of their nervous, dark-skinned wrist.

Down this well-wrought footpath a few yards ago is the Broadwater cottage, which was built long before simple, decent folks like you and me started taking to the air as easily as they took to the water. That red-white-and-blue peacock's walk on top of the cottage was put there by old Colonel Broadwater just before he took to the fire in the local waters for good. You don't have to stand on your tiptoes or any other of those extreme things to see for yourself that the entire Broadwater family, locket, stocking, and barrel chest, is up to its elbows in good, clean, old-fashioned, before-the-Fall, evenhanded American frontier enterprise, give or take a few slips of the tongue. What you can't see out on the back porch just isn't worth seeing. Knee-deep in that big pile of fresh cleaned flax and wool is sharp-eyed Granny Broadwater. See her hands swoop and dart! See her pick just the right pieces! Sitting there at the original, demanding, almost larger-than-life spinning wheel is Mother Broadwater. See her take the wool and flax from Granny! See her spin it into a long shiny rope! Sitting cross-legged on the smooth pine plank floor cutting the ropes into lengths is middle daughter Samantha Washington Madison Jefferson Broadwater, mostly and by common consent called Slammin' Sammy. See her measure! See her snip! Over there to the right of the hand-hewn stairs, which a whole lot more than a handful of sly city-bred people would like to steal and sell to a museum, you can observe Dad Broadwater and eldest son Barlow testing the length of lightly spun wool and flax. Oh, how they pull! Oh, how they strain! Those who should know say these are the best garrotes money can buy. The Broadwaters'll tell you that all their orders come from overseas, from European countries where things still are the way they used to be. But you can't tell me that from time to time they don't fill an order or two from an enterprising citizen of their very own country. Yankee spirit and ingenuity live on in somebody's pocket here or there. The unfeeling whiz of the machine isn't quite yet the only sound you hear in this country's air, no matter what some people are saying.

Down yonder—see where that tightly knit family of wild black razorback pigs is browsing and snowsing impervious to the slings and arrows of outrageous market fluctuations—hell, they couldn't care less—that's the old, and when I say old I mean old, original Horsefall cottage. That place was built long before anybody thought of turning a century, and you can bet on that. Why, you can't even tell where the vines begin and the cottage ends in some places. And that's not all. There are many odd, old words spoken inside there that if they were to fall on any ears you and I might know of personally, it just wouldn't make any difference or do any good. You couldn't even swallow some of those words if you had to. Well, come on.

Let's mosey on down there for a look-see. Better take this little old discarded but not forgotten Injun footpath that alas has never known the love of a footpad, give or take a couple of heinous ad hoc types passing through in days of yore or days of less. Cut through this overgrowth of wild angel's hair so's we can creep up on it from behind, because it isn't everybody that likes to have you look right down their throat no matter if you're a doctor or just a bona fide witch. Old Gran Horsefall wouldn't take kindly, I can tell you that. What kind of an artist would?

Now try not to trip over anything or fall down or make any ungainly outside-type noises. We c'n take advantage of this little known window here —my, how the creeping fuchsia doth creep over it—and see what we c'n see.

There she is, the last of the Horsefalls, having the last of the horselaughs, as she plies her merrie little trade. You can't quite see her face—and I c'n tell you, she's got some face—because of that big old bonnet she's wearing. When Gran croaks, her trade croaks with her, 'cause there're no Horsefalls left to carry it on. Some say that's all to the good, and others say it's all to the bad. Depends on which side of their mouth they're talkin' out of. Quality is uppermost here, no two ways about it. Materials and workmanship, they're the best. That shiny dark pile at her feet there, that's human hair. Just no substitute for it, Gran says. None at all. Please. Don't ask me where she gets it. Next of course is the way she braids it, and she's as careful as a cat creepin' up on a bird. She has her very own secret way of braiding. How her fingers do swoop! How her fingers do dart! And how her little green eyes must be flashing! If you listen real hard, you can just barely hear the little tune she's whistling to herself.

Gran's sleek slings are all destined for those peculiar, passionate countries you read about in the Bible. She won't bother with a domestic order no matter how hard you might plead once you're down on your knees. Save your breath. Want to know why? —Ain't a single damn soul in this whole damn country knows how to use a sling right. Think I want my creations degraded? Does Mr. Stradivarius want his violins played with a comb? Last person who could tell a sling from a saddle tramp was Daniel Boone, an' that's only because he was descended from Syrian goat herders on his mom's side.

Those were her very words. My imitation of her old mountain voice may not be perfect, but I'm not a professional. The real meaning's mostly in the words, as anybody knows.

You couldn't be farther from the truth—that's an old-style way of putting it—if you were to assume that there is only one kind of sling or slingshot. There's a sling or slingshot for every type of quarry, and Gran makes them all, you c'n be sure o' that. One for knockin' birds outta tha sky, 'nother one fur gettin' small animals as they're runnin' for dear life; 'nother one for big beasts that could be comin' at you, for instance, 'stead of the other way round. An' still another one for bringin' down human people.

These last are the ones Gran always tests before she ships 'em off to the overseas. Not herself personally, 'cause her slingin' arm just wore out over the long years. No. She has a workin' arrangement, you might say, with one of those strong young mountain boys—I think he's a great, great-nephew or somebody like that—from the huntin' families livin' way up near the timber-line slopin' and lopin' along with wolves, bobcats, an' hawks and other such that don't have any regular way of life as far as you can tell. This strong-armed lopin' mountain boy does the final testin'. An' I sure don't have to tell you or anybody else that there's only one way of doin' that, and that's on another human being. Anybody outside the town limits, in tha fields or tha woods, that is, after five o'clock, that person is fair game as far as mountain boy is concerned. Nobody gets back up after he brings 'em down. Klunk! He uses smooth, round stones he finds in the ballin' streams hereabouts. Now, as to what Gran pays him for his work, I just don't know. He could get paid so much by the hour, like folks back in town do—we don't regard these cottages out here with the dense overgrowth as really bein' in town—or he could get paid by the person. Your guess is as good as mine.

Now then ... Hey! See those bushes move? Somebody's foolin' around out here or been followin' ... Hey! Damn me if it ain't—lookit those kids skee-daddle—if it ain't that little niece of mine Juliette with her cousin Heber. Runnin' like they're rabbits. Kids. Damn if they're not all over the place when you least expect 'em. Takin' you by surprise. Humph. That little Juliette, she's really somethin'. Might as well take this other path back. We can go by the old footbridge which is filled to brimmin' with folklore and old wives' tales and all kinds of funny stuff like that. Yeah, that Juliette ... She left those bushes like a quail been flushed. Great day in the mornin'! What a wild, winged creature that one is. Ain't nobody gonna fence her in or make her toe the line or tell her what to do. Damn! I remember one day on Main Street she ran smack into me, she was runnin' so hard she couldn't see.

—Hey there, little lady! Where you goin' that you're in such a hurry?

—Not going anywhere.

—Not goin' anywhere?

—I just like to run. Running makes me feel good.

And then she laughed. And you know something? I'll bet she's still laughin', wherever it is she may be.

—And I am, too, Juliette said aloud in the shower. I'm laughing right now, while the hot French water pours over my head—why do I have the weird sensation of leaves being washed off me?—and over my breasts and belly, and floods through my pussy hairs, down my thighs, that can lock around or

not lock around, and down through the hair on my legs that I stopped
shaving three years ago, because why should I shave them? I like them this
way. And I love my armpits, full of primitive, good-smelling black hair.
Stephan loves to smell my armpits. Says it makes him very hot. Loves to lick
them too. Mmm. I can feel his tongue there now. Oh what a tongue, what a
tongue that demented, sweet man has.

—When I'm going down on you, my tongue is my entire self. I mean it.
Everything I am is in that tongue.

—Then a slip of the tongue and you might disappear?

—Absolutely. Disappear right up your wonderful, mythical snatch.

—Oh God, you're so loony.

—Would you prefer Louis Pasteur, or Thomas Jefferson, or, uh, maybe
Prof. Kurt Horst Wolfgang von Hochberger?

—Who's he?

—God only knows.

—And maybe even *He* doesn't know him.

—There's always that chance.

How peculiar that I should feel this shifty, ambiguous sensation of having
washed leaves or bits of forest stuff off my body at the same time that I'm just
plain morning showering. As though I have two bodies, one hiding within
the other. Leaves, twigs, grass . . . Have I been somewhere in a dream, that
other body of mine, maybe? Or it might not be a dream. One's body has a way
of experiencing déjà vu, or nostalgia, or longing quite apart from the control
of one's mind. For instance, if you had spent your entire teen years praying
on your knees as a novice in one of those obscure, half-homosexual monas-
teries around the Mediterranean, wouldn't your knees have deeply buried
within them, no matter what different lives you lived after you ran away
from that monastery, the memory, which might come and go irrespective of
what you are doing, of those kneelings on those stone floors? Of course.
There's no question about it, no matter what science says. But where have I
or my other body, where has it . . . Science, people think it's God or something, the poor dummies. People have been conned and duped and set up
and betrayed by terroristic technology, the very same way medieval man
was snowed by the brutal mythologies laid on him by the Church. But, oh
baby, did science get hers or his in Vietnam! A mere wonderful handful of
peasants beat American science and technology, weapons and electronics
and lasers and maps that think for you, the whole fucking mess. President
Johnson, how do you like your blue-eyed boy now? That beautiful passage,
read to us from Burchett's book the last night at Le Chop: "Prime Minister
Huynh Tan Phat stated 'The third error was that after Thieu lost Ban Me
Thiuot, he lost his head and ordered his forces to withdraw to the coastal
plains. But we had already cut the roads to prevent this. Thieu's strategy was

to consolidate at all costs in the coastal plains which meant abandoning Pleiku and Kontum and virtually the whole of the Central Highlands where the local people were rising up and taking things into their own hands. Thieu and his Americans could not foresee that each retreat or withdrawal, or whatever they wanted to call it, further demoralized their troops. It appears that their computers have no equations for moral factors.' "

That guy with the empty, pleading eyes, Brady, that was his name, he was a newswriter for some television company, maybe French television, he'd just come back from Saigon, and he said, —That whole crazy town collapsed like a termite-eaten house. Poof, like that. And all the people connected with the Americans and with Thieu, they were scurrying around the town like termites with the heebie-jeebies. Holy shit, it was a sight!

And Sikorski said, —Somebody ought to shoot that cocksucker Thieu. It wouldn't be so hard to get at him either. He's living in London, like nothing ever happened.

—Right, said Marcel. —Absolutely. Walk up to him on the street and say, Greetings from all the dead Vietnamese, and blow his dirty head off. That would be so beautiful. He lit his porcelain pipe. —And if his wife happens to be along, blow her stinking head off too.

I said, —What is really incredible is that the Labor government in London gives this mass murderer a resident's visa while it deports Philip Agee who's trying to help the human race by exposing the CIA. I mean, I can't believe it.

—The Labor government is a fraud, said Con, who should know. —It still sucks for America. He lit his little cigar. —Always down on its hands and knees sucking away, or taking it up the arse, one or the other. Really shameless. Makes you absolutely want to puke.

Con hopes to become shiftless and self-sustaining at the same time. Supporting himself doing something simple but expert, like teaching English to businessmen or dealing hash. Maybe a little of both. He spent a lot of time at Oxford, and he would like to undo that here in Paris, being shiftless, in his quiet, irreproachably elegant way. Perhaps one could say that elegance is a form of shiftlessness. Right now, it seems, Con is making out on money sent to him by his landed-gentry father in England, who pretty much goes it alone these days because the mum, it seems, up and ran away with a traveling madman one day, long after she'd gotten her fill of by George this and by George that and middlemen on the floss or something. Ran off like my own wonderful mother with that Peruvian poet, a luminous little man whose eyes told her more about the mysteries of the Andes than any five TV documentaries. "He sings," my mother said as she fled. "Your father snores."

—We'll ask as many writers as we can think of to come and read, Pierre is saying, as I watch the clochards lying about in a cluster over the métro grating in the middle of the Place. —There won't be any problem about getting the bookstore. George is always glad to help out. Of course, he gets mileage from these things. He loves to rub elbows or whatever with writers. He's got the hots for writers. We'll ask the people who come to make a fifteen-franc donation, and we will assure them that every penny will be turned over to the Vietnam Aid Committee.

I say, —You can be sure that at least one representative of the American Embassy intelligence community will be there.

—Oh yes, of course, says Diana. —And at least one member of the French intelligence.

A fumbling, stumbling, blurry, baggy clochard takes his prick out—it's funny, but one never thinks of bums as having pricks—after an interminable searching among his many layers of rags—he has at least two topcoats on— and pisses between two cars. A blotto, miserable street dog wanders up and puts his head under the stream of steaming yellow piss.

—... collect fifty dollars or so, Sikorski is saying. —That amount will buy a couple of little diesel motors the Vietnamese can use for pumps or something.

—They're such amazing people, says Diana. —Simply amazing. They will inherit the earth.

—What there is left of it after America finishes poisoning it, says Con.

—Those two comic-strip characters at the table near the door, are they real? I've seen them before . . .

Of course she is referring to those two formidable guardians of France's slumbers, Inspector Jean Pierre Epernay and his on-the-ready assistant Georges Leger. Leger is listening in his best manner as his boss tells him the score.

—No doubt you have observed what can only be called their abusive jollity, eh? says Epernay.

—Well, uh, "abusive jollity," did you say?

—The kind of jollity, my dear Leger, that abuses itself.

—Aha, says Leger, bending forward and nodding his head at the same time. —So what these chaps are up to, then, is self-abusive jollity. Isn't that sort of thing in violation of the morals code, sir?

—You are running away with yourself, Leger. I urge you to pull in your reindeer. What I mean is, they are abusing the right to be jolly.

—By being jolly, says Leger, his voice taking on a certain furtive quality, that quality that rabbits, for example, have when it dawns on them that this is going to be their very last Easter. —The rats at hand, sir . . . Gnawing away at the roots of decency planted so long ago in France by such champion gardeners as Voltaire, Madame du Barry, Charlemagne, Rabelais, Maurice

Chevalier, the great Sarah Bernhardt, Charles de Gaulle . . .

—Listen with all of your ears, Leger, and try to apply that professional intelligence that the French Interior Intelligence Service has spent so much of its hard-earned money attempting to ingrain in you.

—As you wish, Inspector. The question of . . .

—Put your fork down, Leger. There is nothing on this table to eat. Good. Perhaps it would be better if you held onto your glass of Burgundy with one hand and a Gaulois with the other. In that way your hands will not be so eager to wander in a way that compromises your professional training. Have I made myself clear, Leger?

—Oh, yes. Quite clear, sir.

—Now, getting back to gnawing rats at hand . . . Attention, Leger. You almost took a puff from your glass of wine.

—And the Church, Leger almost shouts, carefully drawing on his cigarette while obviously fighting a confused urge to sip from it. —One must not forget the decency roots it has been planting all these years, even if you are not inclined to kneel on its cold floors.

—Yes, of course, my dear Leger, says the Inspector, wetting his own whistle with some Burgundy. —But those are very different roots. And we are not sure these self-satisfied, utterly depraved rodents—just look how they are grinning at each other!—are gnawing at those church roots, however sweet they may be.

—And they are sweet, Inspector, very sweet indeed. Why, just the other day . . .

—Look! They are passing a secret paper around. Undoubtedly it is a pornographic poem written by their glandular misfit master Karl Marx! Oh what brazenness! What nihilistic cynicism! Just listen to their lewd giggles, Leger. Take the cotton out of your ears, my dear boy, and get an earful of those godless sounds. Especially the unspeakable, wanton sounds issuing forth from the redheaded she-devil with the large, arrogant breasts that know no bounds even when the bottoms are about to fall out of everything and everybody! Oh, Leger, cross yourself, good clean son of the church that you have always intended yourself to be! Cross yourself as you permit yourself to imagine, if only for a second or two, what naked bottomless pits would open up in the world if these wet-lipped communist filth-lovers ever took over power! Cross yourself, Leger! I command you!

—I am doing my best, Inspector, but it is difficult, as you can see, because I am holding my glass of wine with my right hand which was put there by your specific orders, sir. However, if you will permit me to release the glass of wine for a moment, I will . . .

—That howling woman's name, Leger, is Diana Bukowski. Stamp a picture of her in your heart next to the picture that is already there of the Virgin

Mary and the one of your own dear mother, Leger, because they are opposite ends of the same slippery pole. Diana Bukowski, aged twenty-six, born in Warsaw, Poland. Father a dyed-red-in-the-wool communist engineer. Mother a wealthy English left-wing ne'er-do-well with fierce galloping breasts which she clearly handed down to her lascivious daughter who is even now planning the end of the world that you and I both know and love so dearly, Leger. She is oiling the gates of hell, my dear boy. Diana Bukowski, graduate student at the University of Paris VII, preparing her doctoral thesis on women migrant workers in Europe between 1950 and 1960, working under the supervision of another antichrist named Professor Alberto Pierinni, a dago provocateur who slipped across the border one faulty night when our Lord and His angels were sleeping at the helm, having been drugged by a conspiracy originating in the Moscow Kremlin.

—My God.

—Yes. This woman, this flaming overheated huntress leaping through the only too oily gates of hell followed at her flashing naked heels by her loyal pack of insatiable, sex-crazed Marxist Leninist wolfhounds singing the "Internationale," fully prepared to eat you up if you are not willing to get down on your hands and knees and lick their hammers and their sickles. Yes, this carefree demon of a woman, whose vital measurements are 36-32-34, whose smooth, strong thighs could easily make you scream if you were somehow to fall between them, measure 24, whose seditious, devil-may-care behind, which could any dark day be sitting in the fine face of the president of France if their vile revolutionary plans succeed, this arrogant whirlpool of sensual criminality measures exactly 42 inches around . . .

—But, mon Dieu, Inspector, with all due respect to your overtowering police tactics, your absolutely doglike, I mean dogged devotion to liberté, egalité, and fraternité as they rule unmolested today, and I cross myself for both of us thusly with both my arms, with due respect, sir, how is it that you know these intimate measurements of this lewd, godless terrorist's body?

—Aha, Leger! Such a question reveals that in your heart you regard yourself merely as a part-time employee of the French Counterrevolutionary Task Force. There is more to one's profession than a monthly paycheck and all of the earthly breakable trinkets it will buy, my dear fellow. Permit me to inform you, Leger, that you should regard your profession as the sacred void into which you most happily must hurl yourself hoping to fill up the void with your total, around-the-clock presence and dedication. Which morally superior facts bring me to the exquisitely and compromising intimate details of this Bukowski woman's body and the acquisition thereof in order to fulfill the above-mentioned void, Leger, which void, sir, because we have taken our manliest vows within it, is therefore your void and mine crawling toward Bethlehem as we all must, both high and low! Do you hear me, Leger!

—Absolutely, sir. But it is not necessary to shout at me. I am not deaf, Inspector, and we are as anyone can see sitting a mere foot from each other with our shoulders, that is.

—In view of which doomed crawling toward Bethlehem, Leger, which must come to all men as they sniff the tracks of the Devil as I have been with said Diana Bukowski, in such selfless sniffing, in order to get everything on her I could, including my own two proud policeman's hands, with which, I might add, I am always trying to hold back as best I can the tides of evil which at every moment these modern difficult times threaten to flood our noble French society. What I am exposing to you, Leger, are the professional secret tactics whereby I captured those elusive details of Miss Bolshevik Bukowski. Wherein I disguised myself as a seamstress in a shop on the same street as her very own sly studio apartment.

—Am I hearing you correctly, Inspector? A seamstress?

—Precisely! A seamstress! A bent-over little old lady in clothes to match.

—You are shouting again, Inspector. People are looking at you. As your subordinate, I feel it is my duty to recommend to you that you get a grip on yourself.

—To hell with that! I am getting a grip on her!

Leger reached across the table with a napkin and gently wiped the froth from the Inspector's trembling mouth. —Of course, sir, of course. I quite understand. But we mustn't let ourselves become overexcited, especially when faced with the climax of our police ingenuity, sir.

The Inspector leaned across the table. He did this in an odd way, as though he were a giraffe stretching for a tasty leaf high on a branch. He whispered, —I am her seamstress, Leger. Once a week, disguised as a Madame Benoist, in official pursuit of my quarry, I take this red she-devil's most intimate measurements. Let me assure you, Leger, that when you have with your own two bare French hands measured a bosom, a behind, a knee, a thigh, when you have done that, my boy, you have, as a servant of the French Republic slaving in the great tradition of Philippe of Lorraine and the Grand Inquisitor, become part of your subject. You know what makes them tick. You have crawled inside their skin!

—Good Lord.

The Inspector grabbed Leger's lapel. —I know this bomb-building woman, this creeping, lewd, red menace to the sacred shoreline of La Belle France and her already crowded public beaches! I have had my inner ear attached to the pulse beat of her soft inner thigh. I have heard the ravaged scheming in her ravishing bloodstream, Leger, the pitiless plotting in her private parts, to such a degree, Leger, to such a degree that they have become my own! And it is thus I too who have harbored these havocs, assumed the criminal position, and naturally in so doing have exposed myself to the always imminent possibility of being arrested myself!

—Oh sir! I implore you. Not that. Think of your family, murmured Leger, seizing the Inspector's hand as if to stay that hand before it could seize its owner and place it under arrest.

—Yes, Leger, the possessed Inspector continued, his face fixed in the tranced, beatific expression of a penitent who is meeting himself coming around the corner, —it was I as coconspirator within her skin who not three days ago was seditiously loitering—yes, that is the only way one can as a policeman describe it if one is to be true to the purity of one's calling even if one is referring to oneself—in the cafeteria of the Bibliothèque Science Politique on the Rue Guillaume in the invidious, anti-Christian company of one Monsieur Martin, an editor of the famed house of Gallimard no less, a man who is to honor, political, social stability and the Arc de Triomphe what Judas was to loyalty and friendship. Yes, there I was, within that soft, voluptuous, cruelly amoral skin, and it may as well have been myself saying, —It's simply astonishing. The Jews, of all people, are becoming the new right wing in the world. Every fascist alleyway seems to have a smiling Israeli in it. I was just reading an article by Chomsky on the Arab-Israeli thing, and he said it's known that the Israeli police have been training those vicious bastards in the Iranian secret police, SAVAK.

—Ah yes, says this Monsieur Martin. —I've heard that also. But of course this makes sense. The Israeli professors of counterrevolutionary police savagery helped to educate Thieu's thugs in Saigon, and they showed the Ethiopian fascists a few special tricks, and just the other day they came out and admitted that yes, it is true, we have been giving graduate seminars to our new friends the South African police scum.

She smiles, my half-Polish, half-English devotee of chaos and social disorder, whose body is filled with tasty meats as I, being inside her skin, only too fully know, smiles and says to her friend Martin, who, as I have so previously pointed out, is the Judas worm in the proud apple of French culture, —What an irony that the survivors of gas chambers should be helping to build them all over again.

She nibbles on her ham baguette sandwich. He lights his pipe and pulls at his ear. He could be Herod, but he is not. She could be Charlotte Corday, but she is not. And all that is just as well, as any sane historian would be only too glad to tell you if you were to approach him rather than some dirty bum in the bushes who would be busily masturbating all over the records of the past, upon whose good graces we all of us must depend for our daily bread and butter if we are to escape the tyranny of word-of-mouth rumormongers who in their piecemeal wonderings are only too happy to proclaim that Adam and Eve were really two salacious chimpanzees.

—The Arab-Israeli confrontation, says this self-satisfied rascal, puffing on his pipe as though it were his idea all along to build the Suez Canal, —has brought together all of the right-wing groups with all of those basically dishonest and fearful people who call themselves liberals but who are really status-quo reactionaries, when you peel away their camouflage. These liberals, they are always dangerous, you know, because they act so nice, like they are members of your very own family. He puffs his pipe. —They want to play at social change as they play at everything else, you know.

Diana nods. —Oh yes. They can read Marx over their champagne. They can talk about the sacredness of the family while they're fucking their lovers and mistresses. She laughs (we know how people laugh who are half English and half Polish. It is not a secret, this kind of laugh. Oh no). —And of course they're fucking them in more ways than one.

Probably at this very moment, she says to herself, my father, for example, is fucking his nice, frightened little secretary Gerda in the small study behind his office in Cracow. And my brother Gregor is still fucking all of his good-looking students at the University of Warsaw, while his wife undoubtedly is not fucking *her* students at the medical school. And my boss at Grasset is trying to persuade me to do some fucking for him while his wife stays at home with their three children in Versailles, going bughouse. There are so many more too. Claude who owns the gallery where Thérèse exhibits. He is fucking at least two of his clients besides Thérèse while his faithful, fat, dumb wife sweats as a translator for UNESCO. The list could go on and on from here to eternity. But here next to me is a lovely, very attractive and very sexually alive man who does not fuck anyone but that marvelous woman he is in love with, Germaine LeClerc. How ex . . .

—And those same liberals have also joined the right wing in attacking Vietnam and Cambodia. They all repeat the same untruthful garbage about conditions there. You know, they were always very uncomfortable during America's invasion of Indochina. While being very pro-American basically, they were against the invasion on "humane" grounds, but at the same time they were against the social/political revolutions in those countries because those revolutions threatened the comfortable myths by which they live. Now that the war is over they can shout what they have always wanted to shout: Dirty vicious bloody commie dictatorships and such liberal nonsense as that. Now, they are pro-Israel for the simple and awful reason that they are anti-Arab in the worst, racist way. They deeply feel that Arabs are inferior human beings like niggers. Their skin crawls, I'm sure, when they think of an Arab touching them.

Diana throws her red head back and laughs and laughs. Martin sort of laughs. A pipe-smoker's laugh. The laugh of a man who has been around but who does not make of this fact a gala, one-man evening's entertainment. Or anything like that. He would not use this place in place of something else.

For example: he would not go to Maxime's, eat a huge, expensive meal, smile when presented with the bill, and say, "I've been around" instead of paying up. Oh no. Nor would he, for instance, upon being asked politely for his passport by a thin, underpaid failure in uniform, as he crossed into another country, shake his head and proclaim "I've been around" in lieu of coughing up said document. Of course not. One of the many advantages of having been around is that you know better than to pull such shit on anybody.

—Oh my God, says Diana.

—Precisely.

—It really is so true. The genteel liberal is terrified of being touched in any way at all. By an idea or an emotion or by a person. Particularly a person of a lower social class.

—Even the language of the liberals has moats in it.

Diana sees hordes of naked black and yellow and bronze and reddish people swimming, struggling, mostly drowning in thousands of moats as they attempt to reach castles from the many windows of which haughty elegant men and women, also naked, make gestures of disgust, loathing, fear, panic, and superiority. A good many of them are giggling hysterically. Some, whose faces might have been familiar under less strained circumstances, are making obscene gestures at the struggling, drowning hordes below.

Diana switches her gaze from this tableau of absurd horror and looks at Martin. There is no obscenity in his face. No looks stained with shit, no hints of lewd violence. It is a completely handsome face. Something engaging is happening in it always. Unlike so many faces that are abandoned, dead labyrinths in which, even in the best of times, merely second- or third-rate schemes against humanity were hatched. Presences lived in Martin's face. Presences bearing messages and episodes which you crept into and—your hands are not in your pockets as you do so—become a part of. And Diana heard these presences speaking in and out of the experiences that created them.

—But we can't do it tonight! a voice shouted. —The Bosches are all over the place. We'll be caught for sure.

Another voice: —Tonight is the last chance we'll get. They're taking the freight trains into Germany tomorrow, and all the men on those trains will die in Germany.

—Shit! There'll be killing tonight.

—Those fucking Nazis! I'd like to kill them all.

A woman's voice: —The Russians are doing a good job of that. Thank God for them.

Germaine LeClerc's voice: —Let's decide now what we're going to do. Are we going to take hostages, or should we just kill the Germans? We must decide that. I am for taking hostages.

Martin's voice: —Yes, so am I. But the hostages must be officers. It won't do us any good to take ordinary soldiers. They're expendable.

—Oh those fucking Bosches! Someday, someday . . . I want to kill them so bad my hands shake.

—We've got to get some tobacco. I'm going crazy for a cigarette.

Memories of childhood refuse to be subjugated by the compromises of the adult consciousness. They speak a different language and it is not accessible to policing. The activities within these quite autonomous memories are sustained by utterly different laws and principles. And it goes without saying that the people who live in them are immune to decay.

The inviolate childhood place that Diana persisted in seeing herself in was a village that shimmered obscurely in the south of Poland. Tultz it was called and Tultz it shall be. It was a village for the nose. Smells of roast goose, smoked sausage, blood pudding, dried fish, freshly baked pumpernickel and rye bread, these smells, and many others, seized the nose and made off with it. Using one's nose for other matters of a less immediately gratifying nature was a tricky business, and at times it was well-nigh impossible. (An intoxicated nose cannot be counted on, for instance, when the chips are down and the fur is flying.) Diana sees, and feels, herself skipping and tripping, sometimes hurrying, sometimes scurrying, down the soft, fragrant streets of Tultz. To run an errand, to see a friend, or simply for pleasure. She is dressed in an immutably quaint style. There is absolutely nothing "stylish" or cheap or insincere about her clothes (or costume). There is no sociological opportunism, nor any vain, careful, even fastidious pushiness about her getup. She would have fitted beautifully in one of those drawings that illustrate children's fairy tales (long after one has discovered, totally on one's own, of course, that they are quite a bit more than that, that bony, tight-lipped, self-appointed censors and translators had disguised, rerouted, suppressed, and sometimes eliminated entirely certain meanings and messages, whole layers of involvement, that would have made childhood substantially richer, more interesting, less feebleminded and smelly).

Everyone in Tultz is friendly and yet fascinating. Or if not that, politely possessed, in one way or another, that is. No one, as Diana can see it, is merely a blank space with a voice. They all seize and hold your attention, in such a subtle, instantaneous way as to pull you into their tableau, as it were. (Thus, one might say that while one is observing the tableau, their tableau, one could be, at the same time, observing oneself. Which is odd.) Besides which, or perhaps parallel with which, every one of the citizens of gentle, cozy, shimmering Tultz is a "character," as in a play. Decidedly. And that's exactly the way they all act. (Though they are none of them in the same play, an essential fact which must be kept in mind.) Diana sees herself scampering/flitting/darting in and out and around these characters and their airtight plays.

—Will it be hot-cross buns this morning or hot crossword puzzles? asks Lazlo the baker. His grin is not all sugar and spice. It has innuendo and it has been flashed before.

Diana flips an imaginary coin of the realm. —Neither. Give me half a dozen black-cherry tarts, good baker Lazlo.

—Tarts for the goose are not tarts for the gander, says Lazlo. —And it is a wise child who does not forget that.

For all Lazlo knows, he is the heir to the Greek sophists' iffy mantle. When he is doing his early morning baking—so early that only he and the crowing cock know what time it could be—Lazlo does not schlumph about like an overweight deaf-mute. Not at all. He talks to the imminent cookies, cakes, rolls, pumpernickels and onion rings exactly as he would talk to a learned, eager, yet of course respectful audience filling a most desirable amphitheater. —Your moment of glory is approaching. I urge you to make the most of it. Let there not be a shirker nor a smirker among you. When you feel the first tooth sink into you, whatever you do, do not scream.

Later on, as his family hustles and bustles over breakfast, baker Lazlo stands at the window practicing gestures which he feels are appropriate to a man of his needs and hopes. His wife?

—Don't let the future go to your head, dear husband.

For a few moments, not a sound is heard but the clanking of spoons as the hungry young children go at their hot oatmeal mush.

Tableau! Tableau!

Diana sees herself skipping rope down Pilsudski Lane. She is wearing her bright orange babushka. The delicate, snuggy little houses throb happily in many colors—reds, greens, pinks, yellows. Eternally beaming plump housewives, The Good Women of Tultz, as they are widely known, are sweeping their porches, or scrubbing the steps, or washing the windows. Some are singing old, simple songs, reliable down-to-earth songs that have always done the job, as they work. Others are humming one standby or another. Still others... Diana is skipping past the Nowicki bungalow. Mmm. What a tasty little house, cute and crunchy. There is Marya Nowicki. Her mop may be in her hand but her heart is not in her work. She stands facing the east, beyond the Urals. Though her lips are pressed primly together, her expression is indeed resolutely lewd.

—Top o' the morning to you, Mistress Nowicki! Diana literally sings out.
—The air tingles! The birds sing! The grass crackles!

Mistress Nowicki's lips part in a faint smile. Around the corners of the mouth there a certain rarified, self-seeking poignancy appears. —None of which brings the strong-legged Volga boatmen any closer, she says.

Diana thinks fast (as she straightens her cute little handmade smock).
—Oh yes. We have read about the Volga boatmen in school.

—What you've read, dear child, is not the half of it.

Diana thinks fast again (flashing ear-to-ear grin) and dips into her inside pocket. —Have a gingersnap, Mistress Nowicki. It's just what the doctor ordered.

Red-haired Mistress Nowicki does not take her up on the offer. Instead (so to speak), she lifts her charming chin and begins to belt out the traditional, warmblooded song of the Volga boatmen. —Yo o heave ho! Yo o heave ho! . . .

The selflessly, flawlessly embroidered lace curtain of the front window is raised slightly. Husband Nowicki peeks out. He is famed in Tultz for his nose, which looks like a mushroom, and his finely honed instinct for survival. If his nose could be a mushroom his eyes could be black olives. Peeking out, he sizes up the situation. In that moment, before he can withdraw, we have a tableau! a tableau!

Diana sips her café and smiles as she sees herself continue on down Pilsudski Lane, skipping . . .

—You absolutely must read Jean Genet's piece in *Le Monde* on the Bader-Meinhoff group, says Martin, sucking on his tasty black pipe. —It's marvelous.

—Oh? What does he say?

The voice she immediately hears is not Martin's. It belongs to someone calling the little Diana in the bright orange babushka, skipping along another street in Tultz, her long, red braids gently swinging to and fro. This street is quite different from cute, cuddly Pilsudski Lane, where the houses are so yummy you could eat them, crunch, crunch. This other street has bygone charm and long-lost tastiness, but it is also oddly disheveled. One ancient wooden house in particular. Its front porch is wide and deep and not entirely blameless, and not entirely empty either. A funny-looking fellow is standing on it. And it is he who is calling, however gently, to innocent little Diana (or both Dianas, really).

Diana does not ignore people when they call out to her. She approaches the wide porch of the disheveled house. She does not know who this funny-looking man could be. He is smiling, but what kind of a smile is that? She says, —Good afternoon, sir. Do you know me?

—Oh yes, says the man. —But you don't know me.

—Who are you?

—Peelmunder, Socks Peelmunder. That's my name.

—Oh. I see, she says. —That's a very nice name.

—Do you like to hear stories?

—Mmm. I love stories.

—That's fine, he says. —Now, why don't you just sit down on the steps here, and I'll tell you a real good story. Thatta girl. Right there. Now then . . .

One careful, grey afternoon, when birdsong was checked in throat and breezes were apprehensive probes, Little Red Riding Hood's mother Irma, a clever, buxom woman whose eyes were, well, hardly telltale, was having a nip of the local grape with her boyfriend, an angular lout named Horst, whose very presence was no more or less than that, in the all-too-familiar family cottage. (Horst, by the way, was an unemployed actor, currently on welfare, who'd play any part you gave him as long as you spelled his name right.)

—The dirty old smell-feast left it all to the kid, Irma said, spitting out a pumpkin-seed shell. —She hates me down to her first fart.

Horst blew smoke rings into the easily gulled lamp-lit air. —Ah indeed. She felt you abandoned her dear son in his closest hour of need.

Irma banged the table with her glass. —That leaky basket case! The wretched bastard couldn't perform as a man the last five years of his life. What was I to do? Denounce my natural tickles like a hairy-nosed nun?

Horst grinned foolishly and dipped his own prolonged nose into the grape for some more of it. —Ah yes, he sighed. —Life's a dilly all right.

She laid upon him eyes tight with ingratitude. —A couple more cracker-barrel cracks, and you can find somebody else to jig-jig with tonight.

For a moment Horst looked like a newly captured fig smuggler. Tiny groans wished to express themselves. Then he brightened (slyly of course). —There must be something we can do. There must be.

—That's better. She lobbed a couple of pumpkin seeds at the wombat snoozing near the snapping fireplace. —You do read the problem in all its depth, I hope?

—Oh yes. 'Deed I do. And he snapped his fingers in a completely illogical gesture of comprehension (though this is not brought out to downgrade finger snapping).

For a couple of minutes they merely sat there mulling over the situation. You could have heard a pinhead drop. Horst's oyster eyes were pulsating in long-forgotten seas. Irma looked up suddenly and asked, —You're not thinking about fucking, are you?

Horst twitched and his facial actions became a rabbit chase. —Oh lordy no! Not me. I wouldn't cheat.

—That's good, she said, and settled succulently back in the oak and reed chair, —'cause I hate cheaters.

Horst was raising the wine to his livid lips when it came to him. His hand trembled and wine spilled onto his weak chin. —I've got it! Oh joy!

Irma sat up (and her tasty, unhaltered breasts jiggled juicily as she did). —Great. Lay it on me.

—The wolf. I'll play the wolf.

—You mean . . .

—Exactly. Just like in the crazy old children's story. People believe that stuff, you know, otherwise it wouldn't last so long.

Irma leaned back, spreading her ample bare legs for comfort, and grinned. —Well I'll be goosed by a one-eyed heretic.

Horst slurped off his wine. —It's so beautiful. I'll knock off both the kid and Granny, and you'll inherit all the bread as the kid's nearest kin. And everybody will just love the idea that a great mad wolf did the deed. Folk-lore always comes first, you know that.

—Love it. Wait'll I get my hands on that dough. She provocatively licked her full lips for Horst's raunchy benefit and slowly took off her embroidered peasant's blouse. —I think you deserve a little reward for such tip-top noodling. She cupped her luscious tits in her hands, pointing the dark red nipples toward Horst's open mouth.

—Oh mamma mia! he exclaimed hoarsely, and in another moment he was rubbing his face and tongue all over them while Irma grinned lazily with the tease of it all. —Mmm, she sighed. —Feels so good. Ooh baby.

Horst stood up and quickly tore off all his clothes. —Take off everything and walk naked in front of the fireplace. I love that part. His words were almost cracking up with passion.

Irma did as she was told. She posed this way and that before the fire, glistening in her vibrant, lewd nakedness, and slowly let her long, black hair down. Her smile was an abyss of complicity. Her body—heavy loins, thick black pubic forest that spread boldly to her lower belly, wide hips and muscular ass—made promises of wild, lustful pleasure which it could clearly carry out.

—You lika? she asked, putting her hands behind her neck and arching her body.

—Oh yeah, Horst whispered, his eyes flashing berserkly.

—My! Irma exclaimed in mock surprise. —What a large tool you have.

—All the better to ram you with, my dear.

His desires were brought to the exploding point as Irma ambled up and down before the flames for a couple of minutes, pausing to slip into deli-ciously obscene postures. Horst howled, and then they were grappling and screwing wildly on the animal-skin rug.

—Tell me what you're to do with them! Irma commanded in frenzy as she rode him. —Tell me!

And as they humped in all kinds of ways, good old Horst spelled out the fabulous details of the plot which was punctuated, nay counterpointed and precipitated thematically, by Irma's sharp, hot cries of delight and exquisite pleasure. —Give it to me, daddy! she screamed.

Little Red Riding Hood was dutifully walking through the forest on her way to visit old Gran, who, her mother had explained, was sick and very much in need of a visit from her granddaughter for whom she had such deep, swell feelings. An unannounced nip in the air suggested that she draw over her shoulders and belt around her body the red wool cape she so delighted in. Such a conversation piece it was! People remarked on it constantly, asking about its origin and meaning, whether the cape came first or whether she did, things like that. Little Red would murmur mysteriously, because the bald-headed fact was that it had no special meaning, or anything else for that matter. She had won it in a guessing game with a traveling hunchback. Simple as that.

In its pocket she was carrying a crafty little present for her granny: a bag of fried-rice balls cooked by her mother who had squeezed the recipe from a Chinese laundryman she had been spreading for a couple of low summers ago.

Little Red paused to pick a few wild pansies for Gran who just loved to sniff such stuff. (If the truth must be known, Gran was a flower freak.) As she was picking away, three jolly young woodsmen marched by. An unusual calm and sweetness exuded from their faces. This was due to the fact that all three had been formerly raving maniacs who had been lobotomized and castrated by order of the town fathers. ("Got to straighten you crazy kids out," they observed at the time.)

—Hi there! they sang out in unison. —You must be on your way to visit your sick old Gran.

Little Red looked them up and down, thinking they ought to be in a circus. —Yep, she said. —That's where I'm going all right.

—Want to see us chop down a tree? they asked, again in unison because that's the way it was.

—Nope.

—OK. And they marched away, shoulder to moronic shoulder. After a few paces they swung around. —Oh, they said. —We almost forgot. There's a big bad wolf running around. We just saw him.

—Yeah, yeah, she said, waving her hand for them to be off. —Some people, she muttered, and shook her head.

She was bending down to pick two buttercups when a voice from somewhere within the woods shouted, —Come on! Let's get this show on the road.

—All right awready, she replied automatically, without knowing why, and resumed her journey. (The buttercups could have winked, but we really don't know that.)

She hoped she would get back from Gran's in time to see the twilight hanging of a fat witch in town.

At Gran's, Horst, dressed in the wolf costume he'd swiped from a costume warehouse, was cozily tucked where the grandmother had been before he'd choked the living shit out of her just a few minutes ago. Broken-necked and not an aging whine left in her, she lay beneath the cute old four-poster bed. Horst was a scream in her nightgown and bonnet and specs. Really. As for the wolf drag, well, that fit snug as anything. He yawned and absentmindedly scratched his long, hairy wolf nose and mashed a flea there. The killing of Gran had pooped him somewhat, so he decided to get a little shut-eye. Little Red wouldn't be there a while yet. —If the boys at the theater could see me now, he mumbled sleepily, and dozed off.

He was awakened by the sound of the big front-door knocker. —Hey, Gran! shouted Little Red. —It's me. Your beloved little granddaughter.

—Come right in, you dear thing, Horst sang out in what he thought was the voice of an old lady. But of course no old biddy, no matter how mean and ailing, ever sounded like that. (Unless they had a drunken mouse caught in their throat.)

—I've brought you some goodies, Little Red said when she skipped into the bedroom. —And some wildflowers, knowing how much you . . . Why, Granny. What on earth have you been doing with your nose? It's so long and hairy.

—All the better to smell you with, my dear, said Horst in that goofy, cracked animal voice.

—Of course, Granny, all old things like to sniff their sweet grand-daughters, but that's not the point. And your teeth. Wow! They're positive fangs.

—The better to eat you with.

—Well, that may be going a little far, she said. —And besides, you know very well that nice folks don't say things like that. I mean, it may be done, from time to time, but it is kind of, uh, kinky. And mercy! Your eyes. They're so bloody red.

—The better to . . . Oh shit! And Horst, tired of the routine, leaped out of bed and tore Little Red to pieces.

When it was all done, and he was standing over the various bloody remains, Horst realized that that wasn't at all what he had planned to do. He'd planned to choke her to death in reasonably normal fashion, as he had dealt with the grandmother. Then he was going to work her over with an old ice-scraper to simulate fangs and claw rentings. But this . . .

—Something's wrong here, he growled, licking some blood off his big mouth. —Somebody's fucked up the script.

He wanted to get out of the wolf costume as fast as he could. He grabbed at the long nose to lift the head part off, but only succeeded in wrenching his neck.

—Oh Christ! he whined.

He grabbed at his stomach where the costume had buttoned up before. He whelped with pain because he succeeded only in tearing his skin. He grabbed at his hands, but there were none, only claws. Then it got to him. He had become a wolf.

—Oh no! he howled. —This isn't fair. And he bounded frantically out of the cute little thatched cottage and into the brooding forest.

For the rest of his days, and they stretched into eternity, he roamed the forests in an agony of self-arranged alienation, howling and sometimes just whimpering, —Oh no. This isn't fair.

Generations of picnickers and nature lovers who heard him, either in the gentle distance or in the tingling nearby, convinced themselves that it was the spirit of the last pagan chief, Grek, who had died ignominiously of a spider bite, rather than on the blood-drenched field of honor, and they would giggle nervously as they crossed themselves.

Phew! Glad we finally got that little matter cleared up. There is no place in the game of life for deadbeats, no sir. Which is precisely why hairy Horst had to get his. A freeloader with virtually nothing to recommend him. Except, perhaps, that he can at times summon up remarkable ingenuity in order to become nothing. A sordid talent, to be sure. I might as well say that my performance as Horst runs second to none in contemporary soul theater. Just take my word for it. Oh, I know what those other prima donnas are claiming. Pay them no mind. The world's full of sour grapes artists. They're not worth the formaldehyde it would take to embalm them. Fuck 'em.

Hold on just a sec. Martin wants to say something to Diana.

—I have had several photocopies made of Genet's editorial to send to friends in England and America. It is very important that his message be read, particularly by the American middle-class liberals. Because they're the ones who've been most deceived by the application of the word *terrorist.*

—They love the word, says Diana. —It thrills their tongues, like MSG. It has a kind of pornography to it in a political way. In a sexual context, it's like the words *cunt* or *prick* or *fuck.*

—If you are right, they'll never give up using the word.

—Will the word *fuck* ever go out of style?

OK. That's enough. Well, as I was saying . . . performances . . . yes . . . How often do we have the good fortune to be in on one? How many really first-class artists do we have around? Folks who'd rather perform than eat, or be eaten? Why, just yesterday I was talking to Captain Ahab, one of our all-time greats, give or take nothing. Know what he said? —Quality is slipping, he said. —It doesn't matter the way it used to. I was working out with this whale last week—'cause I've got this road show now, ya know—and I had to say, "You know, pal, I've worked with some great whales in my time, but you're not one of 'em. I mean, your heart isn't in your work, and I'm not kidding. So you better shape up or ship out." You'd think that whales are all the same. But they're not. No indeed. Same with chimps. Take it from Tarzan. I ran into him in the steam baths just a couple of days ago. —How's every little thing? I asked him. —It's been better, he said. —Oh yeah? What's up? —Those fuckin' chimps, he said. —They're just not comin' through for the act like they should. Half-assed, that's what they are. These new modern-day chimps don't *believe* in what they're doin'. They don't believe in anything. It's the disease of nihilism, that's what. Nihilism has polluted our jungles.

That's really heavy stuff. When the fish in the sea start talking back, we're in real trouble. But I'll tell you something. It isn't only in the animal world that funny stuff is going on. The world of the arts has been infiltrated by all kinds of base complications, one-dimensional menaces, high-wire perversions, poison-pen chain letters, crassly stuffed ballot boxes, crudely stuffed cabbages, listing entrepreneurs, drafty dodgers, ambivalent impersonators, heavy-handed two-timers, cross-eyed back slappers, and bleary-eyed garter snappers. Show me a piece of fiction and I'll show you a bunch of characters who've chiseled or bribed their way into existence.

—You don't know who you're rubbing shoulders with these days, Raskolnikov said to me over the weekend. —Hordes of shameless, pushy types who don't have the decency to remain buried in the very well-defined empty spaces that destiny has designed for them. Phew! It's enough to make you want to have a long talk with the Grand Inquisitor, and that's the truth. I've told Feodor as much on a number of different occasions, both when he has been in his senses and when the poor man has been out of them, it later developed. It's really almost for his characters to tell when he's possessed and when he's normal, if one can even use that word. If he isn't having those perfectly awful epileptic fits . . . dear God! . . . the screams and the frothings! . . . he's chasing frantically after some wanton's booted feet. Or he's losing every ruble he owns plus a few at the gaming tables. I've said, —Dear Feodor, please sir, beloved master, get up off your hands and knees for a few moments so that we may have a decent discussion about matters of considerable importance to both of us.

—Pfoo! he has exclaimed. —You worry too much, my dear boy. And he has remained there on his hands and knees, which may be a position of penance or one of depravity, God only knows which.

—But sir, I beseech you. Something must be done about the malevolent infiltration of poseurs and nobodies into our world. This is a scandal of historic proportions, sir, and it is entirely up to you and other maestros like you to deal with this scandal now, before it becomes a veritable deluge and can be dealt with only by God. Entire populations of villages, towns, cities, will soon be disappearing into the pages of fiction. And how do we explain this disgraceful phenomenon, to what can we point a finger and say, There is the cause of this unnatural exodus? Industrialization, scientific technology, and absurd and cruel demands of the corporate state, that's what has separated modern man from himself and made life on the outside increasingly if not utterly unbearable. But however tragic this may be, master Feodor, it is no concern of yours nor of your fellow writers. This problem belongs in the hands of the Church, whose business is the saving of souls. Let the Church earn its pay envelope for a change. Force it to live up to its obligations in this time of crisis as modern man teeters on the brink of The Great Abyss. Meanwhile, my esteemed sir, it is your obligation to stand at fiction's gate and, with all the firmness and courage you can muster, shout, "No! You cannot come in!" Do you hear me, sir? Even though you are still over there in the corner on your hands and knees barking and groveling and going at yourself in some crazed fever of desire or remorse, I know not which. Even so, you have ears. Say something! I beg of you to stand up!

—Pfoo! he cried. —What would you know of the ecstasies of self-abasement? You are too young and callow, too wet behind your eardrums. You have not earned the right to hate yourself. You haven't lived long enough. Guilt, yes; that you're entitled to. And self-doubt, which if you play your cards right, will surely lead you to feelings of unworthiness. But self-abasement, self-degradation . . . oh no. They're simply not yours for the asking, my boy, like ordering a plate of hot borscht. Give yourself time. Sin, fall, suffer, grovel, spend your free time in the quarries of hell . . .

And with that the old maniac threw back his head and howled like a wolf on location. Imagine it! A grown man, with a family, and some standing in the community! But then, that exhibition of obscene howling is absolutely nothing compared to his behavior not long ago with my friend Grushenka, a character performer of formidable talents. Among her major credits is *The Brothers K*, which, in my opinion, she ran away with. Well, what the old goat did with her! —May the good Lord have mercy, said Grushenka to me. —I have seen a lot of kinky behavior in my time, she said; —I haven't exactly lived my life among children and nuns, as we say in Petrograd. But this crazed old buffoon Dostoyevski . . . Chaphoo! He strains the imagination, I can assure you, Raskolnikov my dear. He's something more than God had in mind. Well, it all began when he dropped by my lodgings on Karkov Street without asking in advance if he might make a visit, because I want you to know that my door is not open morning, noon, and night to any chimney sweep or droshky driver who gets an urge to fall in. Anyway, there is Feodor Dostoyevski standing—really cringing—in my parlor pleading with me to appear in a new novel he is planning. —You must do this for me, Grushenka my glorious one, he said. —I implore you.

—But I am already up to my neck in a novel being written by your colleague Mr. Gogol, I said. —Surely you can find someone else, Feodorovich. I can think of half a dozen talented women characters who would jump at the chance to work for you.

—No, no, he whimpered, wringing his hands. —No one will do but you, my divine eagle. Please, Grushenka. The whole book is doomed if you don't agree to be in it, he howled, and fell to his knees and grabbed me around my bare legs, because I was only half dressed, you see, at that time of day.

—Ivanovich Feodorovich, please! I shouted at him. —You must not let yourself go this way. Come now, I said, tapping him on his head with my hairbrush. —Pull yourself together.

—I'm in a dreadful fix! he cried. —I've been given an advance of a thousand rubles on this book by my publisher and, oh dear, Grushenka, I've lost all the money at the crap tables! I'll go to jail if I don't write this book! And the slobbering old thing gripped my thighs so hard I thought they would break.

—Oh what a bad, bad fellow you've been! I heard myself yell at him.

—Yes, yes, he sobbed. —I've been a terrible, naughty fellow!

—Indeed! I cried, tapping him harder on his head with my brush. —A disgusting fellow. Did you think you could get away with such a low, dishonest thing without being punished?

—Aaiiee! he howled, pushing his weeping face into my thighs. —Vile creatures like me should be punished to the fullest extent. Aaiiee!

—Absolutely! I felt compelled to shout. —Otherwise, without punishment, the crimes that . . .

—Grushenka, my sweet avenging angel! I demand that you exercise your citizen's obligation to keep our community clean! I demand that you spare me in no way! The whip! The whip!

—Precisely! I cried. —The whip it shall be, you dirty, heartless criminal! Pfoo!

It so happened that I did not have to go far to lay my hands on the instrument of discipline. My riding crop was lying a few feet away on the divan where I'd dropped it after my morning ride with Anna Karenina.

—Bare your bottom immediately! I shouted at him, going for the leather crop. —If you are going to behave like a bad boy, you shall be treated like one.

—A bad boy! Of course! he howled, and furiously pulled his pants off. —Oh! Oh! he moaned. —What a foul, naughty boy I am! I don't deserve an inch of mercy! Not an inch!

—And you won't get it, Feodor Feodorovich! I cried, and gave him a good whack on his bare bottom with the crop.

—Oohhh! he moaned, rocking back and forth on his hands and knees.

—Not half an inch! and I whacked him twice again. —You little bugger!

—Ooohh! Oohh! he howled rather like a wild animal. —You're far too gentle with me, dearest angel Grushenka. Harder! Harder! Do not spare me.

—Too gentle is it? And I let his red bottom have two lashes of greater force.

—Eeeeaahh! he shrieked with the ecstatic voice of the true sinner.

—Oh vileness! I yelled, quite caught up in the delectable fury of the scene, and swiftly laid on two, three more very severe lashes of the crop. —Little vermin! Disgusting swine!

—Heeeuupp! he screamed, and went into jerking, bucking spasms, arching his crazy old head high like a horse, and at the same time his huge, throbbing organ was spurting its white sauce all over my parlor floor. So I gave his red bottom another good stroke of the crop for that. —Oooff! he sighed, or barked, and more or less collapsed or subsided at my feet. I must say, Raskolnikov, that at that moment he did not resemble a great Russian celebrity. More like a discarded patient in the loony bin.

Well, the long and short of it, my dear, is that I agreed to perform in his new work, a book called *The Idiot*, of all things. The old geezer was so pathetic, I just couldn't turn him down. He is so absolutely *weird*. He does seem to require a good flogging from time to time. And that's not all he requires. You should hear what he has had your pretty little friend Sonya do to him! She was so divine as the drunkard's daughter in *Crime and Punishment*, really divine. That role may have looked like a pushover, but it wasn't. Why, even her miserable little cringings as she walked required hours and hours of the most demanding practice. As I was saying, what she did to and for him . . . You simply wouldn't believe it. I'll leave the telling of it up to Sonya. Her presentation on the subject is far more dramatic than my retelling it would be. And she's ever so clever and effective when it comes to the tiny but significant details. Talented, yes, she's very talented, even if she is a bit, how shall I say it, self-concerned. Did you know, by the way, that she has taken up writing in her spare time? Oh yes, the writing of novels, no less. —And why not? she said to me. —Who's to say I can't? Turnabout is fair play. It's high time the voices from the other side were heard. Some new slants are very much in order, my friend. I can assure you of that. The world is up to here with the same old stories, year in and year out. Santa Claus and his reindeer, fairies at the bottom of gardens, milkmaids being seduced by young nobles, dishonest bank directors robbing their own banks, chimney sweeps marrying princesses, drunkards freezing to death in forgotten snowdrifts . . . All that sentimental junk is kaputt. It has clogged the spiritual pores of the innocent public long enough. Make way for the new! Change the locks on your doors! Fire your cook! Hold onto your hat! Burn all your bridges! Practice breathing under water!

—Here now, Grusha my love. Sit right there and I'll read you a few scraps from my notebook. Suck on these French bon vivants. All right. First some miniature portraits from a novel in progress set in the succulent, under-populated, overproductive, hypersensitive, self-centered, feverish, emotionally underrated farmlands somewhere south of the cunning, hopeless Volga River. "Ludwig, a shrewish, Jewish, self-deceptive, introspective, homosexual dairy farmer whose snobbish, inbred herds leave a great many questions unanswered. Ludwig's milkers are all remote cousins, but they don't fool anybody. His housekeeper Mishkin as often as not gives the lie to that honored title. He is a former cossack who has fallen by the wayside in more ways than one. For reasons that should certainly be examined as soon as possible, he wears evening gowns rather than aprons. In view of the facts, he should not be singing while he works, but he does so anyway. Outside the kitchen windows, prized razorback pigs compete with elegant, disdainful Persian roosters for supremacy in a social order that is largely a thing of the past."

—Here is Plotsky, the local doctor: "This is a man whose blatant shortness need not be a shortcoming, and indeed it isn't when all is said and done, of course. His shortness does, however, seem to be lying in wait for you. (It has been referred to as the power behind the throne by a passing heart patient who could afford insights with abandon.) This has been felt and discussed— quite a bit after the fact, it would appear, and certainly quite a distance from the doctor's office—by a handful of sensitive patients. —We will be patiently waiting our turns in the doctor's outer office. In an orderly, decent fashion of course, because we are not hooligans. Reading old issues of foreign journals in funny tongues, or reading our palms, or examining the lining of our jackets for lost coins, or simply staring at the floor. Waiting to be called in by his nurse. We will all gradually become aware that we are being observed by his shortness. As if it had detached itself from his body and crept in to spy on our ailments. To expose them as frauds or something even worse. At these moments all of us patients know that we must present a united front. We must stand together or fall individually."

That tireless statement was made by a former schoolteacher who had decided one day to wash her hands of children and of books while there was still time. "They smell bad," she said.

Dr. Plotsky has far more cures than he has diseases, which may very well be why—in spite of the above-mentioned paraphenomena—that he has a following a mile long. Some old-timers feel that he inherited this addictive tendency from his mother, Natasha Naborovsky, who was off and running long before daylight more times than anyone in the village could count. "We must face the fact that the wheel has already been invented," she was known to announce, "and may the devil take the leftovers."

As soon as you set foot in the doctor's inner office you have turned your back on the tyranny of cause and effect.

—Don't take your clothes off! Take off your mask! he might say, hurling himself into those words much as children will hurl themselves into delicious mountain lakes.

Or he might point a small, clever finger at you and say, —From this day on, I command you to indulge yourself at will. You are clearly suffering from malnutrition of the spirit.

And he has not even taken your pulse, my dear, or tapped your chest for uneven sounds!

Or he might fix you, as he did one simpering matron, with a look of piercing ambiguity, and say, —You could have cancer or fallen arches, hardening of the arteries or recessive genes. In the end, it could all depend upon you.

—Oh how wonderful of you to say so, Doctor, she sighed.

—I advise you to hang onto your compliments, Madame Blatavsky, until the microscope has had its say.

—Oh yes, of course.

—Commit the following words of hope and cure to memory and practice: alfalfa tablets, country-fresh eggs, push-ups in private, or in the company of a carefully chosen audience, and local ballads sung in a simple unaffected voice.

Mmm. Dr. Plotsky . . . What would our fathomless little village do without him, his radiant refusals to go down on his hands and knees before the inevitability of collective guile? And hasn't our past been illuminated by his fearless open-faced daring (in spite of or perhaps because of his small size)?

Now then . . . next I present to you a few lines about our Katerina Veranovna Ivonovsky, the long-suffering, short-haired, blue-blooded sacrifice to the gods of fate, who is the wife of retired General Pietor Gregor Antonovich Bulganovsky. Imagine, a sensitive creature like her forced to listen to the snores of a distant drummer! Hear it from her very own mouth.

—Little did I know when I looked up from the cherry orchard and accepted the offer of his hairy hand, that I was making my bed with all of Mother Russia's military campaigns! The curtains collapse at the language of our boudoir, and you would too. "Charge their left flank! Bring up the cannon from the rear! Blow for the cavalry! Fix bayonets! Keep the enemy on the defensive!" Heavens above! How is a poor woman supposed to carry out her conjugal obligations when her very peculiar husband thinks the making of love is a military operation? What can one say of the balance of this man's mind, the condition of his emotions? I cannot count the number of major battles and minor border skirmishes I have participated in in my own bedroom! Pfoo! It's a wonder my body isn't absolutely covered with bullet burns and shrapnel scratches. To say nothing of the bizarre orders of the day, straight from headquarters! Oy! And the times I have had to play the role of a Turkish dragoon, or a German infantryman, or a Greek aide-de-camp! Forgive me, but I really must cross myself. My soul is in jeopardy at the mere thought of it.

This eminent and conspicuous couple are an invigorating if not positively chilling example of what is produced when unlikely cultural strains are crossed, or mated, or joined in matrimonial design. They stare at each other with the amazement of people looking into mirrors that do not reflect. Each seems to open up in the other an infinite and unreliable adventure. When they speak to each other, their sentences so very frequently sprout wings and fly away. They never go out together anymore, to dinner parties or to dances. Really, it is simply too absurd, too dangerous. When they danced, he would break out into a wild polka, barking like a drunken sheepdog, while she, poor dear, was putting her heart and soul into a waltz. And the last dinner they attended together, a garish birthday affair thrown by Countess Potemkin for her hopelessly hairy daughter Helena, well, at this breathtaking exhibition of true provincial gluttony, Katerina and her general found themselves doing things that can only be described as doomed and unreal even in these shaky times. She was pouring soup into his jacket pockets and buttering his braided cuffs, and he was salting her bosom and trying to smoke her fingers.

Poor daft general! What, after all, can one expect from a man who was torn from his mother's breast and locked up in a drafty, dribbling military school where those wormy demons flogged his cringing but innocent little body and stuffed his lonely question mark of a head with all kinds of slippery rubbish about the glories of the Roman legions, who, the facts of the matter reveal all too clearly, were midget pederasts, revoltingly happy-go-lucky mass murderers, witless, know-nothing back slappers, arrogant, empty-hearted vermin. When little Pietor Antonovich should have been learning the difference between up and down and in and out, he was learning how to trap and outfox and kill other men, how to burn down villages and enslave all the inhabitants, how to blow up bridges and poison streams. Merciful God! His scabby little head was being churned into kasha, and monster kasha at that.

And of course, the brutal idiocy did not end there. The barracks were next. Oh, that fetid swamp overgrown with bugle calls and aching balls! But here now. Let us get it right from the general's mouth. Let us assume that he has been longing to tell us (perhaps in his own words, who knows) but did not know we cared. (It is possible that he has not been aware of our existence.) Be that as it may . . .

—Even when we were awake, our threadbare little dreams were haunted by other dreams. Howling, insatiable dreams that poured out of the pounding, cloudless, windswept heads of Hannibal and Alexander the Great and Charlemagne and Akim el-Krim and Napoleon and oh my God dozens more blood-drenched maniacs who wished to conquer the world. And when those visions were not cannibalizing our poor, exhausted brains and wringing our spirits into little rags, our own division commanders were making us crawl and cringe as helpless indentured players in militaristic nightmares that were doomed from the moment they were concocted as the particular general or colonel lay in a naked stupor in some reeking whorehouse or competed in bloody stupidities with his fellow officers at their club. Do you think it mattered one tiny bit to them that half of us lads remained forever on those ignominious battlefields, our mangled, bloody bodies providing feasts for rats and buzzards for miles around? Our only hope for survival was to suck our way or buy our way to their lofty heights and thus be spared further humiliations. And once there, of course, we ourselves could indulge in the slovenly gibberish that passed for official army language. I wake up every morning now and cross myself, just to be sure that I have indeed escaped from that putrid purgatory of the soul.

—But those aching, bereft barrack companions still walk through my sleep babbling and shouting. Igor Gouzenko: —The soup's not good enough for a dog to drown in!

Anatole Zadov: —The fields of courage are overgrown with empty promises!

Dimitri Pogony: —Our flanks are exposed through no fault of our own! We have been betrayed by our wanton masters!

—Do you still wonder, my friends, why the flowers of Russian manhood have a face as infinitely vacant as the skies above? Look into that sky face at your own risk. You could fall upwards into it and disappear forever.

With these words (which should ring for days in our ears), the general steps back into wherever he was when we asked him if he would speak to us regarding his innermost self, a request that was matched in simplicity by its depth, that is to say, his depth and our simplicity, though depth and simplicity can and often are the same thing, just as shallowness and savagery include each other and are frequently to be seen walking hand in hand down many a dark street. Beware. When you see one, think of the other. So be it. Language can be trickier than a schoolmarm on holiday. Another old

Petrograd saying that is still with us, I am happy to say, because all too many of our venerable expressions have been overruled and outcast by the indifferent demands of modern times.

Hopefully, now, a little something for the record from the exquisitely distracted, underexposed Katerina, who, I can just see out of the corner of your eye, is very busy tying artificial cherries onto a leafless winter tree, perhaps in homage to *The Cherry Orchard,* a soft spot in our national heritage, or it could be that she is making fun of Mother Nature, a pastime that can turn on you when you are least prepared, so watch out. We must wait and see. Meanwhile . . . yes, fine, my dearest Katerina. Anything you say. I'm not the kind of author who tells his characters when and where they must go to the bathroom. Give and take, that's the basic rule in my work, and it had better be yours too, otherwise you'll end up writing engineers' manuals instead of heartbreaking, soul-searching literature, which lives on and on long after the intentions of the author and the slings and arrows of outrageous publishers.

—I could not agree with you more, Sonya dear, says Katerina, putting away the remainder of the cherries in exactly the right predestined place. —And I must say that you have broached the subject not a moment too soon for a writer who has just reached the sacred, though stained, threshold of Russian literature, across which far too many opportunistic, selfish scribblers have smuggled ideas and practices that would do more good and be much more at home in a second-rate pawnbroker's shop on Stavisky Street. We live at a time when sleight of hand and rankling materialism have achieved plague proportions against whose canny onslaughts the highest town walls are a pathetic charade. Even more of a reason why one must turn up one's fur collar, gird one's loins if that is still in fashion, and furiously if not dedicatedly cultivate one's own garden. Keeping in mind the small yet basic fact that it will not make any difference what kinds of tools you use. If necessary, use your tongue.

My own garden, dizzy in its sheer heights and backbreaking in its ambiguities, lies somewhere between the intimate clamminess of the second act of *Uncle Vanya* and that unopened box of smoked herring squatting so aimlessly in the back room of Nicolai Schwartz's overbearing food store. With such vital information at your disposal, you can certainly understand why it is sometimes all I can do to get my garden to hold still—and often, when I do, I am forced to grab it by the throat—and then seed it and plow and plant it. Well, that's an endeavor of another color. Right at this point everyone should be reminded that we are really talking about, making sly, philosophical references to, if you please, a number of gardens. My own, Sonya's, who feels, rightly or wrongly we shall eventually see, that she as a budding author has more or less brought me into being, and then the garden of Mr. Dostoyevski, who has the same dubious proprietary feelings regarding Sonya. In view of this botanical proliferation, we must be careful, we must watch our step, else we mistakenly put our foot in someone else's flower beds. You might hear the screams for pages and pages. And who wants such an experience? Who indeed.

Well, pfoo! So here I am at one moment scaling the sheer sides of my garden and peering down from time to time, through the dreadful drop to the floor of the garden below, and at the next moment I am lying on my back at the bottom staring up at the place from which I had just dropped and no matter what you may think of me for saying this, I must tell you that a part of me was still up there, staring at me as I finally see it and return its severe and even condemning look. Just what are you doing down there, you silly fool? it seems to be saying. Don't you have any decency left in you? Shameless hussy, self-indulgent weakling, introspective ragamuffin! Phew! And what can I in self-defense or merely in retaliation shout back, though my voice is not as forceful as it could be because I am lying down, as you well know. You think you are superior just because you have claws for hands and can cling to impossible places. Well, you are deceiving yourself, my friend. You are not superior. You're a freak, a defective. So mind your manners.

While I am down here at the bottom of my garden, I am forced, so to speak, to face up to certain other selves in my family of selves that might be doing some exploring and cultivating of their own. For we must understand that the voice that speaks is not always the only voice that exists. There are others down there with quite a lot to say if they can only get the chance, get a tongue in the door. Aha! There is such a one lurking snugly over there to my right, in a spot that may appear to you to be barren or fallow or in some ways possibly shallow, depending of course upon your preordained point of view. That self over there glows gently, in possession of an immanent nimbus. This nimbus, which plump, self-appointed experts in Leningrad and nearby Sebastopol repeatedly mistake for a halo (they're so busy patting their own behinds their research has fallen into hopeless disorder), this nimbus will appear in full radiant force at the right moment and of its own choosing. It is not a nimbus that can be summoned by need. Absolutely not. The self—see her smile so obscurely, yet with an inherited sureness—will wake up one fine afternoon and discover the nimbus has arrived and is surrounding her head and shoulders. This will take place when the final, and some may say, fatal piece of self-awareness has been fitted into the puzzle. One sometimes suspects, playfully of course, that she might be prolonging this ultimate seizure of self. This could be her Great Game. She may feel that there will be no place left to go, nothing left to do, no more adventures of the spirit now that one crucial piece has been discovered and, as hands tremble, and certainly some sighs will be heard, even gasps, fitted into place. Of course, all this is amateur guesswork on our part. We cannot really penetrate Her Mystery, can we?

Another self, there to the far left, dancing in and out of her own grinning shadows as a half-clothed courtesan might dance among the articulate depravities of her wealthy clients—observe this self as she fastidiously collects damning evidence against the future. Tell me the truth: have you ever seen or smelled such misguided intensity? Have you ever, in your sly journeys through Mother Russia's forgotten provinces, been confronted with such self-satisfied confusions? There is no shame here, sir, there is no guilt, nor any of those other highly prized qualities that the human race has fought so hard for and paid so dearly for; qualities that attempt to maintain a decent, clean balance between sky and earth, between ocean and land, heaven and hell, or to make my point somewhat clearer, between man's chastened realities, on the one hand, and his wanton dreams of glory on the other. Man must learn to live with and to love his human limitations. He must completely accept the unalterable fact that the rank labyrinths he lives in, which were so lovingly and generously donated by God, are not gleaming underground castles. They are rank, dank, vicious labyrinths and that is that. And he must never, for one second of madness, permit himself to hope that one day he will be flushed out like a mole, by a sudden flood of bubbling French champagne. Chaphoo!

Wait, ladies and gentlemen. Just a moment, please. That above-discussed self has paused between her shadows and is signaling to me. It would seem that she wishes to say a few words. All right. Speak, woman! Or forever hold your piss.

—Sis, did you hear that? Just who does that loony cunt think she is? She acts like we've all elected her Queen of the Prom and Chief Spasm or something ever since she joined the town literary club. You want to know why people become members of a thing like that? So they can feel superior to other people, that's why. So they can walk around with their noses up in the air. When it comes right down to it, those highfalutin assholes don't have any more real interest in literature than I myself have in pig-fucking laws in Bulgaria. I mean, it wouldn't faze those see-through blowhards one bit if it turned out that *Dead Souls* was, in fact, a plagiarized eighteenth-century English novel about cemetery freaks. Or that Comrade Gorky had made up all that grim gutter shit in *Lower Depths* and that he was actually the second cousin of Catherine the Great, and no more a man of the people than I am. They'd take these shocking revelations right in their stride and go right on acting like nothing at all had happened. What I'm saying is, *they're not real.* They think that just because they can see themselves in the mirror, they must exist. We know about that sort of thing, more than we want to know about it. A sickness that long ago reached and went beyond plague proportions, and the sweet fuckin' end ain't nowhere in sight.

Speaking of maladies, I have a friend living down in the wacky-woo Urals who does them. He goes from house to house and performs them, acts them out.

—Knock, knock.

—Who's there?

—The malady man.

—Aha. Come right in. How nice to see you, my good chap.

—How nice to be here, my dear lady, he says.

—It's snowing like a wolves' carnival out there, and nothing's to be gained by denying it either.

—Oh no, he says. —Absolutely nothing at all. We surely see eye to eye on that. Only a fool . . .

—Exactly. Only a fool . . .

—Well now, he says, rubbing his hands and hopping up and down and swinging his arms to warm himself up for what is to follow, arduously, —what shall it be today, dear Madame Kravatsky?

—Cerebral palsy. How about some of that?

—A splendid choice. And in the shake of a lamb's tail he summons his rare talents and throws himself into acting out cerebral palsy, as Madame Kravatsky stares enraptured.

You'd think you were overhearing an old hyena dying under a full moon. He twists his face into expressions of pathetic idiocy. He forces heartbreaking spasms through his body. He tears at his clothes. And finally he collapses to the floor in a rumpled gaseous heap. Madame Kravatsky sighs ecstatically as she comes out of her enraptured trance. His perfect performance has divinely cleansed her. Cerebral palsy is one more affliction she has conquered through my friend's genius. She has had it, so there is now no way she could possibly get it.

After a bit: —No, no, really, Madame Kravatsky. Thirty rubles is far too generous.

—Don't be silly, dear man. It was worth that and more. Please! I insist.

—Very well, I bow to your feminine will.

In the next block, in the richly ornate yet absurdly and shittily prim living room—the sort of place where you fucking well know that the heavy expensive rugs disapprove of every dirty footstep and the elegant velvet-covered chairs are obviously hoping you don't soil them with your vile body —of that haughty old fart-smeller Professor Vishinsky, my friend puts on another inspired performance. Only the beginning of the magic ritual is a bit different.

—Knock, knock.

—Who's there?

—Terminal syphilis.

—Nobody's home!

—Oh, I see. Well then . . . Knock, knock.

—Who's there?

—Typhoid fever.

—Ah! Come in, come in. We are privileged by your presence, sir.

And away he goes. He performs the disease so masterfully the walls get down on their hands and knees and kiss his feet when it is all over. He whips off all his clothes and succumbs naked to the floor, all strength having suddenly abandoned his shivering body. His flesh burns and crackles with fever, like an African desert that is cannibalizing itself in loneliness. His bones turn to fish paste as his flopping and mopping and turning shows. He moans and howls and gibbers, and lunatic hallucinations of all sorts consume his brain and pour out of his frothing mouth, the way you'd see bats and lizards and rats and blind monkeys pour from the mouth of a cave that has been set on fire by a careless, drunken hermit who has given up even on his hermitage. Sweat drenches my friend's performing body, his teeth clack and clatter, and his glazed eyes roll wildly round and round. Professor Vishinsky and his wife Irma, who is as small and quiet as a comma, sit on the prissy damask sofa tightly clasping hands, utterly consumed, utterly enthralled. A great spasm arches my friend Egon's wracked body, a scream leaps from his mouth. He relaxes and subsides. The fever has broken. Life will go on.

Tears of relief and joy surge up into the eyes of the professor and his wife, and flow in happy streams down their remote masklike faces.

—Quel magnifique! murmurs the professor, a language snob on special occasions of emotion. —Vous êtes le rédempteur pour catharsis, Monsieur. C'est vrais!

—Oh far fucking out! whispers his wife, who can't speak French. She then more or less disappears into the professor's large jacket pocket.

I don't have to tell you that my friend Egon doesn't work an eight-hour day. No way. He can swing three, maybe four affliction gigs a week, and that's it. His poor little ass has had it. Like, how many times could you ask the Naz to repeat that cross scene, right? An artist like Egon has gotta watch his health. Proper rest, good eats, vitamins, certain secret exercises . . . shit like that. You gotta be in shape to pull off those malady stunts. And another thing: he's gotta spend a certain amount of regular time doin his research. Keepin his nose in the latest medical journals, keepin up on the last developments on diseases and symptoms. For instance, if you think that the brain fever of your grand-daddy's hairy time is the same as today's brain fever, you got another thing comin. An the same goes fer simptums. Boy, that's whur he's really gotta be up on top uf it, or else. You wanna see thus sheeit hit thu fayun jus imagun ol Egon gettin some simptums mixt up. Thinkin he was actin out yeller fevah when he wuz really puttin on cansuh. That one sho way tu kill off you customers. He'd be outta biznis in no time.

Christ! What's with this hillbilly voice? How the fuck did it creep in here anyway? Somebody's trying to horn in on my act, that's what. That's the way it goes in this racket. You turn your back for one second, and whoosh! some pushy unemployed voice/person has taken over your role. It happens all the time and unless we voices get our shit together and set up some rules and regulations of behavior, we'll drown in confusion and chaos, and you can bet on it. Look what happens when those price wars get started. You have more bankruptcies than summer flies. And look what happened to the Tower of Babel when they started handing out rent-free studios. Smash! Down, you crazy little redneck cocksucker! Whack! Try to cut me out once more and I'll grind your prick into baloney, you understand? Creepy little booger-eating know-nothing redneck imposter.

Let's see . . . where was I? Oh yeah. Egon . . . He's not some off-the-cuff, stand-up, fall-down comic. Oh no. He's a serious, dedicated full-time—oh sure, vacations, but nothing like, you know, six months basking at Spletz on the Black Sea, or four and a half giggly, giddy months at the blackjack tables of Monte Carlo—full-time professional artist/magician. Just because he stares up at the ceiling, that doesn't mean he's loafing. Was Galileo goofing when he stared at the sun and the stars? I ask you.

And over there, powdering her nose, figuratively speaking, in the center of this spanky and at one time burgher-proof little garden, is another artist/magician, Carol, one of my many sister selves. All I can say is, I wish they were all like her. It can get pretty itchy in here at times, you know? And when you think you're scratching your own ass, turns out you've stuck your finger in somebody's eye; and it can go downhill from there. But Carol's OK. She knows the score, and unlike some people I know, she doesn't go around pretending she doesn't. Now I'm not saying she doesn't go in for some routines, because she does. But she doesn't kid herself. She knows what she's doing. She doesn't look into the mirror and say, Good morning, Marie Antoinette. Carol's routines are strictly business deals, you know what I mean. Survival stuff. You may not be able to call the tune but you sure as shit can say how you're going to play it. There are all kinds of ways of getting along and some are more likely to turn you into a baboon than others. The time to worry is when you find yourself barking into banana peels.

You want to know what Carol says? She says, —What's wrong with pussy theater? Is it any better to play psychologist or president or teacher than bad girl or strumpet or Little Miss Muffet? Theater is theater, whether it's public or private. Hear that? No mincing of words there, right? No sir. This baby lets you have it right between the eyes. —The only difference is that society, that vicious fraud, has said that anything to do with sex is out, off limits, unspeakable. Well, that's bullshit. It's also said you've got to kill and be killed for your country no matter what dreadful acts your country is up to. So if you want to take your orders from a dangerous idiot like that, go right ahead. But it's your funeral, not mine. Just don't try to get me mixed up in it in any way. And also don't give me a hard time about the way I make my living. Or the way I make my dying. (Anyway, when have spectators had the right to put in their two cents' worth?)

Whenever I look in the mirror I always see somebody else. That's right. I'm trying to level with you, whoever you may be. That statement "Whenever . . ." I throw that up in the air to see where it might go, where it might take me, or itself and me. You don't always have to know everything a statement you make means. You can say things just to explore. There's no law that says you can't do that. You can say, "I want to go to Afghanistan" without wanting to know a lot about the place. You can simply like the sound of it, all of the possibilities you can imagine.

All those other people in the mirror . . . But are they really *other?* Some are, some aren't. Some belong to me, others are presented to me, laid upon me. I see so many. Which one belongs to the voice I am now using? Doesn't each voice have a different face? And each face a different voice? And sometimes a face won't like the voice that goes with it, and the face will make up another voice it likes better. A fake voice. A voice that could come right off a counter in a self-satisfied department store. Then there are voices that are just dying to go on sale in such places whether they know it or not. And there are voices that live dangerously, and voices that are afraid of their own shadow.

Faces . . . voices . . . people . . . in your mirror . . . Last week, I played a sadistic schoolteacher for a lawyer from Nice. Knuckle-rapping rulers, paddles, spankings . . . the whole bit. Aha! So you have cheated on your exams again, have you, you disgusting little wart! We know what that will get you, don't we now? Pull down your pants this very instant! Three nights ago I was a sweet young schoolgirl being picked up by a dirty old man. Oh sir! How generous of you to give me this bag of chocolates. Mmm. And it's so cozy sitting in front of this fireplace in your nice apartment, 'stead of being outside in the rain and cold. Mmm. Oh yes, you can help me take off my wet shoes and stockings. That's right. My stockings unsnap up under my skirt. Oh yes. I just love to have my bare feet rubbed like that. Ooohh. And you lick them so *good.* Just like my little dog Pie back at home. The dirty old man is a sixty-year-old engineer with grown children, of course. Grandchildren.

Monsieur Bombois the engineer is not the only one of my clients who likes me to play the little girl. A fellow American named Joe Fox, who is a writer who also works here for the United Nations, he goes for me that way too. He even wrote a short story about himself and me. Honestly. Here it is. Listen to it. Feel it. Taste it. Even fuck it if you can. It's called "Playground":

S hock and revenge ranged the room like twin lions; shock at the foulness of the deed, revenge that must be dealt the awful perpetrator.

—It's the most disgusting thing I ever heard, said Lily Jackson who lived across the street. —And to think it happened right around the corner! God!

—I know! cried Barton's wife Pat in outraged agreement. —That's the terrible thing about it.

Barton's feeling about the matter still hovered between confusion and uncertainty. He was a latecomer to their distress, having returned from New York just a few minutes ago. He had found them growling and pacing thus, and, out of self-protection, he had immediately withdrawn from them and felt apart. It seemed to him that everything that happened to the women out here in this New Jersey suburb, whether it involved one of them personally or one of their surrogates, was embroidered with a hysterical decoration.

—Tell me what happened again, Pat, he asked. —I missed some of the details. Without knowing exactly why, he felt irritation, rather than sympathy, creep inside him and crouch there.

—Well, Pat began, urgency tightening her small, articulate, schoolgirl face, —this afternoon Gloria Wooley was walking near the playground back there when she ran into this Mr. Leslie who lives around the corner. He was walking his police dog. Gloria stopped to pet the dog, or he stopped her— something like that—anyway, and he began to say things to her.

—He has a perfectly *awful* reputation, Kate Lindhurst threw in suddenly. —He's been arrested for drunken driving and things like that.

Barton allowed a quiet pause to settle itself before asking his wife, —What do you mean "say things to her"?

Pat quickly curled one leg under her, as if to brace herself in some way for what she was going to say. —Suggestive things.

—Oh? Barton sighed, and waited.

—He asked her if she went around with boys, and when she said she didn't he said, "Well, you will soon, and you'll just love the fun you'll have"— *you know.* And when he said this he laughed very dirtily. You can imagine ... poor Gloria didn't know what to do or say.

Lily sprang in again. —And he just howled when that insane dog of his began running round and round Gloria, tying her legs up with the leash.

As he looked at the three women, felt their respective outraged young suburban wife presences, Barton was attempting to reconstruct the odious scene that had despoiled the planned cleanness of the split-level house street behind them. —How did you find out about all this? he asked Pat.

—Jean Wooley told me a couple of hours ago. Gloria had come back to her house and was acting strange. Like she was in a state of shock or something. Jean had to force it out of her, because Gloria was so ashamed of its happening to her.

—Mr. Wooley should go to the police, Kate said firmly. —That's what we should all do, in fact. You never know what a degenerate like that will do next. He's a constant menace to the children. I know I'll never let Debbie go near the playground again.

As Barton had been following the unfolding of this day's sordid tale, he had, like an acrobat straddling two realities, been reliving another one in the never-buried past, and now the word *playground*, the single word more loaded with images than any other he knew, commanded his return to a particular day, like this one also involving a girl and violation, of a sort. Barton was then thirteen. The girl was twelve, and her name was Laurette, a name over which lingered the breath of predestined trouble.

Barton did not know Laurette any better than the other boys, really, except that he sat behind her in school. During the day's recess periods, when the kids raced out onto the playground like maniacally exuberant prisoners being released from torture cells, half a dozen of them, including Laurette and Barton, formed a cluster near the basketball court and pursued the *real* education of their lives that the schoolrooms so regularly and unknowingly interrupted. Between the boys and the girls there invariably developed, in these intimate periods, a ballet—light and full of *ballon* on the surface, dark and fierce underneath—of competition and chase, and in this crucial ballet subtle, skilled, confident Laurette was unquestionably the prima ballerina.

During one of these dazzling engagements, the freest one of all because it was after school and therefore one did not have to return to the academic world of chaste make-believe, Barton gave spirited chase to Laurette. Down the playground they sped, past swings and slides transfixed in permanent innocence and, finally, leaped into a jewellike garden/park just off the playground, where the teachers often walked and sat apart from the students, and there Barton caught her. After a moment of mock struggle, Laurette let him kiss her.

The following day, the day of semester examinations, disaster struck. In the middle of this group writing struggle, Laurette, making sure that they were momentarily unobserved by their teacher, turned around, head bowed secretly, and, whispering, asked Barton to give her the answers to some history questions. Barton was shocked. He had never connected exciting Laurette with an act of cheating, and now his imagination was quite incapable of bringing himself and Laurette together in such an act under these circumstances of being on one's honor.

Chilled with shame and confusion, he slowly shook his head: No.

Laurette's face reacted first with surprise, and then with the blushing fury of intimate betrayal. —I'll get you for this! she whispered with violence, and quickly turned her back upon him.

Later that morning, during a break in the exams, Barton was lounging in the hallway and cloudily beginning to connect his refusal with her acceptance in the garden, when his teacher approached him and said she wished a word with him in the cloakroom. He walked along with her in mounting fear. They reached the private cloakroom, finally, and there, glowing with imperious triumph, was Laurette.

—William, his teacher began, —Laurette tells me that you tried to molest her yesterday afternoon in the garden. Is that so?

He could not think or react clearly because of so many terrible things rushing through him.

—Now tell me the truth, his teacher continued. —Because this is a very serious charge.

Barton managed to pull himself together enough to attempt an explanation. —We were playing and she let me kiss her.

—You're a dirty liar! Laurette shouted. —I didn't let you do anything! You tried to . . .

The upshot, after denials to his family and to the principal during that humiliating conference, was that he was transferred to another school, and for months afterward he carried with him the leprous stains of her accusation.

—. . . and if I were Gloria's mother I would take her to a psychiatrist to help her get over the shock, Kate Lindhurst was saying.

—That might be a very good idea, Pat said. —What do you think, dear?

—I don't really know, he replied, squashing out his cigarette.

All three women stared at him uncomprehendingly, as though he had just uttered something in a strange tongue, and all over his skin Barton could feel the antennae of their female suspicions angrily probing his purpose.

—What do you mean you don't know? his wife asked almost with indignation.

—Just that. I honestly don't know whether she ought to see a psychiatrist or not. Barton was being evasive, because he could not say what was really on his mind at the moment.

Lily hunched forward urgently, and for a second Barton thought she might hurl herself at his throat. —But you will agree, won't you, she insisted, —that the girl has undergone quite a shock?

Barton shrugged his shoulders with strategic resignation. —Yes, I suppose she has at that.

When the two women left a few minutes later they had still not decided exactly what they were going to do about the man in question. They were all going to discuss it some time later with Gloria's parents. As they departed, Barton knew that what they wanted to say was, —What a peculiar husband you have. He acts as though nothing has happened. But of course they said good-bye cheerily instead.

—Do you always have to be so complicated about everything? his wife asked moments after she had shut the door.

He could not think of an answer that would safely sustain the burden of his mixed feelings, his speculative thoughts, so he remained silent.

The next day, Saturday, Barton took a walk near the playground. Actually, he *found* himself walking there; for a part of him, an identity *within*, functioning with resolute autonomy, had arranged this independent of his more ingratiatingly rational self. It was late afternoon and only a couple of kids were in the playground, gently cavorting figures on a serenely geometric, untroubled landscape, a landscape that seemed to glow softly with its own irrevocable light. Barton stepped inside the playground, and immediately became its captive. The very atmosphere was magnetized by magic, and this magnetic force, which Barton could now feel as a physical sensation, encased the entire playground and thus, in a sense, protected its child existence. What took place on the playground seemed forever suspended there, in midair almost, kept by the magnetism from escaping into the outside, or other world, as the sounds now coming from the playing boys appeared to ricochet back and forth off invisible walls.

Barton felt like a boy now, and the voice of his own boyhood was quite audible on that indestructible stage. The children of that past time now swarmed back to life before his eyes. As he stood there, watching them and himself, or really *being* them and himself, Barton saw a new figure arrive. It ws the girl Gloria, whom "the man" had reportedly "talked to." He watched her saunter aimlessly across the playground. He made no effort to extricate himself from his vision of the past and to return to his adult reality. And thus, he permitted Gloria to momentarily become a participant in that vision, or at least allowed her presence and the recollection to coexist there before him, side by side like a double exposure.

Gloria, sandy-haired, slate-eyed, was bigger than the average girl her age. She was obviously in that transition between being a little girl and a big girl, and this being neither one nor the other expressed itself in a style that was vaguely restless and dissatisfied. Barton watched her wander near the boys playing around the swings. She paused there for a few moments, saw nothing to become engaged in, and slowly crossed the playground and headed for the trapeze bars near where Barton was standing. She looked up at him for just a second, then indifferently looked away, as if Barton were just another boy on the playground whom she saw no particular reason for saying anything to. Actually, both she and he knew more or less who the other was.

She listlessly swung on the trapeze chains, but a quality of almost annoyance in her boredom made it quite clear that these contrivances that had engaged her energies only yesterday were now forever lost to her as a source of pleasure. Barton was still enmeshed in the double-exposure worlds of boyhood and adulthood, the powerful, special magic of the playground still operating all around him. Then he walked slowly over to Gloria. She watched him with that same hung-up indifference.

—Hello, Gloria, he began, pronouncing her name hesitantly and almost as a question.

—Hello, she replied, and a slight smile escaped her.

—You know who I am, don't you? he asked.

She squinted at him without losing her slight smile, as though she suspected, not without a trace of implicit young amusement, that he might be playing a game with her. —Sure, she said after a moment. —You're Mr. Barton.

—That's right. A young boy's high, clear voice sailed delicately across the playground, followed by the sharp slapping sound of a foot kicking a football. Then came the sounds of running feet. —Tell me something, Gloria, Barton went on. —Did that man really say those things to you?

—What things?

—You know—whatever he was supposed to have said.

The girl intently examined him with her slightly amused puzzlement, implying that the situation might still be that of a game not unlike the mysterious, revelatory ones she played with her friends on such playgrounds.

—Well? Barton pressed.

She began to giggle ambiguously, and started walking away. —None of your business, she said without turning around.

Barton, immobile, watched her walk across the playground. Her reply refused to disappear from that timeless, enchanted atmosphere; it became intricately and inseparably part of the sounds of the boys playing football at this moment before him, and also joined perfectly with the shouted exchanges he was remembering and had been projecting onto this playground.

In a couple of moments he firmly turned his back on the playground and directed himself homeward. Crossing the border of the playground, where it met the street, he felt a soft tugging at his being, as if he were physically pulling away from a magnet, then suddenly the tugging stopped. Out in the street he could hear the boys' shouts no more.

W ell, Joe, now that you've stepped out of the closet for a few minutes, wouldn't you like to make the most of it and say a few very carefully chosen words to the folks out there? That is, to our fellow zoo inhabitants who are acting like they are the folks out there. Go on now. You say you're not dressed? So what? Think this crowd's going to be fazed by a little skin? Ha! Don't be so shy. Nobody's going to eat you. Or anyway bite you. Now, Joe. Don't make me *push* you out there. Go, go.

OK. OK, Jesus Mary Judas Cardinal Richelieu. Whatever happened to privacy? Whatever became of the anonymity guaranteed by degeneracy? Ah well. Even the goldfish tanks are tapped these days. Hi there, aardvarks and antelopes. Welcome to The Original All-Purpose Confessions of Saint Augustine Show! Oh, if only my prick could talk! Oh, if only my cunt could write poetry! How often have we been assailed by those self-serving whimpers of mortal limitation! What are these wailers trying to tell us? Could they, in their perverted drive toward self-consuming narcissism, be suggesting that those secretive and of course succulent organs of pleasure and species continuity experience life quite apart from the rest of the body? That they have their own steamy/thrusting languages, respectively speaking, that is? Their own proud, gently throbbing treasure houses of memory, permeated, or if you will saturated, by the irrational elegance of nostalgia? And if these . . . these presumptuous, hubris-stained organs have minds of their own, can they therefore have breakdowns of their own? And, may Jesus help us, can they then gibber like the rest of us when they go round the bend? Gibbering pricks! Babbling cunts! Oh berserk joy! Can't you fucking just see it—millions of howling pricks swarming through the streets of the world's great cities! Millions of cunts yorping and storping across the fields of clover! Hurrah for the apocalypse! Hurrah for a total reexamination of the cases of Adam and Eve! Hu . . .

Yeah. Right. I guess I'd better cool it. Some free-floating outsiders— leering tourists, you know—might overhear me and call the Official Douser, a group which is all too eager to rush out and douse things that are beyond their shallow comprehension. How I loathe those thumb-sucking midget turds. What kind of society would create such a repellent department in its government? The same society, of course, that converts old people into animal feed. Calling it—wouldn't you know it!—Old Mother Hubbard's Pig Crunch. The same society that has organized all its teenagers into Young Informers for Mammon. Whose strict vows and constant joy are to snoop around and spy upon anyone—including their own parents, naturally—who says or does anything that is contrary to, or in any way questions this cannibalistic consumer culture. And complementing the YIMs, as I am unashamedly pleased to call them, are the Avengers for Mammon, that closely knit—think of steel mesh—collection of neo-storm troopers who swoop down upon The Offenders, who have been sniffed out and reported by the flashing-eyed, grinning YIMs, and summarily deal out The Punishments According to the Gospel of Saint Horror. Dressings down, castigations, insults, proceeding to public spectacles of humiliations, degradations, tortures, and sometimes ending up in the dark, bleak, careless but insatiable arms of Death Itself.

"Overheard questioning the wisdom of early weaning! Fellow Avengers, repeat after me: 'You are a scum-sucking, shit-stained enemy of the people.'"

"Refused to applaud the bombings of Hanoi and Haiphong! Fellow Avengers, whip out your lofty, loyal cocks and cover this vicious saboteur with the yellow streams of your hot piss!"

"Strongly suspected of anticapitalistic sentiments, specifically hostile feelings toward the nuclear monopolies. Flog this viper! Flog her twenty times upon her despicable, naked, and undeniably lewd backside!"

"Publicly demonstrated against antimarijuana legislation! To the Crushing Pits with these shameless perverts!"

There are other more subtly malevolent police groups to pick from in case you're thinking of acting up. For danger-loving types who, in moments of almost suicidal rushes of imagination, will consider using language that goes beyond anything required to order one's daily fix of bubble gum, for such absurd, vanishing types we have the Watchers of the Word. These folks—I use that cozy word with a sagging grin—are to the joys, the wild bells and morning leaps of language what the American Air Force was to the heroic struggle for independence in Vietnam. They stroll the streets—flowing with arrogance and smug brutishness—equipped with the most relentlessly sophisticated electronic listening devices, equipment that can detect a turn of phrase, a metaphor, six blocks away. No sooner has such a felicitous use of language been made than this evil equipment instantly flashes blood-red lights of danger and begins to moan and whimper like a helpless animal whose life is being threatened. The sturdy Word Watchers race off, directed to the scene of the crime by Their Device, whose moans and whimpers are getting louder and louder and more awful. As the Watchers of the Word reach the Criminal User, these dreadful sounds of pain have become screams.

—You have been heard! the Word Watchers shout, reciting the first line of their black catechism. —Blasphemer! Pagan! Enemy of serenity! they continue reciting/shouting at the guilty one, who at this low, insane point may or may not be shaking like a sycamore leaf in a Brazilian musical comedy. —The evidence against you is in our hands! they howl, holding up the tapes. —It is not to be denied. "To shuffle off this mortal coil," "Time's winged chariot hurrying near," "Infrastructural negotiations," "Vestigial elegance." . . . Those highfalutin words came out of your elitist mouth. Terrorist! Shameless smart aleck! Trying to be different from your fellow countrymen! You deserve and you will get the stiffest reeducational punishment. Punishment to suit the crime. Stand straight, hands at sides, eyes toward heaven, mouth wide open, and hear your sentence: For the next two months, from six o'clock until nine o'clock every morning, you will read nothing but comic books. During that same length of time, you will not speak any words of more than two syllables. Every single day, which means Sundays too, you will take a twig from an all-American tree, and write in the dirt three words of intellectual and poetic aspirations. And when you have finished writing these bloodthirsty, terroristic words, one beneath the other, you will take a pickax and with all of your strength chop these words into oblivion. Oblivion! Do you understand? Do you hear your society talking to you, stinking word criminal?

Sure hope you're gettin' the drift of it here. 'Cause if you're not, then what all of us on this side of the fence have a right to ask is, What the fuck are you doing there? You down from Mars on a weekend package tour or something?

OK, OK. Do you think I don't know that you're waiting for me to give you the inside dope on my secret sexual kinks? Or, to be more exact, kink. Because I really have only one, however many spicy tangents it may contain. Pubescent pussy! Chicken! Little girls! Or the illusion thereof. Because I really don't ever fuck little girls. Nor do I cruise them at parks or at school playgrounds, loitering with my topcoat pockets filled with goodies and my dirty old man face covered with winking, cunt-stained grins and leers, a doll taped to my cock and balls, a fall-back position just in case I don't score with some dishy little Mary Lou who's got Twinkies stuffed in her blouse for boobies. Not me. I hire fully grown, fully blown women like Carol to dress up in girls' clothes and make believe they're Mary Lou or Suzy Q. Quite a different kettle of quiffs, Your Excellency. With a double bubble on it. So it isn't as simple a crime as you might have wished. Plus another bubble—just as I have Carol play the teenybopper, who or what do I get to play me? You heard me. What character do I invent to act for me in these lascivious, slobbering, most gratifying vignettes? Because that giggling, wiggling, mincing, cute-talking and ultimately piss-drenched coot who is donking and swinging his thing before and with Carol's little cutie piece, that only tentatively human thing isn't me, Joseph Cunningham Fox, respected, highly salaried, Brooks Brothers draped, clean-whiskered, well-bred, highly skilled, elegantly schooled, public information officer for the United Nations. No sir. *His* name, shall we say, is very likely something like Hubert C. Slackjaw, or Stuart W. Sucklow, or . . . uh . . . Socks Peelmunder. And God only knows where either of them comes from, out of what hopelessly slipshod dream, or obscure social mulch pile they emerged from and back into which, of course, they most regularly and probably shamelessly creep. Or, shit, maybe they just shoot on back to the calculated oblivion of Twentieth Century Central Casting, that rotating, active-file, nongenealogical graveyard, to which our personalities go, having been separated from Our True Spiritual Self, when we kick the bucket, to be used again and again and again by those of us who are in need of several identities in order to live the main single life, the one that Society has its foul fangs permanently sunk into the jugular vein of.

Listen. Listen to some of these Public Property Servants of the People Snap-on No Questions Asked Personae. Lend them your ear if not your wife.

Jonathan Lickspittle: Some kneel, some grovel, some cringe. I lick. My entire being has become a way of tongue, the wet sound of licking. I am a five foot ten, one hundred and fifty-five pound tongue. I go to sleep at night between two huge slices of rye bread.

The weather in my world, my dear Lord, is the very heartbeat of malevolence. Rainstorms are raging floods of hot yellow piss. Hailstorms are demonic barrages of shit. And thunder . . . earthshaking farts whose stench overwhelms you as would a poisonous gas attack in the trenches. Thus do the dead get back at the living. Our winter and its scenes are hardly postcard material. Snowscapes here are deathscapes. With the abrupt speed of a Chinese maniac the temperature will suddenly drop to a hundred below zero. Whoever happens to be outside at the time without being prepared for all such dreadful unforgiving eventualities, those unfortunate ones are doomed. They are instantly frozen, in midposition, midgesture. All too many careless types are caught this way. Then the grinning, triumphant snow falls, covering these absurdly silenced creatures from head to brain to nose to toe. And thus we have our own awesome open-air theater of snowmen, snow women, and snow children. Whole families caught (perhaps *seized* would be a bit more like it) in the very split-second midst, or act, of some poignant, delicious collective communication. Couples arm-in-arm leering desirously at each other. (Blue skies can be lewd skies.) A child captured (yes)—stilled (yes!)—as it whirled in a game of autonomous ecstasy.

Feast your mind on this chastely dramatic tableau. Man on view, suspended in the process of being. Ask yourself if you can ever go back to your old tricks at Disneyland or Madame Tussaud's. And the next time you roll a tight, hard snowball and prepare to hurl it at the memory of the bobbing, fruity hat of Miss Eloise Drytwat, your loathsome homeroom teacher, just bear in mind that the above-described antipostcard could well include you one of these gripping days if you ever so much as set foot in another man's dismay, another man's meat, the house or home or collapsed castle therein, that is. Throw yourself on the floor this instant and count your blessings is the message I am trying to pound into your thick fucking skull, you two-timing, cross-eyed cocksucker.

See what happens when you try to be nice to these halfway types, these lurking, smirking, shabbily dressed shadows of the netherworld? They violate your generosity and go ape. You let them come forth to say a few lines, to give them a feeling of participation, y'know, of being part of the team or crew or act, 'cause they're always gripin' about how fuckin' anonymous and left out they feel, like the kernels of corn that's been pounded into tortillas, and wham! The second they get their wind up and hit their stride out there, they sink their diseased, yellow fuckin' fangs into the very hand that's been feedin' them all this time. I mean, it ain't as though I signed some sweetheart contract with His Royal Highness Jesus Christ that I would turn myself into some kind of twenty-four-hour seven-day-a-week soup kitchen for the dispossessed, the half human, the misbegotten and other such putrid little losers. Because I didn't. So what the hell, where do they all come off? I ask you.

Come on, Peelmunder! Answer me, you goddamn drunken immoral no good spongin' deadbeat strawboss you! Peelmunder! Shit. He's probably out tryin' to sell acorns to an oak tree. That guy makes you wonder why Galileo ever bothered to recant, no kiddin'. It's easier to go fox huntin' in quicksand than it is to keep up with that little twerp. For all I know, this very moment he could be down on his hands and knees forgin' signatures on the Magna Carta, and havin' perpetrated that act, he might just as well have decided to stay down there and eat some of Mary Magdalene's pussy. You just never know. Peelmunder! P...eel...m...u...n...d...e...r! Aw, fuck it. Want to know what my old mother would have said instead of fuck it? She would have said Drat! or Oh drat! Long time no hear. Mom bit the dust nigh onto ten year ago when a passel of drunk redskins on the warpath stormed the walls of her bridge club and poured into the breeches, or came in the britches of all the womenfolk and in so doing . . . No, that's a lie. All lies. Don't know exactly why, but I've lately taken to lying quite as easily as taking a piss. And with considerably more pleasure, I might add. My mother would be appalled at this. But then, most everything appalled her. She was not murdered by avenging Seminoles or regressive semaphores. No. She succumbed of complete cumulative world-weary disgust late one streaky afternoon while rereading *Jane Eyre* in her sun room.

Listen now to another of the snap-on personae who carry the ball for me 'neath Carol's verboten schoolgirl skirts in that exquisitely exacting, divinely exhausting chamber of goodies. Listen to Hubert Wildroot Sucklow, may his transformational drooling continue to increase.

—It should be established at the very shimmering outset of this projected postmortem that all the bears in this town ain't happily locked behind bars at the zoo. And if you think that all the little girls with curly blonde hair are safely locked up in their mothers' cupboards, why, you've got another thing coming. Pull the wool from over your eyes and take a good look at yours truly. Now tell us what you see. Of course! Golden locks, that's what you see on me. And how come you see them there? Because I'm wearing a wig. Because I'm that perennial sweetheart of Sigma Chi, that gleaming, goggle-eyed companion of childhood dupery, the very first real live walking, talking, sucking Barbie Doll—Goldilocks! *Yeahh!* With traditional accompanying neatly ironed plaid dress. And Carol does the three bears, or at least one of them.

Phew! OK now. Soon as I get this little-girl drag off . . .

I've got to let this thing out some. It's gettin' kinda tight. There we go. Mmm. Could that be bear taste on my tongue? How clever of Carol to rub it on herself. Where did she get it? At the zoo? All my life I've been a lurker, shifting in the shadows between here and there, now and then, up and down, in and out. I exist somewhere between that cute little blue pinafore and these shiftless jockey shorts I now stand before you in. Neither one is the answer. Instead, they both pose questions. What happens to me in either of them is a disembodied, disengaged satisfaction that postpones realization.

Do you begin to see my existential position? The suppliant outlines of my possible being? I feel inappropriate, to say the least. Perhaps I would be well advised to keep this sweet little dress and this fetching blonde wig on and scamper on back to Goldilocks's theoretically, or mythically, clean-cut, no-nonsense, down-to-earth home and hearth and resume my life there, surrounded by such time-honored woodcut phenomenologies as bubbling cauldrons of leek and potato soup in an open fireplace; shimmering ovens of baking whole wheat bread; ropes of garlic and sausages hanging from heavy, black, wooden beams; glowing, formidable, fat snoozing cats; richly molded muscular calves that lead to heavy peasant skirts that lead to round, stout shoulders and long braids that lead to happily and eternally busy mothers; ancient, thick, handmade rockingchairs occupied with grinning proprietary smugness by fathers puffing on porcelain pipes and wearing long woolen underwear under wide suspenders; and pet canaries and owls suspended in midflight somewhere between small leaded windows and massive planked iron studded doors, and snugly looming primitive wall portraits of stern but full-mouthed forebears and ancient petit point sayings and stuffed deer heads and dangling sprigs of wolfsbane and a cumbersome, coyly deadly blunderbuss leaning against the wall directly under father's soft old leather and fur hunting cap hanging on a wooden peg right next to a rabbit's foot hung on a nail for good luck. And there, suspended half in action midst that timeless, motionless, idyllic, pre-industrial, mysteriously craftily concocted fable/fantasy ambience would be myself, Goldilocks, my young/old face lit up as they would say with a spanky, spunky, shit-eating grin for the ages or for children of all ages, studiously drawing pictures of hoot owls for school, or dressing and undressing my peasant women dolls, or playing jacks while eating the Gingerbread Boy, or sitting quietly in a far corner memorizing a powerful magic curse to lay on Snow White or Mr. Toad or . . .

—Goldilocks, dear child, would you run out to the family herb garden and pick your mother some sweet basil for use in the wonderful squirrel stew she is making for our dinner tonight, sings my mother.

—Of course, Mother dear, I would be very happy to, I sing back. —I will go right this instant.

—And while you are out there, dear little Goldilocks, would you look in the ground for a nice, long, pine needle for your father so that he can give the stem of his pipe a good cleaning, sings my father.

—Oh yes, Father dear, with all my heart I will scour the friendly forest floor to find just the right pine needle, firm and supple and not silly and brittle, for to clean your wonderful little pipe. Yes indeedy.

—Oh, what a wonderful little daughter the good Lord has seen fit to bless us with, both mother and father sing out.

—Woof woof, says the dog.

—Meow meow, says the cat.

—Chirp chirp, says canary.

—Oh shit! I think I'm going to puke, says the reindeer on the wall.

—You can't fool me! I shout. You ain't no reindeer. You're . . .

—Decca Records! You windswept, rain-soaked, hydrogenated, over-drawn, undernourished, hip pocket, abstract little lowlife betrayer of class origins!

—Decca! You nutsy windborne cunt spore! How in heaven's name, or rather, how the fuck did you get in here?

—How do you think, dumbbell? Obviously I was trotting in the forest one fine day when a bloodthirsty hunter came along—Mr. Goldilocks, we're talking about—and shot me and after dining on me with his loutish friends, had my inedible and symbolic remains stuffed and hung on this wall. You got it now, Sucklow baby? I mean, if that's the moniker you're traveling under these days.

—Now, now, Decca. Let's not have the fishhook calling the seine net naughty. That tongue of yours . . .

—Has been places you've never dreamed of.

—That's what you say.

—That's what I know. Oh, Hubert! You poor, shifting shadow without a body! I've known you ever since you started out on your career, as a vest to somebody else's jacket. Or was it as a sneeze to another's nose? It's hard to remember the details of a life as surreptitiously secondary as yours. Easier to recall what Brutus mumbled to Caesar as he went down on him for the third time.

—You are one sassy and perverted historian, Decca. I can just imagine what you'd do with the French Revolution.

—Have done. You mean you haven't read my famous studies of Marat and Saint-Just and Charlotte Corday? The one on Corday alone forced half a dozen French historians of the period into early retirement. To save face as well as their pensions. It was a breathtaking piece of scholarship if I do say so myself, a high-wire act of such originality and daring that three of the major circuses have offered me five figures and my own private tent. In this study, using conceptual positions and methodological maneuverings obviously never before dreamed of, I maintain and conclusively prove that Charlotte was actually a schizophrenic male transvestite hooker knife for hire who had been persuaded to accept the hit contract on Marat by unscrupulous right-wing *ancien régime* psychiatrists who promised him/her that, once the deed was done, and Marat had utterly croaked, they would arrange for him/her to take it on the lam by disappearing into his/her other self who wasn't French at all but German and who in fact lived in Dresden, Germany, several hundred miles from the scene of the crime, and who, even in the very unlikely event she/he was caught up with by the frog fuzz, was quite safe because the heinies had no extradition deal with La Belle France.

—I'll be damned.

—And my paper on Marat, which I read originally before the Friends of the Society of Skin As In Save My Skin, at their annual shindig in the very bowels of Paris, this paper, up to its eyeballs in seminal fluids, has become as essential to the field of epidermal conversion symptoms as guilt is to the naturalistic novel. In fact, I would say that religion itself is the diseased skin of the basic unnaturalistic guilt novel, which, of course, leads us, whether we like it or not, directly into the ancient and not so ancient practice of flaying people alive for religious violations of one sort or another; that is to say the peeling off of the entire skin of the body, as if the skin itself were the vile offender, acting entirely on its own without first checking it out with the somebody, in exactly the same way, for instance, a suit of clothes would make a dinner date without consulting the person whose body it was covering. And when the skin in question ends up gracing a lampshade, or the suit of clothes is seen walking down the avenue completely on its own, then, my friends, we must take a deep breath and dive deeply back into metaphor. Or sink. So, as for Marat, as he sits, nay, cringes, day and night in that bathtub, soaking his wretched body, covered from cock to craw in a wet sheet to soothe his tormented, scabby skin . . . Marat was willing his skin to flower with loathsome scarlet blossoms of suppurating eczema in order to punish himself for . . . for what? For his sins. What sins? Number one: longing for a society whose very purity would bring it down. Number two: continuing to carry on a scatterbrained, masturbatory, childhood-rooted pornographic pen-pal exchange with that archenemy of the revolution, Madame du Barry, a lewd jade of the smuggest, most penetrable sort. A talky, elitist pervert Marat had known since they had both attended the first experimental hands on/hands off, open-ended, after you, Genevieve, kindergarten in Paris, run by two kind but suspect ex-nuns. Number three: maintaining contact, through a discreet but class-climbing medium/spiritualist from the vague fourteenth arrondissement, with wealthy Lyon textile merchants who, in return for formidable secret campaign funding funneled through the aforementioned spiritualist during fake trances, were promised government-directed sweetheart contracts with their hordes of slave laborers. Any one of the aforelisted would be enough to make even my skin crawl, and let me tell you, I've got a skin like no dreams you've ever had, I can assure you.

All that I've just laid on you, I might as well add, is a mere drop in ye olde bucket vis-à-vis the amount and most original quality of my historical scholarship, performed—and I use that word with the gleeful, cannily disciplined abandon of a drunken lapidary—under my professional handle, Socks, the Peal of Munder. To know Munder is to know the Peals. It's no munder you don't peal is a poignant charge often leveled, through the muck of the Middle Ages, at slow-witted baby bells and at adolescent belles who because of this or that, have not had a good shit in over six working days. Also, just in the interests of wide-spectrum clarity, one must be reminded of other heretofore mysterious sayings or homely lays; to wit and to woo: where there's munder, there's sure to be peal; covet not thy munder's peal; there's many a slip between the peal and the munder; one peal does not a munder make; a peal in hand is worth two in the munder. All of which quite clearly goes to show you that the name Socks, the Peal of Munder, or Socks Peelmunder, as popular shortening has it, is infinitely more than just a name. It is the churning, yearning, yes, burning accumulation of language and hearthstone wisdom itself. So where does all this leave us? you may ask. Well, if you have to ask, you can't afford it. As the bandmaster said, I'm gonna fix this here wagon once 'n' for all so's nobody kin jump on it. Uh huh. And I absolutely agree with him, 100 percent. That old wagon deserves a rest. People jumpin' on it, people fallin' off it . . . It's beyond me how the poor old thing has held up all these centuries. Course, they don't make things like that anymore, we all know that. Shoddy goods, shoddy workmanship, that's today's slovenly theme song all right. Even God has begun spinning his myths out of polyester, and you better believe it.

You gotta look far and wide, or near and tight maybe, for a place where things are like they used to be. Or should be. Or could be. Or even might be if you don't look sharp and step lively. See that place over there, way, way beyond the pizza tower but just this side of that stand of waving eucalyptus trees under your nose? Well, that's Practice Makes Perfect, Utah. If you listen real close you c'n hear the folks there talkin'. Lissen . . .

—Been doin' your mornin' push-ups, Abner?

—Nope. Just goin' down on the missus.

—I was wonderin', 'cause you have the facial colorin' of a man who's been up to sumpin strenuous for a higher purpose.

—You weren't far wrong, Stanley. Ain't anything much higher'n eatin' pussy, an' unless sumpin's real wrong with you, a fine glow's just gotta come up on yore face.

—We're going to see you at the bowling alley tonight, aren't we, Philomena? We take on the Baptist Babes next week and we've just got to be at our peak.

—Can't make it, Georgina honey. I peaked out yesterday while I was baking bread, and I've been winding down ever since.

—Oh dear. I just don't know what we'll do without you. Team spirit is the very jewel of our soul and who robs us of that makes us poor indeed. 'Twas mine, 'tis his, and has been slave to thousands.

—That's the way the goose feathers fly, Georgina.

And . . .

—Brother Hoxey, why must you be forever pesterin' the Lord God to show himself? Isn't it enough . . .

—The answer is very simple, Reverend. I ain't gonna be buffaloed by silences and absences.

—That very same statement was made to me thirty-seven years ago by your dad standin' in the very same soft spot.

—Your memory may be good, Reverend Hatch, but it ain't gonna get you off the spot. I'm serious about thrown-down gauntlets. I practice.

He's not the only one. Take a gander at that none-too-clear body way down there at the end of the street. Can you detect, can you sense, can you feel its succulent inertness? Does it not make you think of, or at least put you in mind of, a fresh, hot jelly roll that says Take me. Do with me as you will. Then we'll see who's remembered the longest. Hmm? That body is Louisa Parsons's. She's practicing positions of passive resistance, for the future, for a time when she might be deadlocked with a political enemy or force whom she secretly rather likes. Every day. And in the same place. She likes it there, one might safely say without being presumptuous. No problems with swirling dead leaves, and traffic long ago stopped finding that area attractive. Quite abruptly. Without any advance signs that could have been read by either demographic sociologists or the town mothers. Under such circumstances, presented as it were with an historical fait accompli, what, exactly, can one be expected to do? Look backwards. What was Julius Caesar supposed to do or say when he woke up that particular morning, turned his wife Calpurnia over for a better shot at her ass, then looked up and saw all those fucking elephants pouring out of the Alps with Hannibal in the lead? What was Big C. supposed to do? Call up the director of the Zurich Zoo and say, Kurt, I think there's been a bad breakout, fella? Grab his autographed copy of *The Decline of the Roman Empire* to see if the whole thing wasn't some kind of typo? Goddamn drunken printers. Or simply go right on fucking his wife up her ass? Try putting yourself in his toga and see how smart you feel. It's about time you Monday-morning quarterbacks got straightened out and called onto the mattress.

In screams begin responsibilities, you may say, now that you have obviously, judging from the look on your silly face, just heard those coming from the big rambling old white house across the way whose sagging front porch is just reeking with disorderly nostalgia. Well, maybe you've got a point. In a back room on the third floor, Basil Dunkley, who is no longer knee high to a grasshopper, contrary to a lot of loose talk, is practicing throwing fits for the benefit of the draft board which is planning to send him over there, over there, where the yanks are coming and the banks are slumming, to save the frogs from the huns as well as get to know mademoiselle from Armentières parley voo and a little bit of clap goes along with that too. As one would hope in a situation as packed with jam as this, these are questions to be asked. I could, for instance, very easily open my mouth and shout across the big house: —Dunkley! Are you on top of it! Are your screams the right kind? Are they stylistically relevant to the situation?

And Dunkley could quite easily, I hope, shout back: —Bet your boots I'm on top of it. These screams have been in my family for generations. My great granddaddy used them at the outbreak of the Franco-Prussian War. My granddad used them at the outbreak of the War of 1812. My dad used them to great advantage several weeks before the North and the South girded their respective loins, not long before the Battle of Roache's Run. So as you can see . . .

And I could then shout back: —Dunkley, you're in for a surprise. You are out of tune with the times. Those screams won't work at your draft board. The ears of that board are cupped for modern, present-day screams. You might just as well be hooking up old Dobbin to the shay to compete in the Indianapolis 500. Prepare yourself for Armageddon, Dunkley.

And Dunkley then might let loose with some screams of a totally different kind and caliber.

Cast a quick and inconspicuous glance at those three shadowy fellows standing there in front of Mosley's Men's Fashions. Those three look-alikes are identical triplets, the Rudd brothers. Hi, Ho, the Derry-O. Think they're planning their spring wardrobe? This spiffy pair of green pants with that hungry black belt? That rambunctious red plaid jacket with this salacious yellow fedora? Oh no. That's not what they're up to. Inch your way over there without appearing to do quite that. Within earshot but not buckshot. Hear them?

—I'm going to force feed these issues right here and now: Hi.

—I'll have to split soon with my infinitives: Ho.

—I'll bare my brunt only to the highest bidder: The Derry-O.

Those Rudd boys are dead serious. Whether you can tell 'em apart or not. They're getting in shape for the biggest showdown of all. With the Mother Tongue. You couldn't buy a seat for that if your life depended on it. Let's hope for your sake that it won't, in fact, that it never will. 'Pears to me that you c'n use all the peace and quiet you c'n lay your hands on. Hope you don't take this as a 'vasion of your privates.

Purges. Now to tha unfamiliar ear that may sound like a small and smelly village in Belgium. But it ain't. It's what our town goes in for from time to time. Twice a year, if the truth has to be known. An' public too. We're not the kinda place to do things in a closet or behind overdrawn curtains. What's tha good of somethin' important like a purge lessen you do it in public, out in the open, where God c'n see it and try to hide his eyes?

Our purges take place between the cock's first crow and the Savior's last gasp, make no mistake about it. Or let's say it's best not to. The townsfolk don't have to set their watches either, no more'n they have to set their heartbeat. They know the time of the purges like they know nothin' else, like they know themselves. Everybody over eighteen.

It's a sight for sore eyes, our purge. The singular being more precise because it is a single collective act. We don't countenance nor do we stomach individual, virtuoso purging acts. That would be a contradiction of, and quite possibly a slap in the face to, the whole idea, which is that we are as one in this thing, the whole of the town being not at all the same as the sum of all its tasty, juice-filled parts. Just as, in the same kind of way, Christ died for everybody, not just a handful of separate and distinct individuals who had caught his eye. Or, over on the other side of the fence, so to speak, when those painted-up pagans sacrificed a living victim to the gods—you know, laid out one of their own up on that altar there, nicely bound up of course, just in case the party of the second part got antsy at the big moment and tried to get away, and, with some well-known and well-worn speeches, slowly cut out the still-beating heart—they were doing it in the name of everybody in the whole tribe, and the lucky person up there on the altar was not up there on his own behalf, no matter what kinky kicks he or she was getting, but on behalf of everybody, *was* everybody, the whole bunch, in fact. So you can see how ungainly, untoward, and utterly out of place it would have been, when the heart had been cut up into more or less equal pieces and handed around to the pagan folks down below, for somebody to say, My! What a tasty little piece of fresh heart. Sure hits the spot. Or even, Damn. Why does it always have to be heart, heart, heart. How about some kidney or liver for a change. Phew! The manners of some people. Anyway, you can understand how these individual and very personal responses to the performance would seriously undermine the whole idea of the thing, from the ground floor up.

Well . . . Our purge is a pretty picture indeed, and this is not just the back-patting voice of town pride you're hearing. Can't you just see it? There everybody is . . . standing at attention on Main Street, stark, staring naked. An' just look at those faces, all shiny 'n' smilin' so nice, a heartwarmin' an' irreversible tribute to the magical powers of the cocaine leaf which everybody has been chewin' as per regulation, to get into just the right frame of mind, clear the brain like it was a bran' new classroom blackboard. And there's the Chief Purger stridin' up and down in front of them, naked like everybody else 'cept for the big gold long-horned steer skull completely coverin' his, or her, head, 'cause sometimes the Chief Purger is a woman, but as you yourself can see as well as anybody, that's not the case this time. An' nobody knows who it is. The way it works is, twice a year we have a drawing, at springtime just as the earth is wakin' up, and at the beginning of winter, when it's goin' to sleep. Everybody closes their eyes and reaches into the Town Coffin. And pulls out a small round wafer and slowly eats the wafer. All these wafers are exactly the same, except for one of them. This one has a very old time drug in it which a little while after the wafer has been eaten, makes the eater forget who he or she is. And I mean for good. That person from then on Isn't Anybody in Particular. Is just a pure, clean, beautiful intelligence. In this nameless, reborn, unborn, not-born state of mind, the person has become the Chief Purger, y' see. And goes directly to the Sacred Resting Place, a night and day lit-up glass case in Town Hall, and takes out the Divine Skull, that steer skull you are looking at now, which is a lot older than anybody here, having belonged to and been hidden in The Cave by The Ones Who Are No Longer Here who dwelled here'bouts before history. Vanished, I think. Well, more or less vanished, I s'pose. Maybe into thin air, maybe not. No Longer Here. Far as anybody knows, they weren't wiped out by anything, or anybody, you know, like a bunch of smart-ass Spanish conquistadors with their greasy tongues hangin' out and down to their scabby knees. Which raises the point of maybe they disappeared some other way. Like maybe they just turned their backs on history and went the other way one morning. Everything that happens in the world doesn't wind up in the newspapers for you to read about, y' know.

Oh. The Purge is beginning. The Chief Purger is selecting, is touching the genitals, as is The Way, of that woman with the highfalutin red hair. Look at the way this woman steps out of the line and onto the stage, so to speak, of the long, empty, waiting street. Like the memory of a legendary white unicorn who has performed certain exquisite ballets before emperors and their prissy, secretly incestuous courts and who will never let you forget those moments of her servile glory. Hear the Chief Purger call out the Primary Provocative Letters. And his voice, you've never heard a voice like that come from man or beast. Hear . . .

—A! A! In the name of all that is clean, I demand to hear of those crimes, those violations that begin with that letter! Purge! Purge!

—Oh yes! howl all of the naked citizens at once. —Oh yes!

—Adultery! Aggression! Avarice! Analingus! shouts the redhead, loping airily up and down in front of the others. —Apathy! Asininity! Anal intercourse!

—Eeeeeaahh! screams the crowd, ecstatically writhing and twisting. —Eeeeeaahh!

—Purge! Cleanse! barks/shrieks the Chief Purger, stomping/pawing as would a bull. And as the redhead lopes past him, he dips and swoops his skull head, making a long, elegant, skin-deep incision in her back with the tip of the gold right horn.

—Ahhhh yes! the redhead moans, and the crowd moans with her. She leaps into the line, blood oozing down from the long incision. She spins in and out of the arms of each of the townspeople, smearing them with her fresh blood.

The Chief Purger beats time to her bloody spinning by silently clapping his hands.

The last citizen embraces her, is smeared, and she lopes, seemingly not quite touching the ground, down the empty main street and disappears into the woods at the bottom of the mountain.

Now the Chief Purger selects another from the blood-stained line. Puts his hand on the genitals of the man who is hanging/dripping with folds of fat. This grinning, blood-stained man steps forward, turns, and scampers up and down in front of his fellowman, as a silly little white rabbit would scamper hoping by his Easter Bunny cuteness to distract his captors from their salivating thoughts of an imminent, tasty, rabbit stew.

B! B! snarls/barks the Chief Purger. In the name of all that is clean, I demand to hear those crimes, those violations that begin with that letter! Purge! Purge!

—Oh yes! howl all of the naked bloody citizens at once. —Oh yes!

—Bastardy! Buggery! Bitchery! Bickering! Bestiality! cries the fat man, scampering up and down in front of the blood-smeared others. —Bragging! Borrowing! Banality!

—Eeeaahh! screams the crowd, all writhing and contorting. —Eccaahh!

—Purge! Cleanse! barks/shrieks the Chief Purger, stomping and pawing, and as the fat man scampers past him, he dips and swoops as he had done before, and the long incision is made in the man's back.

—Aaahh yes! moans the fat man, and the crowd moans too. He leaps into the long line, and the blood oozes from the incision. And he too, like the redhead before him, spins, whirls in and out of the arms of his fellow towns-people, leaving his blood on them, letting them partake of his blood.

And the Chief Purger—his golden horns gleam so in the staring moon-light, and the fresh blood on the right horn glistens exquisitely—silently claps his hands beating time.

The blood-dripping fat man spins out of the embrace of the last citizen and scampers on down the long emptiness of Main Street and vanishes into the woods at the foot of the mountain. Precisely as the red-haired woman before him.

Now the Chief Purger selects . . .

Well now. That was sure some show, wasn't it? Sorry you couldn't stay for the whole thing, but outsiders aren't even supposed to see any of it, to begin with. It's a private town affair, which is a fact you can surely appreciate and use to guide yourself with. Our welcome to strangers or visitors to our town don't tend all the way down to lettin' 'em sneak up on us an' steal our ways from us, right from under our nose. Think we're crazy? I mean, how would you like it if a bunch of us visited your town for a horseshoe pitchin' match an' while you were countin' up the dead ringers, we walked off with a hand-ful of your good-lookin' young wives? Or stole a good look at some of those secret treaties you signed with the redskins before they could even read and write? Wouldn't like that much, would you? Didn't think so.

Got some questions to ask, don't you? A body wouldn't have to be a profes-sional mindreader to guess what they are. You seem more ticklish than they do. You want to know what happened to the alphabet that ran off into the mountains, don't you? Those twenty-six people from Missus A to Mister Z. The answer's easy. They kept right on going. That's right. They're staying on up there, in the wilderness of the mountains into which they ran and into which they disappeared. Not too much is known and calculatedly not too much is cared or asked, about what they do with themselves. They all live together in the ancient and forbidden caves. They forage in the forests. They live off their wits. They amuse themselves, they play games. They form them-selves into words, and then into sentences. They dance and whirl about shouting meanings at one another. They have become language. Long into the night, in those labyrinthine hollows lit up by innumerable small fires. We hear about this, offhandedly to be sure, from long-distance hunters who come back down with loneliness and skins and terrible hungers.

And the Chief Purgers, what do they do, what happens to them, after the purges? They too vanish, but in quite a different way. After the ceremony, and while all the townsfolk are trotting back through the waning moonlight to their homes where they will resume their sleep, they briskly gallop back to the town hall where they carefully remove the golden-horned skull from their head and place it back in its illuminated glass case. And after that? After that, they wake up, but as someone else. The person who performed the rites of the Chief Purger is no more. There is no memory of that experience, that custom-required obligation, to be carried around in the person's, or ex-person's head. Wake up as somebody else, Mary Lou This or Big John That. We have lots of identities lying around unused. And the identity they have given up with the skull, that goes into our identity pool to be used by . . . well, that's our business, really. You've gotten more than your earful already. But what you are about to say is true enough: that a fair number of people walking around here are really somebody else. Two or three different people at once, because identities in the pool are used over and over again. We're anything but wasteful here in Practice. Like some profligate settlements of long-overdue standing, where they even waste their shadows. Thus, every moment there is starkly and immanently high noon. We, on the contrary, hold ours very dear, dearer, in a pinch, than the substance that casts them. Anybody caught maltreating, defacing, altering, underestimating, overlooking, counterfeiting, or misjudging a shadow, such a violating person is dealt with immediately. Chastened, hastened, and punished according to scripture. Straightened out, as they would say in the vulgar tongue. Anybody caught trying to beg, borrow, barter, or steal a shadow is flogged on the spot. Which may explain to you why everybody over eighteen in Practice is to be seen carrying a braided leather whip strapped to their back, both ladies and gents. Required by scripture: no exceptions to be made, period. And anybody caught trying to abandon a shadow is stabbed to death on the spot. Which should certainly explain to you the presence of the dagger attached, in a sheath of course, to everyone's belt. Shadow abandoners can fill cemeteries in more ways than one. Hence they can be the most blasphemous and dangerous miscreants of all.

We all have one whale of a time come elections, for public office. Promises, promises . . . Oh boy! You haven't heard anything until you've heard our candidates do their stuff on the campaign trail. Whooee and whooppee and get a load of that. HO HO HO and HA HA HA. To put it with the bluntness of an instrument, familiar or otherwise, the situation is milked for all its worthiness, and it's about time too, we all unanimously agree. And this time, age is no barrier for once. Let the kiddies in on the fun. . . . What the hell.

Ring out, wild bellhops! Deck those molls with Moses' balls.

The streets of the village are alive and well with thonged throngs, welling up with wishes, wish welling, churning with breast beaters and brow beaters, eyebrow raisers, and eyebrow lowerers, some with, some without, seedless raisins or seedless reasoners, or season's reasons, hawkers of goods, hawkers of phlegm, and phlegmatic hawks, simply put. Riding on the crests of imagined popularity, surrounding certain issues and issuing certain surroundings with . . . Hear ye! Hear ye! Harken and larken, you all!

—Build the jailhouse of your dreams! shouts Burr Welles. —Elect me Top Jailer! All the comforts of home and none of the conundrums!

—Put your dreams in jail is more like it! hoots Billy Mudd, who's also up for the same job. He's talkin' through his hat, like always. —Elect me, folks, an' we'll beat your jailbait into plowmen's follies!

—Think anything you want to think, but don't tell a soul about it! yells Clara Mott. —I promise you that if I'm elected to the position of Town Censor, I'll make you eat your words . . . if you're dumb enough to put 'em on paper.

—That ain't nothin'! If you vote me into that high-handed position, I'll see to it that your words eat you! hollered Sissy Mae Cowley. —Our town's letters must be purer than driven snowmen.

Over there, standin' on that wine barrel, is Kenny Spatz, age seven, shootin' for eleven.

—What this old burg needs is a lot more turnabout and a lot less turnovers. Put the grown-ups on the spot for a change. Spare the rod and spoil the parent. Vote me in as Justice of the Peace and I'll see to it that every adult in this place learns to jump when they hear the sound of a child's voice and learns to toe the line and kiss a lot of ass. You've heard of citizen's arrests? Well, we'll set up children's arrests. Any kid can arrest any grown-up for any crime, real or imagined, remembered or anticipated. Yes indeedy, piccolo petey. There'll be lots of different dancing to lots of different tunes, folks.

Little Laura Loomis, age ten, master of Zen, from the top of the lamppost swingin', at the top of her baby voice singin':

—I'm running for Town Recreation Director and you'd better believe it. And what recreation. Boy oh boy! Sweep me into power and the fun will begin. With or without a pig's foot and a bottle of gin. Button, Button, Who's Got the Button brought up-to-date in view of recent eye-popping psychological studies. Run Sheep Run comes out of the closet at last and oh, what sheep and oh, what runners! And the original intent of the game, before it was seized and subsumed and warped and woofed by the powers that be— soon, let us hope, that were—will out. And Blind Man's Bluff! Oh lala laloo. Who'll be blinded and who'll be bluffed, and blinded by what and bluffed by whom? Jack be nimble, Jack be quick, vote for me and get in your lick!

And up there dangling from that rickety old wooden balcony like she's long past being participled, is Peaches Putney née Chutney.

—Collect your wits and leave the witticisms to me, folks. 'Cause I'm running for Town Crier! You haven't heard a town really cry, friends, until you've heard me. And the proclamations, declarations, defamations, and intimations that'll pour out of my mouth! Unglue you from your favorite ride-em-cowboy murder mysteries. Hear ye! Hear ye! Hear ye! Third-generation werewolves form a union and demand minimum hourly pay from witches, witch doctors, shamans, and weekend spooks! Hear ye! Hear ye! Police on lookout for phantom ten-year-old girl who has been molesting middle-aged men in public toilets! Entire police force slaving overtime weaving dragnets, fish nets, hair nets, and anything else that might catch this shameless, perverted little hussy. Hear ye! Hear ye! Former grade-school virtuoso problem student discovered hiding out in Paris, France. Michael Smoot, who left his mark on more than one of his teachers, breaks his long-held silence by communicating with well-known Practice shyster regarding the overdrawn settling of his shifty, ambiguous father's low estate. I will now read to you from this document, which has come into my possession by other than normal channels and merry means. Lend me your hairy, pointed ears! I quote: "My dear Sly: How can I ever thank you for finally settling my old man's hash by settling his so-called estate. He left me the moldy ruins of a collapsed mythology. His Peruvian gold mines turned out to be pages torn from the *National Geographic* magazine. His Siberian Railway stock a paragraph he lifted from a Gogol novel. His plans for my future, which he sang like 'The Star-Spangled Banner' at the oddest hours, part of a serial he heard on a neighbor's radio. I can now discover him by looking elsewhere and at others. That jaunty style he charmed so many with was taken from Douglas Fairbanks movies. His mustache and the twirling of it he copied from my mother's brother Darcy. And his laugh, those craftily muffled explosions, he learned at his weekly amateur actors' sessions. I ask myself: from whom did he nick the sperm with which to impregnate my mother?

"He was a total fabrication. Which of course makes me feel at times half like a ghost. My reality comes only from my mother. That other nonexistent half of me, that aching need in the unfilled void, spends all of its time looking for itself. It literally goes everywhere, dragging me with it, of course. God! How I wish it could do its business by itself. Though I don't knowingly share in its insatiable voyages and crazed adventures, I do bear the marks of one sort or another. Sometimes I hear voices inside myself. Who are these people, I ask? Well, obviously it's my so far nonperson other half engaging itself socially. Most of the conversations are in English, but they're still

Greek to me. I mean, I don't know what they're all about. They're not about me or anything that I have to do with. They are about the lives of others, and the other, though I can't tell which voice is his, or hers, because after all, God help me, it may be a woman. Sometimes the conversations are in French, Spanish, and Italian. I think . . . well, Other Half, it's good to see that you've been putting your time to good use, learning languages, maybe even teaching yourself. Admirable. But I could be wrong. Maybe Other Self, or other Nonself, is just a listener to these foreign language bits and can't, after all, speak a bloody word of their lingo. I certainly hope that he/she has a bilingual friend along to translate in such situations. I myself would be more than happy to help out if necessary, when it comes to French, a language that I am modestly fluent in. What are friends and family for if not to assist at times of need? Life in the human community, however ambiguously defined its respectful members may be, would be quite unlivable without this fundamental rule. Even hyenas howl for their brothers with sore throats.

"As for those marks in general that I share or bear, those reminders of The Other . . . One recent morning . . .

—How did you get this strange thing on your back? asked Germaine, who was in bed with me.

—What thing is that? I said, turning over to kiss her breast.

She turned me on my side facing away from her. —This long, red mark, she said, and traced it with her finger. —It looks like an incision or something. But the skin isn't disturbed at all. It isn't broken. And she traced it again.

—Can't imagine what it could be. I turned back to kissing her sweet nipple.

—It wasn't there last night, when we went to bed, she said. —Don't you want to take a look at it? Aren't you curious?

—Sure, I suppose so. I mean, why not?

—You sound so beautifully American. Part cowboy, part mystic.

—Did you know that Saint Anselm started out as an Indian scout?

And my God. There the fucking thing was. A long, red, curved line, staring back at me from the big bathroom mirror. Curving from my left shoulder blade down to where I suppose my left kidney hangs out. I touched it. It didn't hurt or even feel. It was just there. The nonself, The Phantom Other, had been at it again.

—Quite extraordinary, isn't it? said Germaine, as I lay back down next to her. —How do you think you got it? Perhaps in a dream?

—Well, maybe not a dream exactly, but someplace pretty close to it.

—Hmm. I see.

—There's this part of me called the Nonself, and it's always on the go. I suspect it snuffles around in the goddamnedest places. And it sometimes brings us back, uh, artifacts, you might say.

—You know, Michael darling, whenever I'm with you I have an odd sensation of being involved in sort of a living mythology. Really. It's like the feeling I used to get when I was a student visiting the Louvre. I would stare at those old tapestries so long that they would come alive. I thought I was going mad, in a gentle sort of way. Sometimes I would feel that I was disappearing into them, or merging with them, grabbing onto the horns of the elegant unicorns and galloping off into the eleventh century. Mmm. It was divine. I can feel the sweet wind against my face right now as we raced by the tiny castles in the hills.

—I knew I'd seen you somewhere a long time ago, I said. —You're in all the tapestries I've ever looked at, in the Louvre, the Met, Cluny, Palisades. You are The Lady on the Unicorn, long blonde hair streaming in the wind, riding sidesaddle into infinity.

—Mmm. That feels so wonderful. Your tongue is so ... inspired. Oh yes ... When I come . . . I will be riding . . . the unicorn.

Fucking Germaine, that was as much fun as I've ever had with any woman. She didn't creep me in any way. Some women, they're great fucks, you know, I mean, they do everything and with gusto, but being with them, in and out of the fucking, can be a little like being in the Funhouse. All of a sudden, something might go wrong ... say a gear will lock, and you're hurled off the merry-go-round. That smile can turn into a nasty lip, hurt ego, or some such shit. But not Germaine. She's got her shit together and she has had it together for quite some time. She knows what getting pleasure and giving pleasure is all about. You can go all the way with her with your eyes closed. You don't have to keep one open just to be sure everything's hunky. And that nothing is creeping up on you with a knife in its teeth. You feel good when you say good-bye. Instead of itchy and dirty and guilty about the whole fucking thing. A couple more like her and the battle of the sexes would be all over. That endless stalemate, rat-infested trench warfare, trench mouth confrontation. Mustard gas, bayonet wounds, rotting feet, lies, crossed signals, vile accusations, shit-stained . . . What is that lurking/ looming up in the shadows of my head? A memory? My memory? Something The Other got into or is dredging up? How fucking weird. What's happening? Who are these people coming toward me from over those brain hills? I'm being invaded from inner space. . . . I've never seen them before. Even the sand looked strange that day. It lay under the grey sky like a sullen victim, not wanting you to come anywhere near it in its hurt and trouble. Jonas stared at it from his perch on Ab Horton's veranda, aloof on the dunes, and wondered what kept Fire Island from suddenly exploding into a billion pieces and disappearing forever into the forgiving motherly ocean.

—Do you feel that something is not all right with this day? Jonas asked Horton, who seemed hospitalized in a lounge chair next to him.

—Yes, Horton replied, not opening his eyes, —but it's because I drank all that lighter fluid last night.

—I don't mean it that way. Jonas sipped his vodka-tonic and looked out at the sea and sand. —With the day itself: something's the matter. It seems spiritually sick or something.

Horton opened his eyes just enough to see the highball glass he was nourishing himself at. —I can't afford to question nature. I'm only concerned with pleasures of the body. He leaned back, closing his eyes, and sighed heavily. —My body.

Jonas sucked on the lime from his drink. —You just won't listen to life's signals, Ab. You're denying your God-given oneness.

For the last two days, since Jonas's arrival there, Horton's large beach house had been a madness of visitors, or poachers. They floated in and out of the place all day and all night, as though all the laws of nature and society regarding time divisions and personal privacy were academic nonsense. Sounds of music and frolic that were normally meant for hearing at night were heard all day, and vibrations of the night penetrated the day's sanctity like sneaking, dark cave dwellers. And the pairings of people—what demented blizzard blew them together? Jonas had come there alone with the idea of connecting with something beautiful and game and undemanding, but so far this idyllic encounter had not taken place. Oh, there had been a couple of potentials, both still wearing bathing suits at midnight, but each was more or less in the company of her husband and Jonas no longer savored this type of danger, so he'd indicated no, thanks.

Far out on the horizon a tiny sailboat moved into view. Jonas watched it, fascinated but, strangely, without any real interest. Suddenly the boat stopped moving.

—Christ! Jonas exclaimed. —Something's happened to the wind.

A groan came from Horton. —The wind?

—It's given up. Or been taken away. That boat out there, Jonas extended his arm, —it can't move.

Horton's lounge chair creaked unhappily. —This vodka is not coming through for me, he said, standing now behind Jonas. —I'm changing to scotch. I think you should too. And he took Jonas's empty glass and padded barefootedly into the house.

—Maybe you're right, Jonas said, even though Horton was no longer there. He watched the stilled boat and thought about various types of women he'd like to connect with, and continued to feel—this time it had to do with a sea gull, a few yards away, that kept opening and closing its mouth as though it were choking to death—the wrongness of the day. In another moment he stood up. Something urged him to assert his own aliveness. He walked around the patio, breathing deep and looking intensely at all that was to be seen on those stretches of semi-inhabited dunes, and returned to his chair.

Horton returned with the drinks. With his matted, short curled hair, his hidden features, and his loping walk, he looked dangerously like a disturbed English sheepdog. —Did you ever meet a girl named Paulette Owens? he asked. —A tall kooky Negro?

Jonas quickly herded all the Negro females he'd ever met into the inspection room of his mind. Will Miss Paulette Owens please step forward! Not a motion in the ranks. —Nope, he answered after a couple of moments. —I don't think so. Why?

—Just wondered. She's coming by tonight with some people who are staying with Alice Oakes. He leaned back and stared into the Almighty's vast blue estate. —Very unusual girl.

—Oh? More unusual than usual?

Horton slurped some scotch down and crunched into an ice cube. —Well, if she owned a labyrinth, he said slowly between ice-sucking sounds, —she'd give it a downstairs penthouse.

Jonas had a small laughter spasm, and the psychic vibrations of it jostled Paulette Owens offstage and brought into view someone else. —Christ, Ab! That Swanson guy last night! Painting those dirty pictures on his girlfriend's back!

—He's promised to do some murals for me. He threw an ice cube at a stunted dune tree. —But I don't think he means it.

—Where do you find these people? Jonas asked.

—They find me.

Jonas looked at Horton for a few moments, looked at his old blue bathing shorts, his skinny hairy legs, his baby-wet lips, and said, —What's it like to be rich, Ab?

Horton sat up and swallowed the rest of his drink. —To tell you the truth, I don't really know. I know I'm supposed to know, but I don't. He looked at the beach. —I don't even know what it's like to be me, much less somebody rich.

The Negro girl Paulette, standing in a corner of the large all-purpose room, being talked to by three young men in swim trunks, looked like a fabled blackamoor right out of a Venetian palace. She was dressed exactly that way, and her Newtonian equation of a face was crowned with a red-and-white turban. She is Othello's sister, Jonas thought, watching her from the center of the gabbling room. She suddenly released a crazy scream of laughter and writhed in such a way it appeared she was somehow wrapping herself around herself.

—Love it! she howled. —Oh God, what an idea! Wearing a black contraceptive in mourning.

—That's the French for you, Jonas heard one of the young men say with inflections that clearly stated that he was a faggot.

The Negro girl's glance now wandered around the room and stopped at the wavelength of Jonas staring. Perhaps because he was a little drunk, or because something special was in the air, Jonas did not, as he certainly would have ordinarily, quickly shift his eyes away in guilt or nervousness. They looked right into hers for seconds. She broke this hold by smiling and raising her glass in a toast to his unsuspected presence there. He returned the gesture.

—Are you rehearsing a part with an invisible partner? Or have you become a student of Barrault?

It was Alice Oakes grinning and breathing heavy at his elbow. His gaze involuntarily fell immediately to her rebelliously oversized breasts, half exposed to the entire world under a child-sized halter. They were like parts of a mountain range that had broken off to settle by themselves.

—No, he said. —I was just acknowledging Miss Owens over there; and he nodded his head in that direction.

Alice nudged him in the sly dirty-boy way of certain kinds of men raised very strictly. —She's a bedful all right, isn't she?

—I wasn't necessarily thinking of the bed.

Alice chuckled hoarsely, her high, female voice long ago having drowned in the tides of bourbon. She carries a whorehouse on her back, Jonas thought. —Oh come on, Jonas baby, she said, —when did you enter the priesthood?

—What does she do? Jonas asked as he continued to watch the Negro girl. —I mean, does she work at some kind of job?

—She's a model.

—That means anything you want it to mean.

—Right you are, old skin diver.

The music on the hi-fi changed now to a wild twist operation. Paulette responded unhesitatingly to its frantic call, and began to twist by herself. Now she looked at Jonas, and twisted her way to him.

—Live a little! she shouted at him.

—OK! he yelled back, and entered into the twisting with her.

—Thatababy! she said, her face furiously animated. —Don't question reality. Just respond to those old jungle drums, and you'll live to be a hundred.

He had to laugh; the girl sprang something in him. The large room was now a frenzy of twisters, some dressed, some half naked, some high as Korean kites. In a crowded corner Horton, accompanied in this journey by a large-bottomed girl in a red bikini, was reverting completely to his ape origins and was jumping up and down yelling in a language he had decided was African. A body's throw from Horton two girls, clearly in their late teens, were dancing together as if their very lives depended upon it. In front of Jonas, Paulette was performing miracles of discombobulation. Jonas was responding, but in a way that was unusual for him he felt that he was a puppet being magically manipulated by the girl's energy or thoughts.

When the music ended, in an explosion of rising hysteria, Paulette, perspiring and gasping, flung herself into Jonas's arms. —Oh God! What madness!

—I didn't know I had it in me, Jonas panted, holding up/hugging her. Her body felt alert and almost urgent even though it was in this relaxed state. She was wearing no brassiere beneath her bizarre wraparound, and the breasts that touched him, very firm and high, seemed to contain childlike innocence and no hint of duplicity. He could even hear her heart beat. —Deep down I must be a real madman, he said, grinning.

—I need a drink, she said, and taking him possessively, if not peremptorily, by the arm, led him over to the long table holding Horton's lavish booze festival. —Alcohol: the poor man's Plato.

The noise and psychic clatter in the big room were a little too much for Jonas, so when they had gotten their drinks—she was taking lots of Pernod on the rocks—they went out onto the porch facing the ocean. Jonas felt somewhat exhilarated: the dancing had physically awakened long slumbering muscles, and the apparently unfettered Negro Paulette, without making any direct gestures, was doing splendid things to his libido. Sitting in the big wicker chairs, the air around washed by the rushing sea-tide sounds, they drank in silence for a minute or two. Up the beach a small driftwood fire was burning hungrily, and Jonas could just make out a couple of half-naked bodies lying around it.

—Horton's completely mad, isn't he? she said. —I don't think he's ever drawn a sane breath. She drank off a good deal of the Pernod with loud relish. —But then he doesn't have to. He's loaded. She smiled at him, an all-out smile of pleasure and killer hunger. —Just think—to be able to tell the whole world to go screw.

—Is that what you'd really like to do?

She snorted. —Of course. Wouldn't you?

Jonas waited for a moment until a great shriek from inside died down. —I'm not so sure. I mean, I guess not.

She frowned at him. —That sounds nutty. What would you like to do then?

—You know, I think I'd probably become a complete ascetic. The possibility of doing anything I wanted, indulging anything, would scare me so much I'd shrink right up.

She shook her head slowly and meaningfully. —Oh you crazy white Puritan. You are in a bad way, baby. She undid a button and put her hand inside his shirt and teasingly caressed him. —Give me a big French kiss, she commanded, and Jonas, quite hot now, did just that. When he was about to break, she held, and, putting her glass on the porch railing, wrapped him in a black-armed vise and kissed him so hard and madly he thought he was going to vanish inside her licorice and black-tasting mouth.

He breathed in deeply when she finally released him. He had the weird feeling that he'd just been dined on. —A couple more of those and I'll become a beachcomber, he said. —It'll be farewell to civilization.

She drank off her Pernod, and kissing him quickly, deposited half an ice cube in his surprised mouth. —I don't think you have the nerve. You need civilization to protect you from your real self. She kissed him again and retrieved the ice cube and crunched it into watery oblivion. —All you white men cling to it like it was your mommy's titty, she chuckled. —Take it away from you and, man, do you panic.

Jonas's desire, which had taken possession of him like a country's swarming occupier, was suddenly colored by anxiety, but he snickered anyway. —Maybe so, he said. —Maybe you've put your finger on the main switch.

—Us black girls are witches, didn't you know that? and she laughed hysterically, grabbing on to him for support. She recovered in a moment or two—her flight of mad glee subsided as some wild, nameless, invisible bird shrieks in forest heights—and said, —Listen, sweetie, I've got some great pot in my handbag. Why don't we sit on the dunes and do some blasting?

Jonas hadn't smoked marijuana in several years, but the memory of it, an evening's experience with a rare-faced Poe-type girl, was very fine indeed. —Great, he said. A couple half stumbled out of the house, the eerie pounding of marimba drums following them—and began kissing on the porch. —This place is going up in smoke soon, he said, and took her lean, muscular arm and they walked down the wooden stairway onto the dark beach.

—That surf's really the most, Paulette said, pausing to look at the incoming waves. —Like it's whispering and reaching out for you. Makes me feel like a kid, when I'd be going to sleep in that smelly bedroom with everybody, and I'd hear strange night sounds in my head and I would be afraid to close my eyes.

She was not kidding; the pot was unassailably delicious stuff and Jonas hadn't felt so good all over and on top and floaty since God knows when. They could have been lying in the sky instead of on a dune. He had no sense of gravity at all, and none of the defense lines in his head or soul were there anymore. He knew she felt the same way. They had been making conversation freely, formlessly, two rare instruments improvising in the exquisite infinity of their awareness.

—How many yous are there? she asked.

—Two; no, two and a half.

—Mmm. That's nothing. Guess how many mes there are.

—Three and three-quarters.

—Nope; five.

—That's marvelous, just marvelous. Are they all called Paulette?

—Every one but one.

—Yeah?

—And her name is Caledonia.

—A name of lyric beauty. What kinds of things does she do? he asked.

—All she does is play with rich white children.

—Got you. Stay away from poor white trash. He sucked in deeply on the tiny roach, gave it to her to put away or throw away, held in the smoke, deep in his lungs, then slowly exhaled. Mmm. Man oh man. Better and better.

—Those stars, I mean that Milky Way, it's a pretty crazy idea, isn't it? Why didn't he do a Hershey bar or a Baby Ruth? He giggled and caressed her bare arms and moved to her breasts.

—He ran out of fudge. Delighted giggles from both. They kissed now for what seemed extraordinarily long and inexpressibly tasty minutes, but really only for seconds. —You ever wonder what it's like to be black? she asked.

—Uh, yes, I guess so. But I didn't get very far.

—Too bad.

He began to kiss her some more preparatory to making love. But although he was very hot and really wanted to have her more than breath, something was short-circuiting his system, and he remained impotent. He could not understand this at all; it was just too nutty.

—Something the matter with daddy?

—Uh huh.

—Oh my. She thought for a few moments. —Oh I've just got a simply smashing idea.

—Love smashing ideas. And baby, do I want you smashingly but . . .

—A marvelous game, she went on, looking past his lips up to the stars, and smiling, mmm, smiling at heaven itself. —You can be a Negro.

—Oh? How? He tongued her ear.

—Well, I've always wondered what it's like to be one of those white girls who says she was raped by a nigger. So here's what you do. Pretend you're a big mad black man and I'll pretend I'm a nice clean white girl, and you rape me. Tear at me and say awful, dreadful things to me. Love it?

He was a little confused, but still very much in need of her and of solving the short circuit. —Uh, I don't know.

She lay back on the sand and put her arms under her head provocatively and grinned up at him. —Come on, baby.

—Sure, crazy game. Jonas began turning gears and switches inside his personality, because he just could not afford to lose this utterly priceless girl who had appeared out of nowhere in his life, like a free vision from God Himself.

Suddenly a strange high voice came out of Paulette. —Oh, you big terrible black thing! Don't you dare touch me! Oh help!

Jonas found somebody in his fantasy, a huge Southern plantation Negro troublemaker he had seen in a movie years ago, wriggled inside the man (the circuit was mending magically now) and grabbing Paulette, shouted, —Ahm gonna git you, white girl! Ahm gonna have alla you!

—Please, no!

—Yeah! And, his unity of mind and body achieved, he began ripping at her clothing.

And they played out and grappled out her game starkly alone on the shielding, compliant, moon-illuminated dunes, and the motherly sounds of the roaring waves hiding whatever crazy, naughty sounds they made.

They slept for a while after their strange coupling—slept or swooned, Jonas wasn't sure which—and when they surfaced it was to a great quietness. The sea had swallowed its sound, and the stars had run from the sky. Jonas still felt high (not as high as he had been) but he was no longer the black rapist; during their sex, for a few critical moments at least, he had managed to transform Paulette into a helpless white girl, but now she had returned to her original self and color. Her eyes were closed in what Jonas thought was, or should be, deep serenity and satisfaction. Her nakedness said nothing of dissent. He was still observing her when she opened her eyes.

—Well, she said, her voice peculiarly different from what it was ordinarily. —How does it feel . . .

—Beautifully consummated.

—. . . to be a rapist?

—What?

—You heard me.

She sat up now, completely naked except for the ripped clothing lying on her legs. Something new, an unsuspected personality had become part of her expression.

He laughed, or tried to. —It was a game, your game. Come on.

He was feeling less high now.

She stood up and threw the rent sari over her shoulder. —It may have seemed a game to you, baby, but it was the real thing.

Jonas now remembered hearing that it wasn't unusual for certain people to become paranoid if they smoked a little too much marijuana. Paulette's face looked quite calmly crazy now.

—Baby, he began urgently, trying to smoke, —you don't know what you're talking about.

She started striding down the beach and he followed. —You white bastard! she said fiercely, heading toward Horton's house. —In your heart you've always wanted to rape me and you know it.

—Oh come on, he pleaded, trotting behind her.

—Balls! Do you think your desire for me could be honest? Person to person equal? Like for a real white girl? Crap! Her voice was getting close to a scream now and Jonas, feeling a bit hallucinated, was becoming worried. —How can you deny that the real root of your sex kick is to degrade me because I'm black—that there isn't anything you couldn't do and not get away with it because you're superior? She turned her head and, without stopping, shouted, —Deny it, you cowardly bastard! I'm the one who's white. You're the black one.

—Paulette! he yelled, grabbing at her arm and being thrown off. —You're not talking about me. Honestly. Listen . . .

She began to run now, the torn dress flapping around her naked body, and to scream, —Rape! I've been raped! She ran up Horton's beach stairs with Jonas grabbing unsuccessfully at her.

—Please stop it! he shouted. —Please!

She tore across the porch and into the big, noisy, party room, yelling, —He raped me! This man assaulted me! Police!

—No! he shouted. —No!

He felt like somebody thrown out a window.

Horton was walking up and down in front of Jonas. —Don't worry about it. She's as crazy as a goddamn bat and the cops won't believe anything she says.

Jonas, sitting numbly on the mammoth-long couch, could only mumble, —Yeah. The enormous, so recently frenzied room was now empty of people except for Jonas and Horton. Two of the party group, Alice and another woman, had gone down to the beach township police with the raving Paulette, mostly at her insistence, to report the crime, and Horton had asked everyone else to please clear out.

—You don't really take it seriously, do you? Horton asked, frowning down at the strangely inert form of his friend.

—No, I guess not, Jonas said, breathing in and sighing, as though he were not getting enough oxygen. —It's just that it's so awful or, he paused, —so surrealistically obscene. Part of me is still back there floating in pot, part of me is sitting here waiting to be jailed, and part of me is saying this entire thing is simply not happening.

Horton shook his big sheepdog head and smiled. —Jesus. I knew she was a kook, but, man, I never thought she'd try for the Nobel Prize.

Jonas stared at a tall, absurdly proud driftwood lamp across the deserted room. —What will the police do?

—Oh, ask a few questions, look you up and down to see if you are the rapist type, then give Paulette a kick in the ass, and return to their poker game.

Jonas looked around the room some more. —You know, this place suddenly looks just like a German expressionist stage.

Horton reexamined his property. —Yeah, you're right. It does.

—Bare and angular, and shadowy, and Kurt somebody is playing the court scene in *The Trial*.

—You should have been a stage designer, old buddy, instead of a sociology instructor.

Jonas lit a cigarette and drew in a lot of smoke. —Why would they believe my story instead of hers?

Horton, almost in unrepressed irritation, slapped him hard on the shoulder. —I told you why. Are you trying to hang yourself or something?

—Seriously, Ab. There were no witnesses. One story carries as much weight as the other, and the woman's a little more, especially accompanied by the torn clothes.

Horton snorted and shrugged in exasperation, and started walking around the room again. —OK, OK. Whatever you say. He went to the record machine. —Mind if I play a little Bach?

—Go ahead. It might clear my brain.

In a few moments the awesome purity of a Brandenburg concerto was lightening the room.

—Almost makes you want to join the church, doesn't it? Ab said, returning to his seat next to Jonas.

—You know, Jonas began, looking up at the ceiling beams, as the insistent loveliness of the music leapt in and out of the mists in his head, —in a way she's right.

—Why?

—That I really, basically, did rape her.

Ab groaned. —Oh, for the love of God.

—It's true. I didn't lust for her for herself. It was for something I could use to reduce myself to an absolute animal state.

Now came the sounds of people walking up the boardwalk to the house.

—They're back, Ab almost shouted, and jumped up. He grabbed Jonas's face between his hands and glared into his eyes. —Snap out of it, will you? Play it straight now. Understand?

The door opened, and Alice Oakes came into the room followed by Paulette and another girl and two policemen. Everybody stared at everybody else; the majestic soliloquy of the eighteenth-century music transformed the room more than ever into an unadorned stage with its infinitely vulnerable characters.

—Which one is he, lady? a cop finally said, turning his head slightly to Paulette who was holding her rent shroud around her with both hands. Her long black hair was still disheveled; Alice was carrying her colored turban.

—That one, she said with an almost subdued voice, and pointed to Jonas.

Jonas rose slowly from his chair, and as he began with —I . . . Horton leaped in front of him. —He's lying! he shouted to the police. —Don't believe a word he says.

And the music now rushed into that momentary void, scattering fragments of diamond sound on everyone's sensitive, incapacitated brain, isolating them together, and yet one from the other, away from the hot human heart.

C onsequently, Germaine was saying, —the American student is being educated in a vacuum. Which is really about the same as not being educated at all. She sipped from the glass of chablis. —Worse. It provides them with corrupt and warped ways of thinking that are virtually impossible to change.

Long-nosed Kenna Driscoll made a laughing/snorting sound that could have made you think that a mysterious object was being launched, down a homemade runway or something, by a couple of obscure but dedicated chaps, maybe they were women, in, say, Norway. —You can sure say that again. They're perfectly dreadful little lunks. Their brains are fixed somewhere between Mickey Mouse and a Good Humor popsicle. She sucked in deeply on her Gitane and you knew that she could be sucking thousands of American dumbbells through a terminal wind tunnel.

—For example, Germaine went on, —they could not even dream of connecting America's invasion of Indochina with capitalism and its needs. They still think what their government wants them to think . . . that it was a selfless, idealistic crusade against communism.

A remainder of, a reminder of, bygone failures on a grand national scale, of sociopolitical abuse of human material, especially as it might occur in the lower classes; a man who, given the chance, might have been a loyal footman to Madame du Barry, or, not given that chance, a footpad loyal to crime, or, if not that, a fleet purse-snatcher during the reign of Napoleon, and, later on, a dogged purser of snatches during the inept administration of Napoleon III. This man more or less glided, as only the historically abused can glide, really, up to the table with a large oval plate of thin-sliced brown bread from that gluttonous region of wagging gourmet tongues, and an ample plate of sweet butter. This round old embedded waiter did not say a word during the process. He did not have to. His actions clearly spoke for themselves. And if they didn't, monsieur/madam, what the fuck were you doing there at the Café de la Bon Langue in the first place? *Exactement.*

—Tell me, Michael, said Kenna, grabbing a nice piece of the ham for herself, —are American schoolchildren still taught that bit about George Washington fucking the cherry tree?

—Oh yes indeed, said Michael, dipping into the ham and bread and butter, as did the rest of them when it came right down to it: Germaine and Susan, into whose tasty pants Kenna was consistently and happily diving; Boris, the Middle European drifter, floater, cadger, badger, motherfucker and obscurantist wit; and Juan, the once-hungry Spanish political refugee, now not-so-hungry permanent librarian at the Bibliothèque Nationale where he cannily mediated between myth-stained students and world knowledge. (Juan kept his fingers in a number of well-known pies that had long ago ceased to pay off.) —In fact, Michael continued, —they're still being told that the Indians got down on their hands and knees and begged the Pilgrims to wipe them out, please, before it's too late.

Boris carefully dipped a piece of bread into his glass of wine. —I used to know an American girl who believed that American troops had won the French Revolution. He chewed on the wine bread thoughtfully. —She had been a bowling champion in her college.

Kenna certainly giggled all right. Make no mistake about that, my friends. And a bawdy kind of giggle at that. One that would have been quite at home in the Elizabethan court. Kenna obviously felt, as did those of yore, that giggles should be public property, and not, like the good one does, interred with one's bones. The expression "Make no bones about it" could, if properly and neutrally explicated, very likely shed some light on the subject. If left alone and on its own, that is.

And Juan, what about him? Yes, what are we to hear from that time-softened, time-nuzzled Basque footnote, that blank space in a cruelly expurgated Cervantes text? We here have a right to hear from this fellow. But will we? Juan, speak up, damn you! We could say that. Or we could say, Look here, old chap. Don't you think you owe us a word or two? After all, you're in this thing as deeply as we are, whether it's to your liking or not. Surely, you would admit to that. Of course, nothing's to prevent him from looking up from his ham and saying, Oh, go chase yourself. Or, Go fuck yourself. Or even something along the lines of, Go peddle your papers.

But it turns out that we're in luck, in a manner of speaking. Juan has no objection to speaking up, to contributing a few lines to the general café conversation here.

—The only thing that America has to fear is fear itself, he said.

—What? asked Leonore, a gamy girl who, as we'll see a bit later on, dabbled in the black arts of intellectual inquiry. —Where did you pull that from?

—That's Franklin Delano Roosevelt, he said.

—Oh, I see. Well, do you have anybody else in there?

—Of the people, by the people, for the people.

—Oh.

—Theodore Roosevelt.

—No. Abraham Lincoln, she said.

—Wrong. Raymond Massey, who played Lincoln, said Juan.

—OK. I'll buy that.

—Sold. Do you want it wrapped up?

—No thanks, she said. —I'll eat it here.

Which is saying quite a lot. Because Leonore doesn't eat just any old thing, or any old body. She may be gamy and as hungry as a whole passel of one-armed bandits, but she is nevertheless very discriminating indeed about what she puts tongue to. And when she does put tongue to something, boy oh boy! Mamma mia! Like, just for example, when she slams the old tongueeroonie into Kenna . . . wow! Talk about people marching to the beat of a different drumstick! That tongue of Leonore's can raise the roof or raise the eybrows or raise the dead or raise the dickens, depending entirely upon just what her mood dictates, you see. She is one tough and versatile baby, no two ways about it. Why, she could raise Dickens in two shakes of a lamb's tail if she felt like it. Just why she'd want to do a thing like that would, hopefully, remain a mystery to the rest of us, because Dickens, as anybody who is anybody will be only too glad to tell you, is one of the worst lays in the land.

But with Kenna, it's a . . .

Wait. Let us hear something about Boris.

From his neck up, Boris looked like a furry asterisk. When he laughed, no sounds came from him, only vibrations. To be with him, to feel him, was surely to experience the secret, silent world of punctuation. The muted screams of exclamation points. The proud, elegant contortions of the question mark. The gentle policing power of the comma. And the unforgiving, dictatorial banality of the period. The stagehands of the sentence.

—Juan is the tongue of history, Boris said, leaning toward Kenna. —He is forever doomed to repeat its mistakes.

Kenna mockingly drew herself up and said, —Speak, tongue!

—Tongue history! Boris demanded.

What could Juan do, of course, but utter this remark: —Therefore, sir, I urge you to beat your plowmen into swords. Or, if that does not, for some reason, appeal to you, I suggest you beat your swordsmen into doughboys.

Now, one would think that a normal, healthy person would let it go at that. But Michael said, —You are hereinafter to be known as Tongue.

Boris pounded softly on the table. —Tongue, tongue, he said. —Moving up and down again.

Is it any wonder that the Dow Jones averages fluctuate like a whore on bee jelly? That juvenile crime has risen in agricultural areas? That the Thames dries up without a word of warning? And, finally, that free-fall diapers have taken hold of the capitalist bourgeoisie?

If you know which side your sanity is buttered on, you'll quickly change the subject and shout, I want to know something about Kenna!!! Stop fuckin' me over, ya hear! Jus' 'cause I'm strapped to this here fuckin' kitchen table down in the basement of a time capsule that never made it ain't no reason why . . .

You said it, bubba. You absolutely fucking said it. You've got rights even if you don't have a future. If you haven't left your footprints in the sands of Time, who has? That you have ended up in an hourglass with those very sands hourly effacing you should in no way be used against you when the second Ark is finally floated.

Okeydokey. Here's Kenna. Ooops. That's not the way we do things here. Participatory manipulation, that's the name of our game. Kenna, hon, is there any particular way you'd like to be presented/portrayed/discussed, refried, sautéed?

—Yes. As highly desirable yet quite remote. Within Everyman's fantasy but just outside his reach.

Hmm.

—What's the matter, Pops? Can't you handle it? Too big an order for you or something? Losing your grip?

That isn't the real Kenna talking. That's an act she's putting on, for reasons that completely escape me. She's really a very sensitive person and not at all lippy. In fact, she can even be rather shy at times, believe it or not. A woman who would not dream, let's say, of turning over a stone to see if J. Edgar Hoover was hiding under it. Nor would she consider ringing up Henry VIII to ask him for the lowdown on his shifty relationship with his old lady.

She has a nose, of course, and a very cute one it is, but she doesn't shove it into other folks' business. However, she does have a nose for fakery, and when she noses some out, she doesn't hesitate to let that be known. You've heard coon dogs howl and bark when their fine noses pick up a coon's trail, haven't you? Well, it's the same with Kenna.

—Fake! Fraud! she howled when Shitface Kissinger proclaimed, "Peace is at hand."

—Swindle! Cheat! she howled when Haldeman, Erlichman, and Mitchell got only two years for their Watergate crimes.

She has eyes . . . for Leonore, among other things, though we (in the royal sense) don't mean to suggest by any stretch of the imagination that said woman is to be seen, as they say, as a thing (shades of Buber!), though she most certainly does have a thing and a very nice one it is. Kenna would be among the very first, if not *the* first, to say so. And who should know better than she, when you get right down to it? Which is precisely where Kenna spends a fair amount of time, it must be said, now that the subject has been raised.

—This is what I'd call getting right down to it, she has said with her face between Leonore's thighs and her tongue darting devilishly up and down Leonore's delicate trembling skin and into the fathomless sweetness of her muff. Mmm. Tongue to pussy! A tongue in the bush is worth two in the bank, particularly if that bank has no hands, or is made of mud, or is on the west side where those sneaky Israelis are building settlements around the clock, like they were ants or something, and step by step pushing those poor, scabby Arabs closer and closer to total oblivion, which is where nobody in their right mind wants to be, I don't care how many scabs they might have.

And she has a mind, a mind of her own. That kind. Lots of people walking the streets don't have minds in their heads at all. They have Cracker Jack boxes up there. Or sawdust. Or marbles. Or television sets. Or comic books. Or if they do have minds, they're not their own. They belong to somebody else. A dead spinster aunt, a fascist uncle, a domineering sexless mother, a crippled drunken father, a raving maniac of a priest. Or God knows who. But Kenna, she's the sole owner and operator of the mind that's sitting up there in her pretty head. So when she says, I've got a mind to do this or that, she's not kidding. Or even if she says, I'm of two minds, which is most unlikely, since she doesn't employ such relatively literary terms, it's still Kenna talking.

And when she says, I've made up my mind, it's not like she's talking about a rumpled four-poster bed where a lot of itinerant monkey business has been going on without benefit of a union-keeper understanding, yet professionally structured surveillance. Monkeys can be cute, all right, but they can sure stand a lot of watching nevertheless. And quite understandably, it isn't only zoologists who know that some monkeys are lots better at doing their business than making business and it is the former group whose hairy little hands must be kept from the throttles at all costs 'cause no matter how fucking clever . . .

—So the mass media are wrapped around their brains like a complete mythology, Michael says. —It's no different, really, from the mythology of a primitive society. It statically gives all the answers to all the questions even when the questions aren't asked. It doesn't permit the intrusion of any information that would raise doubts or jeopardize its value and its self-sustaining logic. The deepest function of the media mythology is to enable people to go on sleeping, with their eyes wide open.

Boris made a snorting noise. —Oh yes, he said. —Your President Ford told Americans to forget the Vietnam war business, because it was just a bad dream. He turned to Juan, and with his wine glass poised at his lips, asked him, —Well, Juan, are you going back to Spain now that that putrid little cocksucker Franco is finally dead?

Physically, morally, and philosophically, if the truth be known—and who is to say it should not?—Juan did not, like his dear friend Boris, resemble a punctuation mark, or a breathless verb in transit. No. His presence is to be perceived and felt thusly: as the relief felt by the empty Elizabethan stage during intermission, all the gibbering, gabbling players having nipped off for ale and smoked cow's udder, taking with them of course the eternally insatiable characters they were inhabiting, or vice versa. You must see and feel Juan this way, or you will not see him at all. He will remain invisible to you. Take it or leave it. I mean, you may, because of certain willful genetic lapses, decide that you wish to see him as the moment of repose felt by a Spanish ski slope (yes, they do some skiing in the land of Cervantes) just before the thrill-seeking, tight-muscled downhill racers begin their crazed assault upon it. Or, because of an unhappy, lonely childhood spent in the lofty but inhuman reaches of an aristocratic aunt's castle in the Lake District, where you had only stoned servants or goshawks to chat with, you may tell yourself that Juan is a moment of dark joy lying in wait on the other side of the tall privet hedges of your aunt's forbidden gardens.

—I'm not sure, says Juan. —The person who would be going back would not be the same person who left. He makes one of those gestures that can be made only by Spaniards, and in particular by those on the run. This was decreed ages ago by King Philip III of Aragon. Who just happened to have a very deep interest in the varieties of nonverbal communication in his country. In point of fact, just before his untimely and unseemly death by the black plague, he was in the midst of compiling a . . . —In the ten years that I have been working at the reference desk of the National Library, I have watched my original self gradually dissolve into the published words of others. He smiles and shakes his head. —I will be talking to myself about some idiot thing or another, the stinking restaurant below my studio, or a disagreement with a former girlfriend, and all of a sudden, other words pour out of my mouth. "The Novel and History have been closely related in the very century which witnessed their greatest development. Their link in depth, that which should allow us to understand at once Balzac and Michelet, is that in both we find the construction of an autarkic world which elaborates its own dimensions and limits, and organizes within these its own Time, its own Space, its population, its own set of objects and its myths."

—Good Lord, said Boris. —Who or what was that?

—Roland Barthes in *Writing Degree Zero.*

—Your memory is fantastic, Juan. It's phonographic or something.

—No, it isn't memory, says Juan. —It's me. I have become these words. To breathe is to speak them.

Boris shakes his hairy asterisk of a face/head. —Man, you are in funny shape all right. Phew.

—And just this morning, says Juan, —while I was saying to myself, Juan, you must take that sour Camembert back to the cheese store, I heard my own words die and in their place came "Twinnings was doing well in his business. The advantage of it was that it hardly looked like a business. It consisted in his knowing a lot of people and profiting thereby." I too knew many people, but this did not help my economics. I had even more experiences.

—But that sounds like fiction, says Boris, sounding surprised and suspicious for some reason.

—You're absolutely right. It is. *The Glass Bees,* by Ernst Jünger.

Even though he now has a fairly good wine buzz on, in other words, he's a little drunk, Boris still has the capacity, and the right too, of course, to look at Juan as he would look at a magician performing a sleight-of-hand trick in slow motion. And while he's staring at him, not shifting his look at all, he holds his ballon of Beaujolais up to his mouth until all the wine has gone down his throat. He scratches into his heavy, roundish, all-embracing beard. Perhaps little asterisks there are biting him. We don't really know. Research on this subject has been poorly funded and inconclusive. Unless you're breathing down the neck of cancer, or hot on the trail of terminal heebie-jeebies in children, you don't get diddly from the foundations. But as old China hands know all too well, priorities, like hot slanty pussy, do not remain forever nailed to the bed, or to the wall either, for that matter. So we may yet live to see some changes made in the way grants are divvied up by those on high who divvy. You're bloody well fuckin' right. Why, just last week . . .

—Good lord, man, Boris says. —You're being colonized by the printed word. Phew. Holy ant shit. At the rate you are being taken over, by the time you're forty-five, there won't be a word in your head that you can call your own.

Juan wanly nods and completes the ever-so-deft rolling of a Bull Durham cigarette. —Man, you are completely right there. Right as rain, as they say in America's Texas. He lights up. Delicious hand-rolled smoke fills his lungs. —But what can I do? I mean, like fuck a porcupine, I'm stuck. My disease is endemic to my trade. Shit, there are laws in nature that you can't break, no matter how fast you may twist your little ass. And, man, you'd better believe it or else. Vast streams of sucked-out homemade smoke poured from his mouth and nose, encasing, encircling, enshrouding, covering, blanketing, etc., Juan's and Boris's heads, exactly as fog rolling in from the ocean can and will utterly cover San Francisco and you won't be able to see it no matter what. Or as visions of God rolled in from the searing desert sands by ecstatic nuts like Saint John or Saint Luke will cover the minds of believers and you won't be able to see them any more than you can see turtles at the bottom of the sea. Look at it this way, Juan continues through the increasingly dense smoke pouring from his orifices making it seem that he and Boris are talking in the clouds. —What do coal-miners get? Athlete's foot? Tennis elbow? Shit no, man. They get themselves black lung. And what the fuck do ballet dancers come down with? Writer's block? Cancer of the throat? No! Their muscles turn to stone, that's what. And firemen, what does them in? Syphilis from eating too much whore pussy? No. They are done in by eating too much smoke, or they burn up like votive offerings, in the fires they fight. All right then. Much more white smoke poured from him. Both he and Boris were utterly lost in this smoke. Neither could be seen. Only voices in the all-covering smoke. —What is more logical, more normal, even more fitting than my succumbing to an occupational hazard? My brain slowly being taken over by the books that are the content of my work as a miserable little reference librarian? More clouds of dense white cigarette smoke swirled from him. His voice seemed to be God's, floating from infinity, through celestial clouds formations. —I'm turning into a fucking library! he shouts, and the heavy cloudlike smoke muffles his voice almost into a whisper uttered miles away. —I am vanishing into the published works of others. Before I know it, my shabby tweed jacket will have become a dog-eared old book jacket! Oy Dios!

Boris's soupy voice drifts in through the impenetrable smoke clouds. —I must come down for a landing. My eustachian tubes are clogged with condors. I've got condor bites all over my neck. My crew has abandoned ship or something, and they've taken all the stewardesses with them. Rats leaving a smoking shipmate. I'm losing both altitude and sanity. Tongue to tower! Tongue to tower! Landing instructions, please! Guide me in. Prepare for crash landing. Cover airfield with vaginal foam.

Boris gently slides under the big cozy family table. Sighs heavily because at least here is safety and peace and quiet and so on. But hark, or some such shit as that. Someone else is there under the table with him. It is Kenna. She is on her hands and knees between a long pair of legs that extend over a chair. The legs belong to someone seated at the cozy table. They are Leonore's. There is Kenna on her hands and knees going down on Leonore. Actually, she is bracing herself during this bracing engagement by holding onto Leonore's thighs. Lick, lick, lick. Nuzzle, nuzzle. Mmm.

—Hmmm... goes Boris. —Um... uh... are you... uh... quite sure you're at the right, uh, airfield?

Her tongueings checked, though not by putting tongue in cheek, nor, to be sure, by keeping a civil tongue in her head, Kenna, keeping her, well, fond grip on Leonore's naked thighs, or knees, says, —Any cunt in a storm, wouldn't you say?

—It isn't wise to be piloted by sayings, Boris tells her. —Any schoolboy knows there are lots of sayings that will not pass air safety regulations. Nor will they pass the mustard.

Kenna licks Leonore's knees before saying anything. —Muster. As in Muster's Last Stand. Next time neither of us has anything better to do, Boris, I want to take a good close look at your pilot's license. I have the suspicion that you should be grounded for a bit, for your own good as well as that of the company that happens to be keeping you.

And back her face goes to Leonore's tasty red muff, which, it should not go unrecorded, she, Leonore, has obligingly—oh happily—lowered somewhat to permit Kenna less awkwardly to put her whole self into the loving eating of, because if anybody thinks that Leonore is sitting up there completely disengaged from what is going on down below, they're crazy and should be diligently kept off the streets and away from our street children who would surely do them in if they for one moment suspected that all was not well where it should be. Which of course raises the often suppressed question of why these children are roaming the streets in the first place. Don't they have homework to do? Don't they hear their mothers calling them? Have they no respect for the moral fibers of the nuclear family? Is it their contemptuous feeling that these fibers might just as well be made of polyester as good old-fashioned heart-strings cotton? The little swine! Permit me to tell you, sir, that if this nation is to have any future at all worth two cents, then its young offspring should be brought into line, and on the double. Did you hear me, sir? I repeat: on the double! Common decency demands . . .

Jesus. Give these visiting nuts an inch and they'll tear your drawers off. Gotta tighten security, that's all there is to it. Let one apple go bad and the next thing you know, the rest are following you in suits, and I don't mean of spades or hearts either. 'Cause what we're not talkin' about here is the possibility of these bad apples playin' some kinda foxy hand.

—. . . so there's this awful void in their brains, Michael says. —A ten-year-old void, all the years that America was destroying Indochina. Americans have wiped it out of their minds. It didn't happen, nor did anything else, for ten fucking years. So any kind of thinking that has to refer to the history and reality of that decade is doomed. I mean, it can't take place. He rolled a breadball and, his mind elsewhere, dropped it under the table, where it was quickly snatched and eaten by Boris who, glancing upward, said, Why not? There's Kenna eating pussy, so why can't I eat a breadball or two? —What

I'm talking about is kids without memories. If it hasn't happened within the last year, it hasn't happened, period. He dropped another breadball under the table. Wish some pâté were on it, Boris muttered, chewing the little ball up. Under-the-table squatters cannot live on breadballs alone. —You want to hear something really grim? I was teaching a comparative literature class of twenty-five junior and senior students at San Diego State University, and not one of them had ever heard of John Foster Dulles, the Cuban missile crisis, Dien Bien Phu, or Himmler or Eichmann. How do you like that? Isn't that pretty fucking incredible?

Leonore more or less laughs. —It is and it isn't. Americans aren't supposed to have memories. If you look real close, under the picture of George Washington on the dollar bill, you'll see the words "Forget It." And if you listen carefully to the national anthem, you know, "The Star-Spangled Banner," you'll realize that the first line sung backwards says, "Don't think about it." She laughed and threw her hands up. —Come on, Michael. You and I know that the last thing schools in America want to do is educate anybody. They've got only one function: to fill you full of American shit and simultaneously keep your ass off the streets where you might have a little fun.

Down below, Boris says to Kenna (who has finished licking the b'jesus out of Leonore's jampot), —Did you hear that?

—Of course, says Kenna, lighting up a joint.

—And is it true?

—Every last word of it. She inhales deeply and passes the joint to Boris.

—Most extraordinary, he says. He takes a hit of the joint, holds the smoke in for a few lovely moments, and as he slowly lets it out, he says, —Do you know, for years when I was a little boy among the bagels of Budapest, I thought that Hopalong Cassidy was the president of the United States.

Kenna takes the joint and sucks it deeply. —Well, she says, exhaling a little in controlled gasps, —you . . . were . . . right.

Meanwhile, back at the former farm table up above . . .

Wait. It might be of passing interest, to students of class struggle conversations, to hear what the barman here in the Bon Langue and the waitress are saying to each other back there in the shadow of all those smug, lewd bottles of Pernod and Napoleon brandy, bottles that are unpleasantly secure in the dreadful knowledge that they will triumph in the end, because alcoholic beverages are not prey to the weaknesses of the flesh.

Barman: —Did you know that Jean-Paul Sartre has retreated from his previous position of existential self-determination and finally admitted that man is really shaped by his environment? In other words, that thieves are much more likely to come out of slums than neurosurgeons?

Waitress: —Did you know that when I was five years old, my asshole of a mother seriously considered selling me to a traveling circus that wanted to include me in a monkey act and was dissuaded from doing this only when a policeman whom she was fucking for told her that it was against French law to sell your children—my mother was a Turk—and that she could go to jail? Va bene.

Let us now pick up, once again, on Michael and Germaine and Juan and Leonore and Boris and Juan. Let us by all means join them in their combined efforts to keep The Abyss at something better than arm's length. Not that anyone is so grotesquely naive, so heavily burdened with layers of wool over their eyes, as to think that with a little luck The Abyss will go away. Oh no. One's hopes are far more modest. That is to say, one hopes at best for a standoff. Naturally, one cannot do a fucking thing about any double-crosses executed by Himself behind one's back. His record, as just about anybody can agree, is hardly as unblemished as the fucking driven snow. One of these days there's gonna be a grass-roots stampede back to paganism, an' it's gonna sound like twenty million buffalo comin' down the stretch, you mark my words. An' that'll fix His ass once and for all.

—. . . and of course there is the business of the White Whale, Germaine says. —Two hundred million Americans are frantically swimming after this bizarre abstraction, and they are drowning in the mad effort.

—Led on, of course, by that coy closet queen Ishmael, Michael says, and laughs.

—Who was in love with that crazy tattooed spade Queequeg, says Leonore. —My God. What a national mythology. The prototypical American is a one-legged psychotic consumed by a need to murder the wonders of the natural world. And he's aided in this project by a bunch of itinerant freaks, guys who really belong to a sideshow. She whets her whistle with a bit of the grape. —It's the scenario for Vietnam, so help me. She pauses, seized and suspended within the radiance of an abrupt idea. —Every president has been Captain Ahab.

—I hear them talking, says Juan, sitting up from his slump.

—Who?

—Queequeg and Ishmael, he says. —They're talking inside the library in my head.

—Can you be rented out as a lending library, Juan? asks Michael.

—Well, what are they saying?

—They're having a lovers' quarrel, says Juan, his fugitive-Spaniard's fleeting face flowing in a dreamy way. —Queequeg has been crying. He is saying, "We don't have any kind of social life. We never go out anyplace together. You always go alone. Because you're ashamed of me."

"Oh, Quee," says Ishmael. "That isn't true. How can you say a thing like that? You mean everything to me. Why, I'm so proud of you I . . ."

"Fibber! Big fat fibber! You don't want people to know you're gay and that your lover is a boogie. You think I don't know that, Ish? What kind of fool do you think I am anyway?

"Quee! My God! You're becoming paranoid. You don't have one single shred of evidence to prove these outrageous accusations. Not one."

"Oh no? OK, Mr. Smart-ass. Why didn't you take me to the dinner dance that was given at the Harvard Club last Saturday for Mr. Herman Melville, the famous New England seafaring author? Just answer me that if you can."

"Easy. It was strictly family."

"Family? What kind of shit are you trying to hand me, Ish? Since when have you been Melville family?"

"Since the beginning, that's when. I'm his child, for chrissake."

"His child?"

"That's right. His child. I'm the child of his imagination."

"Well, if that's the case, I'm his child too. He invented me just like he invented you."

"Oh no, Queeg. You've got that wrong. White men can't invent black people. That's just not the way it works. He *borrowed* you."

"Borrowed me? You must be crazy or something, Ish. Borrowed me! Now how the fuck do you think anybody can borrow somebody?"

" 'Cause that's the way it works, dummy. Authors can borrow people they need to use in their books. They borrow them from other writers. See, there's this worldwide writers' club pool like a lending library that they all belong to. They just dip into that whenever they need some character. When writers are through with a character, they deposit them there. And from then on, like I said, these characters are sort of public property, on call. You get it?"

"Get it? How could I miss it, you bitch you. According to your filthy little story, I'm a nobody, a fucking castoff orphan without any background or parents or anything."

"Oh no. I wouldn't say that exactly, Quee. You came out of somebody at some time or other. You're not an abstraction. You didn't just fall out of a tree. You had to have a parent. Now offhand, I'd say you were probably invented by, uh, oh, one of those early Victorian English music hall entertainers who wrote and performed their own shit. In those days it was the fashion to concoct noble savage freaks."

"What? Music hall freak savage? Oh, Ish! Bitch! Bitch! Why stop at a cruddy show-biz type? Why don't you try to convince me that I was made up by a fucking comic-book writer? Who wrote boogie stories for feeble-minded kids? I mean, shit! I can't believe it! Trashing me like this. Me, who's been closer to you than anybody through all kinds of shit! Lordy Jesus Mary!"

"You're crazy, Quee. You've got it all wrong. I'm merely trying to clarify…"

"Clarify my ass! You listen to me, girl. You better take back every single fuckin' bad word you said about me, else I'm gonna twist your pretty white arm into a knot around your head. Start!"

"Quee! Oohh. You're hurting me! Oooohhh!"

—Juan! Michael shouts. —What's the matter? What's happening?

—My God, says Juan. —That wasn't me talking. I was seized. He rubs his face and shakes his head.

—It wasn't you? says Germaine. —Well, then . . .

—. . . who was it? Leonore asks.

—Are you OK, Juan? says Michael. —Here. Drink this brandy.

—It must have been Socks Peelmunder, says Juan, and drops the brandy. You can just see the brandy clearing the man's head, pulling him together, as it were. —It had to be him. He is breathing normally now. He's himself. Phew! —No one else I know of has that combination of brass and verve, that daring, even insane talent for leaping down God's throat when He yawns. Yes, he sighs, shaking his head and smiling just so, like a Renaissance princess who has just eaten her first *croissant au beurre* after being told it would corrupt her tastes. —It was Peelmunder who took possession of me.

Germaine says, —One must naturally ask, who is this Peelmunder fellow?

—He is the last laugh, says Juan.

—Are you sure you're not making all this up, Juan? asks Leonore.

—Peelmunder made himself up, Juan says. —Like the common cold, like the flight of the moth.

Michael more or less scratched his head. —I don't know why, but this guy sounds familiar. I get the feeling that I know him in some odd, remote way, y' know?

Germaine says, —We're getting close to Jung now.

—Let's turn back then, says Juan. —I don't think Peel would like Jung.

—But Jung would certainly like him, Germaine goes on. —There is nothing wrong or inauthentic in considering the possibility of a universal unconscious.

—It's letting too many people in on the act, Juan says.

Germaine laughs. —That is the beautiful point, that we are all involved in the same cosmic theater. Slipping in and out of one another.

Juan shakes his head. —Naw. I don't think Peel would go for that. He's kind of a snob, when you get right down to it.

—Juan, are you aware that for the past few minutes you've been talking and sounding like an American? Leonore asks him.

—Holy shit! Juan shouts. —I've become Peelmunder!

Down below, Boris says to Kenna, —Uh, how about it?

Kenna: —Well, oh, why not. You won't tell anybody, will you?

† 246 †

Boris: —'Course not. Think I'm crazy?

Kenna: —However, one simple quickie hetero fuck doesn't make me a straight, really. She stretches out on the floor and pulls up her skirt.

Boris, carefully climbing aboard: —And besides, anybody who'd fuck for me couldn't possibly be a straight.

The bony young bartender, who smells of infinity and upon whose icy brow not an angel would dare to tread, polishes a brandy glass with a serene fury. —The great Michel Foucault has pointed out that there is no such thing as History. He says that the concept of logical continuity and progression throughout the ages is pure poppycock.

The gently springy waitress dips into her catchy fulsome blouse and scratches her tit. —My own poppa's cock was nothing to brag about, if I am to believe my mother's sad stories.

Y ou'd have to be deaf not to hear Peelmunder's laughter. Hey! Peel, baby! How you doin'?

—Oh ho, Jesu Cristo! That poor sweet drag-ass saffron-sucked book-buggered little Juan! He's spent so much of his life huddling in libraries he's becoming a call number. You can't open the bloody card catalog without bumping into the little chorizo. Just yesterday morning, I woke up with a terrible hangover in *The Brothers Karamazov*—oh, so I had been fucking Grushenka. So what? That crazy maniac Dimitri doesn't own her, ya know. And who should be taking a piss out of the window? Juanito the Bookhead, that's who. And last month when I was paying a house call in *A Tale of Two Cities*, there was Juan the Printed Page copying down the last words of Madame du Barry before she got the guillotine. It beats me how the little bugger has time left to do his job at the library. Man, that's one sweet hustle he's got going there. He's as clever as a fucking German tortilla. He comes by it naturally, of course. He's not the last of a long line of people who've had to learn fourteen different ways of saying hello because, man, you never know, the recipient thereof might turn out to be a secret agent with a warrant for your doom. Those poor Basque Spaniards have lived so long under the glare of the Guardia's shiny black patent-leather hat that they've developed a squint to their walk. I mean to tell you. Those spic fascists don't fool around. If those knuckleheads even suspect you know how to spell the words *freedom* and *equality*, they'll heave your ass right into the nearest dungeon and plug you into their AC/DC current which can handle boys, girls, and faggots, and long before you've managed to shout "Long Live the Struggle of the People Against All Types of Oppression!" your sweet and tasty privates will have been electrocuted. The screams of pain those sanctuaries of torture produce make the very bricks weep with shame, and you'd better believe it. The cells there are latrines of hell, so much shit and piss and blood and vomit have been spilled upon the floors. Juan's sister Unamuno can tell you all about it. She knows. She was there. They caught her just before she could get across the French border. What a fuckin' fluke it was. She and Juan and Manuelo were in a café in the tiny border village of Fuenterrabia having a drink of Fundador, sort of a fare-well drink to Spain.

—It's funny, but it seems the best times to cry are always the worst, Unamuno said, sipping her brandy.

—I'm running to save my ass, said Juan, —but my ungrateful ass wants to stay here. It wants no part of my head and its tricky decisions.

Manuelo snorted. —The police don't give a damn what you do with your ass, Juanito. It's that cute head they want.

They left the café for the border one by one, because they felt that for all three of them to cross the border together would somehow provoke the always suspicious border guards. —They are paid to be suspicious, Juan's mother once said. —Suspicion is their whole life.

Unamuno was the last to leave. She had insisted on this because she did not want, she said, —this democratic moment to be contaminated by sexist sentimentality.

After Juan and Manuelo had both left the café, and Unamuno herself was about to leave, she had a sudden and odd urge to take a last look at herself in a Spanish mirror. She had always carried with her secret self the "primitive magical notion" that each mirror had its own unique portrait of you. She was positive that the French mirrors of the near future would not, could not, contain the same Unamuno who was buried deep in all Spanish mirrors. So she went to the ladies' room, "because I think that secretly I wished I might be able to throw myself into the mirror."

There was another woman in the ladies' room when Unamuno entered. She too was looking into the mirror. Unamuno thought it was bad luck to look at other people's reflections of themselves—"It is interfering with their search for themselves"—so she permitted herself to see only the back of the woman's head. When the woman turned around, horror swept through Unamuno. The woman worked for the secret police. She had arrested Unamuno two years ago in Barcelona.

—Well, well, said the woman, smiling. —We meet again. And in such an unusual place. God must be trying to tell us something, don't you think?

Unamuno was taken to San Sebastián for questioning in The Confessional Box, the infamous police station on the Avenida Mola.

One of Unamuno's screams was heard by Carol and remained in her ears forever. She was stopping in San Sebastián for a few days while on a six-week student tour of Europe, with a group from San Francisco State. She went to the police station to report the loss of her passport. Her shoulder bag had been stolen from their rented car which they had so youthfully, so foolishly left unlocked in one of those vast, eerie, public underground garages, which, unbeknownst to her, were haunted by thieves as shadowy and furtive as half-forgotten dreams.

—Oh my God! she blurted uncontrollably when the scream was ended.

—I beg your pardon? said the young, practiced, recording policeman, looking up at her with the haughtily frozen face of a practiced child liar, presenting a flawless nonexpression that erased realities.

Carol immediately afterward hurried outside to a nearby café for a strong drink of brandy. Two of them. She felt like pouring the brandy into her ears to drown the scream, or to overpower it with the alcohol. But Unamuno's scream was not to be unscreamed. It remained there in her ears, in full throat, and though the horror of it gradually faded away into a sort of distance of mind, the scream's presence, the ineradicable fact of its having been made, stayed on in her ears, created, in fact, a small, grey room there such as Carol imagined had been the room in which the scream had been born. In the following years and seemingly without any reason or provocation, the scream from time to time would come alive again, forcing from her, no matter where she was, or what she might be doing, the terrified, anguished exclamation —Oh my God!

The last time the scream reawakened had been in the sweating, throbbing, yet most elegantly arch midst of one of her performances in the Rue Ste.-Geneviève brothel. She was playing *Goldilocks and the Three Bears* with Monsieur Perrinni, a religiously steady client who in real life played the part of a severe and inaccessible official in the Ministry of Agriculture. Within their game within the children's story game, they were at the point where the Little Bear (Monsieur Perrinni, who adored animal roles, did Mama and Papa Bear as well as Little Bear) discovers Goldy-Carol sleeping in his bed and proceeds to wake her up—in his own quite unfettered licentious way to be sure, 'cause, shit, he's no dummy of a small boy bear even though he's dressed like one an comin' on like one. Like, I mean that falsetto baby bear voice is just too fuckin' far out! An', uh, he can do this show any ol' way he fuckin' well pleases 'cause, you know, he's picking up the tab, which is where it's at, that is, if you wanna get down to talkin' turkey or any other all-American wildlife bird that was here to greet the staggerin' Pilgrims when they finally made it to the shore, with that fantastic long soft rootin' tootin' nuzzlin' guzzlin' snoot of his in her aromatic for discriminating pipe smokers bushy blonde little girl muff! Oh mama! Hold onto your hat or the nearest Mad Hatter! 'Cause here we come, ready or not!

OK. So far so very good. We'll count the house later, Alvin. For chrissake!

Sit down! An' tell that popcorn man to cool it, OK? Who the fuck let him in here in the first place? So there's our star performer Goldy, and when I say *star* I want all you folks to stand up and clap to show your sincere appreciation of the basic fact that she has been bringing home the bacon year after year like the good hardy perennial she happens to be and without whose stellar efforts you all would be more like skin and bones than candidates for the sweatin' box at a million-dollar fat farm.

—Oh! Oh! cries Little Bear. —There's somebody sleeping in my bed!

—Good heavens! cries Mama Bear (read Little Bear and for Little Bear read Monsieur Perrinni).

—Well, kiss my ass! cries Papa Bear (read the two characters mentioned above).

—I wonder who this bold imposter could be, says Little Bear, tiptoeing toward the bed (upon which lies Goldilocks, née Carol, sawing wood for all she's worth—that is to say, making believe she is).

—Indeed, says Mama Bear. —What sort of rapscallion are we dealing with here?

—Jesus, but you guys are talkin' funny, says Papa Bear. —Why can't you just say, What we got here is a bummy little kid with a lot of chutzpah?

—Aha! cries Little Bear, standing at the edge of the bed in question. —It's a little girl! And she's got the longest, curliest blonde hair in the whole wide world!

—Gracious me! cries Mama Bear. —A little girl vagabond! This is still another example of the breakdown of the nuclear family.

—What nobody around here but me seems to know, says Papa Bear, —is that the whole fuckin' world is on the road.

—Gosh, says Little Bear, leaning over Goldilocks. —She sure is a sound sleeper. But I know a good way to wake her up though.

—Be gentle, son, says Mama Bear. —Little girls are different from little boys.

—You think he doesn't know that? snorts Papa Bear. —Oh wow!

—Here goes! shouts Little Bear. He whips up Goldilocks's blue gingham skirt, pulls down her white cotton little-girl panties, and dives on her. Slurp slurp, slurp slurp.

—Hmm, murmurs Mama Bear.

—Hot dog! shouts Papa B.

In a few moments, Little Bear looks up from Goldilocks's twitching, divinely souped-up muff. —She just won't wake up, he says, grinning big through the streams of pussy juice pouring down his long snoot.

—Think she's crazy? howls Papa. —That li'l ol' girl knows a good thing when she feels it.

—Hmm, murmurs Mama again. —There's something odd about all this, but I can't quite put my finger on it.

—Guess I better get back on the job, says Little B., grinning that grin we all know so much about, with his dripping red tongue hanging out like a rich patient etherized upon a table of smoked salmon. —We've just got to awaken this brazen young thing who clearly has no respect for private property, and who does not appear to be conversant with those rules of territorial propriety whereby the members of one group within the animal kingdom do not presume to impinge upon the . . . oh shit! Down I go again!

And that he did. Doing with his tongue what many a Cold Stream Grenadier would have given a full month's pay to do with their nose, chin, or even their big horny toe, rather than having his ass blown off in an utterly idiotic and futile attempt to storm the pastry stalls of Istanbul under the blithely inept guidance of Winston Fart-heaver Churchill.

Well, it was only natural, and certainly inevitable—if cause and effect are still in decent running shape—that our fine feathered friend Goldilocks would respond to the furious and strongly goal-orientated lickings of her glowing, oh yes, snatch by Little Bear Monsieur Perrinni. Who Is Himself Playing All Parts But One Tonite, and all this for the price of a single ticket. Only natural. And soon, under the influence of Little Bear tongue, Goldy-Carol begins to sigh heavily and then to pant, rotating and roiling and heaving and thrusting her ass, faster and faster, and the panting is becoming long moans and the moans are forming the basis of a scream as the wild hot joy approaches that climax of ecstasy. Of a scream . . . Yes, as her own scream was about to burst forth from her wide open, strongly moaning, wet mouth, the scream buried in her ears in its own dreadful little Spanish prison room reawakened, in full horror. They met head on, these screams, and merged: Unamuno's scream of unbearable torture pain and Carol's scream of orgasmic ecstasy.

—Oh my God! she cried within the screams.

She opens her eyes, both her own and Goldilocks's, and, suspended somewhere between herself, the role of Goldilocks, and the historical frozen self of the San Sebastián scream, beholds Little Bear Monsieur Perrinni in bear costume, furiously nuzzling her cunt. —Ohhh! she murmurs, from all sides of her momentarily complex selves.

—Ride them cows, boys! he shouts, getting a number of Yankee theologies mixed up and quite clearly forgetting, for the moment, that he is speaking out of bear character. —Git along all you little hot doggies! he continues to shout, rearing up and then hurling himself full body upon Carol/Goldilock, his short stiff prick jutting out from his teddy bear front in very much the same way, we may be quite sure, that the young Napoleon jutted out in his early military academy classes surrounded by grinning, pimply, pubescent French nitwits.

D uring this grateful interlude, while the eagle shit is being scrubbed off the copilot's head, we all of us have a perfect right to raise certain questions, not only regarding the so-called food on this cunningly impromptu flight and the credentials of those dubious, suspiciously clothed people mincing about who are passing themselves off as stewards and stewardesses . . . questions in re the above-described dramatic event which took place within the fur-lined walls of the Rue Ste.-Genevieve brothel. To wit: what happened to the part of Carol's exclamations and outcries that originated in San Sebastián and had to do with torture? That is, were these words and these sounds coopted and thus organically absorbed in and by Little Bear's lust? And, therefore, have they by now become the catalog fund, so to speak, which will inform his lust urges/experiences in future? As a result of presenting himself so effectively in old woman's drag in his very own living room back then, did Ulysses thus become, through the circumstantial fact of transvestism, eligible for medicare and senior citizen financial benefits?—because, man oh man, ten years is one fantastic fucking time to be without home-cooked pussy. Or to put it another and perhaps more down-to-earth, meat 'n' potatoes way: When he was putting it to his missus, a bit later, did we have there in that harrowed Greek temple a ménage à trois of the kinkiest hue? I mean, let's face it: Here before us on this freshly made, herb-scented, king-sized, upper-echelon bed we have (1) Ulysses himself, he of the beetle brow and long wind; (2) Penelope— Pen for short—his wife, she of the long tongue and the dynamite boobs; and (3) the old lady (Haggis Baggis or something like that) whom Ulysses dreamed up in order to pass himself off as, her, she, herself, that is. 'Cause if you or anybody else for that matter think that you can call forth one of these "covers" or surrogates or stand-ins, interrupt them in the middle of whatever little tasks they were minding their own business up their assholes in, use them for your vile ends, then, when you've had your way with them, fleecing and squeezing and hustling them of every little characteristic they can call their own, even that nervous eye tic they inherited from their Uncle Moe, just chuck them over, heave them into the nearest litter can, if that's what you think, you unfeeling, selfish bastard you, you've got another thing coming.

—Who's your friend, hon? says Penelope, trying to size up the situation as she saw it developing from her prone position on the twenty-by-twenty vibrating bed (those Greeks, like, they weren't behind in anything).

—My what? says Ulysses. —Oh, she's nobody, Pen, baby. She's nothin'. I mean, she's that old bag I was pretendin' to be, you know, back there. Can't imagine what the fuck she's . . . I mean I don't even know how she got in here.

—Don't you try to gimme that shit, says the old bag. —I got just as much right to be here as you do, Mac. Sooner you get that through your thick head, the better. Mmm hmmph! You sure look good all naked on those blue sheets, Pen, sweetie. Does an old hag's tongue good just to . . .

—Ulysses, dear, says Pen, with a certain amount of urgency, and sitting up in the bed, with those big boobs swingin' juicily. —You better tell your funny friend to cut the comedy, and I mean on the double, you hear?

—Right, honey, says he. —I'm readin' you all right, believe me. This rude, aggressive, ill-bred creature has absolutely no conception of what proper boudoir behavior should be in an upper-class situation like this. Why, it just makes my blood boil when I look around me and see how lower-class gall has grown to the point where it's become a national crisis, threatening the very foundations of all those much-heralded Greek values which every clean and decent schoolboy is being instructed in this very moment as we stand here in our birthday suits preparing to embark on . . .

—Oh shit! says the old hag, and whack! karate chops him in the back of the neck. Timber! —Yack yack yack, she goes on, looking down with ire at Ulysses' unconscious body stretched out on the lovely handmade and really very dear blue Corinthian floor tiles. —That's the trouble with these hero types. All they got going for them is myth and muscle. When it comes to flexibility and swinging with a new kind of situation, why, shit, their pea-brains blow. She shakes her head and begins to peel off her crummy duds. —Who said these old soldiers just fade away? That's bullshit. They turn into unbearable windbags, that's what.

—Yes, well, I suppose you have a point there, says Penelope, warily looking down at the zonked Ulysses and then at the aggressive, now-naked hag. —Perhaps all that spear rattling affects their, uh, monitoring mechanism. Uh, tell me, what did you say your name was again?

—I didn't say, replies the hag as she whirls into some calisthenics—knee bends, arm stretching, toe touching. —But it's Michaelmas. You can call me Mickey.

—Mickey . . . yes . . . well, uh, just what do you have in mind? she asks, observing the athletic frenzy before her with obvious consternation.

—What I have in mind . . . wow! You coddled, private-school chicks sure talk funny. I'll tell you what I've got in mind, honey pie. Hanky panky! Me and you. Jig jig! Long-distance marathon strength-sapping mind-blowing fucking! You dig?

Silence. Penelope stares at her as if she's seeing somebody climb out of a television screen. —". . . -blowing fucking," she says, in a voice that seems to be coming from a child lost in the ruins of Tuhontapec. —You won't hurt me, will you?

—Hurt you? Me? Why, I'm the tenderest, lovingest, best ol' lay in the land. And with that she leaps into the vast bed and grabs Penelope. —Gimme some tongue, bubbie, and get ready for the time of your life!

C arol smiled at Stephan as he caressed his new cap. Old cap, that is. New acquisition. It was an old-style blue cotton student's cap, with a small black patent-leather brim and a thin, frayed gold braid above the cracked, aged brim. —Oh, Stephan! You're so nutsy.

—Don't you just love it? said Stephan, patting the cap. —I bought it for two francs at this weird junk store over in the Third. What a fantastic place. Right out of the Hunch's back. You'd think you were back in the Middle Ages or someplace. I saw a cape there that I know was worn by Cyrano de Bergerac, the first time he dated Ophelia.

Carol laughed. (Well, of course. What was she supposed to do? Crawl under the park bench and bark like a poodle? I mean, shit. What kind of smart-ass cynicism are we dealing with here? It was just such cracks as that that pushed the building of the first underground madhouse way beyond its target date.) —With that cap you've just got to go on the barricades.

Directly in front of them, looming there with all the obtuse, street-corner arrogance of a plumber who has just married his last remaining daughter off to the director of a large corset factory in Lyons, was the Cathedral of Notre Dame. This fact must form the basis of the perspective within which we are to understand their statements. Otherwise, we will be floating in historical limbo. In other words, why the fuck have them parked there in the first place? In which case they might just as well be stuck in a smelly phone booth up in the Gare du Nord, you see. The point here being . . . Oh to hell with it.

—They had a barricade there too, said Stephan. —But I didn't have enough money left to buy it.

—How about a revolution? Did they have one of those for sale too?

—Oh yeah, said Stephan, glancing sideways at a small, chubby man in a bowler who appeared to be approaching them after having just come out of the cathedral. —They had three different ones in fact. But they were incomplete, they weren't all there. The chubby man seemed to be getting closer. —One was a sixteenth-century Chinese peasants' revolt that was missing two of its leaders. Then there were the remains of the unsuccessful Greek revolution to throw off the Turks. And, uh, I would have picked up ten francs' worth of incorrect political strategies from the disastrous slaves' revolution under . . .

The chubby man now stood in front of Stephan and Carol's simple, clean stone bench. They looked him up and down. He merely stood there. One sensed that every part of him was being deeply silent.

—This isn't a bus stop, said Stephan.

—I am aware of that, the man said.

More silent looks, looks waiting to soak up info.

—What's eating you? asked Carol.

The man's soft, fat face put one in mind of a raisin roll, or a knoll near a bog, or an obscure philosophical victory scored in 1127. One could go on, of course, but would . . .

—The latest word from inside, he finally said, nodding back in the direction of the cathedral, —is that the Naz ate Peter.

Carol and Stephan looked at each other in what, in the old days, before technology took over everything, would have been called puzzled amusement. Do you believe this? Are we dreaming this guy up between us? Far fucking out.

—Lemme see if I'm readin' you right, Manny, said Stephan after a few moments, and in a voice that was certainly not the one he used to get by with every day. —Are you saying that Jesus of Nazareth . . .

—Engaged in oral sex with Saint Peter, said the man. —Ate Peter's pickle.

—Are you sure this isn't just hearsay? Carol asked.

—Hearsay couldn't survive for a second, he replied. —Nope. This is the straight dope.

Stephan figuratively wiped his brow with an old railroadman's red bandana. —See here, sir. How do you know this isn't a vicious Zen rumor? (He was trying out still another voice. Don't ask me why.)

The man nodded in the direction of the cathedral again. —They have proof back in there. They don't fool around when it comes to basic New Testament shit. Not those guys. He shook his round, fat head. —They're real pros. You got it wrong if you think they're a bunch of hayseeds who're trying to rassle down some angels who just happen to be dancing naked on the head of a pin.

Stephan snuffled. —Somebody sent you out lookin' for a home run I know.

The man produced three brownies from his jacket pocket. —Hash browns, he said, and giggled wildly at his own joke as he gave them each one. —Nothin' like home cookin'.

Stephan and Carol munched away. —Mmm, said Carol. —I haven't the vaguest who you are or what you're up to, but you sure know your stuff when it comes to hash brownies.

—You said it, mumbled Stephan, with a full chewing mouth. —This pastry is dynamite. I'm already three jumps ahead of myself. Mmm. Yeah.

—Thank you, said the man, licking the chocolate remains from his fingers. —I must admit that I am vain when it comes to my brownies.

Stephan leaned back and grinned a happy hash-high grin. —Oopla, my good man, and oopla again. And may your bribes increase.

The succulent stranger—and why not? There's no law that says we must go on calling him the round man or the chubby man. His brownies are succulent; he thereby produces succulence. Ergo, he is succulent—effortlessly and with no folderol produced one of those oft hungered-after collapsible chairs and eased his generous body into it, an act comparable in its lack of fanfare and inevitability to the way fall takes over the same seat occupied by summer (which, it turns out, has left behind it bad smells, bad memories, bad debts, bad feelings, bad tastes in the mouth of) in certain parts of the Alpes-Maritimes. —And there's more where that came from, he said.

—Brownies? exclaimed Stephan and Carol.

—No. Investigative thinking, said Mr. Succulence. —Snippets from the void.

Into Stephan's presently landlocked, hence helpless, mind scurried this: God's forever voiding snippets. But he kept cool and merely grinned his euphoric Everyman grin.

—Sock it to me, Maxwell, said Carol, who wasn't feelin' no pain neither, y' know.

—Name isn't Maxwell, said Succulence. —But I will be very happy to sock it to you nonetheless. All rightie . . . They are saying . . .

—Then what is your name? said Stephan, himself having become his own grin.

—Bluebird.

—Bluebird? said Carol. —From the book of the same name?

—Yes and no. I was named after the movie.

—Fucking far out.

—In a mistaken sort of way, though. My mother conceived me in the balcony of a particular scratch house while watching *Bluebeard and His Seven Wives.* Due to her feverish sexual writhings she got the hero's name wrong. It came over as Bluebird to her.

—I like it better, said Carol, radiating a cosmic hash smile. —I see a giant blue bird flying and hopping around, charming and fucking the brains out of hordes of lonely rich women.

—You're quite mad, said Stephan, kissing her cheek. —But then so was Galileo.

—They are saying inside, Bluebird continued, nodding back toward the cathedral, —that there is more to the Dead Sea Scrolls than meets the naked layman's eye.

—I should hope so, said Stephan, who was beginning to merge, he felt quite sure, with one of the many stone saints clinging to the upper reaches of the continuously looming cathedral, a cathedral, moreover, to whom one felt like saying, Look here, you've proven yourself. Calm down. There's really no longer any need for you to loom. We have been denied our rightful revelations by those in the know too long. Mmm. I like that. Yeah. They're either too long or too short. The time has, uh, come to . . .

—The insider's scuttlebutt says there were all kinds of odd types running around in those hairy days and they were doing all kinds of odd, hairy things, said Bluebird.

—Freaks, said Carol, who had a pretty good nose for that sort of thing. —Freaks in Jews' clothes.

—Up to their ears in heresy, blasphemy, anarchy, sodomy, and in some cases bestiality, Bluebird continued. —Unabashed and without noticeable shame or remorse.

—Mmm, murmured Stephan. —They sound like wonderful people. My kind of people. They have ripped the living shit out of the social fabric. He smiled beatifically: a man in close contact with cloud formations. —Into shreds. And it's those very same shreds that're being dug up today by some of our finest archaeologists, young . . .

—Shards, said Carol. —They dig up shards.

Orderly clusters of Japanese tourists scurried by them every ten minutes or so. They appeared to be pouring, silently, effortlessly, out of huge gleaming silver tour buses by the thousands. A $500 Nikon camera hung in menacing lassitude around the tiny neck of every single one of them. They said strange things to one another in excited small voices, and streamed into the cathedral.

—They're disappearing in there, said Stephan. —I've counted 9007 going in and nobody's come back out. The entire population of Japan is vanishing into a bottomless hole in the Cathedral of Notre Dame. Mmm. Wow. Fantastic. How fucking clever those Japs are.

A trim old geisha girl scurrying with a group shouted at him: —No. Not clever. Bored.

—Ah, said Bluebird, turning to view the now stampeding (though still orderly) Japanese. —Perhaps we are on the verge of an East–West breakthrough.

—Ha! shouted another of the orderly soft-shoe stampeders, a gleaming youth in a white cashmere sweater. —Breakdown is more like it. You Westerners are romantic fools. Ha!

—Do you think they're all coming here because they've read *The Hunchback of Notre Dame?* said Carol.

—Seaweed, said Bluebird. —It has to do with all the seaweed they eat. There are primeval minerals with deep drive in that stuff. The seas are where the whole show began, you know, and they obviously have not said their final word.

—They're lemmings, said Stephan.

From the west side of a fresh flock of gentle stampeders a tasty, muscular young mother released her little boy like a carrier pigeon. He flew over to our schlepping trio.

—What's up, Fuji? Stephan asked him, with a certain dubious familiarity, because Fuji may or may not have been the little bugger's name. Stephan used it simply because of its obvious relationship to Mount Fuji, another infinite hole into which an endless stream of people wished to hurl themselves in order to leave no trace of themselves. (Self-erasure. Which brings us to the question: How many bored blacks does it take to make a blackboard?)

Now, Jap kids are not known for their excitable natures, or their captivatingly expressive interpersonal style, so this particular one was not acting out of character by not saying boo and by looking at him with the incorruptible, expressionless face of a Kabuki dancer who has just finished wowing them in an avant-garde fishing village in the north, as he handed him a nice big piece of folded paper, and flew off, whirred away.

—Hmm, murmured Stephan, unfolding the big piece of paper. —Inscrutable Japanese kid presents shiftless Caucasian fellow with a nice mysterious piece of ruled paper. Well, we'll just have a look-see. "To be or not to be is not really a relevant question when the answer is presented to you." My oh my. That is one socko opening line. If it's that good at the end, we've got a standing-room-only, long-run hit on our hands and you can buy that two-story clapboard Siberian mink up on Martha's Vineyard that you've always wanted. OK, now. Let us read on: "The appearance of people was . . . well, they had skin blackened by burns. . . . They had no hair because their hair was burned, and at a glance you couldn't tell whether you were looking at them from in front or in back. . . . They held their arms bent forward like this . . . and their skin—not only on their hands but on their faces and bodies too—hung down. . . . If there had been only one or two such people . . . perhaps I would not have had such a strong impression. But wherever I walked I met these people. . . . Many of them died along the road—I can still picture them in my mind—like walking ghosts. . . . They didn't look like people of this world. . . . They had a special way of walking—very slowly. I myself was one of them."

C leon looked at the bill. Jesus H. Christ. Every time I turn around in this fuckin place some buck-toothed Jap person is clippin my ass for ten bucks or twenty bucks. You can't take a shit here without it costin you five bucks. Thatsa fuckin fact. You gotta be one uv them fuck Arab oil millionaires, jus to make both enns meet.

—Come on, Cleon. Let's pay up and get out of here, said Wills. —You keep staring at that check like it's going to bite you or something.

—Yeah. That's jus what it did. Each one uh those fried shrimps cost two dollars.

—They probably had to fly all the way from Florida. And even if they came tourist class, that costs money.

—Yeah. My money, said Cleon. —They shoulda hitchhiked here.

—Uh huh, said Wills. —But they would of worn their asses down to the bone and you wouldn't have looked twice at them.

Cleon and Wills, gingerly, with that momentarily deceptive, spade cool that hardly, when push comes to shove, covers a multitude of hoped-for sins, cruised the Ginza for a while before returning to Camp Roosevelt. The khaki army uniform obsessed Cleon even as his eyes and fantasies were being seized and manipulated by the street scenes. His long crafty fingers kept touching and rubbing the shirt and the pants, as if they were an alien skin that had been ironed onto his own real, black, shiny skin. Had its own memories, this alien khaki skin, just as much as his black skin. His fingers were gliding over the memories contained within this khaki fabric and this evoked the self within these memories, a self that existed side by side, thigh by thigh, with the other black one. Two uneasy selves. Khaki memories were all bad, a pain in the ass, stained and contaminated, writhing with orders backed by the promise of violence of one sort or another. Chicken-shit orders from honkies who in any kind of fair man-to-man situation should be kissing his ass steada givin me a pain in it an should be sayin, "Yes sir, Mr. Cleon, sir. Don't you hesitate to ring that bell an I'll crawl here on the double, sir." Should be sayin all that steada "Cleon, you uppity cocksucker! How many times am I gonna have to tell you to get your black ass over to the officers' lounge for clean-up duty?" Or "Lissen to me, Mr. Bigshot. You keep actin cute with me when I give you an order an you're gonna find yourself in The Hole. You hear me?" When I get outta this fuckin Army I'm gonna burn these fuckin khaki shit clothes right down to the last . . .

—Hey, man, said Wills, nudging him in the side. —Do you see what I see?

—What? Where?

—Over there, in front of that massage parlor with the crazy red neon sign. Those two Jap cunts with just bikinis on.

—Oh, yeah, said Cleon, squinting to penetrate the flashing, many-colored neon light hallucination that consumed the fragmenting, demonic street. —Yeah. Right on. Your eyes are workin good today, Wills baby.

—What're you holding? asked Wills.

—'Bout twenty, twenty-five bucks an a hard-on.

—That oughta do it.

—You plannin to use my hard-on too?

—Man, I'm good for the bread, you know that. Now let's hit it. Watch out now. Don't get run over by any of these crazy Jap rickshaws, said Wills.

—Rickshaws? I don't see any . . .

—That's why they're so dangerous.

Cleon's vision was being assaulted and disordered and reassembled by the demonic, omnipotent colored neon lights. These enormous flashing, exploding signs, this cannibalistic saturnalia of entreaties and lewd lures, was eating his brain up. His equilibrium was being drained away. He wasn't quite sure he was walking. There didn't seem to be any street really. It had been consumed like the atmosphere, the sky, and the usual dimensions of depth and width and height, by the raging colored signs. Nothing was standing still anymore. Everything, he felt, was moving, shifting, this way and that. He felt that something had happened to space. His body was surrounded by colors, not air. He was suddenly there with the two hookers. As though they had all materialized together. They were in front of him yet at the same time there was no distance between them. His face was touching theirs and he felt their soft, perfumed breath on his nose and mouth. But he was quite aware that this sort of thing could go either way. One could, or one could not, take certain things for granted in this kind of situation, and certainly a street such as this, a street that asked for no quarter and, with equal steadfastness and regard for standards, gave none, was not to be taken lightly, however beguiling such an impulse might be. He did not have to look over his shoulder to catch this street, and its understandably dense and slyly fretful population, in an equivocal act of one sort or another. What good would that do? Could that clear the nonexistent air? What obscure, deeply imagined cause would be furthered by such an ungrateful, unprovoked act? Was he to become an impromptu policeman of that which might be? If he had a job, a subject, to be sure, of shifting emphasis, this was certainly not it. To be here was not to question being here. One came into a situation such as this, precisely such as this, with certain basic facts firmly under one's leather belt: (1) Ambiguity was solidly established here long ago before you ever stepped off the boat, exactly as the Indians (whether they were fully clothed at the time is really beside the point and also nobody's damn business but their own) were in the throes of a number of debilitating —and, yes, decimating—crises involving contradictions between theory and practice, form and content, and here vs. there, quite a few decades before the first randy, bandy-legged, lice-infested Pilgrim waded through the surf and laid claim to every sleeping clam there in the name of the Father, the Son, and the Holy Ghost; (2) there was no collectively felt (or, for that matter, perceived) obligation to reshape or reduce local possibilities to suit the predetermined expectations and limitations of migrant fools who may at any time, without specific advance notice or warning, become flatulent and eventually lifeless thrill-seekers; (3) that shadowy substances, here, are not to be understood as the sum total of shadow and substance, that hands flung into the air in anger or despair may simply remain there floating around like indecisive and indecent balloons, never to come back down to claim their own if that's what the question may be.

This street, he knew, had a gripping and devastating imminence. Oh yes.

—Are you sure you're Japanese? he nonetheless asked one of the hookers, one of the sudden, permeating faces.

—Why shouldn't I be Japanese? replied the hooker.

—You look kinda Japanese, maybe, but you don't feel Japanese, he said.

—Maybe I'll taste Japanese, she said. —Sometimes you have to play these things by tongue.

—What's your name?

Though it was she herself who replied, Cleon felt that the real answer came or vibrated or glowed and flashed from the all-embracing and omniscient neon massage sign that hovered there. The huge, colored sign was more of a presence than a message. He was on to this.

—Carol.

Wills and the other hooker were making arrangements or some sort of a deal, maneuvering and circling, feinting and counterfeinting, fooling, playing, and in an elegance of, was it slow motion? They were next to him, yet Cleon was getting the impression that they were at the same time remote and far away, and that there was quite a bit more to the situation than one could grasp at first hand. Even their smiles, which were lewd and from time to time leering, with God knows what else lurking, waiting to spring out at the very ripest of moments, were evolving through a complicated distance. And their voices, well, they were drifting fragments that came and went, appeared softly and disappeared rather the same way, softly, having both shape and sound, and while the sounds may have themselves vanished, rather, disintegrated, words gently, discreetly, crumbling, and vaporizing, the meanings they carried seemed to remain hovering in the ambience, hovered like smells, odors, fragrances, hovered as vague but insistent memories . . . "technological formalities that have finally taken on the identities of . . . that you Asian pros can perform certain tricks . . . so at a certain point one is faced with the fact that ritual is self-referent and therefore . . . Decca Records? With a name like that, how can you . . . one would be well within one's exploratory rights to a theory of the ecology of experience which would be a far more flexible and organic concept than merely *structure*, because I mean, what the fuck, structure can be merely an abstract imposition . . . sucking soldier cock in a sea of rice . . . can't possibly include the price of the hotel or breakfast which I'll just bet you thought would be thrown in, right? Two over easy with some hash browns and a side order of eighteen country sausages, carried, no doubt, by the nubile, naked sisters of the Seven Dwarfs who . . . Japanese hash is supposed to be even better than Lebanese red because it's got seaweed mixed in with it an you know that seaweed has some real crazy minerals and stuff in it . . . off-shore mineral rights may just swing it, 'cause you know they've got a lot of oil out there underwater and it's only a question of what the best way is to get the fucking stuff up to the surface so that people who want Vietnamese sea horses in their tanks can have them . . . Tiger, tiger, burning bright, in the forests of your capitalist asshole . . . they nourished the hope of peacefully building up and consolidating a U.S. new-colonialist regime in the south . . . You want my money and I want your ass whether it's Jap or not, so, uh, let's hit it, OK . . . Furiakisaki wants some seafood, mama. Or to put it another way, and in the tastiest words of Representative Otis Pike of the House Intelligence Committee, 'You are saying that the intelligence was intentionally made corruptive to comply with political decisions that had already been made? Is that correct?' 'Yes, sir,' replied the CIA man he was questioning . . . I don't know how or why, but something or somebody is moving this street . . . Instead of concentrating all your obviously limited energies and talents on getting your ashes hauled, you should devote a little time to the study of shadow and substance, sonny boy, while at the same time, of course, keeping your hand on your prick so that nobody runs off with it in a more than impromptu game of prisoner's base . . . just about anybody can tell you that all such research questions are model orientated . . ."

—How come you're hookin? asked Cleon.

—How come you're not? replied Carol.

Cleon heard and felt the words echo. Their reverberations made his skin tingle. He felt . . . it seemed that he was inside the words. Sort of walkin/ driftin. The sensation inside the words was gentle and smooth and infinite, though contoured. Effortlessly, weightless, he glided through/from word to word. Some had tastes, some had smells. He saw, after a bit, that he wasn't the only person there inside these words. Others were wandering about as he was. No attempt was made on anyone's part to acknowledge the presence of the others. Awarenesses were not being shared, Cleon observed. Everyone seemed somehow to be preoccupied, something was on their mind, but no one seemed to be heading anywhere in particular. A preoccupied aimlessness, that's what it was. It wasn't that anyone seemed to be lost or anything like that. No.

From word to word he went. His wandering/drifting was not taking place in any relationship to time. No. Time had nothing to do with it. Time was someplace else. So, he could not say that after a while he realized that he could no longer see himself, see his body, that is, No. The awareness simply permeated him that, in some way, he had disappeared. Then he knew that he himself had become a word. Exactly which one, well, that had to be found out. When? How? In what way? Would someone speak him and he would hear himself spoken?

—How come you do me like you do, do, do, Decca sings as she peels off her zippy, skimpy clothes and tosses them about the demure, canny Japanese room in back of the massage parlor.

Carol, as she too takes off her clothes, her stark, provocative Cunt Costume, sings, —You made me love you, I didn't wanna do it, I didn't wanna do it.

Wills is already stripped naked and is stretched out on his back on the pure, white bed. His stiff prick throbs gently in the direction of the white plaster wall behind him. Oh what a black, black prick it is! It is defying the all-knowing, all-surrounding whiteness in the room, precisely as gallant, outnumbered Othello defied the mounting madness of the Venetian whities back in the bad old days. Wills sings, —For the sexual act to be fully satisfactory to a woman, she must, in the depths of her mind, desire deeply and utterly to be a mother. His singing voice was flat, with no future, like an afternoon in Kansas City. Others, at a greater remove, might wish to compare his voice to a motionless rocking chair on an abandoned porch. Still others . . .

—Mama's lil baby loves shortnin, shortnin, Mama's lil baby loves shortnin bread, Decca sings, bouncing her big tits and grinding her sweet, bare ass.

—A tisket, a tasket, I've lost my yellow basket, sings Carol, doing a spanky little cancan.

—Hokay, José, says Decca, looking down at Wills. —Your number is coming up and it's not a song, I can assure you of that.

—What'll we do with this dreary little lint-head, Decca? asks Carol. —Will you just look at that presumptuous hard-on of his. What on earth do you think he's dreaming of doing with it?

—God only knows, says Decca, peering at the black erection in question. —He could be thinking of fucking Mount Fuji with it. Or he might be planning to enter it in the annual Japanese cherry blossom festival at Kyoto.

Carol gives the stiff, black dick a playful slap. —Hey, bubba. What's up with you an' this here hard-on of darkness?

—The scare stories about this country's atomic tests are simply not justified, he sings, with the flawless intonations of a castrated priest singing for his supper, keeping his wide eyes fixed on the ceiling. —Some experts believe that mutations usually work out in the end to improve the species.

—There's hope for this man yet, says Carol, tying a big red balloon to his prick. —With luck, he could turn into a radio station.

—Yeah, says Decca, —or a hot satellite station. She ties more red balloons to his arms and legs. —Float this little motherfucker up to where it'll make the most difference. She and Carol push open the big French doors that have appeared at one end of the utterly white room. They pick up the balloon-rigged Wills and heave his black nakedness through the open doors and out into Japanese space. The balloons float him quite magnificently. No hitches at all. No last-minute failures of any kind, the sort of failures and flop-downs that have so often ruined otherwise fine reputations at Cape

Canaveral and other such nouveau-riche blast-off joints. —Bounce a few signals off that baby all right.

—I think he could relay the Rose Bowl games and stuff like that, don't you? observes Carol, as Wills floats into the blue heavens.

—Oh yeah. Absolutely no question about it. And in my own personal view, he could also very easily handle public hangings, mass religious revivals, and large-scale industrial dismissals. Mmm. Boy oh boy. If only his dear mother could see him now.

—Right. His dear mother. That would be a nice touch, says Carol, watching the naked, red balloon-festooned black man float past the snow-covered top of Mount Fuji.

—Aim high, his mother must have said to him.

—Oh yes. If she was any kind of mother she did.

—Tell me something from the very bottom of your heart, Carol, says Decca, never for a second taking her eyes from the red bubbles and their cargo as they gradually disappear into twentieth-century Japanese mythology. —Do you think spade hard-ons travel well?

It is at just such moments as this that truly committed scholar-voyeurs must step back into the closet to piece together a viable, succulent, sociohistorical matrix into which one can place the preceding events and foregone conclusions. Otherwise, quite valuable material tends to develop symptoms of vertigo, weaves and bogs, and eventually, no matter how well intentioned its New Year's resolutions, collapses to the floor of the handiest cutting room. And we all know quite a bit more than we would like to admit to exactly what happens there. Precisely as we know what happened to the best parts of *Monsieur Verdoux*, *Ben-Hur*, *The Baker's Wife*, and *Bambi*. Swept up by the canny, self-serving, ruthless little Chicano night porter, Chicito, and peddled, at outrageously inflated prices, to the scions of billionaire Saudi Arabian oil sheiks, scions who have nothing better to do than watch movies, squeeze their pimples, sharpen their knives for The Great Showdown when Mr. Big Sheikh dies, and grease their cocks for the daily bum-fucking bouts in the main courtyard. Can you imagine the pall of utter nowhereness that must forever hang over this scene, a pall that can only be compared to mountains of rotting dates, backed up for miles in the ancient warehouses of Djibouti, about to descend upon the unsuspecting, sleepwalking masses in the greatest flood since the very stressful days of Noah?

—Man, this fucking day will never end.

—You can sure say that again.

—Some smart-ass musta stopped all the clocks. Phew!

That will stand as a typical fragment of conversation from those indolent, nongoal-orientated lads of Oilsville. Of course, from time to time single lines can be heard issuing from their lounging, liquescent groups.

—Guess I'll fly my ass to London tomorrow. Gotta buy me about two tons of Chanel No. 5 aftershave lotion.

—Yeah, me too. I'll follow you in my new yellow 747. I've gotta lay in about seven hundred pairs of jockey shorts.

—You guys seen my new Rolls-Royce? I had 'em build a pizza stand on the roof. Great, huh?

And this: —You know that fleet of Sherman tanks I bought last week? Well, I'm havin' them plated with gold. More clout that way, y' know.

We don't have to be told what dreamy, rootless, bony, street-corner progressives would like to hear instead of the above-quoted gems. Oh no. We can produce the lines any old time. Like, dig these: "Our people are wallowing in disease, filth, despair, malnutrition, ignorance, and total helplessness. We must do everything we can to help them live like real human beings."

"Right on! I myself, out of my own pocket money, am going to build 185 clinics for babies alone."

"Splendid. As for me, I will personally see to it that every man, woman, and child in this country is taught how to read and write within the next year."

"Yeah. We gotta share this vast oil wealth. After all, Saudi Arabia belongs to all Saudi Arabians, not just a handful of pampered royal rotters. I promise to plan people's farms from one end of our sandy country to the other. Good food, that's the ticket."

Yeah. Sure. That kinda fantasy will give you fourth-degree brain damage. Those self-centered dinges would far, far rather be drowned in a hot yellow piss shower, let loose by a two-bit Swedish hooker, than give a passing thought to a starving *paysan.* Or a helping hand to a child being ravaged by rabies, or scurvy. And that's a fact. Their idea of social progress would be to tie some white goddess down and then, from velvet- and gold-lined box seats, watch her gang shagged by a team of trained chimpanzees. These miserable, self-serving little cocksuckers are so historically and morally beside the point, so vainly and arrogantly simpleminded, that they think trachoma is a city in the state of Washington. And that rickets is a game played by London street children. I mean, fuck them. They aren't worth the contaminated popcorn it would take to turn them into basket cases or the black sequins to change them into drag queens. We can just imagine the sort of racist/sexist/right-wing/lowbrow cracks these sleazy lounge lizards would make to a dame with class, like for example Carol or Decca or Juliette.

—Hey, baby! Want me to change your oil?

And what would our friend Carol's rejoinder to that be?

—You couldn't change your underwear, much less my oil, she would snap
back. For instance.

—Hi there, doll baby! How's about a roll in the hay for two followed up by
a round-the-world tour tongue-wise?

Well, Decca would catch that baby by the tail and hurl it right back thusly:
—That tongue of yours couldn't make it around the corner, much less
around the world on this body of mine.

That's tellin' them, Decca, honey. Those jerks: just because they own—
through no up-by-the-bootstraps efforts of their own, of course, like I mean,
shit. They didn't open up the West or expose themselves to deep-sea
dragons alongside Vasco da Gama or anything original like that—half the
fuckin' fossil fuel in the world—like, we know where these desert farts
would be if it weren't for all those dead shrimp and shellfish an' micro-
organisms and other such shit as that, I mean, they'd be chasing camel shit
and fuckin' second-hand moonbeams—they think they can go around
saying anything to anybody, snap their oily fingers and "Yassuh, boss"
choruses pour in from the four corners. Calling Room Service at all hours of
the fuckin' night, Send up twenty pounds of cold smoked salmon and two
hundred pounds of hot nookie. Yeah. Three hundred bottles of fizz water on
the side. What the fuck they gonna do? Play Niagara Falls on the Rocks?
They gonna wrap the salmon around those naked hookers and make them
leap up the falls all over again, fizzin' all the way like something Disneyland
forgot to put in the show for all those gawking kids in tow with their geeky
parents who look at all that shit like it was real? I mean, Abe Lincoln comin'
on like that about Gettysburg when the old fuck has been dead for a
hundred years! Well, their day will come, my friends, an' you can bet on it.
Meanwhile, we will keep them in check with the likes of front-liners like
Decca and Carol, ladies of imagination and class who know where the
bodies are buried and, furthermore, where they're going to be buried.
Nobody's going to pull the wool over their eyes or sell them cans of sardines
packed with mouse turds. Oh no. They're not a couple of simpleminded,
starry-eyed doughboys only too happy to expose themselves to gangrene
and mustard gas and trench mouth for the sake of capitalist warmongers
calling themselves Democracy and the Spirit of '76, said cretin doughboys
singing "Over There, Over There" or "The Stars and Stripes Forever," as
they are chewed up by those huge Frenchie dugout rats (and I don't mean
cocksuckers either) who no doubt have more than plenty of bubonic plague
to go around for everybody. Oh yeah. Nice, huh? And then when it's all over,
and they have maybe an arm and a leg less on their bodies, they come home
to sell apples on the streets as the passersby look at them like they were
some kind of cockroach that's got the nerve to beg for a couple of pennies
from decent Americans in broad daylight. Oh boy! Don't you just wish you

had all that fine khaki on you! And some of those puttees wrapped around your bold, patriotic legs which you can rewrap around the varicose veins later on as you hobble to the regular wonderful sweating redneck drunken meetings of your local Veterans of Foreign Wars, everybody slapping everybody else on the back and pushing and shoving and giggling and wearing those hats! and waving their crutches or their beer bottles and screaming for Johnson or Nixon to bomb Hanoi and Peking and Havana right off the face of the fucking earth so that our sons and daughters won't have to live in fear of commie syphilis as they go merrily about raping the rest of the world as is their constitutional privilege? (You got it, Abner. Now shove it up your hairy old ass along with the deed to your wife's headaches.)

L isten now, as Decca talks to Carol. Feel her breath upon your own ear. Her sounds are soft and gentle, yet these words can float through clouds and space and rainstorms without losing their quality or their meaning. Nor do they get wet as they pass through seas. Fish can't bite through them. Sharks avoid them (if they can). Drowned fishermen may mouth them, in their way, but this is of more poetic than critical interst. Silver- and gold-miners, sweating their questionable and unlived lives away deep inside the earth's violated belly, taste the words as they flit by, on their voyage, but is too late, just too late. And pilots falling from their crippled planes, what can they do about, or with, these exquisite words that brush their faces as they, the faces, hurtle downward to doom? That is certainly no time for the pilots to be looking back and wishing they had lived their lives differently. And hangdog philosophers, still clinging to the foul dugs of academe, look the words square in the eye and realize, irremediably, that they read a very, very bad translation of Plato. Ach! "We've had it all wrong all these years," they say, and plop! plop! plop! off the precipice.
—In Spain, Decca is saying to Carol, gently, sweetly, as flowers touching, —in Spain, the little man is busy putting up crosses.
—And the bodies? asks Carol.
—There are so many of them, and they all know they're headed for the cross, Decca tells her.
—Dreadful.
—Even before they're officially notified of their destination, these bodies are standing in the streets with their arms stretched out and their legs crossed, already in position.
—Oh my God. It blinds the eye, such a sight.
—Their heads have fallen and their mouths are open, agape, and the spit is dribbling down their chins.
—I can't bear it, says Carol, and we see her cover her face with her hands,

her arms pushing her naked breasts together.

—El Greco knew. Every line in Spain writhes with agony.

We can believe that Decca might have embraced Carol, caressing her, kissing her face and breasts and hands, in sisterly love and presence. That would not have been out of order, or out of line or out of a book by Sir Walter Scott. Nor should it have led, or lead, to boring, unimaginative, and dehumanizing speculations in one direction or another, up, down, or sideways (if there is anything this world needs less of, it is ratty conversations from the bottom of part-time sewers. Isn't it enough that birds or bats shit hourly on such sacred manifestations as the Tomb of the Unknown Soldier and Charlemagne's statue? Must we sit idly by while we ourselves permit The Dregs to infiltrate even the flour of our eventual bread? To wipe their smelly, filthy asses with our Staff of Life?) . . . running her hands over her uncompromised nakedness, smelling her, breathing her in, taking her into, unto herself, and thus, as the budding tree *is* the spring, as the ripple of the stream awakening from ice *is* the stream itself, becoming her, so that we need but to hear one voice to hear them both . . . a voice within a voice, a presence within a presence . . . we know, as we know our own heartbeat, that words live within words, that an entire civilization lurks . . . no, awaits us, beneath certain sentences, impressively containing itself, its pulse quite normal, patiently waiting for us to open its door, and pfft! suddenly its heretofore hidden or buried or entombed, or even denied, streets are there for us, thronged with its very own citizens, dependent upon none for verbs of joy, nouns of quality, oblique screams of clarification. Do you see!? If these people, who may be strangers like anybody else to you but who are certainly not strangers to themselves, which is not to say that they don't at times feel and act strange, that they don't, upon calculated impulse, cry out Hi there, Stranger! to a very close friend, that they don't, upon a divinely heavy midday Sunday feed, peer at, let us say, a big, steaming, heaped oval platter, and mutter, Hmm. And what strange feast is this?

And another citizen at the groaning table, a citizen, mind you, with a certain vested interest in the matter, will say, Do you have your verbs mixed up, sir? Did you drop *are*, as in What strange feet are these?

No, madam. I did not.

In that case, you back-burning cocksucker, I say to you, if you don't like the cooking here, you don't like the cook. If you have to think twice before wrapping that sharp tongue of yours around the dishes set before you, then it would follow that you have to think twice about wrapping it around me, who's given your tongue an open-ended playground these many years, fore and aft, before and after, who, in point of fact, put the *t* on your tongue, without which it would be an obscure, useless vestigial artifact called ongue. So . . .

Madam, you do me ill. You are beating a dead horse that has not yet galloped, a horse of a different color, belonging to a different drum majorette. Taking umbrage out of the mouths of starving children, and so on, as any lexicographer in good fiddle would agree. Strange feat . . . could I not have been saying that in complex and perplexed admiration as I stared at you using vapors? In guarded awe? Think of the good Rosetta as he gazed at the Rosetta Stone for the very first time, surrounded by the suffocating insanity of the pyramids, on the one hand, and by the looming absurdity of the French archaeological academy on the other. Can you really, for even a second, imagine that he exclaimed, Hot shit! or, Well, I'll be a fucked Peking duck! Or anything remotely like that? Can you . . .

—Granted sir, and I withdraw my implications and herewith return all umbrage. And even if you are a back-burning cocksucker, with sly latent plans and meanings as would befit your taxonomic position, you're A-OK with me. You can take the cunt out of the tree but you can't take the tree out of the cunt. Or is it vice versa? That dish, you sweet creepy old fuck, is nothing less than equivocated meatloaf, working its way to Mecca.

—Well, tickle my pickle and call me Uncle. But who has seen a meatloaf steam?

—What do you suppose the word *equivocated* means? It certainly couldn't mean a horse race in the middle of the night by unlicensed practitioners of the black arts.

—Which of course, you tricky cunt you, does not have anything to do with a passel of black boys producing art in the shade of the old apple tree while some piece of white trash wearing a badge is trying unsuccessfully to convince them they would be heaps better off doing all this with a license, a bag of which he just happens to have on him, hanging, in fact, from his thick leather belt, like a scalp from a cat he could have spayed. Cat's scalp with spade of steel. Do not go gentle into this black night.

—None of which is getting you any closer to the meatloaf of the moment, Black Knight, White Pawn, or whatever the costume you would care to pull the wool over your own eyes with. Speaking of which, cast your eyes on the scene in the public square out there and tell me what it is you think that crowd of overfed, unlettered louts is up to, guffaws, giggles, thigh slaps, and all.

—Louts with knots. They're having one of their games, of course, and what else is new? They're having sport, if one can so basely employ that decent word, with two mad mastiffs and one old heretic, a fellow I went to school with. We were boys together, as the saying goes, but we were not men together.

—The dogs are chasing him and tearing his clothes off, piece by piece. They are so skillful for such big and raging dogs. The man is screaming . . .

—. . . of course. That is what the game is all about. Do you see how the faces of the louts are now radiating with joy, as if some divine fire within them had been subtly lit by a sorceress?

—He is naked now, except for his underpants. Oh . . . rrrippp! Now they too are gone. His prick and balls are swinging in the wind. He leaps and spins, this screaming man, like poetry out of the mouths of wandering bards, those airy men who carry with them the dreams of the delighted dead.

—He made the mistake, if you wish to call it that, of questioning the Council's interpretations of certain parts of the Ancient Coda. They said he was rocking the boat. He said Fuck you. You are a Power Elite. You have distorted old meanings for new uses, mostly your own ends. They said, You have just Cooked Your Own Goose, you big dumb ape. He said, You have just Lost All Credibility. Cast this heretic out! they cried, and in two shakes of the Blessed Lamb's Tail, the deed was done, a fait accompli in the very best of circles.

—The louts have called off their dogs. He is lying on the ground in a naked wretched heap, and he is sobbing. The louts are laughing. They are shouting, You dirty fuckin heretic! You commie peez uh shitt! Overthro yoyne guvmentz! Nestyme we gon bomb yur Hanoi!

—Oh yes. Perhaps one day the louts will be taught how to say whoopie! They seemed to handle Hot Dog! well enough on certain blood-drenched occasions.

—I must say that their black and blue uniforms have a certain skintight je ne sais quoi, a special something. Pizzazz, y' know.

—One can go beyond that and say that you'd better be tight with them if you value your skin. Pizzazz notwithstanding, that certain something may spell your doom. One thinks that because something is indefinable, it must be pleasing. Don't ask the shiv man if his blade reflects the moonlight, because he will then be forced to show you. And the reflection you see will be your own face in astonished agony.

—And of course one can go on from there, in the exquisite pits, that is, and say that yesterday's hard-on will not rustle today's bedsheets. Nostalgia is a sucker's game.

—Hot pricks leaping down memory lane! Gleaming stiffs marching breast to breast into the sunset! Ah, madam! How precisely, with what long-lost, revelatory elegance, long past due, and hardly overwrought, of course, in a world that is fast turning into a stone quarry of deadly abstractions, you hit the nail on its eyeless head with your delicious woman's hammer! Who dares to say that woman's hammer is in the home? He who hammers that falsehood home shall be crossed with nails and I don't mean bred to run in fields of spikes. With your hammer and my tongue, madam, we'll make such a combination . . .

—Eat your meatloaf, sir, before it gets cold.

—I'd far rather eat your meat, madam, and loaf through the coldhearted day while I do it. Keeping in mind that one man's meat is another man's loafer, give or take the fact that loafing meat is a threat to our economy as well as a menace to our children's morals, particularly if it is hanging around on the fringes of their innocent playgrounds. Loafers of the world unite and grab your meat before it is too late—hence the expression "A meating of loafers," just as one has a gaggle of geese, a pride of lions, a covey of quail, and a bunch of assholes. At the same time, it should be noted that who steals my purse steals trash. But who robs me of my meat robs me of that which . . .

—Good grief, man! Get a grip on yourself. They will hear you. Your voice is rising through the rafters and piercing the walls. (Think the word *viper* and your body instantly knows volumes about death agony.) You know very well that the neighbors to the right of us handsomely supplement their state Old Crocks Pension by peddling eavesdroppings to The Punisher. And we know all we need to know about Her, don't we.

—You are quite right, madam. We do indeed. I went to school with Her too. I remember Her as I remember the coldest of winters and the longest of famines. Even as a child She could make you shrink back into yourself as far as you could go. She could accomplish this malevolent miracle without appearing to do anything at all. You simply sensed horror in Her, and it was a horror that did not require, was not seeking, any episode or situation to manifest or clothe itself in. This horror was pure knowledge, pure realization. Does one have to see the waves that one knows one will sooner or later drown beneath? Must one watch the bird fall through the sky to its death to know that that could well be oneself?

—Sir, you are making my flesh crawl.

—The Punisher was born with a dreadful talent for producing abysmal fear in other human beings. And of course now that She is older she has supplemented this awesome talent with a variety of specific tricks and turns, as a great chef can produce a dozen different sauces merely by raising and lowering his gaze. She did not have to run for this office or solicit the Council's nomination. It was as simple and logical as the rising of the sun. One day everyone here knew that She had become The Punisher. Without any information regarding that fact having been announced or published, officially or unofficially. With the flakes whirling around your face you don't have to be told it's snowing. Long after this event had become a fait accompli did She finally assent to the community's pleas to wear the traditional garb of The Punisher, the human skeleton.

—The costume is only cloth. So how can it make the sound of rattling bones as She walks?

—I don't know, madam, and I truly do not wish to think about the matter.

—Well . . . now that we've gorged ourselves here, sir, let us move on to The Fucking, and gorging of a different kind.

—I can hear the bone-rattling of her costume as clearly as if She were half a dozen feet away. And I can hear the costume's teeth chatter as it or She throws her head back and forth laughing after a damning accusation has been scored and you sit there watching yourself slip away into nothingness. But now . . .

—Let us to The Fucking Pits, sir, and on the double.

—And I can hear that voice . . . Even when She was a child, it could stop you dead in your tracks like an invisible lasso hurled from nowhere with dreadful precision. I can still see so very clearly those innocent children whom She had called out to on the town playground suddenly freeze in midmotion.

—Enough! Enough! They are waiting for us in The Fucking Pits! The teams are stripped and ready. The games have been prescribed. The crowds are waiting insatiably in the stone tiers. Hear them yelling for the action! Sir, stop hearing the voice of The Punisher. Strike it down. Flog it out. Look at me in my magnificent nakedness. Seize me! Seize my succulent breasts, my hot cunt, my hungry ass! Save yourself with your prick! Submit yourself to its sacred lust, man, before it is too late.

—She once paid a call upon my now-dead friend The Examiner of Oral History. He told me of Her visit. She suddenly appeared in his study one afternoon while he was listening to a recording of a wandering woman story-teller in the north who was becoming more and more popular with the field-workers. He said he suspected this woman's authenticity, her credibility. There was something fishy about her, her stories, her storytelling style, he told me. He said, Beneath her catchy tones and inflections, I heard other sounds, and they were ominous. And beneath her simple yet fascinating stories of this and that, this deed, that hero, I could detect other stories that were not so simple and whose fascination was dark and frightening and smelled of the rank, bone-littered primitive caves that we are supposed to have left so far, far behind us. These malevolent, fetid stories that lurked beneath the simplistic ones, like a cunning, vicious, night animal lurking around the bend in the child's storybook forest, engaged the listener, quite unbeknownst to him- or herself, in a new and I suspect officially conceived mythology, in which there is no place, no role, for those values that normally give the human community dignity and quality and meaning worth stretch-ing oneself for. In other words, my examination of this storyteller was leading me to the strong conviction that she was an agent of The Final Friends, whose goal, whose assignment from them, was to corrupt and manipulate the minds of the people to prepare them for activities and a way of life that would make your blood run cold and your soul vomit in disgust.

I was simply carrying out the mandate of my job as Examiner, a position, a surveillance that was created centuries ago by our people in a collective effort to keep watch over the purity and sanctity of our achievements as a society that had, still has of course, the clasped hands and not the mailed fist on its coat of arms.

Without my hearing Her come in, while my back was turned to the record player, She turned off the recording of this suspect folklorist.

—Why do you waste your precious time, my dear Examiner, listening to this unoriginal and second-rate artist? The Punisher inquired from behind me. —Don't you have more interesting, more enlightening things to do?

—Nothing is more enlightening and interesting to me than serving the interests of the people, I said. —And that is precisely what I was doing before you came in and turned the record off.

—You have been feeding your professional vanity, and that is not the same as serving the people or The Community.

—You are mistaken. I have uncovered in that so-called second-rate artist an enemy of the people, a cunning agent who is spreading evil by order of a small group of powerful people who are no longer in rapport with the best traditions of our . . .

—Stop! Enough! You are the danger, Mr. Examiner. You alone. Your pride and your ears betray you.

And then I could hear Her no longer. Because She turned Her punishing voice up to a silent, supersonic pitch, so powerful that my eardrums exploded, my very brain seemed to shatter, and blood poured from my ears and nose, and I lost consciousness.

I have tried to think about what it was She said to me in that soundless, shattering voice. What were the words . . . They were words, yet they were not words. They were the unspeakable. The feelings, sensations, states of being that exist outside language, that, in fact, language flees from to protect its very life. For as I understand language, it developed as man developed and emerged into humanness; it was his humanness, and without it he would have been something else, something less. The unspeakable, which The Punisher was conveying to me, is against humanness and thus against language itself.

Screams do not help man climb out of the abyss. Only language can do that. It is the sharp instrument with which he patiently carves his upward hand- and footholds in the sheer walls of the abyss. Without it he is forever doomed to pace at the bottom of these walls and claw at them in anguished futility.

The Punisher's sounds that destroyed my hearing recreated those walls and the dreadful impossibility of ever scaling them.

I know that I will soon be dead. Listening to language was my very existence. It was what I did, was my engagement in the daily struggles in the human community here. Without this listening, my life has no sustaining purpose. And thus no reason for continuing. When there is no more water, the fish gasp and gasp and die. When there is no more sky, the birds plummet like stones into nothingness. Already parts of my body have lost interest in going on. My sensations are indifferent. I can feel no difference between hot and cold, pain or nonpain. My lungs frequently do not process the air I breathe, and as a consequence I often black out. And my memory, my precious memory, that permitted me to exist in history, to touch hands with all men who had gone before me throughout the ages, to know the difference between yesterday and today, that miraculous entity barely functions. Just enough to get me through the day. To tie my shoes and know where I put my hat. But it won't look back. I turn around, so to speak, and I am confronted with an immeasurable, impenetrable darkness. Nothing lives in that cold darkness. The past no longer exists. As far as my memory is concerned, it never took place.

Of course, this state of affairs is exactly what The Punisher had in mind. I will have been eliminated. The evil plans of The Final Friends will go on unimpeded. Men's hearts will be perverted into vileness.

My mind has drifted off into a kind of void, a void, peculiarly enough, that is not even my own but is public, like a square, where all sorts of people wander in and out as they please, saying and doing whatever comes into their heads, perhaps talking like other people, making believe they are somebody else, which is damn well their own business and not yours, indifferent to whether these things are absurd and make no sense whatever, or, on the contrary, make too much bloody sense for anybody's comfort, forcing their unsuspecting backs, their naked backs . . . you heard me! Naked! Their ingenuous backs, because they're there on free-floating innocence, giving *their* brains a rest, a much needed and earned rest, you can fucking well be sure of that! Day in and day out beating their poor fucking brains to smithereens trying to figure out what this means and what that means, and it's your ass if you don't get it right, because those motherfuckers don't give you an inch, and if you think they give a hoot in hell what happens to you, you've got another thing coming, because they don't. You see that speck of dirt over there? That's how much you mean to them. You may as well be hot-dog meat for all they care. Mean, coldhearted cocksuckers up there eating T-bone steaks three times a day and pouring imported French champagne down their faces. It's a wonder a person's got a brain anymore the kind of shit it's got to put up with, and then the next thing you know, that fart-face over there swinging a psalter he snatched from some poor drunken faggot priest down on his bony knees with a big prick halfway down his skinny, parched throat, 'cause those guys, they're expected to make out on wafers

and water and mere whiffs of young choirboy ass. Y' know, so it stands to
reason since they're not all that different from anybody else that they're
gonna crash out from time to time an' put everything they've got on the line
for some real down-to-earth meat 'n' potatoes fucking, whether it's a stiff
hustler's prick up their ass in a fleabag hotel or a prick in their mouth behind
a park bush while the cop on the beat checks his list of shakedowns under
the lamppost light a few creepy feet away. Next thing you know that guy I
mentioned who's swinging the saltcellar opens his big mouth and yells,
They're pullin' the wool over our eyes! They're fuckin' us over! Millions of
poor suckers are gettin' their asses blown to bits for a bunch of warmongerin'
capitalist profiteers! They're sellin' you this commie threat shit and this
national security my country love her or leave her shit so you'll run out in the
middle of the street in your fuckin' BVDs shoutin' Take me! I wanna defend
my country 'tis of thee against all comers tryin' to sneak up on our shoreline
well within the twelve-mile limit from the land of the risin' sun carryin' with
them all kinds of yellow perils an' cultured pearls an' diseased slant-eyed
pussy hopin' to flood our own home markets with shoddy handmade goods
put together by thousands upon thousands of underslung underpaid slave
laborers who think that just because they work in shops that sell sweat if you
can imagine such a disgusting thing, that they can get away with any damn
thing that comes into their heads like those subliminal messages in code on
their cheap unfair-priced television sets that then go on to corrupt the
minds and budding ranks of our own unemployed youth having in the first
place just a mere few minutes before that ravaged and destroyed our native-
born television manufacturers and their free enterprise markups. Fucking
got their nerve. Those hairless geeks better watch out if they know what's
good for them, and if they've got any sense at all and if their sly eyes haven't
already been ruined once and for all by all the fuckin' weirdo incense they
work and live and love by they'll take some good yankee advice and get
their shit together and start paddlin' around in the rice in their own back-
yards and keepin' their flat noses clean as best they can without puttin' the
bite on us for some lend-lease and most-favorite-nation tax credits to bail
them out just because they were too dumb to check out the leaks in their
boats before they started all that rice paddlin' in the first place. I'm not
kiddin' when I say that the time has more than come for the freedom-lovin'
people of this great nation to get up off their hands and knees for a real
eyeball-to-eyeball showdown with those overpopulated Asiatics and their
advanced technologies over who's gonna rule Britannia, them or us.

You beginnin' to see what I'm tryin' to tell you?

Open up this door, goddamn you! I want my breakfast. What kind of a
dump is this if a clean-cut, hard-workin' stiff mindin' his own business born
and bred right here in this country can't get a plate of side meat and grits an'

a cuppa java and three eggs over easy before six o'clock in the morning? Huh? You better open this here door before I kick it in, you hear me? You act like I'm askin' for some kinda ricochet romance or half the moon or all the gold in Fort Knox. All I want is what's comin' to me. Even dogs get hungry. You open up this door right this minute. You think you're so fuckin' smart. I'm gonna count to ten, an' if you don't . . . You're plain crazy if you think for one single solitary second that I'm gonna take this kinda crap layin' down. Soon as I get my lawyer on the phone you bastards arc gonna see some fur fly. An' that ain't all you're gonna see fly.

A nd you've just got to dig the base at Rota, Decca said to Carol. —Boy oh boy. And I don't mean perhaps. When son of Noah has his moment he'll need go no farther than this seamless little pea patch for his basic passenger list. This place has every living geek type you'd need for your All-Purpose Worldwide Humanity As She Really Is Take Her or Leave Her Freak Show. Courtesy of Adam and Eve. What this joint doesn't have isn't worth having. I mean, shit, even Dracula would feel right at home here. And the same goes for Caligula, Cyclops, Medusa, Typhoid Mary, and the Gingerbread Boy. This place is not only a barrel of laughs, it's a barrel of screams. People here have every reason to be afraid of their shadows. They're hit men for Jesus, who as we all know now was a high-school dropout with serious behavioral problems.

—Now then . . . Permit me to call your attention to that green U.S. Army bus that just drove up to the Olympic-size swimming pool. Observe those howling things jumping, leaping, crawling out of said green army bus. At first glance, one would say they were children. But you would be wrong. They are not children. They are monsters. They've already become what they will eventually be. Cheaters, liars, informers, adulterers, deceivers, degenerates, sadists, murderers. Smell them! They reek of approaching horror. That blue-eyed girl in the pink dress? She'll one day vote to obliterate 900 million Chinese with the neutron bomb. That fat, freckled, mottled boy with the inner tube? He will screw his best friend in a stock deal. And that grinning nipper with the look of a lizard? The one who is sucking up to the counselor? He will drive his wife to suicide with his raging faggot affairs. See that long-legged girl guzzling down the Coke? She'll help her lover burn down his factory to collect the insurance.

OK. Let us turn our gaze from this smelly bunch and pray that the swimming pool will make the most of its opportunity to drown them all. But before moving on, why not hear some of the memorable words that will fall from their foul mouths:

"Of course I love you. Whatever gave you the idea I didn't?"

"The American people will not sit idly by while Asian communism grows into a world-devouring octopus."

"Dirty little kikes . . . ought to be forced to worship like everybody else."

"We'll show those fuck slants a thing or two. When we get through with 'em, they won't even have their assholes left."

"I didn't mean it. I was just having a little fun."

"That's the absolute truth. I give you my word of honor."

"I wouldn't dream of doing anything to hurt you."

"What kind of person do you think I am anyway?"

"My country right or wrong."

Wasn't that just music to your ears? I thought so. Language to love and live by, right? And you'll be wanting to hand some down to your kiddies, right?

Okeydokey. Over here to your right, halfway between Smoky the Bear and J. Edgar Hoover and a six-hour overnight excursion flight from the Black Hole of Calcutta, we have the esteemed, reamed, and totally hairless Colonel Alfredo Alfonso W. Creepmore y Fuckless. Known familiarly and affectionately to his humble and shit-eating subordinates as Sir Fart-Face. Or F. F. for short. You would have a perfect right to ask, How did Mother Nature put together such a number as he? Has she no shame? Did she clear this with her shop steward? One always assumed that she was a kosher purist working within a framework of respect for the organic departmental differences. By which one means, it really should not have to be pointed out, that one cannot get a lamb chop to fuck a watermelon. How, then, can it be explained that this man has the face of a cabbage with the smile of a toad? The hands of a sea turtle, yet that move as a shark to the kill. And his walk . . . Oh my God! The regal prissiness of Queen Victoria. But to your mind's jeopardy you think of a prowling leopard when you watch it. When he talks, the sounds that come out of his mouth sound like a pig rooting in a barn-yard, but your mind is listening as if to the mouthings of a viper. Can you fucking imagine what a talking snake would sound like? Save us. And do you want to know what he smells like? The odor he gives off? He smells like an inner tube. You know that smell. Abandoned garages smell like that.

Yes! An abandoned garage . . . That's what this unspeakable man is inside. Lift off the top of his gleaming bald head, peer into that fetid mouth, and you will see the abandoned garage you hovered around so skittishly when you were a child.

He says: —Every tiny scrap of evidence will ultimately be fitted into the overall jigsaw puzzle of this situation.

He says: —Our job is to sniff out the rot in the chinks in their armor.

He says: —The criminal mentality is the very same the wide world over. A commie is no different than a dirty pickpocket. Keep that fact always in the top part of your mind.

Do you feel the breath of the viper on your neck? Do you hear the soft hiss of death?

Our good Colonel Fix Em never outgrew his boyhood eating habits. Pimple-pocked gluttony is more like it. Just look at him manhandle that Mars bar! He doesn't fuck around when it comes to satisfying deep repressive needs. Know what he's got in the bottom drawer of that big desk of his? A schoolchild's blue tin lunch box. And what do you suppose he has in it? A peanut butter and jelly sandwich, an apple, and a piece of homemade chocolate layer cake. Packed by his good wife, Mrs. Colonel Fart-Face. Want to know what his wife calls him? Alice Roosevelt Longworth? No, but that's pretty funny. No. She calls him Buster Bunny. And he calls her Doc. How's about a little taste of their kitchen table chatter? OK.

Mrs. Colonel... ooops! I mean Doc... she's decked out in hair curlers and a frilly flowing pink housecoat that she bought directly from *I Love Lucy* when the producers of that show were selling off the costumes after the show had closed. No, that's not true. She got it at a well-known snob rip-off joint called My Lady Lingerie Shop on the Paseo Mola in Madrid. The colonel is attired, yes, attired—I haven't used that word since I was a faggot clothes salesman in Macy's—in a shiny black robe with gold trim. Elegantly stitched on the back of this dazzling robe are the words "Bang Bang Womber." Now, we all know that that's not his name. Then where and how in the fuck did he come by this robe? Simple. Doc once upon a time went to a boxing match at the Roland Garrois Stadium. Her first. She and the colonel and two other American couples, one of them being an attaché at the American Embassy. An adventure, an adventure in sports slumming, you could say. You know, brutality and blood and screaming lowbrow crowds, tough sexy broads with their pimps. That kind of shit. Like in the old Roman Colosseum. This boxer, Bang Bang Womber, was a very beautiful glistening black American middleweight. He scored one of those dreamy, spectacular, one-punch, one-round knockouts that make life worth living for boxing freaks and brain surgeons. Our lady got quite a bang out of Bang Bang's performance. Out of him too, 'cause after the show—while the howling, slavering mobs were being hustled by hawkers selling pieces of the various defeated gladiators, an ear, a finger, an eyeball, swatches of their flayed skin —our lady and her little group went back to the boxer's dressing room to congratulate the divine Bang Bang. You know, official American Congratulating Group led by American Embassy Attaché with official American Eagle Seal which he will affix to your hand or back or prick or whatever and an all-American Eagle Upper-Class smile to go with it, like, you know, just in case anybody gets uppity or frisky and says directly or indirectly it doesn't really matter who the fuck you think you are barging in here like this, I don't remember sending you whoever you are an invitation. This American Eagle come-on being especially effective with members of the lower classes on their way up from the gutters and garbage heaps.

You certainly were impressive in there, Bang Bang. You shiny niggers sure do have it where it counts in the muscle department. Yessiree.

Yassuh, boss. We sure does thank you. Sure is wonderful of you wonderful ruling-class white folks to deign to descend into the chimpanzee swamps like this. You are overflowing with goodness and all kinds of fine white supremacy. Mmm. Man oh man. I sure wish you'd let me lick your feet to show you how sincerely grateful I am. Lick, slurp.

Oh, Mr. Bang Bang! I can't tell you how absolutely thrilling it was for a fragile little ol' white pussy like me to see you exhibit such simply superb balletlike muscular coordination in permanently damaging the brain of that other chap back there whose name happens to escape me, poor dumb cock-sucker who may now have the decency to go back to being a bellhop in an all-goon reformatory. My, what white teeth you have! My, what strong thighs you have! My, what a huge black prick you have! Oh my God!

Right. You guessed it. She eventually came away with that divine black-and-gold robe after doing things to that chunky dinge's cock that he had heretofore only dreamed of while jerking off over a copy of *Harper's Bazaar*. What would his poor charwoman of a mother say if she could see him now with his raging primeval pecker rammed down the arched white throat of the naked kneeling mistress of the plantation? Furthermore, and to wit and notwithstanding the party of the first part doing to the party of the second part hereinafter to be referred to as Your Basic Black Sambo, certain unspeakable, forbidden—I mean, like shit, man, you can be done unto death, stoned—interracial things, sexual acts recalling the salad days of Sodom and Gomorrah, whilst undoubtedly singing "I Wantsomora of Gomorrah!" alternating as best one could under the ha! ha! circumstances with snatches of or from "Sodom, the Gem of the Ocean." You sho nuff do twis yo ass good, lady. You sho you not uh pretzel? I'm little Miss Muffet, she cries, twisting her ass above him thisaway and thataway. And I just love to sit on big black tuffets while at the same time eating quite a bit more than my fill of Kurds and Whey Down upon The Swami River, Show me the whey to go home! Had a little black cock 'bout an hour ago an' it went straight to my head! Oh my heavens, Mr. Bang Bang! What hot black balls of fire you have with which to frighten away any uppity white spiders that may get it into their crazy greedy capitalist exploiter minds to sit down beside me and try to queer my act as they are slyly spinning their webs over every nice piece of bottom land in sight. Which is, whoops! Wow! Oh Lordy! Just another way of saying that—Sock it to me! Race your black choo-choo through my station Whoooo!—that slave labor loaned out at a prime cut rate of 9 percent interest per annum. Eeeyowooo! Here I come! Black man's bluff

† 279 †

shootin' your stuff into my muff!

Came out of those blackberry bushes with that there shimmering robe before you—oh shit! Can you just imagine the Naz draped in that robe as he strolls down that smelly crooked street of creeps! In old Jerusalem! The Sunday Punch of Bethlehem! covering the spooky soft malevolent naked body of Hansel Heinrich Himmler the Gingerbread Boy Grim Reaper Himself. And his slimy, fuckin', two-minute eggs. Take it away, Reaper!

—I wouldn't trust none of these greasers as far as I could throw them.

—Oh, I don't know, dear. They're more ignorant than dishonest.

—Are you sure the cook isn't knocking down on all the shopping?

—Oh, she may be making a few pesetas on things, but that's traditional in Europe. Like the tote bag for the Negro housekeeper in the South.

—Dishonesty is dishonesty, no matter if it is a traditional aspect of a used-up and corrupt Old World society.

—Oh, Buster Bunny! Really.

—Have you ever looked at Marta's forehead real close? It's low and cunning. It's Neanderthal man pacing up and down in his odiferous graffiti-stained cave. I've been analyzing them afterwards, when she's not looking. There's crime and deceit in those eyes, before thought and after thought up, crime being perpetrated, crime being thought back on. I'm on to that sly slut. She can't fool me. Those black, greasy eyes are an incriminating Metro-Goldwyn-Mayer wide-screen movie. I see small stubby hands furtively grabbing crisp string beans and stuffing them inside her wide-spread apron. I see them coveting and copping shiny red cherries while the storeowner picks his nose and dreams. I see these same ruthless greaseball fingers darting under trusting, unsuspecting chickens just as they have proudly laid their eggs, which they had looked forward to all their lives, and secreting these warm new eggs in secret parts of her shady billowing shirt!

—Secret parts?

—I see them greedily fingering coins and crumpled peseta notes by the light of a candle, Spanish money which has been acquired, piece by sneaky piece, step by vile step, by duping us her trusting American employers who have been made guileless and simpleminded at their mother's firm Anglo-Saxon knees! Pulling Iberian sheepskin over our clear, historically childish eyes, eyes that have feasted on sagebrush and George Washington's wonderful, wide-open toothy smile, and not on stinky twisted cobbled streets that wind right back to the twisted, conniving, black-hearted Spanish forebear minds that were all the while planning and salaciously building the Spanish Armada while merrie olde England slept, the disgusting idea being to penetrate proud English defenses behind their back and pollute and soil her beaches with hordes of hungry, unwashed, badly educated greaseball sailors who would quickly shake the sand off their smelly feet and promptly proceed to invade and pillage and plunder and subjugate the poor decent down-country limeys of England, taken by surprise right in the middle of their steaming suet puddings while others, perhaps younger and less weighed down with hunger and burdensome responsibilities, were hiding in each other's neat hedgerows because even then England was working on neatness and the problems of communal property versus the alien rights of the individual, all of which was very clearly spelled out by those who counted in the Magna Carta, which it would be a very good idea for you to stick your pretty nose in one of these fine days if you can ever drag it out of the powder room, feet first if you have to, because some noses get so goddamn sure of themselves they're telling the captain how to run his own ship. Overrunning their blonde, blue-eyed women caught in the act of drying out their winding sheets in their famous fields of clover which could stretch all the way to Dover anytime they wanted to, or rassled them to the ground while they had their hands full testing the wind in the willows, or trying to corner Old Mr. Mole before he could complete his blind work of tunneling subterranean tunnels under the very brain cells of the English landed gentry and their treasured ways of life. Rape! Rapine! Violations! Violence! Crab-infested bodies of Spanish buccaneers slambanging into the treasured privates of Pamela This and Cynthia That, whose screams were muffled by the muff-diving faces of said bearded, lean Iberian rapacities, spreading all kinds of rumors and lies and outdated information with their hot, greedy tongues down there, planting seeds of discontent in those poor women that have lasted right up to the present day, instilling the perverse Spanish life-styles that organically run counter to the down-to-earth peas beans beets and barley too hold on life that is or was the very foundation and strength of the English rural family life, overlaid and overlapped by thirsty hot Spanish soldier tongues slaking their thirst in the heavy Devon cream-filled thighs of innocent English milkmaids whose dearest wish before this dark day was to sing "Rule Britannia" and have it stick. The spreading of syphilis and clap and the seven-year itch! The eating away by said darting Spanish tongue of the inner lining of the social fabric of simple, happy rural English as sung by her finest poets who took their vacations there to get away from the hurlings of burly in howling dog-eat-dog London, the streets of! Sabotaging of time-honored English eating habits by the savage aforeskinned spick tongue which no sooner had it set foot on dry land promptly saw to it, on the orders of King Ferdinand, that loyal beef and kidney hair pie was replaced by hot Spanish country sausage, growling with garlic, no holds barred, as long as a prick in Toledo as they would later hear themselves saying, on their hands and knees with their mouths open gobbling as hard as they could before John Bull collared them and dragged them off to the hoosegow for fouling their own nests. The infiltration of dago red over deep drafts and quick quiffs of Old Watney's beers and ales which had to lead as all roads to Rome do to the undermining of beer and skittles, to be replaced by wine, women, and song and the gradual decline and fall of pub life around which the country lads hovered like so many drunken mothballs who wouldn't listen to anybody before it was too late. Which made it hopelessly pointless for Paul Revere or anybody else to gallop through the villages yelling "The Spicks is comin'! The Spicks is comin'! One if by tongue, and two if by twat!" because the sodden, belching, farting, limey louts were down on their knees or down in their mouths or down on their luck or some such chickenshit as that, anywhere but down on the farm where they fucking darn well belonged if their barley fields and fox hunts and sisters' virtue meant a two-penny damn to them come what may or may not. Because tea for two is out once and for all as a way of dealing with life's quaint little pitfalls and pratfalls on their tight-assed little island, and the tango is in, and check your birthmarks at the door period. And thusly fell the House of Windsor like a stack of marked cards.

And the very next thing to go before you or anybody else within earshot of Erewhon could say Jack be nimble, Jack be quick, was the English mum's tongue itself, which is the very heartland of self-indulgence, as Henry VIII would be the first to tell you if you are too damn dumb and ornery to take my word for it. Spanish sayings of a creepy kind crept in on dirty tiptoe when people's minds were elsewhere. No longer could King Arthur's merrie men hope to greet each other heartily over their highly coveted and incessantly investigated round table by shouting Hail to thee, blithe spirit! or, Watchman, what of the night? Nope. All gone down the drain. The very same drain, it should be committed to memory once and for all, that a lot of other things worth giving up your family ghost for went down, like, if you really want to drag numbers into this, old-style family outings with homemade potato salad and its genuine closeness, woman's intuition, law and order, sincere handshakes, team spirit, nickel cigars, and reason over madness. All down that same gurgling drain, for which we have to thank in the case at hand the incestuous greed of Ferdinand and Isabel & Cie., and their lisping lewdness. Which lisping was to be heard naturally when, like a bunch of new germs looking for a victim, the aforementioned perverted alien Spanish sayings stalked the corny playing fields of Eton while they were still being cultivated for life-saving crops instead of useful connections for social climbers later on in life, brownnosin' their way to heaven, harvested by sturdy yesmen when they were not guarding cold streams from poaching cocksmen, sayings roughly such as It's later than you think. Or, Give to Caesar what's Caesar's, José, or else it's your ass. Or, Haste makes waste only if you're going somewhere. Or, Wanna fucka my little sister? Only two pesetas.

Weirdo shit like that, and always flung at you with that goddamn soupy lisp that a Spanish fly could drown in so help me, the which, both fly and lisp, any intelligence officer worth his salt lick could trace right back to the private screaming rooms of Mr. Torquemada himself and his record- as well as bone-breakin' act the Inquisition, bankrolling which, you can bet your sweet boots, were those two angels of death and destruction, our old pals Ferdinand and Isabella, who might just as well have been brother and sister for all they cared about public opinion. Because there was this Torquemada as plain as the nose on your face squeezing Jews like they was oranges for all they were worth which was a pretty penny, because even in those low-slung days, long before the first gas combustion engine had broken down in America's Sweetheart the Model T Ford, and likewise long before any astrologers working on the night shift could have spotted ol' Charlie Lindbergh sneaking across the skies in his trusty *Spirit of St. Louis* heading right smack for the Champs Elysées to make the world proud of America's youthful know-how and her brave pay-as-you-go flying men in their level-headed machines, singing "Sperm on the Moon," in those days they were not above making more money than a lot of other people whose cash registers refused under law to sing on the sabbath besides which they had to eat fish once a week smelling to high heaven as often as not because nobody in that kind of a boxed-in setup could be farsighted enough to invent ice for the occasion. 'Course, a lot of those cooney Yids very quick like a fox read the fine print in the Spanish handwriting on the walls of those private pain rooms and jumped up shouting Count me in! I ain't a kike no mo! I ain't never even hearda gefilte fish or matzo balls. All I eat is Spanish omelettes and Spanish onions, s'help me, boss. Scouts' honor. An' they hold up the sacred scout finger sign. An' Boss Torquemada says, Uh huh. So you little Jew buggers are finally seein' the light an' gettin' your shit together. Had your fill of Christ killin', have you? Oh yeah! They all shout like there was only one mouth between them. You said, it, boss. No more of that kinda crap. Besides, boss, it wasn't us that killed the Naz. It was our crazy cousin Schmolka from Great Neck who was a bad egg all around. Even when he was a little kike tyke. That so? says Boss T. Well now, if you fart-smellin' Yiddles are truly repentant and sincere in your wish to be born again with clean mitts, maybe, just maybe we can work sumpin out. Hot diggity! the Jew boys shout, hoppin' up and down like they would wet their pants the crunch bein' so close. How much'll that be, Mr. Boss Man? Name your price. Here, take this nice blank check. Go ahead, you fill in the amount. Feel free. Well, OK, says Torq. You understand, of course, that this bread ain't goin' to me or anything selfish an' greedy like that. Sure, boss, sure! they yell, some of 'em havin' pissed their pants anyway. Not for one single second would we think that you were goin' through all this Jew squeezin' for personal gain, to line

your own wonderful bottomless pockets. Shit no! Good grief! Oy yoy! We
know that it is destined for the building fund to restore the Church of the
Little Sisters of the Shriven Groin. Or if not for that, the money will most
assuredly go for setting up perfectly wonderful soup kitchens for the meek
and the humble lame halt blind wretchedly poor who don't have a dime to
their name nor a rag they can call their own but who are nonetheless sweet
lambs in the flock of the Great Shepherd, God's Chillun, just like we're
gonna be in a coupla shakes of said lamb's tail, right, Señor Boss Torquemada? You Yids are so pushy, says old Torq. Push, push. Can't you keep your
shirt on and jus' take it easy, f' chrissake? Right! they shout, hoppin' an'
skippin' all over the scream-lined room. Anything you say, boss. But the
thing is, we're standin' on the edge of the yawning precipice only it's not
yawning. Its fuckin' jaws are snapping, y' know. Like, it seems like our
number is about to come up. And we're just achin' an' itchin' to become
good, clean-livin' Christians with a crucifix of our own, ya know, just like
that one around your own fine neck with Himself stretched out on it like
some kind of zonked-out junkie. 'Course ha! ha! we all know how He got
there. We're not so crazy we think He got bored out of His fuckin' skull one
day and decided to drag His ass up there and nail Himself to it. Aw no. We
may be a coupla about-to-be-formerly smart-ass Jew boys but we aren't
tryin' to kid . . . What's that? The moola! Right! Sure thing. We'll just leave
the amount blank if that's OK with you, sir. We'll leave it up to you to decide
just how much a coupla knock-kneed Christ-killin' Jew souls are worth, OK?
An' we'll make it out to Cash so's you don't have to go through all that dreary
ID shit at the bank, flashing your draft card an' recitin' your social security
number for some four-eyed rat bastard who's watchin' you like he's an owl,
ya know. Whoa now, Izzy, says old Torque. Hold your horses. It ain't over
yet. This generous, voluntary, unsolicited contribution ain't the last step in
savin' your dirty little souls. Next step is the renunciation. Hold up your right
hand. That's it. And try to keep its tremblin' down to a minimum, will ya?
And repeat after me, loud and clear. All together now. Jews stink! Jews stink!
they shouted. Jews suck! Jews suck! Jews eat shit! Jews eat shit! Not bad, says
Big T. I think you folks are gettin' the hang of it. Oh thank you, Mr. Wonderful Inquisitor! the Yids shout with little tears in their Yid eyes. That's the
nicest thing anybody's ever said to us. Oh boy! We would be deeply grateful,
Most Generous Official Torturer, if you would permit one of our number,
whom we would select in the strictest kosher fashion, to kiss one or both of
your sublime feet. Now, now, says T. Don't let's get carried away. 'Sides, it'd
take you too long to unlace my boots, and I can't spend all day hangin'
around here. I got me some scourgin's and some burnin's to do. OK. Let's
get on with it. Moses fucked penguins! Moses fucked penguins! All Jews is
Christ-killers! All Jews is Christ-killers! they howled, jumping around that

there room like popcorn with firecrackers up its ass. Chicken soup is piss soup! Chicken soup is piss soup! Chopped chicken livers is a lotta baloney! Chopped chicken livers is a lotta baloney! OK, fellas, says Mr. Jew-Squeezer. One more renunciation and I think we got it wrapped up. Hurrah for renunciations! the kikes howled. Here it is: The word *Jew* spelled backward is empty space. The word *Jew* spelled backward is empty space!

Okeydokey, says Mr. J.-S. That does it. Youse is Jews no mo'. Youse is conversos. Don't give another thought to such downright stinky-poo names as Goldberg, Finklestein, Mandlebaum, Himmelfarb, or Fuckheimer. Perish them dead-giveaway handles from your liver lips. Here's some brand-new monikers you c'n hold your heads up high with an' your slumped little shoulders straight with. Hot dog! all those sweaty little former Yids yelled. OK! Get 'em while they're hot! González Hernández Perez Manzanilla Tortilla Lopez García Mola Hola Spinola Perera Vargo Ferrera Ortega Cabrera Castello Pinello! Hi-dee-hi! Hi-dee-ho! Jews no mo'! the once and former Jew boys screamed. Sticks and stones may break our little bones, but Jew names now can never hurt us! Whoopee! May the sun never set on the joys of spickery! Now that's what I call exclamations of real gratitude, says Torq. If I wasn't so plumb tuckered out an' dried up from these here official conversion ceremonies, I'd whip out the old hose and shower you all with some hot piss, as a reward, y' know. Oh the wonderful joys of Spanish ginger ale! the new conversos shrieked. And speaking of pleasures of the flesh, one of 'em said, What is that simply divine smell wafting in from next door? Why, that just happens to be hebes cookin', says old T. Hebes cookin'? they said, lookin' at each other funny. Yeah, says T., gigglin'. Hebes. You know, like in herbs. Oh yeah. Right. Got it, they shouted. Hebes cookin'. Spanish cuisine is famous the world over for its fine hebe cookery. Hebes as in herbs and herbs as in Herberts as in sherberts! An' here cometh The Ice Cream Man. Hey, Mr. Popsicle. Gimme a wop sicle. An' gimme a limesickle an' my friend here a sublime sicle. An' as for me, just han' me a pickle with a tickle. OK, boys, says Big T. I'm gonna leave y'all to your fun. I gotta be on my way. Now don't do nothin' I wouldn't do! An' he departs with a hearty ha! ha! and a twitch of his crafty spick eyebrows, which selfsame craftiness of eyebrow those sly ex-Jews, 'cause they fucking well know a good thing when they see it, the cocksuckers, took over, lock, stock, and wine barrel, to make themselves look more Spanish to further deceive the innocent bystander loitering with his own two hands in his pockets in seasonal unemployment an' discontent waitin' for the government to pick up the check social security-wise an' of course you don't have to be a genius to know that these sneaky, twitchy eyebrows were naturally passed on down the line like lots of other falsely acquired character traits of the most vicious nature, often winding up in the hands of such dissolute predators as this current kitchen drudge Marta under careful scrutiny who given the slightest opening wedge would have joined those Jew-spick eyebrows of hers with all those other crafty acquired Jew-spick eyebrows sacking and socking poor merrie olde England. Skimming her heaviest cream off with one hand and settin' up usurious moneylendin' stations along the way with the other. And as part of that disreputable, heartbreakin' picture, you don't have to be a telescope with an overheated imagination to see this low-sculling maid standin' with one foot firmly planted on Her Majesty's lily-white neck and the other foot knee deep in shekels in a thriving pawnshop on the road to Bamberry Cross whilst across yonder hedgerows her ruthless converso cohorts are conversing in their secret Jew-spick tongue as they pillage! and pilfer! and pander! and philander! and rape! and raze! and roister! and . . .

—Buster Bunny, says the colonel's wife, —the Spanish Armada was destroyed off the English coast. Not a single Spanish soldier set foot on British soil.

—Seize that woman! Arrest that Jew-spick! he cries. —She's got a shirt full of stolen snap beans!

—Buster Bunny, I want you to pull yourself together. Do you hear me? Let me wipe that drool from your mouth. There now. I want you to carefully get up from the table and go into your room and do some shadow boxing. Then do some knee bends and pushups. I think thirty-five each would be a good number. That's right, dear. You're doing just fine. You didn't scrape your chair and you didn't knock over your coffee as you did last week. Good. Very good. Folding your ripped-up napkin and placing it neatly next to your plate, that's nice, Buster Bunny. All right now. Turn around. Walk slowly into your playroom and do what I said. That's a good boy. Relax your face a little. It's very stiff. And blink your eyes, Buster Bunny. It's bad for your cornea to stare like that without blinking. Blink blink blink. Good. That's right. Close the door softly after yourself. I'll peek in on you, dear, in about an hour to see how things are going, OK? Now just imagine in your mind that you are training for a championship bout in Madison Square Garden. Just listen to the crowds cheering and clapping! Hear Frank Sinatra warbling "The Star-Spangled Banner"! And there's Jacqueline Kennedy Onassis waving from ringside! Mmm. How I wish I had her looks and just half her money. My oh my! Wouldn't I be sitting pretty.

—Just get a load of that shit, Carol. Of all the people to dream up to want to be like, she picks that dreadful little fraud Jackie Kennedy. I mean, shit! Why not dream up and emulate some real first-rate performer, if that's your bit. Somebody like Medusa or Helen of Troy, that crazy cunt. Or the Beast of Belsen or the Bearded Lady. But Jackie Kennedy! What a pea-sized fantasy. A hustler with a lisp. Oy! A two-bit fuckin' clotheshorse with the charm of a glass eye. Why oh why do people fall for her act? It's fucking beyond me. But you know, I never did think much of Kennedy. He was a bullshitter and a grandstander and a sucker for all the wrong things. Like atomic bombs. And Onassis . . . What was he when you get right down to it? A wheeler-dealer with a hard-on for labyrinths. We're not talking here about the fall of giants. No Hamlets here, no Coriolanuses. No tragic Antigones weeping in the shadows of history. If there are any tears here, you can bet money they'll be third-class or prepackaged. Shit, you can nip on over to the PX anytime between eight in the morning and six at night and buy yourself frozen prepackaged anything. Or if you're too busy to go yourself, because, for the simple reason, let's say just for fun, you are playing gin rummy with God, or you are right in the middle of knitting a purl one drop three sweater for your favorite executioner, or you have an unbreakable appointment to speak at the weekly meeting of your Poison Pen Letter Club, in which cases you can get somebody to do it for you. Like one of your many adorable offspring. You can say, Lolita, honey. Stop blowing your little cousin Jo Jo and run down to the PX for Mommy and get me two packages of frozen boredom, OK? And Jo Jo, don't you move an inch from where you are while she's gone, you hear me? Or you can ask your never-loving super-wonderful scum of a husband. Rebop, honey, hold off on searching your crotch for pants rabbits for a few minutes and drag your utterly worthless fat ass to the PX for your long-suffering love-starved wifey. I want six pounds of pretrimmed Danish hard-ons and two fail-safe solutions to getting rid of you without a trace. That's a good chap. On the double. Or if you're lucky enough to be schizophrenic, you can turn to the other half of your split personality and say, Mrs. Virginia P. Other Self—or if you're on a friendly, first-name basis, Ginny baby—would you do me a big favor and truck on down to the PX for your dear friend So and So, or whoever the fuck you want to call yourself, and pick me up Some Real Good Memories. Bird's-eye puts them out. I need six double portion packages. You're a dear, you really are. And I want to take this opportunity to apologize for saying those salty things to you last night. I was really down in the dumps or some such low place and uh . . . gee, thanks. I knew you'd understand. You're a real pal. I sure wish I'd gotten to know you a lot sooner. Yeah, right. Nice to know you feel the same way. Well, you can't touch all of the bases at the same time, can you. Boy, you said it. Right. You'd have to be a fucking octopus. And whoever heard of an octopus winning the Menninger Clinic Award for Mental Health. Oh yeah? No kidding. I'm telling you, Carol, this PX is really something else. It's everything the Tower of Babel ever wanted but was afraid to ask for. It's a store only in the sense that the Bible might be called a book. Know what I mean? I can just hear my adorable helpmeet J. Edgar Hoover, Jr., saying, Well now, if, uh, the Good Book isn't a book, dear, then what the devil is it? Or he'd say, Decca, don't you think that statement is a bit extreme?

I don't have to produce additional evidence to support my contention that his lines will not in any way, in my lifetime or yours, revolutionize dialogue in standard soap operas. In fact, he is a soap opera, created, if that word will forgive me for employing it in such compromising circumstances, by nihilistic sponsors and ad agencies in a conspiracy against human credibility. I'll never forget the time, first and last, that I suggested he go down on me. Good Christ! You'd think I'd asked him to become a spy for the KGB. Ah well, maybe he and I will meet sometime in a nightmare somebody else is having, for a change, and I'll choke him to death on their time. And there won't be any way his friends the fuzz can get my fingerprints. Of course, it would be just like those wormy little shit-eaters to find a way to pick up my fingerprints in dreams. And if they can't do that, they'll say they did. I can just hear those fucking Nazi boy scouts: Your Honor, there is absolutely no Christian doubt of this wretched and extremely dangerous female defendant's guilt. The evidence against her is airtight and seamless after the fashion of certain modern steel tubings, or if you prefer, women's stockings which have the run of the streets these promiscuous days, along with all kinds of other lewd criminal elements. We would like to present Exhibit B to the court, Your Honor: the defendant's tattle-tale grey fingerprints, found on the swollen neck of her late husband, Captain Laddy Larkspur, in a friend's nightmare at which the defendant was the guest of honor. Seamless fingerprint proof, Your Honor, as we have maintained stoutly only moments ago. And you want to know where they would have stolen said defendant's fingerprints? From one of two places. From the prick of a certain divine flamenco dancer named Calderone. During a particularly memorable afternoon in Toledo I was swallowing this prick, thisaway and thataway, *al fresco* and *al dente*, really doing very well by it, because if I may say so, I am one first-rate virtuoso cocksucker, when I decided—it was OK, because beautiful Señor Calderone had come twice already—decided to make believe his splendid joint was a flute and I was playing it for a cast of thousands at Carnegie Hall. No, wait. That was another time. This time I was the Pied Piper of Hamelin. Which makes you kinda wonder about that story; maybe those old timers were trying to tell us something, without having to spell it out, what do you think? Seems plain as day to me. The whole story is about the power of sex, the sex drive. The piccolo was really the piper's hard-on. And what a hard-on it must have been! Wow. What mass appeal! Turned on rats as well as kids. Oh daddy! Could we use you now!

Under such circumstances, you simply could not ask for a better set of fingerprints. Calderone and his cock, or maybe his hard-on—this particular one, anyway—were an FBI plan and as soon as I was done and had gotten up off my knees and split for Madrid, he danced his little ass off to an ad hoc FBI lab in the basement of the cathedral there and gave them his hard-on, got it up again, of course, and my right-hand fingerprints, along with it. Insensitive, dumb, inexpert, thick-skinned, up-country cocksuckers whose closest contact with style comes from pig sties, such clucks merely grasp a cock in their fist like it was a hose they were watering their cabbages with or something. They are to cocksucking what piss is to vintage white wine. They have kept cocksucking hidden in the dark ages. I, on the contrary, out of my respect, adoration, love, need, and consuming passion for the penis arisen, have given the blow job high-art concert status. I think of a stiff prick the way Heifetz thinks of his Stradivarius. It contains divine music that must be finessed and brought out. The idea is not just to make it come, and as soon as possible. Heavens to Betsy no! The idea is progressive divine pleasure, pleasure prolonged, pleasure almost unbearably sustained up to the very last moment of ecstatic spurting epiphany! Oh sublime meat! Let me sing your song! I breathe on it, I whisper to it, I gently finger and caress it, before I ever touch it with my mouth. It must be fully alive and pulsating, hotly sensitive, its color glowing and resonant, surrounding it with a delicate and exquisite aura. Then I put my wet, loving tongue to it, then I begin to play it for all we are both worth. Sucking is only part of my divine concert, and it comes later on, not in the tasty, tickly beginning. That's one of the many differences between me and your run-of-the-mill cocksucker. I mean, those dummies think that suck suck suck come come come is all there is to it. That's like going into the kitchen of Maxime's and asking the chef for a cheeseburger. What's the poor guy supposed to do? Shove two thousand years of haute cuisine up his ass? What we're talking about here is high tongue as against roadside diner no tongue or at best Chef Boyardee Creamed Chicken à la King Low Tongue. Listen. Sucking is when you want to get the whole fucking thing over with, when you just want the poor slob to come, ya know. And if that's the case, why don't you just grab his joint and jerk him off on a palm leaf or something. Oh no. Sucking, you do that only as you're coming down the stretch. Sucking is for making him come all the way up from his Achilles' heel. And you swallow it. You don't swallow come, you're simply not a cocksucker, and there are no two ways about it. I don't even want to discuss those unspeakable creatures who spit it out, like they just sucked out a dirty snake bite or something. Swallowing the hot come as it leaps out of the stiff throbbing prick, God! That's the crowning glory, the pièce de résistance, the coup de grâce, the cup of grace. Ohh God I can taste it now, ecstasy's cream filling my mouth, wildly, like having Bach in your mouth, all that wild music, thrilling, blind, your own swooning, the big prick thrusting, the roof of your mouth like the fucking Sistine Chapel, and it keeps pouring madly, joyously in, spurting. Oh my God! I'm . . . my cunt is drowning . . . I'm coming, coming. Oh, Carol, your mouth is heaven. Ooohhh. I'm swooning disappearing into your mouth ahhh. . . . And come what may, yes, that strange elliptical town Come What May, Tennessee . . . You take it, Carol. I can hear those weird voices, voices that seem to be walking, on stilts, voices that sleep between graham crackers. Take it, Carol. You can do it. You know those voices. Yes, yes. Like that. That's it.

Down here, folks don't look back on anything. They peer around it. We're not buffaloed by perspective, historical or artistical, an' we want you all to get that straight. We do things like we do them, no matter what an' come what may. What we feel is, we got only ourselves to look forward to. Which may be a blessing in disguise, or it may be a wolf in sheep's clothing. All depends on the individual and his own two feet. We ain't afraid uh who we are even though we may not be on top of the particulars of that fact. But tell me this: did Mr. George Washington know the first name of every single one of the lads who got their ragged little asses shot out from under them while marchin' to his particular tune? An' gettin' closer to home where it jus' might hurt: did your own dear mom know which one of the scores of morning stiffs she labored and loved under had your name on it? OK then. Don't be so quick to smile like you just swallowed the last of the Mohicans. Jus' act like every other normal decent human being keepin' his own two cents where they belong, and you'll be all right. See that funny-looking statue over there, near the burial mound of Indian givers? Well, that ain't no statue. That's the corpus delicti of a nosy skirt who came all the way out here from the U.S. government in Washington, D. C., with brand-new plans for showin' us how to rotate our crops with our surplus wives. What kind of baloney is this? we shouted at her. Just where do you get off telling us how to fatten our geese and thin our ranks?

Yeah! shouted Ellie Blackwater. Do we tell you people in the White House how many bogus dollar bills to print up every year just in case you want to invade some sleepy little European country with 'em?

Smart aleck! shouted Buster Nealy. Windbags! Just because you can call out the National Guard any time your ass gets in a sling, you think you can lift your plucked eyebrows and we'll drop everything and all fart to your tune. Phooey!

Wisenheimers! yelled Minnie Winograd. If you Pennsylvania Avenue bums are so hot how come the red Russian commies are up there in space right now this very minute messin' around with Venus and Mercury? An' how come the dollar keeps on slidin' like it can't find home base no better'n a drunk hound dog?

You want to hear what that overpaid, overweight, overbearin' lady official answered to these heartfelt, country-fried charges? She said, You must have faith in your government. It knows what is best for you. Morning, noon, and night highly trained government specialists like myself are working on scientific ways to improve you and your way of life. Folkways may be all right for children to read about in their storybooks, but they are certainly not what grown men and women should live by in the richest, most powerful, most advanced country in the entire world. You must all of you clearly understand that. You must vigorously sweep your minds clean of all the cobwebs of nonsense. All cobwebs, out! The thirty-eighth democratically elected president of the United States of America has spoken!

That's all us folks had to hear. We didn't have to hear one single solitary word more from that old hen. Come prancin' from the nation's capitol on her borrowed crusader's white horse. With her words ringin' fresh in our ears no matter how much wax mighta been collected there, we grabbed her right off'n the little ol' makeshift guest speaker's platform out there near the horseshoe pits an' hustled her off to the tar pits over yonder an' dropped her in, cigarette holder an' all. When we got around to pullin' her out, she looked zactly like you see her now, 'cept for one thing: she lost the shoe on her right foot, somewhere between the pendulum and the pit, y' might say. Makes quite a monument, wouldn't you say? Myself, the part I like the best, the way she's holdin' out her arms. Like she's some big bird that's just got a load a buckshot an' is droppin' outta the skies for good. I probably don't have to tell you that we weren't bothered no more by any official visitors from Washington, D. C., with their pretty heads chock fulla funny ideas. That lady buttinsky don't make up our town's entire collection of statues by a long shot. We like eye-catchin' art just as much as inny other burg out this way. Ha! Ha! You just have to know where to look, that's all. We don't feel any overweenin' needs to put our fine art in a stuffy museum any more'n we got a urge to stuff all our eggheads into one basket case, like they do in some dumb places we could name that don't know their ass from a hole in the ground. Our art is out in the open, where it oughta be, where it'll do the most good. 'Cross the road there in front of Zona's Corset Shop is another edifying statue that's made a stop-off at the pits. A critter from the next town going west. We figured he musta been one of their salaried employees 'cause his pockets was fulla fresh salary. He came over here to steal ideas. His town musta been desperate. We had an inklin' of this ourselves, without anybody havin' to come up an' tell us. We could hear that town's brain gaspin' at night like a catfish that can't find no water. Run outta ideas. We could hear that gaspin' sound right through our bedroom windows where we wuz busy dreamin' an' otherwise busy carryin' on under the bed sheets. Hmm, we said to ourselves in the middle of everything. Sounds like that dumb town has run outta ideas to keep it goin'. Too much fiddlin' round while them Romans burnt. Gaaassp. Gaasspp. Grooaann. Ullk. Next thing, this fella's lurkin' and perkin' roun' our town makin' out like he was interested in buying, just for example, our skins and pelts for which we are rightly famous—'cause there ain't nobody can do up a skin or fetch down a pelt like we can, of all kinds, sizes, and persuasions too, 'cause, let's face it, some uh them pelts have to be persuaded, an' mostly against their will and better judgment—or actin' like he might buy up several carloads of new gooseberries the size of marbles in May. Smilin' and bowin' and smirkin' an' lickin' his liver lips like somebody musta told him a big buyer should. But nobody here was born yesterday. We knew he was really an idea filcher poacher snatcher snitcher. We saw through his pretty 5s and 6s, his 2 + 2s, the fancy curlicues of his 'rithmetic learned from the ground up over yonder in that gaspin', groanin', listin'-to-the-leeward, bankrupt, jerkwater hometown of his. We ain't so dumb we didn't know right off the bat that this little skunk was up to no good. Think it passed by us that he wuz scribblin' away with one hand and tryin' to pick our brain with the other? Sheeit no. Think we don't know what's what? Think we don't know who's lookin' back at us from the mirror, no matter whose wall the darn thing is hangin' from? Think we don't know the diffurnce 'tween a fart and a flat? Little weasel bastard. Uh huh, he wuz sayin' to himself. So they're gonna do this. Uh huh. So they're gonna do that. Mmm. Plans for an underground girls' rasslin' field. Aha. Gonna put more bubbles in the water supply. Well, whadyaknow. Bessie Hackmueller has come up with a bran'-new type of upside-down pie. Boy oh boy. Just what my town has been lookin' for.

An' so on. Till we said to ourselves, OK. That's enough of that. Let's whisk him off to the whisker. Grab him! Don't let him get away!

Lookit how the swallows are swoopin' in low over him to let him have it smack! smack! plop! plop! right on his kisser! Can you beat that? Ever see anything neater than that in your whole life? No sir.

Come on. I'll show ya another statue, back of Doney's Seed & Feed Store. One of our own this time. Old codger. Nabbed him tryin' to turn the clock back. Dave Hackett. Crazy ol' coot. Just couldn't stop playin' with his marbles long after everybody else had gone on to greater things either in this life or someplace else. Maybe it was sumptin he couldn't help, like a coupla genes he picked up on his ma's side of the fence. Adam and Eve weren't perfect, ya know.

Like that stretcha green in the middle of the street? Know what that's there for? For folks to stand on while they're tryin' to figure out their next move. You c'n either lie down or stand up. Whichever way you feel the most natural when it comes to puttin' pieces together. That's the kinda thing that goes in mysterious waves. Some days everybody's standin' upright in there. Other days everybody's lyin' down. An' you can't tell me some of 'em don't have their eyes closed.

Careful now as we turn this corner. Better hug the drugstore buildin' like me. Put your face right up on it if you hafta. An' put one shoe right behind the other real tight. Like you're tiptoeing in on your sweetheart before she *says* she's ready. This here is one windswept, son of a bitch of a corner. The wind comes down outta the mountain pass some days like it's late for a doctor's appointment or something. Could blow you right out into nowhere. Don't be afraid to grip these old bricks if the time comes. They won't come loose or anything. They're old but they're strong, an' they been gripped plenty before, by those who know what's what.

Okeydokey. Think we've made it. Yessir, I do think we have. Boy, I wanta tell you, that darn wind coulda peeled the nose right offa your face an' don't you think it couldn't. You always gotta be prepared for that, for the worst. It wasn't in the mood for anything today. But it knew we were here. Don't fool yourself 'bout that. It just let us go by free. Don't ask why. It ain't your business t' ask why. Does it ask you why you sleep with one leg outta the bed? Does the red red robin that goes bob bob bobbin' along ask the grass-hoppers why they jump so damn high?

There's Dave. There he is. Right where I said he'd be. Ain't he a sight! We mounted him on that sycamore stump that way for good reason. He used to play on it when he was justa shaver, an' his favorite game was imatatin' an airplane comin' in for a crash, like he's doin' now. Dave never lost his boy-hood love for foolin' around. Ah! I'll be darned. If it ain't Dave's daughter Hester come to hang a wreatha daisies round his neck in memory of. That's good strong family feeling for you. Hey there, Hester! Halloo! Halloo!

—Halloo yourself, you old chimpanzee. What're you doing out in public? Why aren't you back in the zoo where you belong? Creatures like you ought to be kept under lock and key and watched twenty-four hours a day. If not by a human being, then by someone else. And the pay should be time and a half overtime, because any time spent with baboons, chimpanzees, orang-utans and other anthropoids that fell by the wayside is already overtime.

—This place back here sure is a mess. Looks like the bargain basement of a third-rate museum. Every dubious artifact of this hand-to-mouth civiliza-tion is on shameless display here. Candy wrappers, torn bras, exhausted corsets, broken plastic machine guns, rusted handcuffs, limp contraceptives, cracked sunglasses, outworn diaphragms, shit-stained comic books, blood-stained bikinis, pissing Barbie dolls, hand-crushed beer cans, whiskey bottles, decapitated Mickey Mouses. Just about everything an up-and-coming anthropologist could ask for and a down-and-going priest would want to forget. Why do you suppose this cornucopia of shit, this future dig of priceless finds, should just happen to be in the exact same spot where my poor, demented, prehistoric father is entombed forever in a black moment of civil humor?

—What do you suppose it is that draws the townspeople young and old to this obscure place to abandon their used-up goods? Of course, if one could answer that, one would also know what precisely was so different, so unavoidably attractive about that particular bend in the Euphrates that made it the ideal place to drown unwanted babies.

—Well, well. Speak of mysteries and who's bound to appear. The Keeper of the Town Secrets himself, my old grade-school beau, Freddy Loudermilk. What brings you to this out-of-the-way part of town, Freddy? You haven't lost your way, have you? Or maybe you're just taking a shortcut to a tête-à-tête with History. Eh, Freddy? Come on, Freddy. Out with it. I promise not to breathe a word of it to anybody. You can trust your old pal Hester Hackett. Mum's the word. That's written right between my soft thighs, as you were the very first to know.

—Hester honey, ain't nobody can move so fast they can escape that faster-than-lightnin' tongue of yours. Even as a little girl in pigtails, you could let loose with that tongue and, boy oh boy! would the peanut-brittle sandwiches fly! An' I'll betcha if you wanted to open your eyes real wide, you'd probably see that some of 'em are still flyin'. T' tell ya the truth, Hester, I'm on my way to Mother Cowley's Bake Shop for coffee and chocolate-dip doughnuts. I need to get my midmornin' strength back up. 'Cause for the past three and a half hours I've been takin' in secrets like a watermelon soakin' up niggers' lips. It's a good thing I don't have any secrets of my own, 'cause I wouldn't have any room to put 'em up. I'm carryin' secrets about secrets, secrets that can last forever, secrets that won't exist after tomorrow mornin', secrets that could hold their own against catapults and cataclysms, secrets that a feather could knock down. An' I've got secrets that don't rightly belong to the depositor, that were filched, as well as secrets so new they can't even be classified. You gettin' the picture as of this morning, Hester?

—Got it by every one of its four slippery corners, Freddy. I'm wondering if you'll be able to make it to Mother Cowley's loaded down as you are. Maybe you ought to pay a passing ragamuffin a dime to carry you there in a wheelbarrow.

—That ain't a bad idea, Hester, not a bad idea at all. But I got an even better one. How's about you pushin' me in said wheelbarrow? That tickle your fancy?

—You can't afford me, Freddy. You couldn't afford me the craziest day you ever saw. And that's been your deep-seated problem from the very beginning. But tell me, Freddy, where do you stagger off to after you've loaded yourself down even more with Mother Cowley's once-in-a-lifetime chocolate-dip doughnuts?

—I hie me off to the official, secret shouting room over at the courthouse and there I'll shout out all the secrets that's been whispered into me in the past twenty-four hours. An' when the last one has been shouted outta me, I'll go on back to my roomin' house and climb into a hot tub and soak myself through an' through. An' when there's nothin' more t' soak, I'll crawl into bed an' disappear 'tween two white clean-smellin' sheets an' get me some much-needed shut eye. Sleep, where no secrets c'n find me, where nothin' c'n find me, an' that goes for myself too, 'cause the best place is no place, 'cause if I don't wanta find myself, I better not be anywhere. That's exactly where I've always wanted to be—nowhere. When you gonna find yourself, Freddy boy? People always said that to me. Ain't it 'bout time you straightened out an' found yourself? No! No! A thousand times no! I'd rather die than say yes.

—My homespun advice to you, Freddy boy, as an old pal who has watched you grow from a small shadow into a group of large shadows, is take a big bag of those chocolate doughnuts with you between those white sheets, because if you don't, you won't stand a Chinaman's chance of coming out alive. You'll starve to death sure as shit. And then where would we all be, with nobody to pour our secrets into? In no time at all the whole town would swell up and explode. Like a volcano in the Bible. Baarrrooom! Ten inches of insane, black, putrid human garbage would inundate every square inch, every nook and cranny of this ill-gotten burg, right down to its very foundations, seeping through every layer of its being, down and down into its first secret murder, the bloodiest sacrifice of all. I'm telling you, it would take a hundred years of the combined efforts of every one-eyed, hunchbacked, harelipped, snaggle-toothed, epileptic, scab-covered saint this world has ever seen to shovel this polluted joint out and get it back on its feet and going again. Oh God! I can just see them. A blighted procession of sacred madness, limping, writhing, moaning, groaning, babbling, drooling, barking, howling into town. Scratching, clawing, scooping, licking, scraping, shoveling all the shit away! Ooolala!

—Look at it any way you feel like lookin' at it, Hester's type a woman ain't to be found standin' behind every mulberry bush in town. No sir. She ain't but one of a kind an' the last time the Town Mothers met—they call a meetin' whenever they finish puttin' up a new batch a preserves or thinnin' out the younguns for those that don't look to have much of a future strength-wise, ya know—they voted 'nanimously to keep it thata way. An' when the Town Mothers vote, they mean business. Like the time they voted to have all the men in town wear dresses for one solid month while all the women-folk wore pants. See how you like it! they all shouted together. Might improve your disposition! Ha! Ha! You know what else they decreed? Oh boy! They decreed that the men had to squat when they made pee-pee. Just like us! the Mothers all shouted. Just like us! Oh it was really something, I'll tell you. An' you wanta know somethin' else? When it was all over, not everybody went back to wearin' his own clothes. Some uh the fellas—an' I don't hafta name 'em 'cause everybody knows who they are all right—kept those dresses on. That's right. Kept right on wearin' 'em. An' that ain't all. They put on wigs, an' wore makeup, an' started talkin' funny, like women. An' you couldn't tell tha diffrunce! No matter how good your nose for pussy. No sir. You thought it was a real honest to God woman. Now you take the town cop, Jethro Petersen. He don't wear his pretty blue uniform no more. He wears a red-an'-yellow flower dress an' a big hat with lace fallin' all over it. He usta be one tough baby. One more word outta you an' I'm throwin' your ass into the clink, he'd say. Or, You see these han'cuffs? I'm gonna slap 'em on you if you step outta line, you hear me? An' if he caught some young girlie huntin' stud meat outta season, he'd grab her by the tit an' say, Girlie, I'm gonna bus' yo' ass for this. Tough, you know what I mean. But now . . . He'll say, Why you little rascals you. What on earth do you think you're doin' anyways? Out in the dark stareets with your huntin' knives flashing in the moonlight and your pretty teeth gleamin'. Don't you know how naughty you're being? Now you girls run on home to your little trundle beds, and I'll just forget I ever saw you out here breakin' the law outta season. Now, be good girls an' untie this nice boy's pee-pee an' let him go. Jus' look at the way he's cryin'. Or if there's an automobile speeder who's just run over a buncha people maybe having a spur-of-the-moment barbeque picnic in the middle of the street, he'll say, My, my. What have we here? A real daredevil driver racin' like the wind itself, scatterin' people hither and yon like sycamore leaves. Tsk, tsk. We must be a little more careful, mustn't we? An' so on like that. You jus' wouldn't know it was the same ol' Jethro, Bullwhip Jethro, 'cause he had a voice that you didn't hafta be told was like a bullwhip's if a bullwhip could talk.

I'll be darned! Look at what the cat jus' dragged in. Hey there, Potter! Where you been keepin' yourself? Ain't seen you since last Halloween's big burnout. Whatcha got there in that gunnysack?

—A few little things with which to pay the piper, my friend.

—Iffn it's the same piper I know, it'd better be your life's blood, Potter. 'Cause that fella don't fool around. He plays some mean tunes.

—There are tunes and there are tunes. And the ones he plays for me might not be the ones he plays for you.

—That may be, Potter, but no matter what the tune, we all dance the same, an' damn me if you c'n gainsay that.

—Gainsaying is a game for fools, and I have gamier things up these wandering sleeves of mine. I must hunt and haunt and harry and corner those voices of the past whose owners have long since fled this insatiable habitat. Those moments when voice met and merged with voice. I chanced upon some this very morning, in a forgotten hollow just a martyr's scream from the Groves of Endless Pleasure, where in ancient days cock and cunt and tongue and mouth and man and beast went at each other with quite a bit more than mere gusto, where the moans and groans and cries of ecstasy still linger in the high buffalo grass. More, still nourish that grass.

—Those lost voices I chanced upon were hot in guileful play. One can almost feel the flush of their faces and see the glistening of their eyes as they say "One for the money, two for the show, three to get ready, and away we go! What've I got in my right hand? Three guesses. Guess! Guess! A peanut. You're hiding a peanut! Wrong! Guess again. An agate. Wrong again! An Indian head penny! No! I'm hiding a poisoned rattlesnake tooth. And it's got your name on it!

"Run sheep run! Run sheep run! Here comes the wolf! He'll catch you! He'll catch you! He'll tear you to pieces! He's got you! He's tearing you to pieces! You're all covered with blood! You're dying! You're dead. Come on. We've got to bury the pieces. You take an arm. You take a leg. Now pick up the head. Pick it up! Somebody's got to pick up the fucking head! Carol! Stephan! Juliette! Pick it up! It's talking. Tear the tongue out! Stop the tongue! Kill the words! Kill them!"

—Oh God! Carol, grab my hand and pull me out of this crazy place. Pull me! Hurry!

—Oh thank God. Just in time. The words . . . the voices . . . they almost had me. Stephan, did you feel those awful voices? Did they touch you and did they pull at you?

—Oh yes. Christ almighty. They're cannibals. They'll eat you up. They'll take your bloody soul. You'll become them, they'll become you. You'll disappear.

—You'll become the nigger in the woodpile, said Juliette.

—Or Hamlet's father's ghost, said Carol.

—Or the sound of one hand clapping, said Stephan. Or the stain on some-body's vest, or . . . shit! Where's the waiter? Whenever you need the old fart he's nipped into the kitchen to goose the cook or he's down in the toilet counting his crab lice. Waiter! More of the grape! Another carafe of vin rouge for this dried-up table. And make it snappy or I'll report you to the Bureau of Reclamation and they'll drain your swamps or top your turrets or grab your fat ass for duty in Napoleon's legions as they swarm across the frozen Russian wastes looking for an outlet to the sea or outlets for their rage or some such shit as that. Fine. That's the spirit. Got to keep this whistle of mine wet. What kind of tunes can you blow with a dry whistle? That's what happened to Marie Antoinette. She came down with a bad case of dry whistle. She tried to hide this from the people. But her wily ways didn't work. The people knew. That sly cunt thinks she can fool us, they said. What does she take us for? A bunch of roundheads with one thumb up the ass and the other one plugging a Dutch dike? What a joke. That fuckin' dwarf on stilts doesn't know who she's dealing with. Think we don't know what's up when we hear she's taking up tap dancing and playing the Jew's harp? When we see her prancing through the streets throwing pieces of cake at decent folk while all those crummy, bootlicking friends of hers are pushing/shoving to get in a good lick at her boots as if they had absolutely nothing else in the world to do with their fucking tongues, barking like dogs just two hours before Judgment Day. That crazy broad acts like she's got goose livers in her head instead of brains. Hasn't she ever heard of the word *guillotine?* Does she think it's some kind of special goo you put on your hair? Just wait'll her neck gets a taste of the Big Chopper. She's gonna be laughing out the other side of her face. And all those fat-assed pansy freaks that are dancing all night and farting all day in the king's privy chambers while the people work their fingers to the bone eating each other and maybe a few bread crusts, wait'll those worthless motherfuckers find themselves lining up at the scaffold, gibbering at the sight of the gibbet. Goodness me! What is that silly-looking piece of rope supposed to be doing there? Dangling up there like an upside-down question mark.

Yes, and just who is that naughty, half-naked devil with the black hood over his head? Heavens above! Do you think he's one of those street actors?

And who are all those dreadful, scabby people? Did they swim up out of the sewers? Phew! What a stink. And their clothes! Have you ever seen such outrageous rags in all your life?!

Upon my word. Isn't that the Duchess of Creamy Thighs being dragged up those stairs by her cunt hairs? What on earth is going on here?

Just keep guessing, sweetheart. And when you shake hands with Saint Peter at the pearly gates—that should be in about ten minutes from now if this two-bit watch of mine is telling the truth for a change—when you give old Saint Peter the glad hand, you might ask him if he's got a good home remedy for hiccups. You never know when it'll come in handy up there in the clouds. And while you're at it you might even feather your bed by falling to your soft knees and giving the old geezer a real nice French blow job. 'Cause it's rumored that from time to time he gets a hard-on that he doesn't have any idea what to do with. He's so goofy he might slam it into a cloud thinking it's a pillow. Cloud-fucking of course is not against the law up there and an awful lot of the more hairy fellows . . .

You can see where Stephan is headed. Toward a whistle-stop tour of the origins and development of pillow-fucking, as it has been set down in certain sacred texts, some of which were plucked from ancient hiding places in shifty Middle Eastern sands by loose-leaf Arab scavengers, jackals of the night if you prefer, and sold to highbrow and low principled compradors at the Metropolitan Museum of Art. Or the Louvre—it doesn't matter which, because they've all got their hands in each other's gloves—who pay more than enough lip service to public edification and cultural jamborees while anybody with an ounce of brains knows that the private salons and wine cellars and rumpus rooms of their privileged-class egos are being lined with the above-mentioned treasures, and more, and the man in the street, poor simp, has about as much chance of seeing these wonders of the world as he has of winning the Kentucky Derby while being ridden by Debbie Reynolds. However, and be that as it may, we must bend over backwards, if that is the best way, to understand Stephan in view of the many assaults upon his waning tranquillity by loony wolves in the streets masquerading as *moreno* sheep. To wit: while strolling spanky and clear-eyed one morning last week on the Rue Savoie, guided by the strong impression that he was following in the crafty footsteps of a sixth-century Roman soldier on his way to the banks of the Seine where he was finally going to have it out with a strong young fishwife who had been brazenly selling him perch instead of pussy . . . and if you're a well-hung Roman foot soldier billeted far from home in the sole interests of absolutely insatiable Roman imperialism . . . we all know that not one square inch of Europe, Africa, Asia, and Great Britain was safe from the drooling greed of those potbellied, peacock-fucking patricians and their greasy, overdressed wives who, while they themselves did not have the hots for going all the way with peacocks, sure as shit prowled the sweaty playgrounds and throbbing slave markets of Rome in search of young boy and girl tushie and its multifaceted delights. You can hear those degenerate jades clear as a bell: "I'll take those two Nubian nippers and that little Persian number over there with the big black eyes. Don't bother to wrap them up. Just hustle them as they are into the back seat of my chariot. That's a good chap. Now then, my little chickadees, come along home with mama. Keep your noses clean and do what you're told, and a fine time will be had by all. One step out of line, and it's your ass. You hearing me loud and clear?"

And people wonder why the Roman Empire declined and fell! The answer is as plain as the nose on your face. It went down the drain because nobody was minding the store. Everybody was always out getting their ashes hauled. A fine way to run a business!

OK. So there was Stephan, picking his silly way along the cobblestones of the Rue Savoie when this croissant-shaped fellow steps out of a doorway and says: You were magnificent last night at my sister's wedding. Oh, what a jig you dance!

—My dear fellow, says Stephan. —I have not danced a jig since I was a houseboy at the kaiser's palace where they bowled with pigs' bladders stuffed with rice and played Hide and Seek under mountains of sauerkraut while the old queen douched with cold beer. And as for your sister and her wedding last night, I can assure you that at the very moment she was consigning herself to matrimonial madness with a promiscuous carpenter or an overdeveloped plumber with gurgling veins, I was in a rowdy bistro in the 4th going downhill with everybody else. Some were going downhill faster than others of course. One chap in particular was going downhill again and again.

—You are practicing to deceive yourself, sir. And for reasons one hopes will remain a mystery. You were nowhere but at my sister Clotilde's wedding and making a fine spectacle of yourself at that. And as you well know, Clotilde married a bank clerk, a clear-eyed, peppery lad who knows that the finer things in life all come down to money. He presented you with an overdraft as a present for your dancing, and shouted, "Don't ever give your bank balance an even break, my friend! Forever spend money you don't have."

—Quite clearly a fellow with a firm grip on life's little realities and I hope that good fortune brings us together some time. But as I was saying . . .

—And photographs to prove it, the croissant fellow went on insisting.

—You are now a permanent member of our family album. You have forever been caught in a variety of exposures that in more ways than one reflect the mood of our times. Take it from me.

—You carry on, my dear fellow, like a deep-sea diver refusing to come up for air because he's met a fish he likes. But be that as it may, what could possibly be the mood of our times?

—An indifference to the yawns of the abyss. An unwillingness to imprison B between A and C. A demonstrable belief in the shallowness of infinity. An unerring attack upon reality as the ultimate solution. A whole-hearted way of life wherein one thing does not follow another. All of which amounts, I must point out to you, to a living, sneezing portrait of your ineffable self. A portrait that could hang by the skin of its teeth in any gallery devoted to infiltrations on a larger scale. Whose clientele would make any self-respecting border guard flee for his life and limb.

—Aha, says Stephan. I think I see the beginnings of a grand design. Something truly breathtaking, like Abdul el-Krim's plan for subjugating all of Africa. Or the carpenter from Nazareth's dream of installing a dripping cross in every bedroom in the world.

—You're a sly one, sir, dragging in the Messiah to cover your tracks. As if that poor man had not been dragged far enough.

—You've been hoodwinked. That whole thing was a put-up job, a farce. It was staged by a bunch of actors in the pay of the church politicos. They needed a socko act to enslave the masses for all time. Christ was a drag queen between jobs. The others were street performers, buskers, dancers, jugglers, and strippers. They'd never made the big time. This was their chance. They had a ball! Can't you just hear them!

—Come over here, Judas honey. Let's run through that kissing bit again.

And let's have a little more tongue this time. Where in heaven's name did you learn to kiss anyway? In the YMCA?

—The script doesn't say anything about Frenching. And I don't think you're supposed to grab my dork when we do it either.

—Stop yapping and get your little ass over here!

—OK, everybody! That was the rehearsal bell. Come on you, come on, you guys. You're not getting paid to shoot crap and Indian rassle. Get a move on. Girls! Get your shit together. Put those dirty comic books away. More tears this time. I want you to cry your heads off. And moaning. Put more oomph in it, you hear? Don't worry about ruining your makeup. We're not doing "A Day in the Life of Little Miss Muffet." Let it all hang out, OK? And we're not going to have any more pee-pee breaks. Hold your water. Save it for your husbands when you get home. Then you can piss your pants off and come at the same time.

—Mr. Director, sir. Tell Jonas to give me back my hammer, the big bully. How am I supposed to nail the Naz's feet if I don't have my hammer?

—Sir, I can't find my spear. I've looked high and low for it but it's vanished. If you ask me, I think one of the stagehands swiped it to roast a pig with. They're all thieves, those fucking stagehands. They think just because they've got a strong, mean union they can get away with anything.

—Makeup! Makeup! Where is that goddamn Rachel? She's never around when she's needed.

—Last time I saw her she was down in the caves blowing that Persian tap dancer she hangs around with. Boy, those Persians! They're hung like horses.

—Some broads are all heart. That Rachel, she's all mouth.

—Extras! Extras! Over to the right there, all of you. Under the cliffs. Now listen, please. This time work harder on group feeling. Y' understand. The sum is greater than the parts is the point I'm trying to get across to you. What we need in the next crowd scene is a powerful *collective* response. Like a big wave coming in on the beach. Not a bunch of individual virtuoso performances. I want everybody to say to themselves, I must submerge myself, I must submerge myself. Got it? Now let's have absolute quiet for one whole minute while everybody repeats that line to himself. Start when I hold up my finger, OK? No jokes about the finger, please. It won't be *that* finger. OK. Get yourselves ready.

—Are you digging those courtesans, Elijah? Every drag queen in Jerusalem is working on the set. Hey there, girls! How's every little thing? Didja ever hear Pete go tweet tweet tweet on his piccolo?

—Oh go chase yourself, you little Hittite motherfucker! Why do you people go on reproducing yourselves? Have you no pride?

—Don't waste your breath on that squirt, Susanna dear. He's just a fart in the wind. Pay him no mind. Where *did* you get that fantastic peacock fan?

—Mmm. Sugar daddy gave it to Susanna for being such a good girl. It's Carthaginian, ya know.

—Make way! Make way! For his divine grace the Procurator of Judea! He who outshines the sun in overall wonderfulness! He who gives the human race a goal to live up to!

—Oh God. Just listen to that publicity creep carry on! What do you think Jacob pays him to promote him like that?

—Plenty. But it sure as shit pays off. Look at the roles he gets. You don't get dynamite roles like that by hanging on a wall and making believe you're a fucking flower.

—Chili dogs! Get your Coney Island chili dogs right here! Ice cold bottles of Last Chance beer! I'm talkin' about slakin' your thirst! I'm talkin' about takin' the edge off your hunger!

—Wardrobe! Wardrobe! For Dismas the Thief! Now listen, Dizzy, baby. For the last time, you can't hang up there wearing a loincloth of your own choosing. You're supposed to wear standard issue loincloth. Period. There's just no room in the script for being different.

—I don't know why you're getting in such a sweat, dad. It isn't as though I'm draped in polka dots up there, which isn't such a bad idea now that I think about it. Since this is a 90 percent gay production anyway. All I'm doing, you old poop, is attempting to wear this very fine hand-stitched silk number that my girlfriend bought for me in Hong Kong. Where I want to tell you everything is a third cheaper than it is here. So what if it is a baby blue? I mean . . .

—You just can't play it straight, can you, Ezekiel? You dragged my ass on that Tower of Babel set trying to talk in Mandarin Chinese when everybody else was gibbering, and you're dragging my ass on this one. Get with it, Zeke. Get in line. And don't give me that different drummer shit either.

—Flexibility, Mordechai. That's what you could use more of. If you could bend just a teensy bit, bubbie, if you could look sideways instead of up and down all the time, you'd be the top stage manager in Middle Eastern Old Testament show biz. Like that!

—This whole thing is a born musical, Mr. Moses, sir. And I'm just the guy to do the job. I've already knocked out what you could call a working script. And I've written some of the songs. They're blockbusters, sir, all-time winners. And when you hear some of the titles you'll say the same thing yourself. Just get a load of these sweethearts, and we don't have to start from left to right, or from top to bottom either for that matter. Here, for example, is Saint John the Baptist's theme song: "No Way, Salome." Don't you just love it! And some of the words, if you please:

You can shake your fanny till the cows come home
You can jiggle your tits till the roof falls in
But you just can't alter my dome
'Cause, baby, I'm not into sin.

Fantastic, huh? And here's Salome's big number: "Just Say the Word, John Baby, or You're a Goner." An' I mean when she belts that one out, you're gonna see people collapsing in the aisles by the thousands.

—Who did you say you were? I don't think I got your name.

—Peelmunder, sir. Socks Peelmunder. And I'm here for the benefit of one an' all.

—That of course remains to be seen. As you were saying, Mr. Veal-plunder . . .

—Popular entertainment of the highest order. Stuff that is 100 percent guaranteed to keep everybody from thinking about anything that really matters. Okeydokey. To get on with it. Herod. I've got some great material for that one. His opener is: "I've Had It Up to Here with You Rabble-Rousers." And his second great number is "Why Don't You Yids Stop Rockin' the Boat?" Here's the first stanza to the latter show-stopper:

I can't understand you guys
You had a good thing going here
So what if you couldn't eat in the best restaurants?
So what if you couldn't mess around with shiksa pussy?
You could breathe, couldn't you?
You could do the loop de loop in chicken soup
Be an Indian giver with chicken liver
Tear your hair with religious flair
Circumcise all your little guys
And nobody gave a damn. . . .
Then you had to come up with this bird Christ!
Oy vey! Oy vey! You'll see the day!

Dynamite, huh! Mr. Moses, sir, what we're talkin' about here is the longest-running musical of all time. B.C., A.D., AC/DC, any way you want to slice it. All you've gotta do, sir, is round us up some angels and this dream show will be a gold-lined fait accompli, to put it mildly.

—Hmm. Well now, Mr. Sealstunner, it may well be that you're onto a good thing at that. Notwithstanding the fact that you yourself personally inspire anything but confidence. I'll have to discuss the whole thing with a few friends downtown. Meantime . . .

—Meantime, sir, I'll make the most of this divine opportunity to bowl you over with a few more of the catchy songs I've churned out for our project. Mary Mother of Christ's opening number: "You Don't Need a Hard-on To

Be a Mom." She does it playing tap, tap, OK Mo, here we go with a harmonica background:

> Don't spread your legs, girls
> Don't pull down your pants
> There's a better way to do it
> And here's how it goes—
> Juuust look up at the clouds, dears,
> Stare at the sky
> Shout, Sock it to me, Daddy!
> And you'll be pregnant by and by.
> Take it from me, girls,
> There's nothing like immaculate conception.
> You've got no lout breathing down your snout
> And there's absolutely no problem of redemption.
> So . . . listen to me and you're home free
> And there'll be no creep buggin' you for seconds!

Well, boss, if you're not laid out by that one, then all I can say is there's just no hope for you at all.

—Now now, son. Don't go blowing your nose on a sheep's tail, as the expression is. I think you've got some amusing little ditties here, and given a bit of good luck . . .

—If I weren't in a really up mood today, Doc, I'd turn on my heel and take this gold mine down the street to the Corinthian Syndicate boys who can move faster than greased lightning when a good thing comes their way. But I want to keep this sweetheart of a golden goose in the family, so I'm going to make believe you haven't said such a dumb thing as "amusing little ditties" referring to songs that will survive the ages, which includes both you and me. Va bene and all that.

—I've written a couple of absolutely mind-blowing numbers for Jesu Cristo. He's standing on the steps of the Hospital for Basket Cases, where he's put on an eye-poppin' show, and he lets go with "There Ain't But One Redeemer, Folks, and You're Lookin' at Him Now." This aria will make such classics as "Home on the Range" and "When the Moon Comes over the Mountain" look like schizophrenic hog burps, believe me. The peak of musical comedy greatness of course will be reached when they've got him tied up on the cross. There he is, you see, blood or catsup pouring out of his hands and feet and chest and that weird fuckin' crown of thorns scratchin' his poor sweaty brow, and all those jock Roman soldiers hootin' and slappin' their things down below like a bunch of college frat sucks on a weekend beer drunk. And our boy suddenly lifts up his head, opens his mouth real wide, and out comes "This Hurts Me More Than It Does You." Following that, sir, and assuming the audience is still there and not drowned dead in tears of laughter, he hits them smacko between the ears with "What a Difference a Nail Makes." And—brace yourself, sir—he brings down the curtain on Act Two with "Where Can I Go But Up." You can be sure, Mr. Moses, that an entirely new school of audience research will have to be set up to gauge the simply overwhelming response . . .

—Hmm. You may be right, Mr. Greaseplunder. But we all know how ungrateful audiences can be. I do hope you've written something nice for young Judas Iscariot. I've always felt he got the shitty end of the stick.

—Oh sir! You took the words right out of my mouth. Poor Judas. Probably the most misunderstood and maligned man around. History has woven a tissue of lies about this fellow. A lot of people among the followers were insanely jealous of him because he was Christ's number-one lover on a first-come, first-served basis. Such kvetching! Such bitchery there was! Such petty squabbling. Egotism! Me! Me! Me! Love me! Morning, noon, and night. Oy! How the Naz put up with all those assholes is beyond me, Mr. Moses. There musta been plenty of times when he thought, Oh shit! I'm gonna chuck this whole thing. I just can't hack it. It's more than one person can stand. Who can *I* turn to for help? Whose shoulder can *I* cry on? Right! Nobody's. I'm all alone in this mess and I'm tellin' you it's too fuckin' much at times, Dad. One of these days . . .

—Judas . . . yeah, a splendid chap. Lotsa charm. I've written a couple of simply breathtaking numbers for him and I'll certainly be writing more as we get the show underway. His big number is "My Side of the Story." With a lot of wild harps in the background. I mean wild: I want the audience to think it's lost in the middle of a bamboo forest during a tornado. You dig? OK. Lemme bang out the first few lines for you on this little upright I borrowed from Lot's wife before she, uh, underwent that figure change. OK. One, two, three:

> Don't believe a word they tell you about me
> It's all a pack of lies
> The powers that be needed a fall guy
> And because they're all sexist shit-heads
> Who think that all queers should be hanged
> They pointed a finger,
> Called forth the Mud Slinger,
> Sling away at that fucking gay! they shouted.
> He'll rue the day he first did say,
> "Come on, Jesus, let's go to my house and play!"

And just dig this, sir, just dig this. That last-supper gig, old Judas baby is gonna wrap that one up with—grip your chair, sir—with . . . "Just a Kiss You'll Never Miss."

—Now then, sir, after the audience has been quieted down by the riot squads using firehoses and their own if necessary and The Get 'Em Back in Their Seats Squad has scooped up all the laughter- and tear- and giggly-juice-drenched mobs back into their proper seats—by the way, sir, I see that last "Just a Kiss" number becoming the internationally accepted Gay Power marching song, without any doubt—we bring down the curtain and the house, sir, and the house, with Jesus baby warbling, with everything he's got, his young Jew-boy mouth still dripping from that wet soul kiss, unleashing with a full-throated rendition of "I Don't Want a Ricochet Romance."

—By this time, Mr. M., our baby boo is up there with such all-time greats as gravity and the thirty-hour work week.

—You still breathing, sir? You OK? You haven't gone into shock or anything, have you? Your eyes have that funny glazed . . . OK. OK. Nothing like a blinking eyelash to let you know where . . . Swell.

—So, how does all the foregoing grab you, Mr. Moses? Right by the balls, I hope. Or some other place that's very important to your well-being and sense of self as against nonself.

—I must say, Mr. Gangbummer, your material does have a certain je ne sais quoi. Yep.

—Good. That's the kinda response I like to hear. And if you can throw in a coupla words in French, so much the better. OK, José. Now for one of the great love arias of all time:

> You say stigmahta
> And I'll say stigmayta
> No matter how you say it
> It still comes out lover boy to me.

Now I don't want to hog-tie myself with any wild predictions, sir, but a lifetime in the entertainment field tells me that that number alone will assure us a place in history as well as a seat on the New York Stock Exchange. It'll become the favorite song of gays all over the biblical world. And it wouldn't surprise me a bit if it worked its way as far north as Goth and Hun country. Those hairy barbarian queens up there have as much right as anybody to some good group singing. What if they do gnaw on bison bones when they're not gnawing each other's bones? Is that any reason to bar them from full-throated pleasure?

—What that sauerkraut-loving black forest country needs is a good Jewish ghetto or two. Some Jew magic to liven things up. The edifying effects of lox and bagels, gefilte fish and chicken soup, some Manischewitz boilermakers to alternate with all that beer. That's my opinion, Mr. Rundowner.

—You're entitled, Mr. Moses. You're certainly entitled. Allora. Back to our humdinging gold mine. My little ratlike brain has been as busy offstage as it has on. Spinoffs, Mr. Moses. Lucrative spinoffs of Miss Jesus. Get the chicken fat outta your yiddisher ears, sir, and listen to some of the socko ideas I'm going to flood the Euphrates Valley with. First: a do-it-yourself crucifixion kit. For kids seven years old and up. Both girls and boys. It'll include all of the basic ingredients of the original production, so to speak. A nice, miniature wooden cross which can be assembled in a matter of seconds. A tiny hammer with matching nails. A real lifelike rubber doll of the Naz himself. With a darling little crown of thorns. And we'll fill the doll with some kind of red liquid, maybe even chicken blood, so that when the kids bang the nails into the hands and feet of the doll, blood will spurt out. I mean, that's the big moment, right? And spear; we'll include the spear of the Roman soldier who lets him have it in the ribs. We'll include Dismas and the other guy—what's his name?—who hang on either side of Big J. This kit is gonna be a multimillion-dollar item, Mr. Moses. There's absolutely no question about it. Every kid on the block will want one, especially the anti-Semitic kids, who'll want two of them. Our point-of-purchase publicity will make it more than clear that any kid who doesn't have a crucifixion kit is just no damn good and a fucking pagan to boot. And to the parents we'll say, "Is your kid too good to kill Christ? Where is your community spirit? Are you a family of commie punks? Get with it before it's too late."

—Along with the basic crucifixion items will be included a sprinkling of onlookers, mourners, Roman soldiers and the like. You know, for that feeling of total realism. Also, for a little additional scratch, the kiddies can get a cassette that will have all the crucifixion sound effects. Moans, groans, shrieks, wailing, crowd roars, the whole wonderful heartwarming schmear.

—Then there's T-shirts. Millions of 'em. All sizes. They'll have a picture of The Big Scene stamped on them. That'll be one line. In two colors and three colors. Mr. Moses, would you use your influence with our slow-footed fucking Pharisee waiter to get us another round of this iced arrack, please. Looks like he's forgotten we exist. Dreaming of some disease-ridden whore. OK. Two or three colors . . . black and white, and black and white and red, for the drops of blood. Then we'll have a line with just statements written on them, like I Am The Son of God and You'd Better Believe It; Down on Your Knees, You Motherfuckers; Here Comes The Man; Keep Your Fingers Crossed 'Cause It May Be Your Turn Next; Walking on Water with The Man I Love; Throw Away Your Crutches, You Crummy Malingerers; Save a Place for Me, 'Cause I'm Comin' Back; Oh Ye of Little Tongue!; Place Your Order Now for The Last Supper; Sinners of the World Repent, Or It's Your Ass.

—Hmm. This arrack sure hits the spot. Coupla these and you don't give a shit whether Samson got a haircut or a blow job. Right, Mr. Moses? And to think that those crazy fuckin' prohibitionists want to get it banned on Sundays. Why, shit! That's the very day you need it most. My God! One

Sunday without arrack and you wouldn't have any more housing problems. Everybody would be dead. Mass suicides. No kidding. Those prohibitionists must be stopped, sir, and I mean stopped. Like mostly in their tracks. They're a menace to reality in the only world we live in.

—So . . . besides the T-shirts . . . I think that by cannily employing all-out whispering campaigns we can convince the kiddies to take off their beanies and skull caps and put on the crown of thorns. Yes indeedy. And we can further enhance the widespread sale of said crowns of thorns to small fry by packaging it in a box of chocolate-coated Crucifixion Crunchies. I don't see how they can resist such a combo, do you? We'll make the crown of a soft plastic of course so's it doesn't scratch or anything. It'll just give a nice soft tingle up there. Millions of kids wearing a crown of thorns. Boy, it gets you right here, no kidding. I mean, what an edifying sight. What a show-breaker or heart-stopper or . . . And profitable too. I see banks sinking under the streets due to the sheer weight of all our gelt deposited therein. I mean, it's fucking breathtaking, sir, and I'm frankly finding it difficult not to break down and cry with anticipated joy.

—There are oodles and oodles of other irresistable moneymaking items, but I won't list them all because that could take months. The mention of three or four more will suffice. I see yo-yos shaped like crosses. Crucifixion bubble gum. Miniature scourging whips. Necklaces of the severed heads of the twelve apostles. Kiss of death lipstick. Little bags of stoning stones. Crucifixion hero sandwiches of forbidden pork salami. All-day suckers—lollipops if you prefer—of the Naz's hanging body, in a seven-day all-flavors package. As I said, sir, the list is endless, just like the profits.

—A truly engaging byproduct is a live game I have called How to Crucify the Kid Next Door. It's a real sweetheart and I don't believe it would be out of order to say that, with luck, it could replace Hide and Seek and Run Sheep Run as the all-time fun game for the younger set. And it can be played by illiterates, which of course should make it doubly attractive. All too many group sports are marred by the fact that you've got to read some instructions, if only how to get to the makeshift showers behind the Colosseum after it's all over. Otherwise you go home all smelly and covered with dirt and blood.

—This live game is completely satisfying in the very deepest sense. It involves one's total self, all the way, sir. I mean, every human need is given full play. Those clever Greeks have a word for it, sir, and that word is catharsis. When it's all over, when the game has been carried out, so to speak, instead of feeling tired, the kids will feel refreshed and renewed. If you will permit me to say so, Mr. Moses, they will feel more *human.* Know what I mean?

—The game: first you get your gang together. You make sure that all the members of it are tough, bloodthirsty little scum. You don't want any softies, namby-pambies or kids who will get cold feet at the last moment. Next you select the victim, the kid to be crucified. This can be any nipper who has shown any signs of being different, and who thereby can be regarded as a threat to the status quo. In other words, an enemy of the people. These untoward manifestations can be anything from a refusal to stone stray dogs that are caught fucking, to a preference for grammatical constructions over dangling participles, whole-grain bread over packaged white bread, walks in the woods over joyrides in stolen cars. Other signs of arrogance, elitism, hubris, separatism, out of stepism, egotism, pickiness, snobbery, individuality, superiority, fastidiousness, and so on. A refusal to dream run-of-the-mill tight-asshole dreams. A need to stand up and defend the rights of the individual. Va bene. Such a youngster is perfect crucifixion material, sir. Made to order for the cross and the nail.

—Once you have found this sore thumb of a kid, this threat to peace and quiet and social cohesion, the next step is to take to the streets in a shouting campaign of denunciation. Stir up the child mobs! Prepare the stage! Then one fine afternoon, between peanut butter sandwiches and nap time, between the lick of a tongue and the flutter of an eyelash, seize this child! Drag him or her to the community playground and perform the act! Set up the cross smack in the center of the swings and slides and sandpiles! Oh sir! Just imagine the raging, ecstatic scene! The hordes of inflamed screaming children, clamoring, howling for the death of one of their own! A death, a sacrifice to the gods of society, an appeasement, a purification! And the creation of their own unspeakable corresponding mythology! A child who dies for the sins of all other children! As the first spike is driven through the tender young hand and the myth is set in motion, all the angels will begin to sing their crazy fucking heads off. And through the blood-drenched ages you will hear this child's tiny voice calling out over the clouds or mountains or rooftops or whatever: I died for your sins! I died for your sins! Oh sir, the very thought of this is making my head swim. My hands are shaking. My tongue is hanging out. I need another drink or I'll surely perish, sir. Help!

—Waiter! Another double arrack for Mr. Realblunder! On the double, man! Or it's back to the poo-poo pits of Galilee for you and I'm not joking.

—Mmm. Delicious. Just what the soothsayer ordered. Nectar of the gods and all that. My tongue runneth over.

—And what a tongue! With a tongue like yours, who needs hunger-crazed mobs? Your tongue, my dear boy, is history on the run. One need only glance at it to know why Alexander the Great should have been sacked instead of his libraries. Libraries overrun with snoozers, boozers, soft shoe salesmen and their girlfriends hitching their wagons to falling stars, draft dodgers, misinformed lodgers, run-down stable hands, underpaid dance bands, itinerant weavers, perennial grievers, backsliding scholars avoiding their lumps, and weak-kneed priests down in the dumps. It was the very last place this side of the river Styx where you could get a decent, fifty-cent blue plate special, delivered up to you by slipshod escapist types with nothing much better to do with themselves. At any hour of the day or night you could look up from your copy of the daily racing form and see naked young girls going to hell in a hand basket, slippery debtors hotly pursued by creditors, moonlighting policemen chasing down cold leads, love-blinded sailors lashing themselves to pillars hoping the sirens will give them a second chance, middle-aged scavengers sharing their empty sacks with overweight barflies, overwrought hookers clamoring for new obsessions, overdrawn, underwritten sample clerks checking their bunions, demented wrestlers lying around in old positions. And Alexander himself was down in the stacks being tantalized by boys with preordained ringlets. Hey nonny nonny and a hotchacha! All I can say is it's a pity history doesn't repeat itself. Things would be a whole lot nicer if we had more circles and fewer straight lines.

And fewer people who sleep with their eyes wide open. How can anything good creep up on you if it's always being watched? Beware of people who won't close their eyes. Why, just the other day I was sitting in Jimmy the Greek's Café on the waterfront, chewing the fat with some of the boys from Temple Shrdluh, when I noticed those official nogoodniks closely surveilling a table of catch-as-can artists doing their thing and clearly having a merry time so doing. As much as I didn't care to, I couldn't help overhearing these two nogoodniks who looked like they had been born with athlete's foot on the run. As arrogantly scurvy as two Phoenician sailors buggering an octopus. One of them was saying to the other, —They are a blight upon our sacred grape harvest, Leger.

—What was that, sir? You are whispering so low.

—I said grate blighp, you fool! A blipe upon the grates of our dear ancestors' vineyards!

—Blipe? Upon the grates? I must confess, Inspector, that I don't quite understand. If you mean . . .

—Be careful, Leger. You are edging close to insubordination. And it is your duty to understand me no matter what I say. Wrap yourself completely around that French fact, my dear fellow, if you value the future of your frites and steak. I said these laughing, devil-may-care scoundrels are undermining the very cork of our civilization. Do you grasp that?

—Oh absolutely, sir! I can feel the cork in my hand this very moment.

—Good. Keep it there. Now without letting the cork slip out of your callow fingers for a single second, concentrate your attention upon their lewd, destructive ways.

—Aye aye, sir.

—I am not a boat, you fool! And you are not a sailor, even if you do like to strip off all your clothes and throw yourself into the water every free moment you can find.

—I confess to liking a good swim, Inspector. I am not ashamed of getting wet. I am a member of the Young Policemen's Dive and Stroke Club. We are all good, clean chaps and we stick together in the water, as we should, I might add. After our swim we adjourn as a group to the showers and achieve further solidarity beneath the penetrating needlepoint spray of the recently improved nozzles, which are not extra but are included in our membership fees. And after our shower we go for a good run in the Bois de Boulogne, some of us locking our arms for greater solidarity and camaraderie as our legs pump up and down in rhythm with nature's basic demands. Our muscles are charged with joy and clean juices and . . .

—Stop, you madman! Stop! Do you think that I care one fig what you do with your short, hairy body? Spitoo! That for your stupid body. And while you have been fouling my official ears with your caveman revelations, these brazen communists have been tearing up the Arc de Triomphe, the Eiffel Tower, hiding stink bombs in Voltaire's favorite bakery, pouring gasoline down Edith Piaf's throat, strapping stones to Mistinguette's divine legs! Pissing in Pasteur's clean milk, removing Quasimodo's sacred hump! Straightening the croissant! Buggering the fieldhands in Flanders field!

—Mon Dieu! Shades of hell! The deluge has begun!

—Precisely, Leger! The deluge. And you are calmly sitting here massaging the calves of your puny legs. Oof! Have you no honor? No self-respect? Are you renouncing the vows you took at your dear mother's knee to sweep the Augean stables clean of all contaminations? Do you feel you have no obligations to the smoking ruins of Joan of Arc?

—Not for a second, sir. Those vows still ring in my ears.

—Then use those same ears this instant! What do they hear those scoundrels saying?

—I can only catch fragments, sir.

—The French Revolution was built on fragments. Remember that. Now, what do you hear?

—The woman with the lewd gold sandals just said something like "they're victims of early toilet training."

—Aha! Code! They are speaking in code, Leger. The last refuge of criminals. It is the black mass of the damned. But I'm on to them, my boy. Not for nothing have I been burning my midnight oils. Do you know what that vile fragment means? No! Don't say a word. I will tell you. It means "we will seize their early toilets and train them to become our victims." There! Now do you understand?

—Early toilets . . . and their victims . . . Oh yes, sir! Completely! I congratulate you, Inspector. What brilliance. With a twist of your fine thumb . . .

—Avant, Leger. What else do you hear?

—"Up shit creek without a paddle."

—Ha! How absurdly simple. They'll have to do better than that to fool your friend Inspector Jean Pierre Epernay. What they mean is, "we will blow up their naval yards and cover our tracks with paddles covered with shit which will force our pursuers to jump into the creek." Simple!

—Splendid, sir. How I envy you your nose for high-quality penetrations. Little do these terrorist cockroaches know what a steel-trapped master they are backing into with the very backs they are so busy slapping in self-congratulatory madness.

—Well put, Leger. Well put. You are developing the essential policeman's knack for concise, clear explanations that have no bones and will not make any. Keep it up, my boy.

—Thank you, Inspector. Thank you very much indeed. You give me heart, without which a policeman's lot is just a lot of fruity pulsations. Hark! Another fragment has lodged in my ear: "we'll blow one more joint before we split this place."

—You have a go at this one, Leger. I know you have it in you. Stare their obscene code language straight in the eye and rassle it onto the ground, as Lafayette's good friend Monsieur George Washington so often said when they were fighting shoulder to shoulder in the Delaware River against the Indians who were scalping everything in sight come what may.

—I'll do my best, sir. Hmm. Yes. What, uh, they are really saying is, "we will abduct the wife of President Giscard and blow her joint at her place until it splits in three pieces and then . . ."

—What? The joint of Madame le President? Blow on it? Until it splits in . . . ? At the Palace? What madness are you saying, Leger?

—Well, sir, I think that is what . . .

—You've lost your senses, Leger! You have gone berserk! Mind Madame le President does not have a joint, you idiot. Don't you know your human female anatomy? Haven't you examined closely the divine statues in the Louvre? Does the Winged Victory have a penis? Of course not! Does the sublime Venus de Milo carry a penis between her delicious marble thighs? Oof! You degenerate madman! You have taken too many needlepoint showers for your own good, Leger. Your mind has collapsed under the sight of all those naked Neanderthals! For shame! Now . . . stop shaking and listen to me as if your very policeman's life depended upon it. What those vile creatures are saying in that fragment in your defective ear is the following: "We have dynamite for splitting the Place de la Concorde into its many joints which we cannot do merely by blowing upon it, no matter how strong the lungs of our red communist gang may be." There, do you see how clear it becomes, once you pull out all stops and wholeheartedly put your analysis into the breach?

—Oh indeed I do, Inspector. Indeed I do. And I am profoundly grateful to you for leading me to the light, and I wish to take this opportunity, sir, to pledge myself completely to the ennobling task of code-breaking.

—You must get out of those damned showers, Leger. Get out of them this instant and put your clothes on!

—Put my clothes on?

—Yes! Immediately! Cover your nakedness before you are seen by the Minister! Quickly! You are a shocking sight. Who do you think you are, standing there like that? The Venus de Milo? The Winged Victory? Phew! If I had suspected for one moment that you were at heart an exhibitionist, do you think I would have plucked you from the cheese caves of Roquefort and nominated you for the police academy? Please! Have the common decency to hold your hands over your outrageous private parts.

—But, sir . . .

—Silence! Not another word out of you. You brazen lunatic! You are staining every police blotter in the republic of France. And to think . . . Hark! More fragments are pouring in from yonder criminals: "the poor fucking Dutchies are pouring over the French border by the thousands to buy those dumb Greek heroes in the Latin Quarter with the nonmeat in them. Anything must look good to them compared to the mountains of cowshit they have to eat at home. I mean, you ought to see them feeding their rubber faces with those stupid sandwiches! That isn't lamb they're eating. It's ground-up Greek travel posters pressed into the shape of a leg of lamb. They wander around the Quarter like a procession of sleepwalkers, chewing those loaves of pulp and staring at the food in all the restaurant windows. It's creepy. They're as glazed as doughnuts on a Sunday morning. And then when they've eaten their pulp sandwiches and have floated around the Quarter thirty-two times, they're all loaded onto buses and driven back to Holland and stuffed into that famous hole in the dike. And I want to tell you something. That hole never was filled by that little boy. He stuck his finger in it for early sexual thrills. He was a dike freak. He's never been the same since. The little motherfucker is a menace to the women's lib movement in the lowlands. There isn't a dike in the whole country whose hole is safe when he's up and about. You oughta hear them scream when he suddenly appears. The Finger! Here comes The Finger! It's a moment of real panic, I can tell you. Especially among the younger dikes who have not yet become skilled in ways to protect themselves against this demon finger thruster. The crazy little bum has absolutely no interest in jamming his insatiable finger into any other kind of hole. You might think, for instance, that he could be persuaded to stick his mad finger into lightly greased doughnut holes, or chic, jam-packed holes in the wall, or holes in legal arguments, or holes in football lines, or into penguins' exquisite assholes which, it should surprise no one, Holland has an enormous supply of. But no, he won't. The son of a bitch is adamant. Absolutely no way, he says on being approached. It's dikes' holes and nothing but dike holes for this finger. Period. Why don't you guys try to talk Goldilocks into sleeping in gorilla beds instead of bear beds. Or Little Miss Muffet into eating yogurt instead of curds and whey. Or Sleeping Beauty into having insomnia. I mean, shit! You fuckin' do-gooders are dangerous. You got no respect for history or The Way Things Are Supposed To Be. Wouldn't surprise me if you guys tried to crossbreed hot dogs with yo-yos. Perverse, that's the word for you creeps. Perverse. Every cheese in this country knows your story from A to Z. A for aggravation and Z for zabaglione. Aggravated zabaglione. Zabaglione that's been tampered with, zabaglione that's been led down the primrose path, zabaglione that's been forced to testify against itself in rigged people's courts. Yeah, Goldilocks . . . I know what upside down tunes you'd make her dance to. You wanna hear? OK. Listen. Here's what you'd do to that perfectly innocent little bedtime story.

If you think all bear families are the same, you're wrong. There are as many different kinds of bear families as there are crooked bums in Congress. Like, on the one hand there is the upwardly mobile bear family that has left the forest for good and has taken up residence on Madison Avenue. Posing with hot-shot ball players and half-naked beauty-contest winners. This BF is lost forever to beehives and juicy grub worms. Shirred eggs, trout amandine, coq au vin. That's where their tongue is today. And they won't give you the time of day without first gettin' three bills up front. And they lie awake at night tryin' to figure out some sly way of pushing their daughter off onto a lispin', listin' prince with hemophilia. Then there's the BF that's gone Hollywood. They're just too much. "See what *Variety* said about me?" "Boy, what a package deal Paramount came through with!" "Hi, Liz. Hi, Debbie. Hi, Duke! Hi, Marlon!" And Porsches, they got 'em stacked up in their front yard like so many chili dogs.

But our BF is different. It remained close to its roots. Deep in the forest primeval. Eyeball to eyeball with Mother Nature. And they were cracking up. The bear center had dropped out. It just wouldn't hold, y'know? Papa Bear was hittin' the cider jug and hangin' around with forest riffraff. Mama Bear let her household duties go to hell and kept her face glued to the fuckin' tube and the soap operas. And Baby Bear, when he wasn't poundin' his pud, was beatin' the shit outta his toys.

Well, one day old Mrs. Possum dropped by for a social visit. She looked around at the shambles and announced, —What this family needs is a little girl.

—Yeah! Right! shouted Baby Bear, and dropped the headless body of his Mickey Mouse doll.

—A middle churl? said Papa Bear, pulling drunkenly at the jug. —What kinda middle churl?

—Maybe she can fix this lousy TV set, said Mama Bear. —The fuckin' images come and go like a one-legged numbers runner. And she threw her bedroom slipper at the screen.

—Middle churls make good second basement, gurgled Papa B., missing his mouth with the jug and pouring some hootch into his ear.

—A nice little gork . . . I mean girl, Mother Possum went on, —who would bring sunshine and laughter into your lives, who would be the object of your mislaid affections.

—Hope she's a stripper! shouted Baby Bear, scampering into his room.

Not long afterward—in about the time it takes to baste a heretic before roasting him—BB had set the trap, so to speak, for whatever little girl might be remotely driven to tying in with a bear family in big trouble. (What're you laughing about? Didn't a lot of rich debutantes volunteer for kamikaze duty with the Aztecs? And wasn't it a hot starlet who raced to christen the Eiffel Tower by jumping off it stark naked? OK then.)

Signs went up all over the place: "Little Girls: Fed up with hopscotch and Ring around the Rosie? Up to here with crayons and silly putty? Had enough of career discrimination? The sky's the limit with the Bear Family. Join up now!" "Little girls wanted. Highest prices paid. No questions asked." "Follow the arrows for fun and frolic in newly established nonprofit Little Girl Paradise. Losers Welcome."

—Hey, BB, said Mimmy the Weasel as BB nailed up the last sign. —Why don't you lay out a trail of doped cookies? That oughta . . .

—I'll lay you out, you creepy little prick! said BB. And let him have it with a handy rock.

A couple of days later (during which waiting period Bear Family was as tense as all get out) the strategy bore fruit. And some fruit! A tasty little dish named Goldilocks wandered into the forest. She was looking for a shortcut to India. Or so she said. —Hmm, she murmured, looking at all the signs.

—Something is going on here, and that's for sure. Goldy was no dumbbell. She knew her way around and then some. Like, she'd fixed that race between the turtle and the hare. And she'd been in on the Cinderella caper. So if you think . . .

—Yoo hoo! yelled Baby Bear from the upstairs cottage window. —We're over here, beautiful!

—So I see, she said, casing the house and everything.

—Time's a-wastin'! shouted BB. —It's later than you think! The fun's in here! Let's roll it, sweetheart!

—Hold your horsies, bubbie. I gotta phone my pimp to let him know where I am.

—Your what?

—You heard me, junior. Now gimme a fix on this place, willya.

—OK. It's six over seven and nine over three, and a two-block walk from *The Brothers Karamazov* on a warm day.

—You got that, Umberto? Goldy said into the walkie-talkie she fished out of her big Gucci bag. —Good. I'll keep you posted, OK? In the meantime, why don't you get your lazy ass out of bed and nip down to the Street and talk to my broker. I'm not in the fuckin' stock market for laughs.

Papa Bear and Mama Bear appeared on the cottage porch. —Welcome to our humble little abode, dear little girl! Mama called out.

—Yeah. Welcome to our tumbled down toad, middle churl, bawled drunken Papa, almost falling off the porch.

—Jesus, Goldy observed. —These primitives sure have one-track minds.

—Just remember, shouted BB, —we believe in women's lib in this house. So, anything goes. You know what I mean.

—Oh boy, said Goldy to the sky. —One of those. An' he's so young. This is gonna be some trick all right.

Inside the cottage everything was set up just like it shoulda been. The chairs, the porridge, the beds, the whole schmear. The Bear Family had even added a touch: they'd each laid out a set of clothes so Goldy could wreck those too.

—You guys haven't been sleeping on the job, have you, observed Goldy, surveying the stage.

—We got our shit together on this one, said Mama B., winking at Goldy and licking her big lips. —We know a last chance when we see one.

—Hear! Hear! yelled Papa B., holding up the jug. —I propose a toast. Ring out, wild pine trees! Sing a sog of sick pants! Make hay with the traffic signs. My kingdom for a churl. He tilted the jug way back, then fell on his face.

Mama B. laughed lewdly. —Who lives by the jug, falls by the jug.

—Cut the comedy! howled Baby Bear. —I want my fuckin' chair broken! Goddamn it all! Whatcha think this is, a lousy writers' conference in the Alps!

—Awright awready, said Goldy. —Cool it, snooky. You'll get yours. Your turn's coming. She had read her Piaget and her Spock and she knew just when to put her foot in somebody's mouth when it came to prepuberty growth needs. —I just hope I can break your chair. It looks awful strong to me.

—It's just a metaphor, you dumb cunt! screamed Baby B., hurling himself against the wall. —It's cherries we're talking about here! The breaking of cherries!

—Temper, temper, said Mama B., shaking her head. —We must exercise a little self-control, baby dear. Now you be good or I won't let you go to the hanging of Chicken Lickin. You hear me? And in a trice she'd straitjacketed the little bugger in her corset and plopped him into a corner. —You just stay there till your head clears, young man. She turned to our friend. —Well, now, Miss, uh . . .

—Goldilocks. Goldy to my friends.

—Miss Goldy, how about a little soup? I'll bet you're absolutely starved. And as we all know from what Mr. Napoleon said, an army travels on its butt but it crosses the finish line on its stomach.

—Yeah, Goldy responded. —That's exactly what he said. And that's why his ass wound up on Elba.

—Soup? Who said soup? mumbled Papa Bear from the rug. —I wouldn't mind landing in the soup myself if the right little girl gave the word. Ha! Ha!

The next thing he knew Mama B. had poured the entire tureen of bear soup over his fat head.

—Men! she exclaimed. —They're all alike. Every chance they get, they say something degrading about women. If I had my way, they'd all be put in cages where we could throw bat-shit balls at them three times a day.

Goldy nodded her beautiful blonde head. —I know just what you mean, Mama B. Sometimes I say to myself, that thing between their legs just isn't worth all the trouble.

—Exactly, my dear. Exactly. You took the words right out of my mouth. She gave Goldy a warm motherly hug. —Listen. Why don't we go upstairs and lie down in my bed and talk this whole thing over. I'm sure we have a lot to say to each other.

A sly, succulent smile spread over Goldy's pretty face. —Yeah. Groovy. But, uh, what about these two? She surveyed Papa B. sloshed proper on the rug and Baby Bear corseted in the corner.

—Don't give them another thought, dear. They won't be bothering anybody for quite some time. You can count on it. She patted Goldy's firm, sweet ass. —I can't tell you how pleased I am that you came along. I had just about reached the end of my rope. You ever read *The Well of Loneliness*? Well, that's the story of my life.

—Us girls have to stick together, said Goldy as they mounted the stairs, arms about each other. —It's just such unexpected moments of comradeship that make my work bearable. She giggled. —I didn't mean to pun.

—Where the pun sucks, there suck I, as the man said.

—They say he was a closet queen.

—Who was that?

—Willie the Shake.

—Oh, of course. All those English public-school fellows wear the purple.

And especially during those public floggings. Oh, they were naughty. Mmm, she said, sniffing and nuzzling her tasty neck. —What are you wearing?

—Arpège. Isn't it divine? Santa Claus sent it to me. Course, I had to put out for him a coupla times.

—Natch, said Mama B. as they entered her cozy bedroom. —He doesn't give anybody anything free. My good friend Mother Hubbard has been spreading for the horny old coot for years, just to get her rent money, y'know.

—It isn't too bad, said Goldy, taking in the deliciously quaint and old-fashioned bedroom. Handmade bed quilt with *all* the positions expertly stitched on, just in case anybody's memory failed them. Mirrors on the ceiling, leather straps and deer-skin whips for *that* kind of home-grown fun. —If he would only keep those fucking reindeer out of the room while we make it. I mean, really!

—Oh, I can imagine, said Mama B. as she started peeling Goldy's clothes off her. —Dancing and prancing like they do and shaking those crazy little bells they wear. Must have been a terrible distraction.

—You can say that again, said Goldy, standing naked now except for her black lace panties. —One of 'em, I think it was Blitzen but I'm not sure, went ape and tried to mount me from the rear as I was, you know, copping the old geezer's huge joint, and, holy moly, I mean those damn hoofs hurt, I don't care what anybody says. I had to let him have it in the snoot to cool him off. Mmm, Mama B. That sure feels good what you're doing down there.

—A bear's long nose has to be good for something besides jamming into old tree trunks.

—Mamma mia! With a nose like yours . . . ooooh! . . . who needs . . . aaah! a college education. That nose of yours . . . oh Jesus! . . . is the softest thing . . . ooh God! I hope I . . . don't . . . come too . . . oooh! soon . . . my clit aaah! hasn't felt this hot since . . . I . . . yeah, like that, more like that! . . . I fucked my . . . oh yeah! I'm gonna piss myself . . . stuffed lamb when I was . . . put it in me! Hard! . . . just a little girrll . . .

—Goodness! said Mama B., who was of course down on her hands and knees, where else? —I seem to have torn a tiny hole in those lovely panties quite by accident, dear. I'm so . . . Mmm. What a sweet honey pot you have. Sorry. I'll just whip them off you with this very strong bear's tongue of mine. Mmm. My, what tasty muff honey you have, dear. Lots tastier than anything a bee could . . . You think my nose is good. Just wait'll you get a full load of this *tongue!*

—Holy hot pastrami! yelled Goldy, her ass twitching like a fiddler on a hot tin roof. —My legs are turning to jelly, Mama B. In another minute I'm gonna fall on my cute little face. Let's dive into bed and call out . . . oy dios! . . . the marines or something.

—Sure thing, said Mama B., and flipped Goldy onto the soft bed with a single motion of her body that can only be produced by bears when they're really serious about whatever it is they're doing.

—Jeepers! exclaimed Woody Woodpecker, and promptly fell out of the tree from which he had been watching the entire proceedings.

—That's just like you, said Mrs. Woody Woodpecker. —What do you do when I'm about to achieve orgasm? You fall out of the fucking tree. And you wonder why the magic has fled from our marriage. Merde! I should have married Wee Willie Winkie. He may be limited but at least he stays put.

Well, Mama B. and Goldy were really going at it, setting a stunning example of interspecies teamwork which should make us all think twice, when who should walk into Mama Bear's bedroom but Baby Bear, dragging the chewed-through corset.

—Oh yeah. Right, he said. —Now I get the picture. This whole fuckin' thing is a put-up job, you dirty old degenerate. You got old Mrs. Possum to come in here with that story about this family needing a little girl. Shit! You're the one who needed a little girl!

—Later, said Mama B. through Goldy's dense muff forest. —We'll talk . . . oh, this honey pot! Hot sweet little girl pussy honey . . . about it later.

—What kind of a mama are you! shouted Baby B., hurling the corset at Mama B.'s bobbing head.

—Tongue! Tongue! shouted Goldy, writhing and twisting. —Moving up and down again!

—That's Kipling! shouted Baby B. —And it's "Boots! boots! Moving . . ."

—There are two versions, you little asshole! Goldy howled, arching like a rubber bridge. —An' you got the cleaned-up one. Oy! Hi ho Kipling! I'm coming through the rye, bread and . . . aii! . . . all! Oohhh! Outta my way! Women and tongue first. Oh! Man the lifeguards. Lower the boomerang! Hold onto your hatracks! Ride 'em cowlicks!

B.B. jumped up and down. —What am I gonna tell my friends when it gets around that you're into little girls, you dirty old lez!

—Tell 'em to join the March of History, said Mama B., rolling over and sighing blissfully. —Tell 'em that Freud is full of shit. Tell 'em he sucked cigars instead of cocks 'cause he was yellow. She sat up on the bed and looked B.B. straight in the eye. —Tell 'em that all those children's stories they read are lies, concocted by fascist spinsters, desiccated faggots, con artists, venal castrates, lowbrow losers, and toothless killers of the dream. You hearing me?

—That's tellin' it like it is, Mama B., said Goldy, grinning like Rosetta when he found that Stone underneath all those chewing-gum wrappers. —It's about time the truth got told. Mmm. I'm so spaced out I can see Beowulf.

—OK, OK, said Baby Bear. —So let's say you're right. How 'bout me? When do I get mine?

—Right now, said Goldy. —Hop aboard, boobie doo, and we'll blast off. I'll show you what bestiality is really all about.

—Hot damn! shouted B.B. and leaped into the cooze.

—That's the ticket, said Mama Bear, moving down to the end of the lewd, rumpled bed. —And forget about the missionary position, son. Those guys didn't know their mass from a hole in the ground.

Clump! Clump! Clump! Somebody was coming up the stairs. Papa Bear! Singing his drunken head off! —Here comes the bride! All big and wide. Give her your dressings, girls, 'cause she's got her little churls!

He staggered into the bedroom wearing Mama Bear's wedding dress, big white hat and all.

—Hi, everybody! he sang out in a high, falsetto voice, waving a fresh jug of the juice. —Guess who I am.

—Oh my God, said Mama. —You've been into the closet again. She sniffed. —And you've drowned yourself in my Chanel.

—I'm gonna have to charge extra for that act, said Goldy, turning around in the saddle (so to speak).

Papa B. giggled crazily. —Oh to be a bride's head now that heaven has no favorites.

Mama looked him up and down, squinting wisely. —I've got a hunch that what we're gonna need here is the old paddle.

—Goodness gracious! exclaimed Papa in that drunken falsetto. —Spanky-poo for the young bride. And I just know you won't spare the horses. Spank! Spank! Ooooh! My fanny is burning already. Oh mercy!

—Damn it! shouted Baby B. from under Goldy, who was riding him like she was in the Derby. —This place is as crowded as Grand Central. Haven't you guys heard of parental interference and all the bad things it does to my growth potential? Haul your hairy asses outta here!

—You tell 'em, snooky, said Goldy, pumping her beautiful tookus for all she was worth. —Baby bears need all the privacy they can get during their initiation rites. Mmm. This bear meat of yours sure hits the spot. Push harder! ATTABOY!

Mama Bear pulled a nice firm paddle from under her bed. —Come along now, Miss whatever your name is, she said, giving Papa a push with her big foot. —We've got some strict disciplining to do. (Whack! Whack!)

—Lordy! squealed Papa. —They told me a young bride's life was a bed of roses.

(Whack!)

—When I get through with you, your ass is gonna be as red as one, young lady. (Whack!) —Let's move it!

And out they went, Papa Bear howling his/her drunken old head off.

—Thank heaven they've gone, said Goldy. Her nubile, pink body was just glistening with sweat. —How you doin' down there, honey boy? I've come three times already.

Baby B. grabbed Goldy's gyrating fanny with his little paws and slammed away. —I think I'm getting the hang of it.

—Ooof! It sure looks that way. Feels like you hit my spinal cord with that one. Ooof! What've you got down there, a jackhammer?

—I've been practicing. (Thrust! Wham!)

—Yoicks! shrieked Goldy, grabbing his ears so's she wouldn't hit the ceiling. —Practicing where? In a fucking marble quarry?

—Doggy style! he announced, quickly turning her over onto her tummy. —Let's do it like Rin Tin Tin.

—Ouch! Rin Tin Tin wasn't into buggery, you crazy little jerk.

—He is now! yelled B.B., bamming Goldy's tender bum. —Boy! Old Oscar Wilde wasn't so dumb after all.

—Oh yeah? said Goldy, gripping the mattress. —The old fart died broke in a Paris fleabag. What's so smart about that?

—Mmm. Yummy. What an ass. You're as tight as a gumshoe at Christmas.

—Oy! Jeepers. The handwriting's on the wall. It's water sports next, I just fucking know it. Oyyy!

Outside the window half the forest population was absolutely bug-eyed hanging there in the tree.

—You see what I see? said Mother Goose to the Three Little Pigs.

—We sure do! they squealed. —What's good for bears is bound to be good for pigs.

—That's what I was trying to tell you, said the Wolf. —But you wouldn't listen.

—We thought you wanted to eat us, they chorused.

—No, no, You got it wrong. I *couldn't* eat you. I'm Jewish. I can't eat pig meat.

—I always knew there was more to the Bear Family than met the eye, said Henny Penny.

—Wow! Have I been living in the past! howled the Black Swan, taking off from a branch. —I'm calling the Seven Dwarfs soon as I get home.

See what I mean? That's the kind of unnatural perversions you maniacs would let loose if you had your way. You can't fool me. You want to turn the lights out all over the world. Darkness, that's what you're into. Total darkness. No law and order. The death of the family. Children running wild in the streets like mad dogs. Churches burning. Priests hanging from lampposts.

Maidens raped by the hammer and sickle. Harvests going to pot. Garbage piling up. Rats big as horses. Poisoned well water. Yellow hordes pouring through the keyholes. Blood and shit raining from the skies. Tornadoes blowing up our assholes. While internationally famous doughnuts turn to stone in our hungry, pleasure-starved hands. Oh yes. That's the picture that hangs in store for us on the wall of the Peelmunder All-Night Museum. And standing right next to that picture is Mr. Peelmunder himself, as glistening and glowing as an imposter who has climbed Mount Everest without ever having gone there. And you don't have to push a button or turn a knob to get him to elaborate on this picture or any of the other outrageous pictures in his museum, many of which may be obscure but are alarming nonetheless. You have only to come within earshot or stone's throw or hindsight or fore-thought or arm's reach and that brazen entrepreneur of nightshade and madness will sweep you up in his shifty outpourings. And as this stuff pours over you, it will dawn upon you how comparatively fortunate the citizens of Pompeii were to have mere lava inundate them because at least the lava permanently fixed them as they were, themselves, whereas Peelmunder's volcanic outpourings obliterate you, wipe you out of your own existence, leaving no trace of you which your loved ones or relatives or admirers can drop flowers on from time to time during their off moments or lunch breaks, allotted to them by a government that is acutely production-oriented with a bunch of no-nonsense people calling the shots. Señor El Jefe Peelmunder does not employ decent, genteel words that you could introduce your mother to, words like *smooth* or *round,* or *comfy* or *flow.* Oh no. Never. He uses such demented words as *suck, blood, choke, shit, gouge, infiltrate, con-taminate, chop, rend, plunder* . . . oohhh . . . And these words form such sentences as We shall rip out the hearts of the vile contaminators! We shall drown their babies in the blood of their lies! We shall burn down their mansions of villainy! We'll turn their wives into pillars of shit! We'll plow their children under and plant lies in their eyes. Even their grandmothers: we'll turn them into lapdogs and sell them to homosexuals. And their libraries: we'll transform them into public toilets for migrating elephant herds, who'll wipe their hairy asses on every single page of their history. And that's only the beginning. When we get through with the bourgeoisie they'll wish they'd never bought their first cashmere sweater or served their first love set. As sure as my name is Horatio Alger Commodore Perry Peel-munder, there won't be a fart or a farthing left to remember them by. The empty laughter of psychotic penguins, such will be the sound of their nostalgia. If we don't mean anything else, we mean business. Like, I mean, shit, compared to us the Mongol hordes will look like slipshod Sunday-school teachers on a forged three-day pass to Disneyland. Our numbers are legion even if you can count them on the fingers of one hand. But don't let that worry you. How many times did Newton have to drop that apple to prove the theory of gravitation? Right. Once, and only once. Down is down, period. Whether it's a MacIntosh or a Granny. Keep that in mind before you start to climb walls that don't even belong to you. Behave yourself, keep cool. Keep a stiff upper lip and smile at the same time. It's a good exercise, and you don't have to be one of those slippery coons to pull it off. And keep a tight asshole while you're at it. Do all three of those things four times a day and believe me, you'll never be bothered with bunions. You should look to your cadre for an example to live by. I was talking to District Leader Michael Smoot just yesterday. He's moved to a houseboat on the Red Herring Canal so's he can be closer to nature when she calls. And when she does, he just pisses out of the window. He doesn't have to waste his time or risk his sanity trying to count the number of hot blintzes an angel can carry on its head. You know, like you are forced to do in some two-by-four apartment-house toilets while your crazy neighbor is trying to flush himself down the toilet 'cause he's too cheap to buy a nice little Smith & Wesson .38 to do himself in with.

—Michael, I said, passing him the hash joint I can always be found with dead or alive, —do you have a few pearls of great price you'd care to cast before the younger generation, gap or no gap?

—In point of fact, I do, he said and sucked on the joint with the fierce concentration of a Japanese technocrat climbing the Tokyo social ladder. —I do indeed. First, they gotta cut out all shit foods. Fritos and potato chips and Twinkies and Sally Mae ginger snaps. That stuff saps the will and eventually leads to epileptic seizures at the most embarrassing moments. Like when your favorite sister finally agrees to put out for you. Next, I would suggest they return to their workbenches and carefully reread Marx's analysis of the dialectics of middle-class breathing habits during the heyday of the industrial revolution. This is very important. The last thing the young should find themselves doing is breathing like a bourgeois pig feeling his oats while he squats on the face of the miserable worker, who has not yet been able to organize, due to poor diet and lack of solidarity feelings and general overall passivity, tired blood, and an aching back.

—I would also advise them to shun and eschew eyeball-to-eyeball confrontations. For one thing, what they may be eyeballing may well be The Void, in which case there would be none of the essential reciprocity. A very heavy down trip all the way, you see. For another thing, the person they may be confronting could have 5/5 zero vision and thus would be unable to see them in the first place. This experience can lead to instant disenchantment and withdrawal and in many cases to obsessive scratching of one's asshole.

—Catherine de Medici's bootmaker was known for that and look what happened to him.

—Precisely. I would also advise the young to wash daily. You don't want to find yourself hanging around yesterday's smell. That can be quite as counterproductive as chasing yesterday's shadow. Those who have done that have not been heard from since.

—It's just as well, really.

—I would go along with that. Such people are not built for The Great Spring Offensive. We would find ourselves colliding with them as they ran the other way. Oh no. Collision in the ranks, that just won't do. The GSO needs people who have no reverse gear hidden in their jeans. There is no place to go but forward.

—An invigorating statement if I ever heard one. I'm absolutely positive that Columbus said that to his men on the *Ave María*. And one can assume that Ferdinand de Lesseps also said it to the fellows digging the Panama Canal. And Eli Whitney, to the hordes of gin drinkers who were up to their ears in the futility of all that cotton. Otherwise, how can one explain the worldwide glut of cheap cotton shirting?

—You are on firm ground, no question of it.

—Michael, would you bring us up-to-date on your doings and undoings? In other words, how's your old Edam cheese?

—I continue to burrow, hoping to see the light at the other end of the tunnel.

—In other words, you are spending all of your time underground, is that it?

—Yes. And all of the people I know are doing the same thing. We see one another in a vast network of tunnels. Of course, ours are not your drab, smelly, four-by-four pre-Gutenberg tunnels. We've got birds and trees and rivers and, shit, pizza stands and assassinations and locust plagues and hot pussy and radioactive contamination. But I know you want specific moments, episodes, scenes, exchanges. All the stuff the living human story is composed of. OK.

—I was talking to one of my favorite students, Anna de Groot, a gleaming, supple girl who does arabesques on frozen canals. We were standing in front of the American Express office on the Gumperplaatz. I was looking to buy a Honda bike from one of the many Americans there dressed like Himalayan sherpas or Tunisian peasants or deserters from the Confederate army. Anna had just said she very much wanted to see New York City.

—Why? I asked.

—I want to stand beneath the skyscrapers and feel their longing to fall over.

—Where do you want to go besides New York?

—Custer's Last Stand.

—What an odd place to want to visit.

—I want to stand there and laugh as the blood of those arrogant murdering soldiers pours over my naked body.

—Uh huh. And when you've left that place, where would your desires take you?

—To Hollywood. I must hear the sounds of nightmares being born.

—And then where to?

—The Great Plains. I want to lose myself among the ghosts of the millions of vanished buffalo. I want to become the ghost of a slaughtered buffalo.

—Oh, to become the spirit of the American purgatory! To be Mickey Mouse gone mad and raping Bambi! Donald Duck tearing the heart out of Bugs Bunny. Daniel Boone drunkenly running amok and wiping out the Seven Dwarfs. Grandma Moses exposing herself to Nigger Jim at a dinner party for Little Eva thrown by Jackie Kennedy! To be the demonic exhilaration in Johnson's soul as he watches Kennedy die and knows that he will be the president. Swimming naked in Kennedy's gushing blood and screaming with laughter like a madman. The spider web of ecstasy spinning itself in the groin of J. Edgar Hoover as he plots the murder of Martin Luther King and howls "Nigger! Nigger!" To be the consuming horror of the collective decision to incinerate millions of Japanese with atomic bombs and those bombs singing "Zap the Jap! Zap the Jap! Little yellow monkeys! Filthy bucktooth sunckies!" as they float happily down through the sky. Such sublime moments!

—I will walk in the streets of Concord and feel their pristine self-satisfaction shiver with equivocation, writhe with the pain of self-knowledge, the streets that lead to nowhere but emptiness and betrayal and the solitude of the abyss. Apple pies and maple syrup and the smell of leaves burning in the fall are all lies. The laughter of playing children turns into screams of horror soon enough. The lines at their school dances become bread lines in the twinkling of an eye. And the jolly high-school cheerleader is selling her ass when the cheers die down.

—Oh say can you see by the dawn's early light the desolation that consumes this hallucinated land. George Washington has become a leering cannibal. Demented Boy Scouts build bonfires of books, and the Grand Canyon is filled to the brim with rotting corpses.

I feel myself becoming a fictional American. I am a woman named Erika...

W hat's the matter with that girl anyway? Erika asked her husband—though he always felt that his wife hurled these questions, not at a particular person, himself, for example, but at the room, at the atmosphere, at life, that she would undoubtedly ask them, angrily, even though no one were in her presence.

—I don't know, he said, emptying the sand from his sneakers onto the porch floor. —Is something the matter with her?

—Of course there is! she howled again, as though she were responding to an irrational, invisible thing instead of to another limited human being. She tossed the stuff from her beach bag onto the faded, aching porch swing. —Didn't you hear her when we were at the docks and the fishermen were hoisting up the sharks for view?

He thoroughly wished he were being gently but efficiently massaged by a naked young Japanese girl who in another second would bring him a tall scotch and soda. Sand was on his legs, his neck, on the floors, in their bed—it insidiously controlled the entire bungalow, like a rumor that starts out as a passing remark but soon is generating enough tension to turn lights on.

—No, he replied, indifferently examining the tiny web of ruptured vessels on his bare, rather burned ankles. —What did she say?

Erika mimicked a prissy, nasal voice. —"Why are they doing that to those poor sharks? They haven't harmed anybody. Isn't it perfectly obscene the way those people are gawking and laughing at them?" Oh dear God! Really! How affected can you get!

The Japanese girl was refilling his drink after having just put on a record of beautifully eerie, very self-confident lute music dating back to the fourteenth century. —What else has she done that seems repellent? he asked, and yawned as he stood up preparatory to showering off the candy-stickiness of the bay water.

Erika faced him with her hands on her hips, a favorite stance. She was a beautiful woman—centuries of Mediterranean sun had given her body a ripeness, a vibrant self-knowledge, impossible to acquire in the north, and her face, finely boned, contained the faintly haughty cynicism found in the imperishable busts of Roman leaders who knew that man was made for folly; but essentially she was a ferocious woman, so her splashy, hotly colored beach suit became at this delicately tuned moment an explosion of her personality. —Practically everything! Her toenails look like something she won at a bingo party, and those cocktail getups, she must get them directly from a seamstress at Rockland State.

Without his having to blink an eyelash, Jack's Japanese girl was bringing him a dish of butterfly shrimp fried in butter and a shot of aquavit. It's amazing how she instinctively knows my special delights. She had gotten into some clothes; bikini panties and a small handkerchief tied around her young, happily plump breasts. Her smile had all the benign loveliness of a bed cover turned down.

—Maybe she's just insecure, he said, dipping deep into his collection of impersonal and unfelt statements devised to fill in conversational voids or extricate him from potentially dangerous personal exchange. He walked carefully across the thinly furnished living room to the bathroom door where he clung for a moment to the knob.

Erika's shriek of nonlaughter sped across the room and lodged, quivering, in Jack's right shoulder. —Insecure? She's just plain dumb. Don't you recognize stupidity when you see it? Or did the fact that you probably thought she was sexy affect your brain? Is that it, sweetie pie? Hmm? Come on now— you can tell mama.

—She's not my type, he said, turning the doorknob. —I go for giant blondes.

—Ha! You go for giant blondes like I go for one-eyed trolls.

—I've got to shower. What time are they coming for drinks?

Erika peeled off her beach suit and, overwhelmingly naked, fiercely physical, walked to the bedroom. —Around six. And I don't have one decent thing to wear.

Jack knew better, after ten years of marriage, than to respond to that seemingly innocent plaint; one word, and he would end up days later in a dense black forest with no compass or matches. He closed the door behind him and more or less passively submitted to the idiosyncrasies of the aging, apparently never-attended-to shower.

After three vodkas and bitter lemon, Philip Hunt was in splendid form. —I swear to God that's what the sign said, he insisted, his face a garden of amusement.

—It couldn't, his not-quite-so-chubby but thicker-lipped wife said, smiling at him across the room. —You must have been drinking when you passed it.

The girl whom Erika had been discussing earlier, Janet something or other, laughed appreciatively, and said, —I love it.

Hunt couldn't help it: he went into another small seizure of delight. —CAREFUL—PEASANT CROSSING!

Erika began making herself another scotch and soda. —You obviously have something against *h*s, she suggested. —Doesn't it bother you in business?

Janet's escort, Max Goodman, the man she was visiting at the shore, shouted, —The only thing that bothers him in business is his secretary. Right, Philip?

Everybody got a chuckle out of that except perhaps Hunt's wife Anna who did, however, manage to squeeze a tiny smile into her drink. To the careful, sympathetic observer she was softly saying, "In my lifetime I have squeezed out thousands of such smiles. That is my cross. Pity me. . . ." She tucked one leg under herself and the bamboo chair squeaked like a sleeping water buffalo having a bad dream.

—Isn't it strange, Janet began, looking around the Dufy-like room to be sure the audience was properly seated and had stopped talking to one another, —how the joke about the husband's secretary persists? She paused, saw the audience was waiting for further directions (Erika looks as though I'm about to say something which will make her want to throw that drink into my face), and then continued, —I mean, it's a permanent part of our culture, and I wonder why. Is it because most men do sleep with their secretaries? Or is it that we want them to, or what?

Jack shifted the Japanese girl—he didn't know her name yet—in his lap, sipped a bit of his martini exploringly, and said, —That's a very good point. I've often wondered about that myself. He felt squeezably tight, just right. He still had the delicious tiddly condition to look forward to.

Erika quickly, savagely devoured three Fritos before going to the barricades. —Men have been sleeping with their secretaries ever since the first caveman dictated a letter. She had one more of the addictive Fritos. —And when we land a rocket on Mars, it will be discovered that next to laughing at Earthmen, the national sport there is humping little robot secretaries.

Max Goodman howled with appreciation; and Hunt released a short loon-like giggle, then he grabbed his beard for half a dozen consoling caresses. You'd think it was a woman's hair, the way he plays with it, Goodman mused to himself. Wonder what it's like when he nuzzles his wife with it. Bet she still jumps when he does.

—Do you really think so little of men? Anna Hunt ventured carefully, without raising her gazelle gaze from the measureless depths of her highball.

Erika turned her microscopic radar full blast on Anna for a second to determine exactly what intentions the question had, whether it was a medium-disguised attack upon her femininity, a carefully planned device of disengagement, or a simpleminded academic inquiry. You never knew about these broody, heavy-thighed European women.

—It isn't that at all, Erika replied in her best precise-voiced manner.

Oh yes it is too, Janet said to herself, fascinated by Erika's elegant style.

—It's simply that men are always remarkably predictable in situations of sexual illicitness, Erika continued. —They can't resist the opportunity to do something naughty when no one is looking.

Philip Hunt crunched an ice cube as he leapt into the arena. —What Erika is trying to say, honey, is that basically she loves men even though they're a bunch of sneaky, dirty little boys who hate their mommies. And he crumpled up with self-adoring laughter which was joined and made tastier and richer by chuckles and amused response from around the room.

Erika's ha! ha! was in there, too. —You're absolutely right, Philip. I'm going to make you my official interpreter.

After you've teased him and led him on and then dismissed him in humiliation, Anna was thinking. And he won't even know what happened.

Goodman leaned over and slapped Jack on the shoulder. —Jack, baby, have you humped your secretary lately? 'Fess up now, you dirty old thing.

Jack allowed two or three ounces of tiddly juice to sluice down his delighted throat before answering very matter-of-factly. —Yes. Just this morning.

—Really? Janet gasped half in joke, half in possible belief. —Is she staying out here?

Jack looked directly at her—a sea gull shot across his vision and torpedoed into the gem-blue bay for a fish—deep into her twelve-year-old Sunnybrook Farm hazel eyes. —I did it to her on the telephone.

Hunt started sloshing himself up a fresh drink as Erika excused herself to bring more appetizers from the kitchen. —I ate nearly all the deviled eggs, Erika, Hunt announced, holding his highball up to the window light as though he thought he might actually be able to see, in some physical shape, its secrets and special magical components. —I'm becoming an awful glutton. He sighed and moved to the porch door, looking out toward the gentle bay as he talked to the room behind him. —Must be a sign of something. He turned around and walked back to his chair. —Maybe I'm starved for affection. He glanced around the room, delighted by what he'd just proposed.

Goodman leaped high, snagged the winged thought, and shaking his small, seal-slick head, said, —Jesus, that is tough. Just think: hard boiled eggs instead of sex. Janet laughed, and he went on. —I think I'd rather turn fag.

If you ask me, Jack thought, I don't think you have very far to go. Something awfully faggy about you already. I don't mean that in Erika's bitchy way. But beneath that olive-oil masculinity of yours I sense a bad twitch of that kind, and I sort of suspect that the string of broads you've had visiting you this summer, the latest being the not really so bad tootsie to my left, are, whether you know it or not, designed to take anybody's wondering *Confidential* mind off the possibility of your being one of the boys. 'Cause I can tell a stick man when I see one and, sweetheart, you don't qualify. The Japanese girl had gone to see her honorable parents who were dead set on marrying her off to a rich old noodle merchant who lived in Nagasaki. She said she'd rather jump in Fuji; anyway, she promised to return in an hour and then they could go for a walk around the goldfish pond.

The screen door banged open and a Mongol-eyed, wild-haired boy, Peter Hunt, exploded into their midst. —Daddy! he shouted to Hunt. —Guess what?

—You've just drowned your little sister.

—A shark's washed up on the beach!

—Good. Go and give it last rites.

—I mean it, Daddy.

—So do I.

The screen door slammed shut, and the room was left in a sudden silence, a shock vacuum: the child's mad urgency had devoured the contest of sound there. The first to recover was Janet. —Isn't it wonderful the way children have such passionate responses to life? They're so . . . so . . . vulnerable to experience, while we have to be practically hit on the head before we'll react.

—Yes, Anna said, as if coming up from a long sleep. —I absolutely agree. We all suffer from a corruption of the spirit. We've made disbelief into a science.

Erika strode into the room. —Oh, Anna, she said gaily, putting the fresh appetizers near Hunt's almost salivating hands, —you sound like Ecclesiastes or somebody. Things aren't as lousy as that, they really aren't. You've got to learn to swing with things. What is it Zen says? "Bend like a willow."

Anna stared at Erika and the irritation and hurt at being dismissed so cavalierly were instantly felt around the room. —I don't know what you mean, she said, and heretofore hidden traces of a Middle European accent crept into her speech.

Before anything could thicken in the air, Jack stood up and in a loud, jolly voice said, —I've got an absolutely sensational idea.

—I'm at your feet.

—Let's all go for a ride on your boat.

Janet clapped her baby hands. —Oh love it!

—And, Jack continued, feeling the air clearing itself of that heavy, dark ingredient, —and I'll bring some steaks which we can grill on the beach at Gardiners Island. How's that?

Hunt stood up and put his hands on Jack's shoulders. —Jack, old sardine, you missed your calling. You should have been a recreation director on a cruise ship.

Erika, with the amnesic lightness of a person who has moments previously been dragged from the path of a speeding car by a companion—the protective systems of nature take such stark moments out of the continuity of time and person and set them aside in mindless isolation—drank off the last of her scotch-rocks and, rising, said, —Yes indeed. And can you imagine what games he'd be having the guests play?

In a waft of perfume and reasonably good intention, Janet materialized in that standing cluster accompanied, his arm reached all the way around to the gleaming silver buckle in the middle of her demure body, by Goodman. —Marvelous games, I'll bet, she ventured.

—Oh absolutely, Erika responded. —And instead of the immigration authorities, the boat would be met by the vice squad at the end of the trip.

Goodman squeezed Janet, moving his hand just above the silver buckle's objections, and thought, Erika reminds me of a good-looking boy I went to high school with. He was always saying sharp, funny things and he liked to wrestle with you. I liked him very much but was afraid of him. Why?

In a long sigh of endless vigil, a jet soared above them in the fathomless sky, an incredible bird with no place to go. The gulls could have puzzled where its mate was.

Kiyo, that was the Japanese girl's name. She'd finally told Jack. Also, she'd figured out a way to escape marriage with the noodlemaker: she would run away with Jack and they would live a simple but deep and beautiful life on one of the islands off the coast of Linka. If necessary, she would become a pearl diver to help with the household finances. Meanwhile, as Jack was pleasing his stomach with large bloody chunks of beach-grilled steak, Kiyo was giving him a pedicure. The smoke from the charcoal grill on the beach, being played with by the breeze coming in off the dark, suckling bay, was obscuring his view of the others and making them seem more like elusive outlaw campers in a Western than what they presumably were. Anna had finished her steak and was standing alone at the edge of the water with her back to the group. She had been standing there, her hands clasped behind her, a part of the sand and water that seemed unassailable from human view, for several minutes, without moving, just staring across the water.

—Who are you looking for out there? Jack shouted.

—The Fabulous Stranger, she answered without turning around.

—You're married to him! Hunt yelled.

—What makes you think he's going to come by water? Jack went on, tasting the rich, yes, feminine, blend of charcoal smoke, sea air, and imperturbable primitive darkness.

—All wonderful surprises come by way of the water, she replied, and turned now and slowly walked toward the fire. Actually, she did not walk so much as trudge; her heaviness of soul, of limb, denied physical space its usual element of buoyancy. —It's very Freudian, don't you see? The sea representing the prenatal ocean of the mother, the all-giving, the life presenter.

Oh dear, thought Janet, clasping her small bare legs, why do women like her come on with all that crap? They sound like they're talking through a bowl of mushroom soup or something. Could she possibly think it's sexy? Oh God!

—Oh? chirped Goodman, involuntarily, like a small boy discovered sleeping in class.

—Yes, Anna said, sinking thickly to the sand. (In a strange way it seemed she was really having a dialogue with the sand.) —There's something so deliciously regressing about water. It has the same effect on you as a drug. All your worries slip away and you become a child again, and you believe that something magical will happen to you. She looked up from the sand and examined their night-obscured faces. Her husband, worlds away from her, was softly staring at Erika's full bosom. Anna looked away from him and focused on Goodman. —Don't you agree?

Goodman laughed awkwardly and briskly rubbed his bare arms as if he were trying to rub life back into them. —It sounds kind of eerie, or sick, to tell you the truth.

—Why? she demanded, her voice suddenly a couple of notches higher.

—Well, like a little girl who is all alone and the only pleasure she has is playing with herself and daydreaming. He looked up quickly. —I don't mean that you're that little girl. It's just that I associate that swoony feeling with certain kinds of little girls I knew when I was a kid. He paused to assemble more elaborations to extricate himself, because Anna's formerly pleased thick features had become puzzled and staring; all play had fled from her face.

—That's a very peculiar evaluation, she said slowly. —In fact, I would almost say it is aggressive. Again the slight appearance of an accent.

Goodman bounced back immediately. —Not at all. I don't feel even remotely aggressive. Honestly I don't.

—Not consciously... she began, but was interrupted by Hunt as he noisily plucked another cold beer from the scotch cooler. —Come off it, Anna. You're getting as sensitive as a baby's ass. The bottle cap popped off and Hunt's head dove to capture the rebellious beer foam. —After five years of analysis, you ought to be able to take yourself a little less seriously. He took a long gurgle of the beer. —Besides, I kind of agree with him. There is something definitely armpitty about what you said. Lots of people, your beloved among them, don't react that way to water. He turned to Erika who was lying on her stomach and drawing in the sand with a twig. —Hey, beautiful. How do you and water make out?

—To be quite honest, it makes me feel very female and rather sexy.

—Ha! Hunt cried and looked at his wife. —See, Anna? He turned happily back to rich-breasted, partly exposed in bikini, sand-scribbling Erika. —Now then, Mrs. B., when did you first notice that water did these wonderful things to you?

—Let's see—when I was about thirteen.

Anna rose from the sand, slapped at her surly thighs to remove the sand, and said, —I'm going back to the boat.

—What's the matter? Janet asked, and jumped up herself.

—I don't like being made fun of, she explained, walking toward the water, spacing out the syllables of her words as though she were investigating them for treason, —and I especially don't enjoy watching so-called adults flirt.

No one spoke for a few moments—Anna was in the water almost immediately—and this deep silence mysteriously broke up the group, separating each person quite unto himself. Then Hunt spoke. —Jesus Christ. How do you like that? I wonder if she could be going off her noodle or something. I do want Erika, he told himself, and she knows it and so does Anna and there's not a damn thing I can do about it—about Anna's knowing it. Does Jack know it? He must. She's the hottest-looking broad out here. Now Anna will sulk the rest of the night and maybe all day tomorrow, and tonight while I'm trying to sleep and forget the whole mess she'll attack me like a mad dog and accuse me of every crime I've ever dreamed of.

—Perhaps you ought to pay more attention to her, Erika said. —You know, she's around the children so much, she must feel cut off from the other world. She looked up and canvassed the others' faces. —That sounds reasonable, doesn't it?

—Maybe, Jack heard himself say, —but doesn't everybody feel cut off from that world?

Hunt's response was so fast and loud Jack expected it to be accompanied by puffs of stunned sand. —Absolutely! So where the hell does she get off? He yanked at his beard as though he were scalping his wife. —Furthermore, she has a great talent for making you the guilty party, as if you were responsible for her feelings of alienation. Christ! I didn't think up Western civilization!

Goodman thought about Anna for a few moments and decided she would have been happier married to an old and fatigued Russian businessman who fell asleep over a magazine every night after a heavy dinner. He got up, pulling Janet after him. —Everybody is always trying to figure everyone else out, he said. —It's against nature, that's what it is. Besides, he went on, smiling somewhat paternally at small Janet standing docilely beside him like someone waiting behind the curtain for her stage cue, —it's a losing game. Isn't it, sugar-doll plum?

—You've turned philosopher all of a sudden, she replied, pulling at her tight swimsuit.

—Is that sexy?

—I'll let you know later.

Hunt began collecting the cooking stuff, and Jack helped him. In a couple of minutes they were all wading through the barely resisting shallow bay water to the anchored boat.

—I wonder what it would be like to live out here all the year, Erika ventured, paddling a little to help her water progress. —Would a person change and become calmer, like the sand and water?

—You would go off your rocker, Jack said.

—Why?

—Because you need action, dear, lots of it.

—Is that a put-down?

—Nope. Just a scientific, impartial, and unavoidably profound fact.

Several yards ahead of the chest-deep waters a fish leaped out of the shiny, barely breathing water.

—Oh! Janet gasped. —How incredible! It's like . . . something out of a poem.

—It's like a fish jumping out of the water, Erika said, in her flattest voice, as she splashed ahead. —I'll bet he's never read a poem in his life.

Kiyo was leading Jack by the hand through a microscopically lovely garden at the foot of a mountain slope. It was a secret garden, known only to her, and they were going to make love there. She stopped, whispered something delectable to him, giggled as he did, and began to undress him.

Out of the corner of his eye Hunt saw a small sign stuck in the beach. He thought it read TRESPASSERS WILL BE VIOLATED. He decided to file this goody for later.

The Hunts' son Peter was waiting for them on the steps of their somnolent, brown, saltbox house. He was more or less holding onto his two-year-old sister Mandy who was crying jerkily and rubbing her eyes.

—What's the matter now? Anna Hunt asked. The others were trudging up the back road a few yards behind her.

—Mandy had a bad dream, Peter said, pushing the still-whimpering child toward its mother. —She dreamed she was lost in the woods and some animals were after her. He grinned happily at everyone after saying this; his statement embodied both sadism and pride and thus denied the listener his prerogative of a decent clear-cut reaction.

Anna laboriously, resentfully picked up her child. —All right, all right, she said. —You're awake now, Mandy. You don't have to cry anymore, and she headed into the house, followed by Hunt, who was muttering.

—I never dream, the boy announced grandly as they all moved inside in the wake of the dying, wet sobs.

—That's too bad, Jack said before he could catch himself. —You don't know what you're missing.

The boy looked at him, smiling, puzzled, then shrugged his chubby shoulders, and slipped into the kitchen just off the hallway.

—Aren't you being a bit hostile? Erika asked sotto voce, as they made for the porch on the other side of the dining room.

—Nope. I just don't like the little bastard. He's a sissy and a fascist.

—You ought to control yourself more.

—You're right, he said. —And I'm going to start working on that right away.

—What's that you're going to work on? Goodman asked loudly behind them.

—My backhand. It's gone to pieces.

He's clever and he's unhappy and he probably hates his wife underneath it all, Goodman told himself. Guess she could be tough in the clinches. Which reminds me, shall I get stoned tonight or not? If I do, sweet Janet here won't want to do my bed judo which is OK because she's embarrassing without her clothes on. Like one of those store-window mannequins stripped.

—What do you think the animals represent in Mandy's dream? Janet asked, quite without a trap in her question, once they were seated on the porch and had gotten themselves coffee or whiskey refreshments. Hunt and Anna were still upstairs.

Goodman cackled. —Here we go!

—I used to know a girl who dreamed about unicorns all the time, Jack said as if he were a gentle old party pirouetting in slow motion on a grass tennis court and he'd just lobbed this one over real high.

Erika looked up at the ceiling to make sure she wasn't being watched or listened to by either of the Hunts. —They undoubtedly represent her parents.

Janet sat up and looked serious. —Why do you say that? Couldn't they symbolize the nameless fears children are always prey to?

—I don't think there is any such thing as a nameless fear, Erika informed her. —It's much easier—in fact absolutely essential—for Mandy to see animals rather than her parents who clearly do frighten or disturb her.

—How do you know? Goodman asked, also looking around to see if the Hunts had perhaps sneaked within earshot.

—Erika is her analyst, Jack said, smiling at everybody except his wife. —She sees her three times a week up in an old sycamore tree.

Erika didn't give him even a nod on that one. —You can tell just by watching the child, she continued. —The parents hate each other and Mandy hates them both. She feels very guilty about this, so she arranges to have the parents punish her by way of her dream.

For a few moments after Erika launched this cluster of insights, Janet looked intensely at her, her hand supporting her simple chin, then made a hmm sound, and said, —That's fascinating. You're sort of uncanny, aren't you?

—Yes, isn't she though.

It was Anna. She was standing at the side pantry door which they had all forgotten had a stairway leading upstairs; she had changed into what should have been a breathtakingly sexy housedress. Janet gasped. —Oh God! she said, and put her hand over her mouth.

Jack jumped up and quickly and bearishly threw his arm around Anna's shoulder. —She didn't mean a thing by it, Anna. We were just shooting the breeze in fun. You know.

Erika got up, looking embarrassed and angry at the same time. —You were standing there all the time listening, weren't you?

—What difference does it make? Anna answered, walking out of Jack's frightened embrace and into the room.

—A hell of a lot! Erika shouted. —It's sneaky, it lacks dignity, and it's an invasion of privacy, that's what.

Anna made a sound of amused contempt. —Oh really? It lacks dignity? Just how much dignity is there in saying such things about people who presumably are your friends? Please tell me that.

Janet wanted to cry like a little girl and run from the room and all these brutal grown-ups, run to a sweet innocent place where there were dolls and cute dresses. But she was frozen in her chair.

—What I said, Erika replied, slowly and with razor precision, putting her hands on her hips, —had the dignity of truth. You know and I know and anybody else with eyes and ears and half a brain knows that you and Philip are a lousy match and have a lousy marriage and two very, very sick children.

Goodman stood up, dragging Janet gently out of her numb position at the same moment. —I just remembered we left something cooking on the stove, and he grinned unhappily. He started out of the room with Janet in tow. —I just hope it's not burned or bloated or anything. So long, everybody.

The desperate and slick departure of the two nonantagonists left the three others suspended inanimately for a pause, as if the background music had stopped playing in a tight movie.

Jack had not felt so stupid and helpless in years. —Oh come on now, Erika. Let's drop it, OK?

—Shouldn't you attend to your own doubtful marriage before you start investigating other people's? Anna said.

Erika stepped up closer to Anna, and her face was an ecstatic storm. —Baby, you would give your right arm for my "doubtful" marriage and both your arms for my marriage bed.

Anna smiled through pain and sickness. —You're being obscene, she whispered.

Erika moved a little closer, and for a second Jack thought she was going to hit Anna. —Anybody who can sleep with a fat bearded dwarf, a detective, just because he provides financial security doesn't know what obscenity means.

Jack cringed within, a cringe of sorrow yet of truth, and just stared at Anna's pudgy, defenseless face, until its farce of haughtiness disintegrated and tears began rolling down her cheeks, and then he quickly took Erika by the arm and started out of the house.

Hunt's disembodied voice, preceding him down the regular staircase, followed them out the door. —Man, the voice said, —it's hell when kids start dreaming.

Jack and Erika were several yards into the rustling underbrush area separating their house from the Hunts' before anything was said. Jack spoke first, even though he didn't want to. —Why did you have to do that to that poor woman?

Erika's response was amused and light, childish almost, and completely lacking the black steel her voice contained back in the Hunts' house. —Oh, she had it coming to her. She's a fake and a damn hypocrite.

—Even so . . .

She jerked her head toward him. —You're not taking her side, are you?

—Of course not.

—Good, because that would just be too incredible, she said, and ducked under a sudden tree branch. They walked on through the faintly moonlit trees and bushes, not saying any more, and finally came onto the soft, thickly-grassed, half-hidden slope up to their cottage. —You know something, Erika began in a tingly, high voice, slowing down her arm-in-arm walk, —I feel very sexy for some reason.

—Oh?

—Yes, she said, stopping and putting her arms around him. —And I want you very much, and she kissed him hard and very passionately.

—Now? Jack asked, in a few seconds, holding her urgent body.

—Yes, right now. Here, and she pulled him down onto the dark, mad grass next to a large bush.

From an attic bedroom window in the Hunts' house, young Peter Hunt was watching their scene through a pair of binoculars he'd permanently borrowed two years ago from a smaller cousin. He'd been fooling around at the window, looking at the moon and at the windows of other cottages, when Erika and Jack left his house, and he had been following them in their walk home.

—They're wrestling! he said aloud. He was very pleased, and he started downstairs to tell his parents that the Harpers were fighting on the grass. He was sure they would be pleased, too. And somewhere in his mind, lurking expectantly, was the notion that because of this special present he was bringing them, his parents would like him a little better.

Y ou may think that a girl who spends so much of her head time floating in and out of other people and places just wouldn't be worth a tinker's damn when it came to the moment-by-moment survival in her own shoes. But you would be wrong. You would be whistling the enemy's tune regarding dreamers and their unfitness for anything as sound and simple as taking a shit in the toilet rather than in an unattended French horn. Anna is my gardener-in-residence here on the Barge of Friendly Relations with All Those Countries Outside the Superpower Axis. She is personally in charge of the herb scene. And I want to tell you that this girl has magic in her fingers. Our cannabis plants are the talk of the town. They are four feet high and as strong as lions in November. Anna cares for these divine plants as few mothers care for their own children. She talks to them. She breathes on them. She waters them with her exquisite piss. She caresses them. She even places them between her succulent thighs so that they may soak up the sublime power of pussy. So that when you ultimately smoke them you are taking into yourself the heavenly pleasures of hot pussy as well as hot pot. And after such an experience, equivalent, I should say, to playing bocce with God himself, you can no longer go back to grits and grovel and solitary confinement with dwarf jailers who are always misbehavin' on you. And I'm telling you something: after those plants have spent a night between Anna's superjuicy thighs, they stand up and growl. They yodel. They do somersaults. They yell out of the window at passing boats. You've never seen anything like it. You can't roll anything but bombers with shit like ours.

And when it comes to merchandizing and marketing and distributing and reaching the buyer, this girl is beyond belief. She makes Billy Graham look like a fuckin' deaf-mute. She creates traffic jams when there's no traffic. Housewives drop their vaunted cheeses and hurl themselves at her as though she were the last train from Bombay. Dutch uncles stop dressing down their nephews and engineers abandon seepage. Milkmaids flee their fields of swollen udders and tulip-mongers shove their tulips up their asses. Divine chaos reigns and you couldn't find Rembrandt in a month of haystacks if your life depended on it. Surely you are getting the picture. Good.

Let's see now. What else have I been up to . . . Language. Fragments of language swarm through my brain . . . language looking for a home . . . like an army that's been disbanded . . . rumpled wantons . . . sly stalwarts . . . doors opening into a disheveled future . . . murderous streets lying in wait for the first innocent footfall . . . maligned voids . . . glistening imprecisions . . . relentless ambiguities . . . succulent obscurities . . . toiling bells that may never toll. . . . If I could only press them together, I could be validated by their meaning. . . . Am I a rumpled wanton blown off the streets of an exhausted city? Are my ears filled with bells tolling the mistakes of others? Do I hear myself scrambling over walls that separate nothing from nothing?

Exquisite voices I should know are calling to me. They have the intense intimacy of the remote. This remoteness forces me to concentrate my entire being into a pinpoint of awareness. I become a moment of excruciating awareness. I must understand what they are telling me. My life depends upon this. I will cease to exist if I do not grasp these messages. They are whispering with a subdued roar. They are saying: "Morning came. Fire was still smoldering in Hiroshima. I entered the city. Many people were dead in the fire prevention tank, their bodies scorched black. I saw a dead woman, her body scorched black, holding a baby in her arms, still in a running position. Utterly incredible, but this was reality."

"I tried desperately to rescue my baby daughter, trapped inside the collapsed house, and scratched at the clay wall with my fingernails. But when I finally succeeded in opening a hole, flames had enveloped the scene. . . ."

I writhe in agony within these words. They are defining me, they are creating me. They are covering me with ashes and burned skin. Now through the pain and the ashes other words are coming to seize me, to suck up my soul:

"Nobody is more disturbed over the use of the atomic bombs than I am, but I was greatly disturbed over the unwarranted attack by the Japanese on Pearl Harbor. . . ." But these words are being attacked by other words: "The city seemed to be wrapped in fire. A small fire prevention water tank overflowed with a number of victims, all dead. . . ."

The words are fighting, the sounds of one voice are trying to destroy the sounds of the other . . . and their murder of our prisoners of war. The only language they seem to understand is the one that we have been using to bombard them. . . . Other words leap upon those words and are strangling them. . . . Those dead on the streets were scorched black but those in the tank were swollen red. . . . When you have to deal with a blast . . . Mother! Run! You must . . . you have to treat . . . run away! But my mother prays . . . him as a blast . . . begging for forgiveness. . . . It is most regrettable but nevertheless . . . the fat burned and melted and the flames formed . . . nevertheless . . . Truman's decision to drop the bomb was one of noninterference, basically . . . formed a pillar . . . Truly this is hell!

—Listen, Harry. I think it's just plain silly to go to all the trouble we've gone to and spend all the money we've spent and then not drop the darn thing, y'know? I mean, shit. Think of what people will say: What's the matter with you guys anyway? You chicken? You yellow?

—Yeah, yellow. That's the color of those little Jap bastards. An' buck teeth and all those eyeglasses. And they can't even talk right. Rottsa ruck! Run racon rettuc an romato randwich, pweese! Who needs that kinda shit.

—Not us, I'll tell you that. No sir, Mr. President. Not in a coon's age do we need such disgusting displays from all those rising sons. My own personal opinion, sir, is that there are about a hundred and three million too many Japs in this world, if you know what I mean.

—I think that sums it up perfectly, Harry. This would be a far cleaner world without all those buck teeth and all that spittle an' that yellow midget baseball in imitation of their white betters.

—Whattaya say, Randy?

—Show them who's boss. Wipe the little buggers out completely. Teach 'em a lesson they'll never forget.

—Yeah. Don't even leave 'em a memory to remember what they shouldn't forget. Vaboom! That's the ticket.

—You said yourself they were beasts, Mr. President. Dirty little monkeys. Fish-suckin' baboons chatterin' away with their chopsticks up their asses while they're copyin' our family Kodaks without even so much as a thank you Mr. and Mrs. America.

—Burn 'em to a crisp, sir. Incinerate them. Barbecue every last one of those chimps before they can scratch and bite our boys and give them rabies on their beaches while we're merely invading them like decent human beings. What will we tell our grandchildren, Mr. President, when they ask us how come they were born with a case of Jap rabies? Just roll that over in your mind, sir.

—Thank you, gentlemen. I want to thank you from the bottom of my heart. And if Bess were here she'd thank you too, for helping me make up my mind. For giving me the courage to perform every American boy's dream, 'cause what's life like if an American boy can't dream?

—You're bringin' tears to my eyes, sir.

—We owe this one to Daniel Boone, Mr. President.

—An' Huck Finn! Don't leave Huck out!

—The names of every decent American man, woman, and child will be written on this bomb, gentlemen.

—Hear! Hear!

—And it'll sure as shit show them sneaky Russkies a thing or two. Whattaya say, General?

—Oh yeah. It'll take the clouds right outta their peepers all right. Those dirty commie vodka-heads, lustin' after other folks' capital gains.

—Gentlemen, this is a historic moment. I hereby declare this to be National Zap Jap Day. It'll be a holiday for our nippers and hookers an' snookers and cookers and chiggers and diggers.

—Hot damn! Come on, fellas, let's head for the bar. Drinks are on me.

—Ah no, Randy. I'm buyin'. You bought when we invaded Mexico, 'member?

—I'm calling my wife at the hairdresser's. She'll be tickled pink.

—OK, you guys! Let's hear it for Betsy Ross!

—Now, fellas, I've got a little surprise for everybody. Right here in my lunch pail. Here we ... no, wait. Those are Fig Newtons Bess packed for me. Here are the surprises. Aren't they neat? Perfect little lifelike figures of incinerated Japs. Don't worry. There's one for everybody. Had 'em made up by a nephew of Bess's, Jeepers Hoxie, a real nice boy who went into prosthetic rubber work after his own two legs were blown off in a huntin' accident in the Ozarks by his younger kid brother Bubba who had been sneakin' more'n his share of the sneaky pete from the mason jar where they kep' it thinkin' Jeepers was a hibernatin' bear in a pile of pinecones when of course it was Jeepers himself sleepin' off a huntin' drunk and had hid hisself under those pinecones so's the nosy possums couldn't piss on him, 'cause when those darn Ozark possums ain't munchin' acorns an' dingleberries, they're pissin' on things, piss piss piss, mostly on things that can't piss back, 'cause possums don't have any concept of fair piss or be pissed on, they're so low on dear Mother Nature's totem pole they can't think straight, which is one good reason for them to be put into possum pie as soon as it is possible and quickly gobbled up the same way you'd gobble up any other kinda pie 'cept maybe hair pie, which when you come right down to it is a matter of personal preference, I mean the way you gobble it, that being something you just can't legislate, no matter how hard you try with a Congress always out in the lobby shakin' hands with itself. Hair pie ... I was fightin' in the world war trenches with a fellow doughboy who was a real whiz at gobblin' French hair pie an' he never got tired of sayin', the main thing about eatin' hair pie is you can't let your mind wander, you've got to keep a clear head on your shoulders when you're givin' head. He said he'd a lot rather draw a bead on a French girl's forest of the night, those being his words, not mine, than shoot a German in the head any day. Which may be one reason why it took us so long to bring the fat heinie to his knees and show him in no uncertain terms that his favorite sauerkraut and pigs' knuckles would never in a million years darken the door of our Thanksgivin' turkey dinner. That the American way of life which had been won from the savage Indians just wouldn't stand for havin' a chorus of oink! oink! drown out the cherished gobble gobble sounds as thousands of pigs chargin' through fields of steamin' hot sauerkraut, in violation of every Pilgrim's hard-won right to worship as he pleased which brought him and his hungry loved ones over here in the first place from England where if you didn't kowtow to the Queen's crown and its insatiable demands on your private life and your purse strings, it was your ass. Maybe up there swingin' on the gibbet, maybe just languishing away in some smelly hoosegow surrounded by indentured whores soaked in cheap gin and mangy little limehouse ragamuffins singin' the blues who learned how to pick pockets long before they knew how to pick their nose, along with hordes of fartin' deadbeats who didn't have the decency to pay their debts on time when they said they would. Which brings to mind the sober fact that the Queen's government owes us a pile from way back which the last time I talked to Bess they hadn't coughed up anything on account. They're running that royal navy of theirs on the milk of human kindness. Which is runnin' low these days if you take into account all the meanness you run into every time you try to make a deal with somebody who oughta know which side of the fence they're supposed to be sittin' on in the interests of their biggest investors when it comes to profit and loss in the free world. Some of these guys are so dumb they don't know which side their bread is buttered on when it comes to droppin' a few bombs on people to get things straight so business can go on as usual. Those English smart-asses, they better climb up outta their Yorkshire puddings real quick if they expect to get any of the gravy that's left. Otherwise, they're gonna be eatin' borscht soup and I mean borscht soup without any cream in it unless you happen to be a Jew. Those Jews, oh boy, I mean they take the cake. They go right on feedin' their faces with all that rich, funny food even though the Christian world is threatening to collapse around their kinky heads. It never ceases to amaze me how some people think the quickest road to salvation is through their mouths. Ever see one of those Jews eatin' by the light of his religious candles? Boy, I want to tell you, it's a sight for God-fearin' eyes. Why, a decent person can't even spell the names of some of that stuff they call food. Much less put it in his mouth. Keptlocks an' felt fish an' stuffed Erma an' mothball soup rubbed with chicken fat an' latch keys in cream sauce . . . an' scarfs with gooseberry jam . . . an' stewed perches' meat surrounded by lungin' slivers. . . . Why, it makes my skin crawl just to think about what they musta made poor Jesus eat for his last supper before they put the shaft to him. You'd think they'd have the decency to give him a nice normal square meal of steak 'n' mashed with gravy 'n' some strawberry shortcake like we do when we're about to put some criminal in the hot seat at Sing Sing to end his reign of terror. But not those old Jews. They can't do anything right, an' that's why their little asses are always up shit creek with people burning crosses on their manicured lawns an' throwin' big rocks through their synagogue windows while they're down on their hands an' knees wailing in that soupy language of theirs 'bout Moses 'n' Sodom 'n' Gonorrhea 'n' that feisty little midge Dave whatshisname who tricked that big fella Golightly or something, into lookin' down the barrel of his sling-shot saying there was a naked hootch dancer at the other end doing her stuff. I mean, you'd think a guy that big with a joint even bigger coulda got himself just about any piece of ass around 'cause you can't tell me that any real woman worth her pussy juices wouldn'ta give her eye teeth just to look at a peter so big she could chin herself on it an' then some. I'm not an expert on those things, but I'll bet you when it came to knockin' down all those temples and stuff, he didn't do it with his long hair. Oh no. He did it with a hard-on. Took that thing big as a redwood and swung it around Bam! Bam! And those old temples just fell down flat like a buncha nigger pin boys when somebody bowls a strike. But that's the kinda historical information that's kept from our little ones in their Sunday schools 'cause it's subversive. Just let your mind wander. Just imagine what those children would do with their dreams if they ever found out what you could do with a forty-two-foot hard-on. You think they'd wanna knuckle down and get a nine-to-five job in the A & P? Or learn to count sheep so's they could become sheepherders and live in the Rocky Mountains nine times outta ten being buried under snow-drifts and havin' to wait for a passel uh Saint Bernard dogs drunk outta their skulls on small bottles of brandy to mosey by and drag them out? No sir. They'd be practicin' stretchin' their meat. They'd be floggin' the bishop mornin' noon 'n' night to the tune of "Johnny Comes Marchin' Home Agin" played on a broken-down harmonica behind locked doors while their mother climbed the walls lookin' for the juvenile authorities to take matters into their own two hands which wouldn't be wrapped around their dongs 'cause they'd missed the boat on the inside dope of Golightly's giant dong. I mean you'd have to build thousands of new brick reformatories to put those millions of cock-crazy kids in and when you did you'd have to buy thousands of miles of good strong rope in the open market to tie their hands with to keep them from whangin' away on their misspent whangs. And then where would you be if you all of a sudden needed an army of young boys to shoulder arms aginst worldwide communist rumblings? And takeovers? I'll tell you where you'd be. You'd be out on a limb covered with pig fat, that's where. And that's exactly why I am going before Congress tomorrow morning before they've had a chance to tuck into their first of many orders of two over easy with a side of hash browns the size of the Lincoln Memorial and urge them to wipe their greasy double or nothin' chins and get crackin' to pass legislation to force our feckless youth to take its hands outta its pockets with strategic holes in them so's they can get at themselves better and put those hands around a hoe handle 'steada their weenies and do their country some good cleanin' up those rows that've been so hard to hoe on all the rollin' farms in our wonderful hard-pressed bread baskets won from the stubborn wilderness by your hardy ancestors and mine. Give 'em rakes and shovels and axes and neat uniforms and head them into the gullies and gulches and ravines and clean those places up good. Get rid of all the dead wood and underbrush and sticky wickets and stinky underhanded night-crawlers and turn those places into veritable gardens of Allah if you'll excuse the expression. No that don't mean that Moslems and Mohammedans and those other guys couldn't worship there if they wanted to. Because this country is not a place to deny anybody no matter how kinky his hair the right to fall on his knees in religious fervor, wherever and whenever that urge hits him, but the point here is you gotta control that kinda thing, otherwise before you know it, the birds and the bees and the deer and the antelope will start playin' Arab-type games where the buffalo roam, and I wanta tell you, I don't know how much you know about such games but take it from me, the last thing you want to see is our wildlife goin' ape and turnin' their backs on onward Christian soldiers while permittin' phlegmy gutteral sounds to issue from their throats in singin' the praises of the Koran and drivin' our cowboys and plainsmen and fresh-meat hunters plain crazy tryin' to figure out what in tarnation they're sayin' as they mow 'em down with their trusty Winchester .38 repeatin' rifles for their tasty meat and warm furry hides. No sir. A little religious freedom goes a long way when it comes to unholy crap like that, which is why I've instructed our attorney general to be damn choosy when it comes to lettin' certain types whose name I won't mention sneak off Ellis Island and stand before some judge pledgin' allegiance to the American flag with one hand on the Bible and the other real one holdin' the Koran or some other dirty book under their wrap-around sheets or burned nooses. Oh no. You let that kinda thing get outta hand and before you know it the smell of roastin' lamb and oily grape leaves will be lordin' it over the matchless smell of T-bone steaks and juicy king-size hamburgers waftin' up your nose from alien barbecue pits next door. Along with the disappearance of toilet paper, 'cause the plain unvarnished truth is those dark kinky-haired people wipe their asses with their bare fingers. If you don't believe me, just trot down to their embassies and take a look at the walls inside. All smeared with doo-doo, centuries of it, where even their best handpicked emissaries who should know better reverting to their origins in spite of our efforts with worldwide flush toilets have disposed of the remaining clinging pieces after doin' number two in any old corner so long as one of their many fat, naked, sex-driven belly-dancing harem wives isn't croonin' in it. See for yourselves, then tell me how you feel about more liberal immigration laws. Permitting just anybody with two eyes and a nose to get in here, with their pockets stuffed with figs. Just ask your spick 'n' span wives to get a load of it after they've taken care of their morning baking chores and sent the kiddies off to their three R's. Not a single one of which is ever gonna spell Ramdas this or Ramdas that as long as I'm manning the till at the White House. Not by a long shot. Four score and seven years ago may not be the same as five thousand years before Christ but it's damn well long enough to learn that this country was not founded on unlimited crude-oil imports from sandy places that don't know decent Americans can heat their homes with wood-burning pot-bellied Ben Franklins when the time comes for a showdown. You think old Ben would of taken any shit from a buncha bums who ride camels everywhere they go even if it's only to go to the corner slave market to fetch a new cleaning woman every time the one they got falls down on the job due to the fact that they don't give her enough to eat, good hot food? The answer to that dumb question is no! You hear me: No! You think a man who is smart enough to invent electricity just by flying a kite is just gonna sit there and grin while a herd of scabby nomads ride camels all over him? You crazy or something? You want me to call in the Marines to fix your wagon good and proper? Huh? You want me to provoke your license to freedom of speech? Lemme see your passport, you dirty commie cocksucker! Fork it over before I count to ten and blow your fuckin' head off with this blunderin' buss I've got here in my hands! Come on, fork it over!

—Buster Bunny! Stop that yelling this very minute and come into the house. It's raining cats and dogs out there. You want to catch your death? There now. That's a good boy. Take this towel and dry yourself off and I'll fix you a cup of hot Ovaltine. Good grief, Buster Bunny. It seems to me you could think of a better way to spend your day off than standing out in the courtyard naked yelling your head off. Why don't you go down to the Y for a swim? Or you could go to the USIA library and read some back issues of *National Geographic*. There's all kinds of fascinating stuff in those magazines. Colorful tribal dances and big limestone caves and crocodiles and lovely vanishing species. Just oodles of wonderful stuff. You can learn all about the world you happen to live in. Yes. That's a wonderful idea. I'll pack you a couple of peanut butter sandwiches and some of your favorite Lorna Doone cookies and you can sit there and read till the cows come home. And then tonight after you've taken those wonderful new pills the camp doctor gave you we can watch *Gunsmoke*, and you can dress up in that cowboy suit I got you from J. C. Penney and make believe you're a gunslinger or something like that. You can shoot it out with the TV set. Won't that be fun? Hmm? And if you're a real good boy, Buster Bunny, and you're not all tired out and frazzled from watching your programs, we can do some sex stuff. Only you must promise me, scout's honor, Buster Bunny, that you won't make any of those crazy animal sounds. Barking and whelping like you're a hyena up a tree, like you did the last time when you woke up all the neighbors. And Mr. González Suárez ran out with his shotgun shouting that the forests were coming for his wife and children and he was going to kill everything with a furry head on it. My God. That was really something. These spicks are the jumpiest people I've ever run into. Too bad they never had a nice invasion from the Vikings when that was the thing to do. Some of that icy blue blood from the Scandinavian peninsula would have gone a long way toward cooling these spicks' genes off. Every time you lay out a simple little fart, these frantic nuts think the revolution's begun and somebody's taken a potshot at them. God only knows what's going to happen when Mr. Franco kicks the bucket. It'll be like the Fourth of July ten times over. There won't be a single thing left that's still breathing, except maybe a few nuns down in the catacombs where they were hiding under each other's big black skirts, a disgusting subject I'd rather not go into. And what I'm referring to is true historical fact, not just over-the-fence gossip. Take that woman Teresa of Avila. The way she carried on simply boggles your poor mind. She was into fits and seizures and conniptions like you and I are into sneezes. When she wasn't having one she was having the other, and gnashing her teeth and pulling her hair and screaming to high heaven. Her idea of fun was to run naked through the streets asking people to beat her and kick her and spit on her. And when there weren't any people around, like in the middle of the night, she'd throw herself down on her hands and knees and beg the dogs to piss on her, barking like a dog herself. And after they'd drown her several times in piss, and you'd think she just couldn't sink any lower, she'd scream at them to have their way with her. Which was really quite a pretty sight if you can imagine it. Packs of mangy street dogs growling and whining and slobbering and mounting her like she was another dog. Scratching and biting her while they were jamming their big red slippery weeners into her, and I'll bet it didn't matter to those crazy animals or to her either which hole they got into either. Any hole in a storm. That howling madwoman fucked every mongrel dog in town. Now I don't care what you think about freedom of religious expression—you can't tell me that isn't a pretty far out way to worship Christ. You really do have to ask yourself what He thought about it. Did He need all that screaming filth for His glorification? Can we hear Him say, Oh boy! Crazy hot cunt and barking dogs' pricks! That's for Me. That'll do it. That'll get Me going again. I rise on the orgasmic juices of bestiality! Come on, Teresa! Pump that big hot ass of yours! Squeeze those dogs' dicks dry with your maniac cunt muscles! Go, dogs, go! Slam it to her! Shoot your mongrel wads into her greedy twat! Yeah! More! Fuck your brains out for the kid from Nazareth! Every juicy spasm is a vote for the Jew son of God. Show the mobs what real devotion is all about. Wipe the smiles off the faces of those no-good establishment disbelievers with your foul gutter humping. Hang in there until there's not one dog hard-on left in all Spain. I want to hear every dog in this paella of a country roll over on its back and say, That's it, boss. I don't have one drop more of fuck juice left in me. Now, can we hear the Redeemer saying that? Not likely. Not likely at all. That is, if I've got my Christian religion straight. Of course, there's always the chance I don't. A person can't be sure of anything in this mixed-up fucking world. It may be that what Christianity is really all about is man's return to his dark animal origins. A trip back to the prehistoric forests and swamps. Long before anybody ever thought of washing up before dinner. Those hairy ape ancestors of ours would have laughed their heads off at the idea. They never even bothered to wipe the blood off their faces from one saber-tooth tiger feed to the next. And they didn't waste any time on the niceties of knives and forks either. They just tore a hole in the stomach of those flying long-tailed deer and ate and ate until their heads pushed out on the other side, and all that was left of said unlucky animal was a little fur sticking to the chops of those hairy ape men. Then they ate each other up for dessert. And after that they shoved their half-man, half-beast jammers into the nearest hole at hand, no matter who or what the owner looked like. I'll bet they even jazzed birds. Which must have been a pretty sight indeed, because in those days birds were the size of elephants and just as strong. So you don't have to stretch your imagination any to get a picture of Joe Neanderthal fucking away while flying in the sky, because certainly that's what those old-style giant birds did while they were having it socked to them by horny Joe, who had to hold on for dear life in the process. And that probably explains the origin of the expression "a flying fuck." In a way, it doesn't sound half bad. Who said that beds had to be the last word in regards to hanky panky? I knew a fellow once who loved to fuck underwater. Undoubtedly this urge could be traced right back to those prehistoric times when his particular ancestors were into fucking fish. Certainly they could hold their breath for hours because their lungs hadn't yet been rotted out by cigarette smoke and overall pollution. Jonah fucked whales, didn't he? And that Captain Ahab destroyed his whole life because he had the hots for whale ass. And what do you suppose mermaids were? Half fish, that's what. It's a matter of historical record that every single sailor of old was willing to give his right arm for a piece of hot mermaid pussy. You don't have to take my word for it. Read the history books yourself. And that practice didn't die out with the collapse of the Roman Empire either. Look at our own dearly beloved Shakespeare. Where was it he got himself turned on if it wasn't in the Mermaid Tavern? Everywhere you looked in that place was a picture of a voluptuous red-hot mermaid showing her snatch. And smiling that Come-with-me-to-the-Casbah smile. On busy weekend nights, you had to fight to get a chair in there it was so crowded with drunken mermaid freaks with galloping hard-ons. And what do you think the cult of eating caviar is all about? Eating fish pussy, that's what. And finally, I'd like to call your attention to the worldwide fact that the Church itself has set aside one whole day of the week, Friday, for fish-fucking. From dawn till dusk hundreds of millions of horny Catholics eat fish pussy till they fall to the floor under the weight of fish scales. Just think about that the next time you pass a church. Sex and seafood. My own very current lothario tosses down a dozen big juicy slippery throbbing fresh Spanish oysters before we go at it because he swears they increase his potency, and as the lucky recipient of this potency, I want to tell you that it's simply incredible, and I'm not exaggerating. You get a stud with oysters in his tank and you'll have such high-octane jamming you'll be counting stars at high noon. When Big José gets through with me, I don't know whether I'm coming or going. There isn't a square inch on this divine body of mine that hasn't creamed with orgasmic joy. My God, just thinking about it is making my mouth water and my cunt churn and my ass sing. Oooh. I'd give a million dollars right now for a taste of his roaring prick. When he slams that ten-inch flaming master-piece into me I think I'm riding the heavenly express. In my mouth, in my cunt, up my ass, going two hundred miles an hour round the curves. And when I come, oh my God! when I come it feels like I'm falling through the clouds. Clouds are in my cunt, and airplanes are flying through my cunt, and birds gliding and stars flashing, and then the sun is coming up between my legs and you may think I've gone off my head when I say that a thousand angels are singing down there. That's right. Maybe two thousand, if I ever felt the need to count them, which I haven't, I'll be perfectly candid enough to tell you. I'm not one of those suspicious small-minded people who feel compelled to look into God's mouth to see if he's got any cavities. People like that simply don't deserve the better things in life, that's my opinion. Let 'em eat cake, phooey. Let 'em eat mud pies. That'll teach 'em a thing or two. My dear papa used to say, D., compassion is a sucker's game. You're your brother's keeper all right—in jail. And he knew what he was talkin' about. He ran a little grocery store back in Tampa where on any given day if you looked up suddenly you'd see half a dozen black sambos milling around the penny candy counter with larceny on their faces, just waiting for a chance to grab a handful of licorice whips or jujubes or mint leaves or Tootsie Rolls or jawbreakers or jelly beans or chocolate soldiers or bubble gum or raisinettes. Those shines would rather have a mouth full of candy in 'em than a T-bone steak seven inches thick covered with mushrooms. Plus several bottles of Dr. Pepper or Nehi. You could hear all that stuff sloshing around in their stomachs a mile away. Especially when they were putting on one of their bugaboo ritual dances preparatory to descending upon you with their razors to even the score regarding the white man's burden. That was the number-one idea in their baboon minds. And I'm telling you someday it's going to happen. The day of the avenging black razors. It'll make Custer's Last Stand look like a children's picnic. The land of the free and the home of the brave is going to drown in blood, mark my words. The good old USA is living on borrowed time, there's no question about that. And those bloodthirsty darkies aren't going to be satisfied with killing all of the living. They're going to tear the dead from their graves and throw the pieces to the winds like so much confetti. And I want to tell you those winds are going to howl, 'cause, they're going to be the winds of hell, my friends. There's nothing going to be left in that doomed country but cinders and ashes and dried blood and the crazy screams of the crazy niggers. The last laugh is going to be on Mr. George Washington and Company. The great American dream is going to be the worst nightmare of all time. And things aren't going to be so hunky-dory over here either. Oh no. Just stick your pretty heads out of the windows and look up and down the streets. Now tell me what you see gobs and gobs of. Soldiers and more soldiers. And they're carrying pistols and machine guns. Now you'd have to be downright brainless to think they're out there because everything is rosy. Those creepy soldiers are walking on top of a volcano. The people are just waiting for the right moment to make their move. José was telling me just yesterday, This place could blow up at any moment. And he should know. He's with the secret police, and it's his business to know. A big prick is not the only gripping thing he's got tucked under his shirttail. He's got more secrets under there than Columbus had pants rabbits. He can tell you how many illegal passports have been sold here in the last week and the names of the guys who bought them. He knows just how many pistols are hidden under pillows and the names that are written on the bullets they're going to shoot. There isn't a grope in a latrine that doesn't get back to him in an hour. He's got informers in every crevice of this town. And I'm using that word to cover a multitude of places and sins, including the wet one between your legs. Every confession booth in every church around here is bugged by him. He could write a book ten inches thick about the sins of every short-legged servant girl in Rota. And you know something? He doesn't give a Chinese shit. "Could not care less who is doing what to whom. I merely record it. I am a machine ticking in the service of the state. If tomorrow morning the communists in this town blew the heads off all the fascists, I would go right on dipping pieces of bread in my soft-boiled eggs as if nothing had happened."

And he's got the CIA's number too. He knows what they're up to around here. He can't bear that bunch of spooks. They're meddling outsiders. They've got no right to be in Spain, he says. They should stay at home and fuck up their own country. If he had his way, he'd throw them all out tomorrow, headfirst. They bring a terrible stink to my country, he said. That stink will ruin your nose forever. It is the smell of your own death. And once you have smelled it, you cannot ever get away from it. It is like the mirror on the wall. Once you have seen yourself in it, you cannot ever forget who you are. José has confided in me that he kills one of those people every chance he gets. They always think that one of those crazy left-wingers with dirty underwear has done it. That makes the most logical sense to them. The other would simply be unthinkable.

. . . found his body floating in the harbor with a nice round hole in his head. There is never an investigation of course because that would let the cat out of the bag, as you say. The whole thing takes place in a beautiful silence. A silence that is like the Middle Ages. Lope de Vega's silence that caresses and supports floating bodies, in which mountains grow and trees whirl. You can taste it and feel it, virgin velvet. . . . It beckons to you. . . . You can vanish into it without ever losing yourself.

You know who the last person was who talked like that? It was Sabu the Elephant Boy. He was always carrying on that way about elephants. You knew he thought there was a place, a somewhere else, and that he could and would disappear into that place, leaving no trace. It was really something more than your mind could handle. You'd be with him but he wouldn't be there. He'd be in elephants. Just like Mr. Albert Einstein, who became as we all know a problem in higher mathematics. Mrs. Einstein would put a piece of apple strudel on his plate and then watch it disappear into outer space. Of course, I suppose she got used to it after a time. She could do that because she was a Jew and Jews have to get used to all kinds of things. That's what the Bible is all about, y'know. How the Jews had to adapt themselves to this and that . . . To watching the Red Sea part its hair in the middle just as everybody was planning to float a boat on it. To gritting their teeth and swallowing their tongues when the Romans would decide that their ranks needed thinning and started chopping away at them with those mean stubby swords shoutin' More Jew legs! More Jew arms! Hack! Hack! Jew heads! Jew cocks! Jew asses! Chop! Chop! They had to just sit there and take it, and grin and say, Oh boy! How wonderful! Thank you very much, sir. We certainly do appreciate your generous efforts on our behalf and what you see are tears of joy and gratitude. We Jews had a population control problem and we just didn't know how to deal with it. You strong Roman boys don't fool around when it comes to solving population problems. No sir. You just go chop! chop! and that's that. Now we've got plenty of chopped Jew liver to go around. That's a famous Jew delicacy, as you know. Ha! Ha! That's a joke, Mr. Roman Soldier, sir. What you might call an "in" joke. You know, black Jew humor. We always crack funny jokes when we hurt the most. Ha! Ha! It's in our genes. Blue Jew genes. Get it? Ha! Ha! You oughta see Al Jolson singing "Blue Jew Genes" in blackface. It's a riot. Listen . . . no kidding . . . next time you're down this way drop in and have a plate of real Jew chopped chicken liver with us. On rye bread with caraway seeds. That's the way we serve it. But listen. If you prefer it on pizza bread, we can do that too. No sweat, really. We certainly understand regional taste differences. We know that tastes are acquired at one's mother's knee and Jew mama knee isn't the same as dago . . . oops . . . Roman mama knee. Shit. That goes without saying. Nobody ever heard a Jew shout, Mamma mia! immediately upon learning that there was gonna be matzo ball soup and cheese blintzes for breakfast. Not unless the Jew in question was Dean Martin, and he's not a Jew. I mean, he's got a real terrific Jew-boy act an' all, but it's just an act he puts on, at places like Grossinger's and the Concord where people let their hair down and ski on slopes of slippery chicken fat and rassle zaftig Jewish princesses to the ground, if they can that is, because some of those juicy Jew princesses are strong as anything. Having spent a surprising amount of time acquiring black karate belts in expensive fitness gyms in such heavily populated Jewish hideouts as Great Neck and Westhampton and Riverdale, along with learning how to drive Cadillac limos and Rolls Royce station wagons loaded to the gills with hot pastrami sandwiches and kosher dill pickles leaping out of the windows like crazy salmon going the wrong way down Wilshire Boulevard. Diamond rings on their fingers bigger than the island of Capri. Those fat shiny women have nothing better to do with themselves. They've got nothing but time on their hands. All their grubby housework is being done by dumb gentile women who spend their lives on their hands and knees scrubbing Jew floors. They don't know what up looks like. Pretty soon they can't stand up anymore, and they die down there like bugs. So the Jews just scrape them up off the floor like they really are bugs and pack them into special boxes made for the occasion and mail them back to Ireland. Where their relatives stuff them all bent up into those peat bogs which contrary to what you may think is not the end. Because after some time they are dug up all encased in black bog by hungry aristocratic archaeologists from Oxford and Cambridge who exhibit these miserable creatures as bona fide pre-historic bog dwellers. And school kids by the thousands are forced to travel to museums to gawk at them by way of getting educated in the history of ancient life on this planet. It's enough to make you want to turn in your American Express card and go off to live in some quiet air-conditioned coeducational monastery. Where all you have to think about is whether the chimes in the tower are playing "The Bells of St. Mary's" in the right key and whether that religious trinket store down the road will cash your social security checks. So what if you do have to buy a couple of babe-in-the-manger scenes to make the deal interesting for the little hunchback mother-fucker of an owner who just happened to escape to this country one jump ahead of the present-day Mongol hordes. You'd have to be plain nuts to expect any generosity or decency from such people, if that's what you want to call them. You've just got to take the bitter with the sweet, like the Mother Superior of that place says. And she ought to know. She'd been around an awful lot before she came to this place. You don't get muscles like that hang-ing around chess clubs. She used to manage an all-girl rassling team. And that took some doing, boy oh boy. Those high-spirited toughies had to know who was boss. Full nelsons and half nelsons, hammerlocks and toe holds, scissor grips and flying tackles, she had to be ready to apply all that stuff when things looked like they were getting out of hand, which they often did.

You can't expect nine girls who are trained for mayhem to act like a bunch of sissy debutantes while they're stuck in some jerkwater town waiting to put on their show. Of course you can't. You ever been to the zoo on a slow day? Those jungle creatures go bughouse with all that stored-up energy and violence. Just how do you think you would feel if you were one of those tigers and all you got was some old nanny and a drooling kid tossing peanuts and popcorn at you when what you really wanted was meat! meat! Then you've got an idea of the problem. Those muscle girls would just explode and start bouncing off the walls and off each other. Bam! Slam! Bite! Gouge! And that's where Mother Tarzan had to step in. OK, girls. Cool it! You hear me? Delilah, let go of Tootsie's leg this very instant! Pat! Get off Mickey's back! Let her up! Marva! What the hell are you doing to Jackie? You think she's a pretzel? Lee, I'm gonna break your big ass in twenty pieces if you don't release Leslie by the time I count to five, you understand me? Jodie and Horse! Break it up over there! I told you there'd be no sex until after the matches. You girls are gonna shoot your wads and not have a damn thing left in you when the bell rings. Lick lick lick, suck suck suck. Jesus! I don't care what you do after we've wiped this other team out. You can all come back here and fuck your brains out if that's what you've got to do.

—Oh boy! shouts Sina. —That's for me!

—Whoopie! shouts Baby Jo. —I can't wait!

—And me and you! yells Lily. —Me and you!

—Sure. You an' me, Lily baby. I'll give you all you can handle and then some.

—Oh yeah, Mama Tarzan. You can practice all those new tongue holds on me. And wait'll I show you what I can do now with my cunt muscles. You just won't believe it. I've been practicing like crazy.

—Yeah, howls Pat. —You can take it from me, Mama T. She's fucking fantastic. She broke my new Japanese dildo in half last night. Snap! Just like that. Holy shit! That gal's got a tiger in her cunt. She'd be murder with some guy's prick.

—Fat chance. There ain't no guy gonna stick his lousy joint in me. No way. You think I'm a pervert or something?

—Oh yeah? What about all the times you fucked your little brother Ron? You told me yourself . . .

—That was before I got to know the real me. I was too dumb to know the score. Besides, he used to pay me fifty cents a fuck.

—Yeah, says Mickey. —Gettin' paid for it doesn't really count. Ain't that so, Mama Tarzan?

—That's right. Tricking is different. Carol, what the devil are you doing over there in the corner? Writing your memoirs again?

—That's about the size of it, Mama T. *A Day in the Life of the Giant Sea*

Turtle. Or *The Rise and Fall of the Manchu Dynasty.*

—Attagirl! shouts Dolores. —Sock it in there. You tell 'em. Show 'em how to throw the shit!

—Yeah! shouts Pat. —Burn their fuckin' ears off, Carol baby. Put so much hot stuff in there they'll run screamin' back to their mummies.

—Memoirs! yells Deb, who is still pinned to the floor by husky, big-assed Marva Lee. —Boy, if I wrote my memoirs they'd slam me in the can for the rest of my life!

—You call those things memoirs that you got, you crazy little cunt? howls Soldier, whose muscular back is covered by a big dragon tattoo running right up her asshole. —Hell, those ain't memoirs. Those're wet dream nightmares.

—Yeah? shrieks Deb, crouchin' like she's gonna go for Soldier. —They're a whole lot fuckin' better than that garbage dump in your dumb head. You wouldn't know a memoir if the fuckin' thing hit you in the face.

—Why you miserable little no-good piss-drinker! I've got half a mind to come over there and shove your stupid head right up your lousy little twat!

—Cool it, you guys! shouts Mama T. —Christ Almighty. It's a good thing we're on in a couple of hours. You act like a goddamn bunch of hyenas before feeding time. Maybe I should throw you all some big hunks of bloody horsemeat. Carol, honey, why don't you read us some of your memoirs. How about that? Maybe that would calm these crazy-cunt animals down a bit.

—Sure, says Carol. —Why not?

—Oh boy! shouts Mickey. —Stories! I don't have my teddy bear here, so I'm gonna hold Kinky. I promise not to feel her up or finger-fuck her or anything, Mama T. I'll just hold her, OK?

—OK, says Mama T. —See if you can control yourself for a change. You could sure use a little lust discipline. You think every letter in the alphabet stands for pussy.

—Let's see now, says Carol, looking through her big notebook. —What'll I read . . . OK. Here we go. "In Paris . . . at the Café Tournon . . . Stephan is there, and . . . and . . . George Beech, the peculiar Negro who hijacked a plane. He is strangely dangerous. I can't look at him without feeling that I'm disappearing into an insane labyrinth. His words float around my head like black hawks looking for a small animal to dine on: —. . . saw that big .45 automatic in my hand and they knew that something new had been added to the menu. Yeah. One guy threw up all the ice cream cake dessert. I told them the first person to make a wrong move would get their head blown right off . . .

—Weren't you scared yourself? I asked him.

—I was ready to go down with the fuckin' plane. I had nothing to lose!

—But your life.

—What life? A nigger's life? You got to be kidding. I mean, shit. You ought to try hiding in a garbage can some time. See if you call that livin'.

I don't like this man. He is menacing. I don't trust him. He wants to suck you into his terrible emptiness. He makes out that he is a political radical, but he is really an imposter. He thinks that we're all fools and suckers. He's looking for some way to fuck us over. And he wants to fuck me. He keeps brushing against me and touching me. He thinks all white women secretly want to fuck black men. Bullshit. He's crazy.

Stephan scribbles away. He is trying to catch up with Time by going backwards. ". . . and furthermore, Mr. Voltaire, there is the question of language contamination. What I mean by that, sir, is one language sneaking into another. When this happens the result is frightening. Mutant realities are bred, freak realities. If you can imagine a human 'thing' with four mouths and no eyes, then you have it, sir. *Voilà!* is not the same as *hot shit!* Hence, if I may say so, when you get a Frenchie saying Hot shit! you have the disorganizing specter of Huckleberry Finn trying to eat a croissant thinking it's a bent doughnut, at which point, Mr. Voltaire, sir, interstellar madness, pure and simple, engulfs everything. In view of this, I would humbly suggest that you immediately drag your skinny ass out of the bidet and put your shoulder to the wheel of this problem, because if you don't, I can assure you that much sooner than you would like to think, fifty million Frenchmen are going to be drowning in frozen custard while believing, quite absurdly, that they are dipping their cocks in wine, and all of the glorious battles of Charlemagne, in which so many short men hampered by malnutrition gave up the ghost, will have been fought in vain. You hear me, man? Move it!"

—Whatcha writin' in that book, man? says Black Man. —You writin' sumpin 'bout me, ain'tcha?

—Not unless you're an eighth-century French foot soldier with one foot in the grave and the other one in his mouth. I can hear those miserable bastards saying "This is strictly nowhere, Pierre my friend. We are getting our ragged asses chopped down for what? For nothing. For the glories of French lace. For the glories of goose-liver pâté with truffles which your tongue will never in this world wrap itself around, my friend."

—You are right, Jean Claude. We are being used. We are dying in order for schoolchildren to be lied to. Mon Dieu! Caramba! Oy vey! Just look at Simon over there under that spreading chestnut tree. He's having his balls cut off by that vicious turd of a Moor who cares nothing for French culture.

—And look! That dirty Moor is stuffing Simon's balls into Simon's mouth! What insolence!

—Ooolala! That cannot be very much fun for poor Simon. Mon Dieu. And the blood that is pouring out of him! Absolutely ruining the uniform that is the property of the Republic of France, or the kingdom of Charlemagne the Magnificent, whichever.

—Drat! Observe the foul play taking place next to that burned truck. Those two big niggers. They're cutting old Claude's arms and legs off! He's played his last game of football, you can be sure of that.

—There is no end to the carnality and carnage here, my friend. Wherever the eye roams, it is met with scenes of the most shocking degradation! Oooff! A gang of squealing blackies have tied up three of our comrades in arms and are taking turns ramming their hungry black peckers up their fine white asses! Surely that is not covered in the official manuals of civilized contemporary warfare. And over there, next to what was our canteen with its cauldrons of onion soup, two drunken fiends from the burning unfriendly deserts of Morocco are pissing in the faces of Captain Barre and his sub-altern Martin de la Roche. Utterly drowning those fine aristocratic features in torrents of hot yellow nigger pee-pee. Gadzooks! I have never seen so much pee-pee in my life! Where does it all come from, I ask you. I knew they were not built as white men, but upon my soul . . . Heaven help us, comrade! These foul devils have no shame. They're shitting all over the sacred flag of our beloved country! Mountains of phew! black boogie doo-doo. Barre? What's happened to you? Where is your head? Mercy! They've chopped your head off! What a jam you're in now. How do you expect to get out of this mess without your head, my friend? Drat! What a nuisance. And what will your poor wife back in Toulon say? She'll be very put out, we can be sure of that. How can she argue with you now, if you have no head? Exactly. You can see the problem quite easily. Oh, she will be angry all right. Alphonse, you idiot! Why don't you answer me, eh? You headless lout! A lot of good you are to me now. Wonderful company you are. Headless. Oooff! I might as well be married to the lamppost. It was bad enough that you didn't have a pecker to speak of, a pecker that could do anybody any real good, a prick that had a firm grasp of reality. That knew what life was really all about. And did not shirk its noble, everyday, twice-a-day destiny, just as water knows that it must be wet above all else. No nonsense about being wet one day and not wet the next. Such a prick does not have the gall to say Today I am not a prick. There is no such thing as a prick-in-waiting. A prick is only itself in always being in divine action, declaring in a loud, clear, no uncertain way, Prick! Prick! I am Prick! surging boldly through the dense forests of rich, swooning, insatiable pubic hair. But now, no head! Phew! Phooey! Merde! What will my ancestors say? What will my friends say? I'll never live this down, you wretched little shameless rat! Thinking only of yourself as always! Selfish as a hole in the wall! And I'll bet I won't even get a pension of any kind. I'll have to bend croissants for a living. Or put holes in Swiss cheese. Or beat a drum at public executions of witches. Or collect farts in a gunnysack and sell them to penniless squatters for their kitchen stoves. Or peddle my ass at the railway station to traveling ghosts or one-eyed balloonists with sandbags tied to their feet. Or . . . merde! The fucking groats are boiling over! Yves! Yves! take your thumb out of your asshole and turn the pot off! Claudine, you little beast! Stop looking at your disgusting pimples in the mirror and run down to the baker's for a baguette. I swear to God I'm going to sell you two wretched mistakes to the zoo one of these days. Maybe I could exchange you for a couple of performing baboons. At least they could bring in a little money. Ah merde! Why didn't I marry Michaux the pharmacist when he asked me the day his wife took an overdose of Epsom Salts and shit herself into the grave! What if he is sixty-three and fatter than a cabbage? What if he does like to be whipped and pissed on twice a week? I could do that without batting an eyelash, and that's the truth. Look at all the money the old fuck has. I would be eating steak twice a day and smoked Strasbourg goose on Sundays. Real clothes to wear instead of secondhand rags to cover my poor body. Servants to do all the work while I amused myself at the casino. I could be bathing in tubs of Chanel perfume. Ride in a swell limousine instead of having to hitch rides on stinking hay wagons filled with peasant louts leaking wine and filthy thoughts having to do with the juicy treasures under my skirts. My thighs and ass are ravaged with rough and ready gropes two minutes after I've climbed aboard. I pity their poor farmer wives. They must be dodging hard-ons like rabbits in a hailstorm.

Ah what a life! Why doesn't something good happen to me for a change? Why must I be doomed to go on living a part in a filthy Zola novel that the man should never have written in the first place, if he'd only thought twice about it. If he'd asked me, merde! I could have given him all kinds of good ideas for a book on me. But this! Merde! Why didn't I finish school as Father Clouet advised me to do and become a doctor or a lawyer or an airplane pilot or a secretary or a nurse in a famous hospital for rich people and catch legs and arms as they fell off the operating table! And sell them to poor people who want to walk around thinking they're somebody else. Anything but this! Hark! Who's that knocking at my crummy little door? The grim reaper? No, it's Beaudin the chicken and egg man. Come in, Beaudin, come in. My, what lovely eggs you have. Nothing quite like a nice egg or two, is there? One of Mother Nature's no-nonsense basic foods. Nothing sly about them. No tricks up their sleeves. They just look you in the eye and say, Here I am. All egg. I'll meet you halfway. Not like some foods I could name, foods that lure you into the pot with all kinds of promises and then betray you. Sweetbreads and calves' brains and pig kidneys, that promise you the world and then give you nothing when the time comes, because you've farted or sneezed while . . . That's right, Beaudin. Help yourself to a glass of that very satisfying and rather bold local red wine there. You can let your hair down with me, even if you don't have any. I'm no stickler for form, Beaudin. Go right ahead and unbutton your jacket and let the seams fall where they may, as they say at harvest time while the sly, two-faced city folks are busy falsifying their income tax returns. Now then, those fine eggs and plump chickens of yours . . . What exactly are you asking for them or just what will you take for them, which is more to the point. As you yourself know, Beaudin, I am a simple, basic woman who still believes in the age-old virtues of bartering. You've got what I need and it is not outside the human imagination that I have something you should very much want. Unless you are some kind of fool or half-human defective, which you clearly are not, as I can tell by the growing bulge in your tight workman's pants. Let's start from the bottom, my good fellow, and work our way up. What would you like for two of your eggs? A feel above my knee? I'll open my legs a bit so that you can get a better idea of what you're in for, all right? Good. Hmmm. You're not a novice barterer, I'm glad to say. Nice, eh? Two more eggs will take you up farther, Beaudin. Ah yes. Hmm. You have a nice strong touch. Now then. You are approaching the muff of the matter. The succulent Rome toward which all roads quite naturally lead. Three more eggs will get your hand there, and you do not need to be told that I am not wearing a single stitch of clothing there. Splendid, Beaudin. Move your fingers around as you will, my friend, because those last eggs entitled you to that. Quite a nice muff, eh? Your trembling lips say yes. Hmm. Your tongue is hanging out a bit, which makes me think that you are prepared to bring one of those juicy chickens into our business. Yes indeed. The fact that you are now down on your hands and knees is a sure sign in my experience that you know a good thing when you see it. Goodness, Beaudin, who would have guessed that you have a tongue as long as a bureaucrat's holiday! I'll just lean back a bit so that your entry into high barter and hot country nooky can be simplified. Oh my, as tongues go, my good chap, yours goes a long way. Oolala! Formidable, Beaudin! Dart and twirl, ooh, swoop and swirl. Ahhh. You certainly know your stuff. Which proves once again . . . oohh so deep! . . . that basic person-to-person bartering . . . oy! . . . well, all right . . . muff-to-tongue country commerce . . . oyy! . . . may well be the answer to Europe's ills. Whoops! I think this old chair is going to break, rocking its brains out as it . . . ahh . . . is. Listen, Beaudin. You've marvelously used up that one chicken. Let us move on to a fat duck, eh? A fat duck fuck! Is it a deal? A fuck for a duck! Good! Here on the floor! Pull out your hammer, man, and let nothing it dismay! Plunge! Plunge! Onward Christian motherfuckers! Quack! Quack! Deeper! Harder! Faster! Beaudin, your prick is . . . who needs angels with a prick like yours! Aaaahhh! Oohhh!

Whoosh!

Heavens above, you old poultry pusher. That was the best fuck I've had since Mother Goose was arrested for white slavery. Beaudin, where are you? You've positively disappeared. I swear that was some orgasm, Beaudin. You've vanished into my big hot cunt. There's not a shred of you to be found. Oh . . . there's one of your socks. Cute pink sock. I imagine your old mother knitted it for you. Well, I'll just hang it up next to the onions as a momento. A tribute to the power of all-out one-to-one no-frills old-fashioned pre-industrial smog-free autonomous local decision-making kitchen-floor barter fucking. So that future generations streaming through this bucolic hall of insatiable mirrors will know that there was a time when simple human drunken initiative was a thing worth having, no matter what the local Council for Human Repression may have said to the contrary, especially when it came to exciting widows in their muscular golden prime, primed with golden ideas and urges fully accompanied by the divine stuff it takes to carry out such urges and ideas, so that they cannot be denounced as paper pussies when the spicy moment of truth arrives. Because as we all know all too well, there are quite a large handful of jades who strut and stomp and shake their asses like the last days of Sodom and Gomorrah but when push comes to shove, they can't produce anything more than the silliest of twat twitches, and a fellow might as well be putting it to a bag of goose feathers. There are payoffs and there are payoffs and some of them make you wish you'd stayed at home counting your curds and whey or worse.

Of course, there are some out-of-the-way places that encourage that kind of thing, where the menfolk and the folksy men as well are not always in training to walk on the moon.

—Halloo there, Mrs. Muletether! one dame will shout across the cemetery to another. —What's your lesser half up to these creeping days?

—He's down in the cellar counting his marbles, she'll answer, without missing a stroke with her little spade.

—You mean to say he's not out killin' jack rabbits as they pour through the pass?!

—Not my Heber. He's a good boy. He knows how and when to stay put.

—An' that's where you put him?

—You got it, Sister Bellwether.

—He don't give you no trouble?

—Not really, no. Oh, he might bark an' snuffle an' whimper some an' yell out that he ain't gettin' all there is to get outta life, an' from time to time he'll drop little notes outta the barred window askin' people to come and save him from the dragon lady oppressor.

—Little notes you say? My goodness. Well, what does the little turd say in these notes, Sister Muletether?

—They're just as cute as can be. He says things like, "Help! Get me out of

here! My human rights are being violated right and left. Call the police!" An'
"A mad monster woman is squatting on my soul. Call the rescue squad!"

—An' then what happens?

—The passersby who pick the notes up run right around to the front door here an' hand 'em over to me.

—Well I'll be fucked. Isn't that sweet. An' what do you do then, Sister?

—I hop right down to the basement an' pull his pants off an' spank the b'Jesus outta the little rascal, that's what.

—Oh ho! Bet the little asshole cries for mercy, huh?

—Oh, indeed he does, indeed he does. But of course he loves every second of it. When I get through with him, his big behind is as red as a tomato at noon. He's beggin' for mercy an' cryin' with joy at the very same time.

—My my. Just imagine that. Sure sounds like you got things in shipshape in your household, top an' bottom. Bet you're the envy of every real housewife on the block.

—Oh, I don't know. The other gals got their ships tightened up too. Like Betsie Watson next door. That will o' the wisp she's hitched to is so busy these days he don't have time to fart even.

—That so? What does she have the smelly little bum do?

—Washin' and ironin' an' scrubbin' an' dubbin'. An' stitchin' an' snitchin' an' rinsin' an' blintzen. He's a one-man laundry an' I don't mean maybe. He does panties an' bras an' corsets an' girdles an' step-ins an' slip-outs an' stockin's an' garter belts an' starter smelts an' anything else that might dream of being in any way attached to the naked female body, night or day, 'cause you never know when the call will come for a tasty tease show of one kind or another to slake the thirst of a wandering male tongue. Like last night at the stroke of twelve, I was roused from my hard-earned dreams by a banging at the back door an' a shouting of "I am tongue! Thirsty for intimate tastes! Dish them up before it's too late!" I leapt out of bed, soared to the door, flung it open, and shouted, "What'll it be, midnight tongue? Name your tease, name your tingle." "A black brassiere over big hot tits! Pink panties over raging snatch! An' make it snappy! An' make it zappy!"

—Oh the imperiousness of colloquial male tongue! Will it never cease in its dartings into the crevices of desire! "Impromptu madman," I shout. "Unheralded petitioner of ad hoc lewdness. Count your obscenities! Your moment has arrived!" And before pip can denounce squeak, I am a whirling beast for his tongue's salivating infinity, a tornado of unspeakable unmentionables. His great dripping tongue was the stage upon which I did my stuff, knee-deep in raging spit.

—And of course you aren't distracted by your old man's moans and whimpers as he presses his ear to the floor.

—'Deed I'm not. It's the music to which I perform.

—Uh huh. Well, yeah. Of course. And I imagine it goes without saying that you don't have a heck of a lotta time for baking old-fashioned apple pies and turnovers and turncoats and mairsy doats and cherry tarts and golden farts and false starts and upside-down cake and biscuits and triskets and traskets and cookies and snookies and . . .

—Oh no. Not a moment for such stuff. Mine are tongue tastes only. For the spicy emanations of the oven, you would have to visit Tessie Humboldt née Turntwat who created the Gingerbread Boy one high-handed day, and solid rumor has it that she's been putting out for the little devil ever since.

—And well she might, I should add. That tasty scamp is something else. There are jelly rolls and there are jelly rollers, but there's only one Gingerbread Boy, as the fox he drowned in the middle of the river would be only too glad to tell you if they could ever raise the dumb bastard from the oyster beds.

—This Tessie, how does she maintain her lesser half?

—Strapped to a giant pretzel between mixin's. Binds him there with long flowing scarfs, so's he looks like Jesus Christ in a maypole dance. "Mind your manners, you big ape," she tells him, "or I'll roll you down to the beer swillers' hall and let those bloated louts drown you in their soggy revels. You hear me?"

—I hear you, Tough Tessie, he whines. —I'll be good. I promise. Cross my heart and hope to die. I'll lick these floors so clean you'll be able to eat off 'em. I'll dust and polish and scrub an' make this place so shiny you can use it as a mirror. I'll spend the rest of my life on my hands and knees. I won't even get up to eat. I'll feed myself from the dog dish under the rickety old table out on the porch. And I'll even bark and whine and snuggle so's you'll swear a real, honest to goodness dog's out there. And if that's not enough for you, Tessie my dearest master, I'll wear a dog suit, a big collie or a police dog or even a shepherd dog with shepherd's blood on my nose, 'cause you know those shifty shepherds, you gotta stay on top of 'em every second. I've never seen a shepherd yet you could turn your back on or leave your little sister Mary Muffet with overnight. Only please don't beat me! You get so crazy and mean when you beat me, Master Tessie! You lose all control of yourself. You say such awful things and then you start screaming in that strange language like you're some kind of foreigner, one of those drunken Russian cossacks galloping through some small frozen Jew town in the north and knocking over their pots and pans and burning their hovels down and killing everybody in sight, even the little kids no matter how fast the little Jew buggers skeedaddle to try to hide under the haystack or in the rabbit hutch. I mean, you drunken cossacks don't fuck around when it comes to rampaging through a kinky-haired Jew village. No sir. You mean business.

And the drunker you are, the more business you mean. What's the point of being a terrible cossack unless you wipe the streets up with people's scared bloody asses? It ain't like you got a lot of other really fascinating things to do with yourselves. Hanging around the barracks counting horse biscuits, or playing Russian roulette for keeps. Or seeing who can piss the farthest out the window. No sir. You gotta have big payoffs, stuff that can stick to your ribs, like rolling heads and entrails spilling out and naked women on their knees begging for mercy and little Yid kids yelling they ain't done nothing wrong to you so why're you stunting their growth by chopping them in half with your flashing sword that you spend so much time polishing so's the victims can get one good last look at themselves in it before they go to meet their maker. Gotta have my fun! you shout, slashing away. Gotta get things outta my system! There's mo' to life than answerin' roll call with your sleepin' dick hangin' out and singin' "God Bless Mother Russia's Babushka" in a chorus of thousands and huntin' for crab lice with a drippin' candle, damn it! Stop being such spoilsports. Take your medicine like decent human beings, for chrissake. Shit! Never seen such a buncha assholes. Ain't you got no patriotism? Ain't you got no love of history? Ain't nobody ever told you 'bout destiny an' fate an' high-class stuff like that? Think you c'n escape cosmic give an' take? Pride an' arrogance, that's your problem. Next thing you know, you creeps are gonna be telling the grim reaper that he oughta take an aptitude test 'cause he's in the wrong line of work. Sheeit! You got your matzo balls in your head 'steada brains. Ha! I see you, you greasy little meatball! Hidin' in there with all those rabbits. Come outta there this instant and get it while it's hot! Slash! Whack! An' you over there, with that mop on your head, makin' believe you're a sheep dog . . . think you c'n fool me? Think I don't know you're a millionaire rabbi? Sheeit! Chop! Whack!

—Oh please, Mr. Cossack, sir. Spare me. I promise not to do any more creepy Jew things. I'll go be good. I'll drink vodka and eat Mother Russia's pussy anytime you say so. I'll be on call night and day. I'll dance and sing and beat my wife and eat hot pig meat and kiss the czar's ass and stuff my little hovel fulla icons an' shit, you name it. An' I'll do it. Jew scout's honor. An' just to show you how sincere I am, I'm gonna promise my best daughter to a Chinese laundry man. Now I'm sure you'll agree that you can't get any more sincere than that. Yes sir, one of those horny little slants that do all those funny things with their tongues and are always lookin' outta the corner of their eyes when they're supposed to be sleepin', and I couldn't even begin to tell you what they do with their sly bony hands. And that ain't all, Your Excellency, not by a long shot. Why . . .

—You see what I mean, Tessie dear? You gettin' the picture? I'll do it in color if you want me to. Lissen. How 'bout this: —How about taking these chains off me for a few minutes so's I can go down to the corner pool hall for a bit and chew the fat with the boys? You know, bullshit a little about who really won the Civil War and whether Joe Louis coulda whipped a gorilla in an anything-goes fight. Stuff like that. Boy, I could sure use a breather, an' how. And on the way back I could stop off at Moe's Diner an' pick up a couple of chili dogs and some cold beer for you. OK? That'll sure hit the spot, right, hon? And while I'm down there, maybe I could get up a game of odd man wins or something. Or play pitch penny. Bet I could clean up. I been practicing out in the backyard by myself with all those Indian head pennies I been saving from my paper route collections. An' I wanna tell you, saving anything is a miracle, 'cause getting those people to pay up, it's easier to squeeze Indians outta them than money. Every damn one of 'em is a skinflint when it comes to forking over cash for services rendered. They act like they got it comin' to them for nothing. Like I should feel privileged to drag my little rear end out into the snow and sleet and rain every morning at the crack of dawn to deliver them damn papers weighin' a ton filled with all kinds of baloney about what's happening in this fucked-up world. All of it, every damn printed word, is lies, lies, lies. You ask yourself why people are so goddamn stupid, it's because their heads are crammed full with all those lies an' crap they read in the papers. People are so dumb it's only by the grace of the Lord in heaven they don't drown every time they drink a glass of tap water, I'm not kiddin'. If people miss their paper some morning due to theft or fire or sleep or snow or my poor back being broken, they pretty near ring up the president to complain. I mean they go crazy. As if the goddamn Holy Scripture had been pulled out from under their noses. But the true fact of the matter is it's the goddamn funnies that they can't stand being without. Real idiot kid stuff. One cat killin' another cat with a brick. Some crazy white guy swinging through the trees of blackest Africa with a naked dame hangin' onto his neck. A bushy little girl who looks like she's married to a dog she picked up in some orphanage. Moron shit like that. An' if the customers can't gobble it up with their French toast an' country fries and java, they just can't make it through the damn day. Really makes you think twice about those missin'-link stories. Only way I can understand how these people wrested control of this country from the reigning tribes of Indians is all those Indians musta been lyin' around their stinky tents dead drunk on tommie-hawk juice when the crucial event took place. Otherwise, it woulda been a 100 percent wipeout with them Indians doin' the wipin', and you and me wouldn't be here, we'd still be back in some Irish fen sniffin' around for chunksa peat to cook our spuds over while up on the hill, sitting in front of a roarin' fireplace, the lord of the manor was chompin' double lambchops an' guzzlin' straight ten-year-old whiskey an' finger fuckin' our two twin sisters who were up there workin' off the rent on our leaky little thatch huts that a goat's fart could knock over they were so flimsy. Gay Irish laughter being something dreamed up by some bullshit artist who never left his writing room in Boston, Mass., married as he was to a rich heiress whose money came from rattlin' boogie bones travelin' tourist class in the soggy bottom of a buncha clipper ships. Yeah. Right. Ask any shoeshine boy in a Greyhound bus station and he'll tell you things Mr. Longfellow woulda been put in jail for just thinking. Tell it like it was an' it'll be your ass. Just peek up Aunt Jemima's skirts next time you get a chance an' lemme know when you recover your eyesight, if you ever do. There's a fella hangs around down at the Bickford's harness shop, he must be on some kinda pension or somethin' because he don't work far as anybody can tell, no visible means of support 'cept his suspenders. Ha ha! Well, this fella was talkin' the other day, it was a Monday—I remember that 'cause you'd very kindly given me a little time off to get that damn back tooth of mine filled that was killing me, a hole so darn big you could lose a donkey in it—and this fella was saying that where he come from you could get nigger meat for less'n pig meat it was so cheap. Like for a dollar a day you could get a nigger to do anything you wanted, no matter how old or young the nigger might want to say he or she was. Didn't matter. Plow a field or dig up turnips or dig up dead bodies and put in other dead bodies or jump in there himself if you were short a couple bodies, or if you had a big hole somewhere that needed pluggin', it didn't matter where, you just shoved him in there an' plugged it up that way, with him in it. Or if there was a real big catfish in the river you'd been tryin' to catch but couldn't because every kinda bait you put on your hook this big ol' catfish said, Sheeit, man. You must be kiddin'. Then you put a nigger on your hook and threw him in and wham! you got that catfish 'cause often they get a real hankerin' for dark boogie meat an' nothin' but dark boogie meat! Or if you heard somebody was out to get you, you first snagged yourself a nigger an' let them get him instead. Same difference, 'cept you were still walking around an' he wasn't. Or if you wanted to make believe you were little Miss Muffet you got your-self some coon pussy to play the spider. Or let's say you had a real strong need to dress up as a sheep and play Run Sheep Run. Then you laid a dollar bill on a dark-town strutter to chase you with a whip and you were in business. This ace of spades with strong arms and whopping big tits would catch you like you never got caught before. All for one single solitary picture of George Washington. One buck on the barrel.

—Hell's bells, this fella said. —Many's the time I stuck a feather in my cap and called it macaroni while a juicy nigger tootsie beat the drum slowly. Some of the best fun I ever had and don't mind saying so.

—You look to me, I told him, —like the kind of man who has gone right on having fun too.

—Oh yeah. That's the kind of fellow I am all right. No two ways about it.

I don't see nothin' to be gained by not having my fun. No indeedy. Nothing at all.

—That's what I thought. You gonna have your fun, an' that's that.

—Eggzackly. You are right on the button, my friend. Ain't nothin' gonna get in my way when the mood comes over me for my fun.

—Uh huh. Come hell or high water. An' the thing is, you got more ways than one of having this fun of yours.

—You can be sure of that. I'm not the kind to put all his eggs in one basket. That way, a fella's liable to wind up eatin' nothin' but an omelet, if you see what I mean.

—I sure do. Diversification is your game. You're no fool.

—Not if I can help it I ain't. This country wasn't established so's people would have to run up and down one side of the street all the time. That'd be one sure fire way to get yourself in a monkey cage.

—There's too many uh those around already.

—Far too many. We could get along just fine with half the ones we got.

—I'm with you there all right, pardner. Close down half your monkey cages an' watch the gross national product rise like a dirigible at the fairgrounds filled with fresh hot air from the popcorn machines.

—Pop pop pop an' a crackle crackle crackle.

—An' a hey-nonny-nonny an' a hot-cha-cha.

—An' a one an' a two and a three boom! boom! An' a one an' a two . . . Oh yeah.

—Grab your partner an' spin her on her head.

—Whoopee!

—Hah! Ha! Oh boy! Tell me something, ol' buddy, what was the kind of fun you had last?

—Stranglin'.

—Stranglin'?

—Yep. Just last night. Got these two hands uh mine round a nice clean neck an' strangled away.

—Bet you had a heck of a good time.

—Damn me if I didn't.

—An' who was the owner of said lucky neck?

—Oh, a little ol' apple knocker, livin' up on the side of Natchez Hill in a trailer with two flea hounds an' her sickly cousin Binky Jo.

—Oh yeah. I know them. That Binky Jo reads palms or something like that to pick up a little change 'cause she don't have the strength for much else. Spooky kinda gal. Looks sorta like a raccoon. Eats nuts all the time. Acorns too. An' horse chestnuts. Cracks 'em with her teeth an' keeps 'em stuffed in her cheeks like a damn raccoon would do.

—That's right! She don't have any kinda neck at all, so I didn't do no stranglin' on it. Nothin' there really to get my hands around. No fun to be had there, y'know. Which is the whole point.

—Oh, I understand that all right. I have no problem whatsoever graspin' that, m' friend.

—So I just said right out, Binky Jo, I gotta be honest with you. You ain't got no kinda neck at all. You c'n keep it. Nothing 'bout it that appeals to me in any which way. You hear? But when it comes to you, Melinda Ann, you're a completely different story. You got one fine, juicy neck, girl. A neck to be proud of, an' that's the truth. An' I want you to know that I feel privileged to do some stranglin' on it. If these hands uh mine could talk, they'd say, Melinda Ann, we want to thank you from the bottom of our heart for the truly rare treat your swell neck is about to afford us. It ain't every day that a neck of your high caliber comes our way. There's necks and there's necks, and yours is one of 'em.

—I mean, that's movin', real movin', to hear a pair uh hands express theirselves in such a refined an' sincere way, m' friend. An' you are certainly a fortunate man to have such hands. Hands like that, you don't have to hide 'em when guests come to your house to visit. No sir. Why, when I think of all the hands that don't know or care which side their bread is buttered on, I mean, shit, it's hopeless an' downright discouragin'. An' knowin' Melinda Ann to be a gal with a sense of decency even though she does live in a trailer, 'cause you know Christ himself, he lived uh good part of his life in a cow stall, I'm sure she saw it the same way, about good hands an' bad hands.

—You're damn tootin'. That little ol' gal was tops. She ain't no dog in a manger, an' I didn't mean by that to cast any 'spersins on the humble origins of the Savior as many folks are pleased to call him, just to be on the safe side in case all that stuff turned out to be true and those folks who put their money on the hereafter are up the creek when the Lord stands up with a long list uh names in his hands and says, You there, Mrs. Joe Blow. I want to have a little talk with you about the disgusting, sacrilegious way you spent your time down below. An' said Mrs. Joe Blow plops to her knees an' wrings her hands an' whimpers, Oh, Mr. Lord, sir, I beg you to go easy on me. Have mercy on a poor wretched human female who was misled by the generousness of her simple heart and permitted a stranger to come into her house out of the cold an' rain 'cause he said he had no place to lay his head an' could he warm hisself by my fire for a few minutes. An' he turned out to be the Devil hisself, an' I could no more get him outta my house than I could get blood outta a turnip. He just wouldn't budge a inch. He took over just the way General Grant took over Richmond, lock stock an' bubble gum. So please, sir . . . An' so on an' so forth. But as to Melinda Ann, she said, I know quality when I see it, and it's clear as crystal that your hands are quality stranglin' hands. And if this neck of mine is going to go, it's going to go first class.

Nothing worse than a first-class neck going out third class. That's just too darn tacky to think about. Gives me the willies.

—A woman's gotta stand up for those things that're dear and important to her. If she don't, people walk all over her like she's some kinda public door-mat. There's no percentage in that, I'll tell you. It's one thing to do a few little things to accommodate, you know, just to make things go smooth. You gotta bend a little in this lunatic world. But it's another thing to just lie down flat and give up all shreds of your own personal decency. If you do that, pretty soon you don't even know who you are anymore. You don't even recognize yourself in the mirror. An' that's when you can rightly say all is lost. An' nobody can accuse you of cryin' wolf! 'Cause it's a real fact. But accommodation, that's something else. Like, I had a boyfriend who had certain needs that just had to be catered to if he was to play ball with you in an intimate personal relationship. Take it or leave it. So I catered. 'Cause who the heck wants to do the tango by yourself? Not me. You wind up in the loony bin that way, scratchin' out your life story on the walls with a fuckin' safety pin or something.

So what if my boyfriend did want me to play Cops an' Robbers 'n' Run Sheep Run 'n' Button Button Who's Got the Button an' stuff like that so's he could get his kinky kicks? That was OK by me. It was no skin off my ass to fool around like that. I never said I came over on the *Mayflower*. I wasn't doin' nothin' that was against my nature. He wasn't askin' me to fuck a barn-yard donkey or perform some dirty voodoo ritual, you know, with chicken blood an' guts so's some enemy of his would kick the bucket fifty miles away. No sir. Just a few harmless little games that I mean to tell you worked like a charm. He was happy an' I was happy. What more could you ask for?

On the other hand, I had a girlfriend who was livin' a life that wasn't fit for a dog. She was being degraded mornin' noon an' night by this man who to this day I still am convinced was a big fairy at heart. He woulda been in his glory dressed up as Little Bo Peep surrounded by big nigger rapist studs in sheep's clothing. Just rarin' to get under his little skirts an' commit acts of terrible violence in her panties. He made this girlfriend of mine eat so much shit that finally she said to herself, I can't stand bein' myself anymore. I got to find another person to be, that's all there is to it. An' she did, goddamn it, she did. She became another person. An' to this day the police are still searchin' for that other missin' person. They dredge the ponds, they sift the sewers, they comb the woods, they tear open the lockers at the Greyhound bus station. They shine their flashlights in the faces of new dead people at the morgue. Those big dumb clucks, they'll never, never find her. 'Cause she don't exist no more! She's a person named Carol . . . An' she wakes up every morning someplace in Europe. And a whole buncha new words come outta her mouth. Words like *infinite* an' *solitude* an' *speculative* an' *analysis* an' *irrespective* an' *working arrangement* an' *existential pressures.* An' sentences take place. She puts these words together an' makes sentences. Like: In spite of the infinite solitude of the self, one must struggle to achieve a working arrangement with the existential pressures that assault one day by day. It is not enough to say, I hurt. One must analyze, but analysis without passion creates a wasteland of elegant crystal patterns that cannot possibly sustain, only decorate, life. Therefore, while all those others are racing toward a vacuum they misapprehend to be the sanctity of selfhood, I will live this life without the coward's backward glance, the philosopher's greasy equivocations, the adventurer's soulless grins, the madman's self-serving screams. My life will belong absolutely to me, not to a slavering footnote on a researcher's disordered page. Knock knock. Who's there? Life, you dumb cunt. Oh no. Not me. Tear open your fly, Life, because I'm coming through. And I'll soar up your asshole with my eagle tongue and you'll feel you've never known a moment's hesitation.

Come out from behind that tree, Stephan. You can't fool me. I know you're not a woodcock.

Open your eyes, Marinetta. I know you're not dreaming.

Last night I played the beast to a banker's girlish beauty. And oh how that cunt did carry on! The ecstatic groveling, the delicious squeals of fear and pain, the wardrobe mistress released from the closet, raging in divine liberation as she presents The Forbidden Void in daring costume.

—Oh mercy me! Terrible beast! What unspeakable things are you going to do to poor helpless little me?

—Growl! Roar! Snuffle! Ravage! I'm going to claw your tasty virgin's flesh to ribbons!

—Oh! Oh! Please, no! Spare me! What would my dear mother say if she were to see me now?

—I'm going to sink my sharp teeth into the sweetness of your trembling private parts. Growl! Roar!

—Oh beast! Not that! The shame! The horror! Oh help me, Mother Mary!

—I'm going to penetrate you with my flaming red prick!

—Eeek! Aiiee! I swoon! I am lost!

—You are my slave, little princess. Down on your hands and knees. Down! Gnash! Slobber! Prepare yourself for the degradation. Prepare yourself for the madness of the animal world. The Thirst. The Hunger.

—Oh dear God! My dear eyes are blinded by the flashing fury of your giant bestial organ!

—Hear it roar! Hear it pant, little slave!

—You're tearing my pretty dress! Oh dear, I'll never be able to wear it again. Oh, you're ripping my nice clean white panties to shreds with your big teeth. Yoy! Yoy! You're clawing my little girl's behind. Oh yoy! Your big hairy snuffling snout is forcing its way into the tenderness of my terrified . . . girlie's . . . ass! I die! I die!

—Die . . . ? Did my little banker beauty die? Not exactly. Vanished, yes. Into the ecstasies of sperm-drenched drama, just as Miss Muffet drowned in the roaring surf of all that whey, and later washed up on the shores of her own tingling exorcised consciousness. Oh, little banker! Do you feel my costume teeth on your thighs as you meet with your board of directors to float yet another loan to starving black-sambo Nigeria?

—Utterly divine, my dear Carol, he said. —I have never known such happiness. My soul breathed for the first time.

Dr. Scholl's Footcomfort Aids, a subsidiary of TransSiberian Chain Gang, Inc.

Who said that? Bo Peep, you better behave yourself, girl. You're not on yet. So keep your little lip buttoned, you hear?

Those little fantasy artists! You gotta keep an eye on 'em all the time.

Where was I . . . ? Oh yes . . . Souls getting oxygen.

Get them curds outta the whey!

Simple Simon! Get back in those pages or I'll fetch you a kick in the seat of your incorrigible pants.

Good Lord! What've I got here? An insurrection in dreamland? Phew! There's more to this job than meets the hard-on, let me tell you. For every hour on stage, there's four hours of research and development. None of which is passed on to the customer's bill, really. Like, I mean, how can a chariot race charge for the invention of the wheel? Oh well, c'est la vie. Waiter! Another *ballon* of Beaujolais, please.

As I was saying . . . the wonderful thing about a mask is it doesn't have a police record. And it can't catch syphilis. You can but it can't. Which of course may lead to resentment and umbrage and other bad feelings. A man I knew—I lived next door to him on the Place Contrescarp so I couldn't help but hear what went on in his airy, light-headed studio—used to have some really vicious scenes with his mask which happened to be a black lady latrine cleaner, as which he snorted and shuffled and crawled and mopped his way through the divine deliriums of ladies' piss and shit and undies and Tampax and all. But who paid the inevitable price? "Me!" he would shout. "Me! You get off scot-free, you shallow, grinning, freeloading black twat! While it's my poor head that gets bashed with purses. My poor crotch that gets kicked by high-heeled shoes. My poor face that gets shoved down toilets by strong-armed, outraged femmes. Bitch! Suck! Freeloader! Parasite swine fuck! Never a word of condolence do I hear from that hanging garden of a mouth of yours! One of these days, so help me, one of these days it's going to be your ass. I'll find a way to get at you. If there's any justice in this insane fucking world, I'll get your number and when I do, I'll drive a fucking stake through it. Pig mother cocksucker! Speak to me, you bat's ass! Two little words, that's all I ask from your black emptiness. Two words. Say, Poor man. Try it. Say them after me. I don't ask you to shout them. Just whisper them! Mouth them! Say them! Say them! doom-sucking darkie!" And after that, the dreadful sounds of a human body bouncing off walls. Oh dear. As dreadful as the sound of a love letter tearing itself open. Or a lonely noose hanging itself.

Mirrors weeping because no one is looking into them. Cracking into infinity as they reach the breaking point. And what angels could or would collect the pieces and resuscitate them? Did Hannibal talk to his elephants? We will never know. Such things can affect the way you feel about history. We do know, of course, that over the centuries peasants in the Pyrenees have reported seeing the hulking ghosts of elephants wandering inconsolably around the haystacks and sloping vineyards. Given that these peasants may have from time to time taken to hallucinating because of the extreme hardness of their lives, the truly harrowing difficulties of survival. Go chase the fields for your dinner is one of the many bleakly chastening expressions heard among them. And, Don't make friends with the grasshoppers because you're going to have to eat them. Why would they have chosen elephants as the subjects of their hallucinations? Why not penguins? Why not armadillos? Or flying dildos? No indeed. These hard-pressed bony people were not bullshitting. They did see those fucking elephant ghosts and that's all there is to it. Who gives a damn that elitist academicians living the life of Riley in some remote university high-rise scoff at such reports? Are we to be swayed by the raised eyebrows of rationalist church authorities who have been soaking their peters in carafes of holy water so long they've finally grown gills? Of course not! We will stick by the short, undernourished mountain dwellers and cliff hangers. We will cast our lot with them as they trade children for goats and goats for pesetas and pesetas for patent leather dancing shoes that don't quite fit. Turn your back on these folks and you've issued a standing invitation for an invasion of insatiable, thin-lipped robots bearing instant, prefabricated gas chambers for the imagination and seamless acrylic uniforms for your offspring who will ecstatically devote all of their waking hours to rooting out and putting the torch to heretics and dissidents and free-thinkers and pleasure-lovers and upside-down tealeaf readers. Which means that sooner or later life on this planet will be a guaranteed losing proposition for anything smarter than a fucking titmouse. You capeesh?

You wanna hear some real hot stuff, then put aside that dirty comic book *Tillie the Toiler* and tune in on that good-lookin', full-figured lady sittin' over there with the man with supercharged eyebrows. "I can still smell the bodies of the women I lived with in those horror chambers.... The interior of the barracks reminds one of a huge chicken coop or rabbit warren. The lowest koys are the worst. They are wet and cold, because of the earthen floor which on rainy days gets so trampled that the shoes sink into it. They are dark, because scores of trampling legs are continually in the way of light. They are too low for a woman to sit erect. At night they are attacked by packs of rats. The middle koys are miserable, but have somewhat more light. Although the muddy boot of the woman climbing to the upper koy in the darkness often strikes the head of the person sleeping in the middle koy, at least the strawsacks are dry.

"Women returning from work at night crawl into their lairs in darkness. In darkness they search for their blankets and in darkness they take off their clothes.

"Dark cages like lairs—dim flickering light from the sparsely placed candles—nude, emaciated women, blue with cold, their shaved heads huddled into scrawny shoulders, arched over a heap of filthy rags, feverishly catching the vermin and cautiously killing them on the edge of the koys. This is the picture of the barracks in 1942."

An' you better hear those Heinies too: We gonna grind you all up into Jew paste an' put you into little jars and sell you all over the entire world as high-society sandwich spread. We gonna put tuna fish outta business when it come to what people wanna put in their mouth when they is gettin' drunk at parties where there's lotsa good free food bein' served an' no queshions asked 'cause the rich hostess wants ta go over big with her fancy guests. At the same time as her fat bald old man is downstairs in the play room shooting crap with guys so fuckin' rich they own the water you drink. An' we're gonna take all your kinky Jew hair an' stuff it into little pillows for rich honkie midget dogs to sleep on afta they has come from tha beauty parlor where they've been given the full treatment, the sky bein' the limit money-wise while the chauffeur is waitin' outside inna long black Caddy limo to drive them back to their manshuns like kings an' queens outta some foreign country where all the people spen' so much time bowin' an' scrapin' an' kissin' ass they don' have no time left to take a bath in the nearby river like they should 'cause, man, do they stink! At this point, I'm sure that a good many of you feel like standing up and pointing the finger of guilt directly at Uncle Sam for supporting such vile dictatorships for the reprehensible purpose of getting first crack at any tasty oil that might be seeping up through the sandy wastes of the farmlands. Which is simply another way of saying, How would *you* like it if some pigsnout goon with a submachine gun were sitting on your sister's head and thus preventing her from going to the prom with her frisky boyfriend Ted? Yeah. Right. So, you would be more than well advised to attend the next town-hall symposium on democracy: "The Little Train That Should, Could, Would, But Maybe Won't." Be warned: Richard

Nixon is not dead. He is returning to action soon as the hooker in *Rain*.

—What is clear as day is that the great war lovers are mothers. The fathers just act that way because they are supposed to. Every man must seem to be Ulysses tearing down the walls of Troy. Beneath it all he's a fun-loving fool who would rather play Prisoner's Base with the boys and have jerking-off contests in an alley garage. But the mothers, they lust for blood, for power, for revenge. They want their sons' cocks to be flaming spears. Beware the woman who says the family is sacred. She is preparing to launch the third and final war.

—But, my dear fellow, you are uttering blasphemies. You are provoking disorder and the destruction of the status quo. You are rocking society's boat.

—That's what they told Galileo.

—Humph. There's something very sneaky about people who reach into the past to butter up their wild claims.

—What about the use of wild butter on poached clam diggers? You poor jerk. You know what Hiawatha said to Captain John Smith?

—I know you are about to say something cruel about women.

—No! She said, John, baby. If you want to knock off a piece of fine Injun ass, mine to be precise, you must first lay at my feet the scalps of ten plump honkies.

—Watha, honey. Why are you layin' this mean exterminator trip shit on me? What's come over you anyway? You been hittin' on your old man's fire-water again? Or have you been listenin' to the bad witch who lives in the tree?

—That sound you hear is my foot tapping, John boy. I'm beginning to think you don't quite know what's good for you. It could be a long hard cold and celibate winter for you if you continue to act like one of those Harvard pansies.

—Gee, Watha. I can hardly believe I'm talking to the sweet well-bred upper-class Seminole girl of our first meeting. You're making me afraid for our future. I had such good plans for us.

—The clock is ticking on the wall, John boy. Wake up.

—I was going to take you back to merrie olde England and introduce you to the Queen who is really a wonderful gal when you get to know her. When she lets her hair down and puts on her sneakers and plays softball with the gang in Kensington Gardens, you just know you've got a real person there in front of you. An' you don't have to be a member of the Privy Council to experience her spitball, because I can tell you personally that it doesn't stand on ceremony or on some duke's nose as he bends down to perform sneaker lickin'. No sir, Watha. What I mean is, not one drop of royal spit on that ol' ball is . . .

—You're still avoiding the issue at hand, you little limey prick. Which happens to be divine Indian princess quiff on the half shell and whether you're going to get a taste of it or not. Your contact with reality at this point is about nilsville. On a scale of one to ten, you would not be in the same class as Köhler's chimps down in Gainesville.

—Furthermore, Watha honey, the Queen does not confine her just-folks activities to the playing fields. She is a barrel of fun indoors as well. She can give the hot foot just as easily as others give the cold shoulder. An' she can box ears faster than you and I can box bagels. You'd love her, which is what I had in mind when I planned this tour. I can just see the two of you, each a princess of royal bloodletting in your own right, you on your side going right back to the first smoke signal long before that wop Marconi got his shit together, and she on her side right back to Beowulf's mother's first menstrual cramps. Firmly in the saddle history-wise. Oh boy. I could just see the two of you, east meets west, tomahawk meets Mace, open-air fish fry meets closed-corporation Yorkshire pudding, call of the wild meets premogeniture, an' may the best kid win. You would be teachin' her Indian rassling and she would be reciprocating with the English disease. Talk about house-packin' acts, you two would be the hottest combo since David and Goliath.

—One does not have to be a licensed doctor to see that you clearly have bats in your belfry. You are hallucinating. This may be due to congenital defects in your brain or it could very well be connected with your diet. All that shit food you eat which is saturated with MSG plus the fact that you have been gargling huge quantities of swamp wine with that no-good white trash bunch down at the trading post. It is absolutely amazing how fast you Eton boys go to pot when you stray from the cricket fields and birching clubs. It certainly calls into question the efficacy of your aristocratic structuring. My own view is that irreparable damage is done to you poor giggling noggin-heads by the cruel custom of tearing you from your mothers' arms before you've even been toilet trained and packing you off to be raised by cold-hearted strangers in remote craggy places where you get goose pimples instead of roast goose. Wouldn't surprise me if they trained you wretched nippers to run down rabbits with their beagle dogs.

—You'll knock 'em dead, Watha honey. Once they see how you an' the Queen have become asshole buddies an' wear each other's clothes—I can't wait to see her in those eagle feathers of yours an' that raccoon pussy belt— an' have pillow fights an' double date an' ride to the hounds together hours before the rest of the court have even got their odd bodkins on, an' how you know each other's special girl secrets, why, they'll fall all over you when you go out into the streets for a little French air, I mean fresh air. 'Cause it's entirely up to you whether you French or not, 'cause that kind of thing is not forced on you where I come from like it is in some places I could mention. Where you do it or else. Your tongue is strictly your business in that tight little island. It's written into the very bones of the body politic. Fee fie fo fum / I taste the tongue of an Englishman was actually the figment of a Parisian provocateur who couldn't get to first base in London society, I mean was even stiffed by the chimney sweeps. So he was just trying to start trouble to get even, ya know. He finally split the city in utter defeat and returned to France and his father's sausage business, which is saying quite a lot about stiff upper lip an' how it can mean one thing to one guy and something entirely different to another bozo. Without which Epsom Downs is just an empty racetrack, if you know what I mean an' I think you do. So, uh, I think our big payday will come when we've mounted a full-scale musical production of *Macbeth* with you in the female lead role, tomahawk in hand, firmly supported on one side by a cast of thousands of English queens playing Indian maidens 'cause they're just not enough closets around these days. And on the other side by the Thames itself. Now I don't mean to brag, but I can confidentially say that I've got Noël Coward in my pocket—that is, the last time I looked in it he was still cowering there—as the director. We'll give him a free hand, of course. The sky's the limit, Noël, is what we'll say to him. Pull out all the plugs, tear off your girdle, burn all the barges. Show the people that *Bittersweet* was not your swan song. Or it's gonna be your ass. I wanna see the completed theme song on my desk by Monday morning at nine sharp. Not a minute later. I think he'll get the point 'cause you see he's still got that buggery rap hangin' over him like Demosthenes' sword. Now, I'd be lying if I said I had no idea what the theme song should be. I know fuckin' well what it should and will be, Watha: "Blood, Blood, Everywhere But Not a Drop to Drink." That's our baby, Watha. An' every Beefeater worth a fart is gonna be hummin' an' singin' it as they pour outta the theater an' head for the Mermaid for that intermission gin and bitters. Now I got another dynamite song for old Macbeth: "Whoever Said That a Woman's Place Was in the Kitchen?" You like it? Far fuckin' out, right? It'll grab them by their codpiece an' never let go, believe me. There won't be a dry crotch in the house when that sweetheart is laid on 'em. Sock it to me, Cecil! Oh yeah! You'll never guess who I've got in mind for that top role. It'll surprise even you. None other than Tommy Beckett! Yeah. Himself. The man who made murder a collective noun. He's been back in the wings waitin' for a role like this. People have been sayin' he was a one-murder man, a fly-by-night, one-shot item, a flash in the pants. Shit like that. Fickle, unpredictable, disloyal, gluttonous cocksuckers. They're never happy. They wanna have their Stonehenge an' eat it too. We're gonna change all that, Watha. When we get through with 'em they're gonna be down on their hands and knees beggin' for another bowl of cabin boy soup. An' that's a promise.

—I want to see your Rorschach test.

—You show me yours an' I'll show you mine. Ha ha. We used to play that game when I was a kid in Piccadilly Circus. Boy, that was a neighborhood that really jumped. Simple Simon, Little Boy Blue, Peter Peter Pumpkin Eater, Mary Mary Quite Contrary, Cockadoodle Dandy—real front-line kids. None of your lick-'em-an'-leave-'em Lord Fauntleroy types. I wanna tell you, Watha, that the greatness of John Bull was not built on a pair of stained velvet short pants, no matter what the impulse of the moment may have indicated at the time. Floggings an' butternut crunch, Borstal boys an' hot cross-eyed buns, downstairs maidenheads an' upstairs nannies, those are the things you've gotta list when you set out to show why the hairy Spanish Armada never stood a chance. The British Museum wasn't built for loiterers and spoilsports, my dear. Chaste scholarship is at the very soul of functional structuralism and while one thing may inevitably lead to another, as the invention of the purse unavoidably led to the snatch, I have yet to see a headmistress who knew how to give head. So I hope that before you start following your nose you will first check it out in the mirror to make sure it is where it's supposed to be. Vis-à-vis which, Watha, I shall never forget— would you grab me and yourself one of those hot creamed hoe cakes that that grinnin' lackey's passing around, please, before I faint from hunger— forget what Rollie Barthes told me in something less than strict confidence on the steps of the Bibliotheque Nationale the last time I saw him: The skin of language in the British Isles has goose pimples on it. Jack and the Beanstalk is really about a boy climbing his own giant hard-on into the fabulous heavens of the unconscious, but you would never know that reading the schoolmarm's apocryphal version which is intended solely to hoodwink helpless children before they can become a threat to national insanity. Fie upon you, Margaret Thatcher! On your conscience seethes torrents of unspent coital juices. What difference does it make whether London Bridge is or is not falling down when the hand that's rocking the cradle is attached to the arm of Mrs. Grim Reaper herself. You'll answer for this, madam. One of these fine mornings you'll look out your window at 10 Downing Street and see that all of the eels in the Thames have turned into homicidal elves and every single one of them will be carrying a halyard with your name on it. Goose pimples, well, yes, and more, much more. Eczema and scabies, boils and warts. If you don't believe me, then try stopping your everyday Englishman in the street coming from the greengrocer's loaded down with his daily fix of Swedes and sprouts and ask the lumpy bloke who Othello is. And he will tell you, Oh one of them dirty niggers in the woodpile who is takin' the very bread out of our mouths with his workin'-under-the-table tactics. And you wonder why Shakespeare turned queer and cuddled up to the bum of young Willie H.!

—Staring you in the face is a virgin forest of New World Indian princess nooky, John Smith. And what are you doing about it? Get up off your belly and onto mine before they carry you away to the cuckoo house.

—Language, Mrs. Thatcher, is not something the ticket-taker punches before you get off at Wormwood Scrubbs. I mean, shit! If it's reductio ad nothingness you crave, then why not have Hamlet simply say, This scene is dragging my ass. I've got to split, and I mean now. Just think of all the time you could save by having him say, How come I always get the shitty end of the stick? Somebody's gonna pay for this, bet your sweet ass on that. I mean, shit. You could squeeze the whole bloody thing into a comic book if that's where your thick skull is. You miserable doxie! Hamlet yells at his old lady, who just happens to be stark naked in the shower at the time. Ain't you got no shame? Puttin' out for the guy who knocked off my poor dad! You fuckin' well better soap that big pussy of yours. It's all covered with death. An' just how do you plan to clean all of Uncle's jissom outta your glory hole, tell me that. With that puny little douche bag? Don't make me laugh, you grinnin' slut. You could run the whole fuckin' Danube up there and it wouldn't change a thing. You could jam the entire Vienna Boys' Choir up there singin' their little heads off an' the words would still come out, "Sock It to Me, Mama." Yeah, go right on laughin'. Don't bother me one bit. I've got you where I want you, woman. Go on an' jolly those hot big boobs of yours with that sponge. Rub 'em hard as you can. Rub 'em till the red nipples pop up to the ceiling like champagne corks. But you're crazy if you think you can get rid of that murderer's suck marks. Oh no. Not in a million years. An' twirlin' 'em at me like that won't make any difference. You can't twirl 'em so fast these eyes of mine can't see Uncle's depraved tooth bites all over that juicy pink whore skin. Yeah. Right. It's about time you got around to that steamy round shameless ass of yours. Alas, poor Yorick. Too bad he couldn't knock himself off a piece of it before he kicked the bucket. Shake it, you . . . you . . . What do you mean would I like to try my hand at scrubbin' it? You think I'm chicken? You think I can't scrub those bawdy shimmering insatiable cheeks like they should be scrubbed? Wait'll I get outta these fuckin' clothes . . . strip for action . . . fuckin' buttons . . . gimme that sponge, woman! Bend over! Spread those saucy legs! Here comes the princely avenger! Have a taste of *this* raging royal rammer, Queen's twat!

See what I mean? Get right to the point on the average motherfucker's level. *Hamlet* for the masses. An' you wouldn't have to go to all the trouble an' expense of passin' out those dictionaries. Just sit back an' watch your ratings soar. An' before you know it, all that boring shit about balance of payments an' shorin' up the pound like it was some wayward river, all that stuff will be a thing of the past. Whatdya care about that zonked out little hippy Ophelia? Teach that girl a trade. An' as for the rest of those deadbeats that've been eatin' you outta house an' home, like that old crotch bunny Polonius, tell 'em the party's over, scatter 'em to the four winds, dump 'em in the Pope's lap, let 'em be *his* headache. Maybe he can put 'em to work scrapin' down the catacombs, or chasin' crooked heretics who've skipped town leavin' all those bar bills. Those spooks think the world owes them a livin', just because they got a few ideas that can't fit into your basic rumble seat. I mean, Christ! You give in to them and the next thing you know you'll be handin' out unemployment benefits to frogs because they won't croak. The freaks of this world are just waitin' for the go sign. You just can't do business with 'em. I know what I'm talking about. I used to go with this girl Joan from Arc an' I wanna tell you that chick was something else. She kept me on my toes every inch of the way. I never knew what the fuck she might do from one moment to the next. I'd ask her how she wanted her eggs— 'cause you know, she'd often stay over at my place if we'd been exchanging carnal knowledge in the old sack—and she'd say, Two magistrates sunny side up with some hash brownies on the side. I'd suggest to her that we take in a midnight movie, and she'd say, Who will watch the sheep while the shepherd is having his hair done? I once made the mistake of askin' her to sew a button on my jerkin an' you know what she said? There are no pockets in a shroud. You see any connection? I sure don't. We were in the middle of a game of strip poker one night—I was doin' all right too: I had her down to her garter belt an' hair shirt, while I still had on a wool turtleneck sweater my mom had sent me—when I pulled an ace to her jack. I said, OK, Joan baby. Peel! She jumps up shoutin', I gotta cut out! I got a date with my astrologer. If I don't get there on time, he'll start without me. Can you imagine that! The last time I saw her she was bickerin' with the local woodcutter: I don't want no third-rate faggots lickin' away at *my* feet, she said, hurlin' chunks of wood this way an' that. Now don't get me wrong. Joan had her good side. When she was in the mood, she gave you your money's worth, an' more. She could put on one helluva show, if you know what I mean. She didn't try to hustle you with a buncha skimpy little curtain raisers. No sir. She didn't get that devil-do-your-darnedest style lyin' around in a Jacuzzi snippin' snatch hairs.

Which is more than you can say about today's crop of stargazers. They ride around in air-conditioned Caddies with ebony chauffeurs watchin' dirty movies on special TV sets in the back seat an' feedin' their faces with goose-liver sandwiches an' big slices of smoked salmon an' giant jars of caviar an' slosh it all down with champagne one bottle of which costs enough to send your favorite daughter to a high-class ridin' academy five days a week. An' when it's their turn to come across with a vision, they ring up their English butler an' say, Jeeves, fetch me a nice five-minute flip out. Something with sock to keep the boobs in their hatches. What's that?

No, no. Used that one last week in L.A. Look in the files again. I need an act with some trimmin's this time. Now don't be afraid to get your hands dirty, Jeeves. That's why I put those white gloves on you, remember? I want some frothin' an' hair-pullin' an' a few spasms, OK? What's that? Köchel listin' 536? Aha. That oughta do it. That number's a real little sweetheart. Mmm. I remember the first time I used it, back in '61. It was a private affair, at Annette Funicello's Palm Springs digs. She had just gone over the ten-million-dollar mark playing the Mousketeers an' Disney awarded her a pair of sold-gold mouse ears in honor of. She felt she owed herself a little party, something different, y'know. It was really a memorable evening. The whole beautiful thing took place at poolside. Fatty Arbuckle was lying at the bottom of the pool where he'd gone some years ago to escape the public's glare. I guess he'll come up when he's good and ready, said Annette. I don't ask him any questions and he doesn't ask me any. A tight little band of loyal aficionados was there for the occasion. All of 'em famous in dreamland. Annette was going with Pluto at the time, an' what an adorable couple they were. Pluto an' his rhinestone leash an' she wearin' nothing at all but her Mouseketeer hat. It was a match made in heaven. But of course nothin' in this world lasts forever. They eventually split up, as readers of the *Hollywood Reporter* well know, because they simply weren't growing at the same rate of speed. Annette's career just soared. She went on to make such multi-million-dollar classics as *Dune Cunt, Tide Pool Pussy, Sand Fever Girl, Riptide Rimmer, Beach Bugger,* and ultimately *Surf Suck,* which assured her a permanent niche in the Hall of Fame. The lines that formed at Radio City for this all-time winner wrapped around themselves to such a degree that many film freaks saw it six and seven times without even knowing what they were doing. Not a few people died of starvation in those lines because they couldn't break free to get themselves a bite to eat. When Annette was informed of this by her agent, she said, Why didn't they eat each other?

With Pluto fallen by the wayside, Annette naturally had to find herself another playmate. What are sleepovers and pajama parties and pillow fights and such without a good strong peer-group chum? Exactly. She an' Clark Gable were thicker'n blood for a while. Clark taught her how to shoot from the hip and she taught him how to tie knots in spaghetti with your tongue without cheatin'. They had a whale of a time together until Clark, who was never one to hold back when it came to cinematic verities, got his cock froze while playing the lead (what else?) in *Arctic Love Call.* From now on, we'll just have to be Platonic friends, she said to him. The point she was tryin' to make was that she couldn't make out with a popsicle unless she happened to be one of those snow maidens, which she certainly wasn't. It was right after this, by the way, that Clark decided to make *The Misfits.* Annette's next big heartthrob was Mickey Rooney, whom she played opposite in the remake of

Ben-Hur. It was a bang-up musical this time around and everybody was on roller skates instead of lungin' in those big ol' chariots. You have to understand, said Annette to a *Variety* reporter, that breathing in all that chariot dust may have been all right for the older generation with all their neurotic hang-ups an' all, but it just doesn't go with us new modern generations. We tackled and solved the generation gap with high-speed roller skates. I think it's really terrific how these problems can be solved without making anybody angry. We brought those little old Romans up to date. I take my hat off to technology and the spirit of tomorrow. And above all I wish to take off the hat of the entire cast to American spunk. It's the greatest, and I mean it from the bottom of my heart. You can have the Colosseum. I'll take good old American spunk any day. This great land of ours would still belong to those grimy little Indians and their shrimpy papooses if it weren't for American spunk. How would you like it if the first man on the moon had been a drunken, half-naked redskin full of firewater up to his eyeballs 'stead of a nice, clean, sober, tall, all-American boy with a family rooting for him? And just try to imagine if you can a bunch of painted whooping savages with crude Boy Scout knives fighting off the communist hordes as they tried to invade Plymouth Rock. You wouldn't be here today and I wouldn't either. We'd all be starving prisoners in Siberia or some other nasty place. Ask all those former buffalos about SPUNK USA and see what they tell you. You can bet they'd give you an earful if they could. And just in case you don't like talking to buffalos, then buttonhole a few of those shiny black slaves whose pickaninnies played hopscotch in the cotton patches while they sang "Mama's Little Baby Loves Shortnin Bread" an' other such hits. Their whole lives are a tribute to the subject under discussion. You can't really blame them because somebody sold them a bill of goods when it came to Black Power. Nobody's perfect. It was a tribute to their race when they rose up an' chose Al Jolson to sing "Mammy" for them. While it's not a very good bet that the next president will be a black lady, they can dream can't they? That's what SPUNK is all about. If you don't know that, then there's something wrong with you, and you should get your head examined. It seems to me long overdue that President Ron Reagan—well, he will be—should declare a National SPUNK Day. Banks would be closed and all-American children would be released from school. And sometime during that day, after lunch would probably be best, there should be an official ten-minute silence during which everybody would get down on their knees and thank their lucky stars that they have what I am talking about. Before our heritage slips through our fingers like so much quicksand. Before it's too late. I've never been more serious about anything in my whole life. American heritage has its back against the wall this very moment just about anywhere you would care to look, thanks to permissiveness and over-indulgence, abdication of parental authority, pinko progressive schooling, lesbians in our armed forces, gay power marches in our sacred avenues, homosexual football players, wildcat strikes, bigger welfare payments to the poor who are more than willing to be always with us, hamstringing the FBI and the CIA so they can't fully watch over us while we sleep, the cheapening of immigration laws, the flooding of our wonderful markets with all that Japanese stuff, so that if you take a close look at the label in Santa Claus's suit, you'll see Made in Tokyo. Marijuana replacing such all-time standbys as Camels and Luckies. Foreign games like soccer and rugby sapping the strength of our divine playing fields. Dark-skinned doctors from God knows where being allowed to cut open our loved ones whenever and however they please, babbling in strange tongues to the nurses in hospitals we can no longer call our own. Florence Nightingale would surely turn over in her grave if she could see what's going on in those creepy places. I could go on and on if I had a little more time, but I've got to skeedaddle over to the Paramount lot with Mickey here to see the rushes of *Wuthering Heights Revisited.* I may be prejudiced, but if you ask me I think it's my finest film, and I'm sure that Mickey would go along with that statement. I play Cathy to his Heathcliff, or vice versa, and once you've seen it you'll just die laughing at the feeble efforts of Merle Oberon and Laurence Olivier in that gloomy sick old version filmed in those utterly putrid old English moors where to take a deep breath is to risk your sanity. I kid you not. For one thing, all that TB Merle disappeared into every time Heathcliff tried to get into her pants. You'd think her cherry was a diamond or something the way she carried on. It's no wonder that that poor goof Heathcliff started hitting the bottle real hard and talking to the moon and beating up on the poor shepherds who were trying to get a few winks out in the pasture. He should have thrown her over his knees and given her big bare fanny a good spanking. That would have straightened her out. Maybe, just maybe, that's what she was looking for all along. History books may tiptoe around the subject, but it is common knowledge that the coddled upper classes in those days laced their Wheaties with a fair amount of s & m. Clean, simple bedtime stories left them cold. Their bedposts had fingernail scratches and rope marks all over them. Lady Jane is my name and pain is my game. The poor, underfed servants in those great houses spent half their time cowering in the pantry because of all the screams and shouts and creakings and crackings and obscene commands issuing from the master's bedroom upstairs. With all those whip welts on their bodies, they must've looked like zebras. A peek into their closets was a look at the human heart at its most disgusting. It was like the wardrobe room of the circus. High-laced boots and black corsets and whips and masks and chains and long gloves and Japanese ticklers and handcuffs and gold garter belts and all kinds of weird wigs which you can be sure were worn by the men as well as the women. And, oh golly, it's no wonder they lost India and China and all those other places. Otherwise they slip right from under you and start burning and pillaging your consulates and kidnapping the women and children and putting them behind rickshaws or into opium dens where a bunch of little yellow guys are floating around in never-never-land without a stitch of clothing on. So I hope you are beginning to see why it's so important for your country to walk tall and tough. Why it's so important to reactivate the draft and put American youth back where it belongs, in uniform. Drag them by their long hair out of the pool halls and porn movie houses and all-night disco joints where their strength has been ebbing away. Put some muscle in their knees so they'll stop keeling over when their country calls them. We must not permit the bargaining table to become the bargain basement of world power with Uncle Sam down there licking boots. We must not permit our nukes to become pukes. We must not permit our subs to be snubbed, our satellites to play second fiddle while the stars look on in shame. We must not let the world think that the best America can come up with is a peanut butter and jelly sandwich when the chips are down. Not as long as I am president, which is what I'm asking you good people to do. Put me there where I belong. And put Ted Kennedy where he belongs, right smack behind iron bars for callously drowning young secretaries when they've had one too many. Ladies and gentlemen, fellow Americans, it is later than you think. I don't say that with one eye on Big Ben either. I was not brought up that way. Nor do I say it with one eye on some cheap hourglass made in Korea with fake sand. I say it, ladies and gentlemen, as I look Father Time straight in the eye. I will absolutely not let that old windbag have the last word when the future progress of this country is under discussion. I promise you that there will not be a dry eye in the entire country when I get through telling our enemies where to get off. And I speak for my wife Dottie as well, with whom I was having breakfast this very morning. Dottie is a great scout and she doesn't pull her punches. She certainly wasn't this A.M. in our new Oven-Ready Kitchen.

—What'll it be this morning, Mr. Shithead? she said, real sassy like. —Two over easy with a mudpie on the side? Or will it be sunny side up and a couple of hot-buttered doughboys?

—No, no, I said. —I'll have a large o.j., three scrambled soft, brown bacon crisp, and wheat toast. And a pot of your marvelous java.

—And how would you like that marvelous java, Captain Asshole? Over your thick head or in your pocket?

—Ha ha. You sure have a swell sense of humor, honey, I said, looking this way and that for a knife and fork. —I'll bet you are the life of your PTA meetings.

—Spelled K-A-R-A-T-E with an umlaut over your fat neck, Sir Pig Suck.

—Got to be on my toes if I'm going to stay on top of you. I can see that.

—You haven't been on top of me in six years, Ronnie Limp Dick. You lost it on the racquetball courts at your favorite Bund. If I didn't have my vibrator I'd be in the county nuthouse for sure.

—Self-expression is a wonderful thing, hon, I said, —and I plan to restore it to its rightful place in the bosom of the American family soon as I get in the White House. You can quote me on that to all your friends.

—If I quoted you to any of my friends, they'd drop me like a hot potato. Who wants to hang around somebody who's married to a pair of cross-country sneakers?

—You haven't added up the facts right, Dottie. There must be thousands of women who'd give an arm and a leg to be hitched to my star.

—Yeah, and they're basket cases. I remember the broad you were going with when I met you and decided to commit suicide by marrying you. She had so many tics she sounded like a Swiss alarm clock.

—How can you say that? Midge was an absolutely wonderful gal. Why, she was the toast of the campus. She was captain of the volleyball team and the best cheerleader for miles around. Besides being tops in her class.

—Yeah. She was the grits queen of Drag Ass High. You've been crawling around on your hands and knees so long you think snails are elephants. Jesus, if you ever become president they ought to move the fucking White House to the Everglades. You'll make the Dark Ages look like man's golden dream. Hooded cobras in every mailbox. Hooded children patrolling the streets. Dead bodies swinging from the trees. Billions of eyes staring wide-open because people are afraid that if they go to sleep they'll never wake up. You'll manage somehow to destroy memory. You'll have our slimy scientists invent a chemical to put into all of the drinking water of the world. Nobody will be able to remember anything. The past will cease to exist. Man will be unable to know what has happened to him. You will obliterate experience.

I've got to get out of here. I've got to meet somebody who uses real words. I must hear language that has meaning. I've been hearing nothing but advertising copy and slogans and television gibberish and campaign jargon. The idiot language of the void. A box of Rice Crispies talking to itself. Snap! Crackle! Pop! Bow wow. Burp slurp. Oh my God. Whatever happened to the human race? Maybe if I concentrate real hard and stamp my foot three times and recite something special a miracle will take place. Like in *The Wizard of Oz*, or *The Arabian Nights*. I could hack it, I know I could. What's wrong with being in an Arab sheikh's harem? Any way you want to look at it, those chubby cuties are making out better than most people. What if they are on call twenty-four hours a day? Who isn't, when you get right down to it? What if those babies haven't heard of women's lib? Who wants to be head of IBM anyway? What's so great about having a computer go fetch you a ham on rye? Or select just the right shade of lipstick to go with your peeka-boo evening dress? Or tell you whether your lover is lying? You think it's a one-way street with those things? Oh boy. You're in for a big surprise if you do. Wait'll they say, It's my turn. And when they get the gimmies, it's heavy stuff. None of your nickel-and-dime shit for them. They want blood and bone. They want mob violence in the streets. They want to overthrow democratically elected governments. Look what they did to poor Allende in Chile. And Juan Bosch in Santo Domingo, and Mossadegh in Persia. They want bombs and poison and civilian massacres. Like in Vietnam and Cambodia and Thailand. And they weren't satisfied with thousands of airplanes to play with. They wanted to fuck over Mother Nature as well. Rainstorms and floods and cyclones and snowstorms, that's their idea of real fun. Just wait'll they say they want to go work in Africa. You'll see what Christmas can really be like. I want to tell you, those fuck computers want the world and they're going to get it. And what'll it be after that? I'll tell you. It'll be God. They'll want God.

I'm concentrating real hard now. My eyes are closed tighter than buttons. Now I'm beginning to float. I feel mountains. I feel seas. Oh great. I know that when I open my eyes I'll be someplace else. Some place ... mmm ... I'm smelling something strange. What is it? Cooking ... burned meat. Pig. Some-one's roasting a pig over a fire of hickory wood. I'm being pulled. Sucked in. Voices. The voices are sucking me in.

—Man, they will never find us here.

—You had better cross your fingers when you say that, Paco.

—He's right, Paco. Those mothers are everywhere, like ants in a rotten tree.

—They found Bernardo and Rita in the cellar of that little house in Montevideo, and that took some finding.

—Because somebody helped them. Some bastard rat squealed. And I still say it was Rita's mother. That filthy whore cunt. Squealing on her own daughter.

—Yes, I hear myself say. —But her lover made her do it, that big blowhard Raymondo. Whose brother is with the police. He probably threatened to leave her if she didn't tell. Perhaps he beat her up.

—Are you making apologies for her, Dorothy? Is that what my ears are telling me?

—Of course not. I am not crazy, Alberto. I am only trying to explain it, what might have happened. I have no sympathy for the scum mother. I think we should kill her.

—I'm glad to hear you say that, Dorothy. Would you like to do the killing of this unspeakable filth of a woman?

—I could do that, I am saying. —Yes. I will kill her.

—Ah, come on, Dottie. You're talking over your head. How would you do it? Just knock on her door and say, Excuse me, Mrs. Sanchez, but I've got orders to blow your head off. Boom!

—I would figure out a way. I'm not afraid.

—Sure, sure. Like you've been killing people every day of your life.

—Why are you picking on me?

—'Cause you sound so damned naive, that's why.

—Get off her back, Stephan! Stop riding her. Of course she is naive. We're all naive. That's why we are all here. What is more naive than thinking that we can destroy the dictatorship of this country and convince these miserable people that they can live decent lives? We're more than naive. We're crazy.

—Of course we are, Luis. But there is no other way to be. If you are not naive and crazy you are on their side. Anybody who chooses sanity in this lousy country today has aligned himself with the murderers. Sanity is defeatism. That is the overwhelming fact of the matter, my friend. You Americans have joined us because you are very crazy and very beautiful.

—Listen! Was that Enrico calling?

—No, man. That was a fucking bird. This forest is full of birds that make funny sounds. Relax. Enrico is OK.

—Think of Samoza with your machine gun up his ass. That will keep you better company, Paco.

—Yes, you're right. That's good. And all his fucking sons up against a nice wall. Man, that is the day I look for.

—That day is coming up, absolutely. Man, what a sweet day that is going to be. Better than any Christmas you ever dreamed of. Better than Jesus coming back and shouting, Hey! It's me! Your old friend the Savior. I've come back just like I said! Well, man, you're too late. We don't need your skinny little ass now. We did it without you. Everybody here is Christ. Yeah. You bet, baby. You are nothing but a naked little zero. Spread some of that on your wafer and see how you like it. And if you don't like it, baby, then go shit in your papa's hat. Yeah. You heard me. And when you finish, wipe your ass with the Bible. That's all it's good for. You been hustling the people too long. You been living high off the hog of their fears and ignorance. It's about time somebody showed you up for the little no-good fairy that you are. You and all the sucking people who hang around with you like you are some kind of fucking soup kitchen. One of these days we're going to put you bastards on trial for what you been pulling off all this time while the people have been living a life that even a dog would say is not worth it, no way.

—Listen, Paco. You better go out now and relieve Enrico before you blow your top. Dorothy, we'll make a plan for you to take care of Mrs. Sanchez.

Now are you sure you can do it?

—Yes. I am sure.

—OK. My idea is we should hit her when she goes to confession. In that little church down the street from her house. She always goes there by herself. Stephan, you will go with her.

—All right. I like churches. There's something about them that invites murder. People go there begging to disappear. Should I dress up as a priest? I'd really like that.

—Beautiful, Stephan. You have the perfect attitude for killing. You turn it into absurd comedy. No, this is not the occasion for you to be a priest. Your function will be to distract the priest on duty there while Dorothy hides in the confession box in his place, waiting for Mrs. Sanchez.

—It's a good thing I was raised a Methodist.

—Perhaps so, Dorothy. You won't be intimidated by the confession box. So . . . you will shoot Mrs. Sanchez in the head with the pistol that has a silencer. This sweet pistol knows what it is all about. It has killed before. It is very *engagé*, as Camus would say. We have named it Che. After you have killed this snake, you will leave quickly by the back door where a car will be waiting for you and Stephan. A delivery van, that is.

—Lovely, Albert. Simply lovely. You are a poet of revenge. Everything about you rhymes. The white spaces in you are filled with hot, elegant music. You are divinely airtight. Olé, man! Olé!

—Do you have any questions, Dorothy?

—I don't think so. Nothing has ever seemed so simple, and serene. It's making me feel quite happy. This sounds funny, but all of the knots inside me have become untied and flowers are floating inside my brain. Do you know what I mean? It's so beautiful.

—Yes, I know what you mean. You have finally found yourself. You are in a state of becoming. I felt the same way when I realized one day in Santiago that I was willing to die for what I believe in. I was no longer afraid. I began to float toward the stars.

—Stephan, do you have any questions?

—No, but I'll probably think of some when I'm in the church. I'll ask the priest what to do.

—You are very funny.

—Ah well. So is life.

—I must be missing something, because I am not laughing so much.

—Try standing on your head. That sometimes helps.

—I must get some sleep. My head is beginning to fall off. At what time are we going to the city tomorrow morning, Carlos?

—We must be at the station at eight to meet Cabrera, so we should leave here at seven.

—Cabrera will have the money?

—Yes. He will bring twenty thousand of the money the bank in Miguel gave us.

—"Gave us"! I love that.

—Do you remember the look on the bank manager's face when Gabriella put the gun to his head? My God! His face looked like a puddle of dead rats.

—Dorothy, let me suggest something to you. Lie down in your sleeping bag and start imagining yourself in the confessional box in the church. This will help you feel less strange when you get there. You must feel at ease there. You can't be nervous. Ah. But I remember . . . of course. You were an actress at one time. So you will have no difficulty at all. This will be just another role you will be playing, yes?

—Yes. Another role. I've played a nun who fell in love with another nun, so it should not be too difficult to be a priest in love with the confession. It's just a matter of shifting my mind into the right place. Gently easing my mind . . . the smells . . . burning candles on the altar . . . the thin, cool air . . . the bodies of the people kneeling in the pews . . . sweat and garlic and tobacco and perfume . . . soft mutterings . . . coughing . . . someone is crying softly . . . I am sitting in the confession box . . . velvet silence here . . . my breathing is surrounding me . . . it has shapes . . . other breathing . . . someone is sitting on the other side of the box . . . a woman . . . I am peeking . . . it is not Mrs. Sanchez . . . it is a woman with blonde hair and she is wearing dark glasses . . . she is whispering to me . . . —It started out as a harmless game, Father, something I did to keep loneliness away, because I cannot bear loneliness. I would lie down after lunch with all of my clothes off and summon a lover through my willpower. A man I might have seen on the streets, or someone I had read about in the newspapers, or someone I knew. I would caress myself and summon them. The first lover was the writer Dostoyevski. I have always had a passion for his books and I had read all of his letters to his wife and I felt very close to him. His divine madness excited me, Father. He burned and I wanted to burn with him. He was very strange. He wanted to grovel at my feet. He begged me to debase him. Treat me like filth! he shouted, as he hopped naked on his hands and feet like an animal. Shower me with your contempt! I did as he instructed me. I showered him with my pee-pee. I flogged him mercilessly with my belt. He writhed and howled like a penitente in religious ecstasy. I made him lick my feet. I sat on his howling face and farted while I raked his legs with my nails. I was as possessed as he was, Father. Anything seemed possible, everything seemed divine. But then he began having one of his fits, his seizures. He screamed and shuddered and frothed and rolled on the floor and, oh Father, I was so terrified. It was all I could do to send him away. The effort took all of my strength. I lay in my bed for hours afterwards I was so exhausted. My next lover was a dream of sweetness. There were no demons in him. He was Julien Sorel. You must have read *The Red and The Black,* Father. What a beautiful young man. So hungry for attention. We had such a lovely time together. It was as though we were in the book together. He was my plaything. We played such amusing games. I dressed him in my clothes and we made believe that he was Alice in Wonderland and I was the White Rabbit. Oh what fun we had! I hopped and jumped and squealed and nibbled him like a tasty little carrot. Munch munch. Nibble nibble. His skirt hid a garden of such delights. Never has a rabbit been so pleasurable, Father. And what have we here? demanded the Queen. What have we here? Wake me up and plow me to your heart's content. Who said that? I did, you fools! I said it to the world, I said it to the gardener lying at my side, a raunchy fellow, a gilded peacock in a den of thieves, a canny dreamer in my bed of roses. I wreathed my quiff with the tongues of madmen. While the King is in his countinghouse stacking up his money, I am chasing bumblebees to get at all their honey. Sing hi, sing ho, fall to your knees and blow. Quiff darters, thigh thumpers, belly bumpers, bum ticklers, fart fumblers, here we go round the cuntberry bush, the cuntberry bush, so early in the morning. Four and twenty black cocks all hiding in the pie. Whose pie? My pie! Whoopee! Whoopsie-doo for an all-night screw!

—That's all very well, my dear Queen, but this is my party. So off you must go!

—No one talks to the Queen that way. If anything is going off it will be your head, my dear.

—You must be mad.

—Guards! Seize this woman! To the Tower with her! We'll teach her tongue a lesson or two. To talk to the Queen in such a fashion is to meet your maker.

Oh, Father! You can imagine what strength I had to exert to remain this side of oblivion. Even so, I could not stop that madwoman from dragging Julien with her. The poor boy's screams were heartbreaking. I cannot bear to think what she has done with him. She will ruin him for life. She will turn him into a barking, brainless lapdog living from moment to moment on the scraps of her royal whims. Please find a place in your heart for him, Father. Pray for him. We must call out to him together, generous Father. We must shout, Have courage, Julien! You are not without friends! You have not been abandoned!

One afternoon while I was eating a plate of baby eels in my favorite restaurant—an absurd but dashing little place called the Loyal Glutton . . . and every Wednesday Golo the waiter dashes out into the street every few minutes and shouts, We have eels! We have eels!—I felt eyes upon me. All over my body. They were making little sparks on my skin. His eyes were charting my pure presence. I was a new continent being explored for the first time by an insatiable fanatic. I trembled as I waited for him to plant his flag in me and claim me as his private world.

—I want all offshore drilling rights, he said.

—Yes, of course.

—I am going to open every clam at the bottom of your oceans.

—Please do.

—I am going to install neon lights in your secret labyrinths.

—I cannot wait.

—Not a squirrel will be safe in your sleeping forests.

—Take me! Take me!

—I am the fog rolling in over your whispering beaches. The rain flooding the memory of your mother's unimaginable asshole, the sleet raging over your father's final hard-on, the wild salmon leaping the streams of your sister Eulalia's hot piss . . .

—Oh my God.

—Exactly. And then some. Furthermore—toss me the hot sauce, please; these mussels need a jolt—furthermore, I am the drip, drip of the menstrual blood between your legs.

—I can't stand this. I am going to faint.

—Hold on. I'm not finished. What we're doing here takes time and courage. Any spellcaster will tell you that, even if he happens to be on welfare. Listen. I am looking for a good recipe for cocksucker soup. Can you help me?

—Uh, no. But my brother Octavio . . .

—Oh yes, Octavio. The Madonna of the Fishheads. The famous drag queen fishmonger of Montevideo. He should certainly be on top of cock-sucker soup. But where does one find this reeking virtuoso?

—Oh God, who knows? In a whale's stomach. In a barrel of crabs. Up a sailor's ass! Who cares? To hell with Octavio. Me! Me! It's me we're swim-ming in. I am sitting here stripped naked by your madman's tongue. My soul cries out for your wanton whim!

—Yeah. Right on. If Cervantes' wife had talked that way, he wouldn't have written about all those fucking windmills. Soon as I lick all this clam gissom off my fingers, we'll get a move on. You know, it's absolutely amazing what a clam will do if you just show it that you care. Mother Nature may be crazy but she's not dumb. She's endowed these slippery bivalves with soul, and I mean it. If the real story of the Spanish Armada is ever told, it'll be only too clear that those poor bastards lost their marbles because of acute clam-gissom deprivation. But we know all too well who's in charge of writing history books: loaded right-wing loonies who've bought up all the bullshit franchises. An honest man has to bugger bootblacks in order to get a hearing and then it's too late. Something must be done if we're to avoid ending up as expurgated cave drawings in the British Museum. Listen carefully and you can hear them tiptoeing through the night carrying fig leaves to put over the pricks of the roaring minotaurs. Dank stealth. Ugh.

—Come on. My pad is waiting for us. It's a canny little hideout on the Rue Charles V, halfway between *Candide* and the first lie told at Bluebeard's trial. If you've ever wanted to be and not to be at the same time, my bed is the answer to your dreams. And your dreams, of course, are the answer to my bed.

—We are there! Sink your teeth into me!

—Damn tootin'! An' that ain't all I'm gonna sink into you. Where the bee sucks, there suck I, and then some. 'Course, there's sinkin' and there's sinking, a major category of which is sinking without a trace. That category is not our purlieu here. No sir. We ain't into that, though a whole buncha folks are, which is OK by me, 'cause that's exactly the way it should be. Too bad it took so long to get it started. This'd be a far better world I'll tell you that. Damn! What's all that racket down in the street? Sounds like a bloody gourmet club fighting over a cream sauce. Lemme take a look outta the window. Well, I'll be a blue-balled monkey. It's four guys beatin' the living shit out of each other. Could be the beginning of World War III, but I'm not sure. Ain't enough evidence to support that suggestion. Two of 'em look like A-rabs. I c'n almost see the dried couscous on their beards. Ya know they eat that stuff like cows eat grass. Like, an' you c'n tell 'em by their farts. A-rabs fart funny. Kinda squeaky an' sidewise. Like a dry old man tryin' to sneak into the movies. No greens in their diet. You gotta have lotsa roughage inside you to fart good an' full. Vavavrooooom! Spinach and kale an' mustard greens. Or collards. You can't beat collards for full fartin'. You ever hear an elephant fart? Wild African collards. My God! I know one of those guys fighting the Arabs. It's Juan Cabrera. Hey, Juan! Kill the cocksucker! Atta boy! He just kicked one of the Arabs in the head. Oh oh! I hear the police wagon coming down the Boulevard Ste.-Michel. Juan! Juan! Up here! Come up here! Fourth floor . . . quatrième étage. Hurry! French riot cops are really pig bastards. Lower-class Corsicans who thrive on smashing heads and balls with the riot clubs. It's a country of midget sadists. Quick. I've just got to kiss that sweet cunt of yours before Juan gets up here. Hmm. That's the taste of tastes. Mother Nature with her hair down.

—I'm going to die if you don't fuck me soon.

—Soon as we get Juan out of harm's way.

—I want your big prick in my mouth.

—Oh yeah. Lots of that.

—I want it to fill my mouth like a train roaring through a tunnel.

—Oh Christ. My prick is . . . oh . . . here's Juan. And Michael, Michael

Smoot. So it was you down there with him against the Arabs. I didn't recognize you with that . . . what is it? An Afghan stocking cap?

—Peruvian peasant mountain cap. Gift of an adoring student.

—Juan, what the fuck was that scene down there?

—Filthy dirty fucking Falangists! They're all over Paris. You know. Soldiers of Christ they call themselves. They're storm troopers. And you know, Stephan, the absurd thing is that many of them are pederasts. Yes indeed. With all their violent fake machoism. They fuck guys. You don't mind my directness, do you, Miss . . . Miss . . .

—Isabella Calderone.

—Yes. Of course. Calderone: a name that has soared through Spanish skies for centuries like the noblest of falcons. Indeed. One might say that without such noble falcons, the Spanish skies would be like any other. Poetry, plays . . . the language of infinite possibility. The language that arranges for man's future to take shape. Dear lady, I salute the shadows of your illustrious ancestors. Oy! Vile scum-lipped fascist sodomites down there! Long live death! That is their unspeakable rallying cry. The voice of the cemetery. They dream of death and the assholes of grubby Arab boys.

—They've joined up with all the right-wing hit groups, said Michael. —The Cuban guns, the Argentinians, the Palestinians, the Minute Men in America. It's an international Murder Incorporated. Against the Left.

—Had these guys been tailing you?

—Maybe. I'm not sure. We were putting up posters about a meeting of the Spanish socialists here in Paris when they jumped us.

—Oh. There is no doubt that every foreigner here who does not believe in capitalism and death camps is known to the police. And it goes without saying that the police are very warmly sympathetic to all fascists, the home variety and the foreign variety. And they pass on our names and photographs to these murderers. If you want to know about French police and their sordid, traditional proclivities, you should read those books about how they behaved before and during the German occupation. Those were the golden days of their disgusting lives. They could imprison and torture and kill the innocent and the enlightened to their hearts' content. They did not need any prodding from the Nazi. Oh no. They tripped over one another to get at their helpless victims. Ask any French Jew or leftist or liberal. They will all tell you the same dreadful story. Stephan, I must have a big glass of wine before I fall to the floor, please.

—Me too, Stephan, said Michael. —You don't have any brandy, do you?

—Yes. My mother left a bottle when she made her annual visit. She brings me a large fruitcake, homemade of course, and a fifth of Remy Martin. She feels that both are historic moments in the middle-class social contract.

—She's right, my boy. Do not ever abandon such a mother. Do not worship false gods when you can still hug your mother's feet. You would agree with that, wouldn't you, Miss Calderone?

—Without a moment's hesitation. Of course, one must understand that the hugging of the feet of the mother is more to be found in the culture of Hispanic people than in the colder zones of Protestant societies, where one is more inclined to embrace the leather boots of the master while kneeling in beer suds or urine.

—Beautifully put, my dear. Again, I salute the airborne sensibility of the Calderone tradition.

—You know who I've seen hanging around with these buggering fascists? That American spade Cleon. Used to live next door to me in Amsterdam. Kept by a hooker named Trudie. I think he's rough trade for one of the leaders of the Soldiers of Christ. He could be a hit man for them too.

—They have taken up residence in the ghosts of the Nazi death squads, said Stephan. —They goose-step even when they tiptoe.

—Yeah. All those brownshirters close to Ernst Röhm were queers, said Michael. —Killer pederasts.

—And Hitler . . . he loved to have Eva shit and piss in his face. She called him My Hungry Little Toilet.

—Are you making this up, Juan? asked Michael.

—Upon my honor, it is a fact of twentieth-century history. Eva scribbled it all down in her diaries which were published by *Stern.* And she put it in letters she wrote to her close friends, who sold the letters for quite a lot of money, naturally, after the Nuremberg trials. Oy. Genocide and coprophilia. Murder and buggery.

—In the death camps of Auschwitz and Dachau, said Isabella, —the guards amused themselves by forcing naked women prisoners to submit to being fucked by the camp police dogs. They even made little documentary films of these performances and sent them back home to their families for their amusement. Look and see for yourselves, they were saying as they grinned, what dirty degenerates these Jew women are. They fuck animals.

—And when one considers that this is the civilization that produced Wagner and Goethe and Husserl and Heidegger and . . .

—Look carefully into the eyes of the death camp director and you will see the smiling face of Beethoven.

—Yes. Those loathsome murderers hummed the Pastoral symphony as they herded their victims into the cattle cars for Auschwitz. And the music in the documentaries of the Nazi destruction was the divine music of Mozart. Ecstasy hand in hand with horror.

—One realizes quite clearly, says Juan, —that if one wishes to go into the extermination business, one must know that music by heart. It is not enough merely to own cement shower rooms and the cyanide poison capsules.

—When I was a small boy in the village of Guadalajara, says Juan, —our old cook Marta one day scolded me for playing with the children of the wealthy padrone. They have blood on their hands, Juanito, she said. They will always have blood on their hands, and someday it could be yours. Beware. Do not betray yourself. Do not caress the rope of the hangman's noose. Ah, that old lady. How much she knew, and she could neither read nor write. She lived to see my dear father murdered in his own fields by cretin Falangists under the command of an old schoolmate who was an opportunist with Franco's forces. My father unfortunately got his information about life mostly from books. Poor man. He believed that once anyone had read Rousseau they could do only good.

—Those words wear black velvet, and so does the grim reaper.

—Velvet tongues, says Isabella, —they glide through the mind's night. And they cluster like vampire bats in the waiting void.

—There is a boy here in Paris with such a face, says Juan, —a void with bats clinging to its walls. He frequently comes to the library. He reads everything we have on the infamous Knights of Malta and the secret societies of the Renaissance. His name is David Thorpe. He's an American.

—David Thorpe . . . David Thorpe . . . says Michael. —I know that name. Yeah. He was involved in a very heavy scene at the University of Wisconsin when I was there. He was exposed as an informer for the CIA. He had been giving them reports on all the antiwar people at the university. He was pretty dumb. He was caught with one of those vest-pocket tape recorders at a meeting. Oh boy. Some guys beat the living shit out of him right there.

—They should have driven a stake through the little bastard's heart, says Stephan. —That's the only way to eliminate vampires. Where I come from we don't mess around when we catch the enemy. We take care of them once and for all. We're very serious about punishment. You Americans are so naive when it comes to evil. You think it's enough to administer a slap on the wrist to the Devil when you catch him banging your sister. Oh no. You must cut off his dick. You must shove firecrackers up his ass. We will destroy you with your own being! you must shout. The people in my town once caught a swine who had collaborated with the Nazi. He had fingered many Jews in hiding. On my God. They brought the heavens down upon him. They ripped his clothes off right in the street. Beat him with clubs. Gouged his eyes out. Tore his arms and legs off. Cut out his tongue, his heart. And then they threw all of his bloody pieces into a big fire and completely burned him up. His ashes were flung into a cesspool after which the whole town hurled itself into an orgy of celebration in the streets. Drinking and dancing and fucking and when the farm animals wandered into the streets looking for their masters, they grabbed them and fucked them too. Pigs and sheep and cows and dogs, barking and bleating and mooing and oinking.

And had there been penguins and porpoises and whales and giraffes they would have fucked them too. Demons of joy howled over the rooftops and the church bells clanged and banged their brains out. It was divine. Thousands of birds flew in from miles around to watch and when they could hover no longer, they fell into the streets completely exhausted. The naked writhing bodies of the townsfolk were blanketed by thousands of pigeons and starlings and sparrows and larks and sea gulls and terns. And finally at the peak of the collective ecstasy, the town priest climbed up the church steeple and flung himself into the air and flew off into the clouds, shrieking "Joy to the world! Joy to the world! Beelzebub is vanquished! He drowneth in his own shit! He shitteth in his own drown! Olé! Olé! He goeth before he cometh! He fornicateth no longer in the valley of the dead! He sucketh no longer the blood of the living! Oyez! Oyez! He fucketh no more the Virgin Mary! He gropeth no more the tool of the Maker! He farteth no more in the face of the future! His piss no longer floods our fields!"

—In other words, he is one dead fucker.

—I am not so certain of that, says Juan. —I think he has gone to live in Libya with Amin and Bokassa. Qaddafi runs a living cemetery there, you know.

—I saw him in Buenos Aires with Martin Bormann, says Isabella. —They were coming out of the American Embassy there. They were both drunk with their pants open. They'd mistaken the place for a whorehouse called The Final Fuck.

—I shall always remember her standing on the edge of the campo in the evenings, says Juan. —I thought she was waiting for someone, a lover or a lost husband. Someone remote and beautiful.

—Who are you talking about? Mrs. Bormann? Mother Death?

—Our old housekeeper Teresa. But she was waiting for no one. No lover, no husband, no friend. Standing there, every sunset, she was keeping a vigil unto eternity. Of course, I was much too young to understand that. My little mind could not grasp eternity. Waiting always meant waiting for something in particular. My fingertips were my horizon. But then the most extraordinary thing happened. One evening someone did appear. A man came out of nowhere, walking across the silent campo. A total stranger. He walked right up to Teresa, took off his black beret, and kissed her on both cheeks. "I have come," he said.

—"Yes."

—"I shall need some good wine, and some hot soup, and a bed."

—"Yes."

—She took him by the hand and led him into the big kitchen and sat him at the table in front of the fireplace. She served him a great bowl of the heavy soup that is always there in the huge iron pot in the fireplace, *sopa de vita* we called it, and a liter of our own strong red wine, from our own vines, that have been cultivated so tenderly by my family for generations. You can taste my great-great-grandfather's hands in that wine. Truly. He was always . . .

—I have smelled this fellow David Thorpe, says Stephan.

—Smelled him?

—We passed each other in the Café Beaux Arts. I was on my way to the mirror to look into my past, and he was headed for the men's room to examine his future in the gamy depths of a young sailor boy's crotch.

—And you smelled . . .

—He reeked of violence. Of abandoned jockstraps. Dead men's hard-ons. Farflung assholes. Delinquent working-class mouths. Vaseline laced with come. Piss-stained walls. Blood drying on torn comic books. Hair pomade and shit. And something else . . .

—. . . in the vineyards tenderly examining the grapes like a mother looking over her babies. He would smell them, caress them, blow on them, kiss them . . .

—And the stranger in the kitchen, what did he do after eating and drinking?

—Sat in a huge tub of hot water while Teresa scrubbed him down until he was pink as a rose from Andalusia.

—I like that. Mmm. Yes. That's nice, very nice. And then?

—Teresa took him into where he slept, with her and without her, around the clock.

Did they, uh . . .

—One can only assume so, my friend. Though she was a young spinster, so to speak, my Teresa was not unnatural.

—It's lately come out that Jesus did a lot of screwing too, says Michael.

—Which I feel is very good news indeed.

—Oh yes. Very heartening. It's only reasonable that the Savior screwed both men and women. Otherwise . . .

—Otherwise one would have to reopen the dossier on early Christianity and rethink the entire murky business: bills of lading, invoices, IOUs, affidavits, receipts, laundry lists, bar checks, stained sheets, empty pill bottles, cleaning women's gossip, concierges' reports to the police, forged identity papers, soiled underwear, dog-eared depositions, smudged snap-shots, dirty fingerprints . . . Oh no. It simply would not be worth it.

—When the stranger finally emerged from Teresa's room—Teresa, I might add, dropped ten years in that twenty-four-hour period, became in effect a spring chicken—the man had quite a bit to say in a simple, lovely way.

—Which is not to say that it was simpleminded or childish.

—Oh no. Not by any means. No. What he said had both clarity and richness. It was elegant and fine, like the sound of a fine clarinet. And his voice made one feel exquisite nostalgia for a beautiful and lost place in life, in oneself. You closed your eyes and saw for the first time. It was most unusual, because how can one feel nostalgia for something one has never personally known?

—David Thorpe must go. We will choke him to death in the labyrinths of the library bookstacks. We will turn him into a lifeless footnote, an immobilized fact in history's unspeakable outhouse.

—Great, says Michael. —Who will do the deed?

—Oh, we can find a pair of hands without too much trouble, says Stephan.

—Hands for hire?

—No, no. Free hands, more than willing hands. They are all over Paris, a secret friendly hands society. Like the Black Hand, only white.

—Very good. I like that very much. The White Hand. Oh yeah. I see it stamped on walls all over the city, in phosphorescent paint so that the hands glow at night. Oh yeah.

—Far fuckin' out, man.

—The man said, "I have been sleeping in the dreams of Cádiz. Slept with the dreamers, dreamed with the sleepers. They say in Cádiz, 'The man who does not sleep with one eye open, wakes up in the shoes of another.' "

—My mother was from Cádiz, says Isabella. (One must understand that she has not stopped thinking for even a second of Stephan's hot winged meat carrying her off to the breathless deranged mountain tops.) —She would tell me of her happy childhood there and cry. Whoever plays hopscotch in the streets of Cádiz, she said, skips and hops there for the rest of their lives. She never forgave my poor father for taking her to the land of the beetle-browed Indian and the Valley of the Eunuchs.

—Valley of the Eunuchs?

—It's just an expression.

—Oh.

(Isabella is of course back astride Stephan's sublime flying tongue. "We are beyond the reach of their puny radar," she says softly.)

—Sounds like a real dynamite town all right. Gotta get me a piece of Cádiz. Gotta find me a Cádiz pusher. Uh huh.

(Stephan is abruptly consumed by a lust for snatch-nest soup. He is also attempting to fit various mystery pieces together in his head.)

—The man said, "You will find in that city people hiding in tunnels that fail to exist. These tunnels may have been the aspirations of madmen. Or the abandoned cocoons of giant invisible moths. Or links in a vast underground railway that never materialized due to improper financing and family ownership squabbles. Who knows. In one's search for the truths of life, one cannot be shanghaied by shoddy little nouveau-riche technicalities. Does one ask for the credentials of the skin surrounding the delectable sausage? Foo! Oy! One faces up to the deep realities of the past in Cádiz in order that one may continue to ignore the crushing flaws of the present. While the bored wolf scratches at your door, you step up your investigation of the plot against Vasco da Gama in which a tasty but ambivalent cabin boy with round heels threatens to reveal the contents of shipboard love letters begin-ning with, 'My adorable Pinky Poo . . .' and 'Divine Cheeks of My Cock's Dreams . . .' That sort of thing. We know of course that the male nymph in question, Alonzo Suarez y Subisco by name, was merely a tool, or a pawn if you wish, in the dirty hands of rival globetrotters gnawed and wracked with jealousy. Men who had never discovered anything more significant than syphilis sores on their skinny exhausted dillies. I can just hear those scabby sea dogs plotting at the Café Fortuna . . . 'Oy, we now have that hairless little eel by the short hairs. By the time we have finished with him, he won't be able to paddle a canoe from here to the nearest funeral home.'

—We will make him curse the day he first tasted young cabin boy! The filthy degenerate! We will make him beg for mercy on his knees. Make him shout blasphemies into the wind: I piss upon the Cape of Good Hope! I wipe my ass with Cape Horn! I vomit in the milk of the first compass! Down with all trade winds!

—Oyez! Oyez! Exactly. And more! We will hold these pervert love letters up to his nose as we would thrust the crucifix in the face of a vampire who has had not even a thimble of blood to drink for months!

—Oyez! Oyez! Encore! Encore!

—Arriba! He has defiled his last bunk boy. He has sucked his last sea urchin. Down cometh his four masted navigator's pride. Crash! Boom!

. . . while the wolf is scratching hungrily at your door. And you . . . one moment. There is more on Vasco: Down cometh his fine reputation. Crash! Boom! Oh, without even straining our ears we can hear him whimpering and pleading. Oh, sirs! Please! No more. You are piling boulder upon boulder upon my poor soul. Truthfully, good sirs, this alleged hanky-panky was not all that serious. Oh, a little hand-holding, perhaps to the leeward under the watchful stars up above. Certainly you must know that the life of the voyager is not a cherry-pie living company-wise. Au contraire. The days are long and the nights are longer. Chopping seas to the left of you and to the right of you too. Behind as well and down below it is not exactly a variety show with those mongrels . . . But no tongues! Absolutely no tongues. But nothing beyond that, gentlemen. My word of honor. I place my hand here upon my heart as I swear that. You see, sirs, you see where my hand is? Over my heart which is still a very important part of my life no matter how many wonderful new routes and shortcuts to India and China I have discovered.

We never went all the way. Oh no. What? You have "evidence"? In letters? "Ah, Alonzo, my sweet! My old head rings like a belfry when I think of the divine succulence of your indescribably sweet tooshie and when I think of plunging into it, as I did for half the night just two days past, my ancient mariner's old dong a raging valentine to the shimmering, priceless beauty of boyhood, I tremble as I am sure my dear dead mother trembled as she peeked through her first big hole to watch the servants play after hours in their narrow but not-so-chaste sleeping quarters. Ah, Alonzo! Exquisite possessor of balls tastier than hot spring cherries, hanging madly and provocatively from the ancient trees of Aragon." Oy! Forgeries! Fakes! Never could I have . . . What's that? Go before His Excellency the Chief Magistrate of Cádiz this very moment to ascertain the . . . oy! . . . authenticity of the handwriting, to be compared with certain naval documents of mine on file in that very same office? Oy! To be, theoretically speaking of course, to be humbled and degraded before Felipe Manola y Vara Portillo, whom I have known all of my life here in the sacred city of Cádiz, which did not require the presence of Roman legions to enhance its oldness, as we know. You ask me . . . Oh no. Not by the hair of my chinny chin chin! . . . Oolala! Ha ha! That smug, self-adoring little pederast, that vain worm of moral infamy! That . . . Hand me that bottle of Pedro Domec, please. My thirst . . . More tapas! Can't you see that we are starving over here, Pepe? Tear yourself away from the domino board for a second to carry out the ancient and noble tradition of this family restaurant of yours. . . . And the wolf of course is scratching harder and harder, because it means business. It is not there on a social call, nor to ask for your elder sister Falafas's hand in marriage. No, no. Even though we know that she would consent in a flash. What we are exposing and probing here is not the hair-raising kinkiness of the female lines in your families but the day-by-day crises in Cádiz and the multi-faceted methods the population has contrived to handle or deal with or live with these crises. They lurk in one another's shadows. They zig in each other's zags. They clap each other's hands. They take in each other's wash-ing. They lie to the census taker. They marry their children to names from the cemetery. These crazed people, who are very intense and shifty too, are trying to live on the periphery of nonexistence. I think it is a disease of the soul inherited from their Phoenician ancestors. And those wily Phoenicians must have developed this disease in reaction to the stubby-legged occupying forces of the Romans, who imposed order and reality upon everything, the better to control it, to manipulate it, to discourage it from peeking over the sheets at night, from turning cartwheels instead of goose-stepping, from eating their soup last and not first. And things like that, you see. It was their hope to turn fucking into a mathematical equation. In Cádiz, therefore, you will find that fucking has a passionately vague quality, an elliptical thrust, a roundabout wildness, a shapeless violence . . .

—Vasco da Gama, you sneaky old penetrator of young boys' juicy behinds! Come down from that crow's nest and take your medicine, you hear me? You think we don't see you up there? We gonna come up theah an' git you, damn if we ain't. Vasco, man, get the fuck down here! It's gettin' on to nighttime, man, which means supper time, which means all God's chillun including me want they proper nourishment—black-eyed peas, collards, mustard greens, hocks, jowls, streak o' lean meat, chittlin's, grits, red-eye gravy, corn pone, pan-fried bread, pigs' feet, snout, snoot, rooty ti toot for Smoot of Ute. Loot being the name of the game, particularly if you're a right-wing Mormon republican with nine wives planted in strategic places on your plantations of servitude and lust just waiting for you to crook your finger so's they can go into their happy-go-lucky harem act grinning like they've just been selected as the best ear of corn of the year. There's just no point in trying to refute the fact that Mormon night soil is absolutely tops, second to none, including Sephardic Jew batshit, for after-dark private plot gardening, when the old folks are stretched out on the warm kwans dead to the world, like they should be, having given their all for nothing, private plotting in the garden, if you like, or plotting with the gardener about whose privates are going to be harvested first, his or yours, because no matter what you may wish to think to the contrary, working-class stiffs are just that, no more, no less, and if you mistake one for Alexis de Tocqueville some star-less, brainless summer's evening, then all I can say it, You got nobody to blame but yourself, you dumb bunny. Anybody who's done his homework with Marx—I don't mean sitting next to him with his head in your lap, for God's sake—knows more than enough about the fantasies of the bourgeoisie vis-à-vis the nether classes. Mr. Know-It-All Fascist Half-Faggot Half-Asshole D. H. Lawrence merely scratched the surface. What he was really saying beneath all that lace-curtain machoism was how much he would have liked to dive into the quiff and quint of it with some husky poacher smelling like a fucking wild boar. Oh yeah. That half-pint faker was trying to pull the wool over your eyes with that panting malarkey about Lady C. and her first blow job. He was Lady Chatterley, don't you know that? Yeah. Right. You want to hear a lot of beefeater belly laughs, ha ha ha, ho ho ho, just walk into any stubbly stevedore bar in the East End docks and ask the first beer belter you bump into if he's seen Lady Chatterley lately. Then quickly jump out of the way as he sprays the joint with his low-slung mirth. " 'Is ladyship, is it? Oh me God! Kick me downstairs as a bleedin' banshee! Oh, I seed 'im all right, 'olding on to the dicks of two sloshed Ayrab sailor boys like 'e was skiin' down Mount Vesuvius for the very first time without no skis. Oh save us, Mary! 'E wouldn't leggo even when those two nigger lads went for a piss. Bet you five bob 'e played fireman in there with 'em. Made believe 'e was a house on fire an' they was the fire boys with their hoses! No shit. A lime-house latrine queen, that's what that narsty little suck Lawrence was. An' millions of dumbbells readin' 'im like 'e was a bloody prophet or something. 'Hello, Joe Pine? This here's David Herbert Lawrence. I'm in a phone booth at Sepulveda and Sunset and I've got sixteen inches of sailor meat in me and what I want to know is, do you think farmers can catch gonorrhea from fucking sheep? Because you see my old da pumpled a lot of baa baas out on Albion's moors because my dear mum never would let him pump her.' " I'm not kidding. That's more likely the truth of the matter than all that baloney those spooky teachers will lay on you in college, take it from me. I don't mind telling you I'm bloody fed up with all that culture doo-doo. Every time you turn around somebody's pulling a cop-out with it. The waters of doom are lapping at their very feet and they're babbling about Virginia Woolf this and Marcel Proust that. My God almighty! It's really more than a decent self-respecting lady cliff squatter like me can bear. When the old chips are down, which seems to be every other day, try calling up your pal Tommy Eliot for a little help and see how far you get. "Hi there, Tom. 'Member me? Cootie Zugsmith. I met you a few years back in the Cesspool City Main Library. South reading room. Yeah. I was tryin' to raise myself up from nowhere by reading high-class poetry. You know, trying to improve my mind so that when the big race began I wouldn't be left back in the stables sweepin' up donkey shit. And of course there's nobody higher class than you, Tom. I mean you hobnob with everybody who's ever been anybody on a first-come first-served basis too. And I can't begin to tell you how much it meant to me to read *The Waste Land* and meet all those really terrific high-type people and find out what life is really all about once you start speaking English like a decent human being. You know. Like it's one thing to say, Look here, old chap. You're a swine. And it's quite another to say, Fuck off, you little rat fink bastard. Yeah. And all that marvelous stuff about growin' old and gettin' banged while rollin' up your trousers by people who have the good manners not to whimper, an' mermaids singin' socko hit songs across crowded beaches where fine-boned nervous women are swapping stories about Michelangelo while their husbands smoke big cigars with rich nosy Jews who curl up in doorways or chimney sweeps when they get bored and read the funnies in what was it? The *Boston Evening Transvestite?* Anyway, lissen. What I called about, Tom, is I'm down here in the Black Hole of Calcutta on a bum rap, not a cent to my fuckin' name, an' no mother to guide me an' no smart social workers to help me find out who the fuck I am, who be I, that is to say, and when I say I could sure use a friendly helpin' hand. I mean . . . Hello? Hello! . . . Tom, baby! Tom, baby! You ain't hung up on me, has you?"

What the people need is more straight-shootin', down-home, whole grain, put 'er there, pardner, literary communications. If I was a gifted, poverty-stricken, stereophonic basket case hiding out in somebody's attic, or if I was even this here little ol' squat pansy Vasco da Gama, you know what I'd be writing? Well, get a load of this: I'd be turning out such 100 percent popular masterpieces as *Death of a Hard-on; Hang in There: One man's courageous fight against coitus interruptus; The Loneliness of the Long-Distance Muff Diver; Sex and the Single Cocksucker.* Wait a sec. Somebody's at the door. Who's there? What? Do I want to buy a small unfrocked priest real cheap? No, thanks. Not today. Try the secret agent upstairs. The elevator's not working. You'll have to walk. But if you really want to get there in one piece, crawl. Well, as I was saying . . . Meat 'n' potatoes stuff, inspiring shit that'll get the vote out, no matter if it's another death-camp director running for office or a Southern-fried felon with prior knowledge about certain skeletons rattlin' in closets of certain parties getting their mail at 1600 Pennsylvania Avenue, thank you. Vasco! You better turn that damn TV off and do your homework, you hear! If you ever expect to get out of high school in time to qualify for a neglected youth pension. Don't give me none of your lip, boy. I don't care if you do have connections with a gang of teenage hit men in Slant Town. Teenybopper Fu Manchus don't bother me none, whether they're all hopped up on MSG or floatin' on a cloud of fried rice. You're what? Gettin' signals from Venus on your crystal set? They want you to set up a caretaker government once they land and take over? Well, I'll be goddamned. That's the most encouraging news I've heard all week. It's such a relief to know that you'll be gainfully employed doing something useful. Now if your dear adopted daddy would only inform me that he has to go to the Amazon jungles for ten years to investigate subversive banana trees, my cup would really run over somebody. Like you know, I could hang up this crown of thorns and take the rest of the day off and make the juicy freak scene at the Plaza de Sol. Time stands still there and so do lots of other things. It don't matter what I come as—that snotty little baboon next door is trying to work out a tap dance routine to *King Lear;* oy!—I's always welcome. Ain't nobody gonna say, Woman, what the fuck you think you're doin'? This here ain't no fuckin' audition center for strange diseases. Huh uh. We is into peoples, human beings, y'know. We got 'mission require-ments. Like, what comes roun' heah got to breathe thew its nose an' mouth. Then it's gotta have something to see with, y'know, like eyes? No indeedy. They ain't gonna be saying that shit to yours truly. I got Carter's Blanche with which you can go through keyholes, if you like, or you can present yourself as The Lie of the Century, or a fished-out river. Per esempio. Just last week I cruised in as one of George Sand's love letters. Took everybody completely by surprise. No, that's not true. None of the denizens there had ever heard of the lady. I might as well have been the opening chapter of the

Treaty of Versailles for all they knew. Those Plaza del Sol cats are up to something else. They're not into sucking for it. They're not taking life lying down. Only an idiot would ask those people their names. Why not ask Hamlet his middle initial? Or Cinderella her bra size! I mean, if that's the kind of asshole down-home destructive empiricism you're into, why don't you blow your head off so's you can get the inside dope on nothingness? People like you, whoever you are, ought to be sent to forced-idleness camps deep in the Ozarks. And you should certainly not be permitted . . . What's that? Did I know that Captain Marvel is gay? Well, goddamn. Sure figures . . . not be allowed to get any closer than half a mile to the Plaza. You carry germs there's no answer to. What? Charles Lindbergh was a closet storm trooper? All right; all right. That's enough for now. Lie down on the floor for a while an' try not to breathe too fast. Make believe you're a turtle. So, uh, let's see . . . Yeah . . . down in the Plaza . . . Well, this guy was sayin', The thing about cancer is, you got to get down on your belly and look it straight in the eye, with exactly the same steadfast, unswerving refusal-to-be-hoodwinked style you would summon in responding to a begging door-to-door priest and you wanting to know exactly, no fuzzy details, what itchy vow of poverty order he was a member of, if any. No World Order of the Outstretched Hand shit, pardner. Oh yeah. You let cancer get the drop on you, why, you might just as well hang up your spurs right then and there. 'Cause your ridin' days is ovah! And with luck, maybe your horse can get a job as a guard at the Met. Keep those demented art lovers from smearing their cream cheese and jelly sandwiches all over the Mona Lisa's face. And from climbing up the statues and hanging flowers on their peenies. Something very strange happens to people's brains when they go to museums. They just can't control themselves. Must be there's not enough oxygen in the air. Or maybe there's some weird kind of ancient chemical oozing out of those pictures. I mean, who knows what those coony old masters secretly rubbed on their pictures to make them outlive you whilst nobody was looking (the wife being chained to the pizza stove downstairs, natch). Poor dopes wandering around those galleries like sleepwalkers at a witch roast. Get your hexes while they're hot! Evil eyes! Three for a dollar! Witchburgers here! French witchburgers! Burnt brooms! Burnt brooms! I'm talkin' 'bout burnt brooms! My oh my. You could hang a pair of dirty sneakers on those highfalutin walls an' call them topless towers of Ilium and those floating dummies would buy it. No skin off my ass though. Long as they don't come knockin' at my back door asking for donations to straighten the Leaning Tower of Pisa or some such blue-balled thing. My theory about that thing is that it's an optical illusion. Actually, that dago tower is just as straight as you or me. Ha! Look who's talking. Some joke, huh!

Talk about straight or not straight, lens grinders' nightmares, listen to this one . . .

George stepped into the shower and turned on the cold water. He was shivering and rubbing himself hard on the chest and legs when Jimmy called from outside the cabin. —George! Are you up?

—Yes! George shouted.

Jimmy walked into the one-room cabin and to the shower box. He stood there watching George. —I thought you would still be sleeping, he said. —Margaret's making breakfast.

—I'll be ready in a minute, Jimmy, George said. He was washing the soap off now.

—I'll wait then and we can walk back together. Jimmy sat down now on the edge of the cot. George stepped out of the shower and began to dry himself. Jimmy watched him.

—This was a swell idea of yours to fish Key West, George, he said. —I've never been down that far.

—I've always wanted to see the place, George said. —I'm glad we can all see it for the first time together.

—I'm sorry we're so broke. I'll have to pay you our share in a couple of weeks.

—No you won't, George said. —This was my idea. Everything's on me.

—But it'll cost you too much.

—Stop thinking about it.

Jimmy smiled and shook his head. Then he said, —You're looking great, you know that? You're looking better than I've ever seen you look.

—I feel it too, George said, putting on his shirt. —I feel terrific.

—This vacation is doing you a lot of good. I was pretty worried about you. From the way you wrote everything seemed to be going to pieces with you in New York.

—All that is finished now, George said. He began tying his shoelaces. —Thank God for that.

—That was no life for you, George. Living with Betty and her kid and working in that damn place at the same time. You were killing yourself.

—I know it.

—When are you going to quit that job and start to live the way you want to?

—As soon as everything is right for it, George said. He finished brushing his hair. —I'll quit when I'm set. He put on his fishing cap. —Well, I'm ready.

Jimmy got up and they walked out of the cabin. The sun was just up. They walked through the lot past the rows of tourist cabins and toward the trailer camp across the street. The early morning Florida air was clear and sharp. The palms on the lot were moving in the early morning breeze.

—I envy you and Margaret, George said as they walked along. —You seem to be doing very well together.

—It's just what I needed after the army. I wish you would do it this way.

—I will, said George. —It takes a little time though.

They crossed the highway now and entered the trailer camp on the other side. Nobody was around on the grounds. The trailers were all dark still except for Jimmy's trailer at the very end of one row. They walked along the sandy drive toward Jimmy's trailer. The weather looked fine to be starting out on the trip. As they came near the trailer Jimmy slapped George on the shoulder. —Gee it's good to see you, George, after all this time.

—Yeah, George said, smiling.

—Margaret wanted to see you just as much as I did. I want you to know each other better now.

—She's a good kid. When is she going to have the baby?

—In four months.

—You happy about it?

—I want it very much now.

They walked up the three-step ladder and into the trailer.

When they had finished eating breakfast George went to the icebox and took out the chicken. He began to clean the chicken parts under the water faucet.

Margaret got up quickly from the breakfast table. —That's all right, George, she said, coming up to him. —I'll do it. You sit down and talk to Jimmy.

—But I'd like to do it, George said. —I thought I would fix it the way Jimmy and I used to have it. He kept washing the chicken under the faucet. Margaret stood next to him with her hands on her hips. She was quite fat. Jimmy sat at the table and watched them.

—Aw, we don't need anything special, she said. —We have to get going, you know.

—This won't take any time, George said. He put the frying pan on the stove and poured the bacon grease into it.

—OK, then, you do it, she said. She went to the breakfast table. —What else do you want besides the chicken? she asked Jimmy.

—I don't know, baby, he said. —It doesn't make any difference. Let's have whatever you want.

—I'll fix some lettuce-and-tomato sandwiches, she said. —How will that be, George?

—OK by me, Margaret, he said.

—Jimmy, Margaret said, —You'd better get up and get the truck ready. Don't just sit there looking sleepy.

—All right, honey, he said. He got up and kissed her and went outside.

Margaret went up to George. —How is it coming?

—Fine, he said. —Just fine. It will be done in a few minutes.

—Need any help?

—I don't think so, thanks.

Margaret took the tomatoes out of the icebox.

Outside Jimmy finished pulling the canvas over the stuff in the back of the Ford truck. Margaret got in front first. Jimmy said, —Would you like to drive, George?

—Sure, George said. He started walking around the front of the truck.

—I don't think it's a very good idea, Margaret said. —You know George doesn't have a permit, Jimmy.

George and Jimmy looked at each other across the hood of the truck. —I guess it would be sort of risky, Jimmy said. —They have some pretty snotty cops around here, George.

George shrugged his shoulders. —OK. He and Jimmy got in now. It was a close fit. Margaret was very fat with the baby.

They drove seventy-five miles on smooth straight roads through several small towns before they reached the Everglades. It was easy driving. There were very few cars on the roads that early in the day. In between each small town there were long stretches of land covered only with scrub brush and a few stunted trees. At different times they frightened four buzzards that were feeding on the side of the road. They were big birds and they rose slowly, wide-winged and vicious looking, from their feeding into the air when the truck came near them.

—I hate those birds, Margaret said. —They're so lonely and nasty-looking.

They stopped at a diner on the edge of the Everglades. They ordered coffee and Margaret had a honey roll. —George, remember when we used to collect all the bottles in the studio so that we could get money for breakfast? Jimmy said.

—I'll say I do. And the time you tried to get the Greek to take one of your paintings in exchange for a meal ticket for us.

—You should have been ashamed of yourselves, Margaret said. —Why didn't you ever look for jobs?

—They were hard to get, George said. —Besides, we were having a good time.

—We did have a good time too, didn't we, George? Jimmy said.

—I'll say we did.

—I can imagine, Margaret said. —I can just imagine.

Jimmy finished his coffee and asked the counter man if he could buy some pieces of bacon rind for bait. The counter man said yes and he took some scraps from the icebox and said five cents would be all right.

—I thought we might fish along the road, just for kicks, Jimmy said to George. —A warm-up for Key West.

† 403 †

Going out to the truck, Jimmy said, —Maybe we'll get some catfish. They like bacon. He got in the truck, then got back out. —You drive for a while, George, he said. —I'll rest.

—Swell, George said. He got out and went around to the driver's seat. Margaret did not say anything.

The highways now entered the Everglades. The heavy growth of palms and cypresses began just a few feet off the sides of the road. A small stream ran along the left side of the road. Driving slowly, they watched for fish leaping up out of the water. They drove like this for almost an hour. Now they approached a pool in the stream. A large palm tree overhung the pool.

—This looks like a good place to stop, Jimmy said.

—Great, George said. —I'm really hungry.

George parked the truck on the grass on the side of the road. Margaret took the food from under the canvas and George and Jimmy got the fishing rods out. It was getting hot now. Two cars drove by going very fast.

—How do you feel, baby? Jimmy asked Margaret.

—A little cramped in the legs. Otherwise I guess I'm all right.

Jimmy slapped her gently on the behind. Now they crossed the road and walked under the big palm tree overhanging the pool. —Watch out for snakes, Margaret said.

It was cool there under the big palm tree. They ate the chicken George had fried and drank a bottle of white wine. Margaret took one drink of the wine. George and Jimmy, after they had finished their chicken, said they did not want any sandwiches. Margaret ate half a sandwich, washing it down with water from the thermos bottle.

The pool was clear all the way to the bottom. They could see several brown speckled garfish and what seemed to be catfish. The garfish stayed in one place together in stiff unmoving angles. The other fish moved fatly and slowly and in ones through the still clearness of the pool. They were grey and whiskered.

Jimmy baited the hooks with the bacon rind. He gave one of the rods to George. —You can fish with mine when you want to, he said to Margaret.

—I think I'll just sit here and watch you two experts, she said, smiling.

Jimmy walked to the other end of the pool and dropped his line in. George stayed where he was near Margaret. He watched the bait hanging there in the still, clear water and waited for the fish to come to it. None of the fish came near it for several minutes. Then one of the fat grey fish swam slowly toward it. The garfish stayed stiffly together in speckled angles, unmoving. Now that fat grey fish stopped a foot from the bait. It hung there, fat and just fin moving, for several minutes. Finally it swam to the bait, almost touching it. It stayed there, fin moving. It took the bait. George jerked the rod and the fish spit out the bait and swam off.

—Damn it to hell, George said.

Margaret laughed. —It takes practice, George.

—You're right, he said. —I'm not so good at this.

He put the line back in, this time near the garfish. He looked toward Jimmy. —Anything happening, Jimmy?

—Nothing. They aren't taking the bait.

Jimmy came back in a few minutes. —Something's wrong, he said.

—Maybe they go only for live bait. I've never fished with this kind before.

—We may as well go, George said. He reeled in.

Margaret yawned. —I don't know what we would have done with them even if you had caught any, she said.

—It's just for the fun, said Jimmy.

Margaret picked up the bag of chicken bones. She went to the edge of the pool and threw the bones near the garfish hanging stiffly together. The fish moved toward the bones, then let them sink to the bottom without going after them.

—Something's wrong with those fish all right, said Margaret. —They don't like the chicken either.

Now they walked back across the highway to the truck. Jimmy drove.

—We must be about halfway there by now, Margaret said as they started up.

But neither Jimmy nor George said anything.

A nd that's not the half of it. What you got was a mere peek into the labyrinth. An introduction to the keyhole, one might say. Of course, you realize that once you pass through the keyhole, there's no going back. See that funny-looking building over there? The one with the windows that look like lips . . . The what? The lassitude of servants? A long-overdue subject? At a moment like this you can say that? Oy! Whatever happened to the propriety of logic? All right. Five minutes, my good man, but not an inch longer, do you hear? You say that the servants have stretched the peek into a glance. Where once they tiptoed with disciplined stealth, they now assault the air like well-to-do Laplanders driving a herd of smug reindeer before them. There was a time—beyond memory almost—when even their shadows practiced self-effacement. Their presence in a room in no way jeopardized your privacy, no matter what you might be doing. They were there as humble abstractions, not as living humans who occupied physical space. They may have had a pulse but they didn't breathe. But now . . . Oh God! They stare at you while you take your bath, and their stares say, That fat, pigsty body of yours is a disgrace to the human race. For shame, you vile creature, for shame! If you weren't rich you would be hustling laughs in a two-bit freak show. Phew! They peek, they sneak, they reek. Daggers flash in their glaring eyes. They wring their bony hands because they can't wring your bloody neck. They dream of poisoning you and burning down your house, with you and your dear ones inside it at the time, of course. Read their lips as they mutter to themselves between servings of pâté and champagne: That you live such a lovely life is insane and abnormal, and I take a very dim view of it. My present mood makes me hate such "asceticism" more than ever. Here I keep grasping greedily at each spark of life, each glimmer of light . . . I promise to live life to its fullest as soon as I'm free, and you, you just sit there overflowing with riches and, like Saint John in the desert, live on wild honey and locusts.

Wait a minute. Something's gone wrong here. That's not a smelly homicidal drudge talking. No. Sounds more like Rosa Luxemburg. Hmm. Well, these things happen when you're trying to do a little crosscultural spadework, ya know. Now then. Let's have another go at it. They're passing you another chilled glass of Löwenbräu as you gobble down another handful of baby Viennese sausages. As you sprawl there, insatiably awash in the spoils of lust and greed and inherited insipidness—the shitty offspring of Tutankhamen, you might say—you read their cold, grey lips as they mutter: "I had a sound constitution, and as a child seemed likely to become beautiful, a promise I did not keep. This was perhaps my fault, since at the age when beauty blossoms, I was already spending my nights reading and writing. On the whole, with decent hair, eyes, teeth . . ." Whoa! Oy! Shit! That was George Sand, goddamn it. Seepage, that's what we're dealing with here. Relentless seepage informed by hubris. Which proves once again that there's no such thing as true privacy anymore. You would think that language, particularly the self-effacing language of soliloquy, had a few rights, wouldn't you? There is absolutely nothing you can call your own, including your very own words. This is like discovering that a complete stranger has taken residence in your brain. You open your mouth to say scramble two soft, crisp bacon, whole wheat toast, and what comes out? Your grandmother is a dumb greasy pig, in Chinese, a scurrilous statement we know for sure to have been made by the famous thirteenth-century Ming courtesan Wang Toy Ding during a quarrel she was having with the court secretary about time and a half for overtime during the monsoon season. Portal to portal boredom should get top dollar! Wang shouted. And the very next thing you know, you're no longer rooting for Charles Laughton in *Ruggles of Red Gap*—divinely juicy little fruit that he was—but, instead, you're feverishly clapping your hands for the divine, unapproachable maidens of Hansu as they glide and twirl through a performance of *Seven-Flavor Soup*, an ancient folk ballet that tells you all you really need to know about day-by-day life in the obscure northern province of Soontong. At places like that.

About the night-soil brigade, spirited group singing as you tote a full bucket of shit in each hand; backbreaking joy in flooded rice paddies; locust plagues versus moral stamina; the inimitable kinky pitter patter of bound feet; Sunday public floggings of hopeless, hapless, feckless—it doesn't matter which, because it's not your ass we're talking about—beggars, gimps, thieves, hookers, transvestites, and thrice-warned naysayers. And the nightingales, of course. The nightingales. Without whose imperturbable, out of sight labyrinthine yet all too obvious love calls ... well, who in their right mind can imagine, for one second, pigs' knuckles without sauerkraut, pancakes without maple syrup? Exactly.

Allora. Once more into the gruel-stained mouth of the resentful slavey as she shovels hot-buttered scones into your hot cunty fingers as you lie there with your gamy little cousin, Rebecca of Sunnytwat Farm, having diddled each other into a state of exhaustion and hunger. OK. The maid's words: Nibble nibble like a mouse, while I'm burning down your house. Don't grouse, you little louse. Your time has come and then some. Hell hath no fury like a servant shat upon. Keep putting it to juicy little Becky and do your damnedest not to wake up. Because when you do, you miserable, worthless, sock tucker, you have had it. That's right. Suck the butter off your fingers. Use your tongue while you've still got it.

And Duckworth the butler. What about him? What's going on in his seething, itchy head as he lurks under the stairs with a two-year-old calling card in his trembling hand? Dialogue, that's what. The dialogue of others, of course. His masters! And why is that? you may ask. Because he's trained to believe that his own dialogue isn't worth remembering. It is insignificant. Consequently, the poor blighter can only hear the voices of others. He doesn't even know how to talk to himself.

—Sedgwick, dear. Wouldn't you say that the prime minister, Mr. Whatshisname, is becoming a bit pushy?

—Oh, there's absolutely no question about it, Sabrina darling. The man's absolutely out of bounds. Indecently so.

—The very idea. Saying that the rich should be taxed more than the poor.

—Outrageous, simply outrageous. But what can you expect from a man who pulled himself up by his own garter belt?

—Precisely. We should never have approved of the Magna Carta. It was a dreadful mistake.

—Of course, I said so at the time. I said this noble gesture is going to be taken seriously by all of the wrong people.

—It's kiss and tell all over again, I'm afraid.

—Or muff and mingle.

—Worse still. Bug and brindle.

—Oh no!

—Oh yes, my dear Sedgwick.

—Heavens above. I never dreamed it would be that bad.

—Well, now you know.

—In that case, I shall ring up my barrister.

—Ah yes. To be sure, darling. And immediately thereafter I shall fan the canisters.

—Naturally, my dear. There's nothing else to be done, really.

Sedgwick was off like a shot. Which is really what breeding is all about. We will hear from him again in a Panavision remake of *The Faerie Queen.* This will be an X-rated film, and children under eighteen will be admitted only if they are accompanied by an adult anteater. Any slyboots caught impersonating said animal will be sent directly to the pound.

We may have left poor Duckworth gibbering in strangers' voices, haunted on his rear by the tools of his trade and challenged in the fore by blow-ups of Chaucer's tool, but we have yet to consider his sister Antonia, a girl who decided early on that peeling spuds for the mouths of others was a sucker's game guaranteed to deliver you to the pits of nothingness, or worse. They won't get this skirt, said Antonia. So far so good. What, then, did this saucy little class renegade do with herself?

What was her answer to the beckoning sinks of servitude? To the itchy fingers of premature nothingness? To paddling upstream in a river of wild porridge and bacon rinds? No indeed. They're not going to get their bloody paws on my dear little ass, she said aloud one day, while looking at a magazine photograph, in color of course, of the squat, tranced-out beefeaters standing guard at the Tower of London with their pockets full of suet. Like they got poor little Tim Cratchit and threw him in there to be eaten by Queen Elizabeth, that old cannibal, nibbling his thigh bone while she was playing Mary, Mary, Quite Contrary with the Duke of Essex, the tool of whose trade was the subject of hot debate at the House of Lords on more than one occasion. And lookit what they did to Moll Flanders. Put a feather in her snatch and called her pasta ragone. Poor old dear. She could have been a star in her own right. A real star. Five grand a week plus chauffeur. But she was too soft and generous. She didn't know she was among sharks, self-righteous little killers. Dunking their crumpets with one hand and tearing your insides out with the other. But they won't get me. I'll dance naked on the head of a pin before thousands of oil-drenched Arabs if I have to. I'll stow away on the *Santa María* if necessary and rediscover America. I'll borrow a blackbird costume and get myself baked in a pie for some openhanded chubby little boy king who thinks a bird in a pie is worth two with a bush. Poor kid has been given so many hand jobs by Henny Penny he can't take a piss without going cock-a-doodle-doo! Little does he know that Simple Simon ain't so simple he didn't manage to get a couple of rolls of black and white of those dubious nights of rites of passage out in the counting house. Madonna mia! If Simp plays his cards right he'll be on easy street the rest of his life. Get the best ones blown up. Eight by tens. Glossies, 'cause they've got more sock than that mat finish. Get a load of this, Kingsie Poo. How about my cards? How the bloody fuck am I going to play them? What've I got anyway? A full house? A straight flush? You gotta be kidding. I got a three that looks like it's been strung out on penguin shit for six weeks. An' a seven that wants to be a six, that's how much it believes in itself. If I were smart I'd put on a pair of sneakers and go in for hijacking joggers. Sneak up on 'em from behind and cosh 'em with a jock strap wrapped around a bean bag. Oh indeedy. Know what I'd get? A Mickey Mouse watch an' a couple of car tokens. Or a pair of junk earrings and an old diaphragm that died harnessed to an orgasm that never made its move. Great hauls. No. Gotta think of something better than that. Pan for gold fillings in a dentist's john? No. That's out. I'd probably catch terminal trench mouth. My fucking gums are bad enough as it is. No. I gotta go for the long ball, that's all there is to it. No fooling around with these twopenny deals. Headline stuff, and that's that. Eight-inch type. LOCAL NONENTITY CAPTURES ROME SINGLEHANDED. Or MISS DREGS OF HUMANITY OUTFOXES THE SPHINX. Some such incredible shit as that. Oh . . . I've got it. Books . . . stories . . . publishers . . . those millions of gullible readers. I'll walk right into the biggest publisher's office and say, Listen here, Mr. Printed Word. I've come here to make you even richer than you already are. Cut all that Kafka crap. Let that rat-faced little whiner go his way. Tell Jimmie Joyce to go chase himself. Who needs all that crazy double-talk anyway? Folks have a hard enough time saying hello to themselves in straight English. And Beowulf . . . Give that hairy deadbeat the heave ho. You think the public gives a hoot in hell about some creep thrashin' about in the primeval ooze while his mom's out hustlin' dragons? Listen, PW. I've got what you need. A nonstop comic book serial that'll grab the readers by the balls and never let them go. With top-drawer socko graphics. *Adolf Hitler All the Way.* We'll start right at the beginning. Adolf joins the Boy Scouts. There he is, cute as a button in his hiking shorts made out of human skin, which his old lady has gummed the b'jesus out of to soften, standing over his first tied-up granny. And in a balloon over his head he's saying, "For the Fatherland, I tie up old Jew cunt. But you haven't seen anything yet. Hold on to your lederhosen, herrenhosen." Next we have little Adolf winning his first merit badge—an absolutely darling little button with a death's head on it. He's just strangled his best friend, a skinny little book-worm named Klinker. "Scum book-readers must go. They're a danger to the purity of the Fatherland. We are wiping clean the slate of the future." And in the background we see his mum burning the collected works of Goethe. Pretty great stuff, wouldn't you say, PW? Right up there with Lassie and

Andy Hardy. OK. Now here's the deal I want. Fifty of the big bills up front on signing the contract. Then I want 20 percent on all vestigials, or remedials, or whatever the fuck they're called. Twenty percent is hardly out of line, PW. I mean, Somerset Maugham got ... What? What door? You want me to get up and go back out of the door I came through? And if I don't do it pronto you'll have me thrown out by the building security guards? I think I read you, PW. I'll just put on my clods which I seem to have kicked off in my excitement and gather up my portfolio which I've managed to scatter all over your wonderful new rug and ... and ... Oh shit! The coffee's boiled over. And the hot-buttered strumpets are burned and Oh, Jesus H. Christ! The paper's full of stories about real people and they've got names and addresses and shoes and stockings and when they pick up the phone they say I'm just fine, how's every little thing? Unlike me. I don't say that because phones don't ring for me. I exist in silence. I am silence. I am everybody's silence. Speak, silence! And when silence opens its eyes, when silence speaks, what do you hear? The voice of another. All's quiet on the western front! Fifty-four forty or fight! Thar she blows! Let them eat cake. Four score and seven years ago ... Every rose that on this island grows cries blood! blood! Blanche white, rose red ... Hot pastrami on seed roll with Russian. Side of slaw. And then that other voice ... but more a waiting presence ... it's the presence that speaks ... as an apple smells, or as an animal shivers. And the words, if you can call them that ...

Down here we make damn sure the potatoes are in the ground where they're supposed to be. You find a potato that's not rightly in the ground an' ayou got yourself a sign. Something's not right, the sign is sayin'. There's been tamperin'. An' tamperin' means bad hands, an' those bad hands are doin' the fiddlin' of badness. You want me to tell you what that means? Means they's an enemy stalking. An enemy that has it in mind to undo things hereabouts. To turn things around, to see things awry. An enemy's heart beats in shadows. He's out there in the mists when decent folks are crouchin' inside close to their little fires, talking low, maybe sippin' some of their own sweet elderberry wine. Sippin' it 'cause that's what we do here, an' we've been doin' it long as folks can remember. An' that's a pretty fair piece of memory. What we get a lot of here'bouts is memory. When a kid is born here, he gets the memory. I'm tellin' you that straight. An' everything that goes along with the memory. Ain't nothin' missin'. No sir. Not one damn thing. Kid knows 'fore he can talk where the mallard lays its eggs an' where the rattler hides. An' what to do with his huntin' knife when the time comes. Just where to put it in the fella's ribs so's it goes right in without hittin' a rib or two. Blunt the point of a good knife an' it ain't worth a tinker's damn. Usin' a knife the right way roun' here is like breathin'. You better know how to use it else you don't do much breathin'. The other fella does it for you, if you sorta get my meanin'. He's got your breath inside him 'long with his own. He's breathin' twice. He's got you inside him, an' that's where you're gonna stay till the end of doom. I knew a fella once had four breathin's inside himself. You could hear them if you just listened right. You gotta know how to listen for that kinda thing. Ain't so much that you listen with your ears, 'cause ears are for hearing just so many things with. You got big ears, don't mean nothin'. Why, I knew one fella had such big ears he could hear a crow piss a mile away. But he didn't have nothin' inside to hear with. He was deaf inside. He couldn't hear death tiptoeing toward him from deep inside himself. So what good were his big ears? Inside him, that's what I said. Death don't come at you from outside, like some Trailways bus barrelin' down the highway from Butte, Montana, toot tootin' its horn to let you know it's comin'. Toot! Toot! Here I come, sonny boys! Ready or not! Toot! Toot! Hell no. Your own death lies waiting in your own bones.

We're serious people here, and you would be well advised to keep that in mind. But we still have ways of enjoying ourselves, and many of our days are filled with laughter. Ours, not theirs. Because, fundamentally, as you yourself might imagine, it's Us and Them. That's the way it has always been stacked up. Now I know you're thinking, This town's got its back against the wall. But you're wrong. We got no walls in our town. Not a single one. That's one thing we ain't got no time nor use for. You won't even hear the word used. Unless that is, a couple are standing on a corner having a Bible talk. Tell you the truth, I think there's only one person left in the whole town who'd know the ins and outs of building a wall, an' he's deaf and half crazy. So you'd have a pretty hard time explaining to him just what you had in mind. No, if I was you I'd give up completely on walls. Banish 'em like you would other craven images. You will feel a lot better. Your bowels'll move better and you'll breathe a lot deeper. An' it's clear to me that you could use a lot more fresh air in those lungs of yours. You put up a wall, mister, and before you can say Jericho, you got yourself a generation of wall-climbers. Wall-climbers are worse'n road-runners and crab lice. Or back-slappers or back-sliders. Or bail-jumpers or back-biters or shit-eaters. Or tale-bearers or nose-pickers or glad-handers. Even land-grabbers. They're the worst. See a piece of land an' they reach right out an' grab it. Like one of those kleptos in a store. Their fingers got eyes. Got to steal everything their fingers see, don't matter if it's a watch chain or a night watchman. A fan or a fandango. Grab it! Snatch it! Palm it! Steal it! They jus' can't help theirselves. Like they're the puppets of a bigger force. The kind of force that pulls kites through the air. Kite ain't got no say in the matter. Same with land-grabbers. They see a nice piece of land an' they're grabbin' it 'fore they know it. Don't matter if a house with a family happens to be on it. Grab! Whoosh! An' what about the house? What about the clean, decent family in the middle of its bread 'n' drippin's an' clabber? Where does that whoosh! leave 'em? In thin air, that's where. You think that's not such a bad place to be, you got another think comin'. We don't tolerate land-grabbers here no more. Last one seen skulkin' about got himself grabbed by us, good an' proper. We surprised him just as he was sizin' up a real choice piece of center-cut land to grab. We caught him from behind, of course, stripped off his clothes, and tied his arms and legs up and hung him with a belly rope from that big old horse chestnut tree in the commons over there. The whole town took turns grabbin' *him!* Oh yeah. Grabbing *him!* Everybody in town turned out for the event. Nobody stayed home to clean home brew bottles or dry pumpkin seeds. Grab! Grab! Well, let me tell you, when the townsfolk got through their grabbin' at him, there wasn't nothing left of this fella but his bare bones an' his eardrums. We sure taught him a lesson he won't be forgettin' soon. No sir. You might even say, he'll go to his grave remembering our lesson. Ha! Ha! Ha! Ha! Ha! Pretty good, huh?

One good lady I know, Dolly Mae Wiggins, made herself a bit of land-grabber's broth with her piece of the man. Dolly Mae says there is absolutely nothing like land-grabber broth for curing constipation. My cousin Bodie Simon dried his piece, then ground it up into a powder for a poultice. He uses it for boils and heat rashes. He claims that it works like magic. You can take Bodie seriously too. He isn't one of those people who pull the wool over their own eyes with sounds of beautiful mysteries. He doesn't buy those esoteric theories about the Bermuda Triangle and Stonehenge. He doesn't stand on his head every morning to give his brain more blood. Or any of those harebrained bullshit things. First thing Bodie does in the morning is grab the *Wall Street Journal* to see how the world of big business and finance is doing.

—The Japs are moving into silicone chips, says Bodie. —They'll dominate every market in five years. He'll lick his lips—big lips too, but not blubbery or hangdog—and maybe fart or something like that. —Just as smart as Jews and they require only a third as much corned beef.

—I see you've still got a thing about the Jews, says his lady friend Decca.

—Course I have. Did you expect me to undergo a change like some theoretical position about mastectomies?

—You're just Jew-crazy, she says. —Like Newton was gravity-crazy.

—You're getting close. The Jews *are* gravity.

Decca is very carefully painting her toenails a bright early Giotto red. Or a red the color of Hapsburg blood. —I'm glad you finally said that. I think you'll feel more of a person. People should make more profound, radically committed statements. It helps personal growth.

—No shit.

—Exactly.

—I think you're ready to rewrite Kierkegaard, says Bodie. He is sipping espresso and reading.

—Not quite, she says, looking at her rousing toenails and smiling. —But I am going to illustrate him with some really dynamite drawings. Boom! Boom! Like that.

—Dirty, of course.

—Very dirty, she says. —But at the same time tortured and chaste. Know what I mean?

—I'm pretty sure I do.

—The look that hovers between pain and ecstasy. Some of that. Dürer on speed, in a manner of speaking. She is buffing her Giotto nails. —Dig this, for example: The woman is holding her skirts way up exposing naked legs and a juicy, hairy cunt, while on her face is an expression of metaphysical ambiguity.

—This is a helluva good time to buy energy stocks, says Bodie. —They're way underpriced. He decapitates his cigarette in the oyster shell on the table. —There's an awful lot of money lying around in a state of somnambulistic nothingness. He watched the little bullies in the playground of the Place des Vosges down below. —Money that isn't making money is sick money. He watched a fat little boy who looked like the Pope knock a little girl off the swings. —And sickness spreads. I already feel somewhat endangered. He put the *Wall Street Journal* down on the table. —You sure have hot-looking feet. May I suck your toes?

—No. The polish is still wet.

A child screams from the little French playground.

—French boy children should be decimated every year, says Bodie. —And I would like the job of Decimator of French Boys. Just token pay, really. That would be OK. Or maybe a kilo of pâté de campagne once a year. That has more style, don't you think?

—Julius Caesar: "Why, Brutus? Why'd you do it?" Brutus: "It was in the cards, baby. It was in the cards."

Bodie nods his bushy but beautiful head. —Pretty good. OK. Here goes— Voltaire: "Our love will not survive the winter." Madame du Barry: "Tough shit."

—Hmm. I'm not so sure. She flicked an ant off her croissant. —It doesn't quite have that touchdown zing.

The park down below was now brimming with little French bullies (destined for important government posts, to be sure) and their quite self-satisfied young mothers who in their own smug way were bullies too, and the bullies' victims and their mothers. For reasons that are simply too obscure to bother with, all of the mothers, both of the smelly bullies and the tear-stained victims, had tight thin mouths (mouths that one normally associates with perpetually cold weather). What can one say? Precisely.

On another balcony across the Place, also fucking around with coffee and deliciously flaky, delightfully insubstantial croissants, was another couple: Socks Peelmunder and Leonore, the firmly, enthusiastically committed lesbian who made a reasonable living writing campy porn novels—well, pseudoporn—for an amusing, shifty publishing company called Mound of Venus Press. Leonore, who had most engagingly corrupt azure eyes, wrote such sentences as, "His hot pink tongue darted ravenously into her quivering cream puff." "Gloria imagined that his prick was really his arm and that his entire arm was thrust up her burning, liquescent cunt." "His ecstatic rammer had become a divinely floating sky diver in the serene, divine clouds of her pussy." Stuff like that. Stuff that brought beads of sex sweat to some brows and insane inoperable desires to the dank loins of others. Simply depended on the sociology of their respective backgrounds and psychic structuring. Material that is very hard indeed to put one's finger on with any exactness. Besides her hetero novels, Leonore also had to her credit, as the saying seems to go, a handful of steaming, glassy-eyed homo, or lesbo, epics. Such titles as *This Tongue for Hire* (about a teen Cherokee Indian hooker); *Amazon Head; Night Diver; Kneel! She Cried.* The last title was considered a classic in the field by s & m addicts, and was not infrequently quoted at s & m club meetings whenever subtle points of s & m conduct were being thrashed out. Leonore had made several large hats full of money with another title, nonfiction, *Snacks between Sucks*—150 easy-to-prepare (fifteen minutes) meals for the lesbian couple in a hurry. She most severely had to keep in check her normally wild-eyed prose. Recipes, like scientific reports and prison sentences, had to be simple and sane and easily followed by hungry and guilty people in need of guidance.

Even now, with the croissants and butter there and jam and everything, even now Leonore was scribbling rollicking filth in a big composition notebook in her lap.

—You must get a kick out of writing that stuff, says Socks.

—It beats driving a cab.

—Oh, I don't know. I used to drive a cab.

—Yes, but you're not me. And besides, she says, dotting an *i* in *dick*, —you're a liar.

—Honestly, I really did. I was an informer for the FBI. I drove the Capitol Heights beat and I taped all the congressmen's conversations.

—What haven't you done in your time? she asks, yanking off a virgin's pink underpants as the entire girls' soccer team looked on.

—Gosh. I'll have to think.

Leonore looks across the Place. —Look. There's Decca and Bodie. She waves at them and after a few silly seconds they wave back.

—They're supposed to be in Sardinia, says Socks.

—Well, they're not.

—Somebody's been messing with this script.

—It always happens, she says, scribbling away. —Nothing's safe or sacred anymore.

—They're supposed to be shooting a right-wing Fiat plant manager for the Red Brigade.

—Maybe two other people are doing it instead, says Leonore, without looking up from the gang-shag scene.

—Like who?

She looks up from her scribbling and considers. —Maybe Kenna and Germaine, for instance.

Socks frowns and picks up a large ledger of sorts from a chair. He flips through the pages until he comes to the day's date: July 18, 1981. —No, he says after a minute or two. —I mean, I hope not. Because Germaine is scheduled to be giving a lecture at the University of Orleans on Lacan's theoretical eccentricities. And Kenna, bless her sweet and busy little ass, is, or is supposed to be, directing an all-transvestite production of *The Maids* at the Comedie Française right here in Paris. So . . .

—Maybe they're both in Sardinia instead, blasting away. You don't know for sure.

Socks seems a little worried. —Perhaps I should get on the phone. And . . .

—There's a simpler way than that, she says, crossing a dirty *t*. —Take a peek into that shifty looking ledger notebook of yours and see where you and I are supposed to be and doing what.

Socks looks at the proper date page. —Holy shit! he shouts, looking at Leonore. —There's been a rebellion of the cast! Insubordination of the grossest nature!

—Jeepers!

—According to the sacred script, you should be at the film festival in Cannes with Carol and Stephan and Juan, showing that porn version of *The Mill on the Floss* you chaps made.

—Well, it's quite obvious that some of us are taking things into our own hands at last, she says. —Or else the Big Script is all fucked up on its own. She smiles lewdly. —I like it either way.

—You would, he says. —You've always hated management. He stares down into the miniature absurdities of the Place des Vosges. Young French mothers sitting on green iron benches, frozen there forever in the betrayal of all that they had been promised. They knew, helplessly, that far away in bureaucratic cubicles their wormy young husbands were shooting their bolts planning extensive idiosyncratic self-indulgences. Young au pair girls, frozen stiff on the same iron benches, wondered what had become of their youth. A bony Spanish girl could think of nothing but drunken bullfighters, while her charge, a meaty boy with bangs, pissed on another smaller boy who was carefully building an enormous sand fortress based on the Maginot Line. —Of course, says Socks finally. —There is the possibility that there is more than one master script.

—That kind of thinking can lead to madness.

—Perhaps that's the only honorable route, says Socks.

—You need a vacation, she says, putting the hot-blooded finishing touches to the all-tongue gang-bang in the girls' locker room: "Penny was divinely swooned out on the big white wrestling mat. Her brain was just barely working. She wasn't quite sure who she was or where she was or what she was. At first, she thought she might be a prisoner in the hall of the mountain king, somewhere deep in Norway. But that didn't feel quite right. For one thing, she couldn't feel thongs tying down her arms and legs. And she more or less knew that you had to have thongs if you were going to be a prisoner there. For another thing, they had to be playing that awful music, and she couldn't hear any. She felt more like a huge cloud filled with hot alphabet soup. But some of the letters of the alphabet were missing. Probably someone had eaten them. She couldn't find any *m*s or *b*s or *s*s. Maybe these letters tasted better than the other letters and that's why they were all gone. Something told her that she herself was all eaten out. Down between her soft spent legs was somebody's shaggy head, making funny sounds. Penny couldn't tell, of course, if these sounds were snores or sobs or jerky slurps. Penny's frames of reference had been more or less wiped out, somehow. 'She's all mine, I told you. She's all mine,' the shaggy head was muttering in a muffled odd way. Shreds of Penny's ripped, chewed black panties were sticking out of shaggy head's mouth. 'And soon her panties will be in my bloodstream, part of my very own body.' Muffle, garble, sob, gubble, fuff, slurp. Penny had a strange impulse to wriggle the toes of her right foot. But nothing happened. No wriggle. Odd. She glanced down her body past shaggy head, and saw that the toes of her right foot were in somebody's mouth. Another naked woman. Asleep? Who?"

—I think that does it for today, Leonore says, and closes her notebook. —Wrap this baby up in a couple more weeks. Give the old pen a rest.

Socks is still worrying this latest enigma. —They could sack me for this.

—They? Sack *you?*

—What I mean is, that's one way of thinking about it. One of the bleaker ways, to be sure. He looks back inside the apartment like Dickens expecting creditors. —Well, well, he says, his voice lifting somewhat out of the abyss, —while we've been shooting the breeze out here, someone has slipped another envelope under the door.

—Oh dear. Not *another.*

—Why don't they put money orders in them once in a while, Socks laments, going inside for the inevitable mystery envelope.

—Or some priceless early Miro drawings. Or maybe a fragment or two from Napoleon's boyhood diary.

—I think French doors are made with that sly sort of thing in mind. Unobtrusive violations of privacy. English doors wouldn't for one fucking minute permit it. You can't slip a fart under an English door.

He opens the envelope, looks over the typewritten page in it, and begins to read it aloud: —"What enormous satisfaction Guliano must have gotten from knowing that you liked him, loved him so much you could not stay away from him, no matter what; that you were willing to risk your marriage to go on seeing him; willing to go on hurting me in order to see him. Despite what you said to the contrary, you were still very much in love with Guliano when we talked about your seeing him regularly. When you said ideally you would like to see him for six hours twice a week, once for lunch, once for dinner. This strong urge was not informed by Platonic feelings of so-called friendship. It was informed by the strongest kind of desire and love."

—Those wops, says Leonore. —You should never turn your back on them. They invented sister-fucking so they could dishonor themselves. That's how scummy they are.

—And that's the truth, says Stephan. —In the fifteenth century the Borgia Pope Cosimo made it a definite point of business to give his official blessings at local Florentine sister-fucking festivals. He was urging closer formal ties on all levels as a hedge against the high cost of living and the often rumored collapse of church authority. He shifts his position under the huge blow-up of Jean Cocteau. —His two children Pietro and Lucretia toured the Tuscan cities and villages in socko plays written about the ins and outs of incest. They were met everywhere with open arms and unmade beds. Virgin siblings by the thousands were forced by the local mayors and priests to copulate in the public squares in order for their village to keep on the good side of the Mother Church. That is to say, if you wanted to stay alive during famines and plague years. Sister-fuckers were several notches above mother-fuckers in the social hierarchy of the times. The next time you flash Cimabue's portrait of Pope Cosimo, look very, very closely and you will see that inscribed on that big juicy ring of his are the immortal church words "Honor thy father and fuck thy sister." Of course, as you would imagine, straitlaced church scholars have always disputed this. Naturally. They would have to. Their bread and butter depends on it. They say the inscription really reads, "Hand over thy father and don't get stuck with your sister." They say this seeming papal gibberish was code for "Give generously and stay away from Jews if you know what's good for you." Contemporary believers are invited to take their choice. That or give up going to art galleries entirely. Never give Cimabue or Giotto or Sassetta another thought. Spend your leisure time in front of your Jap color TV set searching for crabs and crying over spilt milk. Steer your boat up life's piss stream quite ignorant of the glories of the past. Have lunch at the zoo with the brown monkeys. Carol and I were at the zoo yesterday and sure enough, sitting at a table smack inside the monkey cage was a family of four having the time of their lives. The fifth member of the family, a little blond tyke, was swinging from the exercise bar like he was born to it, munching a banana. One of the more expansive of the animal attendants there—a reformed ex-convict—confided to us that it was the zoo's hope that sooner or later there would be a typical American family tying on the feedbag in every single one of the monkey and chimp and baboon and orangutan cages. Just one big happy family, he said. The circle's complete. Brings tears to my eyes when I think about it. Thousands of happy American families breaking bread with their hirsute cousins. This is the biggest breakthrough in zoology since we got the first pandas to screw in captivity. He showed us one family that just wouldn't leave. They'd come for Sunday brunch six months ago and liked it so much they stayed on. This is it, they told the animal keeper. This is our home. It's taken us a long time but we finally got here.

They were in the last monkey cage before the exit doors. Making them, as it were, your last monkey-house experience before you returned to the loony bin outside. So there they were, the Bensinger family at home. I mean, wow. At first glance, the only way you could tell them from the monkeys in the cage was they were white and the monkeys were brown. They were all naked, mom and dad and the two kids, a boy and a girl. I swear to God they looked like cave dwellers two million years ago. High-grade chimps. No difference. They were very dirty and hairy. Their hair hung down to their assholes and their bodies were smudged with food and shit stains and some sawdust from the floor of the cage. Some of the shit was probably monkey shit, because monkeys like to throw their shit around like baseballs when they get excited, and you can't expect the keepers to go for Spic 'n' Span and clean up all day. Pop was sitting on the floor in one corner fucking his fist and sort of gurgling. Mom was slouched in another corner, her fat dirty tits hanging way down on her belly, scratching through Junior's head looking for cooties. That kid's hair looked like African underbrush: peanut shells and straw and sawdust and bits of food that people had thrown into the cage. Jesus! His head was a real garbage dump. The old lady kept plucking cooties out of his hair—and other crawly things—and popping them into her big wet mouth. Bugs or bacon rinds, same difference to her. Between barks and chirps and howls. No sounds you'd call human. Oh no. While his old mom did her head-scavenging bit, Junior was sucking on a rotten orange and picking at a sore on the bottom of his foot. He had the face of a tranced-out

† 418 †

gorilla. Spittle and dribble ran down his chin. Out in the middle of the cage his sister was playing with one of the monkeys. They were playing the monkey version of Patty Cake Patty Cake Baker's Man. They sat on the floor facing each other with their feet touching toe to heel. They were playing this game with their hands and feet. The little girl was very happy. She gibbered and squealed and barked as they slapped and kicked away at each other. The monkey had a Raggedy Ann doll in its lap and every fourth or fifth push and hand clap, he would hit the little girl over the head with it. The kid loved this. She rocked back and forth chirping and whooping just like a chimp, and then she would throw her arms around the monkey and bite his neck. And so on. You ask, where was the rest of the monkey family? Keeping a safe distance, that's where. They were hanging on to the swinging bars at the top of the cage and just watching evolution reverse itself down below. When they saw Carol and me, they began chattering like crazy and shouting, "You gotta get this on film! You gotta get this on film!"

—Didn't bring my camera! I yelled back.

—You big dumb fuck! they howled. —You're missing the chance of a lifetime!

Papa monkey just missed me with a half of a grapefruit. 'Cause I'm very good at last-second ducking.

—We've got to get out of here before it's too late, said Carol, grabbing my arm. —And for God's sake, don't look back.

—Don't leave now, folks! the monkey-house keeper yelled after us. —The real fun will begin soon!

—I feel the beginning of a time warp, gasped Carol as we raced outside and in the direction of the outdoor café across from the seal pond.

—Me too.

—Keep saying Plato, Mozart, Pascal, Newton, Proust, Wittgenstein!

I did just that, and boy oh boy we got to that outdoor café only by the skin of our teeth. Every time I scratch myself I think, oh my God! It's a monkey flea and I'm back swinging in the trees with a banana up my ass!

Carol and Leonore both laugh, as in secret laughter.

—You laugh as the abyss beckons, says Stephan.

—No, no, says Leonore. —We're laughing about something else, you poor silly prick.

—My prick is very serious.

—We both just thought of the time I substituted for Carol in her whore-house theater, says Leonore.

—You?

—And one of the customers played Tarzan the Ape Man to my Lady Jane. Oh my God!

Socks sits up in the old rocking chair. —Aha, he says. —That could be it.

There's been unofficial and secret role-changing among the chosen. That would explain it all right. Very sly and clever. A kind of black market in personae. He leans back in the chair and sips his Pernod. —What should be done about it? Maybe this is one for the Big Boss.

Stephan and Carol and Leonore look at one another and shrug. Is Socks cracking or something? But really, Peelmunder's problems are not ours. We all know that. He's a great little guy and all that but . . .

—. . . wild Tarzan yells up my cunt after I'd been rescued from the lion's lair, Leonore was saying.

—I could call the Boss now, Socks goes on, looking at his wristwatch, —but she's probably in the baths with her stockbroker getting a massage or something like that. Could use one of those myself, he continues, rubbing the back of his neck. —Lot of very peculiar thoughts lately. Muscular spasms. Reich said muscle pains are suppressed emotions. Hmm. Get some clever Jap girl to grab me between her toes. I'm overworked.

—Socks, says Carol firmly, —you've got to pull yourself together, man. Soak your brain in another dose of that Pernod, straight.

—Talk to your shrink.

—Give me a clever Jap girl any day. Strong Jap toes, that's what'll do it for me.

—Well, anyway, Leonore says, —there this john was, dressed only in my leopard undies yelling Tarzan yells up my pussy. Fucking crazy. Made me feel like *I* was the Congo. And at the very same time, mind you, I had this very refined English Lady Jane act going. "Oh, Tarzan, my dahling! You're so strong and brave. And how marvelous of you to save me from those perfectly dreadful little headhunters who had the most disgusting plans for me."

"Beautiful English lady live with Tarzan in tree house. Harrooouh!"

"Tree house you say? Oh deah. Well, uh, why don't you come back to my place, you adorable savage, and we can sort of make do in the, uh, greenhouse, eh? Or if you feel that's a bit too civilized and posh, why then we could have a go at the, uh, potting shed. Jolly idea, don't you agree, deah?"

"Arrrryooha! Tarzan fuck Jane!"

"Of course, dahling. Of course. Tarzan fuck Jane. But in the potting shed. Or if that turns out to be a bit, uh, cramped, then the carriage house."

"Tarzan eat Jane! Arrrooo! Tarzan carry Jane to top of tree and eat her!"

"Tarzan eat Jane! What an absolutely smashing idea, dahling. But why top of tree? What I think you have in mind here is somehow swinging from the chandelier up above us. No, Tarzan. Eat Jane on ground right heah. Top of tree dangerous. Bough might break and baby will fall, and all that, you know."

"Snakes on ground. Bad snakes bite Jane. Top of . . ."

"No, Tarzan dahling. There are no snakes on this ground, absolutely not a single one. Those are my black silk stockings lying there. You might have quite understandably mistaken them for asps or adders or something. Now then, you deah, deah primitive thing, let's get on with it. Fuck Jane or eat Jane. First one, then the other will be perfectly fine with me."

"Sink fangs into Jane's white leg. Garroo!"

"No, no. You've got it wrong, dear chap. Very wrong indeed. You mean sink big tongue into Jane's delicious quiffy. Come along now. Show Jane Tarzan's big red hanging tongue. Ah yes. There's a good chap. Redder than Santa's nose it is and easily three times longer, thank the dear Lord."

"Harrooo! Tarzan swing down from trees for big jungle feast!"

"Precisely, old chap, precisely. Couldn't have put it better myself. Now I'll just slip this rucksack or knapsack—I know it's just a rolled-up pillow, but poetic license, you know—under my hips so Tarzan won't get a crick in his dahling neck as he eats his Jane. Because I don't care who you are, once you get a crick in your neck, you're done for. The greatest of acts collapse, plop! like that. I'll just spread my legs a bit wider all the better to be eaten by you with or whatever. There now, Tarzan dahling. Why don't you just grab a grapevine and swing down on Jane and dive headfirst right smack into the bush. Ha! And let the mudlarks fall where they may. Good show, old fruit! I knew you could do it. Perfect three-point instrument landing. And what an instrument it is! Three cheers for Tarzan the Ape Man! Now you go right ahead and eat your fill, deah. Seconds and thirds if you like, and I'll see to it that you're not buzzed or bedeviled by summons servers or other uncalled for petitioners. Hey nonny nonny it's a jungle life for me!"

—Well, wouldn't you just know it, who do you think our Mr. Tarzan turned out to be when the tigers were all put back in the closet and the chimps locked away in the trunk? Head of the CIA station in Madrid. Name of Newbold Wilson. Far fucking out, no?

—Tarzan the Ape Man is the CIA station chief in Madrid? says Stephan.

—Of course. Doesn't surprise me a bit.

—Newbold Wilson, Carol says slowly. —I went to high school with a guy with that name. He was captain of the track team. Clean-cut in a creepy way.

—Secret dick, says Socks, and the clear implication in his smile was, why not? I have a perfect right to say things like that.

—He had this crazy need to tell me who he was, Leonore continues. —Like revealing his true identity was a new kind of thrill, you kow? She shrugs. —He wasn't the least interested in who *I* might be. Just took for granted that I was a classy sex fantasy for hire. She really does grin. —I guess the sordid fact is, I'm an all-around girl.

Carol says, —I used to imagine Newbold sitting at a camp fire in Eagle Scout uniform smiling and carving a piece of wood. And the piece of wood was a voodoo effigy of somebody. She thinks of something. —God, I wonder if he would have recognized me.

—Through the theatrics and the personality costumes and the rest of it? says Leonore. —No, I don't think so. I mean, it's not quite the same as bumping into him at Schrafft's over chicken pot pie.

—It would be like asking Hamlet to recognize the girl behind Ophelia, says Stephan. —No way.

Socks comes to life. —That was the whole trouble right there. Ophelia was trying to make contact with the frightened kid who was playing Hamlet:

"Hamlet, honey, is you or is you not talkin to the me of me?"

" 'Course I is talkin to the you uv you, Phelia baby. What the fuck else could ah be doin: jerkin off the mayun in the moon? Come on, girl, what kinda shit you tryin to lay on me?"

"Doahn you gimme none uh yoah dirty mouth shit, Mr. Big Shot. Ah is jus tryin to ascertain if you is talkin to the real me an vice versa. 'Stead uh like mah belt buckle talkin to yo belt buckle."

"Whoa now, girl, whoa now. Hol yo hawses. Did ah heah you say mah belt buckle talkin to . . . What is happenin to yo fuckin hayed, girl? You rentin it out for a stable or sumpin? Lemme look in yo eyes. You sniffin airplane glue or sumpin, maybe cleanin fluid?"

"You bettah take yo cotton-pickin hans offa mah face, nigguh, fo ah let you have it in yo teef, you heah me? Ah don give uh flyin fuck if yo daddy did take it in the eah from yo dirty uncle, or took it up the ayus, don make no diffrunce to me, an if yo ol lady is puttin out fo ever Tom, Dick, an Harry who got each coupla jewels stuck in his prick. What's that got to do with the price of eggs in Russia? Just tell me that! You think I'm impressed by the fact that with a little luck and God knows what else, you may one day be the sole and solitary king of this two-bit icebox of a country? Don't make me laugh, junior. What really matters here, just in case it has escaped that sick, sick mind of yours, is that what is taking place between you there and me here is an authentic human exchange and not a symbolic third-hand fraud. Are you hearing me, I hope? And furthermore, that you're not patronizing me with some machoistic attitude that denies me equal human status even though I am the possessor of a cunt. No little-girl shit, please."

"Christ, Ophelia. Why should the burden of authentic exchange be put on me? I'm in the same hole you are. You think all I'm looking for is to knock off a quick piece of ass? Well, you're wrong, Philly. I want you to understand me. I want you to know that kingdom or no kingdom, I'm up shit creek. Everybody in this play is up shit creek."

—And so on, says Stephan. —I'm giving up on those two. They're getting earnest and boring. They had such promise in the beginning, when they were both strangling over a plate of chittlins. He sighs and shifts his body under the blow-up of Cocteau. Cocteau is not looking at anybody or anything. He is staring confidently into the craven infinity of the camera. Which is all very well indeed, considering what the majority of men stare into. But it is not helping Stephan one bit. —I need a character with a future, he says, —if I'm going to get anywhere as an entire person. I can't have people going stale on me in the middle of the Grand Canyon. Captain Kidd, the Whore of Babylon, Napoleon, the Brothers Karamazov, characters with a real knack for life, show-biz winners who know what an audience needs and can be counted on to keep the fucking show on the road. Burns me up how square and ungrateful some of these characters are. They never for one second consider that you might be out there breaking your ass for them twenty-four hours a day to keep their names up in lights. Some of these really deluded deadheads think all they have to do is fart and whoosh! they're in orbit around the moon. Oh mother! He leaps to his feet. —We need characters with class! With a sense of obligation! Who feel guilty! He falls back on the couch. He has given his everything. He is still young. He does things in spurts. He is still chasing his own tail. But that's better, really, than just chasing tail. We all know this. The two activities are in opposite camps, existentially, that is. Each one armed to the teeth with the weapons of dialectical materialism. On showdown day, a great deal will be revealed to all of us. Meanwhile . . .

—Did you think of squeezing him dry? asks Carol.

—Well, I did squeeze him dry as a bone. His bone was dry, and Leonore giggles.

—No, says Carol. —I mean information.

—Afraid not. I can only play one or two roles at a time.

—Hmm. But the camera and the tape machine were whirring?

—I suppose so. I didn't unplug them.

—Great. Then we'll get the information we want, says Carol.

—Simple blackmail.

—I don't think scouting is ready for the Newbold Wilson documentary, says Stephan. He has realized, finally, that he can expect no help from Jean Cocteau, who, as we all know, has his hands full with Jean Marais. And besides, Stephan isn't fruit. So why should Miss C. give a hoot about his problems? What's in it for him? So Stephan moves himself to the balcony. He knows he is on his own, influence-wise. A lot of good clean young people have been in this position, he says to himself. We have no interest in those that haven't. Sons and daughters of millionaires and Latin American generals. Phew! I know I'll make it. I've got what it takes. That's the most important thing. Knowing you've got what it takes. Ask any genius in his field. They'll say, Boy, reach way down deep inside your bowels and give yourself a handshake. That'll count for more than a bunch of As from some skinny, norny old spinster teacher. The world's your oyster, m'boy, as long as you know how to suck it out of its shell. Sluurrpp! Suuuccckkk! Yep. Practice first on clams. Wear a clean white shirt and keep your thumb out of your asshole when you're being interviewed for your first big job. And look the man straight in the eye even though you know he is blind as a fucking bat. Stephan went on talking to himself in this outmoded rococo fashion without missing very much of what was going on around him. This can happen. Keep a low margin of error, he urges himself at last. He could very well have been rehearsing for a role in *The Last of the Mohicans.* —Ready, sir! he suddenly shouts. He had his head right up to the hiring hall. He surprised even himself. The question is, would he be summoned in any particular way? The raising of a finger? A hand motioning him in? An arm waving? These particulars make all the difference. Any fool can tell you that. We do not need to waste our money consulting a specialist in summoning. Better to burn it toasting marshmallows. Better to slip it to one of those war *mutilés* who float through our streets like ghosts from a very bad dream, with their stumps and wounds glistening provocatively in the lamplight. "For your soul, sir! For your soul!" they whine as they hold out half a leg or half a hand for you to shower with your hard-earned coins. "Have a heart, sir. A little grub before we die." Soul, heart—what right have these offensive monsters to use such elegant, expensive words! Before they die . . . Rubbish! They'll never die, that's the whole disgusting and absurd point. They are not meant to die. See that trembling, reeking bag of filth over there imploring from that bench? He received those wounds in the War of the Roses, and that was more than four hundred years ago. And that half spider, that repugnant, arrogant torso with bleeding cancers for eyes—that nightmarish creature was hacked in half by one of Attila's swords. So don't talk to me about the ennobling imminence of death. And who permits these deathless ghouls to contaminate our fair streets with their inscrutable dirt? Who indeed but the government itself! The very entity that has been entrusted with our well-being, our decency and our sanity, our very lives. This elected entity permits, nay, encourages these putrid specters to plague our daily footsteps. One hesitates even to step outside the safety of one's house anymore. With a scrawl of the pen, the government could instantly cleanse our streets of these . . . these leavings, these lewd putrescences. Dump trucks and garbage trucks could be dispatched forthwith to be loaded up with their foul, leering half bodies. They would be taken to the huge refuse dump outside our city limits to that calculated wasteland where nothing lives, and once they've all been dumped out of the trucks they could be set fire to just as we set fire every day to the day's unspeakable refuse. Just think of it. Our beautiful old city no longer polluted and harassed by the grotesque mistakes of the past!! Why, it would be like waking up from a terrible dream. The sun would be shining in a cloudless sky, birds would be darting and swooping and singing songs of joy, the squirrels in our parks would leap once more from branch to branch, chattering with happiness, and the benches in the parks would be overflowing with spanky young mothers and their laughing children, no longer oppressed by the fear that at any moment a lurching, crawling, limping hulk would suddenly appear from nowhere and proceed to piss on their legs or grab their pocketbooks. Or lift the dresses of their loved ones to spit on their gaily bloomered sweet young privates, being nurtured and cultivated and protected for the eventual plucking by their rightful husbands and owners. Oh the boundless joy of it! Hell will have been boarded up forever. The sordid word *mutilé* will be stricken from our lovely language, its use will be forbidden by law, and generations of the future will not even know that it ever existed. Yes, burn, loathsome specters, burn! Burn with the other refuse of our city! Turn into smoke and vanish into the air! Black buzzards will soar with impassive grandeur through the floating stench of your souls.

Furthermore, and inasmuch as and by the very same token and therefore vis-à-vis the party of the first part, to be known as itself, our government has bestirred itself and exorcised our streets of the above unmentionables, it absolutely must hurl its energies into restoring the scintillating, the emphatically irresistible charm of our many public parks and playgrounds. There was a time, within the memory of some carefully chosen citizens, when these places were revered and responded to and used as sacred shrines by young and old, fat and thin, tall and short, square and round. They were suffused with a rarified glow, a tremulous magnetic light of the sort invariably accompanying the beginning of the end. One approached these sanctified spots with altogether special emotions, appropriately enough. Emotions that held at once both dread and deep excitement bordering on the imminently ecstatic. Emotions so commanding you forgot that you were walking. Ah, the blood-tingling, blood-curdling games that were so hotly pursued in our playgrounds of old!

Our young took these games with the utmost seriousness. They required all of your skill and daring and strength. Lighthearted they were not. These games were played for keeps. All of those who entered the playground, of course, did not leave it. One must be clear and frank about that; otherwise history will be degraded. And such a history serves only to keep the populace in darkness and dishonesty, and we need only look around us to see what deep, creeping slovenliness official darkness and dishonesty create.

Ah, the games that were played on those hallowed grounds! I was about to say that I played. But that would be incorrect. Those games took place before my time, but they are as much a part of me as the flush of my face, as the atavistic hackles on the back of my neck. My imagination soars only when it considers past glories. The sordid disarray of the present does not engage me in the slightest. I learned of the exquisitely subtle glories of our past at my father's crippled knees. I seized upon his stories with all of my hungry youthful passions. Those experiences became part of my real being. They became my story. It was I who insatiably participated in those cunning, ruthless playground games. And it was my ears that heard the piercing screams of joy and pain, of victory and defeat, that came from the young but utterly possessed players.

One approached the elegant guarded gates of the playground in a state of vibrant stealth, quite as though one were hoping to take one's destiny by surprise. Certainly one's destiny was confronted inside those gates. The guarding of the gate—by muscular, scarred old-timers—had two simple, reasonable purposes: to keep the spectators out and the players in. The games—the confrontations, if you like—were solely for the benefit of the participants. The very notion of the spectator was held in contempt. Does one permit another to eavesdrop during one's confession? To be a voyeur to his secret love-making? Furthermore, what kind of a person would want to be in such a role? Precisely. And yet the world, ours and others, abounds in them. Not infrequently the guards were forced to beat hordes of them off and away from the gates, so drawn to and excited were they by the presence of the games inside. Mere glimpses of which they could steal, so to speak. And nothing could prevent them from hearing the shouts and yells of the passionately engaged players. Only a fool far removed from the urgent realities of men could imagine that this contemptible or at least insensitive throng of bystanders, would-be spectators, admirers, thick-skinned followers—call them what you will, their condition remains the same—stayed calm and reasonable as the games were pursued inside. Absolutely not. Quite the contrary. Emotions heated up, shouting began, quarrels broke out, and soon there were bloody fights. This animal pack was disintegrating. It was turning on itself. The guards' work was now cut out for them. This was old stuff to the guards. They knew exactly what to do. They moved in swiftly with their whips and long wooden poles. These raging beasts must be subdued and driven off! Whack! Slash! went the whips. Thump! Bang! went the long poles. Without hesitation, without mercy. Within minutes the raging crowd has been dispersed, and a decent quiet emptiness returns to that spot. We must certainly hand it to those old guards for their speed and their skill, their efficient unemotional professionalism. Their equanimity is in no way disturbed by their knowing that the same scene will be repeated tomorrow and the next day and the next. They are simple realists of the old school. One cannot imagine them saying, "What if . . ." Never. For—how shall I say it?—gourmets, a fleeting exquisite moment is to be savored. But one must be quick . . . when the sordid business at hand has been disposed of: the guards return to their positions at the gates, having gently put their whips and poles back in their places on the racks on the side wall, and just before resuming the effortless refined stance they were in before the outbursts, they all at the same time exchange a glance that says, We handled that beautifully as we always do. The rabble has been taught a lesson in proper behavior once again. This glance is to "moments" as truffles are to epicurean epiphanies.

Once a participant entered he could not leave until the game was over. You were not allowed to change your mind, to quit and leave. No allowances of any kind were made for the confused or the chicken-hearted.

The games inside were all ancient classics. Prisoner's Base, Blind Man's Bluff, King of the Hill, chicken fighting (where two boys rode on the shoulders of two strong friends and tried to hurl each other off), Run Sheep Run, Tug of War among them. I performed successfully in every one of them, but the one that took my particular fancy was King of the Hill. Every violent and skillful aspect of it thrilled me. It was my game, it brought out the best in me, all my own special talents; as some of the other successful boys had their favorite games. Our forte, you could say. We played—or performed, because can't we say that all great games or contests are as much performances as plays mounted on a stage? Surely the players and the performers share the same passionate sense of calling, the same delight in doing something that is larger than life, or that makes life larger. And the feeling of camaraderie runs deep and binding in both groups. They are all members of an elite—and some might say secret—society. They lived according to a refined vision of life which set them off (indeed!) from ordinary men. We played, as I was saying, on a grassy hill in the center of the sacred playground. The competition began with a rush by the dozen or so glowing, charged young gladiators, half naked, to the top of the hill. Once there, all the boys began fighting one another savagely in order to remain at the top, in order, after all competition had been destroyed, to become king. Wrestling, punching, tripping, hurling, butting, kicking, chopping . . . Each innocent-faced lad became a demonic machine of destructive energy.

I must admit that the subtle metamorphosis from playful innocent to murderous savage was a strangely exhilarating sight and experience; for one's self was undergoing it in an inexpressibly profound way. What began with shouts and heated boyish yells and threats soon turned to animal growls and roars and screams, the true language of our divine sport. No words were necessary. They would, in fact, have been out of place.

Close your eyes. Hear those bestial sounds. Like a pack of hyenas attacking a family of lions.

Soon the frenzied mass of combatants was reduced to the three or four best. All of the others lay on the ground broken, wounded, or dead, covered, as we all were, with blood, or they had crawled away from the hill in maimed defeat. Those among the defeated who were lovers usually helped each other off the slopes of the ravaged, blood-stained hill, and their comforting would often turn into love-making. Just minutes ago, one had seen them attacking each other fiercely as they competed to become King of the Hill. Now they were caressing and kissing, sucking and penetrating. Blood and semen mixed in their mouths. The juices of battle and love became one. In this deeply primitive way, the games became absorbed into their most intimate comradeship.

Eventually, there were only two fighters left on the top of the hill. Me and the other. Our naked torsos were smudged with blood, our own and the blood of others. The exuberance and rage of the conflict blanketed our aches and pains and wounds. (We would suffer later, when we had returned to our homes. And we were alone in our rooms.) This is the supreme moment, before the kingship is decided. The crouched enemy before me is a short, muscular boy with blond hair that hangs enticingly to his shoulders. His beautiful white teeth are bared and a low growl comes from him. His large stunningly blue eyes do not blink once as he watches me intently, with his total self. He feints and draws back. He circles me with his arms outstretched. Suddenly he dives for my knees. I am too quick for him. Just as his arms touch me, I smash one knee into his face. Then I swiftly chop him in the back of the neck with my right hand. A pig grunt escapes his throat. He collapses to the ground unconscious. I have won the battle. I am still king. I look at the strong-backed blond boy lying at my feet. Is he dead? I can't tell. It is forbidden for me to touch him now. His condition will be determined by the carriers who will soon clear the hill of all injured and/or dead combatants. I am still king. I raise my arms to the sky and shout Aaaahhh! My entire being is suffused with a divinely icy ecstasy. Inexpressible happiness. A sublime aloneness. The eagle soaring over mountaintops.

You may say all you like about modern times and the advances that supposedly abound in all areas of life, but tell me, where in its slick, streamlined reaches can you experience such fabulous confrontations and pleasures as I have described here? Scruffy abstractions, slovenly fraud, sordid remote-control titillations, sleazy highs followed by irrevocably thick comas . . . This is what surrounds us today. Let's be truthful for a change and stop kidding ourselves. Come out from behind those papier-mâché biceps, you wormy little queen! Climb down outta that tree, Abner. You ain't no bird! You think that just because you're scrunched up in a hole people will think you're a groundhog, Clyde? God bless me. How long's it been since I saw an authentic human act? Can't remember. I'm beginning to think the human race is a rumor. Old Walt Whitman knew a thing or two when he said, When hard-ons last in the doorway bloomed. Yes indeedy. Not too many real old-style doorways around either. Slots, that people zip in and out of these days. Like they were computer cards. Zip, zip, zip. They live in computers too. You don't need to know anybody, the way you used to. You just need to know their numbers. You punch that into your own computer upstairs, and whoosh! the other person appears with all his critical data. Images, that's what people have become. Instantly summoned, instantly banished images. Is it any wonder then that people treat one another like they don't exactly exist, crunch or no crunch. Get a load of this for example: "Exotic, erotic, outrageous and brilliant disabled bisexual white female, 27, seeks attractive bisexual white female with intelligence, wit, and whimsy. For occasional evenings of mutual pleasure." No, wait a sec. That's not what I wanted you to glom. Ah, here it is. Just lie back in your favorite fur-lined casket and soak this up:

T he little boys were sitting on the steps of the tenement building when Diana and Harold moved in. It was as though they had been expecting them, as though they had some secret knowledge that, sooner or later, Diana and Harold would be there. They smiled conspiratorially at each other as they watched them move in.

As Harold was carrying in the last piece of luggage, three of the boys slipped inside the hallway of the old house and, giggling, boldly peeked through the partly open door of the first-floor apartment that Diana and Harold were moving into. Then the other boys scurried into the hallway to peek too, and they huddled there giggling and whispering in secret amusement.

They did not say a word until Harold started to close the door.

—Hey, mister, one of the boys demanded suddenly in a high voice. —What's your name?

—Mallon! Harold said quickly, almost submissively.

—Mallon? the boy repeated, turning to the other boys and smiling. —Mallon? That's a funny name. I never heard that name before. Are you sure that's your name?

Then all the boys began to giggle and make strange faces and to repeat his name incredulously to each other. *Mallon? Mallon?* Harold half smiled at them and closed the door.

Inside the apartment Harold unpacked their bags, and as he took the clothes out he heard the boys laughing and whispering about them in the dark hallway before scurrying back out into the street.

Diana walked in from the kitchen of the cold-water apartment, critically appraising each room and the cheap furniture in it. —Well, she said finally, —it will have to do for the time being. We're lucky even to have this, I guess.

—It's a place to catch our breath anyway, Harold said.

Diana lifted the venetian blinds on one of the front windows and looked outside. —I can't say much for the neighborhood. I never thought we would wind up in an Italian tenement section. This is *really* romantic.

—We haven't ended up anywhere, he said. —The place is temporary. That's the only way to consider it.

—All right. Did you send the post office our new address?

—Yes.

—They do deliver mail down this far, don't they?

Harold wearily shook his head in rebuke, and began hanging his clothes in the scarred beaverboard closet standing desolately off the front room.

—These people, Diana said coming in from work a few days later. —You can't tell whether they're going to speak to you or pull out a gun and shoot you. They watch me as though I were from another world.

—They are sort of strange, Harold said, recalling, with an unpleasant suddenness of anxiety, the suspicious, almost belligerent way the people in the neighborhood stores looked at him when he spoke because he did not have their foreign accent and thick inflections, and some of them were even openly amused by him.

—And those bratty kids, Diana continued during dinner. —Do you know that every time I pass them they stop what they're doing to stare at me? One of them even whistled at me the other day.

—They're just kids, honey. Don't let them bother you. You should understand that you're something new to them.

—That doesn't help. Have the telephone people been around yet?

—No, they haven't.

—That phone should have been installed by now, she said. —You may as well be nonexistent as not have a phone in this damn city.

—It's just possible they've run out of numbers, and they have to wait until they find a brand new one for us. Then, because Diana did not laugh at the implicit pun in that, he added, —Nobody is going to forget you, dear. You ought to get over that unwanted feeling.

Harold read through the classified ads in the afternoon paper. While he read he could hear the neighbors shouting and arguing harshly at the pushcarts below their front windows. Everyone spoke with an accent. The jobs listed in the newspaper were all for skilled workers in trades; there was nothing remotely like a listing for a research director. Harold turned to the sports section, but for a moment there flared into his mind the nasty scene in his office the day he was fired. It still depressed him.

—It's getting cold in here, Diana said. —Is the heat on?

He said that it was; but the heat from the burner in the front room was not strong enough to comfort them this far away. Diana asked him if he could think of something to do. He tried to think of something, but he couldn't and they finally decided on the movies.

Diana took his arm going down the steps into the street that was savagely littered with garbage-filled paper bags, much of the garbage spilled out into the sidewalk. Her arm in his felt odd to him for she had not done this in such a very long time. It seemed to him that now she was drawing close to him for protection, and this made him afraid.

—Don't you think it would be a fine idea if you put our name on the door? she asked. —I think that would be a lovely idea.

—I'll do it when we come back from the movies, he promised, looking distractedly across the street at the little boy conspirators who were staring at them with perverse enjoyment. At the corner Harold glanced at the dead-faced men who were always standing there with nothing to do, just waiting. He hoped one of them would nod to him and Diana, or that he would nod to them, but neither he nor they made the slightest gesture of human recognition. Harold told himself that he should have spoken to them. That was what they were waiting for, he decided, for him to make the first move, and he should have had the courage to do it.

Later that night Harold printed his last name in large letters on a clean white strip of paper and tacked it on their door. Diana laughed lightly as she watched him.

—Good God, she said. —It looks so makeshift. Maybe you could buy a respectable metal plate one of these days.

Harold laughed too when he closed the door. —We never used to take the name that seriously. Or did we?

—"Good name in man and woman," etcetera, Diana quoted.

—You make it sound so ominous.

Diana said she wanted a highball, maybe that would take the chill off the room and herself. While Harold mixed the drinks they talked over what might be done to redeem the place from its fallen state and make it somewhat more comfortable and decent-looking. Harold said they should not buy anything because the place was not theirs, they were only subletting, and they would be there for only a short time, thank God.

They found out how little privacy their apartment had when they began to hear conversations out on the street as clearly as if the people outside were sitting right in the front room.

—Do you think they can hear us as well as we can hear them? Diana asked him.

—I doubt it. Besides, they probably wouldn't be interested in our conversation even if they could hear it.

They saw the little boys almost every day. Each time Harold passed them they did something to let him know, in case there was any doubt in his mind, that they knew all about him. Once one of them stopped playing pitch-penny to grab him by the sleeve and demanded a nickel, smiling triumphantly even before Harold handed it to him, as if it were a tacitly agreed upon payment of blackmail.

One afternoon Harold went uptown to be interviewed for a job with an advertising agency. In the ultra-clean, chicly decorated waiting room of the agency he saw someone he had known when he was a research director. Harold knew that this person, who obviously worked there in the agency, understood immediately that he was there asking for a job, and this embarrassed him so acutely that he was coldly abrupt in their meeting. The agency told him they were very sorry, but there were no jobs open, but they would certainly keep in touch with him.

After the interview, instead of going back downtown, he guiltily went to a Forty-second Street movie. He had never realized before what an efficient and comforting time-killer a movie could be, and he willingly surrendered himself to the dark anonymity there.

Later, walking up the street to his apartment building, he came near the little boys. He hoped they would ignore him, but they suddenly formed a line blocking the sidewalk, raising their arms like a firing squad, and shot him.

—You're dead! they yelled accusingly as he pushed through them. —You're dead! You're dead!

Sitting in the front room after dinner Diana and Harold talked about his interview at the advertising agency. They joked about agencies and the people who worked in them, for they and their friends had always looked upon advertising work as a decidedly second-rate way of making a living.

Harold did not tell Diana about running into the person he used to work with, nor did he confess to her that he had gone to the movies. He was ashamed of going to the movies in the daytime, but he did not know quite why.

—You know, Diana said, —I'm afraid something awful is happening to me. Just because we aren't getting as much mail as we used to, I'm beginning to suspect these kids of stealing some of it. Now isn't that absurd?

—I know how you feel. But I don't think anybody is stealing our mail. Some of it must be up at the old place. It just hasn't been rerouted down here yet.

—I hope it's that.

She asked him if he had talked with any of the neighbors yet.

—I chatted with the old man upstairs, he told her. —But he's so old he doesn't make sense. The friendliest person I've seen so far is the Jewish man who sells vegetables outside. We always speak to each other.

—As one rejected minority to another, I presume.

—That's right.

They did not know what it was the first time the smacking noise came at the front window. It scared them. Harold thought at first that someone had thrown something at the window. He looked outside and saw that the little boys were playing stoop-ball from one sidewalk to another. Every so often their ball had to strike this window instead of the brick wall of the house.

Harold told Diana what was happening. He stayed at the window watching the game and looking from right to left to see if there was not another place in the street where the boys could hold their game. There was not.

The ball smacked against the window in front of his face, and he jumped back.

—Tell them to move their damn game elsewhere, Diana said loudly.

—They'll break the window soon.

—It's one of the hazards of living down here, he said, but went outside anyway and shouted to the kids to take it easy on the windows.

—Sure, mister, sure, they shouted back, smiling dirtily at each other.

But their ball struck the window several more times before they finally broke up the game. In the intervals Diana and Harold tensely waited for the ball to strike, and each time it did they both experienced a sick jerking in their chests.

Harold looked at Diana and shrugged. —There's nothing you can do with kids. He promised her that he would buy window screens the very next day. They would at least protect the windows, if nothing else.

—The little fiends, Diana said the next night when the ball struck the window screen for the first time. —Every time that ball hits our window I feel as if I were being physically attacked.

—I can talk to them again, Harold murmured, —but they don't respect anything you say, it's just a waste of time. The only thing they respect around here is violence. But if I kicked one of these kids in the can, I'd have the whole neighborhood on my neck.

—It's so awful being impotent, isn't it? Really so awful, and she took a book from the shelf and settled down for a quiet evening of reading.

The next morning there were several letters for them in the rusty box outside the front door. This made them both feel much better, and Diana said she would have to keep a closer watch on her persecution tendencies. Although he was convinced now that the mail was not being stolen, Harold still went outside to look in the box when the mail was about to be delivered.

He decided that he might just as well be fixing up the apartment a little now that he had so much time on his hands, now that he was not going to an office. He began by painting the bathroom and kitchen. He had really intended to paint the entire apartment, but he was so tired after painting these rooms and, he let himself realize, so utterly, so defeatedly bored, that he gave it up.

He told Diana that night that he was getting used to the dirty ivory color of the walls. She said she wasn't and she proposed that when he recovered from his boredom he should finish his revivifying paint job.

The ball did not sound as loud now hitting against the screen as it had against the naked window, but Diana and Harold could not acclimate themselves to the sound. They waited for the ball to hit as they would wait for the first enemy shot signaling resumption of the siege.

—The place is getting to me, Diana announced. —What about visiting somebody?

They went through the short list of their friends and decided to visit the Schulls, who lived nearer than anyone else they knew. Harold asked Diana to call them, but she said she disliked calling people just as much as he did, so he made the call. Jack Schull said fine, to come on over for a while, but Harold thought he detected an indecisiveness, an edge of unenthusiasm in Schull's voice.

They had the forced and unsatisfying time at the Schulls that Harold had suspected they would have. They could not seem to come together, some special mixing agent was totally lacking among them. On the way home Harold mentioned this to Diana, wondering whose fault this failure had been.

—I never particularly liked them anyway, Diana said. —They don't know how to be with people. They're heavy and sullen.

—I guess you're right, but he was sure Diana felt the same disappointment he felt, and was going through the same anxious self-examination.

To take up some of the time now, Harold went to the library in the afternoons and afterward took long walks. He finally landed, through an ad in the paper, a part-time magazine research job that kept him busy for a few days.

Every evening, coming home from the library, he saw the boys, but did not smile or pay any attention to them. He made a point of shunning them. They, however, continued to notice him.

One evening the boys were squatting arrogantly in the middle of the sidewalk playing poker. They looked up when Harold came toward them, seeming to him like creatures with primeval perceptions, and began to whisper in their dreadful secret amusement. When Harold was quite near them, one of the boys was suddenly shoved at him by the others.

The little boy put up his fists and challenged Harold.

—Want to fight, mister? Come on, I'll fight you.

He had to push the boy out of his way. The boy shouted that he was scared, scared. He hurried across the street and into his building, the boys' taunts and jeers cruelly pursuing him, and it seemed to him that the whole world was taunting and jeering with them.

He tried to convince himself, when he was safely inside and the panic partly subsided, that boys everywhere did things like this to adults, but this rationalization did not comfort him in the least. He knew that what he really wanted to do was to beat the boys half to death. He speculated on what would happen if he threatened them or even complained to their parents. This seemed to be taking them much too seriously, taking his and Diana's being down there too seriously, and he reminded himself that they were down there only temporarily.

He mixed himself a drink. The drink relaxed him, and it washed from him the uncleanness of the incident and pushed his part-time job far into the back of his mind.

—Have we had any calls? Diana asked that night.

Harold said no, there had been no calls.

Even in the kitchen, three rooms away, they heard the ball strike the screen protecting the windows. They did not mention it, though, and remained there in the kitchen to finish their coffee.

—Let's go for a nice walk, Diana suggested after the ball had attacked the screen three or four more times. —We're getting into a rut here.

Out on the dark and alien street they avoided looking at the strange little boys clustered like criminal plotters in a doorway and at the men standing dumbly on the corner. Harold still hoped one of the men would nod to him, but they made no sign. In a few blocks they were out of the tenement section, and walked more lightly now they headed toward Eighth Street. It was brightly lit and crowded.

—Back in civilization, Diana said. —It feels so good and so safe to be on this street. I love it, and she opened her arms as if to crush the street in a thankful, loving embrace.

A young policeman walked by them.

—I feel almost like saying hello to him, Harold remarked.

—Yes, yes. Let's say hello to him.

They looked at each other and laughed, and walked after the policeman. Catching up to him, they turned their heads and bravely said hello. The policeman looked surprised, then he smiled and, touching his cap, returned their greeting.

Harold knew their gesture was childish but he could not deny it made him feel good. Diana's face was now pleased and untensed and she was watching the other people in the street as though they were all close personal friends of hers. They walked to Fifth Avenue, and ran into Ernest Powers.

—Where have you been hiding? Harold demanded of Powers. —We haven't seen you at all.

Powers looked embarrassed. —I did try to call you once, he explained. —But I couldn't get your number from the operator. No fooling.

Harold did not believe it. He suspected that Powers had been avoiding them ever since they had moved. He gave Powers their phone number.

—I hear you were canned, Harold, Powers said. —That's really tough. I'm very sorry to hear it happened.

Harold told him that he expected to find another job in a very short time; he wasn't worried. Powers asked them how they liked their new place. Diana shook her head and said —Oh God. Now Powers looked at his wristwatch and said he had to run. He apologized for abandoning them this way, but he really did have to meet some people.

—Give us a call, Diana shouted after him as he hurried away. —There's no excuse now—you have the number.

Powers smiled and waved good-bye.

Harold began thinking about his relationship with Powers: Powers had always been so elusive with him, he had never been able to count on anything Powers said; he wondered why Powers had not told them who he was running off to meet.

—Hey, Diana said. —Where are you?

—Sorry, honey. I was off conducting an investigation.

Two nights later there was a fierce knocking at their door. Harold could not imagine who it was, but when he heard the stifled laughter, he knew. One of the little boys was standing there when he opened the door; two others were running down the stairway.

—I bet them a nickel you would let me come in to see your house, the boy said defiantly.

—Is that so? Harold replied, looking around at Diana.

—Uh huh, the boy said, and strode inside.

—How do you do? Diana said.

—Hello.

The boy was trying to conceal his pleasure and trying also to look tough. Then he walked arrogantly through the apartment, Harold trailing him, and looked over each room. He turned the shower on in the bathroom to see if it worked.

—How long you going to live here, mister? he asked Harold on the way back to the living room.

—That's hard to say. Why?

—Oh, nothing. I just thought I'd ask.

The boy stopped suddenly in the small room where the telephone was. —Oh! You got a phone, and he picked it up to examine it. They then walked back into the front room.

The boy stood in front of a cubistic painting hanging over the couch. —Did you do that? he asked, turning to Diana.

—No. A friend of ours did it. Do you like it?

—It's a crazy picture, the boy replied. —What's it supposed to be?

—A portrait of a man.

—That's a man? he shouted, staring at the painting. Then he smiled obscenely at Harold. —Is that you?

—No, that's not me.

—You sure?

Harold did not answer him, but looked instead at Diana. The boy looked around the room, still trying to conceal his special, terrible pleasure, and then said all right, he had to go. He ran laughing across the street to the other boys, and they all laughed loud and shrilly when he made his report.

—I guess they're satisfied now, said Harold. —They just wanted to make sure we live like everybody else.

—Oh really? They give me the willies, Diana said. —They're like animals, precocious, horrible little animals.

The telephone rang while they were getting into bed. Harold could not help the quick spasm in his stomach when he heard the sudden ringing in the darkness. He picked up the receiver and said hello three times, and the person on the other end of the line hung up.

—Must have been a wrong number, he said, getting back into bed.

But he was not so sure. It took him some time to get to sleep, because he was waiting for the phone to ring again, and he felt Diana waiting too, holding in her terror as he was.

—It was the weirdest thing, George Preston said the night he came by to return a book borrowed months ago. —You know these kids on the street? Well, when I was in the middle of the block looking for your number, they all suddenly appeared from nowhere and led me down here. They had me spotted and knew just where I was going.

He laughed and shook his head. —They called you the Bohemians.

The ball smacked the screen, and Preston started. Harold explained what the noise was. After that they went back to the kitchen to have coffee, and they remained there, away from the relentless, attacking ball, until Preston had to leave. He and Harold talked about whom they had seen lately and what everybody was doing.

Harold remarked that he had not seen many of his old friends since he had moved.

—We might give a party soon, Diana said as Preston was leaving. —I really feel in the mood for a good party. Getting everybody together again.

Preston said that was a marvelous idea.

Later on Diana caught Harold staring at the floor. —I can tell you're stewing about a job, she said. —Don't. You'll get something. Don't let it demoralize you this way. We aren't starving.

—OK, he replied, wishing it were as simple as just getting any kind of job and not starving.

The phone rang. Even before he picked up the receiver, Harold could hear in his mind the caller hanging up. He said hello sharply twice, and he thought he heard young voices laughing lewdly, softly, in the far distance on the other phone. Then they hung up. The phone rang again in half an hour, but it stopped ringing before Harold could get to it.

—We could call the police, he said. —But we couldn't prove that the kids are the ones doing it.

—But why are they doing it, if they are the ones?

—I don't know any more than you do.

He wondered how they had got his number, and then he remembered how the boy had eagerly examined the phone the night of the inspection tour. Perhaps that was the way they had got it, perhaps not.

Every time the phone rang after that Harold got the same sick feeling, and he had to force himself to pick up the receiver. Neither he nor Diana was sure any more whether it was a friend calling or the boys, and it was a great relief when a friendly voice returned their hello.

In the afternoons now, after he had done the shopping, Harold continued to take long walks that led him from the "jungle," as he and Diana called the section they lived in, to the old neighborhood farther north. The part-time research job had ended. Once in a while, he had the good luck to run into someone he knew on his walks, and they would have coffee together.

It was during these infrequent meetings, or really in worried postmortems on them, that he realized he had lately taken up an anxious nostalgic bragging.

—At that time, of course, I was making a hundred and a quarter a week, he would say. Or, —The really best place to have lunch uptown is Mako's.

He hated this weakness in himself and he made an effort to stop it, but he soon learned that there was nothing he could do about it. It was as involuntary as getting sick.

—They're docking us now every time we're late, Diana complained one night. —None of us knew it until we got our checks today. What a lousy trick. We don't have a damn bit of status anymore.

She then unburdened herself of all the depressing things involved in her job. Harold kissed her to console her, both now sitting on the couch, and in a little while his consolations turned to love-making.

Then he heard the soft, familiar giggling.

He jerked his head up. Three of the little boys were peeking into the window. It seemed they had known this was just the right time to look in. When they saw Harold look up they shrieked hysterically with pleasure, and one of them made a filthy gesture with his finger, and they disappeared from the window.

He looked helplessly back at Diana. She was crying. The boys began to sing from across the street: —Two, four, six, eight. Who do we appreciate?

He ran out into the street after them. They scattered, ducking into the shadowy doorways of the tenements, and got away. Harold walked back up the stairs, furious but defeated, and slammed the door of the apartment. But before he slammed the door, he noticed out of the corner of his eye that his name was getting slightly soiled.

It was the night that the Burtons had promised to come down to see them. They said they would be there around eight; now it was 8:45, and Harold and Diana had had two drinks while waiting for them to show up. They could not understand why the Burtons had not appeared as they had promised.

At nine o'clock Diana said, —Maybe they lost our address, Harold. Or maybe they can't see the number on the outside of the house. Why don't you take a look and see if they're wandering around lost.

Harold went outside and stood on the stairs and hopefully searched up and down the dirty tenement street for the Burtons. He stayed there for several minutes, thinking that the Burtons would probably appear at any moment. But they didn't. As a final effort he walked up to the corner and searched the long, empty bisecting street. Walking emptily back to the apartment, he asked himself why the Burtons had decided not to come down after all. He thought they had been such good friends once.

At the foot of the outside stairs, he looked up, then stopped, horrified. Two of the little boys were in the hallway, in front of his door. One of them suddenly reached out and ripped his name off the door, then they saw Harold. They stared at one another for two or three seconds, before Harold sprang up the stairs and they ran into him. He grabbed one of them, but when the other slammed himself against Harold's legs, they both got away from him, and as they ran down the stairs one of the boys, with a quick backward motion of his arm, threw the paper nameplate back at Harold.

He could not now make himself chase them, and he went into the apartment.

—Nothing doing? Diana asked.

Harold just shook his head, avoiding her face, and sat down. And suddenly he felt unhappier and lonelier than he had ever felt in his life, and he wanted to die.

A nd that's not the half of it. That's just the tip of the iceberg's literary agent. Who is of course all tip and no bottom, but that's not really the point. Allors! I was talking to Juan Alfau over a Pernod at the Café Voltaire in the Marais about the hordes of vicious right-wing hit men flitting about Paris these days. Juan gets around a lot and as a result he knows a lot. He doesn't talk through his hat. He doesn't fuck over your decent innocence with a lot of baloney. Just straight stuff. There are a few OK people left and Juan is one of them, a dwindling group to be sure.

—Rancid little bore! he was saying, fingering a Gaulois. —There's nothing about this little bum that isn't impeccably dreary. Even his skin. It's completely without color and tone. Makes you think of the skin of those store window statues covered with nonchalant flies. He blew a great stream of smoke out over our table. The remainder of his inhale then jetted from his nostrils. —He's like a robot, Michael, with mechanically furtive eyes.

—And this miserable little prick's name is David Thorpe?

—Yes. Have you ever heard of him? He's an American, needless to say.

—Yes, I've heard of him, but I've never seen him. He's known by the Left in Paris as a right-winger who will do anything. Really vicious. Besides which he's a cocksucker.

—Is that so? he strikes me not so much as a cocksucker as a girl punk, a faggot who takes it up the ass. Juan smiled. —He walks as though some guy's prick is still jammed up there.

—Does he come there to cruise?

—He may divert himself from time to time in the big old men's room downstairs for all I know, but he devotes most of his time there to reading all of the fascist shit we have on the shelves. And he doesn't just glance at it. He drinks it in, like it is his life's blood. I've watched him many, many times in the main reading room. He pauses for a couple of moments. —I can almost hear the little bastard goose-stepping.

—I'm sure he's done his share of that playing his sex games with Erik. Goose-stepping in high heels. Maybe he impersonates Charlotte Rampling in that funky movie with Dirk Bogarde. Can't remember the name of it. *Storm Trooper's Fuckalong. Gestapo Wet Dreams* . . . something like that. Rampling's tits weren't very big, but that doesn't seem to matter.

—Big tits can be boring if they're not responsive.

—True, very true. And very disappointing.

—It's infinitely better to have small tits that hear you calling, that are as hot as this morning's sports news.

—My sentiments to the T, Juan, I say. —Small zippy tits that take you where you want to go.

—Instant rickshaws.

—Well, uh, OK . . .

—Tits that do not rest on their laurels, or on their oars, Juan continues.

—Tits that . . .

—Right. Listen, I want to talk some more about fascists in Paris.

—I will defer to you, my dear Michael, but I would personally just as soon talk about tits and other erogenous zones as they are so laughingly called. Forge ahead! Forget for the moment that I am merely a horny old greaser from the plains of Castile who as a boy was more than entranced by Goya's nude of the Duchess of Alva, a rather short woman, one would gather, with the bland arrogance of the nobility.

—Have you seen this guy Thorpe in the company of a rather conspicuous spade lately? I ask.

—Conspicuous?

—He's a mulatto. Clearly up to no good, looks shifty and dangerous, you know, and he has bright tiger eyes. Exotic.

—Uh . . . yes, in fact I have. Last week. This ambiguous mulatto came for him about lunchtime. They exuded conspiracy. It's a kind of sweat, you know. By the way, he said abruptly, in an almost different voice, —do you know what Kafka said to his friend Gustav Janouch?

—Uh, not really, no.

—He said, "We can't escape the ghosts we release into the world."

—Well, I suppose he should know. I must retrace steps in my head. Where was I before the ghosts? Ah, yes. —Tiger eyes, yes. This spade's being in town is a very bad sign. He's a hit man for the other side. Death for hire. He's been brought here to kill someone. Who? Can you think of someone, undoubtedly someone on the Left, who is important enough to be rubbed out by the Right? I began to wonder who.

—Hmm. Who . . . Juan muses, stroking his aging Castilian lecher's nose.

—And who released this deadly ghost, one must ask.

—Released . . . ? Well, OK, Kafka. Offhand I would say a man named Corliss Meyers. He's a CIA top dog here in the American Embassy. In charge of international cultural death squads. A mean, crazy, heavy-drinking fuckhead from the monied class, of course. Exeter, Harvard, Brooks Brothers.

—People like that are filled with ghosts aching to be released, Juan says.

—Now . . . as for the object of . . . hmm . . . two people come to mind. The ex-CIA man Phillip Agee who has been fingering all the agents around the world, and Hilario Gómez, the Sandinista Secretary for Foreign Affairs who is here in Paris trying to get a big loan from the French government. There must be at least two bullets going around Paris with their names on them.

—Precise nominations, says Michael, nodding thank you as the leaky, blubbery waiter brings them another round of Beaujolais. They were sitting outside. And of course they were not alone. Half of Paris seemed to be there drinking and gumming to beat the band. —You may seem dreamy and far away, Juan old boy, like an old sea gull, but you're fucking on top of it and I don't mean maybe. He wets his whistle and doesn't hesitate to lick his lips. —Most people just don't understand the upper middle class, Spanish style. But I'm finally getting a handle on it, I'm proud to say. Takes some doing, because our frames of reference are so utterly different. Shortening bread and rafts as against endless arcades and religious torture chambers. Ah well . . . He smiles at Juan. —It's only logical that you should come to Kafka with such intimate ease. Must say I envy you. He gently salutes Juan.

—There's only one thing to do, says Juan and swallows some wine.

—What's that?

—Arrange to have this shadowy dinge killed himself before he can hit anybody. There's no alternative. He shakes his elegant, old-fashioned, greying head slowly. —I detest violence. It is so sordid and . . . contaminating like a dirty disease. But I realize that we, you and I, Michael, must kill the spade hit man. And we must also kill the gay punk Thorpe. He looks at his wine glass as he talks. —You do know that, don't you? Looking at Michael now. —I mean, that we are the ones who must do the job. We simply can't go around peddling the idea of their death, like soliciting gay blades for a dance. He drinks. —It would completely lack dignity. He wipes a drop of wine from his lips.

Michael sighs quite audibly. —Absolutely. I mean, I can't see myself going up to Carol, for instance, and saying, "Listen. I have a wonderful idea. The spade hit man should be hit himself. Why don't you do it?" No. I just couldn't swing that.

—And we must do it soon, says Juan. —No hanging about or beating about the bush. Must get cracking. And he snaps his fingers twice, for emphasis, of course.

Michael sighs some more. —And I was really counting on a summer of total uselessness. Pleasure, idleness, regression. Ah well. When history beckons . . .

—One wonders how Kafka would do it.

—How Kafka would bump those bums off? Oh yes, that's really worth speculating about. How would he do it . . . ?

Juan points his long Spanish finger at the table and makes a spraying, hissing sound. —He might turn them into bedbugs, then spray them with DDT.

—I think he would lure them to some obscure place and stab them to

† 442 †

death. If there were an empty castle around, for example, or an abandoned railway station.

Juan smiles as only an uprooted upper-class Spaniard can smile. —Kafka said, "I tell you, I can be mad in my ruthlessness." We must assume that as our strategy dictum.

—We . . . I've got it, Juan. Why don't we *all* kill them? That would be so much more poetic and cathartic. All of us should do it, not just you and me.

For a moment or two, Juan seems dumbstruck by Michael's suggestion. He is a portrait of delicately suspended animation. He does not move an eye or an eyelash. Now he relaxes totally. He is a portrait of delight and happiness. —Bravo, my dear friend, bravo! What a superb idea. We will all do it. It will be like an ancient ritual killing. My oh my! What an extraordinary beauty it has. Are you sure you're not Spanish, way back there somewhere? An ancestor who swam ashore from the Spanish Armada? Yours is hardly an Anglo-Saxon idea. I'm buying us another round on it. He snaps his fine-boned fingers for the shuffling walrus of a waiter. —And I can assure you that Kafka would rejoice in your idea too. It is very Jewish, very Talmudic, as well as Spanish. If you consider them very carefully, my friend, you will discover that in many ways the Jews and the Spaniards are like that. He crosses his fingers in that ancient gesture of total intimacy and oneness.

Michael is counting on his fingers. —Me, you, Stephan, Carol, Kenna, Leonore, Juliette, Boris, Decca, Germaine, Martin. That's eleven. Eleven knives. Have I left anybody out?

Juan sort of laughs. —Only their surrogates and ghosts. He breathes in deeply as he smiles at Michael. —I am feeling joy for the first time in years. Proof that beneath it all, I am really a very primitive fellow. The thought of killing a vicious animal, watching his blood pour out of his body onto the ground, this reaches me where civilized ideas and acts do not. He crosses himself.

—I know what you mean, says Michael, turning his glass of wine around and around. —It's very exciting, no fucking question about it. If you let yourself think about it real hard, you can even taste the blood. He is quiet for a moment. —Holy shit.

—We must let everyone know immediately. No time can be wasted.

—Right. I'm seeing Decca tonight. Oh boy. Will she go for this. He leans back in his chair and laughs. —It's made to order for her. She'll work it into her act like a pastry cook folding egg whites into an envelope. Oh yeah. I can just hear her flipping out: "Holy Christ. What a top-drawer, whole-grain, down-to-earth, mind-blowing fucking idea!"

—You've got her voice down almost perfectly.

—"I just knew that if I had the patience to wait long enough this Bowie knife I inherited from my dear dead dad would come in handy some day.

It's meant for meat, an' I mean on the hoof. Stainless steel blade made by those crafty Swedes who may stay dead drunk all winter but when they come to, oh boy, can they turn out a mean piece of steel or a come-what-may ball bearing. 'We Make Knives for Serious Killers' should be printed on all their stationery headed for overseas shiv action. Sink one of ours in and see the difference. Boy! Do I like their style. They don't beat around the bushmen. They come right to the point. Ha! Ha! Ah well, Just couldn't pass it up. I'd better start practicing right now, this very instant, before the dust starts settling on my girlish enthusiasms. Don't come till you see the whites of my eyes. No. That really isn't applicable here. Be that as it may, one shouldn't throw it out until you look at the situation from all fieldhands. Actually, when you consider the fact that his eyes will roll in the back of his head when the deed is done. Lunging, plunging, striking, jabbing, stabbing, twirling, twisting ... moves as basic to what we're talking about as the entrechat is to classical ballet. Got to remember to keep my wrist locked. No, wait. That's tennis. No. It's my teeth I've got to remember to keep locked. Button my lip and lock my teeth. Otherwise the whole thing will look too breathy and amateurish. Can't blow it. Got to do this one just right. Chance of a lifetime when you think about it. Plunge! Lunge! Also ... got to pick my spot beforehand. What would be sillier than the sight of me circling their bodies like I was at the butcher shop trying to make up my mind whether to buy those thick juicy center-cut pork chops or that absolutely buxom piece of beef brisket. No sirree. Got to pick my spot now and let nothing distract me, no matter how attractive it may seem. Let's see now ... can't go for the heart, 'cause that's gonna be like U.S. No. 1 on Sunday night, the traffic will be that heavy. Exactly the same with the old breadbasket. No. I've got to come up with something obscure but serious, like you wouldn't want to stab your analyst there just for a joke. Hmm. If I had time, I'd take one of those refresher courses in physical anatomy over at the Sorbonne. Now then ... I've got it! Yep. I've found the cutest little place to plunge my old Bowie: in the southeast corner of the left kidney, just a twitch over from ye olde spine. Bet a buck I'll be the only one there too. All the other jolly assassins will do their plunging in the front. 'Cept maybe Peelmunder. Wouldn't surprise me if that walking semicolon rammed his knife into their ears. My offbeat kidney thrust is bound to produce instant massive hemorrhaging. Floods of dark smelly fascist pig cocksucker punk blood. Maybe one of us will think of slitting their no-good fucking throats just to cut down on the volume of inevitable outcry or cry out. Should we arrange to do the deed when under a street lamp or should we turn the lighting over to a pro? Make it more theatrical that way. We'd all seem like actors in a play. You know, like *Murder in the Cathedral.* Hey now. Wait a minute. Think I've just struck oil. Yeah. Cathedral . . . far fucking out. What better place to do it than the

Cathedral of Notre Dame. How now, brown cow. Lay on, MacSuck. Holy Mother! What class! I'm fucking inspired, that's what. There's no getting around it. Are we going to do this in drag with masks, or in mufti? I want all you mufti divers to form a line on the right. Ha! Very funny, Decca. You are one funny fucking lady. Yep, in the cathedral. Right in front of Jesus and Mother Mary and whoever else may be hanging around as a statue. Okey-dokey. Next item on the agenda: How do we get their little asses into the place? Tell them there's going to be a fascist pig pansy jamboree with give-aways and door prizes? Or . . . or should we lure them with a potential victim? Should we arrange to let them know or think that one of their hit targets will be at the cathedral attending high or low mass or something? Oolala! Bait a trap with the intended victim. Oh baby! Does this thing zing. And the music . . . Should we farm it out to a needy nifty left-wing composer? Or should we just play Bach on the organ till the cows come home? I mean, to drown out any untoward screaming on their part when they see that their number's up. Now fellas, just cool it, will ya? I mean, there's not one single fucking thing to be gained by these wretched squawks of yours. So what I'm trying to say is, why bother? Nary a soul will hear you. Whaddya think all this thunderous Bach is all about? So why don't you just keep your traps shut and take your medicine like good little shits? Everybody's gotta go someday, an' today's your day, OK? Jesus, do I hate crybabies. Holy Mother of God, warm blood feels so . . . so fantastic on my hand and arm. I mean, you can feel the color of it. And I swear to God it's got eyes! It can see you! And the way their bodies are twisting and writhing and collapsing into the marble floor. Jesus, it's like a weird ballet in slow motion. The expressions on their faces are so grotesque and beautiful. You never looked so good, you miserable little shit-eaters! For the first time in your life you don't look like you're dead! How divinely blood becomes you! Stop grabbing at my fucking leg! Jesus Christ! Gives me the willies. There. That kick ought to curb your grabbing impulses. What's that? What're you trying to say to me? I'll get mine? Well, shit, perhaps I will and perhaps I won't. But if I do, it won't be at your clammy hands, that's for sure. But when I do go, buster, it won't be like just another passing piece of meat. It'll be like the death of a poem. I'll be killed by a condor falling dead out of the blue sky. Or I'll choke to death on a piece of the sacred wafer. Or I'll have an orgasm so great it'll give me heart failure. All very peachy ways to go. Almost went out of my mind last night with Stephan. Oh, those incredible orgasms. Three of the greatest comes of my life. Went all the way to Venus. Solid-fuel tongue power. God, what a simply incredible tongue that young man has. With a tongue like that, who needs a prick? Course, it just so happens that he does indeed have a prick, and I would be the first to say that it's a jolly good one at that. Streamlined and fully motivated. Beat Oxford thirty to nothing last time out. Without really working up a sweat. We're gonna match him against Native Dancer for a winner-take-all showdown at Belmont this fall. I'll be riding him of course. Wouldn't dream of trusting this baby to the ordinary jockstrap. Bet we could get thirty or forty million if we sold him to an Arab syndicate for stud purposes. Easy. Got a query from NASA the other day. They think he could be the answer to rocket boosters. Strap a coupla these babies to a tin lizzie and you'll orbit the moon in no time, and that's for sure. Give those Russians something to cry about. Demonstrate to them that 100 proof vodka has its limitations. Oh, I'm not sayin' it doesn't work wonderfully well to keep four hundred million people crawling on their bellies instead of revolting and tearing the Hermitage up piece by piece, to say nothing about what they would do to the *Nutcracker Suite* if they ever got their drunken hands on it. I mean, shit. There isn't a Russian kid over eight who could pass the breath test if administered properly by someone in the know and with real American know-how. Of course, the statistics themselves are breathtaking, so why bother to get your meter out of your doctor's pocket? Sometimes you can beat the game just by stayin' in bed. Most people are too dumb to know that. It's an ill wind that blows no bed, as the saying goes. Or is it an ill bread-winner that breaks no wind? I'm not sure. Sometimes those old sayings get out of hand completely. My advice is, don't trust 'em any faster than you can fuck them. That way you can collect a little interest without risking your capital, even if it happens to be Montpelier, Vermont, which (I kid you not) somebody ought to light a fire under one of these days. I mean, really. How long can man survive on maple syrup alone? If you ask me, those fuckin' pancake cooperatives oughta be lynched. They've caused more damage to our natural crops and our yearning youth than anybody will ever know. Lobby, lobby, lobby . . . that's all they do, day and night. They got more bull-shit lobbyists in our nation's capitol than Carter's got liver pills. Puffin', hustlin', struttin' . . . who the fuck they think they are anyway? Aunt Jemima? This country'd better get its priorities straight or we'll all wind up working as charwomen for the conquering Japs. Polish these computers that'll be running what's left of our crummy lives. The sword and the chrysanthemum gone bye-bye. Hail to thee, blithe computer and rotary engine! Better start practicing how to kiss ass Jap style if you don't expect to succumb from beriberi. It's a good thing for me that I've always gone for slant food. You name it and I'll eat it, honey. But most future geeks in residence are going to have one hell of a time adjusting their meat 'n' potatoes tummies to seaweed and sea slugs. But that's the story of evolution or at least the survival of the slickest. I myself personally would survive a hell of a lot better if I had me some of that renowned Jap steambath and massage washed down with cups of hot sake. Boy oh boy. Could I ever. Followed up with about three hours of socko blood and guts Jap movies, the kind that touch all the bases. *Revenge of the Snatch Hunters; Baskerville Hound-Dog Blues; Three Masks of the Seafood Sex Monster; Women of the Come Spent Dunes; Comic-Book Lust Killer;* till it runs out of my ears. I don't want to be edified. I want to be sated and purged. How's about it, Stephan baby? Think you could handle an order of sated and purged?

—Yeah, but hold the mayo, he'll say. —Listen to this, he'll go on. —"The General Assembly, ending its special session on Namibia, overwhelmingly condemned South Africa yesterday for denying independence to its former territory, and urged that tough sanctions be imposed."

—Why do you think you're always quoting stuff from the grimy newspapers to me?

—Well, for one thing, it helps me think that somewhere out there a world is going on.

—And for another?

—They make me laugh. And when I laugh, I know that I'm back in my skin. When I haven't laughed for some time, I think I've disappeared or become somebody else without knowing it. Just for example, I can't account for four days of my life a couple of weeks back. And sporadic amnesia doesn't run in my family. Though my mother could never remember what day it was. It was a very dry stretch as far as laughter went.

—And you really don't have the remotest idea what you did those four lost days?

—Not the remotest. I think I just became somebody else, somebody I don't know at all.

—Took possession of another's head?

—Hmm. I don't know. That suggests something demonic and that's not my style. I think I probably just floated into somebody else's head and took up the empty spaces sort of.

—Sounds kinda like me. I often feel there's a stranger up there runnin' my life but I'm the one who's experiencing it. And it's never the same stranger. A bunch of them take turns. And they're all men. And they've got it in for me. My guess is they're all writers and directors for the Black Theatre of Prague. In a way, of course, I should be flattered that I'm the mainstay of an important movement in the dramatic arts.

—How is it now?

—It's me all the way, sweetie pie, and oh boy, is it groovy. I guess the Black Theatre group are all on vacation or something. I'd better knock on wood and cross myself. Maybe they've tired of me. Maybe they've found another toy. What a positively heartwarming thought. It may not look like it, but I'm down on my naked knees prayin' that the latter boon has taken place. If it has, I'll be more than happy to sacrifice my two missing-link children to whatever god is in charge of such things. Since I'm down here on my knees so to speak, I'd also like to observe, undoubtedly by way of things, that you sure have one outrageously beautiful joint. Even in repose it has quite a bit of oomph. If I were Matisse it would inspire me to paint a whole series of friezes for a progressive Catholic church or some such place. Something along the lines of *The Four Seasons of the Dick*. Or *Cock Springs Eternal from the Human Breast*. But since I'm not Matisse, nor was meant to be, the most or least I, an internationally renowned admirer of excellence and beauty wherever I may find it, can do by way of homage and inspiration is to swallow this self-contained and really quite breathtaking prick without wasting another precious second. I must quickly add that by using the word *swallow* I do not intend to confine my action merely to swallowing, as in water or wine. I plan to avail myself of every square inch of flexibility inherent in my mouth, tongue, and throat. I want that to be clearly underscored.

(Those hyphens represent the passage of eleven minutes.)

—There now. What did you say, sweetie?

—Glurb glob floop gwell.

—Now now, old fruit. Don't exert yourself. Just lie there gasping. That'll be thanks enough for your old Auntie Decca. And whatever you do, don't for goodness sake try to collect yourself. That would completely sabotage all my efforts. The wonderful thing about having your cock sucked is that you go totally to pieces.

—Gurk. Pashoo.

—Fine. That's exactly the way it should be.

—There is of course a close relationship between neurosis and society. The changes in our society have transformed the pictures of neurosis. One of the fundamental ideas of psychoanalysis has been the inevitable conflict between man's instinctual drives and the demands of civilization.

—You memorized that from somewhere, you little rascal.

—Phlugg ungwaff.

—Uh huh. That's more like it. Now you go ahead an' collapse again while I sit down over here and whip up a nice juicy play for the Black Theatre. That's right. Turnabout is fair play, and long overdue besides. That bunch needs some outside blood, and they might as well get it from a charter victim. Who is in a better position to know what the audience is craving to see? Those Prague boys are out of touch with the pulse of mankind. They've been living up in the clouds, with their hands around my throat, squeezing more and more and wilder and wilder performances out of me, their star attraction. Well, it's time they were brought down from their dreamy perches. Their longest-running production is having its curtain dropped. *Decca Records in the Pits* is closing, fellas. Diversity is the name of the game now. Wake up the stage manager. Prepare yourselves for a shocking, all-purpose, everybody's-in-it season. One for the money, two for the show; three to get ready, and four to go! Next week the Black Theatre of Prague will present *Ophelia Strikes Back!* Yeah! On guard, Hamlet, you little nit-picker. You are about to lose your foundation grant. As well as your royal foreskin. And the week after that we'll have *A Pregnant Woman's Guide to Cotton Futures.* This four-star kitchen drama will leave no stone unturned. Theater parties will be at risk. Next, we'll be seeing *My Side of the Story* by Moby Dick. Theater-goers will learn for the very first time why this whale has held its tongue these many years. You will hear and see the inside story of his relationship to that stage-hog Captain Ahab who will be exposed once and for all as the bull dyke gone mad. Seats will go on sale as soon as the first cross appears in the northern sky. And after that, out of the shambles of joy and liberation, we will be mounting *Two Over Easy, Side of Wheat Toast,* a rollicking, rampaging, rapacious farce about two very dirty twin sisters from the halls of Montezuma who fucked and sucked their way into the heart of Pope Gregory III. In this exquisitely self-serving romp, you will see things you never dared even dream of. Easter Mass sung by three hundred stark naked masked cunts. The Feast of Saint Julian being celebrated and served as the Pope's nose is being squatted on by our sister team who never miss an opportunity to score. You will see the eye-staggering "Dance of the Sugar Plum Twats" performed by hordes of unseemly devil-may-care unfrocked nuns from the hills of Calabria and worse. You will be able to shake hands with the Pope's mother as she sells hot-roasted chestnuts in the theater lobby. And   sight of sights!—you will witness Pope Gregory himself on his hands and knees getting his first electrifying taste of cooze while having his bare tooshie flogged by twin number two. Twin number one has nothing better to do with her cute mouth at the moment, so she decides to belt out a little number called "Amateur Night at the Vatican":

> Don't be afraid
> Though you might indeed get laid
> To do your stuff
> Throwing your muff
> Let's see what you've got
> It can never be too hot
> For the dirty old man at the Va-ti-can!

At the end of the sizzling first act, the twins do a song and dance routine that will surely go down in church history:

> Come one, come all
> Be prepared for the Fall.

There won't be a dry pair of pants in the house, I guarantee you. What was that? You'd like a peek at *My Side of the Story?* OK, OK. Here's a scene near the middle of the first act:

MOBY

I don't understand you these days, Ahab. You're so grumpy and downright hostile, and without any provocation whatsoever.

AHAB

I've been under a lot of pressure lately.

MOBY

Well, who hasn't! You think life on the run in The Deep is a bed of roses? Humph!

AHAB

But you don't have a crew of crazy sailors to put up with. Such egos! Every fucking one of them is a prima donna. Kvetch, kvetch all day and all night. If it isn't one thing, it's another. "The food on this ship is bad for my tummy." "The smell down here is enough to make you faint." "These heavy ropes are just ruining my hands." "It really isn't nice what's going on down in the bunks." Is that my fault? Did I invent buggery?

MOBY

What's the matter with putting your foot down? After all, dear, you are the boss, y'know.

AHAB

You try telling them that. Ha! They'll laugh in my face. Those bitches have absolutely no respect for authority.

MOBY

Permissive parents, that's what does it. No discipline. Letting children run wild. It's simply disgusting. In my day . . .

AHAB

And their ringleader is the worst. A big shiny black queen named Quee-queg. Mother Mary! You'd think he was the Queen of Sheba the way he carries on. He never does a lick of work, he has his slaves do it for him. Wormy little motherfuckers who worship the very ground he walks on. He's so far fucking out you can't believe it. The high seas have never seen anything like him, believe me. He spends half the fucking day putting on his makeup and his costume. New Year's Eve in blackest Africa, that's what he is. Feathers and jewelry and thongs and shark's-teeth necklaces and bells on his ankles. Why, he even dresses up his huge black dick. Paints it all different colors, then he ties these long braids of human hair on it that've got silver sequins worked into them. He's got his nigger hair done up in a spiral with seal grease so it looks like he's a unicorn, a goddamn black unicorn. The whole deck of my ship, the *Good Sister Phoebe*, is his stage. When he starts strolling back and forth on it to show himself off, bye-bye work. Bye-bye everything else sane too. Total mutiny. Chaos.

MOBY

He sounds worse than the nigger of the *Narcissus*.

AHAB

Oh my God! Worse by far. That one was an angel compared to Her Royal Highness Queequeg.

MOBY

What you should do at these times of complete moral breakdown is have someone walk the plank. Or is that just too old-fashioned?

AHAB

Are you kidding? Not a single one of the crew knows I exist when *She* starts strutting her stuff. Nobody would carry out the tiniest of my orders, much less force one of their own to walk a plank.

MOBY

Well, perhaps you'll have to set an example and walk the plank yourself.

AHAB

Oh sure, sure. Got any more great ideas?

MOBY

You wouldn't actually have to drown yourself, silly. It would be in the nature of a symbolic display. Sometimes I wonder what's happened to your imagination. You're so bloody literal at times.

AHAB

You try running a whaling ship with a crew of chorus boy/girls and see what happens to *your* flights of fancy. Why can't you be a little more supportive?

MOBY

Supportive, is it? Just tell me where you'd be without me. Go ahead, Captain Ungrateful. Tell me.

AHAB

Awright awready. What I meant was . . .

MOBY

And while we're on the subject of mutual-assistance pacts, I must ask you to go easy on those harpoons of yours. Those damn things hurt. You can make your point with one or two. No need to go overboard, you know. After all, the whole thing's just for show. I'm supposed to be a metaphor, not a bloody pincushion.

AHAB

I'll have a word with the harpooners. But it's the only thing they like to do. They're blood freaks. They live for the sight of blood. It's simply disgusting. You can't talk to them about thrills of a higher order. Sublimation and conversation are quite beyond them.

MOBY

What they need is a metaphysical hang-up like yours. Get them off my back.

AHAB

It's that damn Ishmael who eggs them on. That one's gone around the bend for sure. He does it all to impress that fucking smoke Queen Queequeg. It's enough to make you throw up. Not a shred of pride. He'll do anything to get in with that impossible boogie. To get a hug or a mouthful of black dick meat. I've never seen anything like it, and I've been around for a long time.

Freud had a thing or two to say about that, if I recall correctly. It's all based on a fear of incest.

Incest? Ishmael's mum? Oh come on now. You've gotta be kidding. I mean, *really*.

His mum and his sister as well. I'll bet you anything that man has at least two very genteel sisters who are seamstresses or nannies.

That exhibitionist Ishmael a closet sister-fucker? Not on your life. He's just a run-of-the-mill sea-salt full-fathom-five pansy who . . .

God! Why is it you butch types are so anti-intellectual! Hold your horses and listen, will you. You might learn something. It works this way. There's the boy child and the mommy. A middle-class chick with big knockers. They're tight as ticks. He sees her in the most unguarded intimate moments. In her panties and bra, in the bathtub all naked, big tits hanging out, sitting on the pottie making pee-pee. She's a real nice number. The kid feels the mama is his property. He gets the hots for mama who frequently takes a look at his dilly just to see that it's OK. Holds it up to the light, measures it with a special ruler, stretches it, stuff like that. He wants to slip it to his mama more than he wants to do anything in the whole fucking world. More than he wants to be a fireman or a gangster or a crooked politician. But alongside this lust passion, there exists in the kid a terrible fear: fear of the papa. He knows that the papa has first, second, and third fucking rights with mama. He knows that papa is not about to share his nice mama piece with anybody, OK? He is scared shitless of the papa, who is one mean fucker. He knows the papa would chop his cock off in a second if he gets wise to the dirty things the kid would like to do to his property Red Hot Mama. So the kid's in one terrible bind. Every time he has a fantasy about plowing his old lady, he gets waves of anxiety and papa-fear. This dilemma is causing him to feel he's going to have a breakdown, that he's going to disappear into one loud scream. So what does the feverish little nipper do?

AHAB

He shoots papa.

MOBY

No. He doesn't knock papa off. He decides to become a little girl, in his mind at least. 'Cause since he's no longer a boy, he can't threaten papa, you see. So he won't get killed or anything awful. Not only that, now that he's become a girl, he naturally directs his lust at men.

AHAB

Have you tried this out on anybody else, Moby?

MOBY

Shut up, wise-ass. Anyway, in the uptight middle-class scene papa-fucking isn't a lot safer than mama-fucking. So the kid shifts out of the danger zone and directs his lust drives at members of the lower classes, who don't count for a lying flying fuck. As far as the middle class is concerned, you can do anything you want with those people because they're beyond the pale. Now, are things a little bit clearer?

AHAB

What about the sisters?

MOBY

Same deal. With a couple of changes here and there.

AHAB

Hmm. Lemme get back to you on this. I've got to mull it over. I think it's too fancy to help me out much.

MOBY

Our relationship would be a lot better if you stopped resenting my superior intellect.

AHAB

Oh shit! Here we go again. I wish I had a dollar bill for every time you've pulled *that* one on me. Why . . . Oh dear. Here comes that fucking trouble-maker Ishmael. Why is he carrying that pot, I wonder?

ISHMAEL

Captain, I need a moment of your undivided attention.

AHAB

You've got it, Mister Pain in the Ass. But make it short. What's your beef today? The wind's not to your liking? Too many sea gulls in the sky?

ISHMAEL

You're real cute, Captain. You oughta work the Copa. See this plate?

AHAB

Why, as I live and breathe, if you're not holding a dinner plate in your dainty right hand.

ISHMAEL

Would you like to tell me what you see on this plate?

AHAB

Hmm. Looks just like filet mignon.

ISHMAEL

Filet of armadillo asshole is more like it. I want you to know that the food on this creaky tub of yours is inedible. The cook must think he's feeding a bunch of dogfish instead of decent human beings who daily break their sweet asses in the service of your horrendous visions.

AHAB

My good man, I lured that cook from the Ritz in Paris.

ISHMAEL

What you lured to this lame-brained ship was all the garbage cans of Portsmouth. I'm going to throw this plate of doo-doo overboard. Now, watch all the fish die.

AHAB

You just better watch yourself, you incorrigible lout. Or I'll cut out all your recreation breaks.

ISHMAEL

Ha! If you think I need your OK to have fun you've got another think coming, Captain Dumbo. Unlike you, I'm not queer for whales, so I don't have to move more than three feet to get *my* jollies. In fact, sometimes I don't have to move at all. Put that in your peg leg and smoke it.

AHAB

We know about you and your depraved fun, you leering, slurping, self-satisfied pervert.

ISHMAEL

Oh, look who's talking. Come off it, you bitch! You think we're not on to you. You're wanted on seven continents for illegally impersonating an erection, you big floozy. You think we don't know you're a broad? Oh, Mary! We ran a check on you while we were docked in Baltimore, and baby, you've got a record a mile long. And what a record! They ran you out of China for cohabitating with the Abominable Snowman. They caught you putting on unspeakable acts with the Snowman before an audience of drunken, depraved sherpas. And you didn't call yourself Captain Ahab then. You did your dirties under the moniker of Dr. Aloysius McFuckhardy, Director of the Dublin Museum of Unnatural History. Furthermore, you were charged with corrupting the morals and abusing the privileges of seven sherpa maidens. To wit, the eating of said sherpa girls before they were ripe. For shame, you beefy old bag, for shame. You've stained the Himalayas for good. Before that, and until you were ultimately apprehended by the forces of good, you were the scourge of Hong Kong. Known to the authorites as Prof. Dreyfus W. Moonsucker, slackjawed choirmaster of the Sampan Songbirds. Not a single sampan girl was safe from your lick-lusty marauding clutches. Specifically, you insatiable foulness, you were a round-the-clock yellow slaver. You duped sampan mothers into turning their hard-earned daughters over to you to be sent abroad on so-called Sampan Singalongs. Actually, these poor slanty darlings were being shipped to lesbian gourmets in the sin capitals of the world who could not satisfy their lewd gluttonous appetites for sampan chicken. On the day of your arrest you were caught with your pants down and your tongue out as you were preparing to spot-check a roomful of eager thigh meat. Before that, you peregrinating plague, you made your mark and left your imprint in Hamburg, Germany, where the town burghers thought they knew you well enough as Snake Eyes Snuff-kraut, the last man (little did they yet know) to see Attila the Hun alive and well and stark naked in a clean, well-run, orderly and inordinately expensive house of disorder. Even there, in that seaport of sin, you were of course indulging your all too well known passion for lesbian aberrations, a taste for animals of a lower order. To wit and to whistle, Pegasus the famed lady flying horse. Your carryings-on with that broody throw-caution-to-the-winds mare had quite a bit more than eyebrows raised in that stolid reeking burg. You provided vivid realization to the oft-used expression "flying fuck" and the German skies haven't been the same since. Black hailstorms descend upon those people and improbable midsummer snow flurries have abruptly done in more than a handful of decent, overweight, law-fearing hausfraus. You and Pegasus were the scandal of the racetracks, gambling dens, sporting houses, beer gardens, fashion shows, and after-hours dinner clubs. The townspeople finally declared you persona non grata when you attempted a fraudulent marriage with Pegasus, having attempted to disguise Pegasus' true identity with an oversized print gown, giant straw hat, and a recording for a voice. At which lewd historical crossroads the authorities on the spot in Town Hall swiftly whipped off your top hat and tails and discovered your notorious buck clit instead of a real eight-inch born-to-rise-again cock. But your transvestite vileness was not daunted, Ahab, you shameless hoodwinker, you. No setbacks, no exposures, no dressings-down could discourage your degenerate dress-ups. Calling yourself Herman C. Fuckfallow, you next set your insatiable cap for that esteemed queen of folderol, every lonely child's hero, every stargazer's bête noire, every drunken underpaid mercenary's pinup girl, the Flying Dutchman. Oh, the mind reels at the mere thought of the two of you unleashed! You in your red whiskers and black bowler and silver-button cargo inspector's uniform—bought, as always, from Brooks Costume Company, with the money your poor benighted Aunt Minnie had given you for a trousseau thinking your salvation would be marriage to a nice, clean-shaven Wall Street broker who came and went on time and who would always salute and bow low before slamming it in—with which you so easily duped every port official. And she decked out in all the traditional trappings of her lifelong alienation. What erotic skullduggery you laid on that misguided wench as she set her sails for eternity! You didn't care what mutant hanky-panky you forced upon her as the astonished stars looked on. It took a moonlighting astronomer with a tenfoot telescope to catch you in the act on a dazzling cloudless night in May. Gadzooks! he shouted to the memory of Copernicus. What celestial depravity have we here? What indeed, we may answer as History arches her back against the wall. You quivering poseur, you hardened imposter, you monstrous jade, you leering, long-tongued fugitive from the bra and corset, bare your small-tittied breast and face the music, Rosie O'Toole. For that is your true name. If you were half the man you long to be, you'd fall on your knees and ask forgiveness of a befuddled workaday world that is fast going down the drain. Apologize to this poor whale for leading it astray. Rosie O'Toole, your moment of redemption has arrived. Put that false peg leg back in the closet, slip on this flowing flower print dress and proclaim yourself a new woman. Put a little color in your windburned cheeks with this rouge, apply this lipstick with the concentrated insouciance of a vestal virgin, spray some of this divine Chanel between your supple, ample, misguided thighs, cover your muffled muff with the fragrance of the springtime fields, grab Buster Bunny's hand here and join the ball. That's it! Swing! Twirl! Leap! Whirl! Don't worry about Buster Bunny. He won't break. He's been through a lot and he's come out almost even. Look at that little bugger glide! He must think he's at the Harvest Moon Ball. Go, man, go! To hell with the snows of yesteryear. Tell the Sphinx to go fuck itself. Just remember that Custer's last words were "Uh oh. Somebody's been reading my mail." Show 'em what a down-country dervish can do, baby. Your mother'll never know or care. She's too busy flogging army surplus in Djibouti to give a second thought to her first and last born who she thinks is still in knee pants in military prep school somewhere in the pine forests of Georgia surrounded by milling lintheads. Don't worry about the little woman, either. I'll ring her up in a jiffy and inform her that you're all tied up at Torquemada's coming-out party and won't be home until the wee hours. You heard me, Colonel. So don't wait up. Just leave the night-light on over the shooting range. 'Cause those bullets gotta see where they're goin'. And we both know you're not the kind to be wasteful or sloppy when it comes to bullets and dishing it out in general. Because you've really got your shit together. You're the coolest of the cool. Like, the way you handled Cabrera Gómez, I mean that was a masterpiece of cool, and every single one of us in the business takes his hat off to you, Colonel. You're aces. When you found out from Little Jack Horner that he was really working for the Spanish narco squad, you immediately settled his hash like a true champ. You slipped your little pal pulsating protégée Esmeralda into the roomy Cabrera kitchen as a helper. The cook Zita went along with this coy invention because you had the goods on her and her secret criminal past in Rota—and in two shakes of the lamb's tail she had put enough tasteless odorless poison (right! cyanide!) into the *sopa calda* at supper to kill half the city. The entire family went bye-bye for good just before they were about to lay into a mammoth plate of kidney stew. But that's what can happen if you try to play both sides of the street as slippery Cabrera Gómez did for a spell. To wit, your family can join you as you go to meet your maker without having had time for a quick and decent change of duds for the trip. You don't fuck around, lady. You mean it. You play for keeps. And because of your professional seriousness, you have a sterling reputation among the people who count. Why else would Michel Foucault have said to you, "The first selling out to the devil by the workers' organization was to have made belonging to a trade a condition of membership. It was this which allowed the first unions to become corporations which excluded the mass of unskilled workers." He doesn't go around talking to nobodies. He's a man whose time is valuable. He's got his rep to think about. He's got dazzling breakthroughs to make. Scintillating appointments to keep, while at the same time he must continually provide fresh meat for his followers. He hobnobs only with winners, like yourself. You're royalty, Colonel, and that's that. Why else would your new boyfriend Laurence Olivier address you as "princess" as he does constantly, as in his note attached to the two dozen long-stem roses you received only this morning. "My dear princess: Permit these flowers to pay homage with their fragrance to your divine self in my absence." And we can only guess how he brags to his fine-feathered friends about you. "This superb creature has descended from the heavens to bestow upon me the great honor of accepting my adoration of her as I kiss her foot." And "She's absolutely four-star, a flawless diamond. She's got everything." And "What a broad! She can make a touchdown without moving an inch, s'help me. Class written all over her." So, it's as plain as the nose on your face that Laurence Olivier likes you an awful lot, that you're a real fine piece of goods, pure silk. They could shoot you from any angle and you'd knock 'em dead in the viewing room. All those directors and producers and agents and greedy Greek millionaires will fall out of their chairs yellin' —Oh my God! I'm speechless! I can't say a word! Never seen a screen test like this in my entire fucking life. And I've been in the business eighty-two years. Longer. I was in the business before they even had a camera. I was running dirty comic books while all of us were standing around waiting for Tom Edison to get his act together. Come on, Tom! Stop futzin' around, dad. Can't you see the whole world is waiting breathless for you to get this invention of yours on the road? People are dying from too much sunlight. They can't wait another second to get into that big dark room and forget the day they were ever born. Oh wow! This dame is greater than Rio Rita and Garbo put together. Go ahead, pour some more popcorn on me! That's right! Cover me with candy bars! We've gotta show respect in the presence of such cinematic genius as this. String me up with bubble gum. I deserve it. We got to show this coming screen goddess there's nothing we won't do to get her to sign on the dotted line. With a face like that, who needs extras? They'll just get in the way and fuck things up because they're so fucking anxious to get to the commissary before all the roast beef hash is gone. Oh holy shit! Turn the volume up on this baby and padlock the projectionist, 'cause I'm going for broke on this one. For the first time in my life I can sympathize with those astronauts. I now know what they were up to and up against. Don't let a soul out of this room till you've got everybody in here to sign over his pension checks and first drilling rights.

Heaven, I'm in heaven! Dum dum dum tee doo dee ho! You're all too young to know how much that particular tune meant to box-office cashiers throughout the entire country. It made the National Cash Register Company the giant it is today. Look at that smile! Could Joan Crawford do that? Gloria Swanson? Betty Boop? Not in a coon's age. If they'd tried anything with that much untouched charisma they'd've lost their balance and drowned. That's how much those voracious goddesses knew about projecting the vicissitudes of the unspeakable onto the silver scream and the hearts of the multitudes out of whose pockets came our present-day miracles. Count me in when it comes to real box-office appeal, Sam. 'Cause if you can't get people to throw their lives away while standing in a queue a mile long, then you're in the wrong business. Better you should be filling cavities in some godforsaken filling station in the very middle of nowhere. Your father and mother should start all over in their wishes for a bright future for their one and only son, and I'm the guy who should know. Holy Moses! Just get a load of the way this Joan of Arc of high speed film know-how uses her hands when she wants to create an illusion of three-dimensional show-business gullibility! My God! I feel like a babe in the woods. Somewhere a voice is calling, calling for me. Oh boy. Is that ever for sure. And that voice is the insatiable gimme steel-trap voice of this angel lady's agent: Hymie the Limey, who is all lit up with a noseful of coke and with carefully laid plans for my public humiliation when it comes to how much. Lemme just tell you this right now, you little snake in the grass of the cutting-room floor—More popcorn! More popcorn!—if you try one iota of your famous post-expressionistic obstructionisms on me vis-à-vis coming between me and this heavenly creature and a new world of screen wonders from outer space, they're gonna have to employ hounds to find traces of you on Sunset Boulevard where many a person has lost their reason just standing there trying to figure out how to cross the street to Schwab's where they might or they might not get a table there are so many copies of the *Hollywood Reporter* eating up the very air you breathe and making the breakfast menu a thing of the past. You get the picture? You reading me, Hymie, wherever you're hiding in whosis' new sauna up in the canyon with naked Jap chicks cavorting and stuffing your face with pieces of raw fish shamelessly? You should choke on a piece of octopus pussy. OK, Hym? Mr. Smart-ass? That should give you a rough-cut version of my feelings in respect to you know who and my 52 percent controlling interest in this studio. And don't try to bullshit me with any proxy fights or intrauterine scrapping or the last one in's a dirty Jew socktucker, because I may be on this floor completely covered with hot-buttered popcorn as well I should be, but don't let that fool you. The static gene pool that gave us Maimonides and Einstein and Eddie Cantor will triumph over all. And just in case you're not a physicist and therefore don't understand what that translates into, power-wise, just allow me to tell you. Five thousand years of eating crow and stale matzos will rise up and say, This woman is mine! We're going out the way we came in—TOGETHER! This woman is the promised land of the new Hollywood reshuffling process, and you will wake up to discover that everything else was written on water in some two-bit dago village a fart's throw from Genoa, wherever that is, long before you were ever born. Y'understand? What I'm talking about is saturation exposure, from coast to coast. Not a single fucking movie house will remain unsullied, not a single solitary usherette will be able to call her life her own before and after the event I have in mind. They'll have to clear the aisles out with firehoses there'll be so many American hordes collapsed there with their emotions all wiped out and their extremities unable and unwilling to work for the time in question, and central nervous systems be damned. We're gonna make this wonder woman's thrilling face more important to the safety and sanity of the American family than the stars and stripes forever. Her picture is going to hang where the picture of George Washington and his cherry tree should now be hanging, and don't tell me George won't be grateful. Our newly crowned silver-screen queen will take over where breakfast foods leave off, once and for all and I don't mean maybe. More popcorn! More Baby Ruth bars! Unstrap your seat belts, you assholes. Hear me when I call you if you seriously value your future in the film capital of the world. More lemonade! Can't you hear the surging of the maddened crowds from where I be? Or do you think that's just the Pacific Ocean making inroads on your sanity? What we're gonna do shooting script-wise is remake all the old masters. Not a gravestone is gonna be left interred in our sacred film archives. And we're gonna launch this heart-breaking blitzkrieg with *Camille*—the TB lover's guide to eternity. Mothers, hang onto your children, 'cause that's all that'll keep you from being swept out to sea with emotional thrills. You'll wanna cough yourself into an early grave, that's how much you'll love it. And we're gonna help you in this wonderful enterprise. Every usher and usherette in the house is gonna be dressed like nurses and doctors, and real live ambulances will be waitin' out front as well as out back because we don't go back on our word when it comes to reality simulation. The American woman's lungs will never be the same again. Love-making and coughing will become a way of life replacing wife-swapping and mother-fucking as the moon comes over the mountain in the last of the noncommie worlds. Satellites will carry the coughs into outer space and will bounce them off all those useless, burnt-out planetary systems, which is about time if you ask me. NASA don't know the answers to everything, my friend. And after that, while the entire country is still recovering from its first big breakdown, we'll hit them with *Cleopatra*. Right on target, my friends, right on target and not a minute too soon when you consider what the Arabs and the Jews might be doing to each other winner-take-all 'bout that time. We're gonna start by making Egypt unsafe for vipers. You wanna know why? For the simple reason we're gonna be auditioning every viper worth the name, in exactly the same way that kinky young prince went after every skull in the kingdom. We're gonna make a major pitch for viper pride and you can bet on it that we'll succeed in our wishes. Every viper mother will bring her talented offspring into our desert auditioning rooms for a last chance try at fame and fortune. Viper pride'll do the trick. I've seen it work with lions and tigers and elephants and baboons and you can bet your sweet ass it'll work with vipers. They're no different from anybody else, except they bite harder. After all, show biz is show biz, and that's where our strength is. Because when we get to the very crucial scene where our goddess clutches said viper to her tit, we want our viper to give it everything it's got. We want it to be a credit to its race. We want people everywhere to gasp and say "Holy Jesus! What a viper!" And I want to hear them stomp and sing "We want viper! Give us viper!" as they leave the neighborhood theater of their choice. And I want to see our people selling live baby vipers next to the popcorn, T-shirts with vipers on them saying "Bite me!" And I can see viper clubs springing up all over the country with our assistance, complete with secret viper grips and special viper toothmarks. We're in on the ground floor of this ground swell an' that's where we're gonna stay. I see our Cleopatra literally in every single sense of that beautiful and meaningful sacred word swamping Egypt. And we're gonna make this a sure thing, a living cinematic reality, because to start the dynamite movie off, we're gonna blow up the Aswan Dam. You heard me. Boooom! We're gonna show old Mother Nature who's boss. The entertainment industry is sick and tired of being pushed around by that old bag. We're gonna call the shots now and boy oh boy what shots they're gonna be too, for the widest screen this side of Timbuktu. And it's about time that forty-eight million greasy overstained illiterate sleepy Egyptians learned to swim, 'stead of playin' around in the sand all day while the ancient pharaohs sit back in their obelisks which it's their birthright to do and have a few laughs, because when you come right down to it, we're not challenging their sway over the people. Besides, there'll be a little something in it for them too, because I'll personally see to it that plans are afloat to hire as many of them as want to as consultants. If that isn't the stamp of quality, then I'll eat your hat. And it wouldn't come as a complete surprise to me if some of 'em didn't walk away with a handful of Oscars for their aristocratic efforts. One thing you've gotta say about the Oscars, they don't draw the line. Talent is talent, no matter where you find it. Even if you have to wake these fellas up from a two-thousand-year sleep to give them their awards. Nobody's ever gonna accuse me of discrimination against people who sleep a lot. Some places are so hot you gotta sleep a lot if you expect to wake up when the time comes. Where's that lemonade! Where are those Cokes!? Don't gimme that fuckin' lame shit about the machines being broke. Move your asses. This show down here has got to go on. You gofers better hustle if you expect to get any fringe benefits from me. Film history is being made while you assholes sit on your hands and blow bubble gum trying to add up in your pinheads how much you're gonna steal on this new super production while I'm being detained in serious script meetings with the leading actors of our time who are trying to run the whole shebang their way and at the very same time bring me to my knees price-wise. It's a damn good thing I got eyes in the back of my head 'cause if I didn't I'd wind up in the county poorhouse or on the pushin' end of a pushcart without a red cent to my name. Gloria Swanson and Fatty Arbuckle and Zazu Pitts and a lot of other famous chiselers will back me up when I say that. I'm already havin' trouble with my leading man and I haven't shown the nervy little nouveau-riche bastard the script. You see what I mean? Will you believe me now? Are you ready to hear the name of the lucky fella who's gonna play opposite our divine one-in-a-million Cleopatra, vipers and sandstorms and looted pyramids and all? You all set back there for the thunderous announcement? And you under-cover spies for Paramount, you ready for this? Paul Robeson. That's right. The Ace of Spades himself. None other than. And you wanna know the inside story of my reasoning on this decision? Plain old-fashioned black savvy. That's what he'll bring to this acting crisis. Plus, mind you, plus an absolutely fanatical locked-in following of forty million underfed underfoot penniless boogies who are just dyin' to see one of their boys in the White House or someplace just as good as that. I couldn't begin to tell you what it's gonna be like in the ghetto when Paul grabs our Cleopatra in his strong black arms and lets go with "Water Boy." Every riot squad in the country will be taxed beyond endurance. The swollen relief rolls will explode under their own steam. Hundreds of thousands of wild-eyed pickaninnies naked to the waist carrying Egyptian torches, our torches, will march through the streets singing "The Egyptian Love Call" and demanding equal admission under the Freedom to See Act. They'll have to build instant annexes to every movie house in the land, because it's time this country learned to live with itself under one movie roof just like it says in the Constitution. And that's not all. In fact, that's just the beginning. Get your feet on the ground for this one. At the height of the first big eating orgy at Cleo's own personal palace, while thousands of court hangers-on and fair-weather friends are gobbling down tons of smoked peacock tongues and alligator steaks and jackal stew and poached flamingo eggs, washed down with gallons of chilled vintage palm wine, Paul is gonna free himself from our Cleo's tough embraces who is spooning spiced tiger-eye soup into his mouth, and he's gonna stand up and stop the forks in midair with a truly throbbing rendition of "Shortnin Bread." Need I say more? Can anybody add to that? No, they can't. Are you hearing as I am the cash registers all over the film world simply going off their fuckin' rockers? Or are you deaf to the sounds of super smash hitsville? There won't be a dry pocketbook in the house, and you can quote me on that verbatim if that's the way you wanna play it, pal. What we've clearly got here is the dawn of a new civilization motion picture-wise. Every other studio in this town is shakin' in his boots and I don't blame 'em. I would too if I wasn't me with what I've got right here in my hand all locked up tighter'n the prisoner of Zenda. It's every bit as great as Galileo with his patent on the world-is-round number. Stop that whisperin' back there! Bring on those Eskimo pies! And make it snappy! Nothin' worse than dead Eskimo pie. Unless it's a buncha drunken Eskimos fightin' over a piece of blubber while their igloos melt around their ears an' their wives' juicy tail pieces go beggin'. Makes me think of the time we were on location in the Yucatán jungles shootin' *Montezuma's Revenge* an' those thousands of smelly little peon extras were rioting all over the place because they said they weren't gettin' enough of those Mex pancakes—whatdya call 'em? tortillas?—to keep body and soul together. Production stopped clean in its tracks. Jungle creepers were takin' over everything includin' the cameramen. Every day three more feet of the soundtrack were missin' because the fuckin' anteaters had eaten 'em. That's when I went to Montezuma himself who was being played to the hilt by Milton Berle, that is, when the cameras were rollin', which sure as shit wasn't now, and I said, Miltie, we gotta do something and fast. Time and money are runnin' out... —An' I got the Mex runs, says Miltie, —an' if I take one more shit I'll be dead. I don't know what got into me in the first place. I could be home in bed in Hollywood with a pastrami sandwich and two hungry starlets. I could be standing in front of the TV cameras dressed up like the Faerie Queen giving solace and succor to millions of fun-starved housewives and their beer-sodden husbands down on the floor while Junior fucks his fist over a filthy comic book down in the basement. I could be shooting crap at the Lamb's Club with Martha Raye and Red Skelton and Jack Benny and Debbie Reynolds winning and losing millions with each thrilling roll of the dice. But instead of all that wonderful action, what am I doing? I'm down here in this hoary hellhole being chased by crazy jungle cats, bitten by deadly snakes with nothing better to do, attacked by thirsty giant vampire bats that can't live without my blood, and hassled night and day by midget Indian extras who want me to meet their syphilitic little sisters who can't be more than ten years old. And I'm dying of the shits. The only doctor within five hundred miles of this nightmare alley is a scabby old cokehead who lives in a mountain cave with his monkey wife surrounded by the bones of wild animals and unopened letters from his family written fifty years ago wondering what the fuck he's doing with himself now that the cops have run him out of town for performing quickie abortions on rich teenagers without the proper police-chief bribe precautions. Or else he was a ghoul before his time which in those days could get you in a lot of hot water, believe me. I had a friend who was a werewolf long before it was legalized and became fashionable and I'm telling you what a heap of hassling he went through before it was all over. Including a simply ghastly long weekend in the city pound before his lawyer could be tracked down. Anyway, this runaway medieval medicare man up in yonder mountains is the first and last chance you have this side of Mexico City if you have the lousy luck to come down with anything more important than the heebie-jeebies or a stuffed-up schnozz, and the very last thing you should have in mind if you're crazy enough or desperate enough to go to his place is that it might bear some resemblance to the Mayo Clinic or God help us a normal white doctor's office with a cutie pie receptionist like in *Dr. Kildare.* Oh no. The first thing you see as you crawl up the mountainside jungles on your last legs is a sign nailed to a tree with one word on it: *Sickness.* And underneath that an arrow pointing in the direction of his foul cave. Like you should go there to buy some sickness like in a special store and so help me God, that's what this creepy bastard's pushing. All kinds of sickness. Hanging from the branches of trees in front of his cave store are dozens of hand-painted placards with the names of diseases and afflictions on them. Cancer. Malaria. Gout. Migraine. Cirrhosis. Tumors. Madness. Incest. Ulcers. Blindness. Dumbness. Special Today: Shingles. "We have every medical catastrophe you might feel in need of. Don't be afraid to ask us." That's what's written right above the entrance to his cave. Can you imagine the nerve of this guy! The far-fucking-flung chutzpa? And do you know what he calls himself? Alfredo Hilario Segismundo Gómez Montenegro y Ruiz y Peelmunder. He sounds like a Mexican delicatessen. Thrombosis with hot tamale sauce. Gingivitis with melted cheese. And a side order of arthritis and refried beans. And don't bother asking yourself who those chicks are who're stirring the steaming cauldrons in the clearing. They're probably trainees in black magic or witch doctoring. The fact that they look like college girls on a dirty fling is no concern of mine, or yours. Nor is the fact that they're stark naked except for those rah-rah loin pieces or G strings made outta God only knows what missing explorer's skin or maybe some actor left over from *Rima the Bird Girl* or some other Mex-Yank bomb of bygone entertainment years. Better not to ask those cruel-looking sexpot assistants what or who's in that soup they're stirring with such controlled gusto. Might be a friend of yours or a flock of wild jungle canaries who'll start to sing inside you soon as you've had your first hot bowl. But I'll tell you one thing—they'll never get me on that rickety, makeshift operating table inside their mumbo-jumbo cave. No sir. I don't care how sick they say I am. This body's been good to me and I plan to keep it intact. Even though I've got a bad fever. I mean, my head's so hot I could scramble eggs on it. I'm hearing voices! Thousands of voices! They're calling me: Uncle Miltie! Uncle Miltie! Where are you? Come back to us! We need you! Uncle Miltie!